HARD TIMES

HARD TIMES.

FOR THESE TIMES.

Charles Dickens

edited by Graham Law

broadview literary texts

823.8
DIC

50503010978080

Canadian Cataloguing in Publication Data

Dickens, Charles, 1812-1870
      Hard times

(Broadview literary texts)
Includes bibliographical references.
ISBN 1-55111-075-X

I. Law, Graham. II. Title. III. Series
PR4561.A2L38 1996   823'.8   C96-930155-3

Broadview Press Ltd., is an independent, international publishing house, incorporated in 1985.

North America:
P.O. Box 1243, Peterborough, Ontario, Canada K9J 7H5
3576 California Road, Orchard Park, NY 14127
Tel: (705) 743-8990; Fax: (705) 743-8353
E-mail: customerservice@broadviewpress.com

United Kingdom:
Turpin Distribution Services Ltd.,
Blackhorse Rd, Letchworth, Hertfordshire SG6 1HN
Tel: (1462) 672555; Fax: (1462) 480947
E-mail: turpin@rsc.org

Australia:
St. Clair Press, P.O. Box 287, Rozelle, NSW 2039
Tel: (02) 818-1942; Fax: (02) 418-1923

www.broadviewpress.com

Broadview Press is grateful to Professor Eugene Benson for advice on editorial matters for the Broadview Literary Texts series.

Broadview Press gratefully acknowledges the financial support of the Book Publishing Industry Development Program, Ministry of Canadian Heritage, Government of Canada.

PRINTED IN CANADA

Contents

Introduction

In many ways *Hard Times* is profoundly untypical of Dickens's novels. Its narrative content is alien. The story originates in a single fixed idea rather than a set of striking characters or images. The action is set in the alien industrial landscape of the North-West of England rather than the familiar streets of London and the South-East. It begins in the clear cold light of the contemporary world rather than the mists of history or childhood memory. Its narrative form is unusually concentrated and compressed. The novel is short and fills only one volume of the three required for the standard Victorian 'Library Edition.' It has a relatively brief list of dramatis personae and dramatic settings. It offers almost none of those exuberant scenes which are superfluous to the plot but which create the sense of abundance in the Dickens world. In short, uncharacteristically in *Hard Times* Dickens does not attempt to synthesize a complete imaginary world whose contours can reflect external reality only in an indirect, distorted way. Instead he comes as close as he was capable of doing, to producing a novel of ideas, a social novel, which seeks to engage directly and analytically with contemporary political issues.

Briefly, the issues in question were the physical, moral and social condition of England after several decades of rapid industrialization, and the appropriate private and public responses to it. In addressing them, Dickens was engaging in a genre of writing that had been in existence for around a quarter of a century and in fact was shortly to lose its impetus as booming trade and local government policies together began noticeably to bring an end to the most extreme cases of urban squalor and unrest. The genre existed in both discursive and fictional varieties, with a considerable degree of overlap: the former is most characteristically seen as the debate on the 'Condition-of-England question', which is opened by Carlyle in his 1829 essay 'Signs of the Times'; while the latter usually takes the form of the 'industrial novel' prevalent in the 1840s.

Yet it was far from the case that Dickens's contribution represented the last word in the debate, although high school and university courses in literature have too often given that impression. What Dickens had to say in the novel was polemical and controversial and provoked extreme responses. Some who felt themselves under attack in the novel, like Harriet

Martineau, reacted with anger and derision (App. C 9);[1] others, like John Ruskin, who shared Dickens's hostility to the currents of the times, greeted the novel with extravagant praise (App. C 11); many of the greatest and longest-standing admirers of his comic genius, however, were puzzled or repelled by the stridency of the tone (e.g. App. B 8). Later, though there were exceptional voices such of those of George Bernard SHAW (Preface) and G. K. CHESTERTON (pp. 164–5) who praised the novel's social or moral vision,[2] for most of the hundred years following its publication *Hard Times* remained among the least regarded of Dickens's fictional works. After the second world war, however, the novel rapidly became one of the most studied and discussed of Victorian documents, a development for which we can offer an explanation on three different levels. The first is the powerful influence of the Cambridge critic, F. R. Leavis, passionate advocate of the intellectual and social importance of English studies, on a whole generation of university English teachers who entered the academy during the post-war educational boom. In his stern gallery of the masterpieces of modern fiction *The Great Tradition* (1948), LEAVIS singled out *Hard Times* as the one work by Dickens 'possessed by a comprehensive vision' (p. 228). The second is that the novel's attack on mechanical methods in education dovetailed neatly with the post-war emphasis on creativity and freedom of expression. The third is simply the novel's reduced length and clear symbolic and narrative organization, which give it an enormous advantage over the looser baggier monsters which tend to make up the Dickens canon, when it comes to selecting course and examination texts in educational institutions.

The aim of this edition of the novel is above all to help general readers, inside and outside those educational institutions, without the time or the facilities to consult the original documents, to read *Hard Times* in the context of the contemporary debate to which it belongs.[3] To do so is not

---

1.   Citations in this form refer to the contemporary documents collected in the Appendices to this volume.
2.   Capitalized citations in this form refer to entries in the Bibliography to this volume.
3.   For a more extended discussion of the debate on industrialism than that in the sketch in the following pages, see Graham Law 'Industrial Designs: Form and Function in the "Condition of England" Novel' in *Studies Presented to Professor H. Yamanouchi*, edited by George Hughes & Takahisa Takahashi (London: Boydell & Brewer, Forthcoming [1997]).

only to achieve a surer grasp of the novel's strengths and weaknesses but also to begin to engage with a vitally important stage in modern English social and intellectual history. As interdisciplinary approaches to historical texts take hold, encouraging a synthesis of the insights from social studies, philosophy and literature, and as students are increasingly likely to read Dickens under the rubric of Cultural or Women's Studies rather than Victorian Literature, critical editions need to cast their nets more broadly. In addition to the more familiar features of a chronology of the writer, and textual or explanatory notes, this volume contains extensive appendices of contemporary documents, which include extracts from key discursive and fictional contributions to the debate on industrialization. In what follows, this introduction will attempt a brief overview of the relevance of those documents to the study of *Hard Times*, focusing both on the content and the style of the novel, and beginning from a consideration of the title.

★ ★ ★

'Hard Times' is a consciously misleading title. Several contemporary reviewers complained that they had not been given what they were led to expect (e.g. App. B 6 & 8), yet evidence survives that Dickens chose the title with a good deal of forethought and at an early stage in the novel's composition (see App. A 4a). The most common connotation of the phrase, then as now, is a temporary period of adversity for an individual or group because of changed economic circumstances. As a number of popular ballads from the 'Hungry Forties' suggest (see CRAIG pp. 11–2), it was used particularly to describe the hardships of agricultural or industrial workers, and the associated conflicts with land and factory owners, during those periods when demand for labour slackened due to periodic downturns in the business cycle or to the introduction of new machinery. This was indeed to be a central theme during the 'northern' episodes of Mrs. Gaskell's novel *North and South* (1855), which was serialized in *Household Words* almost immediately after Dickens's novel (App. D 6c). Mrs. Gaskell had been concerned that Dickens's work would preempt her own, but he was quick to reassure her that his own interests were different and that the story would not involve a strike (App. A 4n).

More generally, Mrs. Gaskell's theme had been a prevalent one in earlier industrial novels written during the 'Hungry Forties' themselves. In *Michael Armstrong* (1840), Frances Trollope, mother of Anthony Trollope, and author in her own right of a popular sequence of social novels, had broken new ground in attacking the northern factory owners for their inhumane treatment of child labourers (App. D 2). But Gaskell's novel *Mary Barton* (1848), centering on the effects in Manchester of the catastrophic cyclical depression of 1841–2 which gave such a strong impetus to the Chartist movement, and Charlotte Brontë's *Shirley* (1849), with its substantial subplot concerning the hardships suffered earlier in the century by Yorkshire woolen-mill hands on the introduction of new machinery and leading to the Luddite disturbances, are the key documents here (App. D 6a–b & 7). The positions of both Gaskell and Brontë can be characterized broadly as Christian Humanitarian or Philanthropist. Unlike Dickens, for whom Coketown remains irreducibly exotic, both write intimately about the communities in which they live, and attempt to convey sympathetically and truthfully the material and psychological condition of northern industrial workers with the aim of challenging the prejudices of their bourgeois readers. Both recognize the long-term social benefits of technological progress, but accuse the mill owners of hard-heartedness in refusing to accept responsibility for the short-term effects on their workers' livelihoods. Both insist that the relations between masters and men are to be governed not merely by the economic law of supply and demand, but by Christ's teaching concerning love for one's neighbour.

Arthur Helps had taken this line in his influential book *The Claims of Labour* of 1844 (App. C 5). Indeed, this is not too far removed from the position Dickens takes in his own journalism, so that Harriet Martineau once labelled him 'the humanity-monger in "Household Words"' (App. C 9). This can be represented by the piece 'On Strike' reporting on the extended and bitter conflict between masters and men in the Preston textile industry during 1853–4 (App. C 7), and based on a brief visit to the town in search of copy for *Hard Times* at the end of February 1854 (see App. A 4d). There, though the Christian colouring is not so apparent in the rhetoric, the key notes are sympathy for the good-natured restraint of the workers, the sense of waste both in material and psychological terms, and an emotional appeal for human reconciliation. Yet, despite the title, this theme is almost entirely absent from the novel itself. In *Hard Times*, there is little real sense either of the cyclical nature of economic activity or of the antagonism between social classes. Although Bounderby, with his cant about silver spoons and venison soup, is a caricature of the callous master, while Stephen is the model of the long-suffering man, and although in their conversations together in Bk. I Ch. 11 and Bk. II Ch. 5 we witness inhumanity and injustice in action, finally neither is shown to be representative of his class—Bounderby's egoism and Stephen's sorrow both have their sources in private rather than public life. Gradgrind's is the true voice of the manufacturing interest in the novel, as Slackbridge's is that of organized labour, and there is no need for a reconciliation between them because the two are shown to share already the same hard, self-serving values.

There is then the further possibility that by his title Dickens intended to imply that adversity and conflict were not merely temporary side-effects of a phase of industrial development requiring human charity to lessen their consequences, but that as a mode of economic production industrial capitalism *per se* was deeply or permanently antagonistic to social harmony and common welfare. Today we are most likely to associate this idealistic viewpoint with Marxism, and it is indeed to the textile industry of Lancashire in the 1840s that we can trace the origin of Marxist thought. Friedrich Engels, the radical twenty-four-year-old son of a despotic German factory owner, was sent to Manchester to supervise his father's business interests at that time, and wrote a powerful indictment of the material and social conditions he encountered in the growing industrial towns (App. C 6). He was already an acquaintance of Karl Marx and the two later collaborated on a number of key socialist documents, including the *Communist Party Manifesto* of 1848. Though Engels's *Condition of the Working Class in England* was not translated into English until the 1880s, the content and style of his argument would not have been entirely alien to contemporary English readers, for condemnation of the social disruption caused by the factory system was widespread during the early phases of industrialism on both extremes of the political spectrum, not only from Radicals like William Cobbett, utopian socialists like Robert Owen, and Chartists like Francis Place, but also, as Raymond Williams has shown, from Tory constitutionalists as various as Edmund Burke, Robert Southey and Samuel Taylor Coleridge (see WILLIAMS pp. 3–29). P. Gaskell's *Artisans and Machinery* (App. C 3) provides a typical though restrained example from the 1830s.

In the industrial novels of the 1840s these views are reflected, though in a less extreme form, in the work, on the one hand, of Christian Socialists like the Anglican clergyman Charles Kingsley, and on the other of the then leader of the Tory Reform Group 'Young England' and later Prime Minister, Benjamin Disraeli. *Helen Fleetwood* (1841), which like *Michael Armstrong* attacks the abuses of child labour in the Lancashire textile mills but which extends the argument to a wholesale condemnation of the dehumanization and Godlessness of life in the industrial towns, is a pioneering work by 'Charlotte Elizabeth', a devout evangelical who would have angrily rejected the label of socialist (App. D 3). Kingsley, on the other hand, after 1848, the year of revolutions in Europe and the final violent flaring of Chartism in England, wrote over the signature of 'Parson Lot' in the reformist journals *Politics for the People* and its successor *Christian Socialist*. His first two novels *Yeast* and *Alton Locke* give sympathetic portraits respectively of the agricultural poor in the south of England, and the sweated tailors of the London garment industry (App. D 8a–b). The Christian Socialist position, while rejecting the secular philosophy and sometimes violent means of the Chartists, expresses a remarkable sympathy with both their material grievances and their political objectives, including the extension of the franchise to the working man. Outer social revolution is subordinated to inner spiritual rebirth, but self-governing workers' associations based on cooperative principles are advocated and promoted as an alternative mode of production to competition and capitalism.

Disraeli's 'Young England' group, on the other hand, is reactionary in its rejection of urban industrialism. It regards the Reform Bill of 1832, which extended the franchise to those citizens accumulating wealth from industry and trade, as an error, and wishes instead to reform the landed aristocracy and the established church and restore their Mediaeval obligations. Manufacturers are only approved if they are prepared to undertake similar feudal responsibilities towards the workers in their employ. The common people are to be relieved from their misery, but must relinquish claims to political rights and accept permanent social subordination. Disraeli had already published a number of 'fashionable novels', and in the mid 1840s turned to the political novel to present this idealistic programme before a wider public. *Coningsby* (1844), which principally concerns the social obligations which should accompany wealth, and *Sybil*

(1845), which addresses the conflict between rich and poor, are the main results (App. D 5a-c). There is obviously a world of difference between the supercilious wit of Disraeli's conservatism and the passionate intensity of Kingsley's radicalism, but there are many points of similarity between their visions of the social disintegration and alienation concomitant with industrialization, and often the latter's Christian cooperative artisans' workshops come to sound not too different from the former's Mediaeval Monasteries.

And, as will be readily apparent, Dickens's novel really has little in common with either position, although the Victorian historian Macaulay once famously condemned the novel for its 'sullen socialism.'[1] There obviously are narratorial passages, generally towards the beginning of the novel and most notably in the openings to Bk. I Chs. 5, 8, and 10, all of which 'strike the key-note' of the novel, Coketown itself, where the industrial landscape is described in a grim, deterministic way, as uniformly stunting and distorting the lives of all those who live there. But, as Raymond Williams again has pointed out,[2] the action itself denies this, for Rachael and Stephen's wife, say, or Louisa and Tom, have each been raised in the same environment but turn out in very different ways. Similarly there are moments when Stephen's words, notably in conversations with Rachael or Bounderby, seem to accuse the factory system itself of valuing people lower than machinery, though, as we shall see, perhaps the most telling attack was cut from the manuscript before publication. But, even if we find difficulty in defining the outer limits of reference of Stephen's own personal keynote 'Aw a muddle!' (p. 292), it clearly cannot be restricted to the intrinsic character of industrialism.

On closer examination of the Coketown 'key-note' passages noted above, it becomes apparent that the industrial landscape and the factory system are seen merely as surface consequences rather than the underlying cause of the hardness of the times, and indeed only one among a

---

1. Thomas Macaulay, in his Journal, 12 August 1854, the day the serialization of the novel concluded in *Household Words*. See *Life and Letters of Lord Macaulay* (1876; Oxford: Oxford University Press, 1978) edited by G. O. Trevelyan, Vol. II Ch. 13 p. 307.

2. See 'The Reader in *Hard Times*', collected in his *Writing in Society* (London: Verso, 1983) pp. 166–74.

plurality of such effects. Others notably are the various public responses to and attempts to ameliorate the process of industrialization, including those by government, by the churches, and by philanthropists. And it is important to remember here that contempt is expressed not only towards the 'red tape' of parliamentary commissions and Blue Books and tables of statistics, but also towards practical and progressive national or local programmes, such as those introducing elementary teacher training or municipal libraries and parks, or those fostering sound principles of industrial design or discouraging the abuse of alcohol and narcotics. The underlying problem is clearly understood to be that social philosophy which was already becoming dominant by the beginning of the Victorian era and known, after the principle of utility ('It is the greatest happiness of the greatest number that is the measure of right and wrong') of its founder Jeremy Bentham,[1] as utilitarianism. The hardest name in the novel, Gradgrind, is reserved for the spokesman for the principle of utility; he is the main villain of the piece. Bounderby and Harthouse, the other members of the novel's demonic trinity, are only bit players.

The vital question remains of how just and accurate Dickens was in his caricature of utilitarianism in the figure of Gradgrind. The safest way to approach this complex problem is to suggest that for Dickens utilitarianism is a single, unitary system of thought, whereas even the simplest level of social analysis reveals two rather different trends. The distinction between them is primarily but not solely historical. The followers of Bentham were described as 'Philosophical Radicals', but it was clearly a very different thing to be a Radical before and after the passage of the Reform Bill of 1832. Major progressive achievements of the new parliament under its extended franchise included the Municipal Corporations Reform Act of 1835 and the repeal of the Corn Laws in 1846. The former encouraged the development of responsible local government in the new industrial towns and the beginnings of an effective response to their profound problems of public health, safety, and welfare. The latter removed the distortions in trade in favour of agricultural landowners and against

---

1.   Preface, *A Fragment on Government* (1776; Cambridge: Cambridge University Press, 1988) ed. J. H. Burns & H. L. A Hart, p. 3.

the manufacturing interest, which had inflated the cost of bread to the urban and rural poor. Before 1832 the central aim of the Radicals could only be the removal of the bias toward the landed aristocracy enshrined in the English constitution. After 1848, a key role was to resist oligarchic tendencies among the representatives of industrial capital. This meant both going back to sort out the manifest faults and inadequacies of earlier utilitarian legislation such as the new Poor Law of 1834 and the Factory Act of 1844, as well as looking forward to ways of meeting the legitimate democratic demands of the Chartists.

The earlier utilitarianism then was more firmly linked to those bourgeois and manufacturing interests known later as the Manchester School; it tended to see legal and social reform as the removal of obstructions to the operation of the market, in other words, it believed in *laissez-faire*; its mode of thought tended towards mechanism, as we can see from the detail of Bentham's own methods of calculating happiness, or, more influentially, in the iron-clad laws of the new school of political economy led by David Ricardo; and its harsh moral tone was sometimes reminiscent of the puritanical intolerance of contemporary evangelicalism. These tendencies can be seen collectively in the theories of population control propounded by Thomas Malthus in *An Essay on the Principle of Population* (1798; significantly revised 1803), which lent themselves to popular parody and misconception (see HOUSE pp. 69–76). Here they are represented by the voice of Andrew Ure in *The Philosophy of Manufactures* (1836), an encomium on the scientific and social progress represented by the factory system (App. C 2).

Within industrial fiction also there are a number of voices speaking clearly for this earlier utilitarianism. The principal one is that of Harriet Martineau, who could make a strong claim to have founded the genre. Rejecting her early Unitarian beliefs, from the 1830s she took up the utilitarian cause with a similar puritanical fervour. Between 1832–4 she issued twenty-five slim didactic novels illuminating the basic theories of Smith and Bentham, Malthus and Mill, for the moral and material benefit of the lower classes (App. D 1). They are not always as dry and unappealing as they sound in brief summary, and rapidly brought her the literary success and social influence which she required to give free rein to her sometimes wayward reformist zeal. Also of interest here are two popular melodramas by women writers, *William Langshawe, the Cotton Lord* (1842) and *Jane Rutherford, or the Miners' Strike* (1854), which are unapologetically partisan in pleading the cause of the long-suffering industrialists in the face of the ignorance and malice of their workers' representatives (App. D 4 & 9). Both include cloak-and-dagger scenes representing Trade Union rituals and demagoguery which are interesting to compare with those in Disraeli's *Sybil* and Gaskell's *Mary Barton* (App. D 5c & 6a), as well as with Dickens's portrayal of Slackbridge in Bk. II Ch. 4 and Bk. III Ch. 4. The former also features an aggressively self-made mill owner in striking contrast to Bounderby.

As can be seen from these dates, what we have termed the 'earlier' utilitarian trend did survive within the radical movement until after the mid-century, but it was clearly a declining force at the time Dickens was writing, which was precisely when the 'later' trend was defining itself. Here the central figure is that of John Stuart Mill, the model son of Bentham's right hand man, the austere Scotsman James Mill. Key documents are: Mill's essays 'Bentham' and 'Coleridge' (1838 and 1840, published in the *Westminster Review*, the journal of the philosophical radicals founded by his father and Jermy Bentham in 1824), in which Mill controversially distanced himself from the mechanistic aspects of Bentham's thought (App. C 4a); and the *Principles of Political Economy* (1848) which, in addition to serving as an admirable textbook on classical economics, considers the future of democratic institutions in the light of the demands of the Chartists (App. C 4b); and of course his *Autobiography* of 1873. Under the guiding influence of Mill, philosophical radicalism thus began: to divorce itself from narrow manufacturing interests and to recognize the legitimacy of universal adult suffrage (women as well as workers); to see that reform could be viewed as enlightened intervention by the state to promote the common good; to balance the demands of strict logic with those of human sympathy; and to avoid the intolerant tone, associated with evangelical Christianity, which had hindered so greatly the development of elementary education in the 1840s (see HAMMOND pp. 179–216.). We can find no representative of this new mode of utilitarianism within industrial fiction, but it is difficult not to regret, along with the reviewer in the *Westminster Review*, that Dickens himself finally did not quite have the capacity to fulfil that role with *Hard Times* (App. B 7).

For, in so far as Dickens's novel is an attack on the limitations of the early utilitarianism, it is entirely consistent with his own best instincts of 'sentimental radicalism', in Walter Bagehot's phrase,[1] and with the political position he adopts publicly in the 1850s in his journal *Household Words*. But, although Malthus and Martineau do indeed often seem to be the specific butt of the satire at a number of points in the novel,[2] in the end the novel shows no recognition of the distinction I have briefly sketched here. In context, it would have been impossible for an informed contemporary reader not to have taken the jibes at Political Economy scattered liberally throughout *Hard Times* (e.g. pp. 86, 93, 126, & 240), or, more specifically, the attack on developments in elementary education in the person of Mr. M'Choakumchild (Bk. I Ch. 2 p. 47), as directed at the author of *Principles of Political Economy* or his ideas. And in so far as Dickens's attack is directed at Mill and the emerging later mode of utilitarianism, it is in serious danger both of reflecting popular prejudice rather than considered opposition and of antagonizing those who should have been his closest allies. Though there is no evidence that Dickens was acquainted at first hand with Mill's essays on Bentham and Coleridge, it is remarkable on how many occasions in *Hard Times* he comes up with criticisms of Benthamism which Mill had there either made himself or had dealt with under the heading of popular misconceptions.[3] And, from a

---

1. See 'Charles Dickens' *National Review* October 1858, a review of the 1857–8 Chapman & Hall *Cheap Edition of the Works of Charles Dickens*, reprinted in *Estimations in Criticism* (London: Andrew Melrose, 1908) ed. Cuthbert Lennox p. 192.

2. Malthus is mentioned by name only on p. 59 (one of Gradgrind's younger children is named for him); but the satire on statisticians' insensitivity to death by starvation and drowning (p. 94, where Sissy tells Louisa of her mistakes at M'Choakumchild's school) and Bitzer's comments on the improvidence of marriage (p. 150—see W.B. Hodgson's reaction to this passage in App. C 10) are surely directed at his theories of population, or at least popular understandings of them. Martineau is not mentioned by name, but the reference to 'leaden little books' (p. 86—see the explanatory note) must be aimed at her *Illustrations of Political Economy*.

3. For example, the criticism of the action of Junius Brutus in having his own sons executed for treason as utilitarian, which twice is made implicitly in *Hard Times* (see notes to pp. 174 & 296), was countered by Mill in 'Bentham' (1838); see App. C 4a. More generally, if we can anticipate our argument a little, it appears likely that Dickens, unfamiliar with the original writings of Bentham, Malthus, Ricardo or J. S. Mill, was drawing heavily on the caricatures of them made by Carlyle. For

letter to his statistician friend Charles Knight after the completion of the novel where Dickens writes of 'the real useful truths of political economy' (App. A 4v), we understand quite how much he had to take back to mend fences with his political neighbours.

These points can be illustrated further by looking at a considered response to Dickens's satire by the economist W.H. Hodgson in his contribution to the series of lectures on education at the Royal Institution of Great Britain in June 1854, while the novel was still running in *Household Words* (App. C 10). There, not only does Hodgson demonstrate directly how wide of the mark Dickens was in offering the self-interested calculations of Tom and Bitzer as the key-note of contemporary utilitarian thought, but he also suggests indirectly how reactionary a position Dickens was taking in the novel by choosing to laugh at, rather than critically encourage, the Victorian task of developing public policies and facilities for education, health, and safety. Indeed, in his other role as editor of and writer for *Household Words*, that was precisely what Dickens was intending to do. In the angry confrontation which occurred shortly after the appearance of *Hard Times* between Dickens's journal and Harriet Martineau (a former contributor—see STOREY [1993] pp. 67–8) concerning the provisions of the 1844 Factory Act on the fencing of industrial machinery for the protection of the work-force, where Dickens and Henry Morley attacked and Martineau defended the position of the Lancashire mill owners (App. C 8 & 9), there is little doubt not only that *Household Words* had the better of the quarrel but also that their mode of argument is a better and more coherent reflection of contemporary utilitarian thinking than Martineau's own.

What then were the pressures that made Dickens depart so far from the principles espoused in his recently-founded journal when he belatedly

---

example, the satire on Bitzer's self-interestedness on p. 148 ('his only reasonable transaction in that commodity would have been to buy it for as little as he could possibly give, and sell it for as much as he could possibly get; it having been clearly ascertained by philosophers that in this is comprised the whole duty of man—not a part of man's duty but the whole') surely is lifted from Carlyle's '"To buy in the cheapest market, and sell in the dearest": truly if that is the summary of his social duties, and the final divine-message he has to follow, we may trust him extensively to vote upon that ...' *Latter-Day Pamphlets* No. 1.

took up the challenge of redefining the industrial novel? The shortest answer is the powerful but untimely influence of Thomas Carlyle, to whom the novel is inscribed, whose seminal essay of 1829 attacking the mechanistic spirit of the age, 'Signs of the Times' (App. C 1a), is undoubtedly to what Dickens was referring in his full title 'Hard Times: For *these* Times', and whose voice is so often heard above Dickens's own in both the intellectual content and the rhetorical style of the novel. In the 1830s and 1840s Carlyle's challenging social critique carried great authority, and there is hardly a contribution to the debate on industrialism that we have been retracing that does *not* reveal his influence to a greater or lesser extent. Marx and Engels's concept of the cash nexus as the dominant mode of human relations under capitalism, Disraeli's choice of the Mediaeval monastery as his model of healthy social institutions, and Kingsley's tone of moral outrage can all be traced back with equal directness to Carlyle's writings, most notably *Chartism* (1839) and *Past and Present* (1843), two works which return to the 'Condition-of-England question' first raised in 'Signs of the Times' (App. C 1b–c). The philanthropy of Helps and Gaskell and Brontë also borrows many of its attitudes and details from Carlyle's condemnation of industrial society. And later Victorian social idealists such as John Ruskin and William Morris of course owed much to Carlyle's early writings. But though Carlyle was undoubtedly both philosophical and radical, and had early on received considerable support from the *Westminster Review*,[1] the metaphysical and religious cast of his thought and the emotive and prophetic mode of his rhetoric were diametrically opposed to the utilitarian calculus. From as early as 1829 onwards, Carlyle had argued that England's sickness could not be healed simply by the intervention of public bodies but only through the willing return of the people to the paths directed by divine law. But after 1848, there was a marked deepening of his pessimism about the possibility of change and his contempt for government institutions. In the eight *Latter-Day Pamphlets* of 1850, his tone became harsh and shrill, as he raged against

---

1.   According to *The Wellesley Index to Victorian Periodicals, 1824–1900*, edited by Walter E. Houghton in 5 volumes (Toronto: University of Toronto Press, 1966–1989), Carlyle published a total of eight articles in the journal, the first in 1831 and the last as late as January 1855 (Vol. V p. 139).

the evils of democracy and the need for the rule of the 'Strong Just Man.' Apart from the qualified approval of Marx and Engels, the pamphlets were received with almost universal disapprobation in a Victorian England about to prepare for that symptom of national self-confidence known as the Great Exhibition.

Before concluding, we need to illustrate the extent and the effect of Carlyle's influence on *Hard Times* in terms of its narrative content and style.[1] Firstly, one of the novel's main organizing structures can be traced back to the Scotsman's prophetic utterances. What I have called the novel's 'demonic trinity' of Gradgrind, Bounderby, and Harthouse is undoubtedly a direct personification of Carlyle's triad of Mechanism, the Gospel of Mammonism, and the Gospel of Dilettantism (that is, respectively, the godless creed of utilitarianism, and the self-interested values of the industrial capitalist and the landed aristocrat built upon it) which we encounter repeatedly both in *Chartism* and *Past and Present*. Against these powerful economic, social and intellectual forces, Dickens, of course, unlike Carlyle who appeals to the power of the living God, can only counterpoise what he understands as the better side of human nature, affection, forbearance, and fun, embodied in the novel by Sissy, Rachael, and Sleary. These clearly relate to that home-made creed of Dickens which CAZAMIAN has called 'the philosophy of Christmas' (pp. 117–47), and in the narrative economy of the novel they have that power from negative capability which allows them to triumph. That many readers of *Hard Times* have felt a deep incommensurability between these opposed forces is not merely related to the differences between their ideational content, but also to their disparate rhetorical provenance.

Secondly, we can see Carlyle's influence on the controlling metaphors of the novel. As a quick glance through the explanatory footnotes will suggest, there is an abundance of biblical references in the text. Echoes of the King James Bible or the Book of Common Prayer in mid-Victorian discourse are of course commonplace, but the frequency of occurrence here is unusual for Dickens, being more what we might expect from an

---

1.   For a more detailed demonstration than that in the following paragraphs, see Graham Law 'Industrial Relations: Carlyle's influence on *Hard Times*' in *Humanitas* (Waseda University Law Society) 34, February 1996, pp. 1–34.

evangelical writer like 'Charlotte Elizabeth.' A pattern begins to emerge from these references which suggests that they are often filtered through the densely biblical prose of Carlyle, whose Calvinistic background remains most evident in his rhetorical style. The pattern is at its clearest in the agricultural metaphors which head the three books of the novel and which were added after the magazine serialization: 'Sowing', 'Reaping', and 'Garnering.' These derive ultimately from the Synoptic Gospels in the New Testament of the Bible—compare especially: Matthew 6:24–34 ('Ye cannot serve God and mammon'), where the metaphors occurring in verse 26 illustrate the superiority of spiritual over material values; and Matthew 3:11–12/Luke 3:16–17 (John the Baptist on the Messiah) or Matthew 13:24–30/Luke 8:4–15 (The Parable of the Sower), where there is an apocalyptic emphasis on the punishment of sin and the rewarding of virtue, i.e. the saved are gathered into God's garner and the damned are burnt as chaff. But there are prior instances of Carlyle's using these metaphors in precisely the same way,[1] and the threat from Mammonism and the imminence of the apocalypse are the keynotes of *Chartism*/*Past and Present* and *Latter-Day Pamphlets* respectively. In a similar way, Dickens's repeated representation of Political Economy as a mill-stone grinding exceedingly small (e.g. pp. 92, 126, & 314) or Members of Parliament as national dustmen (e.g. pp. 223, 231, 240 & 314) borrows much of its colouring from Carlyle's railing against the 'dismal science'[2] or the Augean stables of the 'National Palaver.'[3] Even metaphorical grace notes like the comparison of Gradgrind to a 'galvanizing apparatus' (p. 42)[4] and his

---

1. See, for example, *The French Revolution* (1837) Vol. I Ch. 6 §3.

2. The phrase first occurs in the essay 'Occasional Discourse on the Nigger Question' (1849): 'The Social Science—not a 'gay science', but a rueful,—which finds the secret of this Universe in 'supply and demand.'... what we might call, by way of eminence, the *dismal science*.'

3. See, especially, *Latter-Day Pamphlets* (1850) III 'Downing Street' and IV 'New Downing Street', although the phrase 'National Palaver' is found much earlier in, for example, *Chartism* Ch. 9 and *Past and Present* Bk. III Chs. 13–4.

4. Compare 'Society, long pining, diabetic, consumptive, can be regarded as defunct; for those spasmodic, galvanic sprawlings are not life; neither indeed will they endure, galvanise as you may, beyond two days' in *Sartor Resartus* (1831) Bk. III Ch. 5; or similar examples in *Past and Present* Bk. II Ch. 15 ('dead or galvanised Dilettantism') and Bk. III Ch. 12 ('[factory workers]... restless, with convulsive energy, as if driven by Galvanism').

philosophy to a 'little mean excise rod' (p. 247),[1] prove to have almost exact precedents in Carlyle. And even the seemingly most casual of one-off references can often be traced back to his words.[2]

Thirdly we can see Carlyle's influence in the rhetorical mode of the novel. The sardonic tone which surfaces in *Hard Times* on many occasions, particularly towards the beginning of the novel, owes much to Carlyle's voice. This is evident, for example, in the metaphors of the mill and the dustheap already mentioned, but we can illustrate it most effectively by a couple of examples of apostrophe (the rhetorical device of direct address to a personified figure by the narrator). The striking passages on p. 47 beginning 'Say, good M'Choakumchild ...' and on p. 192 beginning 'Utilitarian economist, skeletons of schoolmasters ...' are in marked tonal contrast to that at the close of the novel ('Dear reader! It rests with you and me ...' p. 315). The reconciliatory tones of the final paragraph are more characteristic of Dickens's style of narrative address, while the bitterness and aggression of the former two are strongly reminiscent of Carlyle.

The principal effect of the pervasive influence of Carlyle on the novel's content and style is a certain degree of inconsistency of tone, confusion of argument, and blurring of purpose, of which we have already noted a few examples in passing. The most glaring case of confusion in the novel at the narrative level is that over Stephen's promise to Rachael not to join the ranks of organized labour, which is a major turning point in the plot. The account in the manuscript of the promise itself was removed before publication along with Stephen's angry outburst on factory fencing which preceded it (see note on p. 458), although significant unexplained references to it remain in Stephen's speech to his fellow workers

---

1.   Compare *Chartism* Ch. 10: 'Paralytic Radicalism ... which gauges with Statistic measuring reed; sounds with Philosophic Politico-Economic plummet the deep dark sea of troubles.'

2.   For example, the references to the Calmucks of Tartary (p. 132), the Simoom (p. 144), and the story of Sultan who immersed his head in a pail of water (p.152) all have parallels in, respectively: *Chartism* Ch. 10 'Are we Calmucks ...'; *Chartism* Ch. 5 'inanimate Simooms'; and 'Quae Cogitavit' (1833) 'some foolish Mahomedan Caliph, ducking his head in a bucket of enchanted water, and so beating-out one wet minute into seven long years of hardship.'

(pp. 172), in his second interview with Bounderby (p. 178), and in the conversation between Louisa and Rachael in Stephen's lodgings (p. 188). There have been several discussions of the origin of this oversight and why Dickens did not attempt to sort it out during his minor revisions to the novel for the Charles Dickens Edition of 1867–8.[1] One reasonable explanation is that the discrepancy is embedded too deeply in the novel's uncertainties concerning the value of collective action in general and government intervention in particular to allow of such a simple solution. Stephen's arguments and feelings revealed in the deleted passage cannot easily be squared with the derision directed via Slackbridge at Trade Unionism *per se* and via the image of the dustheap at Parliamentary democracy *per se*. And yet evidence of the same complex of ideas remains in Stephen's words to Bounderby on the legitimate grievances of the workers (Bk. II Ch. 5) and in his demands for government action on working conditions and public health just before his death (pp. 291–2).

At the stylistic level, the blurring of focus is most apparent in the metaphorical treatment of the Factory and the Circus, the institutions which represent the deadening force of mechanism and the life-giving force of nature in the novel. It is then unsettling that we repeatedly come across narratorial passages that use one of Dickens's most common rhetorical devices to animate the fabric of the mill and reify the bodies of the performers.[2] Repeatedly we are asked to imagine the factory machinery, smoke, and buildings as elephants, serpents, and fairy palaces (most notably pp. 60, 104, and 144), the very stuff of Circus fantasy,[3] while the

---

1. See: R. B. Woodings 'A Cancelled Passage in *Hard Times*' *Dickensian* 60 (1964) pp. 42–3; Sylvère Monod 'Dickens at Work on the Text of *Hard Times*' *Dickensian* 64 (1968) pp. 86–99; Peter W. J. Bartrip '*Household Words* and the Factory Accident Controversy' *Dickensian* 75 (1979) pp. 17–29; and K. J. Fielding and Anne Smith '*Hard Times* and the Factory Controversy: Dickens vs. Harrriet Martineau' in *Dickens: The Centennial Essays*, ed. Ada Nisbet & Blake Nevius (Berkeley, Cal.: University of California Press, 1970) pp. 22–45.

2. See Dorothy Van Ghent's general discussion of Dickens's use of animation and reification in *The English Novel: Form and Function* (New York: Rinehart, 1953) pp. 127–31.

3. But compare SCHLICKE 1985 pp. 179–80, where it is suggested, unconvincingly to my mind, that these images represent the deformation of the inhabitants' longings for amusement by the harsh industrial environment of Coketown.

riders and clowns like Childers and Kidderminster seem often to be manufactured from bits and pieces (cf. pp. 67–8). Sleary, lumbered from the start with his squint ('one fixed eye and one loose eye') and his lisping voice 'like the efforts of a broken old pair of bellows' (p. 73), is really the most mechanical contrivance in the whole novel. Altogether, *Hard Times*, despite its explicit argument against the role of Fact and for the role of Fancy in human development, is in its own imagery perhaps the least fanciful and most factual of Dickens's creations.

However, a degree of confusion and inconsistency is by no means always fatal to Dickens's fictional enterprise. Indeed, in his more typically profuse and diffuse narrative mode, it seems at worst inevitable and at best a sign of richness and complexity. But in the more single-minded, concentrated, and aggressive mode of *Hard Times* it can hardly be counted as a strength, and it is difficult not to feel that Stephen's 'muddle' gradually becomes more pervasive in the world of the novel in part at least because the author himself is touched by it. But if *Hard Times* functions then in the end less as therapy for and more as a symptom of the disease of early industrial society, we should not be surprised, for, as Raymond WILLIAMS suggests, 'it is a symptom that is significant and continuing' (p. 97). The central conflicts raised directly or indirectly in the novel, between government's duty to intervene to promote social justice and its duty not to intervene to guarantee the liberty of the subject, and between quantitative and qualitative assessments of progress, could not finally have been resolved there, we now know, if only because they are conflicts that remain in the late or post-industrial stages of liberal democracies, whether Britain after Thatcher or the USA after Reagan. Dickens's voice as journalist as well as novelist remains a key one to attend to if we are to understand Victorian society, and studying his interventions in one of the central debates of the period is a more fruitful and enjoyable way than most of entering into its complexities.

Graham Law
Tokyo
February 1996

ACKNOWLEDGEMENTS

I am grateful to the Oxford University Press for permission to reproduce extracts from *The Letters of Charles Dickens: Volume VII 1853–1855* (1993) ed. Graham Storey, Kathleen Tillotson, & Angus Easson.

I would like to thank the staff of the British Library Reading Room, the Victoria and Albert Museum, and the Waseda University Central and Takata Libraries for assistance in locating and viewing materials. Professors Paul Davenport of Hitotsubashi University and Barry V. Qualls of Rutgers University were also generous in loaning materials.

Professor George Hughes of Tokyo University read through the manuscript and offered invaluable advice. Mr. Kazumi Mutoh and Ms. Yuka Aoyagi have assisted me assiduously in checking the text of the novel and the contemporary documents. I also gratefully acknowledge assistance and support on many occasions by members, too numerous to mention by name, of the two electronic conferences in Victorian Studies to which I am subscribed, VICTORIA, run by Patrick Leary of Indiana University, and DICKNS-L, run by Patrick McCarthy of the University of California, Santa Barbara.

A Note on the Text

Hard Times was written at the request of Dickens's four co-partners in *Household Words* (John Forster, W. H. Wills, and the printers Bradbury and Evans) in order to revive the flagging circulation of the weekly journal. Their letter of agreement of 28 December 1853 (App. A 1) shows that Dickens was to retain copyright and to be paid £1,000, not from profits but directly by the other partners in anticipation of the 'enhancement of the value of their several shares.' The length of the work was to be equivalent to 'five single monthly numbers of Bleak House', that is, about a quarter of the length of his previous novel.

As was his practice since beginning *Dombey and Son* in 1846, before starting to write Dickens produced a detailed working plan of the novel, suggesting the length and outlining the narrative and thematic contents of each of the serial parts (see App. A 3). The complete memoranda, dated Friday January 20th 1854, are preserved in the Forster Collection at the Victoria and Albert Museum, London, together with the manuscript and surviving proofs, and are reproduced and transcribed in STONE. According to Dickens's letters (App. A 1b & s), the novel was begun on 23 January 1854 at Tavistock House and completed on 17 July of the same year at the rented villa in Boulogne where Dickens and his family were spending the summer. Dickens's methods of coping with the demands of weekly serialization are described and discussed in detail in BUTT Ch. 7. This was the first time Dickens had written a novel as a weekly serial since *Barnaby Rudge* in 1841; the letters he wrote during the composition of *Hard Times* (App. A 1b–s) repeatedly reveal the intense pressure of the limitation of space that Dickens experienced writing a short, pre-planned work in this form. The story was first published as arranged in *Household Words* in 1854 in twenty weekly parts, as follows:

	Household Words				Present Edition	
Part	Date	Issue No.	Page Nos.	Ch. Nos.	Ch. Nos.	Page Nos.
I	1 Apr	IX 210	141–5	1–3	I 1–3	41–52
II	8 Apr	IX 211	165–70	4–5	I 4–5	53–65
III	15 Apr	IX 212	189–94	6	I 6	66–78
IV	22 Apr	IX 213	213–7	7–8	I 7–8	79–91
V	29 Apr	IX 214	237–42	9–10	I 9–10	91–104
VI	6 May	IX 215	261–6	11–12	I 11–12	104–116
VII	13 May	IX 216	285–90	13–14	I 13–14	117–128
VIII	20 May	IX 217	309–14	15–16	I 15–16	129–141
IX	27 May	IX 218	333–8	17	II 1	143–155
X	3 Jun	IX 219	357–62	18–19	II 2–3	156–168
XI	10 Jun	IX 220	381–6	20–21	II 4–5	169–182
XII	17 Jun	IX 221	405–9	22	II 6	183–194
XIII	24 Jun	IX 222	429–34	23	II 7	194–206
XIV	1 Jul	IX 223	453–8	24	II 8	207–218
XV	8 Jul	IX 224	477–82	25–26	II 9–10	219–231
XVI	15 Jul	IX 225	501–6	27–28	II 11–12	231–244
XVII	22 Jul	IX 226	525–31	29–30	III 1–2	245–259
XVIII	29 Jul	IX 227	549–56	31–32	III 3–4	260–276
XIX	5 Aug	IX 228	573–80	33–34	III 5–6	277–304
XX	12 Aug	IX 229	597–606	35–37	III 7–9	305–315

Each issue of the journal had twenty-four pages of close double-column print without illustrations and was priced 2d; the number from *Hard Times* led off the issue in each case. Following the working memoranda, the length of the numbers increases by around a quarter to a third after Part XVI. Part XX is of double length and comprises the final two of the twenty-one numbers outlined in the working memoranda.

The bound ninth volume of *Household Words* (18 February to 12 August 1854; Nos. 204–229) containing the whole of *Hard Times* in serial form was issued on 16 August 1854 by Bradbury & Evans, priced 5s. 6d. On 7 August 1854 Bradbury & Evans had also issued the novel reset in one volume priced 5s. Though this was advertised as 'carefully revised and wholly reprinted', the only changes of substance were the inclusion of the sub-title 'For these Times' and the dedication to Carlyle, the division of the novel into three named 'books' ('Sowing', 'Reaping', and 'Garnering'), the renumbering of the chapters from one in each 'book', and the addition of chapter titles and running headlines. Dickens also made a number of very minor changes for the revised 'Charles Dickens' edition published by Chapman and Hall in 1868, the last in his lifetime. Significant changes between the manuscript, proofs, serialized version, and volume editions are recorded in the Norton Critical Edition of *Household Words*, edited by George Ford and Sylvère Monod.

The present edition is based on the 'Charles Dickens' edition. Obvious minor errors and inconsistencies have been corrected silently. Number flags in the text mark brief editorial footnotes; asterisk flags refer to the more detailed Explanatory Notes at the end of the volume, which include discussion of significant textual problems.

Select Bibliography

1. Biography and Letters

ACKROYD, Peter. *Dickens.* London: Sinclair-Stevenson, 1990.

FORSTER, John. *The Life of Charles Dickens.* 2 vols. London: Chapman & Hall, 1872–4.

JOHNSON, Edgar. *Charles Dickens: His Tragedy and Triumph.* 2 vols. New York: Simon & Schuster, 1952.

STOREY, Graham, Kathleen Tillotson, & Nina Burgis, eds. *The Letters of Charles Dickens: Volume VI 1850–1852.* Oxford: Clarendon Press, 1988.

STOREY, Graham, Kathleen Tillotson, & Angus Easson, eds. *The Letters of Charles Dickens: Volume VII 1853–1855.* Oxford: Clarendon Press, 1993.

2. Bibliographies and Editions

CRAIG, David, ed. *Charles Dickens: 'Hard Times.'* Harmondsworth, Middlesex: Penguin, 1969.

EASSON, Andrew. *Hard Times: A Critical Commentary.* London: London University Press, 1973.

FORD, George & Sylvère Monod, eds. *Charles Dickens: 'Hard Times.'* New York: Norton, 1966; 2nd edition, 1990.

MANNING, Sylvia. *Hard Times: An Annotated Bibliography.* New York: Garland, 1984.

SCHLICKE, Paul, ed. *Charles Dickens: 'Hard Times.'* Oxford: Oxford University Press, 1989.

SHAW, George Bernard, ed. *Charles Dickens: 'Hard Times.'* London: Waverley, 1913.

3. Literary History and Criticism

BLOOM, Harold, ed. *Charles Dickens's 'Hard Times'* (Modern Critical Interpretations). New York: Chelsea House, 1987.

BRANTLINGER, Patrick. *The Spirit of Reform: British Literature and Politics, 1832–67.* Cambridge, Massachusetts: Harvard University Press, 1977.

BUTT, John & Kathleen Tillotson. *Dickens at Work*. London: Methuen, 1957.

CAZAMIAN, Louis. *The Social Novel in England 1830–1850*. 1903. Translated by Martin Fido. London: Routledge & Kegan Paul, 1973.

CHESTERTON, G. K. *Charles Dickens*. London: Methuen, 1906.

COLLINS, Philip. *Dickens and Crime*. London: Macmillan, 1962.

COLLINS, Philip. *Dickens and Education*. London: Macmillan, 1963.

GOLDBERG, Michael. *Carlyle and Dickens*. Athens, Georgia: University of Georgia Press, 1972.

GRAY, Paul E., ed. *Twentieth-Century Interpretations of 'Hard Times.'* Englewood Cliffs, New Jersey: Prentice-Hall, 1969.

HOUSE, Humphrey. *The Dickens World*. London: Oxford University Press, 1942.

KESTNER, Joseph. *Protest and Reform: The British Social Narrative by Women, 1827–1865*. Madison, Wisconsin: University of Wisconsin Press, 1984.

LEAVIS, F. R. *The Great Tradition*. London: Chatto & Windus, 1948.

MITCHELL, Sally, ed. *Victorian Britain: An Encyclopedia*. New York: Garland, 1988.

NISBET, Ada & Blake Nevius, eds. *Dickens: The Centennial Essays*. Berkeley, California: University of California Press, 1970.

ODDIE, William. *Dickens and Carlyle: The Question of Influence*. London: Centenary Press, 1972.

SCHLICKE, Paul. *Dickens and Popular Entertainment*. London: Allen & Unwin, 1985.

SMITH, Sheila M. *The Other Nation: The Poor in English Novels of the 1840s and 1850s*. Oxford: Oxford University Press, 1980.

STONE, Harry. *Dickens' Working Notes for his Novels*. Chicago: University of Chicago Press, 1987.

TILLOTSON, Kathleen. *Novels of the 1840s*. London: Oxford University Press, 1954.

4. Social and Intellectual History

ALTICK, Richard D. *The English Common Reader: A Social History of the Mass Reading Public 1800–1900*. Chicago: University of Chicago Press, 1957.

BRIGGS, Asa. *Victorian Cities.* London: Odhams Press, 1963.

BRIGGS, Asa. *The Age of Improvement, 1783–1867.* West Drayton, Middlesex: Penguin, 1947.

CHADWICK, Edwin. *The Sanitary Condition of the Labouring Population of Great Britain.* Edited by M.W. Flinn. Edinburgh: Edinburgh University Press, 1965.

HALÉVY, Élie. *The Growth of Philosophical Radicalism.* 1901. Translated by Mary Morris. London: Faber & Gwyer, 1928.

HAMMOND, J. L. & Barbara Hammond. *The Age of the Chartists 1832–1854: A Study of Discontent.* 1930; reprinted, New York: Augustus M. Kelley, 1967.

HOBSBAWM, E. J. *Industry and Empire.* Harmondsworth, Middlesex: Penguin, 1969

KAY, J. P. *The Moral and Physical Condition of the Working Classes Employed in the Cotton Manufacture in Manchester.* 2nd edition. London: J. Ridgway, 1832.

LYONS, David. *Forms and Limits of Utilitarianism.* Oxford: Oxford University Press, 1965.

NEFF, Emery. *Carlyle and Mill: An Introduction to Victorian Thought.* 2nd Revised Edition. New York: Columbia University Press, 1926.

STONE, Lawrence. *The Road to Divorce.* Oxford: Oxford University Press, 1992.

WILLIAMS, Raymond. *Culture and Society 1780–1950.* London: Chatto & Windus, 1958.

WING, Charles. *The Evils of the Factory System.* London: Saunders & Otley, 1837.

WOHL, Anthony S. *Endangered Lives: Public Health in Victorian Britain.* London: J.M. Dent, 1983.

Charles Dickens: A Brief Chronology

1812   Born Charles John Huffam Dickens at Portsmouth, second child and eldest son of John, a naval clerk, and Elizabeth Dickens.

1817   Family moves briefly to Sheerness and then to Chatham, both in Kent.

1822   Family moves to Camden Town in North London.

1824   Father imprisoned for three months for debt in the Marshalsea prison. Employed in a blacking warehouse. Enters Wellington House Academy.

1827   Enters solicitor's office as clerk.

1829   Studies shorthand and becomes a parliamentary and news reporter. Falls in love with Maria Beadell.

1833   Stories appear in the *Monthly Magazine*.

1834   Becomes reporter on the *Morning Chronicle*.

1835   'Sketches of London' appear in the *Evening Chronicle*.

1836   *Sketches by Boz* published in volume form in two series. Marries Catherine Hogarth, daughter of editor of the *Evening Chronicle*. Lives at Furnival's Inn, London. Meets John Forster.

1837   Becomes editor of *Bentley's Miscellany* for two years. *Pickwick Papers* appears in volume form, following publication in monthly parts. Son born, first of ten children by Catherine Hogarth. Family moves to Doughty Street, London. Death of wife's sister, Mary Hogarth.

1838   *Oliver Twist* appears in volume form following monthly serialization in *Bentley's Miscellany*. Visits schools in Yorkshire in preparing to write *Nicholas Nickleby*.

1839   *Nicholas Nickleby* appears in volume form following publication in monthly parts. Family moves to Devonshire Terrace, London.

1840   *Master Humphrey's Clock*, written entirely by Dickens, initially as a miscellany, appears weekly for around eighteen months.

1841   *The Old Curiosity Shop* and later *Barnaby Rudge* appear in volume form following serialization in *Master Humphrey's Clock*.

1842   Travels with his wife in USA and Canada for six months. *American Notes* published in volume form.

1843   *A Christmas Carol* appears as Christmas book.

1844   *Martin Chuzzlewit* appears in volume form following publication in monthly parts. Family move to Italy for around a year. *The Chimes* appears as Christmas book.

1845   *The Cricket on the Hearth* appears as Christmas book.

1846   Acts as founding editor of the *Daily News* for a brief period. *Pictures from Italy* appears in volume form following publication as a series of 'Travelling Letters' in the *Daily News*. Family moves to Lausanne, Switzerland, and then Paris for a total period of over six months. *The Battle of Life* appears as Christmas book.

1847   Begins to assist Miss Burdett Coutts in the running of a home for reformed prostitutes (until 1858).

1848   *Dombey and Son* appears in volume form following publication in monthly parts. Begins to organize and act in private and charitable theatrical performances. *The Haunted Man* appears as Christmas book.

1850   Begins running *Household Words* as weekly journal, owned jointly with Bradbury & Evans. *David Copperfield* appears in volume form following publication in monthly parts.

1851   Father dies. Family moves to Tavistock House, Tavistock Square, London. Meets Wilkie Collins. *A Child's History of England* begins appearing in weekly parts in *Household Words*, continuing for three years.

1852   Last child born to Catherine Hogarth.

1853   *Bleak House* appears in volume form following publication in monthly parts. First public readings from his own works.

1854   Visits Preston, Lancashire, to observe strike by textile workers, in preparation for writing *Hard Times*. *Hard Times* appears in volume form following weekly serialization in *Household Words*.

1855   Moves to France with family for almost a year.

1856   Buys Gad's Hill Place, near Rochester, Kent.

1857   *Little Dorrit* appears in volume form following publication in monthly parts. Organizes and stars in charitable performances of *The Frozen Deep*, a melodrama by Wilkie Collins; falls in love with Ellen Ternan, a young actress in the company. *The Lazy Tour of Two Idle Apprentices* (in parts) and *The Perils of Certain English Prisoners* (Christmas number), written in collaboration with Wilkie Collins, appear in *Household Words*.

1858   *Reprinted Pieces* (articles from *Household Words*) published in volume form. Begins series of public readings for profit. Separates from his wife; issues personal statement defending his behavior in *Household Words*.

1859   Breaks off all links with Bradbury & Evans, buying out its share in *Household Words*, which was then replaced by *All the Year Round*, a similar weekly family journal. *A Tale of Two Cities* appears in volume form following publication as a weekly serial in *All the Year Round* and in monthly parts.

1860   Sells Tavistock House and lives permanently at Gad's Hill Place.

1861   *The Uncommercial Traveller*, papers reprinted from *All the Year Round*, published in volume form. *Great Expectations* appears in volume form following weekly serialization in *All the Year Round*. Begins second series of public readings (until 1863).

1863   Son Walter dies in India. Mother dies. 'Mrs Lirriper's Lodgings' appears in Christmas number of *All the Year Round*.

1864   'Mrs Lirriper's Legacy' appears in Christmas number of *All the Year Round*.

1865   *Our Mutual Friend* appears in volume form following publication in monthly parts. Suffers serious train crash while traveling with Ellen Ternan. 'Dr Marigold's Prescriptions' appears in Christmas number of *All the Year Round*.

1866   Begins third series of public readings (until 1867).

1867   Begins six-month public reading tour of USA. *No Thoroughfare*, in collaboration with Wilkie Collins, published in Christmas issue of *All the Year Round*.

1868   Begins fourth series of public readings (until 1869), leading to physical breakdown. Second expanded edition of *The Uncommercial Traveller*.

1870   Farewell season of public readings in London. First half of *The Mystery of Edwin Drood* issued in monthly parts and left incomplete. Collapses and dies at Gad's Hill Place. Buried in Westminster Abbey.

HARD TIMES.

FOR THESE TIMES.

BY CHARLES DICKENS.

Inscribed

TO

THOMAS CARLYLE

Contents

Book the Third.   Garnering.

Book the First. Sowing[1]

Chapter I.
The One Thing Needful[2]

"Now, what I want is, Facts. Teach these boys and girls nothing but Facts. Facts alone are wanted in life. Plant nothing else, and root out everything else. You can only form the minds of reasoning animals upon Facts: nothing else will ever be of any service to them. This is the principle on which I bring up my own children, and this is the principle on which I bring up these children. Stick to Facts, sir!"

The scene was a plain, bare, monotonous vault of a school-room, and the speaker's square forefinger emphasized his observation by underscoring every sentence with a line on the schoolmaster's sleeve. The emphasis was helped by the speaker's square wall of a forehead, which had his eyebrows for its base, while his eyes found commodious cellarage in two dark caves, overshadowed by the wall. The emphasis was helped by the speaker's mouth, which was wide, thin, and hard set. The emphasis was helped by the speaker's voice, which was inflexible, dry, and dictatorial. The emphasis was helped by the speaker's hair, which bristled on the skirts of his bald head, a plantation of firs to keep the wind from its shining surface, all covered with knobs, like the crust of a plum pie, as if the head had scarcely warehouse-room for the hard facts stored inside. The speaker's obstinate carriage, square coat, square legs, square shoulders,—nay, his very neckcloth, trained to take him by the throat with an unaccommodating grasp, like a stubborn fact, as it was,—all helped the emphasis.

"In this life, we want nothing but Facts, sir; nothing but Facts!"

The speaker, and the schoolmaster, and the third grown person present, all backed a little, and swept with their eyes the inclined plane of little

---

1. See the General Introduction p. 21.
2. See the story of Martha and Mary in Luke 10:38–42.

vessels then and there arranged in order, ready to have imperial gallons[1] of facts poured into them until they were full to the brim.

CHAPTER II.
MURDERING THE INNOCENTS[2]

THOMAS GRADGRIND, sir. A man of realities. A man of facts and calculations. A man who proceeds upon the principle that two and two are four, and nothing over, and who is not to be talked into allowing for anything over. Thomas Gradgrind, sir—peremptorily Thomas—Thomas Gradgrind. With a rule and a pair of scales, and the multiplication table always in his pocket, sir, ready to weigh and measure any parcel of human nature, and tell you exactly what it comes to. It is a mere question of figures, a case of simple arithmetic. You might hope to get some other nonsensical belief into the head of George Gradgrind, or Augustus Gradgrind, or John Gradgrind, or Joseph Gradgrind (all supposititious, non-existent persons), but into the head of Thomas Gradgrind—no, sir!

In such terms Mr. Gradgrind always mentally introduced himself, whether to his private circle of acquaintance, or to the public in general. In such terms, no doubt, substituting the words "boys and girls," for "sir," Thomas Gradgrind now presented Thomas Gradgrind to the little pitchers before him, who were to be filled so full of facts.

Indeed, as he eagerly sparkled at them from the cellarage before mentioned, he seemed a kind of cannon loaded to the muzzle with facts, and prepared to blow them clean out of the regions of childhood at one discharge. He seemed a galvanizing apparatus,[3] too, charged with a grim mechanical substitute for the tender young imaginations that were to be stormed away.

---

1.   Liquid measure appointed by statute to be employed throughout the United Kingdom, in distinction to earlier local standards.
2.   Compare the story of Herod's attempt to destroy the infant Jesus, traditionally known as the Slaughter of the Innocents, in Matthew 2:16.
3.   I.e. a machine to stimulate or simulate life by injecting electrical current, after the therapeutic technique invented by Luigi Galvani in 1792.

"Girl number twenty," said Mr. Gradgrind, squarely pointing with his square forefinger, "I don't know that girl. Who is that girl?"

"Sissy Jupe, sir," explained number twenty, blushing, standing up, and curtseying.

"Sissy is not a name," said Mr. Gradgrind. "Don't call yourself Sissy. Call yourself Cecilia."

"It's father as calls me Sissy, sir," returned the young girl in a trembling voice, and with another curtsey.

"Then he has no business to do it," said Mr. Gradgrind. "Tell him he mustn't. Cecilia Jupe. Let me see. What is your father?"

"He belongs to the horse-riding, if you please, sir."

Mr. Gradgrind frowned, and waved off the objectionable calling with his hand.

"We don't want to know anything about that, here. You mustn't tell us about that, here. Your father breaks horses, don't he?"

"If you please, sir, when they can get any to break, they do break horses in the ring, sir."

"You mustn't tell us about the ring, here. Very well, then. Describe your father as a horsebreaker. He doctors sick horses, I dare say?"

"Oh yes, sir."

"Very well, then. He is a veterinary surgeon, a farrier, and horsebreaker. Give me your definition of a horse."

(Sissy Jupe thrown into the greatest alarm by this demand.)

"Girl number twenty unable to define a horse!" said Mr. Gradgrind, for the general behoof of all the little pitchers. "Girl number twenty possessed of no facts, in reference to one of the commonest animals! Some boy's definition of a horse. Bitzer, yours."

The square finger, moving here and there, lighted suddenly on Bitzer, perhaps because he chanced to sit in the same ray of sunlight which, darting in at one of the bare windows of the intensely whitewashed room, irradiated Sissy. For, the boys and girls sat on the face of the inclined plane in two compact bodies, divided up the centre by a narrow interval; and Sissy, being at the corner of a row on the sunny side, came in for the beginning of a sunbeam, of which Bitzer, being at the corner of a row on the other side, a few rows in advance, caught the end. But, whereas the girl was so dark-eyed and dark-haired, that she seemed to receive a deeper and more lustrous colour from the sun, when it shone upon her, the boy was so light-eyed and light-haired that the self-same rays appeared to draw out of him what little colour he ever possessed. His cold eyes would hardly have been eyes, but for the short ends of lashes which, by bringing them into immediate contrast with something paler than themselves, expressed their form. His short-cropped hair might have been a mere continuation of the sandy freckles on his forehead and face. His skin was so unwholesomely deficient in the natural tinge, that he looked as though, if he were cut, he would bleed white.

"Bitzer," said Thomas Gradgrind. "Your definition of a horse."

"Quadruped. Graminivorous. Forty teeth, namely twenty-four grinders, four eye-teeth, and twelve incisive. Sheds coat in the spring; in marshy countries, sheds hoofs, too. Hoofs hard, but requiring to be shod with iron. Age known by marks in mouth." Thus (and much more) Bitzer.

"Now girl number twenty," said Mr. Gradgrind. "You know what a horse is."*

She curtseyed again, and would have blushed deeper, if she could have blushed deeper than she had blushed all this time. Bitzer, after rapidly blinking at Thomas Gradgrind with both eyes at once, and so catching the light upon his quivering ends of lashes that they looked like the antennæ of busy insects, put his knuckles to his freckled forehead, and sat down again.

The third gentleman now stepped forth. A mighty man at cutting and drying, he was; a government officer; in his way (and in most other people's too), a professed pugilist;[1] always in training, always with a system to force down the general throat like a bolus,[2] always to be heard of at the bar of his little Public-office, ready to fight all England. To continue in fistic phraseology, he had a genius for coming up to the scratch, wherever and whatever it was, and proving himself an ugly customer. He would go in and damage any subject whatever with his right, follow up

---

1.   Prizefighter, barefist boxer. The metaphor is extended throughout this paragraph by the introduction of many items of boxing slang (e.g. 'ugly customer') or technical terminology (e.g. 'up to the scratch') from the London Prize Ring rules then in force.

2.   Medicine in the form of a pellet or thick paste, often used in a contemptuous, figurative sense.

with his left, stop, exchange, counter, bore his opponent (he always fought All England) to the ropes, and fall upon him neatly. He was certain to knock the wind out of common sense, and render that unlucky adversary deaf to the call of time. And he had it in charge from high authority to bring about the great public-office Millennium, when the Commissioners should reign upon earth.[1]

"Very well," said this gentleman, briskly smiling, and folding his arms. "That's a horse. Now, let me ask you girls and boys, Would you paper a room with representations of horses?"

After a pause, one half of the children cried in chorus, "Yes, sir!" Upon which the other half, seeing in the gentleman's face that Yes was wrong, cried out in chorus, "No, sir!"—as the custom is, in these examinations.

"Of course, No. Why wouldn't you?"

A pause. One corpulent slow boy, with a wheezy manner of breathing, ventured the answer, Because he wouldn't paper a room at all, but would paint it.

"You *must* paper it," said the gentleman, rather warmly.

"You must paper it," said Thomas Gradgrind, "whether you like it or not. Don't tell *us* you wouldn't paper it. What do you mean, boy?"

"I'll explain to you, then," said the gentleman, after another and a dismal pause, "why you wouldn't paper a room with representations of horses. Do you ever see horses walking up and down the sides of rooms in reality—in fact? Do you?"

"Yes, sir!" from one half. "No, sir!" from the other.

"Of course no," said the gentleman, with an indignant look at the wrong half. "Why, then, you are not to see anywhere, what you don't see in fact; you are not to have anywhere, what you don't have in fact. What is called Taste, is only another name for Fact."

Thomas Gradgrind nodded his approbation.

"This is a new principle, a discovery, a great discovery," said the gentleman. "Now, I'll try you again. Suppose you were going to carpet a room. Would you use a carpet having a representation of flowers upon it?"

---

1.   Compare the apocalyptic account of the thousand-year reign of Christ and his Saints on earth in Revelation 20:1–15. Figuratively, a Millennium refers to a period of benign government and public happiness.

There being a general conviction by this time that "No, sir!" was always the right answer to this gentleman, the chorus of No was very strong. Only a few feeble stragglers said Yes: among them Sissy Jupe.

"Girl number twenty," said the gentleman, smiling in the calm strength of knowledge.

Sissy blushed, and stood up.

"So you would carpet your room—or your husband's room, if you were a grown woman, and had a husband—with representations of flowers, would you?" said the gentleman. "Why would you?"

"If you please, sir, I am very fond of flowers," returned the girl.

"And is that why you would put tables and chairs upon them, and have people walking over them with heavy boots?"

"It wouldn't hurt them, sir. They wouldn't crush and wither, if you please, sir. They would be the pictures of what was very pretty and pleasant, and I would fancy—"

"Ay, ay, ay! But you mustn't fancy," cried the gentleman, quite elated by coming so happily to his point. "That's it! You are never to fancy."

"You are not, Cecilia Jupe," Thomas Gradgrind solemnly repeated, "to do anything of that kind."

"Fact, fact, fact!" said the gentleman. And "Fact, fact, fact!" repeated Thomas Gradgrind.

"You are to be in all things regulated and governed," said the gentleman, "by fact. We hope to have, before long, a board of fact, composed of commissioners of fact, who will force the people to be a people of fact, and of nothing but fact. You must discard the word Fancy altogether. You have nothing to do with it. You are not to have, in any object of use or ornament, what would be a contradiction in fact. You don't want upon flowers in fact; you cannot be allowed to walk upon flowers in carpets. You don't find that foreign birds and butterflies come and perch upon your crockery; you cannot be permitted to paint foreign birds and butterflies upon your crockery. You never meet with quadrupeds going up and down walls; you must not have quadrupeds represented upon walls. You must use," said the gentleman, "for all these purposes, combinations and modifications (in primary colours) of mathematical figures which are susceptible of proof and demonstration. This is the new discovery. This is fact. This is taste."*

The girl curtseyed and sat down. She was very young, and she looked as if she were frightened by the matter-of-fact prospect the world afforded.

"Now, if Mr. M'Choakumchild," said the gentleman, "will proceed to give his first lesson here, Mr. Gradgrind, I shall be happy, at your request, to observe his mode of procedure."

Mr. Gradgrind was much obliged. "Mr. M'Choakumchild, we only wait for you."

So, Mr. M'Choakumchild began in his best manner. He and some one hundred and forty other schoolmasters, had been lately turned at the same time, in the same factory, on the same principles, like so many pianoforte legs. He had been put through an immense variety of paces, and had answered volumes of head-breaking questions. Orthography, etymology, syntax, and prosody, biography, astronomy, geography, and general cosmography, the sciences of compound proportion, algebra, landsurveying and levelling, vocal music, and drawing from models, were all at the ends of his ten chilled fingers. He had worked his stony way into Her Majesty's most Honourable Privy Council's Schedule B, and had taken the bloom off the higher branches of mathematics and physical science, French, German, Latin, and Greek. He knew all about all the Water Sheds[1] of all the world (whatever they are), and all the histories of all the peoples, and all the names of all the rivers and mountains, and all the productions, manners, and customs of all the countries, and all their boundaries and bearings on the two and thirty points of the compass. Ah, rather overdone, M'Choakumchild. If he had only learnt a little less, how infinitely better he might have taught much more!*

He went to work in this preparatory lesson, not unlike Morgiana in the Forty Thieves:[2] looking into all the vessels ranged before him, one after another, to see what they contained. Say, good M'Choakumchild. When from thy boiling store, thou shalt fill each jar brim full by-and-by, dost thou think that thou wilt always kill outright the robber Fancy lurking within—or sometimes only maim him and distort him!

---

1.   I.e. watersheds, as misunderstood unintentionally by the pupils and intentionally by the narrator.

2.   Ali Baba's slave-girl (often transcribed as Murganah) who pours boiling oil on the thieves hiding in the pots and thus saves her master, in the story from *The Arabian Nights' Entertainments*.

CHAPTER III.
A LOOPHOLE

MR. GRADGRIND walked homeward from the school, in a state of considerable satisfaction. It was his school, and he intended it to be a model. He intended every child in it to be a model—just as the young Gradgrinds were all models.

There were five young Gradgrinds, and they were models every one. They had been lectured at, from their tenderest years; coursed, like little hares. Almost as soon as they could run alone, they had been made to run to the lecture-room. The first object with which they had an association, or of which they had a remembrance, was a large black board with a dry Ogre chalking ghastly white figures on it.

Not that they knew, by name or nature, anything about an Ogre. Fact forbid! I only use the word to express a monster in a lecturing castle, with Heaven knows how many heads manipulated into one, taking childhood captive, and dragging it into gloomy statistical dens by the hair.

No little Gradgrind had ever seen a face in the moon; it was up in the moon before it could speak distinctly. No little Gradgrind had ever learnt the silly jingle, Twinkle, twinkle, little star; how I wonder what you are! No little Gradgrind had ever known wonder on the subject, each little Gradgrind having at five years old dissected the Great Bear[1] like a Professor Owen,[2] and driven Charles's Wain[3] like a locomotive engine-driver. No little Gradgrind had ever associated a cow in a field with that famous cow with the crumpled horn[4] who tossed the dog who worried the cat who killed the rat who ate the malt, or with that yet more famous cow who swallowed Tom Thumb:[5] it had never heard of those celebrities, and had only been introduced to a cow as a graminivorous ruminating quadruped with several stomachs.

---

1.   The star group Ursa Major.
2.   Sir Richard Owen (1804–92), pioneering anatomist and paleontologist.
3.   Another name for Ursa Major, meaning Charlemagne's Carriage.
4.   In the traditional nursery rhyme 'The House that Jack Built.'
5.   In the nursery tale named for its diminutive hero, first found in French in Charles Perrault's seventeenth-century collection of fairy tales.

To his matter-of-fact home, which was called Stone Lodge, Mr. Gradgrind directed his steps. He had virtually retired from the wholesale hardware trade before he built Stone Lodge, and was now looking about for a suitable opportunity of making an arithmetical figure in Parliament. Stone Lodge was situated on a moor within a mile or two of a great town—called Coketown in the present faithful guide-book.*

A very regular feature on the face of the country, Stone Lodge was. Not the least disguise toned down or shaded off that uncompromising fact in the landscape. A great square house, with a heavy portico darkening the principal windows, as its master's heavy brows overshadowed his eyes. A calculated, cast up, balanced, and proved house. Six windows on this side of the door, six on that side; a total of twelve in this wing, a total of twelve in the other wing; four-and-twenty carried over to the back wings. A lawn and garden and an infant avenue, all ruled straight like a botanical account-book. Gas and ventilation, drainage and water-service, all of the primest quality. Iron clamps and girders, fireproof from top to bottom; mechanical lifts for the house-maids, with all their brushes and brooms; everything that heart could desire.

Everything? Well, I suppose so. The little Gradgrinds had cabinets in various departments of science too. They had a little conchological cabinet, and a little metallurgical cabinet, and a little mineralogical cabinet; and the specimens were all arranged and labelled, and the bits of stone and ore looked as though they might have been broken from the parent substances by those tremendously hard instruments their own names; and, to paraphrase the idle legend of Peter Piper,[1] who had never found his way into *their* nursery, If the greedy little Gradgrinds grasped at more than this, what was it for good gracious goodness' sake, that the greedy little Gradgrinds grasped at!

Their father walked on in a hopeful and satisfied frame of mind. He was an affectionate father, after his manner; but he would probably have described himself (if he had been put, like Sissy Jupe, upon a definition) as "an eminently practical" father. He had a particular pride in the phrase eminently practical, which was considered to have a special application

---

1. The tongue-twisting nursery rhyme beginning 'Peter Piper picked a peck of pickled pepper ....'

to him. Whatsoever the public meeting held in Coketown, and whatsoever the subject of such meeting, some Coketowner was sure to seize the occasion of alluding to his eminently practical friend Gradgrind. This always pleased the eminently practical friend. He knew it to be his due, but his due was acceptable.

He had reached the neutral ground upon the outskirts of the town, which was neither town nor country, and yet was either spoiled, when his ears were invaded by the sound of music. The clashing and banging band attached to the horse-riding establishment, which had there set up its rest in a wooden pavilion was in full bray. A flag, floating from the summit of the temple, proclaimed to mankind it was "Sleary's Horse-riding" which claimed their suffrages. Sleary himself, a stout modern statue with a money-box at its elbow, in an ecclesiastical niche of early Gothic architecture, took the money. Miss Josephine Sleary, as some very long and very narrow strips of printed bill announced, was then inaugurating the entertainments with her graceful equestrian Tyrolean flower-act. Among the other pleasing but always strictly moral wonders which must be seen to be believed, Signor Jupe was that afternoon to "elucidate the diverting accomplishments of his highly trained performing dog Merrylegs." He was also to exhibit "his astounding feat of throwing seventy-five hundred-weight in rapid succession backhanded over his head, thus forming a fountain of solid iron in mid-air, a feat never before attempted in this or any other country, and which having elicited such rapturous plaudits from enthusiastic throngs it cannot be withdrawn." The same Signor Jupe was to "enliven the varied performances at frequent intervals with his chaste Shakesperean quips and retorts." Lastly, he was to wind them up by appearing in his favourite character of Mr. William Button, of Tooley Street, in "the highly novel and laughable hippo-comedietta of The Tailor's Journey to Brentford."*

Thomas Gradgrind took no heed of these trivialities of course, but passed on as a practical man ought to pass on, either brushing the noisy insects from his thoughts, or consigning them to the House of Correction.[1] But, the turning of the road took him by the back of the booth,

---

1. Prison, reformatory. The term was in use from at least the sixteenth to the late nineteenth century.

and at the back of the booth a number of children were congregated in a number of stealthy attitudes, striving to peep in at the hidden glories of the place.

This brought him to a stop. "Now, to think of these vagabonds," said he, "attracting the young rabble from a model school."[1]

A space of stunted grass and dry rubbish being between him and the young rabble, he took his eyeglass out of his waistcoat to look for any child he knew by name, and might order off. Phenomenon almost incredible though distinctly seen, what did he then behold but his own metallurgical Louisa, peeping with all her might through a hole in a deal board, and his own mathematical Thomas abasing himself on the ground to catch but a hoof of the graceful equestrian Tyrolean flower-act!

Dumb with amazement, Mr. Gradgrind crossed to the spot where his family was thus disgraced, laid his hand upon each erring child, and said:

"Louisa!! Thomas!!"

Both rose, red and disconcerted. But, Louisa looked at her father with more boldness than Thomas did. Indeed, Thomas did not look at him, but gave himself up to be taken home like a machine.

"In the name of wonder, idleness, and folly!" said Mr. Gradgrind, leading each away by a hand; "what do you do here?"

"Wanted to see what it was like," returned Louisa, shortly.

"What it was like?"

"Yes, father."

There was an air of jaded sullenness in them both, and particularly in the girl: yet, struggling through the dissatisfaction on her face, there was a light with nothing to rest upon, a fire with nothing to burn, a starved imagination keeping life in itself somehow, which brightened its expression. Not with the brightness natural to cheerful youth, but with uncertain, eager, doubtful flashes, which had something painful in them, analogous to the changes on a blind face groping its way.

She was a child now, of fifteen or sixteen; but at no distant day would seem to become a woman all at once. Her father thought so as he looked

---

1.   See explanatory note to p. 55.

at her. She was pretty. Would have been self-willed (he thought in his eminently practical way) but for her bringing-up.

"Thomas, though I have the fact before me, I find it difficult to believe that you, with your education and resources, should have brought your sister to a scene like this."

"I brought *him*, father," said Louisa quickly, "I asked him to come."

"I am sorry to hear it. I am very sorry indeed to hear it. It makes Thomas no better, and it makes you worse, Louisa."

She looked at her father again, but no tear fell down her cheek.

"You! Thomas and you, to whom the circle of the sciences is open; Thomas and you, who may be said to be replete with facts; Thomas and you, who have been trained to mathematical exactness; Thomas and you, here!" cried Mr. Gradgrind. "In this degraded position! I am amazed."

"I was tired, father. I have been tired a long time," said Louisa.

"Tired? Of what?" asked the astonished father.

"I don't know of what—of everything, I think."

"Say not another word," returned Mr. Gradgrind. "You are childish. I will hear no more." He did not speak again until they had walked some half-mile in silence, when he gravely broke out with: "What would your best friends say, Louisa? Do you attach no value to their good opinion? What would Mr. Bounderby say?"

At the mention of this name, his daughter stole a look at him, remarkable for its intense and searching character. He saw nothing of it, for before he looked at her, she had again cast down her eyes!

"What," he repeated presently, "would Mr. Bounderby say?" All the way to Stone Lodge, as with grave indignation he led the two delinquents home, he repeated at intervals "What would Mr. Bounderby say?"—as if Mr. Bounderby had been Mrs. Grundy.[1]

---

1. Imaginary person in Thomas Morton's play *Speed the Plough* (1798), who became the proverbial representative of derided conventional moral and social propriety throughout the nineteenth century.

CHAPTER IV.
MR. BOUNDERBY

NOT BEING Mrs. Grundy, who *was* Mr. Bounderby?

Why, Mr. Bounderby was as near being Mr. Gradgrind's bosom friend, as a man perfectly devoid of sentiment can approach that spiritual relationship towards another man perfectly devoid of sentiment. So near was Mr. Bounderby—or, if the reader should prefer it, so far off.

He was a rich man: banker, merchant, manufacturer, and what not. A big, loud man, with a stare, and a metallic laugh. A man made out of coarse material, which seemed to have been stretched to make so much of him. A man with a great puffed head and forehead, swelled veins in his temples, and such a strained skin to his face that it seemed to hold his eyes open, and lift his eyebrows up. A man with a pervading appearance on him of being inflated like a balloon, and ready to start. A man who could never sufficiently vaunt himself a self-made man. A man who was always proclaiming, through that brassy speaking-trumpet of a voice of his, his old ignorance and his old poverty. A man who was the Bully of humility.[1]

A year or two younger than his eminently practical friend, Mr. Bounderby looked older; his seven or eight and forty might have had the seven or eight added to it again, without surprising anybody. He had not much hair. One might have fancied he had talked it off; and that what was left, all standing up in disorder, was in that condition from being constantly blown about by his windy boastfulness.

In the formal dining-room of Stone Lodge, standing on the hearthrug, warming himself by the fire, Mr. Bounderby delivered some observations to Mrs. Gradgrind on the circumstance of its being his birthday. He stood before the fire, partly because it was a cool spring afternoon, though the sun shone; partly because the shade of Stone Lodge was always haunted by the ghost of damp mortar; partly because he thus took up a commanding position, from which to subdue Mrs. Gradgrind.

---

1.   I.e. he swaggers on the basis of his lowly origins. This oxymoronic epithet is applied to Bounderby on several future occasions (e.g. p. 79).

"I hadn't a shoe to my foot. As to a stocking, I didn't know such a thing by name. I passed the day in a ditch, and the night in a pigsty. That's the way I spent my tenth birthday. Not that a ditch was new to me, for I was born in a ditch."

Mrs. Gradgrind, a little, thin, white, pink-eyed bundle of shawls, of surpassing feebleness, mental and bodily; who was always taking physic without any effect, and who, whenever she showed symptom of coming to life, was invariably stunned by some weighty piece of fact tumbling on her; Mrs. Gradgrind hoped it was a dry ditch?

"No! As wet as a sop. A foot of water in it," said Mr. Bounderby.

"Enough to give a baby cold," Mrs. Gradgrind considered.

"Cold? I was born with inflammation of the lungs, and of everything else, I believe, that was capable of inflammation," returned Mr. Bounderby. "For years, ma'am, I was one of the most miserable little wretches ever seen. I was so sickly, that I was always moaning and groaning. I was so ragged and dirty, that you wouldn't have touched me with a pair of tongs."

Mrs. Gradgrind faintly looked at the tongs, as the most appropriate thing her imbecility could think of doing.

"How I fought through it, I don't know," said Bounderby. "I was determined, I suppose. I have been a determined character in later life, and I suppose I was then. Here I am, Mrs. Gradgrind, anyhow, and nobody to thank for my being here, but myself."

Mrs. Gradgrind meekly and weakly hoped that his mother—

"*My* mother? Bolted, ma'am!" said Bounderby.

Mrs. Gradgrind, stunned as usual, collapsed and gave it up.

"My mother left me to my grandmother," said Bounderby; "and, according to the best of my remembrance, my grandmother was the wickedest and the worst old woman that ever lived. If I got a little pair of shoes by any chance, she would take 'em off and sell 'em for a drink. Why, I have known that grandmother of mine lie in her bed and drink her fourteen glasses of liquor before breakfast!"

Mrs. Gradgrind, weakly smiling, and giving no other sign of vitality, looked (as she always did) like an indifferently executed transparency of a small female figure, without enough light behind it.

"She kept a chandler's shop," pursued Bounderby, "and kept me in an egg-box. That was the cot of *my* infancy; an old egg-box. As soon as I was big enough to run away, of course I ran away. Then I became a young vagabond; and instead of one old woman knocking me about and starving me, everybody of all ages knocked me about and starved me. They were right; they had no business to do anything else. I was a nuisance, an incumbrance, and a pest. I know that very well."

His pride in having at any time of his life achieved such a great social distinction as to be a nuisance, an incumbrance, and a pest, was only to be satisfied by three sonorous repetitions of the boast.

"I was to pull through it, I suppose, Mrs. Gradgrind. Whether I was to do it or not, ma'am, I did it. I pulled through it, though nobody threw me out a rope. Vagabond, errand-boy, vagabond, labourer, porter, clerk, chief manager, small partner, Josiah Bounderby of Coketown. Those are the antecedents, and the culmination. Josiah Bounderby of Coketown learnt his letters from the outsides of shops, Mrs. Gradgrind, and was first able to tell the time upon a dial-plate, from studying the steeple clock of St. Giles's Church, London, under the direction of a drunken cripple, who was a convicted thief, and an incorrigible vagrant. Tell Josiah Bounderby of Coketown, of your district schools and your model schools, and your training schools, and your whole kettle-of-fish schools;* and Josiah Bounderby of Coketown, tells you plainly, all right, all correct—he hadn't such advantages—but let us have hard-headed, solid-fisted people—the education that made him won't do for everybody, he knows well—such and such his education was, however, and you may force him to swallow boiling fat, but you shall never force him to suppress the facts of his life."

Being heated when he arrived at this climax, Josiah Bounderby of Coketown stopped. He stopped just as his eminently practical friend, still accompanied by the two young culprits, entered the room. His eminently practical friend, on seeing him, stopped also, and gave Louisa a reproachful look that plainly said, "Behold your Bounderby!"

"Well!" blustered Mr. Bounderby, "what's the matter? What is young Thomas in the dumps about?"

He spoke of young Thomas, but he looked at Louisa.

"We were peeping at the circus," muttered Louisa, haughtily, without lifting up her eyes, "and father caught us."

"And, Mrs. Gradgrind," said her husband in a lofty manner, "I should as soon have expected to find my children reading poetry."

"Dear me," whimpered Mrs. Gradgrind. "How can you, Louisa and Thomas! I wonder at you. I declare you're enough to make one regret ever having had a family at all. I have a great mind to say I wish I hadn't. *Then* what would you have done, I should like to know?"

Mr. Gradgrind did not seem favourably impressed by these cogent remarks. He frowned impatiently.

"As if, with my head in its present throbbing state, you couldn't go and look at the shells and minerals and things provided for you, instead of circuses!" said Mrs. Gradgrind. "You know, as well as I do, no young people have circus masters, or keep circuses in cabinets, or attend lectures about circuses. What can you possibly want to know of circuses then? I am sure you have enough to do, if that's what you want. With my head in its present state, I couldn't remember the mere names of half the facts you have got to attend to."

"That's the reason!" pouted Louisa.

"Don't tell me that's the reason, because it can be nothing of the sort," said Mrs. Gradgrind. "Go and be somethingological directly." Mrs. Gradgrind was not a scientific character, and usually dismissed her children to their studies with this general injunction to choose their pursuit.

In truth, Mrs. Gradgrind's stock of facts in general was woefully defective; but Mr. Gradgrind in raising her to her high matrimonial position, had been influenced by two reasons. Firstly, she was most satisfactory as a question of figures; and secondly, she had "no nonsense" about her. By nonsense he meant fancy; and truly it is probable she was as free from any alloy of that nature, as any human being not arrived at the perfection of an absolute idiot, ever was.

The simple circumstance of being left alone with her husband and Mr. Bounderby, was sufficient to stun this admirable lady again without collision between herself and any other fact. So, she once more died away, and nobody minded her.

"Bounderby," said Mr. Gradgrind, drawing a chair to the fireside, "you are always so interested in my young people—particularly in Louisa—that I make no apology for saying to you, I am very much vexed by this discovery. I have systematically devoted myself (as you know) to the education of the reason of my family. The reason is (as you know) the only faculty to which education should be addressed. And yet, Bounderby, it would appear from this unexpected circumstance of to-day, though in itself a trifling one, as if something had crept in Thomas's and Louisa's minds which is—or rather, which is not—I don't know that I can express myself better than by saying—which has never been intended to be developed, and in which their reason has no part."

"There certainly is no reason in looking with interest at a parcel of vagabonds," returned Bounderby. "When I was a vagabond myself, nobody looked with any interest at *me*; I know that."

"Then comes the question," said the eminently practical father, with his eyes on the fire, "in what has this vulgar curiosity its rise?"

"I'll tell you in what. In idle imagination."

"I hope not," said the eminently practical; "I confess, however, that the misgiving *has* crossed me on my way home."

"In idle imagination, Gradgrind," repeated Bounderby. "A very bad thing for anybody, but a cursed bad thing for a girl like Louisa. I should ask Mrs. Gradgrind's pardon for strong expressions, but that she knows very well I am not a refined character. Whoever expects refinement in me will be disappointed. I hadn't a refined bringing up."

"Whether," said Gradgrind, pondering with his hands in his pockets, and his cavernous eyes on the fire, "whether any instructor or servant can have suggested anything? Whether, Louisa or Thomas can have been reading anything? Whether, in spite of all precautions, any idle story-book can have got into the house? Because, in minds that have been practically formed by rule and line, from the cradle upwards, this is so curious, so incomprehensible."

"Stop a bit!" cried Bounderby, who all this time had been standing, as before, on the hearth, bursting at the very furniture of the room with explosive humility. "You have one of those strollers' children in the school."

"Cecilia Jupe, by name," said Mr. Gradgrind, with something of a stricken look at his friend.

"Now, stop a bit!" cried Bounderby again. "How did she come there?"

"Why, the fact is, I saw the girl myself, for the first time, only just now. She specially applied here at the house to be admitted, as not regularly belonging to our town, and—yes, you are right, Bounderby, you are right."

"Now, stop a bit!" cried Bounderby, once more. "Louisa saw her when she came?"

"Louisa certainly did see her, for she mentioned the application to me. But Louisa saw her, I have no doubt, in Mrs. Gradgrind's presence."

"Pray, Mrs. Gradgrind," said Bounderby, "what passed?"

"Oh, my poor health!" returned Mrs. Gradgrind. "The girl wanted to come to the school, and Mr. Gradgrind wanted girls to come to the school, and Louisa and Thomas both said the girl wanted to come, and that Mr. Gradgrind wanted girls to come, and how was it possible to contradict them when such was the fact!"

"Now I tell you what, Gradgrind!" said Mr. Bounderby. "Turn this girl to the right about,[1] and there's an end of it."

"I am much of your opinion."

"Do it at once," said Bounderby, "has always been my motto from a child. When I thought I would run away from my egg-box and my grandmother, I did it at once. Do you the same. Do this at once!"

"Are you walking?" asked his friend. "I have the father's address. Perhaps you would not mind walking to town with me?"

"Not the least in the world," said Mr. Bounderby, "as long as you do it at once!"

So, Mr. Bounderby threw on his hat—he always threw it on, as expressing a man who had been far too busily employed in making himself, to acquire any fashion of wearing his hat—and with his hands in his pockets, sauntered out into the hall. "I never wear gloves," it was his custom to say. "I didn't climb up the ladder in *them*. Shouldn't be so high up, if I had."

Being left to saunter in the hall a minute or two while Mr. Gradgrind went up-stairs for the address, he opened the door of the children's study and looked into that serene floor-clothed apartment, which, notwithstanding its book-cases and its cabinets, and its variety of learned and philosophical appliances, had much of the genial aspects of a room devoted to hair-cutting. Louisa languidly leaned upon the window looking out, without looking at anything, while young Thomas stood sniffling revengefully

---

1.   I.e. dismiss her, send her packing (military metaphor).

at the fire. Adam Smith[1] and Malthus,[2] two younger Gradgrinds, were out at lecture in custody; and little Jane, after manufacturing a good deal of moist pipe-clay on her face with slate-pencil and tears, had fallen asleep over vulgar fractions.

"It's all right now, Louisa; it's all right, young Thomas," said Mr. Bounderby; "you won't do so any more. I'll answer for it's being all over with father. Well, Louisa, that's worth a kiss, isn't it?"

"You can take one, Mr. Bounderby," returned Louisa, when she had coldly paused, and slowly walked across the room, and ungraciously raised her cheek towards him, with her face turned away.

"Always my pet; ain't you, Louisa?" said Mr. Bounderby. "Good-bye, Louisa!"

He went his way, but she stood on the same spot, rubbing the cheek he had kissed, with her handkerchief, until it was burning red. She was still doing this, five minutes afterwards.

"What are you about, Loo?" her brother sulkily remonstrated. "You'll rub a hole in your face."

"You may cut the piece out with your penknife if you like, Tom. I wouldn't cry!"

---

1.   After Adam Smith (1723–90), British philosopher and economist, author of *The Wealth of Nations* (1776), which founded the modern study of political economy and *laissez-faire* theory.

2.   After Thomas Malthus (1766–1834), British political economist, known for his theory of population, published in *An Essay on the Principle of Population* (1798).

Chapter V.
The Key-Note

Coketown, to which Messrs. Bounderby and Gradgrind now walked, was a triumph of fact; it had no greater taint of fancy in it than Mrs. Gradgrind herself. Let us strike the key-note, Coketown, before pursuing our tune.

It was a town of red brick, or of brick that would have been red if the smoke and ashes had allowed it; but as matters stood it was a town of unnatural red and black like the painted face of a savage. It was a town of machinery and tall chimneys, out of which interminable serpents of smoke trailed themselves for ever and ever, and never got uncoiled. It had a black canal in it, and a river that ran purple with ill-smelling dye, and vast piles of building full of windows where there was a rattling and trembling all day long, and where the piston of the steam-engine worked monotonously up and down, like the head of an elephant in a state of melancholy madness. It contained several large streets all very like one another, and many small streets still more like one another, inhabited by people equally like one another, who all went in and out at the same hours, with the same sound upon the same pavements, to do the same work, and to whom every day was the same as yesterday and to-morrow, and every year the counterpart of the last and the next.

These attributes of Coketown were in the main inseparable from the work by which it was sustained; against them were to be set off, comforts of life which found their way all over the world, and elegancies of life which made, we will not ask how much of the fine lady, who could scarcely bear to hear the place mentioned. The rest of its features were voluntary, and they were these.

You saw nothing in Coketown but what was severely workful. If the members of a religious persuasion built a chapel there—as the members of eighteen religious persuasions[1] had done—they made it a pious warehouse of red brick, with sometimes (but this is only in highly ornamental

---

1. On developments in Nonconformist movements in the period, see HAMMOND pp. 237–62.

examples) a bell in a birdcage on the top of it. The solitary exception was the New Church; a stuccoed edifice with a square steeple over the door, terminating in four short pinnacles like florid wooden legs. All the public inscriptions in the town were painted alike, in severe characteristics of black and white. The jail might have been the infirmary, the infirmary might have been the jail, the town-hall might have been either, or both, or anything else, for anything that appeared to the contrary in the graces of their construction. Fact, fact, fact, everywhere in the material aspect of the town; fact, fact, fact, everywhere in the immaterial. The M'Choakumchild school was all fact, and the school of design was all fact, and the relations between master and man were all fact, and everything was fact between the lying-in hospital and the cemetery, and what you couldn't state in figures, or show to be purchaseable in the cheapest market and saleable in the dearest, was not, and never should be, world without end, Amen.[1]

A town so sacred to fact, and so triumphant in its assertion, of course got on well? Why no, not quite well. No? Dear me!

No. Coketown did not come out of its own furnaces, in all respects like gold that had stood the fire.[2] First, the perplexing mystery of the place was, Who belonged to the eighteen denominations? Because, whoever did, the labouring people did not. It was very strange to walk through the streets on a Sunday morning, and note how few of *them* the barbarous jangling of bells that was driving the sick and nervous mad, called away from their own quarter, from their own close rooms, from the corners of their own streets, where they lounged listlessly, gazing at all the church and chapel going, as at a thing with which they had no manner of concern. Nor was it merely the stranger who noticed this, because there was a native organization in Coketown itself, whose members were to be heard of in the House of Commons every session, indignantly petitioning for acts of parliament that should make these people religious by main force.* Then came the Teetotal Society,[3] who complained that

---

1.   Compare the Gloria ('Glory be to the Father, and to the Son: and to the Holy Ghost; As it was in the beginning, is now, and ever shall be: world without end. Amen.') in the Book of Common Prayer.
2.   Compare the description of the purifying of the people of God in Zechariah 13:9.
3.   Society devoted to total abstinence from alcohol, founded in Preston, Lancashire, in the early 1830s.

these same people *would* get drunk, and showed in tabular statements[1] that they did get drunk, and proved at tea parties that no inducement, human or Divine (except a medal), would induce them to forego their custom of getting drunk. Then came the chemist and druggist, with other tabular statements, showing that when they didn't get drunk, they took opium.[2] Then came the experienced chaplain of the jail,* with more tabular statements, outdoing all the previous tabular statements, and showing that the same people *would* resort to low haunts, hidden from the public eye, where they heard low singing and saw low dancing, and mayhap joined in it; and where A. B., aged twenty-four next birthday, and committed for eighteen months' solitary, had himself said (not that he had ever shown himself particularly worthy of belief) his ruin began, as he was perfectly sure and confident that otherwise he would have been a tip-top moral specimen. Then came Mr. Gradgrind and Mr. Bounderby, the two gentlemen at this present moment walking through Coketown, and both eminently practical, who could, on occasion, furnish more tabular statements derived from their own personal experience, and illustrated by cases they had known and seen, from which it clearly appeared—in short, it was the only clear thing in the case—that these same people were a bad lot altogether, gentlemen; that do what you would for them they were never thankful for it, gentlemen; that they were restless, gentlemen; that they never knew what they wanted; that they lived upon the best, and bought fresh butter; and insisted on Mocha coffee, and rejected all but prime parts of meat, and yet were eternally dissatisfied and unmanageable. In short, it was the moral of the old nursery fable:

> There was an old woman, and what do you think
> She lived upon nothing but victuals and drink;
> Victuals and drink were the whole of her diet,
> And yet this old woman would NEVER be quiet.

Is it possible, I wonder, that there was any analogy between the case

---

1. Statistical information presented in the form of tables.
2. Opium, usually in the liquid form of laudanum and often sold under proprietary labels such as the popular Godfrey's Cordial, was easily and cheaply available throughout the Victorian period. It was widely used as a sedative for infants as well as a narcotic for adults. Its sale was unregulated until the end of the century.

of the Coketown population and the case of the little Gradgrinds? Surely, none of us in our sober senses and acquainted with figures, are to be told at this time of day, that one of the foremost elements in the existence of the Coketown working-people had been for scores of years, deliberately set at nought? That there was any Fancy in them demanding to be brought into healthy existence instead of struggling on in convulsions? That exactly in the ratio as they worked long and monotonously, the craving grew within them for some physical relief—some relaxation, encouraging good humour and good spirits, and giving them a vent—some recognized holiday, though it were but for an honest dance to a stirring band of music—some occasional light pie in which even M'Choakumchild had no finger—which craving must and would be satisfied aright, or must and would inevitably go wrong, until the laws of the Creation were repealed?

"This man lives at Pod's End, and I don't quite know Pod's End," said Mr. Gradgrind. "Which is it, Bounderby?"

Mr. Bounderby knew it was somewhere down town, but knew no more respecting it. So they stopped for a moment, looking about.

Almost as they did so, there came running round the corner of the street at a quick pace and with a frightened look, a girl whom Mr. Gradgrind recognized. "Halloa!" said he. "Stop! Where are you going! Stop!" Girl number twenty stopped then, palpitating, and made him a curtsey.

"Why are you tearing about the streets," said Mr. Gradgrind, "in this improper manner?"

"I was—I was run after, sir," the girl panted, "and I wanted to get away."

"Run after?" repeated Mr. Gradgrind. "Who would run after *you*?"

The question was unexpectedly and suddenly answered for her, by the colourless boy, Bitzer, who came round the corner with such blind speed and so little anticipating a stoppage on the pavement, that he brought himself up against Mr. Gradgrind's waistcoat and rebounded into the road.

"What do you mean, boy?" said Mr. Gradgrind. "What are you doing? How dare you dash against—everybody—in this manner?"

Bitzer picked up his cap, which the concussion had knocked off; and backing, and knuckling his forehead, pleaded that it was an accident.

"Was this boy running after you, Jupe?" asked Mr. Gradgrind.

"Yes, sir," said the girl reluctantly.

"No, I wasn't, sir!" cried Bitzer. "Not till she run away from me. But the horse-riders never mind what they say, sir; they're famous for it. You know the horse-riders are famous for never minding what they say," addressing Sissy. "It's as well known in the town as—please, sir, as the multiplication table isn't known to the horse-riders." Bitzer tried Mr. Bounderby with this.

"He frightened me so," said the girl, "with his cruel faces!"

"Oh!" cried Bitzer. "Oh! An't you one of the rest! An't you a horse-rider! I never looked at her, sir. I asked her if she would know how to define a horse to-morrow, and offered to tell her again, and she ran away, and I ran after her, sir, that she might know how to answer when she was asked. You wouldn't have thought of saying such mischief if you hadn't been a horse-rider!"

"Her calling seems to be pretty well known among 'em," observed Mr. Bounderby. "You'd have had the whole school peeping in a row, in a week."

"Truly, I think so," returned his friend. "Bitzer, turn you about and take yourself home. Jupe, stay here a moment. Let me hear of your running in this manner any more, boy, and you will hear of me through the master of the school. You understand what I mean. Go along."

The boy stopped in his rapid blinking, knuckled his forehead again, glanced at Sissy, turned about, and retreated.

"Now, girl," said Mr. Gradgrind, "take this gentleman and me to your father's; we are going there. What have you got in that bottle you are carrying?"

"Gin," said Mr. Bounderby.

"Dear, no, sir! It's the nine oils."

"The what?" cried Mr. Bounderby.

"The nine oils, sir. To rub father with." Then, said Mr. Bounderby, with a loud short laugh, "What the devil do you rub your father with nine oils for?"

"It's what our people always use, sir, when they get any hurts in the ring," replied the girl, looking over her shoulder, to assure herself that her pursuer was gone. "They bruise themselves very bad sometimes."

"Serve 'em right," said Mr. Bounderby, "for being idle." She glanced up at his face, with mingled astonishment and dread.

"By George!" said Mr. Bounderby, "when I was four or five years younger than you, I had worse bruises upon me than ten oils, twenty oils, forty oils, would have rubbed off. I didn't get 'em by posture-making, but by being banged about. There was no rope-dancing for me; I danced on the bare ground and was larruped with the rope."

Mr. Gradgrind, though hard enough, was by no means so rough a man as Mr. Bounderby. His character was not unkind, all things considered; it might have been a very kind one indeed, if he had only made some round mistake in the arithmetic that balanced it, years ago. He said, in what he meant for a reassuring tone, as they turned down a narrow road, "And this is Pod's End; is it, Jupe?"

"This is it, sir, and—if you wouldn't mind, sir—this is the house."

She stopped, at twilight, at the door of a mean little public-house, with dim red lights in it. As haggard and as shabby, as if, for want of custom, it had itself taken to drinking, and had gone the way all drunkards go, and was very near the end of it.

"It's only crossing the bar, sir, and up the stairs, if you wouldn't mind, and waiting there for a moment till I get a candle. If you should hear a dog, sir, it's only Merrylegs, and he only barks."

"Merrylegs and nine oils, eh!" said Mr. Bounderby, entering last with his metallic laugh. "Pretty well this, for a self-made man!"

CHAPTER VI.
SLEARY'S HORSEMANSHIP

THE NAME of the public-house was the Pegasus's Arms.[1] The Pegasus's legs might have been more to the purpose; but, underneath the winged horse upon the sign-board, the Pegasus's Arms was inscribed in Roman letters. Beneath that inscription again, in a flowing scroll, the painter had touched off the lines:

> Good malt makes good beer,
> Walk in, and they'll draw here;
> Good wine makes good brandy,
> Give us a call, and you'll find it handy.

Framed and glazed upon the wall behind the dingy little bar, was another Pegasus—a theatrical one—with real gauze let in for his wings, golden stars stuck on all over him, and his ethereal harness made of red silk.

As it had grown too dusky without, to see the sign, and as it had not grown light enough within to see the picture, Mr. Gradgrind and Mr. Bounderby received no offence from these idealities. They followed the girl up some steep corner-stairs without meeting any one, and stopped in the dark while she went on for a candle. They expected every moment to hear Merrylegs give tongue, but the highly trained performing dog had not barked when the girl and the candle appeared together.

"Father is not in our room, sir," she said, with a face of great surprise. "If you wouldn't mind walking in, I'll find him directly."

They walked in; and Sissy, having set two chairs for them, sped away with a quick light step. It was a mean, shabbily furnished room, with a bed in it. The white night-cap, embellished with two peacock's feathers and a pigtail bolt upright,[2] in which Signor Jupe had that very afternoon enlivened the varied performances with his chaste Shakesperean quips and retorts, hung upon a nail; but no other portion of his wardrobe, or other token of himself or his pursuits, was to be seen anywhere. As to Merrylegs,

---

1. After the flying horse of classical mythology; an appropriate place for a circus troupe to lodge in.
2. An item of the clown's ridiculous costume.

that respectable ancestor of the highly trained animal who went aboard the ark,[1] might have been accidentally shut out of it, for any sign of a dog that was manifest to eye or ear in the Pegasus's Arms.

They heard the doors of rooms above, opening and shutting as Sissy went from one to another in quest of her father; and presently they heard voices expressing surprise. She came bounding down again in a great hurry, opened a battered and mangy old hair trunk, found it empty, and looked round with her hands clasped and her face full of terror.

"Father must have gone down to the Booth, sir. I don't know why he should go there, but he must be there; I'll bring him in a minute!" She was gone directly, without her bonnet; with her long, dark, childish hair streaming behind her.

"What does she mean!" said Mr. Gradgrind. "Back in a minute? It's more than a mile off."

Before Mr. Bounderby could reply, a young man appeared at the door, and introducing himself with the words, "By your leaves, gentlemen!" walked in with his hands in his pockets. His face, close-shaven, thin, and sallow, was shaded by a great quantity of dark hair, brushed into a roll all round his head, and parted up the centre. His legs were very robust, but shorter than the legs of good proportions should have been. His chest and back were as much too broad, as his legs were too short. He was dressed in a Newmarket coat[2] and tight-fitting trousers; wore a shawl round his neck; smelt of lamp-oil, straw, orange-peel, horses' provender, and sawdust; and looked a most remarkable sort of Centaur,[3] compounded of the stable and the play-house. Where the one began, and the other ended, nobody could have told with any precision. This gentleman was mentioned in the bills of the day as Mr. E. W. B. Childers, so justly celebrated for his daring vaulting act as the Wild Huntsman of the North American Prairies; in which popular performance, a diminutive boy with an old face, who now accompanied him, assisted as his infant son: being carried upside down over his father's shoulder, by one foot, and held by the crown

---

1. See the story of the Flood (Noah's Ark) in Genesis 6–8.
2. Close-fitting men's coat, originally worn for riding, after the Cambridgeshire town famous for its horse-race meetings.
3. A strange combination, after the creature of classical mythology composed of the upper parts of a man and the lower parts of a horse.

of his head, heels upwards, in the palm of his father's hand, according to the violent paternal manner in which wild huntsmen may be observed to fondle their offspring. Made up with curls, wreaths, wings, white bismuth, and carmine, this hopeful young person soared into so pleasing a Cupid as to constitute the chief delight of the maternal part of the spectators; but in private, where his characteristics were a precocious cutaway coat and an extremely gruff voice, he became of the Turf, turfy.[1]

"By your leaves, gentlemen," said Mr. E. W. B. Childers, glancing round the room. "It was you, I believe, that were wishing to see Jupe!"

"It was," said Mr. Gradgrind. "His daughter has gone to fetch him, but I can't wait; therefore, if you please, I will leave a message for him with you."

"You see, my friend," Mr. Bounderby put in, "we are the kind of people who know the value of time, and you are the kind of people who don't know the value of time."

"I have not," retorted Mr. Childers, after surveying him from head to foot, "the honour of knowing *you*,—but if you mean that you can make more money of your time than I can of mine, I should judge from your appearance, that you are about right."

"And when you have made it, you can keep it too, I should think," said Cupid.

"Kidderminster, stow that!"[2] said Mr. Childers. (Master Kidderminster was Cupid's mortal name.)

"What does he come here cheeking us for, then?" cried Master Kidderminster, showing a very irascible temperament. "If you want to cheek us, pay your ochre[3] at the doors and take it out."

"Kidderminster," said Mr. Childers, raising his voice, "stow that!— Sir," to Mr. Gradgrind, "I was addressing myself to you. You may or may not be aware (for perhaps you have not been much in the audience), that Jupe has missed his tip* very often, lately."

"Has—what has he missed?" asked Mr. Gradgrind, glancing at the potent Bounderby for assistance.

---

1.   Compare 1 Corinthians 15:47: 'of the earth, earthy.'
2.   Stop talking, shut up (slang, now obsolete).
3.   Money, gold (slang, based on the colour).

"Missed his tip."

"Offered at the Garters four times last night, and never done 'em once," said Master Kidderminster. "Missed his tip at the banners, too, and was loose in his ponging."

"Didn't do what he ought to do. Was short in his leaps and bad in his tumbling," Mr. Childers interpreted.

"Oh!" said Mr. Gradgrind, "that is tip, is it?"

"In a general way that's missing his tip," Mr. E. W. B. Childers answered.

"Nine oils, Merrylegs, missing tips, garters, banners, and Ponging, eh!" ejaculated Bounderby, with his laugh of laughs. "Queer sort of company, too, for a man who has raised himself."

"Lower yourself, then," retorted Cupid. "Oh Lord! if you've raised yourself so high as all that comes to, let yourself down a bit."

"This is a very obtrusive lad!" said Mr. Gradgrind, turning, and knitting his brows on him.

"We'd have had a young gentleman to meet you, if we had known you were coming," retorted Master Kidderminster, nothing abashed. "It's a pity you don't have a bespeak, being so particular. You're on the Tight-Jeff, ain't you?"

"What does this unmannerly boy mean," asked Mr. Gradgrind, eyeing him in a sort of desperation, "by Tight-Jeff?"

"There! Get out, get out!" said Mr. Childers, thrusting his young friend from the room, rather in the prairie manner. "Tight-Jeff or Slack-Jeff, it don't much signify: it's only tight-rope and slack-rope. You were going to give me a message for Jupe?"

"Yes, I was."

"Then," continued Mr. Childers, quickly, "my opinion is, he will never receive it. Do you know much of him?"

"I never saw the man in my life."

"I doubt if you ever *will* see him now. It's pretty plain to me, he's off."

"Do you mean that he has deserted his daughter?"

"Ay! I mean," said Mr. Childers, with a nod, "that he has cut.[1] He was goosed last night, he was goosed the night before last, he was goosed

---

1.   Run away, make off (slang).

to-day. He has lately got in the way of being always goosed, and he can't stand it."

"Why has he been—so very much—Goosed?" asked Mr. Gradgrind, forcing the word out of himself, with great solemnity and reluctance.

"His joints are turning stiff, and he is getting used up," said Childers. "He has his points as a Cackler still, but he can't get a living out of *them*."

"A Cackler!" Bounderby repeated. "Here we go again!"

"A speaker, if the gentleman likes it better," Mr. E. W. B. Childers, superciliously throwing the interpretation over his shoulder, and accompanying it with a shake of his long hair—which all shook at once. "Now, it's a remarkable fact, sir, that it cut that man deeper, to know that his daughter knew of his being goosed, than to go through with it."

"Good!" interrupted Mr. Bounderby. "This is good, Gradgrind! A man so fond of his daughter, that he runs away from her! This is devilish good! Ha! ha! Now, I'll tell you what, young man. I haven't always occupied my present station of life. I know what these things are. You may be astonished to hear it, but my mother ran away from *me*."

E. W. B. Childers replied pointedly, that he was not at all astonished to hear it.

"Very well," said Bounderby. "I was born in a ditch, and my mother ran away from me. Do I excuse her for it? No. Have I ever excused her for it? Not I. What do I call her for it? I call her probably the very worst woman that ever lived in the world, except my drunken grandmother. There's no family pride about me, there's no imaginative sentimental humbug about me. I call a spade a spade; and I call the mother of Josiah Bounderby of Coketown, without any fear or any favour, what I should call her if she had been the mother of Dick Jones of Wapping.[1] So, with this man. He is a runaway rogue and a vagabond, that's what he is, in English."

"It's all the same to me what he is or what he is not, whether in English or whether in French," retorted Mr. E. W. B. Childers, facing about. "I am telling your friend what's the fact; if you don't like to hear

---

1.   I.e. a common working man. Like John Smith, the name Dick Jones is the type of ordinariness; Wapping is a dockside area in East London.

it, you can avail yourself of the open air. You give it mouth enough, you do; but give it mouth in your own building at least," remonstrated E. W. B. with stern irony. "Don't give it mouth in this building, till you're called upon. You have got some building of your own, I dare say, now?"

"Perhaps so," replied Mr. Bounderby, rattling his money and laughing.

"Then give it mouth in your own building, will you, if you please?" said Childers. "Because this isn't a strong building, and too much of you might bring it down!"

Eyeing Mr. Bounderby from head to foot again, he turned from him, as from a man finally disposed of, to Mr. Gradgrind.

"Jupe sent his daughter out on an errand not an hour ago, and then was seen to slip out himself, with his hat over his eyes, and a bundle tied up in a handkerchief under his arm. She will never believe it of him, but he has cut away and left her."

"Pray," said Mr. Gradgrind, "why will she never believe it of him?"

"Because those two were one. Because they were never asunder. Because, up to this time, he seemed to dote upon her," said Childers, taking a step or two to look into the empty trunk. Both Mr. Childers and Master Kidderminster walked in a curious manner; with their legs wider apart than the general run of men, and with a very knowing assumption of being stiff in the knees. This walk was common to all the male members of Sleary's company, and was understood to express, that they were always on horseback.

"Poor Sissy! He had better have apprenticed her," said Childers, giving his hair another shake, as he looked up from the empty box. "Now, he leaves her without anything to take to."

"It is creditable to you, who have never been apprenticed, to express that opinion," returned Mr. Gradgrind, approvingly.

"*I* never apprenticed? I was apprenticed when I was seven year old."[*]

"Oh! Indeed?" said Mr. Gradgrind, rather resentfully, as having been defrauded of his good opinion. "I was not aware of its being the custom to apprentice young persons to—"

"Idleness," Mr. Bounderby put in with a loud laugh. "No, by the Lord Harry![1] Nor I!"

---

1.   Common oath of doubtful origin, repeated by Bounderby on pp. 82, 111, & 177.

"Her father always had it in his head," resumed Childers, feigning unconsciousness of Mr. Bounderby's existence, "that she was to be taught the deuce-and-all of education. How it got into his head, I can't say; I can only say that it never got out. He has been picking up a bit of reading for her, here—and a bit of writing for her, there—and a bit of ciphering for her, somewhere else—these seven years."*

Mr. E. W. B. Childers took one of his hands out of his pockets, stroked his face and chin, and looked, with a good deal of doubt and a little hope, at Mr. Gradgrind. From the first he had sought to conciliate that gentleman, for the sake of the deserted girl.

"When Sissy got into the school here," he pursued, "her father was as pleased as Punch. I couldn't altogether make out why, myself, as we were not stationary here, being but comers and goers anywhere. I suppose, however, he had this move in his mind—he was always half-cracked—and then considered her provided for. If you should happen to have looked in to-night, for the purpose of telling him that you were going to do her any little service," said Mr. Childers, stroking his face again, and repeating his look, "it would be very fortunate and well-timed; *very* fortunate and well-timed."

"On the contrary," returned Mr. Gradgrind. "I came to tell him that her connections made her not an object for the school, and that she must not attend any more. Still, if her father really has left her, without any connivance on her part—Bounderby, let me have a word with you."

Upon this, Mr. Childers politely betook himself, with his equestrian walk, to the landing outside the door, and there stood stroking his face, and softly whistling. While thus engaged, he overheard such phrases in Mr. Bounderby's voice as "No. *I* say no. I advise you not. I say by no means." While, from Mr. Gradgrind, he heard in his much lower tone the words, "But even as an example to Louisa, of what this pursuit which has been the subject of a vulgar curiosity, leads to and ends in. Think of it, Bounderby, in that point of view."

Meanwhile, the various members of Sleary's company gradually gathered together from the upper regions, where they were quartered, and, from standing about, talking in low voices to one another and to Mr. Childers, gradually insinuated themselves and him into the room. There were two or three handsome young women among them, with their two or three husbands, and their two or three mothers, and their eight or nine little children, who did the fairy business when required. The father of one of the families was in the habit of balancing the father of another of the families on the top of a great pole; the father of a third family often made a pyramid of both those fathers, with Master Kidderminster for the apex, and himself for the base; all the fathers could dance upon rolling casks, stand upon bottles, catch knives and balls, twirl hand-basins, ride upon anything, jump over everything, and stick at nothing. All the mothers could (and did) dance upon the slack wire and the tight-rope, and perform rapid acts on bare-backed steeds; none of them were at all particular in respect of showing their legs; and one of them, alone in a Greek chariot, drove six in hand into every town they came to. They all assumed to be mighty rakish and knowing, they were not very tidy in their private dresses, they were not at all orderly in their domestic arrangements, and the combined literature of the whole company would have produced but a poor letter on any subject. Yet there was a remarkable gentleness and childishness about these people, a special inaptitude for any kind of sharp practice, and an untiring readiness to help and pity one another, deserving often of as much respect, and always of as much generous construction, as the every-day virtues of any class of people in the world.

Last of all appeared Mr. Sleary: a stout man as already mentioned, with one fixed eye, and one loose eye, a voice (if it can be called so) like the efforts of a broken old pair of bellows, a flabby surface, and a muddled head which was never sober and never drunk.

"Thquire!" said Mr. Sleary, who was troubled with asthma, and whose breath came far too thick and heavy for the letter s, "Your thervant! Thith ith a bad piethe of bithnith, thith ith. You've heard of my Clown and hith dog being thuppothed to have morrithed?"[1]

He addressed Mr. Gradgrind, who answered "Yes."

"Well, Thquire," he returned, taking off his hat, and rubbing the lining with his pocket-handkerchief, which he kept inside for the purpose. "Ith it your intenthion to do anything for the poor girl, Thquire?"

---

1.   I.e. 'morrissed', decamped, ran away (slang, now obsolete, from the traditional morris-dance).

"I shall have something to propose to her when she comes back," said Mr. Gradgrind.

"Glad to hear it, Thquire. Not that I want to get rid of the child, any more than I want to thtand in her way. I'm willing to take her prentith, though at her age ith late. My voithe ith a little huthky, Thquire, and not eathy heard by them ath don't know me; but if you'd been chilled and heated, heated and chilled, chilled and heated in the ring when you wath young, ath often ath I have been, *your* voithe wouldn't have lathted out, Thquire, no more than mine."

"I dare say not," said Mr. Gradgrind.

"What thall it be, Thquire, while you wait? Thall it be Therry? Give it a name, Thquire!" said Mr. Sleary, with hospitable ease.

"Nothing for me, I thank you," said Mr. Gradgrind.

"Don't thay nothing, Thquire. What doth your friend thay? If you haven't took your feed yet, have a glath of bitterth."

Here his daughter Josephine—a pretty fair-haired girl of eighteen, who had been tied on a horse at two years old, and had made a will at twelve, which she always carried about with her, expressive of her dying desire to be drawn to the grave by the two piebald ponies—cried, "Father, hush! she has come back!" Then came Sissy Jupe, running into the room as she ran out of it. And when she saw them all assembled, and saw their looks, and saw no father there, she broke into a most deplorable cry, and took refuge on the bosom of the most accomplished tight-rope lady (herself in the family-way), who knelt down on the floor to nurse her, and to weep over her.

"Ith an infernal thame, upon my thoul it ith," said Sleary.

"Oh my dear father, my good kind father, where are you gone? You are gone to try to do me some good, I know! You are gone away for my sake, I am sure! And how miserable and helpless you will be without me, poor, poor father, until you come back!" It was so pathetic to hear her saying many things of this kind, with her face turned upward, and her arms stretched out as if she were trying to stop his departing shadow and embrace it, that no one spoke a word until Mr. Bounderby (growing impatient) took the case in hand.

"Now, good people all," said he, "this is wanton waste of time. Let the girl understand the fact. Let her take it from me, if you like, who have been run away from, myself. Here, what's your name! Your father has absconded—deserted you—and you mustn't expect to see him again as long as you live."

They cared so little for plain Fact, these people, and were in that advanced state of degeneracy on the subject, that instead of being impressed by the speaker's strong common sense, they took it in extraordinary dudgeon. The men muttered "Shame!" and the women "Brute!" and Sleary, in some haste, communicated the following hint, apart to Mr. Bounderby.

"I tell you what, Thquire. To thpeak plain to you, my opinion ith that you had better cut it thort, and drop it. They're very good natur'd people, my people, but they're accuthtomed to be quick in their movementh; and if you don't act upon my advithe, I'm damned if I don't believe they'll pith you out o' winder."

Mr. Bounderby being restrained by this mild suggestion, Mr. Gradgrind found an opening for his eminently practical exposition of the subject.

"It is of no moment," said he, "whether this person is to be expected back at any time, or the contrary. He is gone away, and there is no present expectation of his return. That, I believe, is agreed on all hands."

"Thath agreed, Thquire. Thtick to that!" From Sleary.

"Well then. I, who came here to inform the father of the poor girl, Jupe, that she could not be received at the school any more, in consequence of there being practical objections, into which I need not enter, to the reception there of the children of persons so employed, am prepared in these altered circumstances to make a proposal. I am willing to take charge of you, Jupe, to educate you, and provide for you. The only condition (over and above your good behaviour) I make is, that you decide now, at once, whether to accompany me or remain here. Also, that if you accompany me now, it is understood that you communicate no more with any of your friends who are here present. These observations comprise the whole of the case."

"At the thame time," said Sleary, "I mutht put in my word, Thquire, tho that both thideth of the banner may be equally theen. If you like, Thethilia, to be prentitht, you know the natur' of the work and you know your companionth. Emma Gordon, in whothe lap you're a lying at prethent, would be a mother to you, and Joth'phine would be a thithter to you. I don't pretend to be of the angel breed mythelf, and I don't thay but what, when you mith'd your tip, you'd find me cut up rough, and thwear an oath or two at you. But what I thay, Thquire, ith, that good tempered or bad tempered, I never did a horthe a injury yet, nor more than thwearing at him went, and that I don't expect I thall begin otherwithe at my time of life, with a rider. I never wath much of a Cackler, Thquire, and I have thed my thay."

The latter part of this speech was addressed to Mr. Gradgrind, who received it with a grave inclination of his head, and then remarked:

"The only observation I will make to you, Jupe, in the way of influencing your decision, is, that it is highly desirable to have a sound practical education, and that even your father himself (from what I understand) appears, on your behalf, to have known and felt that much."

The last words had a visible effect upon her. She stopped in her wild crying, a little detached herself from Emma Gordon, and turned her face full upon her patron. The whole company perceived the force of the change, and drew a long breath together, that plainly said, "she will go!"

"Be sure you know your own mind, Jupe," Mr. Gradgrind cautioned her; "I say no more. Be sure you know your own mind!"

"When father comes back," cried the girl, bursting into tears again after a minute's silence, "how will he ever find me if I go away!"

"You may be quite at ease," said Mr. Gradgrind, calmly; he worked out the whole matter like a sum: "you may be quite at ease, Jupe, on that score. In such a case, your father, I apprehend, must find out Mr. —"

"Thleary. Thath my name, Thquire. Not athamed of it. Known all over England, and alwayth paythe ith way."

"Must find out Mr. Sleary, who would then let him know where you went. I should have no power of keeping you against his wish, and he would have no difficulty, at any time, in finding Mr. Thomas Gradgrind of Coketown. I am well known."

"Well known," assented Mr. Sleary, rolling his loose eye. "You're one of the thort, Thquire, that keepth a prethiouth thight of money out of the houthe. But never mind that at prethent."

There was another silence; and then she exclaimed, sobbing with her hands before her face, "Oh, give me my clothes, give me my clothes, and let me go away before I break my heart!"

The women sadly bestirred themselves to get the clothes together—it was soon done, for they were not many—and to pack them in a basket which had often travelled with them. Sissy sat all the time, upon the ground, still sobbing, and covering her eyes. Mr. Gradgrind and his friend Bounderby stood near the door, ready to take her away. Mr. Sleary stood in the middle of the room, with the male members of the company about him, exactly as he would have stood in the centre of the ring during his daughter Josephine's performance. He wanted nothing but his whip.

The basket packed in silence, they brought her bonnet to her, and smoothed her disordered hair, and put it on. Then they pressed about her, and bent over her in very natural attitudes, kissing and embracing her: and brought the children to take leave of her; and were a tender-hearted, simple, foolish set of women altogether.

"Now, Jupe," said Mr. Gradgrind. "If you are quite determined, come!"

But she had to take her farewell of the male part of the company yet, and every one of them had to unfold his arms (for they all assumed the professional attitude when they found themselves near Sleary), and give her a parting kiss—Master Kidderminster excepted, in whose young nature there was an original flavour of the misanthrope, who was also known to have harboured matrimonial views, and who moodily withdrew. Mr. Sleary was reserved until the last. Opening his arms wide he took her by both her hands, and would have sprung her up and down, after the riding-master manner of congratulating young ladies on their dismounting from a rapid act; but there was no rebound in Sissy, and she only stood before him crying.

"Good-bye, my dear!" said Sleary. "You'll make your fortun, I hope, and none of our poor folkth will ever trouble you, I'll pound it.[1] I with your father hadn't taken hith dog with him; ith a ill-conwenienth to have the dog out of the billth. But on thecond thoughtht, he wouldn't have performed without hith mathter, tho ith ath broad ath ith long!"

---

1.   I'll bet on it, I'm certain of it (slang, deriving from 'I'll wager a pound—i.e. a large sum—on it'). Dickens obviously liked the phrase since it also occurs in *Oliver Twist* Ch. 26 and *Our Mutual Friend* Bk. 4 Ch. 15.

With that he regarded her attentively with his fixed eye, surveyed his company with his loose one, kissed her, shook his head, and handed her to Mr. Gradgrind as to a horse.

"There the ith, Thquire," he said, sweeping her with a professional glance as if she were being adjusted in her seat, "and the'll do you juthtithe. Good-bye, Thethilia!"

"Good-bye, Cecilia!" "Good-bye, Sissy!" "God bless you, dear!" In a variety of voices from all the room.

But the riding-master eye had observed the bottle of the nine oils in her bosom, and he now interposed with "Leave the bottle, my dear; ith large to carry; it will be of no uthe to you now. Give it to me!"

"No, no!" she said, in another burst of tears. "Oh, no! Pray let me keep it for father till he comes back! He will want it when he comes back. He had never thought of going away, when he sent me for it. I must keep it for him, if you please!"

"Tho be it, my dear. (You thee how it ith, Thquire!) Farewell, Thethilia! My latht wordth to you ith thith, Thtick to the termth of your engagement, be obedient to the Thquire, and forget uth. But if, when you're grown up and married and well off, you come upon any horthe-riding ever, don't be hard upon it, don't be croth with it, give it a Bethpeak if you can, and think you might do wurth. People mutht be amuthed, Thquire, thomehow," continued Sleary, rendered more pursy than ever, by so much talking; "they can't be alwayth a working, nor yet they can't be alwayth a learning. Make the betht of uth; not the wurtht. I've got my living out of the horthe-riding all my life, I know; but I conthider that I lay down the philothophy of the thubject when I thay to you, Thquire, make the betht of uth: not the wurtht!"

The Sleary philosophy was propounded as they went downstairs; and the fixed eye of Philosophy—and its rolling eye, too—soon lost the three figures and the basket in the darkness of the street.

Chapter VII.
Mrs. Sparsit

Mr. Bounderby being a bachelor, an elderly lady presided over his establishment, in consideration of a certain annual stipend. Mrs. Sparsit was this lady's name; and she was a prominent figure in attendance on Mr. Bounderby's car, as it rolled along in triumph[1] with the Bully of humility inside.

For, Mrs. Sparsit had not only seen different days, but was highly connected. She had a great aunt living in these very times called Lady Scadgers. Mr. Sparsit, deceased, of whom she was the relict, had been by the mother's side what Mrs. Sparsit still called "a Powler." Strangers of limited information and dull apprehension were sometimes observed not to know what a Powler was, and even to appear uncertain whether it might be a business, or a political party, or a profession of faith. The better class of minds, however, did not need to be informed that the Powlers were an ancient stock, who could trace themselves so exceedingly far back that it was not surprising if they sometimes lost themselves—which they had rather frequently done, as respected horse-flesh, blind-hookey, Hebrew monetary transactions, and the Insolvent Debtor's Court.[2]

The late Mr. Sparsit, being by the mother's side a Powler, married this lady, being by the father's side a Scadgers. Lady Scadgers (an immensely fat old woman, with an inordinate appetite for butcher's meat, and a mysterious leg which had now refused to get out of bed for fourteen years) contrived the marriage, at a period when Sparsit was just of age, and chiefly noticeable for a slender body, weakly supported on two long slim props, and surmounted by no head worth mentioning. He inherited a fair fortune from his uncle, but owed it all before he came into it, and spent it twice over immediately afterwards. Thus, when he died, at twenty-four

---

1.   I.e. like a victorious general entering ancient Rome. The metaphor recurs throughout the chapter—for example, in the comparison of Mrs. Sparsit to a captive princess on p. 80 and the reference to her 'State humility' on p. 84.

2.   I.e. lost their social position due to gambling on horse-races and at playing cards, to borrowing money from Jewish money-lenders, and to being imprisoned as bankrupts.

(the scene of his decease, Calais, and the cause, brandy), he did not leave his widow, from whom he had been separated soon after the honeymoon, in affluent circumstances. That bereaved lady, fifteen years older than he, fell presently at deadly feud with her only relative, Lady Scadgers; and, partly to spite her ladyship, and partly to maintain herself, went out at a salary. And here she was now, in her elderly days, with the Coriolanian style of nose[1] and the dense black eyebrows which had captivated Sparsit, making Mr. Bounderby's tea as he took his breakfast.

If Bounderby had been a Conqueror, and Mrs. Sparsit a captive Princess whom he took about as a feature in his state-processions, he could not have made a greater flourish with her than he habitually did. Just as it belonged to his boastfulness to depreciate his own extraction, so it belonged to it to exalt Mrs. Sparsit's. In the measure that he would not allow his own youth to have been attended by a single favourable circumstance, he brightened Mrs. Sparsit's juvenile career with every possible advantage, and showered waggon-loads of early roses all over that lady's path. "And yet, sir," he would say, "how does it turn out after all? Why here she is at a hundred a year (I give her a hundred, which she is pleased to term handsome), keeping the house of Josiah Bounderby of Coketown!"

Nay, he made this foil of his so very widely known, that third parties took it up, and handled it on some occasions with considerable briskness. It was one of the most exasperating attributes of Bounderby, that he not only sang his own praises but stimulated other men to sing them. There was a moral infection of clap-trap in him. Strangers, modest enough elsewhere, started up at dinners in Coketown, and boasted, in quite a rampant way, of Bounderby. They made him out to be the Royal arms, the Union-Jack, Magna Charta, John Bull, Habeas Corpus, the Bill of Rights, An Englishman's house is his castle, Church and State, and God save the Queen,[2] all put together. And as often (and it was very often) as an orator of this kind brought into his peroration,

---

1.   I.e. a prominent or Roman nose, after Shakespeare's imperious hero. For a further
      reference to Coriolanus in connection with Mrs. Sparsit, see the note to p. 151.
2.   A list of symbols of English national pride.

"Princes and lords may flourish or may fade,
     A breath can make them, as a breath has made,"[1]

—it was, for certain, more or less understood among the company that he had heard of Mrs. Sparsit.

"Mr. Bounderby," said Mrs. Sparsit, "you are unusually slow, sir, with your breakfast this morning."

"Why, ma'am," he returned, "I am thinking about Tom Gradgrind's whim;" Tom Gradgrind, for a bluff independent manner of speaking—as if somebody were always endeavouring to bribe him with immense sums to say Thomas, and he wouldn't; "Tom Gradgrind's whim, ma'am, of bringing up the tumbling-girl."

"The girl is now waiting to know," said Mrs. Sparsit, "whether she is to go straight to the school, or up to the Lodge."

"She must wait, ma'am," answered Bounderby, "till I know myself. We shall have Tom Gradgrind down here presently, I suppose. If he should wish her to remain here a day or two longer, of course she can, ma'am."

"Of course she can if you wish it, Mr. Bounderby."

"I told him that I would give her a shake-down here, last night, in order that he might sleep on it before he decided to let her have any association with Louisa."

"Indeed, Mr. Bounderby? Very thoughtful of you!"

Mrs. Sparsit's Coriolanian nose underwent a slight expansion of the nostrils, and her black eyebrows contracted as she took a sip of tea.

"It's tolerably clear to *me*," said Bounderby, "that the little puss can get small good out of such companionship."

"Are you speaking of the young Miss Gradgrind, Mr. Bounderby?"

"Yes, ma'am, I'm speaking of Louisa."

"Your observation being limited to 'little puss,'" said Mrs. Sparsit, "and there being two little girls in question, I did not know which might be indicated by that expression."

"Louisa," repeated Mr. Bounderby. "Louisa, Louisa."

---

1.   From *The Deserted Village* (1770) lines 53–4 by Oliver Goldsmith (?1730–74), Anglo-Irish poet, playwright and novelist.

"You are quite another father to Louisa, sir." Mrs. Sparsit took a little more tea; and, as she bent her again contracted eyebrows over her steaming cup, rather looked as if her classical countenance were invoking the infernal gods.

"If you had said I was another father to Tom—young Tom, I mean, not my friend Tom Gradgrind—you might have been nearer the mark. I am going to take young Tom into my office. Going to have him under my wing, ma'am."

"Indeed? Rather young for that, is he not, sir?" Mrs. Sparsit's "sir," in addressing Mr. Bounderby, was a word of ceremony, rather exacting consideration for herself in the use, than honouring him.

"I'm not going to take him at once; he is to finish his educational cramming before then," said Bounderby. "By the Lord Harry, he'll have enough of it, first and last! He'd open his eyes, that boy would, if he knew how empty of learning *my* young maw was, at his time of life." Which, by the by, he probably did know, for he had heard it often enough. "But it's extraordinary the difficulty I have on scores of such subjects, in speaking to any one on equal terms. Here, for example, I have been speaking to you this morning about tumblers. Why, what do *you* know about tumblers? At the time when, to have been a tumbler in the mud of the streets, would have been a godsend to me, a prize in the lottery to me, you were at the Italian Opera.[1] You were coming out of the Italian Opera, ma'am, in white satin and jewels, a blaze of splendour, when I hadn't a penny to buy a link[2] to light you."

"I certainly, sir," returned Mrs. Sparsit, with a dignity serenely mournful, "was familiar with the Italian Opera at a very early age."

"Egad, ma'am, so was I," said Bounderby, "—with the wrong side of it. A hard bed the pavement of its Arcade[3] used to make, I assure you. People like you, ma'am, accustomed from infancy to lie on Down feathers, have no idea *how* hard a paving-stone is, without trying it. No, no, it's of no use my talking to *you* about tumblers. I should speak of foreign

---

1. A fashionable theatre in London's Haymarket.
2. A torch or torch-bearer, on sale or hire in the thoroughfares of London before the introduction of street lighting.
3. The arch-covered passage-way in front of the theatre.

dancers, and the West End of London,[1] and May Fair,[2] and lords and ladies and honourables."

"I trust, sir," rejoined Mrs. Sparsit, with decent resignation, "it is not necessary that you should do anything of that kind. I hope I have learnt how to accommodate myself to the changes of life. If I have acquired an interest in hearing of your instructive experiences, and can scarcely hear enough of them, I claim no merit for that, since I believe it is a general sentiment."

"Well, ma'am," said her patron, "perhaps some people may be pleased to say that they do like to hear, in his own unpolished way, what Josiah Bounderby, of Coketown, has gone through. But you must confess that you were born in the lap of luxury, yourself. Come, ma'am, you know you were born in the lap of luxury."

"I do not, sir," returned Mrs. Sparsit with a shake of her head, "deny it."

Mr. Bounderby was obliged to get up from table, and stand with his back to the fire, looking at her; she was such an enhancement of his position.

"And you were in crack society. Devilish high society," he said, warming his legs.

"It is true, sir," returned Mrs. Sparsit, with an affectation of humility the very opposite of his, and therefore in no danger of jostling it.

"You were in the tiptop fashion, and all the rest of it," said Mr. Bounderby.

"Yes, sir," returned Mrs. Sparsit, with a kind of social widowhood upon her. "It is unquestionably true."

Mr. Bounderby, bending himself at the knees, literally embraced his legs in his great satisfaction and laughed aloud. Mr. and Miss Gradgrind being then announced, he received the former with a shake of the hand, and the latter with a kiss.

"Can Jupe be sent here, Bounderby?" asked Mr. Gradgrind.

Certainly. So Jupe was sent there. On coming in, she curtseyed to Mr. Bounderby, and to his friend Tom Gradgrind, and also to Louisa; but

---

1. Fashionable entertainment district.
2. Fashionable residential area in West-Central London.

in her confusion unluckily omitted Mrs. Sparsit. Observing this, the blustrous Bounderby had the following remarks to make:

"Now, I tell you what, my girl. The name of that lady by the teapot, is Mrs. Sparsit. That lady acts as mistress of this house, and she is a highly connected lady. Consequently, if ever you come again into any room in this house, you will make a short stay in it if you don't behave towards that lady in your most respectful manner. Now, I don't care a button what you do to *me*, because I don't affect to be anybody. So far from having high connections I have no connections at all, and I come of the scum of the earth. But towards that lady, I do care what you do; and you shall do what is deferential and respectful, or you shall not come here."

"I hope, Bounderby," said Mr. Gradgrind, in a conciliatory voice, "that this was merely an oversight."

"My friend Tom Gradgrind suggests, Mrs. Sparsit," said Bounderby, "that this was merely an oversight. Very likely. However, as you are aware, ma'am, I don't allow of even oversights towards you."

"You are very good indeed, sir," returned Mrs. Sparsit, shaking her head with her State humility. "It is not worth speaking of."

Sissy, who all this time had been faintly excusing herself with tears in her eyes, was now waved over by the master of the house to Mr. Gradgrind. She stood looking intently at him, and Louisa stood coldly by, with her eyes upon the ground, while he proceeded thus:

"Jupe, I have made up my mind to take you into my house; and, when you are not in attendance at the school, to employ you about Mrs. Gradgrind, who is rather an invalid. I have explained to Miss Louisa— this is Miss Louisa—the miserable but natural end of your late career; and you are to expressly understand that the whole of that subject is past, and is not to be referred to any more. From this time you begin your history. You are, at present, ignorant, I know."

"Yes, sir, very," she answered, curtseying.

"I shall have the satisfaction of causing you to be strictly educated; and you will be a living proof to all who come into communication with you, of the advantages of the training you will receive. You will be reclaimed and formed. You have been in the habit now of reading to your father, and those people I found you among, I dare say?" said Mr. Gradgrind, beckoning her nearer to him before he said so, and dropping his voice.

"Only to father and Merrylegs, sir. At least I mean to father, when Merrylegs was always there."

"Never mind Merrylegs, Jupe," said Mr. Gradgrind, with a passing frown. "I don't ask about him. I understand you to have been in the habit of reading to your father?"

"Oh, yes, sir, thousands of times. They were the happiest—Oh, of all the happy times we had together, sir!"

It was only now when her sorrow broke out, that Louisa looked at her.

"And what," asked Mr. Gradgrind, in a still lower voice, "did you read to your father, Jupe?"

"About the Fairies, sir, and the Dwarf, and the Hunchback, and the Genies,"[1] she sobbed out; "and about—"

"Hush!" said Mr. Gradgrind, "that is enough. Never breathe a word of such destructive nonsense any more. Bounderby, this is a case for rigid training, and I shall observe it with interest."

"Well," returned Mr. Bounderby, "I have given you my opinion already, and I shouldn't do as you do. But, very well, very well. Since you are bent upon it, *very* well!"

So, Mr. Gradgrind and his daughter took Cecilia Jupe off with them to Stone Lodge, and on the way Louisa never spoke one word, good or bad. And Mr. Bounderby went about his daily pursuits. And Mrs. Sparsit got behind her eyebrows and meditated in the gloom of that retreat, all the evening.

---

1.   Probably referring to the stories collected in Grimm's fairy tales and *The Arabian Nights' Entertainments.*

Chapter VIII.
Never Wonder

LET US strike the key-note again, before pursuing the tune.

When she was half a dozen years younger, Louisa had been overheard to begin a conversation with her brother one day, by saying "Tom, I wonder"—upon which Mr. Gradgrind, who was the person overhearing, stepped forth into the light and said, "Louisa, never wonder!"

Herein lay the spring of the mechanical art and mystery of educating the reason without stooping to the cultivation of the sentiments and affections. Never wonder. By means of addition, subtraction, multiplication, and division, settle everything somehow, and never wonder. Bring to me, says M'Choakumchild, yonder baby just able to walk, and I will engage that it shall never wonder.

Now, besides very many babies just able to walk, there happened to be in Coketown a considerable population of babies who had been walking against time towards the infinite world, twenty, thirty, forty, fifty years and more. These portentous infants being alarming creatures to stalk about in any human society, the eighteen denominations incessantly scratched one another's faces and pulled one another's hair by way of agreeing on the steps to be taken for their improvement—which they never did; a surprising circumstance, when the happy adaptation of the means to the end is considered. Still, although they differed in every other particular, conceivable and inconceivable (especially inconceivable), they were pretty well united on the point that these unlucky infants were never to wonder. Body number one, said they must take everything on trust. Body number two, said they must take everything on political economy. Body number three, wrote leaden little books for them, showing how the good grown-up baby invariably got to the Savings-bank, and the bad grown-up baby invariably got transported. Body number four, under dreary pretences of being droll (when it was very melancholy indeed), made the shallowest pretences of concealing pitfalls of knowledge, into which it was the duty of these babies to be smuggled and inveigled. But, all the bodies agreed that they were never to wonder.*

There was a library in Coketown, to which general access was easy. Mr. Gradgrind greatly tormented his mind about what the people read in this library: a point whereon little rivers of tabular statements periodically flowed into the howling ocean of tabular statements, which no diver ever got to any depth in and came up sane. It was a disheartening circumstance, but a melancholy fact, that even these readers persisted in wondering. They wondered about human nature, human passions, human hopes and fears, the struggles, triumphs and defeats, the cares and joys and sorrows, the lives and deaths of common men and women!* They sometimes, after fifteen hours' work, sat down to read mere fables about men and women, more or less like themselves, and about children, more or less like their own. They took De Foe[1] to their bosoms, instead of Euclid,[2] and seemed to be on the whole more comforted by Goldsmith[3] than by Cocker.[4] Mr. Gradgrind was for ever working, in print and out of print, at this eccentric sum, and he never could make out how it yielded this unaccountable product.*

"I am sick of my life, Loo. I hate it altogether, and I hate everybody except you," said the unnatural young Thomas Gradgrind in the hair-cutting chamber at twilight.

"You don't hate Sissy, Tom?"

"I hate to be obliged to call her Jupe. And she hates me," said Tom, moodily.

"No, she does not, Tom, I am sure!"

"She must," said Tom. "She must just hate and detest the whole set-out of us. They'll bother her head off, I think, before they have done with her. Already she's getting as pale as wax, and as heavy as—I am."

Young Thomas expressed these sentiments sitting astride of a chair before the fire, with his arms on the back, and his sulky face on his arms. His sister sat in the darker corner by the fireside, now looking at him, now looking at the bright sparks as they dropped upon the hearth.

---

1. Daniel Defoe (1660–1731), English journalist and novelist, author of *Robinson Crusoe,* etc.
2. The Greek mathematician Eucleides (fl. c.300 BC), famous for his treatise on geometry known as the Elements.
3. See note to p. 81 above.
4. Edward Cocker (1631–75), English author of *Cocker's Arithmetic,* a popular textbook which passed through more than 100 editions and was still in use in the nineteenth century.

"As to me," said Tom, tumbling his hair all manner of ways with his sulky hands, "I am a Donkey, that's what *I* am. I am as obstinate as one, I am more stupid than one, I get as much pleasure as one, and I should like to kick like one."

"Not me, I hope, Tom?"

"No, Loo; I wouldn't hurt *you*. I made an exception of you at first. I don't know what this—jolly old—Jaundiced Jail," Tom had paused to find a sufficiently complimentary and expressive name for the parental roof, and seemed to relieve his mind for a moment by the strong alliteration of this one, "would be without you."

"Indeed, Tom? Do you really and truly say so?"

"Why, of course I do. What's the use of talking about it!" returned Tom, chafing his face on his coat-sleeve, as if to mortify his flesh, and have it in unison with his spirit.

"Because, Tom," said his sister, after silently watching the sparks awhile, "as I get older, and nearer growing up, I often sit wondering here, and think how unfortunate it is for me that I can't reconcile you to home better than I am able to do. I don't know what other girls know. I can't play to you, or sing to you. I can't talk to you so as to lighten your mind, for I never see any amusing sights or read any amusing books that it would be a pleasure or a relief to you to talk about, when you are tired."

"Well, no more do I. I am as bad as you in that respect; and I am a Mule too, which you're not. If father was determined to make me either a Prig or a Mule, and I am not a Prig, why, it stands to reason, I must be a Mule. And so I am," said Tom, desperately.

"It's a great pity," said Louisa, after another pause, and speaking thoughtfully out of her dark corner; "it's a great pity, Tom. It's very unfortunate for both of us."

"Oh! You," said Tom; "you are a girl, Loo, and a girl comes out of it better than a boy does. I don't miss anything in you. You are the only pleasure I have—you can brighten even this place—and you can always lead me as you like."

"You are a dear brother, Tom; and while you think I can do such things, I don't so much mind knowing better. Though I do know better, Tom, and am very sorry for it." She came and kissed him, and went back into her corner again.

"I wish I could collect all the Facts we hear so much about," said Tom, spitefully setting his teeth, "and all the Figures, and all the people who found them out: and I wish I could put a thousand barrels of gunpowder under them, and blow them all up together! However, when I go to live with old Bounderby, I'll have my revenge."

"Your revenge, Tom?"

"I mean, I'll enjoy myself a little, and go about and see something, and hear something. I'll recompense myself for the way in which I have been brought up."

"But don't disappoint yourself beforehand, Tom. Mr. Bounderby thinks as father thinks, and is a great deal rougher, and not half so kind."

"Oh!" said Tom, laughing; "I don't mind that. I shall very well know how to manage and smooth old Bounderby!"

Their shadows were defined upon the wall, but those of the high presses[1] in the room were all blended together on the wall and on the ceiling, as if the brother and sister were overhung by a dark cavern. Or, a fanciful imagination—if such treason could have been there—might have made it out to be the shadow of their subject, and of its lowering association with their future.

"What is your great mode of smoothing and managing, Tom? Is it a secret?"

"Oh!" said Tom, "if it is a secret, it's not far off. It's you. You are his little pet, you are his favourite; he'll do anything for you. When he says to me what I don't like, I shall say to him, 'My sister Loo will be hurt and disappointed, Mr. Bounderby. She always used to tell me she was sure you would be easier with me than this.' That'll bring him about, or nothing will."

After waiting for some answering remark, and getting none, Tom wearily relapsed into the present time, and twined himself yawning round and about the rails of his chair, and rumpled his head more and more, until he suddenly looked up, and asked:

"Have you gone to sleep, Loo?"

"No, Tom. I am looking at the fire."

"You seem to find more to look at in it than ever I could find," said Tom. "Another of the advantages, I suppose, of being a girl."

---

1.   Cupboards.

"Tom," enquired his sister, slowly, and in a curious tone, as if she were reading what she asked in the fire, and it were not quite plainly written there, "do you look forward with any satisfaction to this change to Mr. Bounderby's?"

"Why, there's one thing to be said of it," returned Tom, pushing his chair from him, and standing up; "it will be getting away from home."

"There is one thing to be said of it," Louisa repeated in her former curious tone; "it will be getting away from home. Yes."

"Not but what I shall be very unwilling, both to leave you, Loo, and to leave you here. But I must go, you know, whether I like it or not; and I had better go where I can take with me some advantage of your influence, than where I should lose it altogether. Don't you see?"

"Yes, Tom."

The answer was so long in coming, though there was no indecision in it, that Tom went and leaned on the back of her chair, to contemplate the fire which so engrossed her, from her point of view, and see what he could make of it.

"Except that it is a fire," said Tom, "it looks to me as stupid and blank as everything else looks. What do you see in it? Not a circus?"

"I don't see anything in it, Tom, particularly. But since I have been looking at it, I have been wondering about you and me, grown up."

"Wondering again!" said Tom.

"I have such unmanageable thoughts," returned his sister, "that they *will* wonder."

"Then I beg of you, Louisa," said Mrs. Gradgrind, who had opened the door without being heard, "to do nothing of that description, for goodness' sake, you inconsiderate girl, or I shall never hear the last of it from your father. And, Thomas, it is really shameful, with my poor head continually wearing me out, that a boy brought up as you have been, and whose education has cost what yours has, should be found encouraging his sister to wonder, when he knows his father has expressly said that she is not to do it."

Louisa denied Tom's participation in the offence; but her mother stopped her with the conclusive answer, "Louisa, don't tell me, in my state of health; for unless you had been encouraged, it is morally and physically impossible that you could have done it."

"I was encouraged by nothing, mother, but by looking at the red sparks dropping out of the fire, and whitening and dying. It made me think, after all, how short my life would be, and how little I could hope to do in it."

"Nonsense!" said Mrs. Gradgrind, rendered almost energetic. "Nonsense! Don't stand there and tell me such stuff, Louisa, to my face, when you know very well that if it was ever to reach your father's ears I should never hear the last of it. After all the trouble that has been taken with you! After the lectures you have attended, and the experiments you have seen! After I have heard you myself, when the whole of my right side has been benumbed, going on with your master about combustion, and calcination, and calorification, and I may say every kind of ation that could drive a poor invalid distracted, to hear you talking in this absurd way about sparks and ashes! I wish," whimpered Mrs. Gradgrind, taking a chair, and discharging her strongest point before succumbing under these mere shadows of facts, "yes, I really *do* wish that I had never had a family, and then you would have known what it was to do without me!"

CHAPTER IX.
SISSY'S PROGRESS

SISSY JUPE had not an easy time of it, between Mr. M'Choakumchild and Mrs. Gradgrind, and was not without strong impulses, in the first months of her probation, to run away. It hailed facts all day long so very hard, and life in general was opened to her as such a closely ruled ciphering-book, that assuredly she would have run away, but for only one restraint.

It is lamentable to think of; but this restraint was the result of no arithmetical process, was self-imposed in defiance of all calculation, and went dead against any table of probabilities that any Actuary would have drawn up from the premises. That girl believed her father had not deserted her; she lived in the hope that he would come back, and in the faith that he would be made the happier by her remaining where she was.

The wretched ignorance with which Jupe clung to this consolation, rejecting the superior comfort of knowing, on a sound arithmetical basis, that her father was an unnatural vagabond, filled Mr. Gradgrind with pity. Yet, what was to be done? M'Choakumchild reported that she had a very dense head for figures; that, once possessed with a general idea of the globe, she took the smallest conceivable interest in its exact measurements; that she was extremely slow in the acquisition of dates, unless some pitiful incident happened to be connected therewith; that she would burst into tears on being required (by the mental process) immediately to name the cost of two hundred and forty-seven muslin caps at fourteen-pence halfpenny; that she was as low down, in the school, as low could be; that after eight weeks of induction into the elements of Political Economy, she had only yesterday been set right by a prattler three feet high, for returning to the question, "What is the first principle of this science?" the absurd answer, "To do unto others as I would that they should do unto me."[1]

Mr. Gradgrind observed, shaking his head, that all this was very bad; that it showed the necessity of infinite grinding at the mill of knowledge, as per system, schedule, blue book,[2] report, and tabular statements A to Z; and that Jupe "must be kept to it." So Jupe was kept to it, and became low-spirited, but no wiser.

"It would be a fine thing to be you, Miss Louisa!" she said, one night, when Louisa had endeavoured to make her perplexities for the next day something clearer to her.

"Do you think so?"

"I should know so much, Miss Louisa. All that is difficult to me now, would be so easy then."

"You might not be the better for it, Sissy."

Sissy submitted that, after a little hesitation, "I should not be the worse, Miss Louisa." To which Miss Louisa answered, "I don't know that."

There had been so little communication between these two—both because life at Stone Lodge went monotonously round like a piece of machinery which discouraged human interference, and because of the prohibition relative to Sissy's past career—that they were almost strangers.

---

1.   Compare the teaching of Jesus in Matthew 7:7–12, and the response to 'What is thy duty towards thy Neighbour?' from the Catechism in the Book of Common Prayer.

2.   Official reports of Parliament and the Privy Council were bound in dark blue paper covers and thus generally referred to.

Sissy, with her dark eyes wonderingly directed to Louisa's face, was uncertain whether to say more or to remain silent.

"You are more useful to my mother, and more pleasant with her than I can ever be," Louisa resumed. "You are pleasanter to yourself, than *I* am to *my*self."

"But, if you please, Miss Louisa," Sissy pleaded, "I am—Oh so stupid!"

Louisa, with a brighter laugh than usual, told her she would be wiser by-and-by.

"You don't know," said Sissy, half-crying, "what a stupid girl I am. All through school hours I make mistakes. Mr. and Mrs. M'Choakumchild call me up, over and over again, regularly to make mistakes. I can't help them. They seem to come natural to me."

"Mr. and Mrs. M'Choakumchild never make any mistakes themselves, I suppose, Sissy?"

"Oh no!" she eagerly returned. "They know everything."

"Tell me some of your mistakes."

"I am most ashamed," said Sissy, with reluctance. "But to-day, for instance, Mr. M'Choakumchild was explaining to us about Natural Prosperity."

"National, I think it must have been," observed Louisa.

"Yes, it was—But isn't it the same?" she timidly asked.

"You had better say, National, as he said so," returned Louisa, with her dry reserve.

"National Prosperity. And he said, Now, this schoolroom is a Nation. And in this nation, there are fifty millions of money. Isn't this a prosperous nation? Girl number twenty, isn't this a prosperous nation, and a'n't you in a thriving state?"

"What did you say?" asked Louisa.

"Miss Louisa, I said I didn't know. I thought I couldn't know whether it was a prosperous nation or not, and whether I was in a thriving state or not, unless I knew who had got the money, and whether any of it was mine. But that had nothing to do with it. It was not in the figures at all," said Sissy, wiping her eyes.

"That was a great mistake of yours," observed Louisa.

"Yes, Miss Louisa, I know it was, now. Then Mr. M'Choakumchild said he would try me again. And he said, This schoolroom is an immense town, and in it there are a million of inhabitants, and only five-and-twenty are starved to death in the streets, in the course of a year. What is your remark on that proportion? And my remark was—for I couldn't think of a better one—that I thought it must be just as hard upon those who were starved, whether the others were a million or a million million. And that was wrong, too."

"Of course it was."

"Then Mr. M'Choakumchild said he would try me once more. And he said, Here are the stutterings—"

"Statistics," said Louisa.

"Yes, Miss Louisa—they always remind me of stutterings, and that's another of my mistakes—of accidents upon the sea. And I find (Mr. M'Choakumchild said) that in a given time a hundred thousand persons went to sea on long voyages, and only five hundred of them were drowned or burnt to death. What is the percentage? And I said, Miss;" here Sissy fairly sobbed as confessing with extreme contrition to her greatest error; "I said it was nothing."

"Nothing, Sissy?"

"Nothing, Miss—to the relations and friends of the people who were killed. I shall never learn," said Sissy. "And the worst of all is, that although my poor father wished me so much to learn, and although I am so anxious to learn, because he wished me to, I am afraid I don't like it."

Louisa stood looking at the pretty modest head, as it drooped abashed before her, until it was raised again to glance at her face. Then she asked:

"Did your father know so much himself, that he wished you to be well taught too, Sissy?"

Sissy hesitated before replying, and so plainly showed her sense that they were entering on forbidden ground, that Louisa added, "No one hears us; and if any one did, I am sure no harm could be found in such an innocent question."

"No, Miss Louisa," answered Sissy, upon this encouragement, shaking her head; "father knows very little indeed. It's as much as he can do to write; and it's more than people in general can do to read his writing. Though it's plain to *me*."

"Your mother?"

"Father says she was quite a scholar. She died when I was born. She was;" Sissy made the terrible communication nervously; "she was a dancer."

"Did your father love her?" Louisa asked these questions with a strong, wild, wandering interest peculiar to her; an interest gone astray like a banished creature, and hiding in solitary places.

"Oh yes! As dearly as he loves me. Father loved me, first, for her sake. He carried me about with him when I was quite a baby. We have never been asunder from that time."

"Yet he leaves you now, Sissy?"

"Only for my good. Nobody understands him as I do; nobody knows him as I do. When he left me for my good—he never would have left me for his own—I know he was almost broken-hearted with the trial. He will not be happy for a single minute, till he comes back."

"Tell me more about him," said Louisa, "I will never ask you again. Where did you live?"

"We travelled about the country, and had no fixed place to live in. Father's a;" Sissy whispered the awful word, "a clown."

"To make the people laugh?" said Louisa, with a nod of intelligence.

"Yes. But they wouldn't laugh sometimes, and then father cried. Lately, they very often wouldn't laugh, and he used to come home despairing. Father's not like most. Those who didn't know him as well as I do, and didn't love him as dearly as I do, might believe he was not quite right. Sometimes they played tricks upon him; but they never knew how he felt them, and shrunk up, when he was alone with me. He was far, far timider than they thought!"

"And you were his comfort through everything?"

She nodded, with the tears rolling down her face. "I hope so, and father said I was. It was because he grew so scared and trembling, and because he felt himself to be a poor, weak, ignorant, helpless man (those used to be his words), that he wanted me so much to know a great deal, and be different from him. I used to read to him to cheer his courage, and he was very fond of that. They were wrong books—I am never to speak of them here—but we didn't know there was any harm in them."

"And he liked them?" said Louisa, with a searching gaze on Sissy all this time.

"Oh very much! They kept him, many times, from what did him real harm. And often and often of a night, he used to forget all his troubles in wondering whether the Sultan would let the lady go on with the story, or would have her head cut off before it was finished."[1]

"And your father was always kind? To the last?" asked Louisa; contravening the great principle, and wondering very much.

"Always, always!" returned Sissy, clasping her hands. "Kinder and kinder than I can tell. He was angry only one night, and that was not to me, but Merrylegs. Merrylegs;" she whispered the awful fact; "is his performing dog."

"Why was he angry with the dog?" Louisa demanded.

"Father, soon after they came home from performing, told Merrylegs to jump on the backs of two chairs and stand across them—which is one of his tricks. He looked at father, and didn't do it at once. Everything of father's had gone wrong that night, and he hadn't pleased the public at all. He cried out that the very dog knew he was failing, and had no compassion on him. Then he beat the dog, and I was frightened, and said, 'Father, father! Pray don't hurt the creature who is so fond of you! Oh Heaven forgive you, father, stop!' And he stopped, and the dog was bloody, and father lay down crying on the floor with the dog in his arms, and the dog licked his face."

Louisa saw that she was sobbing; and going to her, kissed her, took her hand, and sat down beside her.

"Finish by telling me how your father left you, Sissy. Now that I have asked you so much, tell me the end. The blame, if there is any blame, is mine, not yours."

"Dear Miss Louisa," said Sissy, covering her eyes, and sobbing yet; "I came home from the school that afternoon, and found poor father just come home too, from the booth. And he sat rocking himself over the fire, as if he was in pain. And I said, 'Have you hurt yourself, father?' (as he did sometimes, like they all did), and he said, 'A little, my darling.' And when I came to stoop down and look up at his face, I saw that he was crying. The more I spoke to him, the more he hid his face; and at first he shook all over, and said nothing but 'My darling;' and 'My love!'"

---

1.   The frame tale in *The Arabian Nights' Entertainments*, where the princess Scheherazade repeatedly uses the suspense of the stories she tells to put off her death at the hands of the sultan Schahriar.

Here Tom came lounging in, and stared at the two with a coolness not particularly savouring of interest in anything but himself, and not much of that at present.

"I am asking Sissy a few questions, Tom," observed his sister. "You have no occasion to go away; but don't interrupt us for a moment, Tom dear."

"Oh! very well!" returned Tom. "Only father has brought old Bounderby home, and I want you to come into the drawing-room. Because if you come, there's a good chance of old Bounderby's asking me to dinner; and if you don't, there's none."

"I'll come directly."

"I'll wait for you," said Tom, "to make sure."

Sissy resumed in a lower voice. "At last poor father said that he had given no satisfaction again, and never did give any satisfaction now, and that he was a shame and disgrace, and I should have done better without him all along. I said all the affectionate things to him that came into my heart, and presently he was quiet and I sat down by him, and told him all about the school and everything that had been said and done there. When I had no more left to tell, he put his arms round my neck, and kissed me a great many times. Then he asked me to fetch some of the stuff he used, for the little hurt he had, and to get it at the best place, which was at the other end of town from there; and then, after kissing me again, he let me go. When I had gone downstairs, I turned back that I might be a little more company to him yet, and looked in at the door, and said, 'Father dear, shall I take Merrylegs?' Father shook his head and said, 'No, Sissy, no; take nothing that's known to be mine, my darling;' and I left him sitting by the fire. Then the thought must have come upon him, poor, poor father! of going away to try something for my sake; for when I came back, he was gone."

"I say! Look sharp for old Bounderby, Loo!" Tom remonstrated.

"There's no more to tell, Miss Louisa. I keep the nine oils ready for him, and I know he will come back. Every letter that I see in Mr. Gradgrind's hands takes my breath away and blinds my eyes, for I think it comes from my father, or from Mr. Sleary about my father. Mr. Sleary promised to write as soon as ever father should be heard of, and I trust to him to keep his word."

"Do look sharp for old Bounderby, Loo!" said Tom, with an impatient whistle. "He'll be off if you don't look sharp!"

After this, whenever Sissy dropped a curtsey to Mr. Gradgrind in the presence of his family, and said in a faltering way, "I beg your pardon, sir, for being troublesome—but—have you had any letter yet about me?" Louisa would suspend the occupation of the moment, whatever it was, and look for the reply as earnestly as Sissy did. And when Mr. Gradgrind regularly answered, "No, Jupe, nothing of the sort," the trembling of Sissy's lip would be repeated in Louisa's face, and her eyes would follow Sissy with compassion to the door. Mr. Gradgrind usually improved these occasions by remarking, when she was gone, that if Jupe had been properly trained from an early age she would have remonstrated to herself on sound principles the baselessness of these fantastic hopes. Yet it did seem (though not to him, for he saw nothing of it) as if fantastic hope could take as strong a hold as Fact.

This observation must be limited exclusively to his daughter. As to Tom, he was becoming that not unprecedented triumph of calculation which is usually at work on number one.[1] As to Mrs. Gradgrind, if she said anything on the subject, she would come a little way out of her wrappers, like a feminine dormouse, and say:

"Good gracious bless me, how my poor head is vexed and worried by the girl Jupe's so perseveringly asking, over and over again, about her tiresome letters! Upon my word and honour I seem to be fated, destined, and ordained, to live in the midst of things that I am never to hear the last of. It really is a most extraordinary circumstance that it appears as if I never was to hear the last of anything!"

At about this point, Mr. Gradgrind's eye would fall upon her; and under the influence of that wintry piece of fact, she would become torpid again.

---

1.   Looking after number one, or acting entirely out of self-interest. The phrase recurs on many occasions in the narrative to characterize the behaviour of Tom or Bitzer, or utilitarian principles in general.

Chapter X.
Stephen Blackpool

I ENTERTAIN a weak idea that the English people are as hard-worked as any people upon whom the sun shines. I acknowledge to this ridiculous idiosyncrasy, as a reason why I would give them a little more play.

In the hardest working part of Coketown; in the innermost fortifications of that ugly citadel, where Nature was as strongly bricked out as killing airs and gases were bricked in; at the heart of the labyrinth of narrow courts upon courts, and close streets upon streets, which had come into existence piecemeal, every piece in a violent hurry for some one man's purpose, and the whole an unnatural family, shouldering, and trampling, and pressing one another to death; in the last close nook of this great exhausted receiver, where the chimneys, for want of air to make a draught, were built in an immense variety of stunted and crooked shapes, as though every house put out a sign of the kind of people who might be expected to be born in it; among the multitude of Coketown, generically called "the Hands,"—a race who would have found more favour with some people, if Providence had seen fit to make them only hands, or, like the lower creatures of the seashore, only hands and stomachs—lived a certain Stephen Blackpool, forty years of age.

Stephen looked older, but he had had a hard life. It is said that every life has its roses and thorns; there seemed, however, to have been a misadventure or mistake in Stephen's case, whereby somebody else had become possessed of his roses, and he had become possessed of the same somebody else's thorns in addition to his own. He had known, to use his words, a peck of trouble.[1] He was usually called Old Stephen, in a kind of rough homage to the fact.

A rather stooping man, with a knitted brow, a pondering expression of face, and a hard-looking head sufficiently capacious, on which his iron-grey hair lay long and thin, Old Stephen might have passed for a particularly intelligent man in his condition. Yet he was not. He took no place among those remarkable "Hands," who, piecing together their broken

---

1.   I.e. a great deal of trouble (idiomatic phrase).

intervals of leisure through many years, had mastered difficult sciences, and acquired a knowledge of most unlikely things. He held no station among the Hands who could make speeches and carry on debates. Thousands of his compeers could talk much better than he, at any time. He was a good power-loom weaver, and a man of perfect integrity. What more he was, or what else he had in him, if anything, let him show for himself.

The lights in the great factories, which looked, when they were illuminated, like Fairy palaces—or the travellers by express-train said so—were all extinguished; and the bells had rung for knocking off for the night, and had ceased again; and the Hands, men and women, boy and girl, were clattering home.[1] Old Stephen was standing in the street, with the old sensation upon him which the stoppage of the machinery always produced—the sensation of its having worked and stopped in his own head.

"Yet I don't see Rachael, still!" said he.

It was a wet night, and many groups of young women passed him, with their shawls drawn over their bare heads and held close under their chins to keep the rain out. He knew Rachael well, for a glance at any one of these groups was sufficient to show him that she was not there. At last, there were no more to come; and then he turned away, saying in a tone of disappointment, "Why, then, I ha' missed her!"

But, he had not gone the length of three streets, when he saw another of the shawled figures in advance of him, at which he looked so keenly that perhaps its mere shadow indistinctly reflected on the wet pavement—if he could have seen it without the figure itself moving along from lamp to lamp, brightening and fading as it went—would have been enough to tell him who was there. Making his pace at once much quicker and much softer, he darted on until he was very near this figure, then fell into his former walk, and called "Rachael!"

She turned, being then in the brightness of a lamp; and raising her hood a little, showed a quiet oval face, dark and rather delicate, irradiated by a pair of very gentle eyes, and further set off by the perfect order of

---

1.	I.e. wearing the wooden clogs common in Lancashire.

her shining black hair. It was not a face in its first bloom; she was a woman of five and thirty years of age.

"Ah, lad! 'Tis thou?"* When she had said this, with a smile which would have been quite expressed, though nothing of her had been seen but her pleasant eyes, she replaced her hood again, and they went on together.

"I thought thou wast ahind me, Rachael?"

"No."

"Early t'night, lass?"

"'Times I'm a little early, Stephen! 'times a little late. I'm never to be counted on, going home."

"Nor going t'other way, neither, 't seems to me, Rachael?"

"No, Stephen."

He looked at her with some disappointment in his face, but with a respectful and patient conviction that she must be right in whatever she did. The expression was not lost upon her; she laid her hand lightly on his arm a moment as if to thank him for it.

"We are such true friends, lad, and such old friends, and getting to be such old folk, now."

"No, Rachael, thou'rt as young as ever thou wast."

"One of us would be puzzled how to get old, Stephen, without t'other getting so too, both being alive," she answered, laughing; "but, anyways, we're such old friends, that t' hide a word of honest truth fro' one another would be a sin and a pity. 'Tis better not to walk too much together. 'Times, yes! 'Twould be hard, indeed, if 'twas not to be at all," she said, with a cheerfulness she sought to communicate to him.

"'Tis hard, anyways, Rachael."

"Try to think not; and 'twill seem better."

"I've tried a long time and 'ta'nt got better. But thou'rt right; 't might mak fok talk, even of thee. Thou hast been that to me, Rachael, through so many year: thou hast done me so much good, and heartened me in that cheering way, that thy word is law to me. Ah, lass, and a bright good law! Better than some real ones."

"Never fret about them, Stephen," she answered quickly, and not without an anxious glance at his face. "Let the laws be."

"Yes," he said, with a slow nod or two. "Let 'em be. Let everything be. Let all sorts alone. 'Tis a muddle, and that's aw."

"Always a muddle?" said Rachael, with another gentle touch upon his arm, as if to recall him out of the thoughtfulness, in which he was biting the long ends of his loose neckerchief as he walked along. The touch had its instantaneous effect. He let them fall, turned a smiling face upon her, and said, as he broke into a good-humoured laugh, "Ay, Rachael, lass, awlus a muddle. That's where I stick. I come to the muddle many times and agen, and I never get beyond it."

They had walked some distance, and were near their own homes. The woman's was the first reached. It was in one of the many small streets for which the favourite undertaker (who turned a handsome sum out of the one poor ghastly pomp of the neighbourhood) kept a black ladder,[1] in order that those who had done their daily groping up and down the narrow stairs might slide out of this working world by the windows. She stopped at the corner, and putting her hand in his, wished him good night.

"Good night, dear lass; good night!"

She went, with her neat figure and her sober womanly step, down the dark street, and he stood looking after her until she turned into one of the small houses. There was not a flutter of her coarse shawl, perhaps, but had its interest in this man's eyes; not a tone of her voice but had its echo in his innermost heart.*

When she was lost to his view, he pursued his homeward way, glancing up sometimes at the sky, where the clouds were sailing fast and wildly. But, they were broken now, and the rain had ceased, and the moon shone,—looking down the high chimneys of Coketown on the deep furnaces below, and casting Titanic shadows[2] of the steam-engines at rest, upon the walls where they were lodged. The man seemed to have brightened with the night, as he went on.

His home, in such another street as the first, saving that it was narrower, was over a little shop. How it came to pass that any people found it worth their while to sell or buy the wretched little toys, mixed up in its window with cheap newspapers and pork (there was a leg to be raffled for to-morrow night), matters not here. He took his end of candle

---

1.   Slide used by Victorian undertakers to remove coffins through the windows of tenement rooms otherwise accessible only by steep narrow staircases.

2.   I.e. massive shadows, resembling the Titans, giants of classical mythology.

from a shelf, lighted it at another end of candle on the counter, without disturbing the mistress of the shop who was asleep in her little room, and went upstairs into his lodging.

It was a room, not unacquainted with the black ladder under various tenants; but as neat, at present, as such a room could be. A few books and writings were on an old bureau in a corner, the furniture was decent and sufficient, and, though the atmosphere was tainted, the room was clean.

Going to the hearth to set the candle down upon a round three-legged table standing there, he stumbled against something. As he recoiled, looking down at it, it raised itself up into the form of a woman in a sitting attitude.

"Heaven's mercy, woman!" he cried, falling farther off from the figure. "Hast thou come back again!"

Such a woman! A disabled, drunken creature, barely able to preserve her sitting posture by steadying herself with one begrimed hand on the floor, while the other was so purposeless in trying to push away her tangled hair from her face, that it only blinded her the more with the dirt upon it. A creature so foul to look at, in her tatters, stains and splashes, but so much fouler than that in her moral infamy, that it was a shameful thing even to see her.

After an impatient oath or two, and some stupid clawing of herself with the hand not necessary to her support, she got her hair away from her eyes sufficiently to obtain a sight of him. Then she sat swaying her body to and fro, and making gestures with her unnerved arm, which seemed intended as the accompaniment to a fit of laughter, though her face was stolid and drowsy.

"Eigh, lad? What, yo'r there?" Some hoarse sounds meant for this, came mockingly out of her at last; and her head dropped forward on her breast.

"Back agen?" she screeched, after some minutes, as if he had that moment said it. "Yes! And back agen. Back agen ever and ever so often. Back? Yes, back. Why not?"

Roused by the unmeaning violence with which she cried it out, she scrambled up, and stood supporting herself with her shoulders against the wall; dangling in one hand by the string, a dunghill-fragment of a bonnet, and trying to look scornfully at him.

"I'll sell thee off again, and I'll sell thee off again, and I'll sell thee off a score of times!" she cried, with something between a furious menace and an effort at a defiant dance. "Come awa' from th' bed!" He was sitting on the side of it, with his face hidden in his hands. "Come awa' from 't. 'Tis mine, and I've a right to 't!"

As she staggered to it, he avoided her with a shudder, and passed—his face still hidden—to the opposite end of the room. She threw herself upon the bed heavily, and soon was snoring hard. He sunk into a chair, and moved but once all that night. It was to throw a covering over her; as if his hands were not enough to hide her, even in the darkness.

CHAPTER XI.
NO WAY OUT

THE FAIRY palaces burst into illumination, before pale morning showed the monstrous serpents of smoke trailing themselves over Coketown. A clattering of clogs upon the pavement; a rapid ringing of bells; and all the melancholy mad elephants, polished and oiled up for the day's monotony, were at their heavy exercise again.

Stephen bent over his loom, quiet, watchful and steady. A special contrast, as every man was in the forest of looms where Stephen worked, to the crashing, smashing, tearing piece of mechanism at which he laboured. Never fear, good people of an anxious turn of mind, that Art will consign Nature to oblivion. Set anywhere, side by side, the work of God and the work of man; and the former, even though it be a troop of Hands of very small account, will gain in dignity from the comparison.

So many hundred Hands in this Mill; so many hundred horse Steam Power. It is known, to the force of a single pound weight, what the engine will do; but, not all the calculators of the National Debt can tell me the capacity for good or evil, for love or hatred, for patriotism or discontent, for the decomposition of virtue into vice, or the reverse, at any single moment in the soul of one of these its quiet servants, with the composed faces and the regulated actions. There is no mystery in it; there is an unfathomable mystery in the meanest of them, for ever.—Supposing we were to reverse our arithmetic for material objects, and to govern these awful unknown quantities by other means!

The day grew strong, and showed itself outside, even against the flaming lights within. The lights were turned out, and the work went on. The rain fell, and the Smoke-serpents, submissive to the curse of all that tribe,[1] trailed themselves upon the earth. In the waste-yard outside, the steam from the escape pipe, the litter of barrels and old iron, the shining heaps of coals, the ashes everywhere, were shrouded in a veil of mist and rain.

The work went on, until the noon-bell rang. More clattering upon the pavements. The looms, the wheels, and Hands all out of gear for an hour.

Stephen came out of the hot mill into the damp wind and cold wet streets, haggard and worn. He turned from his own class and his own quarter, taking nothing but a little bread as he walked along, towards the hill on which his principal employer lived, in a red house with black outside shutters, green inside blinds, a black street door, up two white steps, BOUNDERBY (in letters very like himself) upon a brazen plate, and a round brazen door-handle underneath it, like a brazen full-stop.

Mr. Bounderby was at his lunch. So Stephen had expected. Would his servant say that one of the Hands begged leave to speak to him? Message in return, requiring name of such Hand. Stephen Blackpool. There was nothing troublesome against Stephen Blackpool; yes, he might come in.

Stephen Blackpool in the parlour. Mr. Bounderby (whom he just knew by sight), at lunch on chop and sherry. Mrs. Sparsit netting at the fireside, in a side-saddle attitude, with one foot in a cotton stirrup.[2] It was a part, at once of Mrs. Sparsit's dignity and service, not to lunch. She supervised the meal officially, but implied that in her own stately person she considered lunch a weakness.

"Now, Stephen," said Mr. Bounderby, "what's the matter with *you*?"

Stephen made a bow. Not a servile one—these Hands will never do that! Lord bless you, sir, you'll never catch them at that, if they have been with you twenty years!—and, as a complimentary toilet for Mrs. Sparsit, tucked his neckerchief ends into his waistcoat.

---

1.   See God's curse on the serpent in the Garden of Eden in Genesis 3:14.
2.   Making a network article such as a purse, keeping tension in the thread by wrapping it around the foot; a common form of Victorian needlework.

"Now, you know," said Mr. Bounderby, taking some sherry, "we have never had any difficulty with you, and you have never been one of the unreasonable ones. You don't expect to be set up in a coach and six, and to be fed on turtle soup and venison, with a gold spoon, as a good many of 'em do!" Mr. Bounderby always represented this to be the sole, immediate, and direct object of any Hand who was not entirely satisfied; "and therefore I know already that you have not come here to make a complaint. Now, you know, I am certain of that, beforehand."

"No, sir, sure I ha' not coom for nowt o' th' kind."

Mr. Bounderby seemed agreeably surprised, notwithstanding his previous strong conviction. "Very well," he returned. "You're a steady Hand, and I was not mistaken. Now, let me hear what it's all about. As it's not that, let me hear what it is. What have you got to say? Out with it, lad!"

Stephen happened to glance towards Mrs. Sparsit. "I can go, Mr. Bounderby, if you wish it," said that self-sacrificing lady, making a feint of taking her foot out of the stirrup.

Mr. Bounderby stayed her, by holding a mouthful of chop in suspension before swallowing it, and putting out his left hand. Then, withdrawing his hand and swallowing his mouthful of chop, he said to Stephen:

"Now you know, this good lady is a born lady, a high lady. You are not to suppose because she keeps my house for me, that she hasn't been very high up the tree—ah, up at the top of the tree! Now, if you have got anything to say that can't be said before a born lady, this lady will leave the room. If what you have got to say *can* be said before a born lady, this lady will stay where she is."

"Sir, I hope I never had nowt to say, not fitten for a born lady to year, sin' I were born mysen'," was the reply, accompanied with a slight flush.

"Very well," said Mr. Bounderby, pushing away his plate and leaning back. "Fire away!"

"I ha' coom," Stephen began, raising his eyes from the floor, after a moment's consideration, "to ask yo yor advice. I need 't overmuch. I were married on Eas'r Monday nineteen year sin, long and dree.[1] She were a young lass—pretty enow—wi' good accounts of herseln. Well! She went

---

1. Wearisome, dreary (dialect).

bad—soon. Not along of me. Gonnows I were not a unkind husband to her."

"I have heard all this before," said Mr. Bounderby. "She took to drinking, left off working, sold the furniture, pawned the clothes, and played old Gooseberry."[1]

"I were patient wi' her."

("The more fool you, I think," said Mr. Bounderby, in confidence to his wine-glass.)

"I were very patient wi' her. I tried to wean her fra't ower and ower agen. I tried this, I tried that, I tried t'other. I ha' gone home, many's the time, and found all vanished as I had in the world, and her without a sense left to bless herseln lying on bare ground. I ha' dun't not once, not twice—twenty time!"

Every line in his face deepened as he said it, and put in its affecting evidence of the suffering he had undergone.

"From bad to worse, from worse to worsen. She left me. She disgraced herseln everyways, bitter and bad. She coom back, she coom back, she coom back. What could I do t'hinder her? I ha' walked the streets nights long, ere ever I'd go home. I ha' gone t' th' brigg, minded to fling myseln ower, and ha' no more on 't. I ha' bore that much, that I were owd when I were young."

Mrs. Sparsit, easily ambling along with her netting-needles, raised the Coriolanian eyebrows and shook her head, as much as to say, "The great know trouble as well as the small. Please to turn your humble eye in My direction."

"I ha' paid her to keep awa' fra' me. These five year I ha' paid her. I ha' gotten decent fewtrils[2] about me agen. I ha' lived hard and sad, but not ashamed and fearfo' a' the minnits o' my life. Last night, I went home. There she lay upon my har-stone! There she IS!"

In the strength of his misfortune, and the energy of his distress, he fired for the moment like a proud man. In another moment, he stood as he had stood all the time—his usual stoop upon him; his pondering face

---

1.   Old Gooseberry is the Devil, so the meaning is 'made havoc' (slang).
2.   Trifles, personal possessions (dialect).

addressed to Mr. Bounderby, with a curious expression on it, half shrewd, half perplexed, as if his mind were set upon unravelling something very difficult; his hat held tight in his left hand, which rested on his hip; his right arm, with a rugged propriety and force of action, very earnestly emphasizing what he said: not least so when it always passed, a little bent, but not withdrawn, as he paused.

"I was acquainted with all this, you know," said Mr. Bounderby, "except the last clause, long ago. It's a bad job; that's what it is. You had better have been satisfied as you were, and not have got married. However, it's too late to say that."

"Was it an unequal marriage, sir, in point of years?" asked Mrs. Sparsit.

"You hear what this lady asks. Was it an unequal marriage in point of years, this unlucky job of yours?" said Mr. Bounderby.

"Not e'en so. I were one-and-twenty myseln; she were twenty nighbut."

"Indeed, sir?" said Mrs. Sparsit to her Chief, with great placidity. "I inferred, from its being so miserable a marriage, that it was probably an unequal one in point of years."

Mr. Bounderby looked very hard at the good lady in a side-long way that had an odd sheepishness about it. He fortified himself with a little more sherry.

"Well? Why don't you go on?" he then asked, turning rather irritably on Stephen Blackpool.

"I ha' come to ask yo, sir, how I am to be ridded o' this woman." Stephen infused a yet deeper gravity into the mixed expression of his attentive face. Mrs. Sparsit uttered a gentle ejaculation, as having received a moral shock.

"What do you mean?" said Mr. Bounderby, getting up to lean his back against the chimney-piece. "What are you talking about? You took her for better or worse."

"I mun' be ridded o' her. I cannot bear 't nommore. I ha' lived under 't so long, for that I ha' had'n the pity and comforting words o' th' best lass living or dead. Haply, but for her, I should ha' gone hottering[1] mad."

---

1.   Trembling with rage (dialect).

"He wishes to be free, to marry the female of whom he speaks, I fear, sir," observed Mrs. Sparsit in an undertone, and much dejected by the immorality of the people.

"I do. The lady says what's right. I do. I were a coming to 't. I ha' read i' th' papers that great fok (fair faw 'em a'![1] I wishes 'em no hurt!) are not bonded together for better for worst so fast, but that they can be set free fro' *their* misfortnet marriages, an' marry ower agen. When they dunnot agree, for that their tempers are ill-sorted, they has rooms o' one kind an' another in their houses, above a bit, and they can live asunders. We fok ha' only one room, and we can't. When that won't do, they ha' gowd an' other cash, an' they can say 'This for yo' an' that for me,' an' they can go their separate ways. We can't. Spite o' all that, they can be set free for smaller wrongs than mine. So I mun be ridden o' this woman, and I want t' know how?"

"No how," returned Mr. Bounderby.

"If I do her any hurt, sir, there's a law to punish me?"

"Of course there is."

"If I flee from her, there's a law to punish me?"

"Of course there is."

"If I marry t'oother dear lass, there's a law to punish me?"

"Of course there is."

"If I was to live wi' her an' not marry her—saying such a thing could be, which it never could or would, an' her so good—there's a law to punish me, in every innocent child belonging to me?"

"Of course there is."

"Now, a' God's name," said Stephen Blackpool, "show me a law to help me!"

"Hem! There's a sanctity in this relation of life," said Mr. Bounderby, "and—and—it must be kept up."

"No no, dunnot say that, sir. 'Tan't kep' up that way. Not that way. 'Tis kep' down that way. I'm a weaver, I were in a fact'ry when a chilt, but I ha' gotten een to see wi' and eern to year wi'. I read in th' papers every 'Sizes, every Sessions—and you read too—I know it!—with

---

1.   Fair fall them all—i.e. 'may they all be fortunate' (dialect).

dismay—how th' supposed unpossibility o' ever getting unchained from one another, at any price, on any terms, brings blood upon this land, and brings many common married fok to battle, murder, and sudden death.[1] Let us ha' this, right understood. Mine's a grievous case, an' I want—if yo will be so good—t' know the law that helps me."

"Now, I tell you what!" said Mr. Bounderby, putting his hands in his pockets. "There *is* such a law."

Stephen, subsiding into his quiet manner, and never wandering in his attention, gave a nod.

"But it's not for you at all. It costs money. It costs a mint of money."

"How much might that be?" Stephen calmly asked.

"Why, you'd have to go to Doctors' Commons with a suit, and you'd have to go to a court of Common Law with a suit, and you'd have to go to the House of Lords with a suit, and you'd have to get an Act of Parliament to enable you to marry again, and it would cost you (if it was a case of very plain sailing), I suppose from a thousand to fifteen hundred pound," said Mr. Bounderby. "Perhaps twice the money."*

"There's no other law?"

"Certainly not."

"Why then, sir," said Stephen, turning white, and motioning with that right hand of his, as if he gave everything to the four winds, "'tis a muddle. 'Tis just a muddle a'toogether, an' the sooner I am dead, the better."

(Mrs. Sparsit again dejected by the impiety of the people.)

"Pooh, pooh! Don't you talk nonsense, my good fellow," said Mr. Bounderby, "about things you don't understand; and don't you call the Institutions of your country a muddle, or you'll get yourself into a real muddle one of these fine mornings. The institutions of your country are not your piece-work, and the only thing you have got to do, is, to mind your piece-work. You didn't take your wife for fast and for loose; but for better for worse. If she has turned out worse—why, all we have got to say is, she might have turned out better."

---

1.   Compare the Litany ('From lightning and tempest; from plague, pestilence, and famine; from battle and murder, and from sudden death, Good Lord, deliver us.') in the Book of Common Prayer.

"'Tis a muddle," said Stephen, shaking his head as he moved to the door. "'Tis a' a muddle!"

"Now, I'll tell you what!" Mr. Bounderby resumed, as a valedictory address. "With what I shall call your unhallowed opinions, you have been quite shocking this lady: who, as I have already told you, is a born lady, and who, as I have not already told you, has had her own marriage misfortunes to the tune of tens of thousands of pounds—tens of Thousands of Pounds!" (he repeated it with great relish). "Now, you have always been a steady Hand hitherto; but my opinion is, and so I tell you plainly, that you are turning into the wrong road. You have been listening to some mischievous stranger or other—they're always about—and the best thing you can do is, to come out of that. Now you know;" here his countenance expressed marvellous acuteness; "I can see as far into a grindstone as another man; farther than a good many, perhaps, because I had my nose well kept to it when I was young. I see traces of the turtle soup, and venison, and gold spoon in this. Yes, I do!" cried Mr. Bounderby, shaking his head with obstinate cunning. "By the Lord Harry, I do!"

With a very different shake of the head and deep sigh, Stephen said, "Thank you, sir, I wish you good day." So he left Mr. Bounderby swelling at his own portrait on the wall, as if he were going to explode himself into it; and Mrs. Sparsit still ambling on with her foot in her stirrup, looking quite cast down by the popular vices.

CHAPTER XII.
THE OLD WOMAN

OLD STEPHEN descended the two white steps, shutting the black door with the brazen door-plate, by the aid of the brazen full-stop, to which he gave a parting polish with the sleeve of his coat, observing that his hot hand clouded it. He crossed the street with his eyes bent upon the ground, and thus was walking sorrowfully away, when he felt a touch upon his arm.

It was not the touch he needed most at such a moment—the touch that could calm the wild waters of his soul, as the uplifted hand of the sublimest love and patience could abate the raging of the sea[1]—yet it was a woman's hand too. It was an old woman, tall and shapely still, though withered by time, on whom his eyes fell when he stopped and turned. She was very cleanly and plainly dressed, had country mud upon her shoes, and was newly come from a journey. The flutter of her manner, in the unwonted noise of the streets; the spare shawl, carried unfolded on her arm; the heavy umbrella, and little basket; the loose long-fingered gloves, to which her hands were unused; all bespoke an old woman from the country, in her plain holiday clothes, come into Coketown on an expedition of rare occurrence. Remarking this at a glance, with the quick observation of his class, Stephen Blackpool bent his attentive face—his face, which, like the faces of many of his order, by dint of long working with eyes and hands in the midst of a prodigious noise, had acquired the concentrated look with which we are familiar in the countenances of the deaf—the better to hear what she asked him.

"Pray, sir," said the old woman, "didn't I see you come out of that gentleman's house?" pointing back to Mr. Bounderby's. "I believe it was you, unless I have had the bad luck to mistake the person in following?"

"Yes, missus," returned Stephen, "it were me."

"Have you—you'll excuse an old woman's curiosity—have you seen the gentleman?"

"Yes, missus."

"And how did he look, sir? Was he portly, bold, out-spoken, and

---

1.   See the story of Jesus calming the storm in Matthew 8:23–7.

hearty?" And she straightened her own figure, and held up her head in adapting her action to her words, the idea crossed Stephen that he had seen this old woman before, and had not quite liked her.

"Oh yes," he returned, observing her more attentively, "he were all that."

"And healthy," said the old woman, "as the fresh wind?"

"Yes," returned Stephen. "He were ett'n and drinking—as large and as loud as a Hummobee."[1]

"Thank you!" said the old woman, with infinite content. "Thank you!"

He certainly never had seen this old woman before. Yet there was a vague remembrance in his mind, as if he had more than once dreamed of some old woman like her.

She walked along at his side, and, gently accommodating himself to her humour, he said Coketown was a busy place, was it not? To which she answered "Eigh sure! Dreadful busy!" Then he said, she came from the country, he saw? To which she answered in the affirmative.

"By Parliamentary,[2] this morning. I came forty mile by Parliamentary this morning, and I'm going back the same forty mile this afternoon. I walked nine mile to the station this morning, and if I find nobody on the road to give me a lift, I shall walk the nine mile back to-night. That's pretty well, sir, at my age!" said the chatty old woman, her eye brightening with exultation.

"'Deed, 'tis. Don't do 't too often, missus."

"No, no. Once a year," she answered, shaking her head. "I spend my savings so, once every year. I come regular, to tramp about the streets, and see the gentlemen."

"Only to see 'em?" returned Stephen.

"That's enough for me," she replied, with great earnestness and interest of manner. "I ask no more! I have been standing about, on this side of the way, to see that gentleman," turning her head back towards Mr. Bounderby's again, "come out. But, he's late this year, and I have not seen him. You came out instead. Now, if I am obliged to go back without

---

1.   A humble- or bumble-bee (dialect).
2.   By parliamentary train; from the 1840s every railway company had a statutory obligation to run at least one train per day over each route carrying passengers at a maximum rate of one penny a mile.

a glimpse of him—I only want a glimpse—well! I have seen you, and you have seen him, and I must make that do." Saying this, she looked at Stephen as if to fix his features in her mind, and her eye was not so bright as it had been.

With a large allowance for difference of tastes, and with all submission to the patricians of Coketown, this seemed so extraordinary a source of interest to take so much trouble about, that it perplexed him. But they were passing the church now, and as his eye caught the clock, he quickened his pace.

He was going to his work? the old woman said, quickening hers, too, quite easily. Yes, time was nearly out. On his telling her where he worked, the old woman became a more singular old woman than before.

"An't you happy?" she asked him.

"Why—there's awmost nobody but has their troubles, missus." He answered evasively, because the old woman appeared to take it for granted that he would be very happy indeed, and he had not the heart to disappoint her. He knew that there was trouble enough in the world; and if the old woman had lived so long, and could count upon his having so little, why so much the better for her, and none the worse for him.

"Ay, ay! You have your troubles at home, you mean?" she said.

"'Times. Just now and then," he answered, slightly.

"But, working under such a gentleman, they don't follow you to the Factory?"

No, no; they didn't follow him there, said Stephen. All correct there. Everything accordant there. (He did not go so far as to say, for her pleasure, that there was a sort of Divine Right[1] there; but, I have heard claims almost as magnificent of late years.)

They were now in the black by-road near the place, and the Hands were crowding in. The bell was ringing, and the Serpent was a Serpent of many coils, and the Elephant was getting ready. The strange old woman was delighted with the very bell. It was the beautifullest bell she had ever heard, she said, and sounded grand!

---

1.   The idea that the monarch derives the right to rule not from human sanction but directly from God.

She asked him, when he stopped good-naturedly to shake hands with her before going in, how long he had worked there?

"A dozen year," he told her.

"I must kiss the hand," said she, "that has worked in this fine factory for a dozen year!" And she lifted it, though he would have prevented her, and put it to her lips. What harmony, besides her age and her simplicity, surrounded her, he did not know, but even in this fantastic action there was a something neither out of time nor place: a something which it seemed as if nobody else could have made as serious, or done with such a natural and touching air.

He had been at his loom full half an hour, thinking about this old woman, when, having occasion to move round the loom for its adjustment, he glanced through a window which was in his corner, and saw her still looking up at the pile of building, lost in admiration. Heedless of the smoke and mud and wet, and of her two long journeys, she was gazing at it, as if the heavy thrum that issued from its many stories were proud music to her.

She was gone by and by, and the day went after her, and the lights sprung up again, and the Express whirled in full sight of the Fairy Palace over the arches near: little felt amid the jarring of the machinery, and scarcely heard above its crash and rattle. Long before then his thoughts had gone back to the dreary room above the little shop, and to the shameful figure heavy on the bed, but heavier on his heart.

Machinery slackened; throbbing feebly like a fainting pulse; stopped. The bell again; the glare of light and heat dispelled; the factories, looming heavy in the black wet night—their tall chimneys rising up into the air like competing Towers of Babel.[1]

He had spoken to Rachael only last night, it was true, and had walked with her a little way; but he had his new misfortune on him, in which no one else could give him a moment's relief, and, for the sake of it, and because he knew himself to want that softening of his anger which no voice but hers could effect, he felt he might so far disregard what she had said as to wait for her again. He waited, but she had eluded him. She was

---

1.   See Genesis 11:1–9.

gone. On no other night in the year could he so ill have spared her patient face.

Oh! Better to have no home in which to lay his head, than to have a home and dread to go to it, through such a cause. He ate and drank, for he was exhausted—but he little knew or cared what; and he wandered about in the chill rain, thinking and thinking, and brooding and brooding.

No word of a new marriage had ever passed between them; but Rachael had taken great pity on him years ago, and to her alone he had opened his closed heart all this time, on the subject of his miseries; and he knew very well that if he were free to ask her, she would take him. He thought of the home he might at that moment have been seeking with pleasure and pride; of the different man he might have been that night; of the lightness then in his now heavy-laden breast; of the then restored honour, self-respect, and tranquillity all torn to pieces. He thought of the waste of the best part of his life, of the change it made in his character for the worse every day, of the dreadful nature of his existence, bound hand and foot, to a dead woman, and tormented by a demon in her shape. He thought of Rachael, how young when they were first brought together in these circumstances, how mature now, how soon to grow old. He thought of the number of girls and women she had seen marry, how many homes with children in them she had seen grow up around her, how she had contentedly pursued her own lone quiet path—for him— and how he had sometimes seen a shade of melancholy on her blessed face, that smote him with remorse and despair. He set the picture of her up, beside the infamous image of last night; and thought, Could it be, that the whole earthly course of one so gentle, good, and self-denying, was subjugate to such a wretch as that!

Filled with these thoughts—so filled that he had an unwholesome sense of growing larger, of being placed in some new and diseased relation towards the objects among which he passed, of seeing the iris round every misty light turn red[1]—he went home for shelter.

---

1.   In this arresting image 'iris' means a halo of prismatic colours.

Chapter XIII.
Rachael

A CANDLE faintly burned in the window, to which the black ladder had often been raised for the sliding away of all that was most precious in this world to a striving wife and a brood of hungry babies; and Stephen added to his other thoughts the stern reflection, that of all the casualties of this existence upon earth, not one was dealt out with so unequal a hand as Death. The inequality of Birth was nothing to it. For, say that the child of a King and the child of a Weaver were born to-night in the same moment, what was that disparity, to the death of any human creature who was serviceable to, or beloved by, another, while this abandoned woman lived on!

From the outside of his home he gloomily passed to the inside, with suspended breath and with a slow footstep. He went up to his door, opened it, and so into the room.

Quiet and peace were there. Rachael was there, sitting by the bed.

She turned her head, and the light of her face shone in upon the midnight of his mind. She sat by the bed, watching and tending his wife. That is to say, he saw that some one lay there, and he knew too well it must be she; but Rachael's hands had put a curtain up, so that she was screened from his eyes. Her disgraceful garments were removed, and some of Rachael's were in the room. Everything was in its place and order as he had always kept it, the little fire was newly trimmed, and the hearth was freshly swept. It appeared to him that he saw all this in Rachael's face, and looked at nothing besides. While looking at it, it was shut out from his view by the softened tears that filled his eyes; but not before he had seen how earnestly she looked at him, and how her own eyes were filled too.

She turned again towards the bed, and satisfying herself that all was quiet there, spoke in a low, calm, cheerful voice.

"I am glad you have come at last, Stephen. You are very late."

"I ha' been walking up an' down."

"I thought so. But 'tis too bad a night for that. The rain falls very heavy, and the wind has risen."

The wind? True. It was blowing hard. Hark to the thundering in the chimney, and the surging noise! To have been out in such a wind, and not to have known it was blowing!

"I have been here once before, to-day, Stephen. Landlady came round for me at dinner-time. There was some one here that needed looking to, she said. And 'deed she was right. All wandering and lost, Stephen. Wounded too, and bruised."

He slowly moved to a chair and sat down, drooping his head before her.

"I came to do what little I could, Stephen; first, for that she worked with me when we were girls both, and for that you courted her and married her when I was her friend—"

He laid his furrowed forehead on his hand, with a low groan.

"And next, for that I know your heart, and am right sure and certain that 'tis far too merciful to let her die, or even so much as suffer for want of aid. Thou knowest who said, 'Let him who is without sin among you cast the first stone at her!'[1] There have been plenty to do that. Thou art not the man to cast the last stone, Stephen, when she is brought so low."

"Oh Rachael, Rachael!"

"Thou hast been a cruel sufferer, Heaven reward thee!" she said, in compassionate accents. "I am thy poor friend, with all my heart and mind."

The wounds of which she had spoken, seemed to be about the neck of the self-made outcast. She dressed them now, still without showing her. She steeped a piece of linen in a basin, into which she poured some liquid from a bottle, and laid it with a gentle hand upon the sore. The three-legged table had been drawn close to the bedside, and on it there were two bottles. This was one.

It was not so far off, but that Stephen, following her hands with his eyes, could read what was printed on it in large letters. He turned of a deadly hue, and a sudden horror seemed to fall upon him.

"I will stay here, Stephen," said Rachael, quietly resuming her seat, "till the bells go Three. 'Tis to be done again at three, and then she may be left till morning."

---

1.   See the story of the woman taken in adultery in John 8:1–11.

"But thy rest agen to-morrow's work, my dear."

"I slept sound last night. I can wake many nights, when I am put to it. 'Tis thou who art in need of rest—so white and tired. Try to sleep in the chair there, while I watch. Thou hadst no sleep last night, I can well believe. To-morrow's work is far harder for thee than for me."

He heard the thundering and surging out of doors, and it seemed to him as if his late angry mood were going about trying to get at him. She had cast it out; she would keep it out; he trusted her to defend him from himself.

"She don't know me, Stephen; she just drowsily mutters and stares. I have spoken to her times and again, but she don't notice! 'Tis as well so. When she comes to her right mind once more, I shall have done what I can, and she never the wiser."

"How long, Rachael, is 't looked for, that she'll be so?"

"Doctor said she would haply come to her mind to-morrow."

His eyes fell again on the bottle, and a tremble passed over him, causing him to shiver in every limb. She thought he was chilled with the wet. "No," he said. It was not that. He had had a fright.

"A fright?"

"Ay, ay! coming in. When I were walking. When I were thinking. When I—" It seized him again: and he stood up, holding by the mantelshelf, as he pressed his dank cold hair down with a hand that shook as if it were palsied.

"Stephen!"

She was coming to him, but he stretched out his arm to stop her.

"No! Don't, please; don't. Let me see thee setten by the bed. Let me see thee, a' so good, and so forgiving. Let me see thee as I see thee when I coom in. I can never see thee better than so. Never, never, never!"

He had a violent fit of trembling, and then sunk into his chair. After a time he controlled himself, and, resting with an elbow on one knee, and his head upon that hand, could look towards Rachael. Seen across the dim candle with his moistened eyes, she looked as if she had a glory shining round her head. He could have believed she had. He did believe it, as the noise without shook the window, rattled the door below, and went about the house clamouring and lamenting.

"When she gets better, Stephen, 'tis to be hoped she'll leave thee to thyself again, and do thee no more hurt. Anyways we will hope so now. And now I shall keep silence, for I want thee to sleep."

He closed his eyes, more to please her than to rest his weary head; but, by slow degrees as he listened to the great noise of the wind, he ceased to hear it, or it changed into the working of his loom, or even into the voices of the day (his own included) saying what had been really said. Even this imperfect consciousness faded away at last, and he dreamed a long, troubled dream.

He thought that he, and some one on whom his heart had long been set—but she was not Rachael, and that surprised him, even in the midst of his imaginary happiness—stood in the church being married. While the ceremony was performing, and while he recognized among the witnesses some whom he knew to be living, and many whom he knew to be dead, darkness came on, succeeded by the shining of a tremendous light. It broke from one line in the table of commandments at the altar, and illuminated the building with words. They were sounded through the church, too, as if there were voices in the fiery letters. Upon this, the whole appearance before him and around him changed, and nothing was left as it had been, but himself and the clergyman. They stood in the daylight before a crowd so vast, that if all the people in the world could have been brought together into one space, they could not have looked, he thought, more numerous; and they all abhorred him, and there was not one pitying or friendly eye among the millions that were fastened on his face. He stood on a raised stage, under his own loom; and, looking up at the shape the loom took, and hearing the burial service distinctly read, he knew that he was there to suffer death. In an instant what he stood on fell below him, and he was gone.

Out of what mystery he came back to his usual life, and to places that he knew, he was unable to consider; but he was back in those places by some means, and with the condemnation upon him, that he was never, in this world, or the next, through all the unimaginable ages of eternity, to look on Rachael's face or hear her voice. Wandering to and fro unceasingly, without hope, and in search of he knew not what (he only knew that he was doomed to seek it), he was the subject of a nameless, horrible dread, a mortal fear of one particular shape which everything took. Whatsoever he looked at, grew into that form sooner or later. The object of his miserable existence was to prevent its recognition by any one among the various people he encountered. Hopeless labour! If he led them out of rooms where it was, if he shut up drawers and closets where it stood, if he drew the curious from places where he knew it to be secreted, and got them out into the streets, the very chimneys of the mills assumed that shape, and round them was the printed word.

The wind was blowing again, the rain was beating on the housetops, and the larger spaces through which he had strayed contracted to the four walls of his room. Saving that the fire had died out, it was as his eyes had closed upon it. Rachael seemed to have fallen into a doze, in the chair by the bed. She sat wrapped in her shawl, perfectly still. The table stood in the same place, close by the bedside, and on it, in its real proportions and appearance, was the shape so often repeated.

He thought he saw the curtain move. He looked again, and he was sure it moved. He saw a hand come forth and grope a little. Then the curtain moved more perceptibly, and the woman in the bed put it back, and sat up.

With her woful eyes, so haggard and wild, so heavy and large, she looked all round the room, and passed the corner where he slept in his chair. Her eyes returned to that corner, and she put her hand over them as a shade, while she looked into it. Again they went all round the room, scarcely heeding Rachael if at all, and returned to that corner. He thought, as she once more shaded them—not so much looking at him, as looking for him with a brutish instinct that he was there—that no single trace was left in those debauched features, or in the mind that went along with them, of the woman he had married eighteen years before. But that he had seen her come to this by inches, he never could have believed her to be the same.

All this time, as if a spell were on him, he was motionless and powerless, except to watch her.

Stupidly dozing, or communing with her incapable self about nothing, she sat for a little while with her hands at her ears, and her head resting on them. Presently, she resumed her staring round the room. And now, for the first time, her eyes stopped at the table with the bottles on it.

Straightway she turned her eyes back to his corner, with the defiance of last night, and moving very cautiously and softly, stretched out her greedy hand. She drew a mug into the bed, and sat for a while considering which of the two bottles she should choose. Finally, she laid her insensate grasp upon the bottle that had swift and certain death in it, and, before his eyes, pulled out the cork with her teeth.

Dream or reality, he had no voice, nor had he power to stir. If this be real, and her allotted time be not yet come, wake, Rachael, wake!

She thought of that, too. She looked at Rachael, and very slowly, very cautiously, poured out the contents. The draught was at her lips. A moment and she would be past all help, let the whole world wake and come about her with its utmost power. But in that moment Rachael started up with a suppressed cry. The creature struggled, struck her, seized her by the hair; but Rachael had the cup.

Stephen broke out of his chair. "Rachael, am I wakin' or dreamin' this dreadfo' night?"

"'Tis all well, Stephen. I have been asleep, myself. 'Tis near three. Hush! I hear the bells."

The wind brought the sounds of the church clock to the window. They listened, and it struck three. Stephen looked at her, saw how pale she was, noted the disorder of her hair, and the red marks of fingers on her forehead, and felt assured that his senses of sight and hearing had been awake. She held the cup in her hand even now.

"I thought it must be near three," she said, calmly pouring from the cup into the basin, and steeping the linen as before. "I am thankful I stayed! 'Tis done now, when I have put this on. There! And now she's quiet again. The few drops in the basin I'll pour away, for 'tis bad stuff to leave about, though ever so little of it." As she spoke, she drained the basin into the ashes of the fire, and broke the bottle on the hearth.

She had nothing to do, then, but to cover herself with her shawl before going out into the wind and rain.

"Thou'lt let me walk wi' thee at this hour, Rachael?"

"No, Stephen. 'Tis but a minute, and I'm home."

"Thou'rt not fearfo';" he said it in a low voice, as they went out at the door; "to leave me alone wi' her!"

As she looked at him, saying, "Stephen?" he went down on his knee before her, on the poor mean stairs, and put an end of her shawl to his lips.

"Thou art an Angel. Bless thee, bless thee!"

"I am, as I have told thee, Stephen, thy poor friend. Angels are not like me. Between them, and a working woman fu' of faults, there is a deep gulf set.[1] My little sister is among them, but she is changed."

She raised her eyes for a moment as she said the words; and then they fell again, in all their gentleness and mildness, on his face.

"Thou changest me from bad to good. Thou mak'st me humbly wishfo' to be more like thee, and fearfo' to lose thee when this life is ower, and a' the muddle cleared awa'.[2]* Thou'rt an Angel; it may be, thou hast saved my soul alive!"[3]

She looked at him, on his knee at her feet, with her shawl still in his hand, and the reproof on her lips died away when she saw the working of his face.

"I coom home desp'rate. I coom home wi'out a hope, and mad wi' thinking that when I said a word o' complaint I was reckoned a onreasonable Hand. I told thee I had had a fright. It were the Poison-bottle on table. I never hurt a livin' creetur; but happenin' so suddenly upon 't, I thowt, 'How can *I* say what I might ha' done to myseln, or her, or both!'"

She put her two hands on his mouth, with a face of terror, to stop him from saying more. He caught them in his unoccupied hand, and holding them, and still clasping the border of her shawl, said hurriedly:

"But I see thee, Rachael, setten by the bed. I ha' seen thee, aw this night. In my troublous sleep I ha' known thee still to be there. Evermore I will see thee there. I nevermore will see her or think o' her, but thou shalt be beside her. I nevermore will see or think o' anything that angers me, but thou, so much better than me, shalt be by th' side on 't. And so I will try t' look t' th' time, and so I will try t' trust t' th' time, when thou and me at last shall walk together far awa', beyond the deep gulf, in th' country where thy little sister is."

---

1.   Compare the story of Dives and Lazarus in Luke 16:19–31.
2.   Compare Revelation 21:4.
3.   Compare Ezekiel 18:27–8.

He kissed the border of her shawl again, and let her go. She bade him good night in a broken voice, and went out into the street.

The wind blew from the quarter where the day would soon appear, and still blew strongly. It had cleared the sky before it, and the rain had spent itself or travelled elsewhere, and the stars were bright. He stood bare-headed in the road, watching her quick disappearance. As the shining stars were to the heavy candle in the window, so was Rachael, in the rugged fancy of this man, to the common experiences of his life.

CHAPTER XIV.
THE GREAT MANUFACTURER

TIME WENT on in Coketown like its own machinery: so much material wrought up, so much fuel consumed, so many powers worn out, so much money made. But, less inexorable than iron, steel, and brass, it brought its varying seasons even into that wilderness of smoke and brick, and made the only stand that ever *was* made in the place against its direful uniformity.

"Louisa is becoming," said Mr. Gradgrind, "almost a young woman."

Time, with his innumerable horse-power, worked away, not minding what anybody said, and presently turned out young Thomas a foot taller than when his father had last taken particular notice of him.

"Thomas is becoming," said Mr. Gradgrind, "almost a young man."

Time passed Thomas on in the mill, while his father was thinking about it, and there he stood in a long-tailed coat and a stiff shirt-collar.

"Really," said Mr. Gradgrind, "the period has arrived when Thomas ought to go to Bounderby."

Time, sticking to him, passed him on into Bounderby's Bank, made him an inmate of Bounderby's house, necessitated the purchase of his first razor, and exercised him diligently in his calculations relative to number one.

The same great manufacturer, always with an immense variety of work on hand, in every stage of development, passed Sissy onward in his mill, and worked her up into a very pretty article indeed.

"I fear, Jupe," said Mr. Gradgrind, "that your continuance at the school any longer would be useless."

"I am afraid it would, sir," Sissy answered with a curtsey.

"I cannot disguise from you, Jupe," said Mr. Gradgrind, knitting his brow, "that the result of your probation there has disappointed me; has greatly disappointed me. You have not acquired, under Mr. and Mrs. M'Choakumchild, anything like that amount of exact knowledge which I looked for. You are extremely deficient in your facts. Your acquaintance with figures is very limited. You are altogether backward, and below the mark."

"I am sorry, sir," she returned; "but I know it is quite true. Yet I have tried hard, sir."

"Yes," said Mr. Gradgrind, "yes, I believe you have tried hard; I have observed you, and I can find no fault in that respect."

"Thank you, sir. I have thought sometimes;" Sissy very timid here; "that perhaps I tried to learn too much, and that if I had asked to be allowed to try a little less, I might have——"

"No, Jupe, no," said Mr. Gradgrind, shaking his head in his profoundest and most eminently practical way. "No. The course you pursued, you pursued according to the system—the system—and there is no more to be said about it. I can only suppose that the circumstances of your early life were too unfavourable to the development of your reasoning powers, and that we began too late. Still, as I have said already, I am disappointed."

"I wish I could have made a better acknowledgement, sir, of your kindness to a poor forlorn girl who had no claim upon you, and of your protection of her."

"Don't shed tears," said Mr. Gradgrind. "Don't shed tears. I don't complain of you. You are an affectionate, earnest, good young woman—and—and we must make that do."

"Thank you, sir, very much," said Sissy, with a grateful curtsey.

"You are useful to Mrs. Gradgrind, and (in a generally pervading way) you are serviceable in the family also; so I understand from Miss Louisa, and, indeed, so I have observed myself. I therefore hope," said Mr. Gradgrind, "that you can make yourself happy in those relations."

"I should have nothing to wish, sir, if——"

"I understand you," said Mr. Gradgrind; "you still refer to your father.

I have heard from Miss Louisa that you still preserve that bottle. Well! If your training in the science of arriving at exact results had been more successful, you would have been wiser on these points. I will say no more."

He really liked Sissy too well to have a contempt for her; otherwise he held her calculating powers in such very slight estimation that he must have fallen upon that conclusion. Somehow or other, he had become possessed by an idea that there was something in this girl which could hardly be set forth in a tabular column. Her capacity of definition might be easily stated at a very low figure, her mathematical knowledge at nothing; yet he was not sure that if he had been required, for example, to tick her off into columns in a parliamentary return, he would have quite known how to divide her.

In some stages of his manufacture of the human fabric, the processes of Time are very rapid. Young Thomas and Sissy being both at such a stage of their working up, these changes were effected in a year or two; while Mr. Gradgrind himself seemed stationary in his course, and underwent no alteration.

Except one, which was apart from his necessary progress through the mill. Time hustled him into a little noisy and rather dirty machinery, in a by-corner, and made him Member of Parliament for Coketown: one of the respected members for ounce weights and measures, one of the representatives of the multiplication table, one of the deaf honourable gentlemen, dumb honourable gentlemen, blind honourable gentlemen, lame honourable gentlemen, dead honourable gentlemen, to every other consideration. Else wherefore live we in a Christian land, eighteen hundred and odd years after our Master?

All this while, Louisa had been passing on, so quiet and reserved, and so much given to watching the bright ashes at twilight as they fell into the grate and became extinct, that from the period when her father had said she was almost a young woman—which seemed but yesterday—she had scarcely attracted his notice again, when he found her quite a young woman.

"Quite a young woman," said Mr. Gradgrind, musing. "Dear me!"

Soon after this discovery, he became more thoughtful than usual for several days, and seemed much engrossed by one subject. On a certain night, when he was going out, and Louisa came to bid him good-bye before his departure—as he was not to be home until late and she would not see him again until the morning—he held her in his arms, looking at her in his kindest manner, and said:

"My dear Louisa, you are a woman!"

She answered with the old, quick, searching look of the night when she was found at the Circus; then cast down her eyes. "Yes, father."

"My dear," said Mr. Gradgrind, "I must speak with you alone and seriously. Come to me in my room after breakfast to-morrow, will you?"

"Yes, father."

"Your hands are rather cold, Louisa. Are you not well?"

"Quite well, father."

"And cheerful?"

She looked at him again, and smiled in her peculiar manner. "I am as cheerful, father, as I usually am, or usually have been."

"That's well," said Mr. Gradgrind. So, he kissed her and went away; and Louisa returned to the serene apartment of the hair-cutting character, and leaning her elbow on her hand, looked again at the short-lived sparks that so soon subsided into ashes.

"Are you there, Loo?" said her brother, looking in at the door. He was quite a young gentleman of pleasure now, and not quite a prepossessing one.

"Dear Tom," she answered, rising and embracing him, "how long it is since you have been to see me!"

"Why, I have been otherwise engaged, Loo, in the evenings; and in the daytime old Bounderby has been keeping me at it rather. But I touch him up with you when he comes it too strong, and so we preserve an understanding. I say! Has father said anything particular to you to-day or yesterday, Loo?"

"No, Tom. But he told me to-night that he wished to do so in the morning."

"Ah! That's what I mean," said Tom. "Do you know where he is to-night?"—with a very deep expression.

"No."

"Then I'll tell you. He's with old Bounderby. They are having a regular confab together up at the Bank. Why at the Bank, do you think? Well, I'll tell you again. To keep Mrs. Sparsit's ears as far off as possible, I expect."

With her hand upon her brother's shoulder, Louisa still stood looking at the fire. Her brother glanced at her face with greater interest than usual, and, encircling her waist with his arm, drew her coaxingly to him.

"You are very fond of me, an't you, Loo?"

"Indeed I am, Tom, though you do let such long intervals go by without coming to see me."

"Well, sister of mine," said Tom, "when you say that, you are near my thoughts. We might be so much oftener together—mightn't we? Always together, almost—mightn't we? It would do me a great deal of good if you were to make up your mind to I know what, Loo. It would be a splendid thing for me. It would be uncommonly jolly!"

Her thoughtfulness baffled his cunning scrutiny. He could make nothing of her face. He pressed her in his arm, and kissed her cheek. She returned the kiss, but still looked at the fire.

"I say, Loo! I thought I'd come, and just hint to you what was going on: though I supposed you'd most likely guess, even if you didn't know. I can't stay, because I'm engaged to some fellows to-night. You won't forget how fond you are of me?"

"No, dear Tom, I won't forget."

"That's a capital girl," said Tom. "Good-bye, Loo."

She gave him an affectionate good-night, and went out with him to the door, whence the fires of Coketown could be seen, making the distance lurid. She stood there, looking steadfastly towards them, and listening to his departing steps. They retreated quickly, as glad to get away from Stone Lodge; and she stood there yet, when he was gone and all was quiet. It seemed as if, first in her own fire within the house, and then in the fiery haze without, she tried to discover what kind of woof Old Time, that greatest and longest-established Spinner of all, would weave from the threads he had already spun into a woman. But his factory is a secret place, his work is noiseless, and his Hands are mutes.

CHAPTER XV.
FATHER AND DAUGHTER

ALTHOUGH MR. Gradgrind did not take after Blue Beard,[1] his room was quite a blue chamber in its abundance of blue books. Whatever they could prove (which is usually anything you like), they proved there, in an army constantly strengthening by the arrival of new recruits. In that charmed apartment, the most complicated social questions were cast up, got into exact totals, and finally settled—if those concerned could only have been brought to know it. As if an astronomical observatory should be made without any windows, and the astronomer within should arrange the starry universe solely by pen, ink, and paper, so Mr. Gradgrind, in *his* Observatory (and there are many like it), had no need to cast an eye upon the teeming myriads of human beings around him, but could settle all their destinies on a slate, and wipe out all their tears[2] with one dirty little bit of sponge.

To this Observatory, then: a stern room, with a deadly statistical clock in it, which measured every second with a beat like a rap upon a coffin-lid; Louisa repaired on the appointed morning. A window looked towards Coketown; and when she sat down near her father's table, she saw the high chimneys and the long tracts of smoke looming in the heavy distance gloomily.

"My dear Louisa," said her father, "I prepared you last night to give me your serious attention in the conversation we are now going to have together. You have been so well trained, and you do, I am happy to say, so much justice to the education you have received, that I have perfect confidence in your good sense. You are not impulsive, you are not romantic, you are accustomed to view everything from the strong dispassionate ground of reason and calculation. From that ground alone, I know you will view and consider what I am going to communicate."

---

1.   In popular myth, the husband who hung the bodies of a succession of murdered wives in a locked chamber; the story is best known in the seventeenth-century French version in Charles Perrault's collection of fairy tales.

2.   Compare Revelation 21:4.

He waited, as if he would have been glad that she said something. But she said never a word.

"Louisa, my dear, you are the subject of a proposal of marriage that has been made to me."

Again he waited, and again she answered not one word. This so far surprised him, as to induce him gently to repeat, "a proposal of marriage, my dear." To which she returned, without any visible emotion whatever:

"I hear you, father. I am attending, I assure you."

"Well!" said Mr. Gradgrind, breaking into a smile, after being for the moment at a loss, "you are even more dispassionate than I expected, Louisa. Or, perhaps, you are not unprepared for the announcement I have it in charge to make?"

"I cannot say that, father, until I hear it. Prepared or unprepared, I wish to hear it all from you. I wish to hear you state it to me, father."

Strange to relate, Mr. Gradgrind was not so collected at this moment as his daughter was. He took a paper-knife in his hand, turned it over, laid it down, took it up again, and even then had to look along the blade of it, considering how to go on.

"What you say, my dear Louisa, is perfectly reasonable. I have undertaken then to let you know that—in short, that Mr. Bounderby has informed me that he has long watched your progress with particular interest and pleasure, and has long hoped that the time might ultimately arrive when he should offer you his hand in marriage. That time, to which he has so long, and certainly with great constancy, looked forward, is now come. Mr. Bounderby has made his proposal of marriage to me, and has entreated me to make it known to you, and to express his hope that you will take it into your favourable consideration."

Silence between them. The deadly statistical clock very hollow. The distant smoke very black and heavy.

"Father," said Louisa, "do you think I love Mr. Bounderby?"

Mr. Gradgrind was extremely discomfited by this unexpected question. "Well, my child," he returned, "I—really—cannot take upon myself to say."

"Father," pursued Louisa in exactly the same voice as before, "do you ask me to love Mr. Bounderby?"

"My dear Louisa, no. No. I ask nothing."

"Father," she still pursued, "does Mr. Bounderby ask me to love him?"

"Really, my dear," said Mr. Gradgrind, "it is difficult to answer your question—"

"Difficult to answer it, Yes or No, father?"

"Certainly, my dear. Because;" here was something to demonstrate, and it set him up again; "because the reply depends so materially, Louisa, on the sense in which we use the expression. Now, Mr. Bounderby does not do you the injustice, and does not do himself the injustice, of pretending to anything fanciful, fantastic, or (I am using synonymous terms) sentimental. Mr. Bounderby would have seen you grow up under his eyes, to very little purpose, if he could so far forget what is due to your good sense, not to say to his, as to address you from any such ground. Therefore, perhaps the expression itself—I merely suggest this to you, my dear—may be a little misplaced."

"What would you advise me to use in its stead, father?"

"Why, my dear Louisa," said Mr. Gradgrind, completely recovered by this time, "I would advise you (since you ask me) to consider this question, as you have been accustomed to consider every other question, simply as one of tangible Fact. The ignorant and the giddy may embarrass such subjects with irrelevant fancies, and other absurdities that have no existence, properly viewed—really no existence—but it is no compliment to you to say, that you know better. Now, what are the Facts in this case? You are, we will say in round numbers, twenty years of age; Mr. Bounderby is, we will say in round numbers, fifty. There is some disparity in your respective years, but in your means and positions there is none; on the contrary, there is a great suitability. Then the question arises, Is this one disparity sufficient to operate as a bar to such a marriage? In considering this question, it is not unimportant to take into account the statistics of marriage, so far as they have yet been obtained, in England and Wales. I find, on reference to the figures, that a large portion of these marriages are contracted between parties of very unequal ages, and that the elder of these contracting parties is, in rather more than three-fourths of these instances, the bridegroom. It is remarkable as showing the wide prevalence of this law, that among the natives of the British possessions in India, also in a considerable part of China, and among the Calmucks of

Tartary,[1] the best means of computation yet furnished us by travellers, yield similar results. The disparity I have mentioned, therefore, almost ceases to be a disparity, and (virtually) all but disappears."

"What do you recommend, father," asked Louisa, her reserved composure not in the least affected by these gratifying results, "that I should substitute for the term I used just now. For the misplaced expression?"

"Louisa," returned her father, "it appears to me that nothing can be plainer. Confiding yourself rigidly to Fact, the question of Fact you state to yourself is: Does Mr. Bounderby ask me to marry him? Yes, he does. The sole remaining question then is: Shall I marry him? I think nothing can be plainer than that?"

"Shall I marry him?" repeated Louisa, with great deliberation.

"Precisely. And it is satisfactory to me, as your father, my dear Louisa, to know that you do not come to the consideration of that question with the previous habits of mind, and habits of life, that belong to so many young women."

"No, father," she returned, "I do not."

"I now leave you to judge for yourself," said Mr. Gradgrind. "I have stated the case, as such cases are usually stated among practical minds; I have stated it, as the case of your mother and myself was stated in its time. The rest, my dear Louisa, is for you to decide."

From the beginning, she had sat looking at him fixedly. As he now leaned back in his chair, and bent his deep-set eyes upon her in his turn, perhaps he might have seen one wavering moment in her, when she was impelled to throw herself upon his breast, and give him the pent-up confidences of her heart. But, to see it, he must have overleaped at a bound the artificial barriers he had for many years been erecting, between himself and all those subtle essences of humanity which will elude the utmost cunning of algebra until the last trumpet ever to be sounded[2] shall blow even algebra to wreck. The barriers were too many and too high for such a leap. With his unbending, utilitarian, matter-of-fact face, he hardened her again; and the moment shot away into the plumbless depths

---

1.   A Mongolian people living on the north-west shores of the Caspian sea; there are various transcriptions, the most common today being Kalmuck.
2.   Compare the description of the apocalypse in 1 Corinthians 15:52.

of the past, to mingle with all the lost opportunities that are drowned there.

Removing her eyes from him, she sat so long looking silently towards the town, that he said, at length: "Are you consulting the chimneys of the Coketown works, Louisa?"

"There seems to be nothing there but languid and monotonous smoke. Yet when the night comes, Fire bursts out, father!" she answered, turning quickly.

"Of course I know that, Louisa. I do not see the application of the remark." To do him justice he did not, at all.

She passed it away with a slight motion of her hand, and concentrating her attention upon him again, said, "Father, I have often thought that life is very short."—This was so distinctly one of his subjects that he interposed.

"It is short, no doubt, my dear. Still, the average duration of human life is proved to have increased of late years. The calculations of various life insurance and annuity offices, among other figures which cannot go wrong, have established the fact."

"I speak of my own life, father."

"Oh indeed? Still," said Mr. Gradgrind, "I need not point out to you, Louisa, that it is governed by the laws which govern lives in the aggregate."

"While it lasts, I would wish to do the little I can, and the little I am fit for. What does it matter?"

Mr. Gradgrind seemed rather at a loss to understand the last four words; replying, "How, matter? What matter, my dear?"

"Mr. Bounderby," she went on in a steady, straight way, without regarding this, "asks me to marry him. The question I have to ask myself is, shall I marry him? That is so, father, is it not? You have told me so, father. Have you not?"

"Certainly, my dear."

"Let it be so. Since Mr. Bounderby likes to take me thus, I am satisfied to accept his proposal. Tell him, father, as soon as you please, that this was my answer. Repeat it, word for word, if you can, because I should wish him to know what I said."

"It is quite right, my dear," retorted her father approvingly, "to be exact. I will observe your proper request. Have you any wish in reference to the period of your marriage, my child?"

"None, father. What does it matter!"

Mr. Gradgrind had drawn his chair a little nearer to her, and taken her hand. But, her repetition of these words seemed to strike with some little discord on his ear. He paused to look at her, and, still holding her hand, said:

"Louisa, I have not considered it essential to ask you one question, because the possibility implied in it appeared to me to be too remote. But perhaps I ought to do so. You have never entertained in secret any other proposal?"

"Father," she returned, almost scornfully, "what other proposal can have been made to *me*? Whom have I seen? Where have I been? What are my heart's experiences?"

"My dear Louisa," returned Mr. Gradgrind, reassured and satisfied. "You correct me justly. I merely wished to discharge my duty."

"What do *I* know, father," said Louisa in her quiet manner, "of tastes and fancies; of aspirations and affections; of all that part of my nature in which such light things might have been nourished? What escape have I had from problems that could be demonstrated, and realities that could be grasped?" As she said it, she unconsciously closed her hand, as if upon a solid object, and slowly opened it as though she were releasing dust or ash.

"My dear," assented her eminently practical parent, "quite true, quite true."

"Why, father," she pursued, "what a strange question to ask *me*! The baby-preference that even I have heard of as common among children, has never had its innocent resting-place in my breast. You have been so careful of me, that I never had a child's heart. You have trained me so well, that I never dreamed a child's dream. You have dealt so wisely with me, father, from my cradle to this hour, that I never had a child's belief or a child's fear."

Mr. Gradgrind was quite moved by his success, and by this testimony to it. "My dear Louisa," said he, "you abundantly repay my care. Kiss me, my dear girl."

So, his daughter kissed him. Detaining her in his embrace, he said, "I may assure you now, my favourite child, that I am made happy by the sound decision at which you have arrived. Mr. Bounderby is a very remarkable man; and what little disparity can be said to exist between you—if any—is more than counterbalanced by the tone your mind has acquired. It has always been my object so to educate you, as that you might, while still in your early youth, be (if I may so express myself) almost any age. Kiss me once more, Louisa. Now, let us go and find your mother."

Accordingly, they went down to the drawing-room, where the esteemed lady with no nonsense about her, was recumbent as usual, while Sissy worked beside her. She gave some feeble signs of returning animation when they entered, and presently the faint transparency was presented in a sitting attitude.

"Mrs. Gradgrind," said her husband, who had waited for the achievement of this feat with some impatience, "allow me to present to you Mrs. Bounderby."

"Oh!" said Mrs. Gradgrind, "so you have settled it! Well, I'm sure I hope your health may be good, Louisa; for if your head begins to split as soon as you are married, which was the case with mine, I cannot consider that you are to be envied, though I have no doubt you think you are, as all girls do. However, I give you joy, my dear—and I hope you may now turn all your ological studies to good account, I am sure I do! I must give you a kiss of congratulation, Louisa; but don't touch my right shoulder, for there's something running down it all day long. And now you see," whimpered Mrs. Gradgrind, adjusting her shawls after the affectionate ceremony, "I shall be worrying myself, morning, noon, and night, to know what I am to call him!"

"Mrs. Gradgrind," said her husband, solemnly, "what do you mean?"

"Whatever I am to call him, Mr. Gradgrind, when he is married to Louisa! I must call him something. It's impossible," said Mrs. Gradgrind, with a mingled sense of politeness and injury, "to be constantly addressing him and never giving him a name. I cannot call him Josiah, for the name is insupportable to me. You yourself won't hear of Joe, you very well know. Am I to call my own son-in-law, Mister. Not, I believe, unless the time has arrived when, as an invalid, I am to be trampled upon by my relations. Then, what am I to call him!"

Nobody present having any suggestion to offer in the remarkable emergency, Mrs. Gradgrind departed this life for the time being, after delivering the following codicil to her remarks already executed:

"As to the wedding, all I ask, Louisa, is,—and I ask it with a fluttering in my chest, which actually extends to the soles of my feet,—that it may take place soon. Otherwise, I know it is one of those subjects I shall never hear the last of."

When Mr. Gradgrind had presented Mrs. Bounderby, Sissy had suddenly turned her head, and looked, in wonder, in pity, in sorrow, in doubt, in a multitude of emotions, towards Louisa. Louisa had known it, and seen it, without looking at her. From that moment she was impassive, proud and cold—held Sissy at a distance—changed to her altogether.

CHAPTER XVI.
HUSBAND AND WIFE

MR. BOUNDERBY'S first disquietude on hearing of his happiness, was occasioned by the necessity of imparting it to Mrs. Sparsit. He could not make up his mind how to do that, or what the consequences of the step might be. Whether she would instantly depart, bag and baggage, to Lady Scadgers, or would positively refuse to budge from the premises; whether she would be plaintive or abusive, tearful or tearing; whether she would break her heart, or break the looking-glass; Mr. Bounderby could not at all foresee. However, as it must be done, he had no choice but to do it; so, after attempting several letters, and failing in them all, he resolved to do it by word of mouth.

On his way home, on the evening he set aside for this momentous purpose, he took the precaution of stepping into a chemist's shop and buying a bottle of the very strongest smelling-salts. "By George!" said Mr. Bounderby, "if she takes it in the fainting way, I'll have the skin off her nose, in all events!" But, in spite of being thus forearmed, he entered his own house with anything but a courageous air; and appeared before the object of his misgivings, like a dog who was conscious of coming direct from the pantry.

"Good evening, Mr. Bounderby!"

"Good evening, ma'am, good evening." He drew up his chair, and Mrs. Sparsit drew back hers, as who should say, "Your fireside, sir. I freely admit it. It is for you to occupy it all, if you think proper."

"Don't go to the North Pole, ma'am!" said Mr. Bounderby.

"Thank you, sir," said Mrs. Sparsit, and returned, though short of her former position.

Mr. Bounderby sat looking at her, as, with the points of a stiff, sharp pair of scissors, she picked out holes for some inscrutable ornamental purpose, in a piece of cambric. An operation which, taken in connexion with the bushy eyebrows and the Roman nose, suggested with some live-liness the idea of a hawk engaged upon the eyes of a tough little bird. She was so steadfastly occupied, that many minutes elapsed before she looked up from her work; when she did so Mr. Bounderby bespoke her attention with a hitch of his head.

"Mrs. Sparsit, ma'am," said Mr. Bounderby, putting his hands in his pockets, and assuring himself with his right hand that the cork of the little bottle was ready for use, "I have had occasion to say to you, that you are not only a lady born and bred, but a devilish sensible woman."

"Sir," returned the lady, "this is indeed not the first time you have honoured me with similar expressions of your good opinion."

"Mrs. Sparsit, ma'am," said Mr. Bounderby, "I am going to astonish you."

"Yes, sir?" returned Mrs. Sparsit, interrogatively, and in the most tran-quil manner possible. She generally wore mittens, and she now laid down her work, and smoothed those mittens.

"I am going, ma'am," said Bounderby, "to marry Tom Gradgrind's daughter."

"Yes, sir," returned Mrs. Sparsit. "I hope you may be happy, Mr. Bounderby. Oh, indeed I hope you may be happy, sir!" And she said it with such great condescension as well as with such great compassion for him, that Bounderby,—far more disconcerted than if she had thrown her workbox at the mirror, or swooned at the hearthrug,—corked up the smelling salts tight in his pocket, and thought, "Now confound this woman, who could have even guessed that she would take it in this way!"

"I wish it with all my heart, sir," said Mrs. Sparsit, in a highly supe-rior manner; somehow she seemed, in a moment, to have established a right to pity him ever afterwards; "that you may be in all respects very happy."

"Well, ma'am," returned Bounderby, with some resentment in his tone: which was clearly lowered, though in spite of himself, "I am obliged to you. I hope I shall be."

"*Do* you, sir!" said Mrs. Sparsit, with great affability. "But naturally you do; of course you do."

A very awkward pause on Mr. Bounderby's part, succeeded. Mrs. Sparsit sedately resumed her work and occasionally gave a small cough, which sounded like the cough of conscious strength and forbearance.

"Well, ma'am," resumed Bounderby, "under these circumstances, I imagine it would not be agreeable to a character like yours to remain here, though you would be very welcome here."

"Oh, dear no, sir, I could on no account think of that!" Mrs. Sparsit shook her head, still in her highly superior manner, and a little changed the small cough—coughing now, as if the spirit of prophecy rose within her, but had better be coughed down.

"However, ma'am," said Bounderby, "there are apartments at the Bank, where a born and bred lady, as keeper of the place, would be rather a catch than otherwise; and if the same terms—"

"I beg your pardon, sir. You were so good as to promise that you would always substitute the phrase, annual compliment."

"Well, ma'am, annual compliment. If the same annual compliment would be acceptable there, why, I see nothing to part us, unless you do."

"Sir," returned Mrs. Sparsit. "The proposal is like yourself, and if the position I shall assume at the Bank is one that I could occupy without descending lower in the social scale—"

"Why, of course it is," said Bounderby. "If it was not, ma'am, you don't supposed that I should offer it to a lady who has moved in the society you have moved in. Not that *I* care for such society, you know! But *you* do."

"Mr. Bounderby, you are very considerate."

"You'll have your own private apartments, and you'll have your coals and your candles, and all the rest of it, and you'll have your maid to attend upon you, and you'll have your light porter[1] to protect you, and you'll be what I take the liberty of considering precious comfortable," said Bounderby.

---

1.   Messenger boy.

"Sir," rejoined Mrs. Sparsit, "say no more. In yielding up my trust here, I shall not be freed from the necessity of eating the bread of dependence:"[1] she might have said the sweetbread, for that delicate article in a savoury brown sauce was her favourite supper: "and I would rather receive it from your hand, than from any other. Therefore, sir, I accept your offer gratefully, and with many sincere acknowledgements for past favours. And I hope, sir," said Mrs. Sparsit, concluding in an impressively compassionate manner, "I fondly hope that Miss Gradgrind may be all you desire, and deserve!"

Nothing moved Mrs. Sparsit from that position any more. It was in vain for Bounderby to bluster or to assert himself in any of his explosive ways; Mrs. Sparsit was resolved to have compassion on him, as a Victim. She was polite, obliging, cheerful, hopeful; but, the more hopeful, the more exemplary altogether, she; the forlorner Sacrifice and Victim, he. She had that tenderness for his melancholy fate, that his great red countenance used to break out into cold perspirations when she looked at him.

Meanwhile the marriage was appointed to be solemnized in eight weeks' time, and Mr. Bounderby went every evening to Stone Lodge as an accepted wooer. Love was made on these occasions in the form of bracelets; and, on all occasions during the period of betrothal, took a manufacturing aspect. Dresses were made, jewellery was made, cakes and gloves were made, settlements were made, and an extensive assortment of Facts did appropriate honour to the contract. The business was all Fact, from first to last. The Hours did not go through any of those rosy performances, which foolish poets have ascribed to them at such times; neither did the clocks go any faster, or any slower, than at other seasons. The deadly statistical recorder in the Gradgrind observatory knocked every second on the head as it was born, and buried it with his accustomed regularity.

So the day came, as all other days come to people who will only stick to reason; and when it came, there were married in the church of the florid wooden legs—that popular order of architecture—Josiah Bounderby

---

1.   Compare similar phrases in the King James Bible: 'bread of affliction' (e.g. Deuteronomy 16:3); 'bread of idleness' (Proverbs 31:27); 'bread of adversity' (Isaiah 30:20); etc.

Esquire of Coketown, to Louisa, eldest daughter of Thomas Gradgrind Esquire of Stone Lodge, M. P. for that borough. And when they were united in holy matrimony, they went home to breakfast at Stone Lodge aforesaid.

There was an improving party assembled on the auspicious occasion, who knew what everything they had to eat and drink was made of, and how it was imported or exported, and in what quantities, and in what bottoms,[1] whether native or foreign, and all about it. The bridesmaids, down to little Jane Gradgrind, were, in an intellectual point of view, fit helpmates for the calculating boy;[2] and there was no nonsense about any of the company.

After breakfast, the bridegroom addressed them in the following terms:

"Ladies and gentlemen, I am Josiah Bounderby of Coketown. Since you have done my wife and myself the honour of drinking our healths and happiness, I suppose I must acknowledge the same; though, as you all know me, and know what I am, and what my extraction was, you won't expect a speech from a man who, when he sees a Post, says 'that's a Post,' and when he sees a Pump, says 'that's a Pump,' and is not to be got to call a Post a Pump or a Pump a Post, or either of them a Toothpick. If you want a speech this morning, my friend and father-in-law, Tom Gradgrind, is a Member of Parliament, and you know where to get it. I am not your man. However, if I feel a little independent when I look around this table to-day, and reflect how little I thought of marrying Tom Gradgrind's daughter when I was a ragged street-boy, who never washed his face unless it was at a pump, and that not oftener than once a fort-night, I hope I may be excused. So, I hope you like my feeling inde-pendent; if you don't, I can't help it. I *do* feel independent. Now I have mentioned, and you have mentioned, that I am this day married to Tom Gradgrind's daughter. I am very glad to be so. It has long been my wish to be so. I have watched her bringing-up, and I believe she is worthy of me. At the same time—not to deceive you—I believe I am worthy of her. So, I thank you, on both our parts, for the good-will you have shown

---

1.   Vessels, boats.
2.   A child-prodigy in arithmetic, often exhibited as a curiosity at shows or fairs.

towards us; and the best wish I can give the unmarried part of the present company, is this: I hope every bachelor may find as good a wife as I have found. And I hope every spinster may find as good a husband as my wife has found."

Shortly after which oration, as they were going on a nuptial trip to Lyons,[1] in order that Mr. Bounderby might take the opportunity of seeing how the Hands got on in those parts, and whether they, too, required to be fed with gold spoons; the happy pair departed for the railroad. The bride, in passing down-stairs, dressed for her journey, found Tom waiting for her—flushed, either with his feelings or the vinous part of the breakfast.

"What a game girl you are, to be such a first-rate sister, Loo!" whispered Tom.

She clung to him as she should have clung to some far better nature that day, and was a little shaken in her reserved composure for the first time.

"Old Bounderby's quite ready," said Tom. "Time's up. Good-bye! I shall be on the look-out for you, when you come back. I say, my dear Loo! AN'T it uncommonly jolly now!"

END OF THE FIRST BOOK.

---

1.   The centre of the French textile industry.

Book the Second. Reaping.[1]

Chapter I.
Effects in the Bank

A SUNNY midsummer day. There was such a thing sometimes, even in Coketown.

Seen from a distance in such weather, Coketown lay shrouded in a haze of its own, which appeared impervious to the sun's rays. You only knew the town was there, because you know there could have been no such sulky blotch upon the prospect without a town. A blur of soot and smoke, now confusedly tending this way, now that way, now aspiring to the vault of Heaven, now murkily creeping along the earth, as the wind rose and fell, or changed its quarter: a dense formless jumble, with sheets of cross light in it, that showed nothing but masses of darkness:— Coketown in the distance was suggestive of itself, though not a brick of it could be seen.

The wonder was, it was there at all. It had been ruined so often, that it was amazing how it had borne so many shocks. Surely there never was such fragile china-ware as that of which the millers of Coketown were made. Handle them never so lightly, and they fell to pieces with such ease that you might suspect them of having been flawed before. They were ruined, when they were required to send labouring children to school; they were ruined when inspectors were appointed to look into their works; they were ruined, when such inspectors considered it doubtful whether they were quite justified in chopping people up with their machinery; they were utterly undone, when it was hinted that perhaps they need not always make quite so much smoke. Besides Mr. Bounderby's gold spoon which was generally received in Coketown, another prevalent fiction was very popular there. It took the form of a threat. Whenever a Coketowner felt he was ill-used—that is to say, whenever he was not left entirely alone,

---

1.   See the General Introduction p. 21.

and it was proposed to hold him accountable for the consequences of any of his acts—he was sure to come out with the awful menace, that he would "sooner pitch his property into the Atlantic." This had terrified the Home Secretary within an inch of his life, on several occasions.*

However, the Coketowners were so patriotic after all, that they never had pitched their property into the Atlantic yet, but, on the contrary, had been kind enough to take mighty good care of it. So there it was, in the haze yonder; and it increased and multiplied.

The streets were hot and dusty on the summer day, and the sun was so bright that it even shone through the heavy vapour drooping over Coketown, and could not be looked at steadily. Stokers emerged from low underground doorways into factory yards, and sat on steps, and posts, and palings, wiping their swarthy visages, and contemplating coals. The whole town seemed to be frying in oil. There was a stifling smell of hot oil everywhere. The steam-engines shone with it, the dresses of the Hands were soiled with it, the mills throughout their many stories oozed and trickled it. The atmosphere of those Fairy palaces was like the breath of the simoom:[1] and their inhabitants, wasting with heat, toiled languidly in the desert. But no temperature made the melancholy mad elephants more mad or more sane. Their wearisome heads went up and down at the same rate, in hot weather and cold, wet weather and dry, fair weather and foul. The measured motion of their shadows on the walls, was the substitute Coketown had to show for the shadows of rustling woods; while, for the summer hum of insects, it could offer, all the year round, from the dawn of Monday to the night of Saturday, the whirr of shafts and wheels.

Drowsily they whirred all through this sunny day, making the passenger more sleepy and hot as he passed the humming walls of the mills. Sun-blinds, and sprinklings of water, a little cooled the main streets and the shops; but the mills, and the courts and alleys, baked at a fierce heat. Down upon the river that was black and thick with dye, some Coketown boys who were at large—a rare sight there—rowed a crazy boat, which made a spumous track upon the water as it jogged along, while every dip of an oar stirred up vile smells. But the sun itself, how-

---

1.   A hot, dry wind sweeping across the deserts of Africa and Asia.

ever beneficent, generally, was less kind to Coketown than hard frost, and rarely looked intently into any of its closer regions without engendering more death than life. So does the eye of Heaven[1] itself become an evil eye, when incapable or sordid hands are interposed between it and the things it looks upon to bless.

Mrs. Sparsit sat in her afternoon apartment at the Bank, on the shadier side of the frying street. Office-hours were over: and at that period of the day, in warm weather, she usually embellished with her genteel presence, a managerial board-room over the public office. Her own private sitting-room was a story higher, at the window of which post of observation she was ready, every morning, to greet Mr. Bounderby, as he came across the road, with the sympathizing recognition appropriate to a Victim. He had been married now a year; and Mrs. Sparsit had never released him from her determined pity a moment.

The Bank offered no violence to the wholesome monotony of the town. It was another red brick house, with black outside shutters, green inside blinds, a black street-door up two white steps, a brazen door-plate, and a brazen door-handle full stop. It was a size larger than Mr. Bounderby's house, as other houses were from a size to half-a-dozen sizes smaller; in all other particulars, it was strictly according to pattern.

Mrs. Sparsit was conscious that by coming in the evening-tide among the desks and writing implements, she shed a feminine, not to say also aristocratic, grace upon the office. Seated, with her needlework or netting apparatus, at the window, she had a self-laudatory sense of correcting, by her ladylike deportment, the rude business aspect of the place. With this impression of her interesting character upon her, Mrs. Sparsit considered herself, in some sort, the Bank Fairy. The townspeople who, in their passing and repassing, saw her there, regarded her as the Bank Dragon keeping watch over the treasures of the mine.

What those treasures were, Mrs. Sparsit knew as little as they did. Gold and silver coin, precious paper, secrets that if divulged would bring vague destruction upon vague persons (generally, however, people whom she disliked), were the chief items in her ideal catalogue thereof. For the rest, she knew that after office-hours, she reigned supreme over all the office

---

1.   See Shakespeare Sonnet 18 'Shall I compare thee to a summer's day?'

furniture, and over a locked-up iron room with three locks, against the door of which strong chamber the light porter laid his head every night, on a truckle bed, that disappeared at cockcrow. Further, she was lady paramount over certain vaults in the basement, sharply spiked off from communication with the predatory world; and over the relics of the current day's work, consisting of blots of ink, worn-out pens, fragments of wafers, and scraps of paper torn so small, that nothing interesting could ever be deciphered on them when Mrs. Sparsit tried. Lastly, she was guardian over a little armoury of cutlasses and carbines, arrayed in vengeful order above one of the official chimney-pieces; and over that respectable tradition never to be separated from a place of business claiming to be wealthy—a row of fire-buckets—vessels calculated to be of no physical utility on any occasion, but observed to exercise a fine moral influence, almost equal to bullion, on most beholders.

A deaf serving-woman and the light porter completed Mrs. Sparsit's empire. The deaf serving-woman was rumoured to be wealthy; and a saying had for years gone about among the lower orders of Coketown, that she would be murdered some night when the Bank was shut, for the sake of her money. It was generally considered, indeed, that she had been due some time, and ought to have fallen long ago; but she had kept her life, and her situation, with an ill-conditioned tenacity that occasioned much offence and disappointment.

Mrs. Sparsit's tea was just set for her on a pert little table, with its tripod of legs in an attitude, which she insinuated after office-hours, into the company of the stern, leathern-topped, long board-table that bestrode the middle of the room. The light porter placed the tea-tray on it, knuckling his forehead as a form of homage.

"Thank you, Bitzer," said Mrs. Sparsit.

"Thank *you*, ma'am," returned the light porter. He was a very light porter indeed; as light as in the days when he blinkingly defined a horse, for girl number twenty.

"All is shut up, Bitzer?" said Mrs. Sparsit.

"All is shut up, ma'am."

"And what," said Mrs. Sparsit, pouring out her tea, "is the news of the day? Anything?"

"Well, ma'am, I can't say that I have heard anything particular. Our people are a bad lot, ma'am; but that is no news, unfortunately."

"What are the restless wretches doing now?" asked Mrs. Sparsit.

"Merely going on in the old way, ma'am. Uniting, and leaguing, and engaging to stand by one another."

"It is much to be regretted," said Mrs. Sparsit, making her nose more Roman and her eyebrows more Coriolanian in the strength of her severity, "that the united masters allow of any such class-combinations."

"Yes, ma'am," said Bitzer.

"Being united themselves, they ought one and all to set their faces against employing any man who is united with any other man," said Mrs. Sparsit.

"They have done that, ma'am," returned Bitzer; "but it rather fell through, ma'am."

"I do not pretend to understand these things," said Mrs. Sparsit with dignity, "my lot having been originally cast in a widely different sphere; and Mr. Sparsit, as a Powler, being also quite out of the pale of any such dissensions. I only know that these people must be conquered, and that it's high time it was done, once and for all."

"Yes, ma'am," returned Bitzer, with a demonstration of great respect for Mrs. Sparsit's oracular authority. "You couldn't put it clearer, I am sure, ma'am."

As this was his usual hour for having a little confidential chat with Mrs. Sparsit, and as he had already caught her eye and seen that she was going to ask him something, he made a pretence of arranging the rulers, inkstands, and so forth, while that lady went on with her tea, glancing through the open window, down into the street.

"Has it been a busy day, Bitzer?" asked Mrs. Sparsit.

"Not a very busy day, my lady. About an average day." He now and then slided into my lady, instead of ma'am, as an involuntary acknowledgement of Mrs. Sparsit's personal dignity and claims to reverence.

"The clerks," said Mrs. Sparsit, carefully brushing an imperceptible crumb of bread and butter from her left-hand mitten, "are trustworthy, punctual, and industrious, of course?"

"Yes, ma'am, pretty fair, ma'am. With the usual exception."

He held the respectable office of general spy and informer in the establishment, for which volunteer service he received a present at Christmas, over and above his weekly wage. He had grown into an extremely clear-headed, cautious, prudent young man, who was safe to rise in the world. His mind was so exactly regulated, that he had no affections or passions. All his proceedings were the result of the nicest and coldest calculation; and it was not without cause that Mrs. Sparsit habitually observed of him, that he was a young man of the steadiest principle she had ever known. Having satisfied himself, on his father's death, that his mother had a right of settlement in Coketown, this excellent young economist had asserted that right for her with such a steadfast adherence to the principle of the case, that she had been shut up in the workhouse ever since. It must be admitted that he allowed her half a pound of tea a year, which was weak in him: first, because all gifts have an inevitable tendency to pauperise the recipient, and secondly, because his only reasonable transaction in that commodity would have been to buy it for as little as he could possibly give, and sell it for as much as he could possibly get; it having been clearly ascertained by philosophers that in this is comprised the whole duty of man—not a part of man's duty, but the whole.*

"Pretty fair, ma'am. With the usual exception, ma'am," repeated Bitzer.

"Ah—h!" said Mrs. Sparsit, shaking her head over her tea-cup, and taking a long gulp.

"Mr. Thomas, ma'am, I doubt Mr. Thomas very much, ma'am, I don't like his ways at all."

"Bitzer," said Mrs. Sparsit, in a very impressive manner, "do you recollect my having said anything to you respecting names?"

"I beg your pardon, ma'am. It's quite true that you did object to names being used, and they're always best avoided."

"Please to remember that I have a charge here," said Mrs. Sparsit, with her air of state. "I hold a trust here, Bitzer, under Mr. Bounderby. However improbable both Mr. Bounderby and myself might have deemed it years ago, that he would ever become my patron, making me an annual compliment, I cannot but regard him in that light. From Mr. Bounderby I have received every acknowledgment of my social station, and every recognition of my family descent, that I could possibly expect. More, far more. Therefore, to my patron I will be scrupulously true. And I do not consider, I will not consider, I cannot consider," said Mrs. Sparsit, with a most extensive stock on hand of honour and morality, "that I *should* be scrupulously true, if I allowed names to be mentioned under this roof, that are unfortunately—most unfortunately—no doubt of that—connected with his."

Bitzer knuckled his forehead again, and again begged pardon.

"No, Bitzer," continued Mrs. Sparsit, "say an individual, and I will hear you; say Mr. Thomas, and you must excuse me."

"With the usual exception, ma'am," said Bitzer, trying back, "of an individual."

"Ah—h!" Mrs. Sparsit repeated the ejaculation, the shake of the head over her tea-cup, and the long gulp, as taking up the conversation again at the point where it had been interrupted.

"An individual, ma'am," said Bitzer, "has never been what he ought to have been, since he first came into the place. He is a dissipated, extravagant idler. He is not worth his salt,[1] ma'am. He wouldn't get it either, if he hadn't a friend and relation at court, ma'am!"

"Ah—h!" said Mrs. Sparsit, with another melancholy shake of her head.

"I only hope, ma'am," pursued Bitzer, "that his friend and relation may not supply him with the means of carrying on. Otherwise, ma'am, we know out of whose pocket *that* money comes."

"Ah—h!" sighed Mrs. Sparsit again, with another melancholy shake of her head.

"He is to be pitied, ma'am. The last party I have alluded to, is to be pitied, ma'am," said Bitzer.

"Yes, Bitzer," said Mrs. Sparsit. "I have always pitied the delusion, always."

"As to an individual, ma'am," said Bitzer, dropping his voice and drawing nearer, "he is as improvident as any of the people in this town. And you know what *their* improvidence is, ma'am. No one could wish to know it better than a lady of your eminence does."

"They would do well," returned Mrs. Sparsit, "to take example by you, Bitzer."

"Thank you, ma'am. But, since you do refer to me, now look at me, ma'am. I have put by a little, ma'am, already. That gratuity which I receive

---

1.   Lazy, inefficient, not earning his keep (salt is a conventional metonym for food).

at Christmas, ma'am: I never touch it. I don't even go the length of my wages, though they're not high, ma'am. Why can't they do as I have done, ma'am? What one person can do, another can do."

This, again, was among the fictions of Coketown. Any capitalist there, who had made sixty thousand pounds out of sixpence, always professed to wonder why the sixty thousand nearest Hands didn't each make sixty thousand pounds out of sixpence, and more or less reproached them every one for not accomplishing the little feat. What I did you can do. Why don't you go and do it?

"As to their wanting recreations, ma'am," said Bitzer, "it's stuff and nonsense. I don't want recreations. I never did, and I never shall; I don't like 'em. As to their combining together; there are many of them, I have no doubt, that by watching and informing upon one another could earn a trifle now and then, whether in money or good will, and improve their livelihood. Then, why don't they improve it, ma'am! It's the first consideration of a rational creature, and it's what they pretend to want."

"Pretend indeed!" said Mrs. Sparsit.

"I am sure we are constantly hearing, ma'am, till it becomes quite nauseous, concerning their wives and families," said Bitzer. "Why look at me, ma'am! I don't want a wife and family. Why should they?"

"Because they are improvident," said Mrs. Sparsit.

"Yes, ma'am," returned Bitzer, "that's where it is. If they were more provident and less perverse, ma'am, what would they do? They would say, 'While my hat covers my family,' or 'while my bonnet covers my family,'—as the case might be, ma'am—'I have only one to feed, and that's the person I most like to feed.'"

"To be sure," assented Mrs. Sparsit, eating muffin.

"Thank you ma'am," said Bitzer, knuckling his forehead again, in return for the favour of Mrs. Sparsit's improving conversation. "Would you wish a little more hot water, ma'am, or is there anything else that I could fetch you?"

"Nothing just now, Bitzer."

"Thank you, ma'am. I shouldn't wish to disturb you at your meals, ma'am, particularly tea, knowing your partiality for it," said Bitzer, craning a little to look over into the street from where he stood; "but there's a gentleman been looking up here for a minute or so, ma'am, and he has come across as if he was going to knock. That *is* his knock, ma'am, no doubt."

He stepped to the window; and looking out, and drawing in his head again, confirmed himself with, "Yes, ma'am. Would you wish the gentleman to be shown in, ma'am?"

"I don't know who it can be," said Mrs. Sparsit, wiping her mouth and arranging her mittens.

"A stranger, ma'am, evidently."

"What a stranger can want at the Bank at this time of the evening, unless he comes upon some business for which he is too late, I don't know," said Mrs. Sparsit, "but I hold a charge in this establishment from Mr. Bounderby, and I will never shrink from it. If to see him is any part of the duty I have accepted, I will see him. Use your own discretion, Bitzer."

Here the visitor, all unconscious of Mrs. Sparsit's magnanimous words, repeated his knock so loudly that the light porter hastened down to open the door; while Mrs. Sparsit took the precaution of concealing her little table, with all its appliances upon it, in a cupboard, and then decamped up-stairs, that she might appear, if needful, with the greater dignity.

"If you please, ma'am, the gentleman would wish to see you," said Bitzer, with his light eye at Mrs. Sparsit's keyhole. So, Mrs. Sparsit, who had improved the interval by touching up her cap, took her classical features down-stairs again, and entered the board-room in the manner of a Roman matron going outside the city walls to treat with an invading general.[1]

The visitor having strolled to the window, and being then engaged in looking carelessly out, was as unmoved by this impressive entry as man could possibly be. He stood whistling to himself with all imaginable coolness, with his hat still on, and a certain air of exhaustion upon him, in part arising from excessive summer, and in part from excessive gentility. For it was to be seen with half an eye that he was a thorough gentleman, made to the model of the time; weary of everything, and putting no more faith in anything than Lucifer.

"I believe, sir," quoth Mrs. Sparsit, "you wished to see me."

---

1.   Compare *Coriolanus* V iii.

"I beg your pardon," he said, turning and removing his hat; "pray excuse me."

"Humph!" thought Mrs. Sparsit, as she made a stately bend. "Five and thirty, good-looking, good figure, good teeth, good voice, good breeding, well-dressed, dark hair, bold eyes." All which Mrs. Sparsit observed in her womanly way—like the Sultan who put his head in the pail of water[1]—merely in dipping down and coming up again.

"Please be seated, sir," said Mrs. Sparsit.

"Thank you. Allow me." He placed a chair for her, but remained himself carelessly lounging against the table. "I left my servant at the railway looking after the luggage—very heavy train[2] and vast quantity of it in the van—and strolled on, looking about me. Exceedingly odd place. Will you allow me to ask you if it's *always* as black as this?"

"In general much blacker," returned Mrs. Sparsit, in her uncompromising way.

"Is it possible! Excuse me: you are not a native, I think?"

"No, sir," returned Mrs. Sparsit. "It was once my good or ill fortune, as it may be—before I became a widow—to move in a very different sphere. My husband was a Powler."

"Beg your pardon, really!" said the stranger. "Was—?"

Mrs. Sparsit repeated, "A Powler."

"Powler Family," said the stranger, after reflecting a few moments. Mrs. Sparsit signified assent. The stranger seemed a little more fatigued than before.

"You must be very much bored here?" was the inference he drew from the communication.

"I am the servant of circumstances, sir," said Mrs. Sparsit, "and I have long adapted myself to the governing power of my life."

"Very philosophical," returned the stranger, "and very exemplary and laudable, and—" It seemed to be scarcely worth his while to finish the sentence, so he played with his watch-chain wearily.

---

1. Famous story told by Joseph Addison (*Spectator* June 18, 1711) of an Egyptian ruler who underwent a lifetime of adventures during the few seconds in which his head was immersed in a tub of water.
2. Probably a suite of luggage.

"May I be permitted to ask, sir," said Mrs. Sparsit, "to what I am indebted for the favour of—"

"Assuredly," said the stranger. "Much obliged to you for reminding me. I am the bearer of a letter of introduction to Mr. Bounderby, the banker. Walking though this extraordinarily black town, while they were getting dinner ready at the hotel, I asked a fellow whom I met; one of the working people; who appeared to have been taking a shower-bath of something fluffy, which I assume to be the raw material—"[1]

Mrs. Sparsit inclined her head.

"—Raw material—where Mr. Bounderby, the banker, might reside. Upon which, misled no doubt by the word Banker, he directed me to the Bank. Fact being, I presume, that Mr. Bounderby the Banker does *not* reside in the edifice in which I have the honour of offering this explanation?"

"No, sir," returned Mrs. Sparsit, "he does not."

"Thank you. I had no intention of delivering my letter at the present moment, nor have I. But strolling on to the Bank to kill time, and having the good fortune to observe at the window," towards which he languidly waved his hand, then slightly bowed, "a lady of a very superior and agreeable appearance, I considered that I could not do better than take the liberty of asking that lady where Mr. Bounderby the Banker *does* live. Which I accordingly venture, with all suitable apologies, to do."

The inattention and indolence of his manner were sufficiently relieved, to Mrs. Sparsit's thinking, by a certain gallantry at ease, which offered her homage too. Here he was, for instance, at this moment, all but sitting on the table, and yet lazily bending over her, as if he acknowledged an attraction in her that made her charming—in her way.

"Banks, I know, are always suspicious, and officially must be," said the stranger, whose lightness and smoothness of speech were pleasant likewise; suggesting matter far more sensible and humorous than it ever contained—which was perhaps a shrewd device of the founder of this numerous sect, whosoever may have been that great man: "therefore I may observe that my letter—here it is—is from the member for this

---

1.   I.e. the accumulated specks of cotton waste produced in the mills by the process of carding.

place—Gradgrind—whom I have had the pleasure of knowing in London."

Mrs. Sparsit recognized the hand, intimated that such confirmation was quite unnecessary, and gave Mr. Bounderby's address, with all needful clues and directions in aid.

"Thousand thanks," said the stranger. "Of course you know the Banker well?"

"Yes, sir," rejoined Mrs. Sparsit. "In my dependent relation towards him, I have known him ten years."

"Quite an eternity! I think he married Gradgrind's daughter?"

"Yes," said Mrs. Sparsit, suddenly compressing her mouth, "he had that—honour."

"The lady is quite a philosopher, I am told?"

"Indeed, sir," said Mrs. Sparsit. "*Is* she?"

"Excuse my impertinent curiosity," pursued the stranger, fluttering over Mrs. Sparsit's eyebrows, with a propitiatory air, "but you know the family, and know the world. I am about to know the family, and may have much to do with them. Is the lady so very alarming? Her father gives her such a portentously hard-headed reputation, that I have a burning desire to know. Is she absolutely unapproachable? Repellently and stunningly clever? I see, by your meaning smile, you think not. You have poured balm into my anxious soul. As to age, now. Forty? Five and thirty?"

Mrs. Sparsit laughed outright. "A chit," said she. "Not twenty when she was married."

"I give you my honour, Mrs. Powler," returned the stranger, detaching himself from the table, "that I never was so astonished in my life!"

It really did seem to impress him, to the utmost extent of his capacity of being impressed. He looked at his informant for full a quarter of a minute, and appeared to have the surprise in his mind all the time. "I assure you, Mrs. Powler," he then said, much exhausted, "that the father's manner prepared me for a grim and stony maturity. I am obliged to you, of all things, for correcting so absurd a mistake. Pray excuse my intrusion. Many thanks. Good day!"

He bowed himself out; and Mrs. Sparsit, hiding in the window curtain, saw him languishing down the street on the shady side of the way, observed of all the town.

"What do you think of the gentleman, Bitzer?" she asked the light porter, when he came to take away.

"Spends a deal of money on his dress, ma'am."

"It must be admitted," said Mrs. Sparsit, "that it's very tasteful."

"Yes, ma'am," returned Bitzer, "if that's worth the money."

"Besides which, ma'am," resumed Bitzer, while he was polishing the table, "he looks to me as if he gamed."

"It's immoral to game," said Mrs. Sparsit.

"It's ridiculous, ma'am," said Bitzer, "because the chances are against the players."

Whether it was that the heat prevented Mrs. Sparsit from working, or whether it was that her hand was out, she did no work that night. She sat at the window, when the sun began to sink behind the smoke; she sat there, when the smoke was burning red, when the colour faded from it, when the darkness seemed to rise slowly out of the ground, and creep upward, upward, up to the house-tops, up to the church steeple, up to the summits of the factory chimneys, up to the sky. Without a candle in the room, Mrs. Sparsit sat at the window, with her hands before her, not thinking much of the sounds of evening; the whooping of boys, the barking of dogs, the rumbling of wheels, the steps and voices of passengers, the shrill street cries, the clogs upon the pavement when it was their hour for going by, the shutting-up of shop-shutters. Not until the light porter announced that her nocturnal sweetbread was ready, did Mrs. Sparsit arouse herself from her reverie, and convey her dense black eyebrows—by that time creased with meditation, as if they need ironing out—up-stairs.

"Oh, you Fool!" said Mrs. Sparsit, when she was alone at her supper. Whom she meant, she did not say; but she could scarcely have meant the sweetbread.

CHAPTER II.
MR. JAMES HARTHOUSE

THE GRADGRIND party wanted assistance in cutting the throats of the Graces.[1] They went about recruiting; and where could they enlist recruits more hopefully, than among the fine gentlemen who, having found out everything to be worth nothing, were equally ready for anything?

Moreover, the healthy spirits who had mounted to this sublime height were attractive to many of the Gradgrind school. They liked fine gentlemen; they pretended that they did not, but they did. They became exhausted in imitation of them; and they yaw-yawed[2] in their speech like them; and they served out, with an enervated air, the little mouldy rations of political economy, on which they regaled their disciples. There never before was seen on earth such a wonderful hybrid race as was thus produced.

Among the fine gentlemen not regularly belonging to the Gradgrind school, there was one of a good family and a better appearance, with a happy turn of humour which had told immensely with the House of Commons on the occasion of his entertaining it with his (and the Board of Directors') view of a railway accident, in which the most careful officers ever known, employed by the most liberal managers ever heard of, assisted by the finest mechanical contrivances ever devised, the whole in action on the best line ever constructed, had killed five people and wounded thirty-two, by a casualty without which the excellence of the whole system would have been positively incomplete. Among the slain was a cow, and among the scattered articles unowned, a widow's cap. And the honourable member had so tickled the House (which has a delicate sense of humour) by putting the cap on the cow, that it became impatient of any serious reference to the Coroner's Inquest, and brought the railway off with Cheers and Laughter.

Now, this gentleman had a younger brother of still better appearance

---

1. I.e. attacking pleasure in the name of utility. In classical mythology the Three Graces were the daughters of Zeus, and represented beauty, charm, and grace.
2. Spoke affectedly.

than himself, who had tried life as a Cornet of Dragoons,[1] and found it a bore; and had afterwards tried it in the train of an English minister abroad, and found it a bore; and had then strolled to Jerusalem, and got bored there; and had then gone yachting about the world, and got bored everywhere. To whom this honourable and jocular member fraternally said one day, "Jem, there's a good opening among the hard Fact fellows, and they want men. I wonder you don't go in for statistics." Jem, rather taken by the novelty of the idea, and very hard up for a change, was as ready to "go in" for statistics as for anything else. So, he went in. He coached himself up with a blue-book or two;[2] and his brother put it about among the hard Fact fellows, and said, "If you want to bring in, for any place, a handsome dog who can make you a devilish good speech, look after my brother Jem, for he's your man." After a few dashes in the public meeting way, Mr. Gradgrind and a council of political sages approved of Jem, and it was resolved to send him down to Coketown, to become known there and in the neighbourhood. Hence the letter Jem had last night shown to Mrs. Sparsit, which Mr. Bounderby now held in his hand; superscribed, "Josiah Bounderby, Esquire, Banker, Coketown. Specially to introduce James Harthouse, Esquire. Thomas Gradgrind."

Within an hour of the receipt of this dispatch and Mr. James Harthouse's card, Mr. Bounderby put on his hat and went down to the Hotel. There he found Mr. James Harthouse looking out of window, in a state of mind so disconsolate, that he was already half-disposed to "go in" for something else.

"My name, sir," said his visitor, "is Josiah Bounderby, of Coketown."

Mr. James Harthouse was very happy indeed (though he scarcely looked so) to have a pleasure he had long expected.

"Coketown, sir," said Bounderby, obstinately taking a chair, "is not the kind of place you have been accustomed to. Therefore, if you will allow me—or whether you will or not, for I am a plain man—I'll tell you something about it before we go any further."

Mr. Harthouse would be charmed.

---

1.   A junior cavalry officer.
2.   I.e. preparing himself by reading government reports (see note to p. 92).

"Don't be too sure of that," said Bounderby. "I don't promise it. First of all, you see our smoke. That's meat and drink to us. It's the healthiest thing in the world in all respects, and particularly for the lungs. If you are one of those who want us to consume it, I differ from you. We are not going to wear the bottoms of our boilers out any faster than we wear 'em out now, for all the humbugging sentiment in Great Britain and Ireland."*

By way of "going in" to the fullest extent, Mr. Harthouse rejoined, "Mr. Bounderby, I assure you I am entirely and completely of your way of thinking. On conviction."

"I am glad to hear it," said Bounderby. "Now, you have heard a lot of talk about the work in our mills, no doubt. You have? Very good. I'll state the fact of it to you. It's the pleasantest work there is, and it's the lightest work there is, and it's the best-paid work there is. More than that, we couldn't improve the mills themselves, unless we laid down Turkey carpets on the floors. Which we're not a-going to do."

"Mr. Bounderby, perfectly right."

"Lastly," said Bounderby, "as to our Hands. There's not a Hand in this town, sir, man, woman, or child, but has one ultimate object in life. That object is, to be fed on turtle soup and venison with a gold spoon. Now, they're not a-going—none of 'em—ever to be fed on turtle soup and venison with a gold spoon. And now you know the place."

Mr. Harthouse professed himself in the highest degree instructed and refreshed, by this condensed epitome of the whole Coketown question.

"Why, you see," replied Mr. Bounderby, "it suits my disposition to have a full understanding with a man, particularly with a public man, when I make his acquaintance. I have only one thing more to say to you, Mr. Harthouse, before assuring you of the pleasure with which I shall respond, to the utmost of my poor ability, to my friend Tom Gradgrind's letter of introduction. You are a man of family. Don't you deceive yourself by supposing for a moment that I am a man of family. I am a bit of dirty riff-raff, and a genuine scrap of tag, rag, and bobtail."

If anything could have exalted Jem's interest in Mr. Bounderby, it would have been this very circumstance. Or, so he told him.

"So now," said Bounderby, "we may shake hands on equal terms. I say, equal terms, because although I know what I am, and the exact depth of the gutter I have lifted myself out of, better than any man does, I am as proud as you are. I am just as proud as you are. Having now asserted my independence in a proper manner, I may come to how do you find yourself, and I hope you're pretty well."

The better, Mr. Harthouse gave him to understand as they shook hands, for the salubrious air of Coketown. Mr. Bounderby received the answer with favour.

"Perhaps you know," said he, "or perhaps you don't know, I married Tom Gradgrind's daughter. If you have nothing better to do than to walk up town with me, I shall be glad to introduce you to Tom Gradgrind's daughter."

"Mr. Bounderby," said Jem, "you anticipate my dearest wishes."

They went out without further discourse; and Mr. Bounderby piloted the new acquaintance who so strongly contrasted with him, to the private red brick dwelling, with the black outside shutters, the green inside blinds, and the black street door up the two white steps. In the drawing-room of which mansion, there presently entered to them the most remarkable girl Mr. James Harthouse had ever seen. She was so constrained, and yet so careless; so reserved, and yet so watchful; so cold and proud, and yet so sensitively ashamed of her husband's braggart humility—from which she shrunk as if every example of it were a cut or a blow; that it was quite a new sensation to observe her. In face she was no less remarkable than in manner. Her features were handsome; but their natural play was so locked up, that it seemed impossible to guess at their genuine expression. Utterly indifferent, perfectly self-reliant, never at a loss, and yet never at her ease, with her figure in company with them there, and her mind apparently quite alone—it was of no use "going in" yet awhile to comprehend this girl, for she baffled all penetration.

From the mistress of the house, the visitor glanced to the house itself. There was no mute sign of a woman in the room. No graceful little adornment, no fanciful little device, however trivial, anywhere expressed her influence. Cheerless and comfortless, boastfully and doggedly rich, there the room stared at its present occupants, unsoftened and unrelieved by the least trace of any womanly occupation. As Mr. Bounderby stood in the midst of his household gods,[1] so those unrelenting divinities occupied their places around Mr. Bounderby, and they were worthy of one another, and well matched.

"This, sir," said Bounderby, "is my wife, Mrs. Bounderby: Tom Gradgrind's eldest daughter. Loo, Mr. James Harthouse. Mr. Harthouse has joined your father's muster-roll.[2] If he is not Tom Gradgrind's colleague before long, I believe we shall at least hear of him in connexion with one of our neighbouring towns. You observe, Mr. Harthouse, that my wife is my junior. I don't know what she saw in me to marry me, but she saw something in me, I suppose, or she wouldn't have married me. She has lots of expensive knowledge, sir, political and otherwise. If you want to cram for anything, I should be troubled to recommend you to a better adviser than Loo Bounderby."

To a more agreeable adviser, or one from whom he would be more likely to learn, Mr. Harthouse could never be recommended.

"Come!" said his host. "If you're in the complimentary line, you'll get on here, for you'll meet with no competition. I have never been in the way of learning compliments myself, and I don't profess to understand the art of paying 'em. In fact, despise 'em. But, your bringing-up was different from mine; mine was a real thing, by George! You're a gentleman, and I don't pretend to be one. I am Josiah Bounderby of Coketown, and that's enough for me. However, though I am not influenced by manners and station, Loo Bounderby may be. She hadn't my advantages—disadvantages you would call 'em, but I call 'em advantages—so you'll not waste your power, I dare say."

"Mr. Bounderby," said Jem, turning with a smile to Louisa, "is a noble animal in a comparatively natural state, quite free from the harness in which a conventional hack like myself works."

"You respect Mr. Bounderby very much," she quietly returned. "It is natural that you should."

He was disgracefully thrown out, for a gentleman who had seen so much of the world, and thought, "Now, how am I to take this?"

---

1. The *lares* and *penates*, the divinities presiding over the household in ancient Rome, and by extension the essentials of home life. Here used ironically.
2. List of members of an army regiment, etc.

"You are going to devote yourself, as I gather from what Mr. Bounderby has said, to the service of your country. You have made up your mind," said Louisa, still standing before him where she had first stopped—in all the singular contrariety of her self-possession, and her being obviously very ill at ease—"to show the nation the way out of all its difficulties."

"Mrs. Bounderby," he returned, laughing, "upon my honour, no. I will make no such pretence to you. I have seen a little, here and there, up and down; I have found it all to be very worthless, as everybody has, and as some confess they have, and some do not; and I am going in for your respected father's opinions—really because I have no choice of opinions, and may as well back them as anything else."

"Have you none of your own?" asked Louisa.

"I have not so much as the slightest predilection left. I assure you I attach not the least importance to any opinions. The result of the varieties of boredom I have undergone, is a conviction (unless conviction is too industrious a word for the lazy sentiment I entertain on the subject), that any set of ideas will do just as much good as any other set, and just as much harm as any other set. There's an English family with a charming Italian motto. What will be, will be.[1] It's the only truth going!"

This vicious assumption of honesty in dishonesty—a vice so dangerous, so deadly, and so common—seemed, he observed, a little to impress her in his favour. He followed up the advantage, by saying in his pleasantest manner: a manner to which she might attach as much or as little meaning as she pleased: "The side that can prove anything in a line of units, tens, hundreds, and thousands, Mrs. Bounderby, seems to me to afford the most fun, and to give a man the best chance. I am quite as much attached to it as if I believed it. I am quite ready to go in for it, to the same extent as if I believed it. And what more could I possibly do, if I did believe it!"

"You are a singular politician," said Louisa.

"Pardon me; I have not even that merit. We are the largest party in the state, I assure you, Mrs. Bounderby, if we all fell out of our adopted ranks and were reviewed together."

---

1.   *Che serà, serà*, Italian motto of the family of Lord John Russell (1792–1878), English Prime Minister from 1846 to 1852.

Mr. Bounderby, who had been in danger of bursting in silence, interposed here with a project for postponing the family dinner till half-past six, and taking Mr. James Harthouse in the meantime on a round of visits to the voting and interesting notabilities of Coketown and its vicinity. The round of visits was made; and Mr. James Harthouse, with a discreet use of his blue coaching,[1] came off triumphantly, though with a considerable accession of boredom.

In the evening, he found the dinner-table laid for four, but they sat down only three. It was an appropriate occasion for Mr. Bounderby to discuss the flavour of the hap'orth of stewed eels he had purchased in the streets at eight years old; and also of the inferior water, specially used for laying the dust, with which he had washed down that repast. He likewise entertained his guest over the soup and fish, with the calculation that he (Bounderby) had eaten in his youth at least three horses under the guise of polonies and saveloys.[2] These recitals, Jem, in a languid manner, received with "charming!" every now and then; and they probably would have decided him to "go in" for Jerusalem again to-morrow morning, had he been less curious respecting Louisa.

"Is there nothing," he thought, glancing at her as she sat at the head of the table, where her youthful figure, small and slight, but very graceful, looked as pretty as it looked misplaced; "is there nothing that will move that face?"

Yes! By Jupiter, there was something, and here it was, in an unexpected shape. Tom appeared. She changed as the door opened, and broke into a beaming smile.

A beautiful smile. Mr. James Harthouse might not have thought so much of it, but that he had wondered so long at her impassive face. She put out her hand—a pretty little soft hand; and her fingers closed upon her brother's, as if she would have carried them to her lips.

"Ay, ay?" thought the visitor. "This whelp is the only creature she cares for. So, so!"

The whelp was presented, and took his chair. The appellation was not flattering, but not unmerited.

---

1.   See note to p. 157.
2.   Types of sausage.

"When I was your age, young Tom," said Bounderby, "I was punctual, or I got no dinner!"

"When you were my age," returned Tom, "you hadn't a wrong balance to get right, and hadn't to dress afterwards."

"Never mind that now," said Bounderby.

"Well, then," grumbled Tom. "Don't begin with me."

"Mrs. Bounderby," said Harthouse, perfectly hearing this under-strain as it went on; "your brother's face is quite familiar to me. Can I have seen him abroad? Or at some public school, perhaps?"

"No," she returned, quite interested, "he has never been abroad yet, and was educated here, at home. Tom, love, I am telling Mr. Harthouse that he never saw you abroad."

"No such luck, sir," said Tom.

There was little enough in him to brighten her face, for he was a sullen young fellow, and ungracious in his manner even to her. So much the greater must have been the solitude of her heart, and her need of some one on whom to bestow it. "So much the more is this whelp the only creature she has ever cared for," thought Mr. James Harthouse, turning it over and over. "So much the more. So much the more."

Both in his sister's presence, and after she had left the room, the whelp took no pains to hide his contempt for Mr. Bounderby, whenever he could indulge it without the observation of that independent man, by making wry faces, or shutting one eye. Without responding to these telegraphic communications, Mr. Harthouse encouraged him much in the course of the evening, and showed an unusual liking for him. At last, when he rose to return to his hotel, and was a little doubtful whether he knew the way by night, the whelp immediately proffered his services as guide, and turned out with him to escort him thither.

Chapter III.
The Whelp

It was very remarkable that a young gentleman who had been brought up under one continuous system of unnatural restraint, should be a hypocrite; but it was certainly the case with Tom. It was very strange that a young gentleman who had never been left to his own guidance for five consecutive minutes, should be incapable at last of governing himself; but so it was with Tom. It was altogether unaccountable that a young gentleman whose imagination had been strangled in his cradle, should be still inconvenienced by its ghost in the form of grovelling sensualities; but such a monster, beyond all doubt, was Tom.

"Do you smoke?" asked Mr. James Harthouse, when they came to the hotel.

"I believe you!" said Tom.

He could do no less than ask Tom up; and Tom could do no less than go up. What with a cooling drink adapted to the weather, but not so weak as cool; and what with a rarer tobacco than was to be bought in those parts; Tom was soon in a highly free and easy state at his end of the sofa, and more than ever disposed to admire his new friend at the other end.

Tom blew his smoke aside, after he had been smoking a little while, and took an observation of his friend. "He don't seem to care about his dress," thought Tom, "and yet how capitally he does it. What an easy swell he is!"

Mr. James Harthouse, happening to catch Tom's eye, remarked that he drank nothing, and filled his glass with his own negligent hand.

"Thank'ee," said Tom. "Thank'ee. Well, Mr. Harthouse, I hope you have had about a dose of old Bounderby to-night." Tom said this with one eye shut up again, and looking over his glass knowingly, at his entertainer.

"A very good fellow indeed!" returned Mr. James Harthouse.

"You think so, don't you?" said Tom. And shut up his eye again.

Mr. James Harthouse smiled; and rising from his end of the sofa, and lounging with his back against the chimney-piece, so that he stood before the empty fire-grate as he smoked, in front of Tom and looking down at him, observed:

"What a comical brother-in-law you are!"

"What a comical brother-in-law old Bounderby is, I think you mean," said Tom.

"You are a piece of caustic, Tom," retorted Mr. James Harthouse.

There was something so very agreeable in being so intimate with such a waistcoat; in being called Tom, in such an intimate way, by such a voice; in being on such off-hand terms so soon, with such a pair of whiskers; that Tom was uncommonly pleased with himself.

"Oh! I don't care for old Bounderby," said he, "if you mean that. I have always called old Bounderby by the same name when I have talked about him, and I have always thought of him in the same way. I am not going to begin to be polite now, about old Bounderby. It would be rather late in the day."

"Don't mind me," returned James; "but take care when his wife is by, you know."

"His wife?" said Tom. "My sister Loo? Oh yes!" And he laughed, and took a little more of the cooling drink.

James Harthouse continued to lounge in the same place and attitude, smoking his cigar in his own easy way, and looking pleasantly at the whelp, as if he knew himself to be a kind of agreeable demon[1] who had only to hover over him, and he must give up his whole soul if required. It certainly did seem that the whelp yielded to this influence. He looked at his companion sneakingly, he looked at him admiringly, he looked at him boldly, and put up one leg on the sofa.

"My sister Loo?" said Tom. "*She* never cared for old Bounderby."

"That's the past tense, Tom," returned Mr. James Harthouse, striking the ash from his cigar with his little finger. "We are in the present tense, now."

"Verb neuter, not to care. Indicative mood, present tense. First person singular, I do not care; second person singular, thou dost not care; third person singular, she does not care," returned Tom.

"Good! Very quaint!" said his friend. "Though you don't mean it."

---

1.   Harthouse is represented here and on other occasions as Tom's familiar spirit, like Faust's Mephistopheles, who has power over him and tempts him towards self-destruction.

"But I *do* mean it," cried Tom. "Upon my honour! Why, you won't tell me, Mr. Harthouse, that you really suppose my sister Loo does care for old Bounderby."

"My dear fellow," returned the other, "what am I bound to suppose, when I find two married people living in harmony and happiness?"

Tom had by this time got both his legs on the sofa. If his second leg had not been already there when he was called a dear fellow, he would have put it up at that great stage of the conversation. Feeling it necessary to do something then, he stretched himself out at greater length, and, reclining with the back of his head on the end of the sofa, and smoking with an infinite assumption of negligence, turned his common face, and not too sober eyes, towards the face looking down upon him so carelessly yet so potently.

"You know our governor, Mr. Harthouse," said Tom, "and therefore, you needn't be surprised that Loo married old Bounderby. She never had a lover, and the governor proposed old Bounderby, and she took him."

"Very dutiful in your interesting sister," said Mr. James Harthouse.

"Yes, but she wouldn't have been as dutiful, and it would not have come off as easily," returned the whelp, "if it hadn't been for me."

The tempter merely lifted his eyebrows; but the whelp was obliged to go on.

"*I* persuaded her," he said, with an edifying air of superiority. "I was stuck into old Bounderby's bank (where I never wanted to be), and I knew I should get into scrapes there, if she put old Bounderby's pipe out;[1] so I told her my wishes, and she came into them. She would do anything for me. It was very game of her, wasn't it?"

"It was charming, Tom!"

"Not that it was altogether so important to her as it was to me," continued Tom coolly, "because my liberty and comfort, and perhaps my getting on, depended on it; and she had no other lover, and staying at home was like staying in jail—especially when I was gone. It wasn't as if she gave up another lover for old Bounderby; but still it was a good thing in her."

---

1.   I.e. extinguished his ardour by rejecting his advances (idiomatic phrase).

"Perfectly delightful. And she gets on so placidly."

"Oh," returned Tom, with contemptuous patronage, "she's a regular girl. A girl can get on anywhere. She has settled down to the life, and *she* don't mind. It does just as well as another. Besides, though Loo is a girl, she's not a common sort of girl. She can shut herself up within herself, and think—as I have often known her sit and watch the fire—for an hour at a stretch."

"Ay, ay? Has resources of her own," said Harthouse, smoking quietly.

"Not so much of that as you may suppose," returned Tom; "for our governor had her crammed with all sorts of dry bones and sawdust. It's his system."

"Formed his daughter on his own model?" suggested Harthouse.

"His daughter? Ah! and everybody else. Why, he formed Me that way!" said Tom.

"Impossible!"

"He did, though," said Tom, shaking his head. "I mean to say, Mr. Harthouse, that when I first left home and went to old Bounderby's, I was as flat as a warming-pan,[1] and knew no more about life, than any oyster does."[2]

"Come, Tom! I can hardly believe that. A joke's a joke."

"Upon my soul!" said the whelp. "I am serious; I am indeed!" He smoked with great gravity and dignity for a little while, and then added, in a highly complacent tone, "Oh! I have picked up a little since. I don't deny that. But I have done it myself; no thanks to the governor."

"And your intelligent sister?"

"My intelligent sister is about where she was. She used to complain to me that she had nothing to fall back upon, that girls usually fall back upon; and I don't see how she is to have got over that since. But *she* don't mind," he sagaciously added, puffing at his cigar again. "Girls can always get on, somehow."

"Calling at the Bank yesterday evening, for Mr. Bounderby's address, I found an ancient lady there, who seems to entertain great admiration for your sister," observed Mr. James Harthouse, throwing away the last

---

1.   I.e. dull and boring.
2.   I.e. lived a sheltered life.

small remnant of the cigar he had now smoked out.

"Mother Sparsit!" said Tom. "What! you have seen her already, have you?"

His friend nodded. Tom took his cigar out of his mouth, to shut up his eye (which had grown rather unmanageable) with the greater expression, and to tap his nose several times with his finger.

"Mother Sparsit's feeling for Loo is more than admiration, I should think," said Tom. "Say affection and devotion. Mother Sparsit never set her cap at Bounderby when he was a bachelor. Oh no!"

These were the last words spoken by the whelp, before a giddy drowsiness came upon him, followed by complete oblivion. He was roused from the latter state by an uneasy dream of being stirred up with a boot, and also of a voice saying: "Come, it's late. Be off!"

"Well!" he said, scrambling from the sofa. "I must take my leave of you though. I say. Yours is very good tobacco. But it's too mild."

"Yes, it's too mild," returned his entertainer.

"It's—it's ridiculously mild," said Tom. "Where's the door! Good night!"

He had another odd dream of being taken by a waiter through a mist, which, after giving him some trouble and difficulty, resolved itself into the main street, in which he stood alone. He then walked home pretty easily, though not yet free from an impression of the presence and influence of his new friend—as if he were lounging somewhere in the air, in the same negligent attitude, regarding him with the same look.

The whelp went home, and went to bed. If he had had any sense of what he had done that night, and had been less of a whelp and more of a brother, he might have turned short on the road, might have gone down to the ill-smelling river that was dyed black, might have gone to bed in it for good and all, and have curtained his head for ever with its filthy waters.

Chapter IV.
Men and Brothers

"Oh, my friends, the down-trodden operatives of Coketown! Oh, my friends and fellow-countrymen, the slaves of an iron-handed and a grinding despotism! Oh, my friends and fellow-sufferers, and fellow-workmen, and fellow-men! I tell you that the hour is come, when we must rally round one another as One united power, and crumble into dust the oppressors that too long have battened upon the plunder of our families, upon the sweat of our brows, upon the labour of our hands, upon the strength of our sinews, upon the God-created glorious rights of Humanity, and upon the holy and eternal privileges of Brotherhood!"

"Good!" "Hear, hear, hear!" "Hurrah!" and other cries, arose in many voices from various parts of the densely crowded and suffocatingly close Hall, in which the orator, perched on a stage, delivered himself of this and what other froth and fume he had in him. He had declaimed himself into a violent heat, and was as hoarse as he was hot. By dint of roaring at the top of his voice under a flaring gas-light, clenching his fists, knitting his brows, setting his teeth, and pounding with his arms, he had taken so much out of himself by this time, that he was brought to a stop, and called for a glass of water.

As he stood there, trying to quench his fiery face with his drink of water, the comparison between the orator and the crowd of attentive faces turned towards him, was extremely to his disadvantage. Judging him by Nature's evidence, he was above the mass in very little but the stage on which he stood. In many great respects he was essentially below them. He was not so honest, he was not so manly, he was not so good-humoured; he substituted cunning for their simplicity, and passion for their safe solid sense. An ill-made, high-shouldered man, with lowering brows, and his features crushed into an habitually sour expression, he contrasted most unfavourably, even in his mongrel dress, with the great body of his hearers in their plain working clothes. Strange as it always is to consider any assembly in the act of submissively resigning itself to the dreariness of some complacent person, lord or commoner, whom three-fourths of it could, by no human means, raise out of the slough of inanity to their own intellectual level, it was particularly strange, and it was even particularly affecting, to see this crowd of earnest faces, whose honesty in the main no competent observer free from bias could doubt, so agitated by such a leader.

Good! Hear, hear! Hurrah! The eagerness both of attention and intention, exhibited in all the countenances, made them a most impressive sight. There was no carelessness, no languor, no idle curiosity; none of the many shades of indifference to be seen in all other assemblies, visible for one moment there. That every man felt his condition to be, somehow or other, worse than it might be; that every man considered it incumbent on him to join the rest, towards the making of it better; that every man felt his only hope to be in his allying himself to the comrades by whom he was surrounded; and that in this belief, right or wrong (unhappily wrong then), the whole of that crowd were gravely, deeply, faithfully in earnest; must have been as plain to any one who chose to see what was there, as the bare beams of the roof and the whitened brick walls. Nor could any such spectator fail to know in his own breast, that these men, through their very delusions, showed great qualities, susceptible of being turned to the happiest and best account; and that to pretend (on the strength of sweeping axioms, howsoever cut and dried) that they went astray wholly without cause, and of their own irrational wills, was to pretend that there could be smoke without fire, death without birth, harvest without seed, anything or everything produced from nothing.

The orator having refreshed himself, wiped his corrugated forehead from left to right several times with his handkerchief folded into a pad, and concentrated all his revived forces, in a sneer of great disdain and bitterness.

"But oh, my friends and brothers! Oh, men and Englishmen, the down-trodden operatives of Coketown! What shall we say of that man—that working-man, that I should find it necessary so to libel the glorious name—who, being practically and well acquainted with the grievances and wrongs of you, the injured pith and marrow of this land, and having heard you, with a noble and majestic unanimity that will make Tyrants tremble, resolve for to subscribe to the funds of the United Aggregate Tribunal,* and to abide by the injunctions issued by that body for your benefit, whatever they may be—what, I ask you, will you say of that working-man, since such I must acknowledge him to be, who, at such a time, deserts his post, and sells his flag; who, at such a time, turns a traitor and a craven and a recreant; who, at such a time, is not ashamed to make to you the dastardly and humiliating avowal that he will hold himself aloof, and will *not* be one of those associated in the gallant stand for Freedom and for Right?"

The assembly was divided at this point. There were some groans and hisses, but the general sense of honour was much too strong for the condemnation of a man unheard. "Be sure you're right, Slackbridge!" "Put him up!" "Let's hear him!" Such things were said on many sides. Finally, one strong voice called out, "Is the man heer? If the man's heer, Slackbridge, let's hear the man himseln, 'stead o' yo." Which was received with a round of applause.

Slackbridge, the orator, looked about him with a withering smile; and, holding out his right hand at arm's length (as the manner of all Slackbridges is), to still the thundering sea, waited until there was a profound silence.

"Oh, my friends and fellow-men!" said Slackbridge then, shaking his head with violent scorn, "I do not wonder that you, the prostrate sons of labour, are incredulous of the existence of such a man. But he who sold his birthright for a mess of pottage[1] existed, and Judas Iscariot[2] existed, and Castlereagh[3] existed, and this man exists!"

Here, a brief press and confusion near the stage, ended in the man himself standing at the orator's side before the concourse. He was pale and a little moved in the face—his lips especially showed it; but he stood quiet, with his left hand at his chin, waiting to be heard. There was a chairman to regulate the proceedings, and this functionary now took the case into his own hands.

---

1. Esau who gave up his primogeniture to his brother Jacob because he was hungry (Genesis 25:29–34).
2. The disciple who betrayed Christ (Matthew 26:14–16).
3. Robert Stewart, Second Viscount Castlereagh (1769–1822), English statesman. The reference is to his role in repressing radical movements for Parliamentary reform etc., including his ultimate responsibility for the 'Peterloo Massacre' in Manchester in 1819, in which several hundred peaceful demonstrators were killed or injured when the cavalry was ordered to charge.

"My friends," said he, "by virtue o' my office as your president, I ashes[1] o' our friend Slackbridge, who may be a little over hetter[2] in this business, to take his seat, whiles this man Stephen Blackpool is heern. You all know this man Stephen Blackpool. You know him awlung o' his misfort'ns, and his good name."

With that, the chairman shook him frankly by the hand, and sat down again. Slackbridge likewise sat down, wiping his hot forehead—always from left to right, and never the reverse way.

"My friends," Stephen began, in the midst of a dead calm; "I ha' hed what's been spok'n o' me, and 'tis lickly that I shan't mend it. But I'd liefer you'd hearn the truth concernin myseln, fro' my lips than fro' onny other man's, though I never cud'n speak afore so monny, wi'out bein moydert[3] and muddled."

Slackbridge shook his head as if he would shake it off, in his bitterness.

"I'm th' one single Hand in Bounderby's mill, o' a' the men theer, as don't coom in wi' th' proposed reg'lations. I canna' coom in wi' 'em. My friends, I doubt their doin' yo onny good. Licker they'll do yo hurt."

Slackbridge laughed, folded his arms, and frowned sarcastically.

"But 't an't so much for that as I stands out. If that were aw, I'd coom in wi' th' rest. But I ha' my reasons—mine, yo see—for being hindered; not on'y now, but awlus—awlus—life long!"

Slackbridge jumped up and stood beside him, gnashing and tearing. "Oh, my friends, what but this did I tell you? Oh, my fellow-country-men, what warning but this did I give you? And how shows this recreant conduct in a man on whom unequal laws are known to have fallen heavy? Oh, you Englishmen, I ask you how does this subornation show in one of yourselves, who is thus consenting to his own undoing and to yours, and to your children's and your children's children's?"

There was some applause, and some crying of Shame upon the man; but the greater part of the audience were quiet. They looked at Stephen's worn face, rendered more pathetic by the homely emotions it evinced; and, in the kindness of their nature, they were more sorry than indignant.

---

1.   I.e. asks (dialect).
2.   Fierce, violent, eager (obsolete).
3.   Confused, bothered, worried (dialect).

"'Tis this Delegate's trade for t' speak," said Stephen, "an' he's paid for 't, an' he knows his work. Let him keep to 't. Let him give no heed to what I ha' had'n to bear. That's not for him. That's not for nobbody but me."

There was a propriety, not to say a dignity in these words, that made the hearers yet more quiet and attentive. The same strong voice called out, "Slackbridge, let the man be heern, and howd thee tongue!" Then the place was wonderfully still.

"My brothers," said Stephen, whose low voice was distinctly heard, "and my fellow-workmen—for that yo are to me, though not, as I knows on, to this delegate here—I ha' but a word to sen, and I could sen nommore if I was to speak till Strike o' day. I know well, aw what's afore me. I know weel that yo aw resolve to ha' nommore ado wi' a man who is not wi' yo in this matther. I know weel that if I was a lyin parisht i' th' road, yo'd feel it right to pass me by, as a forrenner and stranger. What I ha' getn, I mun mak th' best on."

"Stephen Blackpool," said the chairman, rising, "think on 't agen. Think on 't once agen, lad, afore thou'rt shunned by aw owd friends."

There was an universal murmur to the same effect, though no man articulated a word. Every eye was fixed on Stephen's face. To repent of his determination, would be to take a load from all their minds. He looked around him, and knew that it was so. Not a grain of anger with them was in his heart; he knew them, far below their surface weaknesses and misconceptions, as no one but their fellow-labourer could.

"I ha' thowt on 't, above a bit, sir. I simply canna coom in. I mun go th' way as lays afore me. I mun tak my leave o' aw heer."

He made a sort of reverence to them by holding up his arms, and stood for the moment in that attitude: not speaking until they slowly dropped at his sides.

"Monny's the pleasant word as soom heer has spok'n wi' me; monny's the face I see heer, as I first seen when I were yoong and lighter heart'n than now. I ha' never had no fratch[1] afore, sin ever I were born, wi' any o' my like; Gonnows I ha' none now that's o' my makin'. Yo'll ca' me traitor and that—yo I mean t' say," addressing Slackbridge, "but 'tis easier

---

1.   Quarrel, disagreement (dialect).

to ca' than mak out.[1] So let be."

He had moved away a pace or two to come down from the platform, when he remembered something he had not said, and returned again.

"Haply," he said, turning his furrowed face slowly about, that he might as it were individually address the whole audience, those both near and distant; "haply, when this question has been tak'n up and discoosed, there'll be a threat to turn out if I'm let to work among yo. I hope I shall die ere ever such a time cooms, and I shall work solitary among yo unless it comes—truly, I mun do 't, my friends; not to brave yo, but to live. I ha' nobbut work to live by; and wheerever can I go, I who ha' worked sin I were no heighth at aw, in Coketown heer? I mak no complaints o' bein turned to the wa', o' being outcasten and overlooken from this time forrard, but hope I shall be let to work. If there is any right for me at aw, my friends, I think 'tis that."

Not a word was spoken. Not a sound was audible in the building, but the slight rustle of men moving a little apart, all along the centre of the room, to open a means of passing out, to the man with whom they had all bound themselves to renounce companionship. Looking at no one, and going his way with a lowly steadiness upon him that asserted nothing and sought nothing, Old Stephen, with all his troubles on his head, left the scene.

Then Slackbridge, who had kept his oratorical arm extended during the going out, as if he were repressing with infinite solicitude and by a wonderful moral power the vehement passions of the multitude, applied himself to raising their spirits. Had not the Roman Brutus,[2] oh, my British countrymen, condemned his son to death; and had not the Spartan mothers,[3] oh my soon to be victorious friends, driven their flying children on the points of their enemies' swords? Then was it not the sacred duty of the men of Coketown, with forefathers before them, an admiring world in company with them, and a posterity to come after them, to

---

1. I.e. easier to call than make out; easier to make accusations than to prove them (dialect).
2. Lucius Junius Brutus, legendary founder of the Roman republic, had his own sons executed for plotting against the state.
3. According to Plutarch, the Spartan mother exhorted her son on going into battle to choose death above dishonour.

hurl out traitors from the tents they had pitched in a sacred and a God-like cause? The winds of heaven answered Yes; and bore Yes, east, west, north, and south. And consequently three cheers for the United Aggregate Tribunal!

Slackbridge acted as fugleman,[1] and gave the time. The multitude of doubtful faces (a little conscience-stricken) brightened at the sound, and took it up. Private feeling must yield to the common cause. Hurrah! The roof yet vibrated with the cheering, when the assembly dispersed.

Thus easily did Stephen Blackpool fall into the loneliest of lives, the life of solitude among a familiar crowd. The stranger in the land who looks into ten thousand faces for some answering look and never finds it, is in cheering society as compared with him who passes ten averted faces daily, that were once the countenances of friends. Such experience was to be Stephen's now, in every waking moment of his life; at his work, on his way to it and from it, at his door, at his window, everywhere. By general consent, they even avoided that side of the street on which he habitually walked; and left it, of all the working men, to him only.

He had been for many years, a quiet silent man, associating but little with other men, and used to companionship with his own thoughts. He had never known before the strength of the want in his heart for the frequent recognition of a nod, a look, a word; or the immense amount of relief that had been poured into it by drops through such small means. It was even harder than he could have believed possible, to separate in his own conscience his abandonment by all his fellows from a baseless sense of shame and disgrace.

The first four days of his endurance were days so long and heavy, that he began to be appalled by the prospect before him. Not only did he see no Rachael all the time, but he avoided every chance of seeing her; for, although he knew that the prohibition did not yet formally extend to the women working in the factories, he found that some of them with whom he was acquainted were changed to him, and he feared to try others, and dreaded that Rachael might be even singled out from the rest if she were seen in his company. So, he had been quite alone during the four days,

---

1.   Expert soldier who leads the file and provides a model for others in the regiment during drills, exercises, etc.

and had spoken to no one, when, as he was leaving his work at night, a young man of a very light complexion accosted him in the street.

"Your name's Blackpool, ain't it?" said the young man.

Stephen coloured to find himself with his hat in his hand, in his gratitude for being spoken to, or in the suddenness of it, or both. He made a feint of adjusting the lining, and said, "Yes."

"You are the Hand they have sent to Coventry,[1] I mean?" said Bitzer, the very light young man in question.

Stephen answered "Yes," again.

"I supposed so, from their all appearing to keep away from you. Mr. Bounderby wants to speak to you. You know his house, don't you?"

Stephen said "Yes," again.

"Then go straight up there, will you?" said Bitzer. "You're expected, and have only to tell the servant it's you. I belong to the Bank; so, if you go straight up without me (I was sent to fetch you), you'll save me a walk."

Stephen, whose way had been in the contrary direction, turned about, and betook himself as in duty bound, to the red brick castle of the giant Bounderby.

CHAPTER V.
MEN AND MASTERS

"WELL, STEPHEN," said Bounderby, in his windy manner, "what's this I hear? What have these pests of the earth been doing to *you*? Come in, and speak up."

It was into the drawing-room that he was thus bidden. A tea-table was set out; and Mr. Bounderby's young wife, and her brother, and a great gentleman from London, were present. To whom Stephen made his obeisance, closing the door and standing near it, with his hat in his hand.

---

1.   Ostracized (origin uncertain but probably connected to the English Midlands city's support for the Parliamentary cause during the civil war).

"This is the man I was telling you about, Harthouse," said Mr. Bounderby. The gentleman he addressed, who was talking to Mrs. Bounderby on the sofa, got up, saying in an indolent way, "Oh really?" and dawdled to the hearthrug where Mr. Bounderby stood.

"Now," said Bounderby, "speak up!"

After the four days he had passed, this address fell rudely and discordantly on Stephen's ear. Besides being a rough handling of his wounded mind, it seemed to assume that he really was the self-interested deserter he had been called.

"What were it, sir," said Stephen, "as yo were pleased to want wi' me?"

"Why, I have told you," returned Bounderby. "Speak up like a man, since you are a man, and tell us about yourself and this Combination."

"Wi' yor pardon, sir," said Stephen Blackpool, "I ha' nowt to sen about it."

Mr. Bounderby, who was always more or less like a Wind, finding something in his way here, began to blow at it directly.

"Now, look here, Harthouse," said he, "here's a specimen of 'em. When this man was here once before, I warned this man against the mischievous strangers who are always about—and who ought to be hanged wherever they are found—and I told this man that he was going in the wrong direction. Now, would you believe it, that although they have put this mark upon him, he is such a slave to them still, that he's afraid to open his lips about them?"

"I sed as I had nowt to sen, sir; not as I was fearfo' o' openin' my lips."

"You said! Ah! *I* know what you said; more than that, I know what you mean, you see. Not always the same thing, by the Lord Harry! Quite different things. You had better tell us at once, that that fellow Slackbridge is not in the town, stirring up the people to mutiny; and that he is not a regular qualified leader of the people: that is, a most confounded scoundrel. You had better tell us so at once; you can't deceive me. You want to tell us so. Why don't you?"

"I'm as sooary as yo, sir, when the people's leaders is bad," said Stephen, shaking his head. "They taks such as offers. Haply 'tis na' the sma'est o' their misfortuns when they can get no better."

The wind began to get boisterous.

"Now, you'll think this pretty well, Harthouse," said Mr. Bounderby.

"You'll think this tolerably strong. You'll say, upon my soul this is a tidy specimen of what my friends have to deal with; but this is nothing, sir! You shall hear me ask this man a question. Pray, Mr. Blackpool"—wind springing up very fast—"may I take the liberty of asking you how it happens that you refused to be in this Combination?"

"How 't happens?"

"Ah!" said Mr. Bounderby, with his thumbs in the arms of his coat, and jerking his head and shutting his eyes in confidence with the opposite wall: "how it happens."

"I'd leefer not coom to 't, sir; but sin you put th' question—an' not want'n t' be ill-manner'n—I'll answer. I ha' passed a promess."

"Not to me, you know," said Bounderby. (Gusty weather with deceitful calms. One now prevailing.)

"Oh no, sir. Not to yo."

"As for me, any consideration for me has had just nothing at all to do with it," said Bounderby, still in confidence with the wall. "If only Josiah Bounderby of Coketown had been in question, you would have joined and made no bones about it?"

"Why yes, sir. 'Tis true."

"Though he knows," said Mr. Bounderby, now blowing a gale, "that there are a set of rascals and rebels whom transportation is too good for! Now, Mr. Harthouse, you have been knocking about in the world some time. Did you ever meet with anything like that man out of this blessed country?" And Mr. Bounderby pointed him out for inspection, with an angry finger.

"Nay, ma'am," said Stephen Blackpool, staunchly protesting against the words that had been used, and instinctively addressing himself to Louisa, after glancing at her face. "Not rebels, nor yet rascals. Nowt o' th' kind, ma'am, nowt o' th' kind. They've not doon me a kindness, ma'am, as I know and feel. But there's not a dozen men amoong 'em, ma'am—a dozen? Not six—but what believes as he has doon his duty by the rest and by himseln. God forbid as I, that ha' known, and had'n experience o' these men aw my life—I, that ha' ett'n an' droonken wi' 'em, an seet'n wi' 'em, and toil'n wi' 'em, and lov'n 'em should fail fur to stan by 'em wi' the truth, let 'em ha' doon to me what they may!"

He spoke with the rugged earnestness of his place and character—

deepened perhaps by a proud consciousness that he was faithful to his class under all their mistrust; but he fully remembered where he was, and did not even raise his voice.

"No, ma'am, no. They're true to one another, faithfo' to one another, 'fectionate to one another, e'en to death. Be poor amoong 'em, be sick amoong 'em, grieve amoong 'em for onny o' th' monny causes that carries grief to the poor man's door, an' they'll be tender wi' yo, gentle wi' yo, comfortable wi' yo, Chrisen wi' yo. Be sure o' that, ma'am. They'd be riven to bits, ere ever they'd be different."

"In short," said Mr. Bounderby, "it's because they are so full of virtues that they have turned you adrift. Go through with it while you are about it. Out with it."

"How 'tis, ma'am," resumed Stephen, appearing still to find his natural refuge in Louisa's face, "that what is best in us fok, seems to turn us most to trouble an' misfort'n an' mistake, I dunno. But 'tis so. I know 'tis, as I know the heavens is over me ahint the smoke. We're patient too, an' wants in general to do right. An' I canna think the fawt is aw wi' us."

"Now, my friend," said Mr. Bounderby, whom he could not have exasperated more, quite unconscious of it though he was, than by seeming to appeal to any one else, "if you will favour me with your attention for half a minute, I should like to have a word or two with you. You said just now, that you had nothing to tell us about this business. You are quite sure of that before we go any further."

"Sir, I am sure on 't."

"Here's a gentleman from London present," Mr. Bounderby made a backhanded point at Mr. James Harthouse with his thumb, "a Parliament gentleman. I should like him to hear a short bit of dialogue between you and me, instead of taking the substance of it—for I know precious well, beforehand, what it will be; nobody knows better than I do, take notice!—instead of receiving it on trust from my mouth."

Stephen bent his head to the gentleman from London, and showed a rather more troubled mind than usual. He turned his eyes involuntarily to his former refuge, but at a look from that quarter (expressive though instantaneous) he settled them on Mr. Bounderby's face.

"Now, what do you complain of?" asked Mr. Bounderby.

"I ha' not coom here, sir," Stephen reminded him, "to complain. I coom for that I were sent for."

"What," repeated Mr. Bounderby, folding his arms, "do you people, in a general way, complain of?"

Stephen looked at him with some little irresolution for a moment, and then seemed to make up his mind.

"Sir, I were never good at showin o't, though I ha' had'n my share in feeling o't. 'Deed we are in a muddle, sir. Look round town—so rich as 'tis—and see the numbers o' people as has been broughten into bein heer, fur to weave, an' to card, an' to piece out a livin', aw the same one way, somehows, 'twixt their cradles and their graves. Look how we live, an' wheer we live, an' in what numbers, an' by what chances, and wi' what sameness; and look how the mills is awlus a goin, and how they never works us no nigher to ony dis'ant object—ceptin awlus, Death. Look how you considers of us, writes of us, and talks of us, and goes up wi' yor deputations to Secretaries o' State 'bout us, and how yo are awlus right, and how we are awlus wrong, and never had'n no reason in us sin ever we were born. Look how this ha' growen an' growen, sir, bigger an' bigger, broader an' broader, harder an' harder, fro' year to year, fro' generation unto generation. Who can look on 't, sir, and fairly tell a man 'tis not a muddle?"

"Of course," said Mr. Bounderby. "Now perhaps you'll let the gentleman know, how you would set this muddle (as you're so fond of calling it) to rights."

"I donno, sir. I canna be expecten to 't. 'Tis not me as should be looken to for that, sir. 'Tis them as is put ower me, and ower aw the rest of us. What do they tak upon themseln, sir, if not to do 't?"

"I'll tell you something towards it, at any rate," returned Mr. Bounderby. "We will make an example of half a dozen Slackbridges. We'll indict the blackguards for felony, and get 'em shipped off to penal settlements."

Stephen gravely shook his head.

"Don't tell me we won't, man," said Mr. Bounderby, by this time blowing a hurricane, "because we will, I tell you!"

"Sir," returned Stephen, with the quiet confidence of absolute certainty, "if yo was t' tak a hundred Slackbridges—aw as there is, and aw the number ten times towd—an' was t' sew 'em up in separate sacks, an' sink 'em in the deepest ocean as were made ere ever dry land coom to be, yo'd leave the muddle just wheer 'tis. Mischeevous strangers!" said Stephen, with an anxious smile; "when ha' we not heern, I am sure, sin ever we can call to mind, o' th' mischeevous strangers! 'Tis not by *them* the trouble's made, sir. 'Tis not wi' *them* 't commences. I ha' no favour for 'em—I ha' no reason to favour 'em—but 'tis hopeless and useless to dream o' takin them fro' their trade, 'stead o' takin their trade fro' them! Aw that's now about me in this room were heer afore I coom, an' will be heer when I am gone. Put that clock aboard a ship an' pack it off to Norfolk Island,[1] an' the time will go on just the same. So 'tis wi' Slack-bridge every bit."

Reverting for a moment to his former refuge, he observed a caution-ary movement of her eyes towards the door. Stepping back, he put his hand upon the lock. But he had not spoken out of his own will and de-sire; and he felt it in his heart a noble return for his late injurious treat-ment to be faithful to the last to those who had repudiated him. He stayed to finish what was in his mind.

"Sir, I canna, wi' my little learning an' my common way, tell the genelman what will better aw this—though some working men o' this town could, above my powers—but I can tell him what I know will never do 't. The strong hand will never do 't. Vict'ry and triumph will never do 't. Agreeing fur to mak one side unnat'rally awlus and for ever right, and toother side unnat'rally awlus and for ever wrong, will never, never do 't. Nor yet lettin alone will never do 't. Let thousands upon thousands alone, aw leading the like lives and aw faw'en into the like muddle, and they will be as one, and yo will be as anoother, wi' a black unpassable world betwixt yo, just as long or short a time as sitch-like misery can last. Not drawin nigh to fok, wi' kindness and patience an' cheery ways, that so draws nigh to one another in their monny troubles, and so cherishes one another in their distresses wi' what they need themseln—like, I humbly believe, as no people the genelman ha' seen in aw his travels can beat—will never do 't till th' Sun turns t' ice. Most o' aw, rating 'em as so much Power, and reg'latin 'em as if they was figures in a soom, or machines:

---

1.   Small island east of Australia, British penal colony until 1855.

wi'out loves and likeins, wi'out memories and inclinations, wi'out souls to weary and souls to hope—when aw goes quiet, draggin on wi' 'em as if they'd nowt o' th' kind, and when aw goes onquiet, reproachin 'em for their want o' sitch humanly feelins in their dealins wi' yo—this will never do 't, sir, till God's work is onmade."

Stephen stood with the open door in his hand, waiting to know if anything more were expected of him.

"Just stop a moment," said Mr. Bounderby, excessively red in the face. "I told you, the last time you were here with a grievance, that you had better turn about and come out of that. And I also told you, if you remember, that I was up to the gold spoon look-out."

"I were not up to 't myseln, sir; I do assure yo."

"Now it's clear to me," said Mr. Bounderby, "that you are one of those chaps who have always got a grievance. And you go about, sowing it and raising crops. That's the business of *your* life, my friend."

Stephen shook his head, mutely protesting that indeed he had other business to do for his life.

"You are such a waspish, raspish, ill-conditioned chap, you see," said Mr. Bounderby, "that even your own Union, the men who know you best, will have nothing to do with you. I never thought those fellows could be right in anything; but I tell you what! I so far go along with them for a novelty, that I'll have nothing to do with you either."

Stephen raised his eyes quickly to his face.

"You can finish off what you're at," said Mr. Bounderby, with a meaning nod, "and then go elsewhere."

"Sir, yo know weel," said Stephen expressively, "that if I canna get work wi' yo, I canna get it elsewheer."

The reply was, "What I know, I know; and what you know, you know. I have no more to say about it."

Stephen glanced at Louisa again, but her eyes were raised to his no more; therefore, with a sigh, and saying, barely above his breath, "Heaven help us aw in this world!" he departed.

Chapter VI.
Fading Away

It was falling dark when Stephen came out of Mr. Bounderby's house. The shadows of night had gathered so fast, that he did not look about him when he closed the door, but plodded straight along the street. Nothing was further from his thoughts than the curious old woman he had encountered on his previous visit to the same house, when he heard a step behind him that he knew, and turning, saw her in Rachael's company.

He saw Rachael first, as he had heard her only.

"Ah, Rachael, my dear! Missus, thou wi' her!"

"Well, and now you are surprised to be sure, and with reason I must say," the old woman returned. "Here I am again, you see."

"But how wi' Rachael?" said Stephen, falling into their step, walking between them, and looking from the one to the other.

"Why, I come to be with this good lass pretty much as I came to be with you," said the old woman, cheerfully, taking the reply upon herself. "My visiting time is later this year than usual, for I have been rather troubled with shortness of breath, and so put it off till the weather was fine and warm. For the same reason I don't make all my journey in one day, but divide it into two days, and get a bed to-night at the Travellers' Coffee House down by the railroad (a nice clean house), and go back Parliamentary, at six in the morning. Well, but what has this to do with this good lass, says you? I'm going to tell you. I have heard of Mr. Bounderby being married. I read it in the paper, where it looked grand—oh, it looked fine!" the old woman dwelt on it with strange enthusiasm: "and I want to see his wife. I have never seen her yet. Now, if you'll believe me, she hasn't come out of that house since noon to-day. So not to give her up too easily, I was waiting about, a little last bit more, when I passed close to this good lass two or three times; and her face being so friendly I spoke to her, and she spoke to me. There!" said the old woman to Stephen, "you can make all the rest out for yourself now, a deal shorter than I can, I dare say!"

Once again, Stephen had to conquer an instinctive propensity to dislike this old woman, though her manner was as honest and simple as a manner possibly could be. With a gentleness that was as natural to him as he knew it to be to Rachael, he pursued the subject that interested her in her old age.

"Well, missus," said he, "I ha' seen the lady, and she were young and hansom. Wi' fine dark thinkin eyes, and a still way, Rachael, as I ha' never seen the like on."

"Young and handsome. Yes!" cried the old woman, quite delighted. "As bonny as a rose! And what a happy wife!"

"Aye, missus, I suppose she be," said Stephen. But with a doubtful glance at Rachael.

"Suppose she be? She must be. She's your master's wife," returned the old woman.

Stephen nodded assent. "Though as to master," said he, glancing again at Rachael, "not master onny more. That's aw enden 'twixt him and me."

"Have you left his work, Stephen?" asked Rachael, anxiously and quickly.

"Why, Rachael," he replied, "whether I ha' lef'n his work, or whether his work ha' lef'n me, cooms t' th' same. His work and me are parted. 'Tis as well so—better, I were thinkin when yo coom up wi' me. It would ha' brought'n trouble upon trouble if I had stayed theer. Haply 'tis a kindness to monny that I go; haply 'tis a kindness to myseln; anyways it mun be done. I mun turn my face fro' Coketown fur th' time, and seek a fort'n, dear, by beginnin fresh."

"Where will you go, Stephen?"

"I donno t'night," said he, lifting off his hat, and smoothing his thin hair with the flat of his hand. "But I'm not goin t'night, Rachael, nor yet t'morrow. 'Tan't easy over-much t' know wheer t' turn, but a good heart will coom to me."

Herein, too, the sense of even thinking unselfishly aided him. Before he had so much as closed Mr. Bounderby's door, he had reflected that at least his being obliged to go away was good for her, as it would save her from the chance of being brought into question for not withdrawing from him. Though it would cost him a hard pang to leave her, and though he could think of no similar place in which his condemnation would not pursue him, perhaps it was almost a relief to be forced away from the endurance of the last four days, even to unknown difficulties and distresses.

So he said, with truth, "I'm more leetsome,[1] Rachael, under 't, than I could'n ha' believed." It was not her part to make his burden heavier. She answered with her comforting smile, and the three walked on together.

Age, especially when it strives to be self-reliant and cheerful, finds much consideration among the poor. The old woman was so decent and contented, and made so light of her infirmities, though they had increased upon her since her former interview with Stephen, that they both took an interest in her. She was too sprightly to allow of their walking at a slow pace on her account, but she was very grateful to be talked to, and very willing to talk to any extent: so, when they came to their part of the town, she was more brisk and vivacious than ever.

"Coom to my poor place, missus," said Stephen, "and tak a coop o' tea. Rachael will coom then; and arterwards I'll see thee safe t' thy Travellers' lodgin. 'T may be long, Rachael, ere ever I ha' th' chance o' thy coompany agen."

They complied, and the three went on to the house where he lodged. When they turned into a narrow street, Stephen glanced at his window with a dread that always haunted his desolate home; but it was open, as he had left it, and no one was there. The evil spirit of his life had flitted away again, months ago, and he had heard no more of her since. The only evidence of her last return now, were the scantier moveables in his room, and the greyer hair upon his head.

He lighted a candle, set out his little tea-board, got hot water from below, and brought in small portions of tea and sugar, a loaf, and some butter from the nearest shop. The bread was new and crusty, the butter fresh, and the sugar lump, of course[2]—in fulfilment of the standard testimony of the Coketown magnates, that these people lived like princes, sir. Rachael made the tea (so large a party necessitated the borrowing of a cup), and the visitor enjoyed it mightily. It was the first glimpse of sociality the host had had for many days. He too, with the world a wide heath before him, enjoyed the meal—again in corroboration of the magnates, as exemplifying the utter want of calculation on the part of these people, sir.

---

1.   Northern pronunciation of 'lightsome' meaning cheerful, light-hearted.
2.   I.e. more expensive loaf sugar rather than the less refined granular form.

"I ha' never thowt yet, missus," said Stephen, "o' askin thy name."

The old lady announced herself as "Mrs. Pegler."

"A widder, I think?" said Stephen.

"Oh, many long years!" Mrs. Pegler's husband (one of the best on record) was already dead, by Mrs. Pegler's calculation, when Stephen was born.

"'Twere a bad job, too, to lose so good a one," said Stephen. "Onny children?"

Mrs. Pegler's cup, rattling against her saucer as she held it, denoted some nervousness on her part. "No," she said. "Not now, not now."

"Dead, Stephen," Rachael softly hinted.

"I'm sooary I ha' spok'n on 't," said Stephen, "I ought t' hadn in my mind as I might touch a sore place. I—I blame myseln."

While he excused himself, the old lady's cup rattled more and more. "I had a son," she said, curiously distressed, and not by any of the usual appearances of sorrow; "and he did well, wonderfully well. But he is not to be spoken of if you please. He is—" Putting down her cup, she moved her hands as if she would have added, by her action, "dead!" Then she said aloud, "I have lost him."

Stephen had not yet got the better of his having given the old lady pain, when his landlady came stumbling up the narrow stairs, and calling him to the door, whispered in his ear. Mrs. Pegler was by no means deaf, for she caught a word as it was uttered.

"Bounderby!" she cried, in a suppressed voice, starting up from the table. "Oh hide me! Don't let me be seen for the world. Don't let him come up till I've got away. Pray, pray!" She trembled, and was excessively agitated; getting behind Rachael, when Rachael tried to reassure her; and not seeming to know what she was about.

"But hearken, missus, hearken," said Stephen, astonished. "'Tisn't Mr. Bounderby; 'tis his wife. Yo'r not fearfo' o' her. Yo was hey-go-mad[1] about her, but an hour sin."

"But are you sure it's the lady, and not the gentleman?" she asked, still trembling.

---

1.   Excited, in high spirits (dialect).

"Certain sure!"

"Well then, pray don't speak to me, nor yet take any notice of me," said the old woman. "Let me be quite to myself in this corner."

Stephen nodded; looking to Rachael for an explanation, which she was quite unable to give him; took the candle, went down-stairs, and in a few moments returned, lighting Louisa into the room. She was followed by the whelp.

Rachael had risen, and stood apart with her shawl and bonnet in her hand, when Stephen, himself profoundly astonished by this visit, put the candle on the table. Then he too stood, with his doubled hand upon the table near it, waiting to be addressed.

For the first time in her life Louisa had come into one of the dwellings of the Coketown Hands; for the first time in her life she was face to face with anything like individuality in connection with them. She knew of their existence by hundreds and by thousands. She knew what results in work a given number of them would produce in a given space of time. She knew them in crowds passing to and from their nests, like ants or beetles. But she knew from her reading infinitely more of the ways of toiling insects than of these toiling men and women.

Something to be worked so much and paid so much, and there ended; something to be infallibly settled by laws of supply and demand; something that blundered against those laws, and floundered into difficulty; something that was a little pinched when wheat was dear, and over-ate itself when wheat was cheap; something that increased at such a rate of percentage, and yielded another percentage of crime, and such another percentage of pauperism; something wholesale, of which vast fortunes were made; something that occasionally rose like a sea, and did some harm and waste (chiefly to itself), and fell again; this she knew the Coketown Hands to be. But, she had scarcely thought more of separating them into units, than of separating the sea itself into its component drops.

She stood for some moments looking round the room. From the few chairs, the few books, the common prints, and the bed, she glanced to the two women, and to Stephen.

"I have come to speak to you, in consequence of what passed just now. I should like to be serviceable to you, if you will let me. Is this your wife?"

Rachael raised her eyes, and they sufficiently answered no, and dropped again.

"I remember," said Louisa, reddening at her mistake; "I recollect, now, to have heard your domestic misfortunes spoken of, though I was not attending to the particulars at the time. It was not my meaning to ask a question that would give pain to any one here. If I should ask any other question that may happen to have that result, give me credit, if you please, for being in ignorance how to speak to you as I ought."

As Stephen had but a little while ago instinctively addressed himself to her, so she now instinctively addressed herself to Rachael. Her manner was short and abrupt, yet faltering and timid.

"He has told you what has passed between himself and my husband? You would be his first resource, I think."

"I have heard the end of it, young lady," said Rachael.

"Did I understand, that, being rejected by one employer, he would probably be rejected by all? I thought he said as much?"

"The chances are very small, young lady—next to nothing—for a man who gets a bad name among them."

"What shall I understand you mean by a bad name?"

"The name of being troublesome."

"Then, by the prejudices of his own class, and by the prejudices of the other, he is sacrificed alike? Are the two so deeply separated in this town, that there is no place whatever for an honest workman between them?"

Rachael shook her head in silence.

"He fell into suspicion," said Louisa, "with his fellow-weavers, because he had made a promise not to be one of them. I think it must have been to you that he made that promise. Might I ask you why he made it?"

Rachael burst into tears. "I didn't seek it of him, poor lad. I prayed him to avoid trouble for his own good, little thinking he'd come to it through me. But I know he'd die a hundred deaths, ere ever he'd break his word. I know that of him well."

Stephen had remained quietly attentive, in his usual thoughtful attitude, with his hand at his chin. He now spoke in a voice rather less steady than usual.

"No one, excepting myseln, can ever know what honour, an' what love, an' respect, I bear to Rachael, or wi' what cause. When I passed that promess, I towd her true, she were th' Angel o' my life. 'Twere a solemn promise. 'Tis gone fro' me, for ever."

Louisa turned her head to him, and bent it with a deference that was new in her. She looked from him to Rachael, and her features softened. "What will you do?" she asked him. And her voice had softened too.

"Weel, ma'am," said Stephen, making the best of it, with a smile; "when I ha' finished off, I mun quit this part, and try another. Fortnet or misfortnet, a man can but try; there's nowt to be done wi'out tryin'—cept laying down and dying."

"How will you travel?"

"Afoot, my kind ledy, afoot."

Louisa coloured, and a purse appeared in her hand. The rustling of a bank-note was audible, as she unfolded one and laid it on the table.

"Rachael, will you tell him—for you know how, without offence—that this is freely his, to help him on his way? Will you entreat him to take it?"

"I canna do that, young lady," she answered, turning her head aside. "Bless you for thinking o' the poor lad wi' such tenderness. But 'tis for him to know his heart, and what is right according to it."

Louisa looked, in part incredulous, in part frightened, in part overcome with quick sympathy, when this man of so much self-command, who had been so plain and steady through the late interview, lost his composure in a moment, and now stood with his hand before his face. She stretched out hers, as if she would have touched him; then checked herself, and remained still.

"Not e'en Rachael," said Stephen, when he stood again with his face uncovered, "could mak sitch a kind offerin, by onny words, kinder. T' show that I'm not a man wi'out reason and gratitude, I'll tak two pound. I'll borrow 't for t' pay 't back. 'Twill be the sweetest work as ever I ha' done, that puts it in my power t' acknowledge once more my lastin thankfulness for this present action."

She was fain to take up the note again, and to substitute the much smaller sum he had named. He was neither courtly, nor handsome, nor picturesque, in any respect; and yet his manner of accepting it, and of expressing his thanks without more words, had a grace in it that Lord

Chesterfield[1] could not have taught his son in a century.

Tom had sat upon the bed, swinging one leg and sucking his walking-stick with sufficient unconcern, until the visit had attained this stage. Seeing his sister ready to depart, he got up, rather hurriedly, and put in a word.

"Just wait a moment, Loo! Before we go, I should like to speak to him a moment. Something comes into my head. If you'll step out on the stairs, Blackpool, I'll mention it. Never mind a light, man!" Tom was remarkably impatient, of his moving towards the cupboard to get one. "It don't want a light."

Stephen followed him out, and Tom closed the room door, and held the lock in his hand.

"I say!" he whispered. "I think I can do you a good turn. Don't ask me what it is, because it may not come to anything. But there's no harm in my trying."

His breath fell like a flame of fire on Stephen's ear, it was so hot.

"That was our light porter at the Bank," said Tom, "who brought you the message to-night. I call him our light porter, because I belong to the Bank too."

Stephen thought, "What a hurry he is in!" He spoke so confusedly.

"Well!" said Tom. "Now look here! When are you off?"

"T'day's Monday," replied Stephen, considering. "Why, sir, Friday or Saturday, nigh 'bout."

"Friday or Saturday," said Tom. "Now look here! I am not sure that I can do you the good turn I want to do you—that's my sister, you know, in your room—but I may be able to, and if I should not be able to, there's no harm done. So I tell you what. You'll know our light porter again?"

"Yes sure," said Stephen.

"Very well," returned Tom. "When you leave work of a night, between this and your going away, just hang about the Bank an hour or so, will you? Don't take on, as if you meant anything, if he should see you hanging about there; because I shan't put him up to speak to you, unless

---

1. Philip Stanhope, fourth Earl of Chesterfield (1694–1773), chiefly remembered as the author of letters to his son and godson offering guidance on social behaviour.

I find I can do you the service I want to do you. In that case he'll have a note or a message for you, but not else. Now look here! You are sure you understand."

He had wormed a finger, in the darkness, through a button-hole of Stephen's coat, and was screwing that corner of the garment tight up round and round, in an extraordinary manner.

"I understand, sir," said Stephen.

"Now look here!" repeated Tom. "Be sure you don't make any mistake then, and don't forget. I shall tell my sister as we go home, what I have in view, and she'll approve, I know. Now look here! You're all right, are you? You understand all about it? Very well then. Come along, Loo!"

He pushed the door open as he called to her, but did not return into the room, or wait to be lighted down the narrow stairs. He was at the bottom when she began to descend, and was in the street before she could take his arm.

Mrs. Pegler remained in her corner until the brother and sister were gone, and until Stephen came back with the candle in his hand. She was in a state of inexpressible admiration of Mrs. Bounderby, and, like an unaccountable old woman, wept, "because she was such a pretty dear." Yet Mrs. Pegler was so flurried lest the object of her admiration should return by chance, or anybody else should come, that her cheerfulness was ended for that night. It was late too, to people who rose early and worked hard; therefore the party broke up; and Stephen and Rachael escorted their mysterious acquaintance to the door of the Travellers' Coffee House, where they parted from her.

They walked back together to the corner of the street where Rachael lived, and as they drew nearer and nearer to it, silence crept upon them. When they came to the dark corner where their infrequent meetings always ended, they stopped, still silent, as if both were afraid to speak.

"I shall strive t' see thee again, Rachael, afore I go, but if not—"

"Thou wilt not, Stephen, I know. 'Tis better that we make up our minds to be open wi' one another."

"Thou'rt awlus right. 'Tis bolder and better. I ha' been thinkin then, Rachael, that as 'tis but a day or two that remains, 'twere better for thee, my dear, not t' be seen wi' me. 'T might bring thee into trouble, for no good."

"'Tis not for that, Stephen, that I mind. But thou know'st our old agreement. 'Tis for that."

"Well, well," said he. "'Tis better, onnyways."

"Thou'lt write to me, and tell me all that happens, Stephen?"

"Yes. What can I say now, but Heaven be wi' thee, Heaven bless thee, Heaven thank thee and reward thee!"

"May it bless thee, Stephen, too, in all thy wanderings, and send thee peace and rest at last!"

"I towd thee, my dear," said Stephen Blackpool—"that night—that I would never see or think o' onnything that angered me, but thou, so much better than me, should'st be beside it. Thou'rt beside it now. Thou mak'st me see it wi' a better eye. Bless thee. Good night. Good-bye!"

It was but a hurried parting in a common street, yet it was a sacred remembrance to these two common people. Utilitarian economists, skeletons of schoolmasters, Commissioners of Fact, genteel and used-up infidels, gabblers of many little dog's-eared creeds, the poor you will have always with you.[1] Cultivate in them, while there is yet time, the utmost graces of the fancies and affections, to adorn their lives so much in need of ornament; or, in the day of your triumph, when romance is utterly driven out of their souls, and they and a bare existence stand face to face, Reality will take a wolfish turn, and make an end of you.

Stephen worked the next day, and the next, uncheered by a word from any one, and shunned in all his comings and goings as before. At the end of the second day, he saw land; at the end of the third, his loom stood empty.

He had overstayed his hour in the street outside the Bank, on each of the first two evenings; and nothing had happened there, good or bad. That he might not be remiss in his part of the engagement, he resolved to wait full two hours, on this third and last night.

There was the lady who had once kept Mr. Bounderby's house, sitting at the first-floor window as he had seen her before; and there was the light porter, sometimes talking with her there, and sometimes looking over the blind below which had BANK upon it, and sometimes coming

---

1.   Compare the words of Jesus to his disciples in Matthew 26:11.

to the door and standing on the steps for a breath of air. When he first came out, Stephen thought he might be looking for him, and passed near; but the light porter only cast his winking eyes upon him slightly, and said nothing.

Two hours were a long stretch of lounging about, after a long day's labour. Stephen sat upon the step of a door, leaned against a wall under an archway, strolled up and down, listened for the church clock, stopped and watched children playing in the street. Some purpose or other is so natural to every one, that a mere loiterer always looks and feels remarkable. When the first hour was out, Stephen even began to have an uncomfortable sensation upon him of being for the time a disreputable character.

Then came the lamplighter, and two lengthening lines of light all down the long perspective of the street, until they were blended and lost in the distance. Mrs. Sparsit closed the first-floor window, drew down the blind, and went upstairs. Presently, a light went up-stairs after her, passing first the fanlight of the door, and afterwards the two staircase windows, on its way up. By and by, one corner of the second-floor blind was disturbed, as if Mrs. Sparsit's eye were there; also the other corner, as if the light porter's eye were on that side. Still, no communication was made to Stephen. Much relieved when the two hours were at last accomplished, he went away at a quick pace, as a recompense for so much loitering.

He had only to take leave of his landlady, and lie down on his temporary bed upon the floor; for his bundle was made up for to-morrow, and all was arranged for his departure. He meant to be clear of the town very early; before the Hands were in the streets.

It was barely daybreak, when, with a parting look round his room, mournfully wondering whether he should ever see it again, he went out. The town was as entirely deserted as if the inhabitants had abandoned it, rather than hold communication with him. Everything looked wan at that hour. Even the coming sun made but a pale waste in the sky, like a sad sea.

By the place where Rachael lived, though it was not in his way; by the red brick streets; by the great silent factories, not trembling yet; by the railway, where the danger-lights were waning in the strengthening day; by the railway's crazy neighbourhood, half pulled down and half built up; by the scattered red brick villas, where the besmoked evergreens were sprinkled with a dirty powder, like untidy snuff-takers; by coal-dust paths and many varieties of ugliness; Stephen got to the top of the hill, and looked back.

Day was shining radiantly upon the town then, and the bells were going for the morning work. Domestic fires were not yet lighted, and the high chimneys had the sky to themselves. Puffing out their poison- ous volumes, they would not be long in hiding it; but, for half an hour, some of the many windows were golden, which showed the Coketown people a sun eternally in eclipse, through a medium of smoked glass.

So strange to turn from the chimneys to the birds. So strange to have the road-dust on his feet instead of the coal-grit. So strange to have lived to his time of life, and yet to be beginning like a boy this summer morn- ing! With these musings in his mind, and his bundle under his arm, Stephen took his attentive face along the high road. And the trees arched over him, whispering that he left a true and loving heart behind.

Chapter VII.
Gunpowder

Mr. James Harthouse, "going in" for his adopted party, soon began to score.[1] With the aid of a little more coaching for the political sages, a little more genteel listlessness for the general society, and a tolerable man- agement of the assumed honesty in dishonesty, most effective and most patronized of the polite deadly sins, he speedily came to be considered of much promise. The not being troubled with earnestness was a grand point in his favour, enabling him to take to the hard Fact fellows with as good a grace as if he had been born one of the tribe, and to throw all other tribes overboard, as conscious hypocrites.

"Whom none of us believe, my dear Mrs. Bounderby, and who do not believe themselves. The only difference between us and the professors

---

1.   The metaphor, an extension of that on p. 157, probably derives from the game of cricket.

of virtue or benevolence, or philanthropy—never mind the name—is, that we know it is all meaningless, and say so; while they know it equally and will never say so."

Why should she be shocked or warned by this reiteration? It was not so unlike her father's principles, and her early training, that it need startle her. Where was the great difference between the two schools, when each chained her down to material realities, and inspired her with no faith in anything else? What was there in her soul for James Harthouse to destroy, which Thomas Gradgrind had nurtured there in its state of innocence!

It was even the worse for her at this pass, that in her mind—implanted there before her eminently practical father began to form it—a struggling disposition to believe in a wider and nobler humanity than she had ever heard of, constantly strove with doubts and resentments. With doubts, because the aspiration had been so laid waste in her youth. With resentments, because of the wrong that had been done her, if it were indeed a whisper of the truth. Upon a nature long accustomed to self-suppression, thus torn and divided, the Harthouse philosophy came as a relief and justification. Everything being hollow and worthless, she had missed nothing and sacrificed nothing. What did it matter, she had said to her father, when he proposed her husband. What did it matter, she said still. With a scornful self-reliance, she asked herself, What did anything matter—and went on.

Towards what? Step by step, onward and downward, towards some end, yet so gradually, that she believed herself to remain motionless. As to Mr. Harthouse, whither *he* tended, he neither considered nor cared. He had no particular design or plan before him: no energetic wickedness ruffled his lassitude. He was as much amused and interested, at present, as it became so fine a gentleman to be; perhaps even more than it would have been consistent with his reputation to confess. Soon after his arrival he languidly wrote to his brother, the honourable and jocular member, that the Bounderbys were "great fun;" and further, that the female Bounderby, instead of being the Gorgon[1] he had expected, was young,

---

1.   The Medusa, one of three monstrous sisters of Greek mythology, who turned to stone all who looked on her.

and remarkably pretty. After that, he wrote no more about them, and devoted his leisure chiefly to their house. He was very often at their house, in his flittings and visitings about the Coketown district; and was much encouraged by Mr. Bounderby. It was quite in Mr. Bounderby's gusty way to boast to all his world that *he* didn't care about your highly connected people, but that if his wife Tom Gradgrind's daughter did, she was welcome to their company.

Mr. James Harthouse began to think it would be a new sensation, if the face which changed so beautifully for the whelp, would change for him.

He was quick enough to observe; he had a good memory, and did not forget a word of the brother's revelations. He interwove them with everything he saw of the sister, and he began to understand her. To be sure, the better and profounder part of her character was not within the scope of his perception; for in natures, as in seas, depth answers unto depth;[1] but he soon began to read the rest with a student's eye.

Mr. Bounderby had taken possession of a house and grounds, about fifteen miles from the town, and accessible within a mile or two, by a railway striding on many arches over a wild country, undermined by deserted coal-shafts, and spotted at night by fires and black shapes of stationary engines at pits' mouths. This country, gradually softening towards the neighbourhood of Mr. Bounderby's retreat, there mellowed into a rustic landscape, golden with heath, and snowy with hawthorn in the spring of the year, and tremulous with leaves and their shadows all the summer time. The bank had foreclosed a mortgage effected on the property thus pleasantly situated, by one of the Coketown magnates, who, in his determination to make a shorter cut than usual to an enormous fortune, overspeculated himself by about two hundred thousand pounds. These accidents did sometimes happen in the best regulated families of Coketown, but the bankrupts had no connexion whatever with the improvident classes.

It afforded Mr. Bounderby supreme satisfaction to instal himself in this snug little estate, and with demonstrative humility to grow cabbages

---

1.   Compare Psalms 42:7.

in the flower-garden. He delighted to live, barrack-fashion, among the elegant furniture, and he bullied the very pictures with his origin. "Why, sir," he would say to a visitor, "I am told that Nickits," the late owner, "gave seven hundred pound for that Seabeach. Now, to be plain with you, if I ever, in the whole course of my life, take seven looks at it, at a hundred pound a look, it will be as much as I shall do. No, by George! I don't forget that I am Josiah Bounderby of Coketown. For years upon years, the only pictures in my possession, or that I could have got into my possession, by any means, unless I stole 'em, were the engravings of a man shaving himself in a boot, on the blacking bottles that I was over-joyed to use in cleaning boots with, and that I sold when they were empty for a farthing a-piece, and glad to get it!"

Then he would address Mr. Harthouse in the same style.

"Harthouse, you have a couple of horses down here. Bring half a dozen more if you like, and we'll find room for 'em. There's stabling in this place for a dozen horses; and unless Nickits is belied, he kept the full number. A round dozen of 'em, sir. When that man was a boy, he went to West-minster School. Went to Westminster School as a King's Scholar,[1] when I was principally living on garbage, and sleeping in market baskets. Why, if I wanted to keep a dozen horses—which I don't, for one's enough for me—I couldn't bear to see 'em in their stalls here, and think what my own lodging used to be. I couldn't look at 'em, sir, and not order 'em out. Yet so things come round. You see this place; you know what sort of place it is; you are aware that there's not a completer place of its size in this kingdom or elsewhere—I don't care where—and here, got into the middle of it, like a maggot into a nut, is Josiah Bounderby. While Nickits (as a man came into my office, and told me yesterday), Nickits, who used to act in Latin, in the Westminster School plays, with the chief-justices and nobility of this country applauding him till they were black in the face, is drivelling at this minute—drivelling, sir!—in a fifth floor, up a narrow dark back street in Antwerp."

It was among the leafy shadows of this retirement, in the long sultry

---

1. Scholarships endowed by Henry VIII at the renowned public school in Central London. Charles Wesley and Lord John Russell were among the famous who received the honour.

summer days, that Mr. Harthouse began to prove the face which had set him wondering when he first saw it, and to try if it would change for him.

"Mrs. Bounderby, I esteem it a most fortunate accident that I find you alone here. I have for some time had a particular wish to speak to you."

It was not by any wonderful accident that he found her, the time of day being that at which she was always alone, and the place being her favourite resort. It was an opening in a dark wood, where some felled trees lay, and where she would sit watching the fallen leaves of last year, as she had watched the falling ashes at home. He sat down beside her, with a glance at her face.

"Your brother. My young friend Tom—"

Her colour brightened, and she turned to him with a look of interest. "I never in my life," he thought, "saw anything so remarkable and so captivating as the lighting of those features!" His face betrayed his thoughts—perhaps without betraying him, for it might have been according to its instructions so to do.

"Pardon me. The expression of your sisterly interest is so beautiful—Tom should be so proud of it—I know this is inexcusable, but I am so compelled to admire."

"Being so impulsive," she said composedly.

"Mrs. Bounderby, no: you know I make no pretence with you. You know I am a sordid piece of human nature, ready to sell myself at any time for any reasonable sum, and altogether incapable of any Arcadian[1] proceeding whatever."

"I am waiting," she returned, "for your further reference to my brother."

"You are rigid with me, and I deserve it. I am as worthless a dog as you will find, except that I am not false—not false. But you surprised and started me from my subject, which was your brother. I have an interest in him."

"Have you an interest in anything, Mr. Harthouse?" she asked, half incredulously and half gratefully.

"If you had asked me when I first came here, I should have said no. I

---

1.   I.e. selfless, altruistic, after Arcadia, the paradisal land of Classical legend.

must say now—even at the hazard of appearing to make a pretence, and of justly awakening your incredulity—yes."

She made a slight movement, as if she were trying to speak, but could not find voice; at length she said, "Mr. Harthouse, I give you credit for being interested in my brother."

"Thank you. I claim to deserve it. You know how little I do claim, but I will go that length. You have done so much for him, you are so fond of him; your whole life, Mrs. Bounderby, expresses such charming self-forgetfulness on his account—pardon me again—I am running wide of the subject. I am interested in him for his own sake."

She had made the slightest action possible, as if she would have risen in a hurry and gone away. He had turned the course of what he said at that instant, and she remained.

"Mrs. Bounderby," he resumed, in a lighter manner, and yet with a show of effort in assuming it, which was even more expressive than the manner he dismissed; "it is no irrevocable offence in a young fellow of your brother's years, if he is heedless, inconsiderate, and expensive—a little dissipated, in the common phrase. Is he?"

"Yes."

"Allow me to be frank. Do you think he games at all?"

"I think he makes bets." Mr. Harthouse waiting, as if that were not her whole answer, she added, "I know he does."

"Of course he loses?"

"Yes."

"Everybody does lose who bets. May I hint at the probability of your sometimes supplying him with money for these purposes?"

She sat, looking down; but, at this question, raised her eyes searchingly and a little resentfully.

"Acquit me of impertinent curiosity, my dear Mrs. Bounderby. I think Tom may be gradually falling into trouble, and I wish to stretch out a helping hand to him from the depths of my wicked experience.—Shall I say again, for his sake? Is that necessary?"

She seemed to try to answer, but nothing came of it.

"Candidly to confess everything that has occurred to me," said James Harthouse, again gliding with the same appearance of effort into his more airy manner; "I will confide to you my doubt whether he has had many advantages. Whether—forgive my plainness—whether any great amount of confidence is likely to have been established between himself and his most worthy father."

"I do not," said Louisa, flushing with her own great remembrance in that wise, "think it likely."

"Or, between himself, and—I may trust to your perfect understanding of my meaning, I am sure—and his highly esteemed brother-in-law."

She flushed deeper and deeper, and was burning red when she replied in a fainter voice, "I do not think that likely, either."

"Mrs. Bounderby," said Harthouse, after a short silence, "may there be a better confidence between yourself and me? Tom has borrowed a considerable sum of you?"

"You will understand, Mr. Harthouse," she returned, after some indecision: she had been more or less uncertain, and troubled throughout the conversation, and yet had in the main preserved her self-contained manner; "you will understand that if I tell you what you press to know, it is not by way of complaint or regret. I would never complain of anything, and what I have done I do not in the least regret."

"So spirited, too!" thought James Harthouse.

"When I married, I found that my brother was even at that time heavily in debt. Heavily for him, I mean. Heavily enough to oblige me to sell some trinkets. They were no sacrifice. I sold them very willingly. I attached no value to them. They were quite worthless to me."

Either she saw in his face that he knew, or she only feared in her conscience that he knew, that she spoke of some of her husband's gifts. She stopped, and reddened again. If he had not known it before, he would have known it then, though he had been a much duller man than he was.

"Since then, I have given my brother, at various times, what money I could spare: in short, what money I have had. Confiding in you at all, on the faith of the interest you profess for him, I will not do so by halves. Since you have been in the habit of visiting here, he has wanted in one sum as much as a hundred pounds. I have not been able to give it to him. I have felt uneasy for the consequences of his being so involved, but I have kept these secrets until now, when I trust them to your honour. I have held no confidence with any one, because—you anticipated my reason just now." She abruptly broke off.

He was a ready man, and he saw, and seized, an opportunity here of presenting her own image to her, slightly disguised as her brother.

"Mrs. Bounderby, though a graceless person, of the world worldly,[1] I feel the utmost interest, I assure you, in what you tell me. I cannot possibly be hard upon your brother. I understand and share the wise consideration with which you regard his errors. With all possible respect both for Mr. Gradgrind and for Mr. Bounderby, I think I perceive that he has not been fortunate in his training. Bred at a disadvantage towards the society in which he has his part to play, he rushes into these extremes for himself, from opposite extremes that have long been forced—with the very best intentions we have no doubt—upon him. Mr. Bounderby's fine bluff English independence, though a most charming characteristic, does not—as we have agreed—invite confidence. If I might venture to remark that it is the least in the world deficient in that delicacy to which a youth mistaken, a character misconceived, and abilities misdirected, would turn for relief and guidance, I should express what it presents to my own view."

As she sat looking straight before her, across the changing lights upon the grass into the darkness of the wood beyond, he saw in her face her application of his very distinctly uttered words.

"All allowance," he continued, "must be made. I have one great fault to find with Tom, however, which I cannot forgive, and for which I take him heavily to account."

Louisa turned her eyes to his face, and asked him what fault was that?

"Perhaps," he returned, "I have said enough. Perhaps it would have been better, on the whole, if no allusion to it had escaped me."

"You alarm me, Mr. Harthouse. Pray let me know it."

"To relieve you from needless apprehension—and as this confidence regarding your brother, which I prize I am sure above all possible things, has been established between us—I obey. I cannot forgive him for not being more sensible in every word, look, and act of his life, of the affection of his best friend; of the devotion of his best friend; of her unselfishness; of her sacrifice. The return he makes her, within my observation, is

---

1.   Compare 'of the Turf, turfy' noted on p. 68.

a very poor one. What she has done for him demands his constant love and gratitude, not his ill-humour and caprice. Careless fellow as I am, I am not so indifferent, Mrs. Bounderby, as to be regardless of this vice in your brother, or inclined to consider it a venial offence."

The wood floated before her, for her eyes were suffused with tears. They rose from a deep well, long concealed, and her heart was filled with acute pain that found no relief in them.

"In a word, it is to correct your brother in this, Mrs. Bounderby, that I must aspire. My better knowledge of his circumstances, and my direction and advice in extricating them—rather valuable, I hope, as coming from a scapegrace on a much larger scale—will give me some influence over him, and all I gain I shall certainly use towards this end. I have said enough, and more than enough. I seem to be protesting that I am a sort of good fellow, when, upon my honour, I have not the least intention to make any protestation to that effect, and openly announce that I am nothing of the sort. Yonder, among the trees," he added, having lifted up his eyes and looked about; for he had watched her closely until now; "is your brother himself; no doubt, just come down. As he seems to be loitering in this direction, it may be as well, perhaps, to walk towards him, and throw ourselves in his way. He has been very silent and doleful of late. Perhaps, his brotherly conscience is touched—if there are such things as consciences. Though, upon my honour, I hear of them much too often to believe in them."

He assisted her to rise, and she took his arm, and they advanced to meet the whelp. He was idly beating the branches as he lounged along: or he stooped viciously to rip the moss from the trees with his stick. He was startled when they came upon him while he was engaged in this latter pastime, and his colour changed.

"Halloa!" he stammered; "I didn't know you were here."

"Whose name, Tom," said Mr. Harthouse, putting his hand upon his shoulder and turning him, so that they all three walked towards the house together, "have you been carving on the trees?"

"Whose name?" returned Tom. "Oh! You mean what girl's name?"

"You have a suspicious appearance of inscribing some fair creature's on the bark, Tom."

"Not much of that, Mr. Harthouse, unless some fair creature with a slashing fortune at her own disposal would take a fancy to me. Or she might be as ugly as she was rich, without any fear of losing me. I'd carve her name as often as she liked."

"I am afraid you are mercenary, Tom."

"Mercenary," repeated Tom. "Who is not mercenary? Ask my sister."

"Have you so proved it to be a failing of mine, Tom?" said Louisa, showing no other sense of his discontent and ill-nature.

"You know whether the cap fits you, Loo," returned her brother sulkily. "If it does, you can wear it."

"Tom is misanthropical to-day, as all bored people are now and then," said Mr. Harthouse. "Don't believe him, Mrs. Bounderby. He knows much better. I shall disclose some of his opinions of you, privately expressed to me, unless he relents a little."

"At all events, Mr. Harthouse," said Tom, softening in his admiration of his patron, but shaking his head sullenly too, "you can't tell her that I ever praised her for being mercenary. I may have praised her for being the contrary, and I should do it again, if I had as good reason. However, never mind this now; it's not very interesting to you, and I am sick of the subject."

They walked on to the house, where Louisa quitted her visitor's arm and went in. He stood looking after her, as she ascended the steps, and passed into the shadow of the door; then put his hand upon her brother's shoulder again, and invited him with a confidential nod to a walk in the garden.

"Tom, my fine fellow, I want to have a word with you."

They had stopped among a disorder of roses—it was part of Mr. Bounderby's humility to keep Nickits's roses on a reduced scale—and Tom sat down on a terrace-parapet, plucking buds and picking them to pieces; while his powerful Familiar[1] stood over him, with a foot upon the parapet, and his figure easily resting on the arm supported by that knee. They were just visible from her window. Perhaps she saw them.

"Tom, what's the matter?"

"Oh! Mr. Harthouse," said Tom with a groan, "I am hard up, and bothered out of my life."

---

1.   See note to p.165.

"My good fellow, so am I."

"You!" returned Tom. "You are the picture of independence. Mr. Harthouse, I am in a horrible mess. You have no idea what a state I have got myself into—what a state my sister might have got me out of, if she would only have done it."

He took to biting the rosebuds now, and tearing them away from his teeth with a hand that trembled like an infirm old man's. After one exceedingly observant look at him, his companion relapsed into his lightest air.

"Tom, you are inconsiderate: you expect too much of your sister. You have had money of her, you dog, you know you have."

"Well, Mr. Harthouse, I know I have. How else was I to get it? Here's old Bounderby always boasting that at my age he lived upon twopence a month, or something of that sort. Here's my father drawing what he calls a line, and tying me down to it from a baby, neck and heels. Here's my mother who never has anything of her own, except her complaints. What *is* a fellow to do for money, and where *am* I to look for it, if not to my sister?"

He was almost crying, and scattered the buds about by dozens. Mr. Harthouse took him persuasively by the coat.

"But, my dear Tom, if your sister has not got it—"

"Not got it, Mr. Harthouse? I don't say she has got it. I may have wanted more than she was likely to have got. But then she ought to get it. She could get it. It's of no use pretending to make a secret of matters now, after what I have told you already; you know she didn't marry old Bounderby for her own sake, or for his sake, but for my sake. Then why doesn't she get what I want, out of him, for my sake? She is not obliged to say what she is going to do with it; she is sharp enough; she could manage to coax it out of him, if she chose. Then why doesn't she choose, when I tell her of what consequence it is? But no. There she sits in his company like a stone, instead of making herself agreeable and getting it easily. I don't know what you may call this, but *I* call it unnatural conduct."

There was a piece of ornamental water immediately below the parapet, on the other side, into which Mr. James Harthouse had a very strong inclination to pitch Mr. Thomas Gradgrind Junior, as the injured men of

Coketown threatened to pitch their property into the Atlantic.[1] But he preserved his easy attitude; and nothing more solid went over the stone balustrades than the accumulated rosebuds now floating about, a little surface-island.

"My dear Tom," said Harthouse, "let me try to be your banker."

"For God's sake," replied Tom, suddenly, "don't talk about bankers!" And very white he looked, in contrast with the roses. Very white.

Mr. Harthouse, as a thoroughly well-bred man, accustomed to the best society, was not to be surprised—he could as soon have been affected—but he raised his eyelids a little more, as if they were lifted by a feeble touch of wonder. Albeit it was as much against the precepts of his school to wonder, as it was against the doctrines of the Gradgrind College.

"What is the present need, Tom? Three figures? Out with them. Say what they are."

"Mr. Harthouse," returned Tom, now actually crying; and his tears were better than his injuries, however pitiful a figure he made: "it's too late; the money is of no use to me at present. I should have had it before to be of use to me. But I am very much obliged to you; you're a true friend."

A true friend! "Whelp, whelp!" thought Mr. Harthouse, lazily; "what an Ass you are!"

"And I take your offer as a great kindness," said Tom, grasping his hand. "As a great kindness, Mr. Harthouse."

"Well," returned the other, "it may be of more use by and by. And, my good fellow, if you will open your bedevilments to me when they come thick upon you, I may show you better ways out of them than you can find for yourself."

"Thank you," said Tom, shaking his head dismally, and chewing rosebuds. "I wish I had known you sooner, Mr. Harthouse."

"Now, you see, Tom," said Mr. Harthouse in conclusion, himself tossing over a rose or two, as a contribution to the island, which was always drifting to the wall as if it wanted to become part of the mainland: "every

---

1.   The image first occurs on p. 144.

man is selfish in everything he does, and I am exactly like the rest of my fellow-creatures. I am desperately intent;" the languor of his desperation being quite tropical; "on your softening towards your sister—which you ought to do; and on your being a more loving and agreeable sort of brother—which you ought to be."

"I will be, Mr. Harthouse."

"No time like the present, Tom. Begin at once."

"Certainly I will. And my sister Loo shall say so."

"Having made which bargain, Tom," said Harthouse, clapping him on the shoulder again, with an air which left him at liberty to infer—as he did, poor fool—that this condition was imposed upon him in mere careless good nature to lessen his sense of obligation, "we will tear ourselves asunder until dinner-time."

When Tom appeared before dinner, though his mind seemed heavy enough, his body was on the alert; and he appeared before Mr. Bounderby came in. "I didn't mean to be cross, Loo," he said, giving her his hand, and kissing her. "I know you are fond of me, and you know I am fond of you."

After this, there was a smile upon Louisa's face that day, for some one else. Alas, for some one else!

"So much the less is the whelp the only creature that she cares for," thought James Harthouse, reversing the reflection of his first day's knowledge of her pretty face. "So much the less, so much the less."

CHAPTER VIII.
EXPLOSION

THE NEXT morning was too bright a morning for sleep, and James Harthouse rose early, and sat in the pleasant bay window of his dressing-room, smoking the rare tobacco that had had so wholesome an influence on his young friend. Reposing in the sunlight, with the fragrance of his eastern pipe about him, and the dreamy smoke vanishing into the air, so rich and soft with summer odours, he reckoned up his advantages as an idle winner might count his gains. He was not at all bored for the time, and could give his mind to it.

He had established a confidence with her, from which her husband was excluded. He had established a confidence with her, that absolutely turned upon her indifference towards her husband, and the absence, now and at all times, of any congeniality between them. He had artfully, but plainly, assured her that he knew her heart in its last most delicate recesses; he had come so near to her through its tenderest sentiment; he had associated himself with that feeling; and the barrier behind which she lived, had melted away. All very odd, and very satisfactory!

And yet he had not, even now, any earnest wickedness of purpose in him. Publicly and privately, it were much better for the age in which he lived, that he and the legion of whom he was one[1] were designedly bad, than indifferent and purposeless. It is the drifting icebergs setting with any current anywhere, that wreck the ships.

When the Devil goeth about like a roaring lion,[2] he goeth about in a shape by which few but savages and hunters are attracted. But, when he is trimmed, smoothed, and varnished, according to the mode; when he is aweary of vice, and aweary of virtue, used up as to brimstone,[3] and used up as to bliss; then, whether he take to the serving out of red tape,[4] or to the kindling of red fire, he is the very Devil.

---

1.   I.e. legion of devils. Compare Mark 5:9.
2.   Compare 1 Peter 5:8.
3.   I.e. the sulphurous fires of hell, in contrast to heavenly bliss; compare, for example, Revelation 20:10.
4.   The rigid following of bureaucratic rules and regulations (such tape was conventionally used to bind legal or administrative documents).

So James Harthouse reclined in the window, indolently smoking, and reckoning up the steps he had taken on the road by which he happened to be travelling. The end to which it led was before him, pretty plainly; but he troubled himself with no calculations about it. What will be, will be.[1]

As he had rather a long ride to take that day—for there was a public occasion "to do" at some distance, which afforded a tolerable opportunity of going in for the Gradgrind men—he dressed early, and went down to breakfast. He was anxious to see if she had relapsed since the previous evening. No. He resumed where he had left off. There was a look of interest for him again.

He got through the day as much (or as little) to his own satisfaction, as was to be expected under the fatiguing circumstances; and came riding back at six o'clock. There was a sweep of some half-mile between the lodge and the house, and he was riding along at a foot pace[2] over the smooth gravel, once Nickits's, when Mr. Bounderby burst out of the shrubbery, with such violence as to make his horse shy across the road.

"Harthouse!" cried Mr. Bounderby. "Have you heard?"

"Heard what?" said Harthouse, soothing his horse, and inwardly favouring Mr. Bounderby with no good wishes.

"Then you *haven't* heard!"

"I have heard you, and so has this brute. I have heard nothing else."

Mr. Bounderby, red and hot, planted himself in the centre of the path before the horse's head, to explode his bombshell with more effect.

"The Bank's robbed!"

"You don't mean it!"

"Robbed last night, sir. Robbed in an extraordinary manner. Robbed with a false key."

"Of much?"

Mr. Bounderby, in his desire to make the most of it, really seemed mortified by being obliged to reply, "Why, no; not of very much. But it might have been."

"Of how much?"

---

1.   See note to p. 161.
2.   At walking speed.

"Oh! as a sum—if you stick to a sum—of not more than a hundred and fifty pound," said Bounderby, with impatience. "But it's not the sum; it's the fact. It's the fact of the Bank being robbed, that's the important circumstance. I am surprised you don't see it."

"My dear Bounderby," said James, dismounting, and giving his bridle to his servant, "I *do* see it; and am as overcome as you can possibly desire me to be, by the spectacle afforded to my mental view. Nevertheless, I may be allowed, I hope, to congratulate you—which I do with all my soul, I assure you—on your not having sustained a greater loss."

"Thank'ee," replied Bounderby, in a short, ungracious manner. "But I tell you what. It might have been twenty thousand pound."

"I suppose it might."

"Suppose it might! By the Lord, you *may* suppose so. By George!"[1] said Mr. Bounderby, with sundry menacing nods and shakes of his head. "It might have been twice twenty. There's no knowing what it would have been, or wouldn't have been, as it was, but for the fellows' being disturbed."

Louisa had come up now, and Mrs. Sparsit, and Bitzer.

"Here's Tom Gradgrind's daughter knows pretty well what it might have been, if you don't," blustered Bounderby. "Dropped, sir, as if she was shot when I told her! Never knew her do such a thing before. Does her credit, under the circumstances, in my opinion!"

She still looked faint and pale. James Harthouse begged her to take his arm; and as they moved on very slowly, asked her how the robbery had been committed.

"Why, I am going to tell you," said Bounderby, irritably giving his arm to Mrs. Sparsit. "If you hadn't been so mighty particular about the sum, I should have begun to tell you before. You know this lady (for she *is* a lady), Mrs. Sparsit?"

"I have already had the honour—"

"Very well. And this young man, Bitzer, you saw him too on the same occasion?" Mr. Harthouse inclined his head in assent, and Bitzer knuckled his forehead.

---

1.   A mild oath, referring to St. George of England.

"Very well. They live at the Bank. You know they live at the Bank, perhaps? Very well. Yesterday afternoon, at the close of business hours, everything was put away as usual. In the iron room that this young fellow sleeps outside of, there was never mind how much. In the little safe in young Tom's closet, the safe used for petty purposes, there was a hundred and fifty odd pound."

"A hundred and fifty-four, seven, one," said Bitzer.

"Come!" retorted Bounderby, stopping to wheel round upon him, "let's have none of *your* interruptions. It's enough to be robbed while you're snoring because you're too comfortable, without being put right with *your* four seven ones. I didn't snore, myself, when I was your age, let me tell you. I hadn't victuals enough to snore. And I didn't four seven one. Not if I knew it."

Bitzer knuckled his forehead again, in a sneaking manner, and seemed at once particularly impressed and depressed by the instance last given of Mr. Bounderby's moral abstinence.

"A hundred and fifty odd pound," resumed Mr. Bounderby. "That sum of money, young Tom locked in his safe, not a very strong safe, but that's no matter now. Everything was left, all right. Some time in the night, while this young fellow snored—Mrs. Sparsit, ma'am, you say you have heard him snore?"

"Sir," returned Mrs. Sparsit, "I cannot say that I have heard him precisely snore, and therefore must not make that statement. But on winter evenings, when he has fallen asleep at his table, I have heard him, what I should prefer to describe as partially choke. I have heard him on such occasions produce sounds of a nature similar to what may be sometimes heard in Dutch clocks.[1] Not," said Mrs. Sparsit, with a lofty sense of giving strict evidence, "that I would convey any imputation on his moral character. Far from it. I have always considered Bitzer a young man of the most upright principle; and to that I beg to bear my testimony."

"Well!" said the exasperated Bounderby, "while he was snoring, *or* choking, *or* Dutch-clocking, *or* something or other—being asleep—some fellows, somehow, whether previously concealed in the house or not re-

---

1.   Striking wooden wall clocks made in the Black Forest (Dutch = Deutsch, i.e. German), popular in Victorian England.

mains to be seen, got to young Tom's safe, forced it, and abstracted the contents. Being then disturbed, they made off; letting themselves out at the main door, and double-locking it again (it was double-locked, and the key under Mrs. Sparsit's pillow) with a false key, which was picked up in the street near the Bank, about twelve o'clock to-day. No alarm takes place, till this chap, Bitzer, turns out this morning, and begins to open and prepare the offices for business. Then, looking at Tom's safe, he sees the door ajar, and finds the lock forced, and the money gone."

"Where is Tom, by the by?" asked Harthouse, glancing round.

"He has been helping the police," said Bounderby, "and stays behind at the Bank. I wish these fellows had tried to rob me when I was at his time of life. They would have been out of pocket if they had invested eighteenpence in the job; I can tell 'em that."

"Is anybody suspected?"

"Suspected? I should think there was somebody suspected. Egod!" said Bounderby, relinquishing Mrs. Sparsit's arm to wipe his heated head. "Josiah Bounderby of Coketown is not to be plundered and nobody suspected. No, thank you!"

Might Mr. Harthouse inquire Who was suspected?

"Well," said Bounderby, stopping and facing about to confront them all, "I'll tell you. It's not to be mentioned everywhere; it's not to be mentioned anywhere: in order that the scoundrels concerned (there's a gang of 'em) may be thrown off their guard. So take this in confidence. Now wait a bit." Mr. Bounderby wiped his head again. "What should you say to;" here he violently exploded: "to a Hand being in it?"

"I hope," said Harthouse, lazily, "not our friend Blackpot?"

"Say Pool instead of Pot, sir," returned Bounderby, "and that's the man."

Louisa faintly uttered some word of incredulity and surprise.

"Oh yes! I know!" said Bounderby, immediately catching at the sound. "I know! I am used to that. I know all about it. They are the finest people in the world, these fellows are. They have got the gift of the gab, they have. They only want to have their rights explained to them, they do. But I tell you what. Show me a dissatisfied Hand, and I'll show you a man that's fit for anything bad, I don't care what it is."

Another of the popular fictions of Coketown, which some pains had been taken to disseminate—and which some people really believed.

"But I am acquainted with these chaps," said Bounderby. "I can read 'em off, like books. Mrs. Sparsit, ma'am, I appeal to you. What warning did I give that fellow, the first time he set foot in the house, when the express object of his visit was to know how he could knock Religion over, and floor the Established Church? Mrs. Sparsit, in point of high connexions, you are on a level with the aristocracy,—did I say, or did I not say, to that fellow, 'you can't hide the truth from me: you are not the kind of fellow I like; you'll come to no good'?"

"Assuredly, sir," returned Mrs. Sparsit, "you did, in a highly impressive manner, give him such an admonition."

"When he shocked you, ma'am," said Bounderby; "when he shocked your feelings?"

"Yes, sir," returned Mrs. Sparsit, with a meek shake of her head, "he certainly did so. Though I do not mean to say but that my feelings may be weaker on such points—more foolish if the term is preferred—than they might have been, if I had always occupied my present position."

Mr. Bounderby stared with a bursting pride at Mr. Harthouse, as much as to say, "I am the proprietor of this female, and she's worth your attention, I think." Then, resumed his discourse.

"You can recall for yourself, Harthouse, what I said to him when you saw him. I didn't mince the matter with him. I am never mealy with 'em. I KNOW 'em. Very well, sir. Three days after that, he bolted. Went off, nobody knows where: as my mother did in my infancy—only with this difference, that he is a worse subject than my mother, if possible. What did he do before he went? What do you say;" Mr. Bounderby, with his hat in his hand, gave a beat upon the crown at every little division of his sentences, as if it were a tambourine; "to his being seen—night after night—watching the Bank?—to his lurking about there—after dark?—To its striking Mrs. Sparsit—that he could be lurking for no good—To her calling Bitzer's attention to him, and their both taking notice of him—And to its appearing on inquiry to-day—that he was also noticed by the neighbours?" Having come to the climax, Mr. Bounderby, like an oriental dancer, put his tambourine on his head.[1]

---

1.   Tambourines were used by street performers both to collect money from onlookers

"Suspicious," said James Harthouse, "certainly."

"I think so, sir," said Bounderby, with a defiant nod. "I think so. But there are more of 'em in it. There's an old woman. One never hears of these things till the mischief's done; all sorts of defects are found out in the stable door after the horse is stolen; there's an old woman turns up now. An old woman who seems to have been flying into town on a broomstick, every now and then. *She* watches the place a whole day before this fellow begins, and on the night when you saw him, she steals away with him and holds a council with him—I suppose, to make her report on going off duty, and be damned to her."

There was such a person in the room that night, and she shrunk from observation, thought Louisa.

"This is not all of 'em, even as we already know 'em," said Bounderby, with many nods of hidden meaning. "But I have said enough for the present. You'll have the goodness to keep it quiet, and mention it to no one. It may take time, but we shall have 'em. It's policy to give 'em line enough, and there's no objection to that."

"Of course, they will be punished with the utmost rigour of the law, as notice-boards observe," replied James Harthouse, "and serve them right. Fellows who go in for Banks must take the consequences. If there were no consequences, we should all go in for Banks." He had gently taken Louisa's parasol from her hand, and had put it up for her; and she walked under its shade, though the sun did not shine there.

"For the present, Loo Bounderby," said her husband, "here's Mrs. Sparsit to look after. Mrs. Sparsit's nerves have been acted upon by this business, and she'll stay here a day or two. So make her comfortable."

"Thank you very much, sir," that discreet lady observed, "but pray do not let My comfort be a consideration. Anything will do for Me."

It soon appeared that if Mrs. Sparsit had a failing in her association with that domestic establishment, it was that she was so excessively regardless of herself and regardful of others, as to be a nuisance. On being shown her chamber, she was so dreadfully sensible of its comforts as to suggest the inference that she would have preferred to pass the night on

---

and as a prop. Donning the tambourine like a hat seems to have been a sign of the end of the performance.

the mangle in the laundry. True, the Powlers and the Scadgerses were accustomed to splendour, "but it is my duty to remember," Mrs. Sparsit was fond of observing with a lofty grace: particularly when any of the domestics were present, "that what I was, I am no longer. Indeed," said she, "if I could altogether cancel the remembrance that Mr. Sparsit was a Powler, or that I myself am related to the Scadgers family; or if I could even revoke the fact, and make myself a person of common descent and ordinary connexions; I would gladly do so. I should think it, under existing circumstances, right to do so." The same Hermitical state of mind[1] led to her renunciation of made dishes and wines at dinner, until fairly commanded by Mr. Bounderby to take them; when she said, "Indeed you are very good, sir;" and departed from a resolution of which she had made rather formal and public announcement, to "wait for the simple mutton." She was likewise deeply apologetic for wanting the salt; and, feeling amiably bound to bear out Mr. Bounderby to the fullest extent in the testimony he had borne to her nerves, occasionally sat back in her chair and silently wept; at which periods a tear of large dimensions, like a crystal earring, might be observed (or rather, must be, for it insisted on public notice) sliding down her Roman nose.

But Mrs. Sparsit's greatest point, first and last, was her determination to pity Mr. Bounderby. There were occasions when in looking at him she was involuntarily moved to shake her head, as who would say, "Alas, poor Yorick!"[2] After allowing herself to be betrayed into these evidences of emotion, she would force a lambent brightness, and would be fitfully cheerful, and would say, "You have still good spirits, sir, I am thankful to find;" and would appear to hail it as a blessed dispensation that Mr. Bounderby bore up as he did. One idiosyncrasy for which she often apologized, she found it excessively difficult to conquer. She had a curious propensity to call Mrs. Bounderby "Miss Gradgrind," and yielded to it some three or four score times in the course of the evening. Her repetition of this mistake covered Mrs. Sparsit with modest confusion; but indeed, she said, it seemed so natural to say Miss Gradgrind: whereas, to persuade herself that the young lady whom she had the happiness of

---

1.   I.e. the desire for the simple life typical of a hermit.
2.   See *Hamlet* V i.

knowing from a child could be really and truly Mrs. Bounderby, she found almost impossible. It was a further singularity of this remarkable case, that the more she thought about it, the more impossible it appeared; "the differences," she observed, "being such."

In the drawing-room after dinner, Mr. Bounderby tried the case of the robbery, examined the witnesses, made notes of the evidence, found the suspected persons guilty, and sentenced them to the extreme punishment of the law. That done, Bitzer was dismissed to town with instructions to recommend Tom to come home by the mail-train.

When candles were brought, Mrs. Sparsit murmured, "Don't be low, sir. Pray let me see you cheerful, sir, as I used to do." Mr. Bounderby, upon whom these consolations had begun to produce the effect of making him, in a bull-headed blundering way, sentimental, sighed like some large sea-animal. "I cannot bear to see you so, sir," said Mrs. Sparsit. "Try a hand at backgammon, sir, as you used to do when I had the honour of living under your roof." "I haven't played backgammon, ma'am," said Mr. Bounderby, "since that time." "No, sir," said Mrs. Sparsit, soothingly, "I am aware that you have not. I remember that Miss Gradgrind takes no interest in the game. But I shall be happy, sir, if you will condescend."

They played near a window, opening on the garden. It was a fine night: not moonlight, but sultry and fragrant. Louisa and Mr. Harthouse strolled out into the garden, where their voices could be heard in the stillness, though not what they said. Mrs. Sparsit, from her place at the backgammon board, was constantly straining her eyes to pierce the shadows without. "What's the matter, ma'am?" said Mr. Bounderby; "you don't see a Fire do you?" "Oh dear no, sir," returned Mrs. Sparsit, "I was thinking of the dew." "What have you got to do with the dew, ma'am?" said Mr. Bounderby. "It's not myself, sir," returned Mrs. Sparsit, "I am fearful of Miss Gradgrind's taking cold." "She never takes cold," said Mr. Bounderby. "Really, sir?" said Mrs. Sparsit. And was affected with a cough in her throat.

When the time drew near for retiring, Mr. Bounderby took a glass of water. "Oh, sir?" said Mrs. Sparsit. "Not your sherry warm, with lemon-peel and nutmeg?" "Why I have got out of the habit of taking it now, ma'am," said Mr. Bounderby. "The more's the pity, sir," returned Mrs. Sparsit; "you are losing all your good old habits. Cheer up, sir! If

Miss Gradgrind will permit me, I will offer to make it for you, as I have often done."

Miss Gradgrind readily permitting Mrs. Sparsit to do anything she pleased, that considerate lady made the beverage, and handed it to Mr. Bounderby. "It will do you good, sir. It will warm your heart. It is the sort of thing you want, and ought to take, sir." And when Mr. Bounderby said, "Your health, ma'am!" she answered with great feeling, "Thank you, sir. The same to you, and happiness also." Finally, she wished him good night, with great pathos; and Mr. Bounderby went to bed, with a maudlin persuasion that he had been crossed in something tender, though he could not, for his life, have mentioned what it was.

Long after Louisa had undressed and lain down, she watched and waited for her brother's coming home. That could hardly be, she knew, until an hour past midnight; but in the country silence, which did anything but calm the trouble of her thoughts, time lagged wearily. At last, when the darkness and stillness had seemed for hours to thicken one another, she heard the bell at the gate. She felt as though she would have been glad that it rang on until daylight; but it ceased, and the circles of its last sound spread out fainter and wider in the air, and all was dead again.

She waited yet some quarter of an hour, as she judged. Then she arose, put on a loose robe, and went out of her room in the dark, and up the staircase to her brother's room. His door being shut, she softly opened it and spoke to him, approaching his bed with a noiseless step.

She kneeled down beside it, passed her arm over his neck, and drew his face to hers. She knew that he only feigned to be asleep, but she said nothing to him.

He started by and by as if he were just then awakened, and asked who that was, and what was the matter?

"Tom, have you anything to tell me? If ever you loved me in your life, and have anything concealed from every one besides, tell it to me."

"I don't know what you mean, Loo. You have been dreaming."

"My dear brother:" she laid her head down on his pillow, and her hair flowed over him as if she would hide him from every one but herself: "is there nothing that you have to tell me? Is there nothing you can tell me if you will? You can tell me nothing that will change me. Oh Tom, tell me the truth!"

"I don't know what you mean, Loo!"

"As you lie here alone, my dear, in the melancholy night, so you must lie somewhere one night, when even I, if I am living then, shall have left you. As I am here beside you, barefoot, unclothed, undistinguishable in darkness, so must I lie through all the night of my decay, until I am dust. In the name of that time, Tom, tell me the truth now!"

"What is it you want to know?"

"You may be certain;" in the energy of her love she took him to her bosom as if he were a child; "that I will not reproach you. You may be certain that I will be compassionate and true to you. You may be certain that I will save you at whatever cost. Oh Tom, have you nothing to tell me? Whisper very softly. Say only 'yes,' and I shall understand you!"

She turned her ear to his lips, but he remained doggedly silent.

"Not a word, Tom?"

"How can I say Yes, or how can I say No, when I don't know what you mean? Loo, you are a brave, kind girl, worthy I begin to think of a better brother than I am. But I have nothing more to say. Go to bed, go to bed."

"You are tired," she whispered presently, more in her usual way.

"Yes, I am quite tired out."

"You have been so hurried and disturbed to-day. Have any fresh discoveries been made?"

"Only those you have heard of, from—him."

"Tom, have you said to any one that we made a visit to those people, and that we saw those three together?"

"No. Didn't you yourself particularly ask me to keep it quiet when you asked me to go there with you?"

"Yes. But I did not know then what was going to happen."

"Nor I neither. How could I?"

He was very quick upon her with this retort.

"Ought I to say, after what has happened," said his sister, standing by the bed—she had gradually withdrawn herself and risen, "that I made that visit? Should I say so? Must I say so?"

"Good Heavens, Loo," returned her brother, "you are not in the habit of asking my advice. Say what you like. If you keep it to yourself, I shall keep it to *myself*. If you disclose it, there's an end of it."

It was too dark for either to see the other's face; but each seemed very attentive, and to consider before speaking.

"Tom, do you believe the man I gave the money to, is really implicated in this crime?"

"I don't know. I don't see why he shouldn't be."

"He seemed to me an honest man."

"Another person may seem to you dishonest, and yet not be so."

There was a pause, for he had hesitated and stopped.

"In short," resumed Tom, as if he had made up his mind, "if you come to that, perhaps I was so far from being altogether in his favour, that I took him outside the door to tell him quietly, that I thought he might consider himself very well off to get such a windfall as he had got from my sister, and that I hoped he would make good use of it. You remember whether I took him out or not. I say nothing against the man; he may be a very good fellow, for anything I know; I hope he is."

"Was he offended by what you said?"

"No, he took it pretty well; he was civil enough. Where are you, Loo?" He sat up in bed and kissed her. "Good night, my dear, good night."

"You have nothing more to tell me?"

"No. What should I have? You wouldn't have me tell you a lie!"

"I wouldn't have you do that to-night, Tom, of all the nights in your life; many and much happier as I hope they will be."

"Thank you, my dear Loo. I am so tired, that I am sure I wonder I don't say anything to get to sleep. Go to bed, go to bed."

Kissing her again, he turned round, drew the coverlet over his head, and lay as still as if that time had come by which she had adjured him. She stood for some time at the bedside before she slowly moved away. She stopped at the door, looked back when she had opened it, and asked him if he had called her? But he lay still, and she softly closed the door and returned to her room.

Then the wretched boy looked cautiously up and found her gone, crept out of bed, fastened his door, and threw himself upon his pillow again: tearing his hair, morosely crying, grudgingly loving her, hatefully but impenitently spurning himself, and no less hatefully and unprofitably spurning all the good in the world.

Chapter IX.
Hearing the Last of It

Mrs. Sparsit, lying by to recover the tone of her nerves in Mr. Bounderby's retreat, kept such a sharp look-out, night and day, under her Coriolanian eyebrows, that her eyes, like a couple of lighthouses on an iron-bound coast, might have warned all prudent mariners from that bold rock her Roman nose and the dark and craggy region in its neighbourhood, but for the placidity of her manner. Although it was hard to believe that her retiring for the night could be anything but a form, so severely wide awake were those classical eyes of hers, and so impossible did it seem that her rigid nose could yield to any relaxing influence, yet her manner of sitting, smoothing her uncomfortable, not to say, gritty mittens (they were constructed of a cool fabric like a meat-safe),[1] or of ambling to unknown places of destination with her foot in her cotton stirrup, was so perfectly serene, that most observers would have been constrained to suppose her a dove, embodied by some freak of nature, in the earthly tabernacle of a bird of the hook-beaked order.

She was a most wonderful woman for prowling about the house. How she got from story to story was a mystery beyond solution. A lady so decorous in herself, and so highly connected, was not to be suspected of dropping over the banisters or sliding down them, yet her extraordinary facility of locomotion suggested the wild idea. Another noticeable circumstance in Mrs. Sparsit was, that she was never hurried. She would shoot with consummate velocity from the roof to the hall, yet would be in full possession of her breath and dignity on the moment of her arrival there. Neither was she ever seen by human vision to go at a great pace.

She took very kindly to Mr. Harthouse, and had some pleasant conversation with him soon after her arrival. She made him her stately curtsey in the garden, one morning after breakfast.

"It appears but yesterday, sir," said Mrs. Sparsit, "that I had the honour of receiving you at the Bank, when you were so good as to wish to be made acquainted with Mr. Bounderby's address."

---

1.   A ventilated cupboard for keeping meat cool and safe from flies.

"An occasion, I am sure, not to be forgotten by myself in the course of Ages," said Mr. Harthouse, inclining his head to Mrs. Sparsit with the most indolent of all possible airs.

"We live in a singular world, sir," said Mrs. Sparsit.

"I have had the honour, by a coincidence of which I am proud, to have made a remark, similar in effect, though not so epigrammatically expressed."

"A singular world, I would say, sir," pursued Mrs. Sparsit; after acknowledging the compliment with a drooping of her dark eyebrows, not altogether so mild in its expression as her voice was in its dulcet tones; "as regards the intimacies we form at one time, with individuals we were quite ignorant of, at another. I recall, sir, that on that occasion you went so far as to say you were actually apprehensive of Miss Gradgrind."

"Your memory does me more honour than my insignificance deserves. I availed myself of your obliging hints to correct my timidity, and it is unnecessary to add that they were perfectly accurate. Mrs. Sparsit's talent for—in fact for anything requiring accuracy—with a combination of strength of mind—and Family—is too habitually developed to admit of any question." He was almost falling asleep over this compliment; it took him so long to get through, and his mind wandered so much in the course of its execution.

"You found Miss Gradgrind—I really cannot call her Mrs. Bounderby; it's very absurd of me—as youthful as I described her?" asked Mrs. Sparsit, sweetly.

"You drew her portrait perfectly," said Mr. Harthouse. "Presented her dead image."

"Very engaging, sir," said Mrs. Sparsit, causing her mittens slowly to revolve over one another.

"Highly so."

"It used to be considered," said Mrs. Sparsit, "that Miss Gradgrind was wanting in animation, but I confess she appears to me considerably and strikingly improved in that respect. Ay, and indeed here *is* Mr. Bounderby!" cried Mrs. Sparsit, nodding her head a great many times, as if she had been talking and thinking of no one else. "How do you find yourself this morning, sir? Pray let us see you cheerful, sir."

Now, these persistent assuagements of his misery, and lightenings of his load, had by this time begun to have the effect of making Mr. Bounderby softer than usual towards Mrs. Sparsit, and harder than usual to most other people from his wife downward. So, when Mrs. Sparsit said with forced lightness of heart, "You want your breakfast, sir, but I dare say Miss Gradgrind will soon be here to preside at the table," Mr. Bounderby replied, "If I waited to be taken care of by my wife, ma'am, I believe you know pretty well I should wait till Doomsday, so I'll trouble *you* to take charge of the teapot." Mrs. Sparsit complied, and assumed her old position at table.

This again made the excellent woman vastly sentimental. She was so humble withal, that when Louisa appeared, she rose, protesting she never could think of sitting in that place under existing circumstances, often as she had had the honour of making Mr. Bounderby's breakfast, before Mrs. Gradgrind—she begged pardon, she meant to say Miss Bounderby—she hoped to be excused, but she really could not get it right yet, though she trusted to become familiar with it by and by—had assumed her present position. It was only (she observed) because Miss Gradgrind happened to be a little late, and Mr. Bounderby's time was so very precious, and she knew it of old to be so essential that he should breakfast to the moment, that she had taken the liberty of complying with his request; long as his will had been a law to her.

"There! Stop where you are, ma'am," said Mr. Bounderby, "stop where you are! Mrs. Bounderby will be very glad to be relieved of the trouble, I believe."

"Don't say that, sir," returned Mrs. Sparsit, almost with severity, "because that is very unkind to Mrs. Bounderby. And to be unkind is not to be you, sir."

"You may set your mind at rest, ma'am—You can take it very quietly, can't you, Loo?" said Mr. Bounderby, in a blustering way to his wife.

"Of course. It is of no moment. Why should it be of any importance to me?"

"Why should it be of any importance to any one, Mrs. Sparsit, ma'am?" said Mr. Bounderby, swelling with a sense of slight. "You attach too much importance to these things, ma'am. By George, you'll be corrupted in some of your notions here. You are old-fashioned, ma'am. You are behind Tom Gradgrind's children's time."

"What is the matter with you?" asked Louisa, coldly surprised. "What has given you offence?"

"Offence!" repeated Bounderby. "Do you suppose if there was any offence given me, I shouldn't name it, and request to have it corrected? I am a straightforward man, I believe. I don't go beating about for side-winds."[1]

"I suppose no one ever had occasion to think you too diffident, or too delicate," Louisa answered him composedly: "I have never made that objection to you, either as a child or as a woman. I don't understand what you would have."

"Have?" returned Mr. Bounderby. "Nothing. Otherwise, don't you, Loo Bounderby, know thoroughly well that I, Josiah Bounderby of Coketown, would have it?"

She looked at him, as he struck the table and made the teacups ring, with a proud colour in her face that was a new change, Mr. Harthouse thought. "You are incomprehensible this morning," said Louisa. "Pray take no further trouble to explain yourself. I am not curious to know your meaning. What does it matter?"

Nothing more was said on this theme, and Mr. Harthouse was soon idly gay on indifferent subjects. But from this day, the Sparsit action upon Mr. Bounderby threw Louisa and James Harthouse more together, and strengthened the dangerous alienation from her husband and confidence against him with another, into which she had fallen by degrees so fine that she could not retrace them if she tried. But whether she ever tried or no, lay hidden in her own closed heart.

Mrs. Sparsit was so much affected on this particular occasion, that, assisting Mr. Bounderby to his hat after breakfast, and being then alone with him in the hall, she imprinted a chaste kiss upon his hand, murmured "My benefactor!" and retired, overwhelmed with grief. Yet it is an indubitable fact, within the cognizance of this history, that five minutes after he had left the house in the self-same hat, the same descendant of the Scadgerses and connexion by matrimony of the Powlers, shook her right-handed mitten at his portrait, made a contemptuous grimace at that

---

1. Taking an indirect course (metaphor from sailing).

work of art, and said "Serve you right, you Noodle, and I am glad of it."

Mr. Bounderby had not been long gone, when Bitzer appeared. Bitzer had come down by train, shrieking and rattling over the long line of arches that bestrode the wild country of past and present coal-pits, with an express from Stone Lodge. It was a hasty note to inform Louisa that Mrs. Gradgrind lay very ill. She had never been well within her daughter's knowledge; but, she had declined within the last few days, had continued sinking all through the night, and was now as nearly dead, as her limited capacity of being in any state that implied the ghost of an intention to get out of it, allowed.

Accompanied by the lightest of porters, fit colourless servitor at Death's door when Mrs. Gradgrind knocked, Louisa rumbled to Coketown, over the coal-pits past and present, and was whirled into its smoky jaws. She dismissed the messenger to his own devices, and rode away to her old home.

She had seldom been there since her marriage. Her father was usually sifting and sifting at his parliamentary cinder-heap in London (without being observed to turn up many precious articles among the rubbish), and was still hard at it in the national dust-yard.* Her mother had taken it rather as a disturbance than otherwise, to be visited, as she reclined upon her sofa; young people, Louisa felt herself all unfit for; Sissy she had never softened to again, since the night when the stroller's child had raised her eyes to look at Mr. Bounderby's intended wife. She had no inducements to go back, and had rarely gone.

Neither, as she approached her old home now, did any of the best influences of old home descend upon her. The dreams of childhood—its airy fables, its graceful, beautiful, humane, impossible adornments of the world beyond: so good to be believed in once, so good to be remembered when out-grown, for then the least among them rises to the stature of a great Charity in the heart, suffering little children to come into the midst of it,[1] and to keep with their pure hands a garden in the stony ways of this world, wherein it were better for all the children of Adam that they should oftener sun themselves, simple and trustful, and not

---

1.   Compare the words of Jesus on the innocence of children in Mark 10:13–6.

worldly-wise—what had she to do with these? Remembrances of how she had journeyed to the little that she knew, by the enchanted roads of what she and millions of innocent creatures had hoped and imagined; of how, first coming upon Reason through the tender light of Fancy, she had seen it a beneficent god, deferring to gods as great as itself: not a grim Idol, cruel and cold, with its victims bound hand to foot, and its big dumb shape set up with a sightless stare, never to be moved by anything but so many calculated tons of leverage—what had she to do with these? Her remembrances of home and childhood were remembrances of the drying up of every spring and fountain in her young heart as it gushed out. The golden waters were not there. They were flowing for the fertilization of the land where grapes are gathered from thorns, and figs from thistles.[1]

She went, with a heavy, hardened kind of sorrow upon her, into the house and into her mother's room. Since the time of her leaving home, Sissy had lived with the rest of the family on equal terms. Sissy was at her mother's side; and Jane, her sister, now ten or twelve years old, was in the room.

There was great trouble before it could be made known to Mrs. Gradgrind that her eldest child was there. She reclined, propped up, from mere habit, on a couch: as nearly in her old usual attitude, as anything so helpless could be kept in. She had positively refused to take to her bed; on the ground that if she did, she would never hear the last of it.

Her feeble voice sounded so far away in her bundle of shawls, and the sound of another voice addressing her seemed to take such a long time in getting down to her ears, that she might have been lying at the bottom of a well. The poor lady was nearer Truth[2] than she ever had been: which had much to do with it.

On being told that Mrs. Bounderby was there, she replied, at cross-purposes, that she had never called him by that name since he married Louisa; that pending her choice of an unobjectionable name, she had called him J; and that she could not at present depart from that regulation, not

---

1.   Compare the parable of Jesus in Matthew 7:15–20.
2.   'Truth lies at the bottom of a well' is a proverbial saying probably first used by Democritus.

being yet provided with a permanent substitute. Louisa had sat by her for some minutes, and had spoken to her often, before she arrived at a clear understanding who it was. She then seemed to come to it all at once.

"Well, my dear," said Mrs. Gradgrind, "and I hope you are going on satisfactorily to yourself. It was all your father's doing. He set his heart upon it. And he ought to know."

"I want to hear of you, mother; not of myself."

"You want to hear of me, my dear? That's something new, I am sure, when anybody wants to hear of me. Not at all well, Louisa. Very faint and giddy."

"Are you in pain, dear mother?"

"I think there's a pain somewhere in the room," said Mrs. Gradgrind, "but I couldn't positively say that I have got it."

After this strange speech, she lay silent for some time. Louisa, holding her hand, could feel no pulse; but kissing it, could see a slight thin thread of life in fluttering motion.

"You very seldom see your sister," said Mrs. Gradgrind. "She grows like you. I wish you would look at her. Sissy, bring her here."

She was brought, and stood with her hand in her sister's. Louisa had observed her with her arm around Sissy's neck, and she felt the difference of this approach.

"Do you see the likeness, Louisa?"

"Yes, mother. I should think her like me. But—"

"Eh! Yes, I always say so," Mrs. Gradgrind cried, with unexpected quickness. "And that reminds me. I—I want to speak to you, my dear. Sissy, my good girl, leave us alone for a minute."

Louisa had relinquished the hand: had thought that her sister's was a better and brighter face than hers had ever been: had seen in it, not without a rising feeling of resentment, even in that place and at that time, something of the gentleness of the other face in the room; the sweet face with the trusting eyes, made paler than watching and sympathy made it, by the rich dark hair.

Left alone with her mother, Louisa saw her lying with an awful lull upon her face, like one who was floating away upon some great water, all resistance over, content to be carried down the stream. She put the shadow of a hand to her lips, and recalled her.

"You were going to speak to me, mother."

"Eh? Yes, to be sure, my dear. You know your father is almost always away now, and therefore I must write to him about it."

"About what, mother? Don't be troubled. About what?"

"You must remember, my dear, that whenever I have said anything, on any subject, I have never heard the last of it: and consequently, that I have long left off saying anything."

"I can hear you, mother." But, it was only by dint of bending down to her ear, and at the same time attentively watching the lips as they moved, that she could link such faint and broken sounds into any chain of connexion.

"You learnt a great deal, Louisa, and so did your brother. Ologies of all kinds from morning to night. If there is any Ology left, of any description, that has not been worn to rags in this house, all I can say is, I hope I shall never hear its name."

"I can hear you, mother, when you have strength to go on." This, to keep her from floating away.

"But there is something—not an Ology at all—that your father has missed, or forgotten, Louisa. I don't know what it is. I have often sat with Sissy near me, and thought about it. I shall never get its name now. But your father may. It makes me restless. I want to write to him, to find out for God's sake, what it is. Give me a pen, give me a pen."

Even the power of restlessness was gone, except from the poor head, which could just turn from side to side.

She fancied, however, that her request had been complied with, and that the pen she could not have held was in her hand. It matters little what figures of wonderful no-meaning she began to trace upon her wrappers. The hand soon stopped in the midst of them; the light that had always been feeble and dim behind the weak transparency, went out; and even Mrs. Gradgrind, emerged from the shadow in which man walketh and disquieteth himself in vain,[1] took upon her the dread solemnity of the sages and patriarchs.

---

1. Compare the 'Dixi, Custodiam' (Psalm 39) from the Order for the Burial of the Dead in the Book of Common Prayer.

CHAPTER X.
MRS. SPARSIT'S STAIRCASE

MRS. SPARSIT'S nerves being slow to recover their tone, the worthy woman made a stay of some weeks in duration at Mr. Bounderby's retreat, where, notwithstanding her anchorite[1] turn of mind based upon her becoming consciousness of her altered station, she resigned herself with noble fortitude to lodging, as one may say, in clover, and feeding on the fat of the land.[2] During the whole term of this recess from the guardianship of the Bank, Mrs. Sparsit was a pattern of consistency; continuing to take such pity on Mr. Bounderby to his face, as is rarely taken on man, and to call his portrait a Noodle to *its* face, with the greatest acrimony and contempt.

Mr. Bounderby, having got it into his explosive composition that Mrs. Sparsit was a highly superior woman to perceive that he had that general cross upon him in his deserts (for he had not yet settled what it was), and further that Louisa would have objected to her as a frequent visitor if it had comported with his greatness that she should object to anything that he chose to do, resolved not to lose sight of Mrs. Sparsit easily. So when her nerves were strung up to the pitch of again consuming sweetbreads in solitude, he said to her at the dinner-table, on the day before her departure, "I tell you what, ma'am; you shall come down here of a Saturday, while the fine weather lasts, and stay till Monday." To which Mrs. Sparsit returned, in effect, though not of the Mahomedan persuasion: "To hear is to obey."[3]

Now, Mrs. Sparsit was not a poetical woman; but she took an idea in the nature of an allegorical fancy, into her head. Much watching of Louisa, and much consequent observation of her impenetrable demeanour, which keenly whetted and sharpened Mrs. Sparsit's edge, must have given her as it were a lift, in the way of inspiration. She erected in her mind a mighty Staircase, with a dark pit of shame and ruin at the bottom; and down those stairs, from day to day and hour to hour, she saw Louisa coming.

---

1.   Like a hermit (see note to p. 214 above).
2.   Compare Genesis 45:18.
3.   The conventional reply of the obedient servant of Allah, based on several verses in the Koran.

It became the business of Mrs. Sparsit's life, to look up at her stair-case, and to watch Louisa coming down. Sometimes slowly, sometimes quickly, sometimes several steps at one bout, sometimes stopping, never turning back. If she had once turned back, it might have been the death of Mrs. Sparsit in spleen and grief.

She had been descending steadily, to the day, and on the day, when Mr. Bounderby issued the weekly invitation recorded above. Mrs. Sparsit was in good spirits, and inclined to be conversational.

"And pray, sir," said she, "if I may venture to ask a question apper-taining to any subject on which you show reserve—which is indeed hardy in me, for I well know you have a reason for everything you do—have you received intelligence respecting the robbery?"

"Why, ma'am, no; not yet. Under the circumstances, I didn't expect it yet. Rome wasn't built in a day, ma'am."

"Very true, sir," said Mrs. Sparsit, shaking her head.

"Nor yet in a week, ma'am."

"No, indeed, sir," returned Mrs. Sparsit, with a gentle melancholy upon her.

"In a similar manner, ma'am," said Bounderby, "I can wait, you know. If Romulus and Remus[1] could wait, Josiah Bounderby can wait. They were better off in their youth than I was, however. They had a she-wolf for a nurse; *I* had only a she-wolf for a grandmother. She didn't give any milk, ma'am; she gave bruises. She was a regular Alderney[2] at that."

"Ah!" Mrs. Sparsit sighed and shuddered.

"No, ma'am," continued Bounderby, "I have not heard anything more about it. It's in hand, though; and young Tom, who rather sticks to busi-ness at present—something new for him; he hadn't the school *I* had—is helping. My injunction is, Keep it quiet, and let it seem to blow over. Do what you like under the rose,[3] but don't give a sign of what you're about; or half a hundred of 'em will combine together and get this fel-low who has bolted, out of reach for good. Keep it quiet, and the thieves will grow in confidence by little and little, and we shall have 'em."

---

1.   Legendary twin founders of Rome, abandoned in childhood and reared by a wolf.
2.   A breed of cow named after one of the English Channel Islands.
3.   In secret, from the Latin *sub rosa*.

"Very sagacious indeed, sir," said Mrs. Sparsit. "Very interesting. The old woman you mentioned, sir—"

"The old woman I mentioned, ma'am," said Bounderby, cutting the matter short, as it was nothing to boast about, "is not laid hold of; but, she may take her oath she will be, if that is any satisfaction to her villainous old mind. In the mean time, ma'am, I am of opinion, if you ask me my opinion, that the less she is talked about, the better."

That same evening, Mrs. Sparsit, in her chamber window, resting from her packing operations, looked towards her great staircase and saw Louisa still descending.

She sat by Mr. Harthouse, in an alcove in the garden, talking very low; he stood leaning over her, as they whispered together, and his face almost touched her hair. "If not quite!" said Mrs. Sparsit, straining her hawk's eye to the utmost. Mrs. Sparsit was too distant to hear a word of their discourse, or even to know that they were speaking softly, otherwise than from the expression of their figures; but what they said was this:

"You recollect the man, Mr. Harthouse?"

"Oh, perfectly!"

"His face, and his manner, and what he said?"

"Perfectly. And an infinitely dreary person he appeared to me to be. Lengthy and prosy in the extreme. It was knowing to hold forth, in the humble-virtue school of eloquence; but, I assure you I thought at the time, 'My good fellow, you are over-doing this!'"

"It has been very difficult to me to think ill of that man."

"My dear Louisa—as Tom says." Which he never did say. "You know no good of the fellow?"

"No, certainly."

"Nor of any other such person?"

"How can I," she returned, with more of her first manner on her than he had lately seen, "when I know nothing of them, men or women?"

"My dear Louisa, then consent to receive the submissive representation of your devoted friend, who knows something of several varieties of his excellent fellow-creatures—for excellent they are, I am quite ready to believe, in spite of such little foibles as always helping themselves to what they can get hold of. This fellow talks. Well; every fellow talks. He professes morality. Well; all sorts of humbugs profess morality. From the

House of Commons to the House of Correction, there is a general profession of morality, except among our people; it really is that exception which makes our people quite reviving. You saw and heard the case. Here was one of the fluffy classes[1] pulled up extremely short by my esteemed friend Mr. Bounderby—who, as we know, is not possessed of that delicacy which would soften so tight a hand. The member of the fluffy classes was injured, exasperated, left the house grumbling, met somebody who proposed to him to go in for some share in this Bank business, went in, put something in his pocket which had nothing in it before, and relieved his mind extremely. Really he would have been an uncommon, instead of a common, fellow, if he had not availed himself of such an opportunity. Or he may have originated it altogether, if he had the cleverness."

"I almost feel as though it must be bad in me," returned Louisa, after sitting thoughtful awhile, "to be so ready to agree with you, and to be so lightened in my heart by what you say."

"I only say what is reasonable; nothing worse. I have talked it over with my friend Tom more than once—of course I remain on terms of perfect confidence with Tom—and he is quite of my opinion, and I am quite of his. Will you walk?"

They strolled away, among the lanes beginning to be indistinct in the twilight—she leaning on his arm—and she little thought how she was going down, down, down, Mrs. Sparsit's staircase.

Night and day, Mrs. Sparsit kept it standing. When Louisa had arrived at the bottom and disappeared in the gulf, it might fall in upon her if it would; but, until then, there it was to be, a Building, before Mrs. Sparsit's eyes. And there Louisa always was, upon it. And always gliding down, down, down!

Mrs. Sparsit saw James Harthouse come and go; she heard of him here and there; she saw the changes of the face he had studied; she, too, remarked to a nicety how and when it clouded, how and when it cleared; she kept her black eyes wide open, with no touch of pity, with no touch of compunction, all absorbed in interest. In the interest of seeing her, ever drawing, with no hand to stay her, nearer and nearer to the bottom

---

1.   I.e. a hand in one of the cotton mills (see note to p. 153 above).

of the new Giant's Staircase.[1]

With all her deference for Mr. Bounderby as contradistinguished from his portrait, Mrs. Sparsit had not the smallest intention of interrupting the descent. Eager to see it accomplished, and yet patient, she waited for the last fall, as for the ripeness and fulness of the harvest of her hopes. Hushed in expectancy, she kept her wary gaze upon the stairs; and seldom so much as darkly shook her right mitten (with her fist in it), at the figure coming down.

Chapter XI.
Lower and Lower

THE FIGURE descended the great stairs, steadily, steadily; always verging, like a weight in deep water, to the black gulf at the bottom.

Mr. Gradgrind, apprised of his wife's decease, made an expedition from London, and buried her in a business-like manner. He then returned with promptitude to the national cinder-heap, and resumed his sifting for the odds and ends he wanted, and his throwing of the dust about into the eyes of other people who wanted other odds and ends—in fact resumed his parliamentary duties.

In the meantime, Mrs. Sparsit kept unwinking watch and ward. Separated from her staircase, all the week, by the length of iron road dividing Coketown from the country house, she yet maintained her cat-like observation of Louisa, through her husband, through her brother, through James Harthouse, through the outsides of letters and packets, through everything animate and inanimate that at any time went near the stairs. "Your foot on the last step, my lady," said Mrs. Sparsit, apostrophizing the descending figure, with the aid of her threatening mitten, "and all your art shall never blind me."

Art or nature though, the original stock of Louisa's character or the graft of circumstances upon it,—her curious reserve did baffle, while it

---

1.   A reference to the grand staircase in the courtyard of the Doge's Palace in Venice, visited by Dickens in 1844 (see 'An Italian Dream' in *Pictures from Italy*).

stimulated, one as sagacious as Mrs. Sparsit. There were times when Mr. James Harthouse was not sure of her. There were times when he could not read the face he had studied so long; and when this lonely girl was a greater mystery to him, than any woman of the world with a ring of satellites to help her.

So the time went on; until it happened that Mr. Bounderby was called away from home by business which required his presence elsewhere, for three or four days. It was on a Friday that he intimated this to Mrs. Sparsit at the Bank, adding: "But you'll go down to-morrow, ma'am, all the same. You'll go down just as if I was there. It will make no difference to you."

"Pray, sir," returned Mrs. Sparsit reproachfully, "let me beg you not to say that. Your absence will make a vast difference to me, sir, as I think you very well know."

"Well, ma'am, then you must get on in my absence as well as you can," said Mr. Bounderby, not displeased.

"Mr. Bounderby," retorted Mrs. Sparsit, "your will is to me a law, sir; otherwise, it might be my inclination to dispute your kind commands, not feeling sure that it will be quite so agreeable to Miss Gradgrind to receive me, as it ever is to your own munificent hospitality. But you shall say no more, sir. I will go, upon your invitation."

"Why, when I invite you to my house, ma'am," said Bounderby, opening his eyes, "I should hope you want no other invitation."

"No, indeed, sir," returned Mrs. Sparsit, "I should hope not. Say no more, sir. I would, sir, I could see you gay again."

"What do you mean, ma'am?" blustered Bounderby.

"Sir," rejoined Mrs. Sparsit, "there was wont to be an elasticity in you which I sadly miss. Be buoyant, sir!"

Mr. Bounderby, under the influence of this difficult adjuration, backed up by her compassionate eye, could only scratch his head in a feeble and ridiculous manner, and afterwards assert himself at a distance, by being heard to bully the small fry of business all the morning.

"Bitzer," said Mrs. Sparsit that afternoon, when her patron was gone on his journey, and the Bank was closing, "present my compliments to young Mr. Thomas, and ask him if he would step up and partake of a lamb chop and walnut ketchup, with a glass of India ale?"[1] Young Mr. Thomas being usually ready for anything in that way, returned a gracious answer, and followed on its heels. "Mr. Thomas," said Mrs. Sparsit, "these plain viands being on table, I thought you might be tempted."

"Thank'ee, Mrs. Sparsit," said the whelp. And gloomily fell to.

"How is Mr. Harthouse, Mr. Tom?" asked Mrs. Sparsit.

"Oh, he's all right," said Tom.

"Where may he be at present?" Mrs. Sparsit asked in a light conversational manner, after mentally devoting the whelp to the Furies[2] for being so uncommunicative.

"He is shooting in Yorkshire," said Tom. "Sent Loo a basket half as big as a church, yesterday."

"The kind of gentleman, now," said Mrs. Sparsit, sweetly, "whom one might wager to be a good shot!"

"Crack," said Tom.

He had long been a down-looking young fellow, but this characteristic had so increased of late, that he never raised his eyes to any face for three seconds together. Mrs. Sparsit consequently had ample means of watching his looks, if she were so inclined.

"Mr. Harthouse is a great favourite of mine," said Mrs. Sparsit, "as indeed he is of most people. May we expect to see him again shortly, Mr. Tom?"

"Why, I expect to see him to-morrow," returned the whelp.

"Good news!" cried Mrs. Sparsit, blandly.

"I have got an appointment with him to meet him in the evening at the station here," said Tom, "and I am going to dine with him afterwards, I believe. He is not coming down to the country house for a week or so, being due somewhere else. At least, he says so; but I shouldn't wonder if he was to stop here over Sunday, and stray that way."

"Which reminds me!" said Mrs. Sparsit. "Would you remember a message to your sister, Mr. Tom, if I was to charge you with one?"

"Well? I'll try," returned the reluctant whelp, "if it isn't a long un."

---

1.   Beer brewed to be exported to India.
2.   The Erinyes, the spirits of revenge in Greek mythology.

"It is merely my respectful compliments," said Mrs. Sparsit, "and I fear I may not trouble her with my society this week; being still a little nervous, and better perhaps by my poor self."

"Oh! If that's all," observed Tom, "it wouldn't much matter, even if I was to forget it, for Loo's not likely to think of you unless she sees you."

Having paid for his entertainment with this agreeable compliment, he relapsed into a hangdog silence until there was no more India ale left, when he said, "Well, Mrs. Sparsit, I must be off!" and went off.

Next day, Saturday, Mrs. Sparsit sat at her window all day long looking at the customers coming in and out, watching the postmen, keeping an eye on the general traffic of the street, revolving many things in her mind, but, above all, keeping her attention on her staircase. The evening come, she put on her bonnet and shawl, and went quietly out: having her reasons for hovering in a furtive way about the station by which a passenger would arrive from Yorkshire, and for preferring to peep into it round pillars and corners, and out of ladies' waiting-room windows, to appearing in its precincts openly.

Tom was in attendance, and loitered about until the expected train came in. It brought no Mr. Harthouse. Tom waited until the crowd had dispersed, and the bustle was over; and then referred to a posted list of trains, and took counsel with porters. That done, he strolled away idly, stopping in the street and looking up it and down it, and lifting his hat off and putting it on again, and yawning and stretching himself, and exhibiting all the symptoms of mortal weariness to be expected in one who had still to wait until the next train should come in, an hour and forty minutes hence.

"This is a device to keep him out of the way," said Mrs. Sparsit, starting from the dull office window whence she had watched him last. "Harthouse is with his sister now!"

It was the conception of an inspired moment, and she shot off with her utmost swiftness to work it out. The station for the country house was at the opposite end of the town, the time was short, the road not easy; but she was so quick in pouncing on a disengaged coach, so quick in darting out of it, producing her money, seizing her ticket, and diving into the train, that she was borne along the arches spanning the land of coal-pits past and present, as if she had been caught up in a cloud and whirled away.[1]

All the journey, immovable in the air though never left behind; plain to the dark eyes of her mind, as the electric wires which ruled a colossal strip of music-paper out of the evening sky,[2] were plain to the dark eyes of her body; Mrs. Sparsit saw her staircase, with the figure coming down. Very near the bottom now. Upon the brink of the abyss.

An overcast September evening, just at nightfall, saw beneath its drooping eyelids Mrs. Sparsit glide out of her carriage, pass down the wooden steps of the little station into a stony road, cross it into a green lane, and become hidden in a summer-growth of leaves and branches. One or two late birds sleepily chirping in their nests, and a bat heavily crossing and recrossing her, and the reek of her own tread in the thick dust that felt like velvet, were all Mrs. Sparsit heard or saw until she very softly closed a gate.

She went up to the house, keeping within the shrubbery, and went round it, peeping between the leaves at the lower windows. Most of them were open, as they usually were in such warm weather, but there were no lights yet, and all was silent. She tried the garden with no better effect. She thought of the wood, and stole towards it, heedless of long grass and briers: of worms, snails, and slugs, and all the creeping things[3] that be. With her dark eyes and her hook nose warily in advance of her, Mrs. Sparsit softly crushed her way through the thick undergrowth, so intent upon her object that she probably would have done no less, if the wood had been a wood of adders.

Hark!

The smaller birds might have tumbled out of their nests, fascinated by the glittering of Mrs. Sparsit's eyes in the gloom, as she stopped and listened.

Low voices close at hand. His voice and hers. The appointment *was* a device to keep the brother away! There they were yonder, by the felled tree.

---

1. Compare the descriptions of the translation of Elijah in 2 Kings 2:11 and of the Second Coming of Christ in 1 Thessalonians 4:16–17.
2. I.e. telegraph wires.
3. Compare Genesis 1:24–5.

Bending low among the dewy grass, Mrs. Sparsit advanced closer to them. She drew herself up, and stood behind a tree, like Robinson Crusoe in his ambuscade against the savages;[1] so near to them that at a spring, and that no great one, she could have touched them both. He was there secretly, and had not shown himself at the house. He had come on horseback, and must have passed through the neighbouring fields; for his horse was tied to the meadow side of the fence, within a few paces.

"My dearest love," said he, "what could I do? Knowing you were alone, was it possible that I could stay away?"

"You may hang your head, to make yourself the more attractive; *I* don't know what they see in you when you hold it up," thought Mrs. Sparsit; "but you little think, my dearest love, whose eyes are on you!"

That she hung her head, was certain. She urged him to go away, she commanded him to go away; but she neither turned her face to him, nor raised it. Yet it was remarkable that she sat as still as ever the amiable woman in ambuscade had seen her sit, at any period in her life. Her hands rested in one another, like the hands of a statue; and even her manner of speaking was not hurried.

"My dear child," said Harthouse; Mrs. Sparsit saw with delight that his arm embraced her; "will you not bear with my society for a little while?"

"Not here."

"Where, Louisa?"

"Not here."

"But we have so little time to make so much of, and I have come so far, and am altogether so devoted, and distracted. There never was a slave at once so devoted and ill-used by his mistress. To look for your sunny welcome that has warmed me into life, and to be received in your frozen manner, is heart-rending."

"Am I to say again, that I must be left to myself here?"

"But we must meet, my dear Louisa. Where shall we meet?"

They both started. The listener started, guiltily, too; for she thought

---

1.   In Defoe's novel, the hero and Man Friday use the protection of a wood to attack a group of cannibals who are about to roast a European prisoner.

there was another listener among the trees. It was only rain, beginning to fall fast, in heavy drops.

"Shall I ride up to the house a few minutes hence, innocently supposing that its master is at home and will be charmed to receive me?"

"No!"

"Your cruel commands are implicitly to be obeyed; though I am the most unfortunate fellow in the world, I believe, to have been insensible to all other women, and to have fallen prostrate at last under the foot of the most beautiful, and the most engaging, and the most imperious. My dearest Louisa, I cannot go myself, or let you go, in this hard abuse of your power."

Mrs. Sparsit saw him detain her with his encircling arm, and heard him then and there, within her (Mrs. Sparsit's) greedy hearing, tell her how he loved her, and how she was the stake for which he ardently desired to play away all that he had in life. The objects he had lately pursued, turned worthless beside her; such success as was almost in his grasp, he flung away from him like the dirt it was, compared with her. Its pursuit, nevertheless, if it kept him near her, or its renunciation if it took him from her, or flight if she shared it, or secrecy if she commanded it, or any fate, or every fate, all was alike to him, so that she was true to him,—the man who had seen how cast away she was, whom she had inspired at their first meeting with an admiration, an interest, of which he had thought himself incapable, whom she had received into her confidence, who was devoted to her and adored her. All this, and more, in his hurry, and in hers, in the whirl of her own gratified malice, in the dread of being discovered, in the rapidly increasing noise of heavy rain among the leaves, and a thunderstorm rolling up—Mrs. Sparsit received into her mind, set off with such an unavoidable halo of confusion and indistinctness, that when at length he climbed the fence and led his horse away, she was not sure where they were to meet, or when, except that they had said it was to be that night.

But one of them yet remained in the darkness before her; and while she tracked that one she must be right. "Oh, my dearest love" thought Mrs. Sparsit, "you little think how well attended you are!"

Mrs. Sparsit saw her out of the wood, and saw her enter the house. What to do next? It rained now, in a sheet of water. Mrs. Sparsit's white stockings were of many colours, green predominating; prickly things were in her shoes; caterpillars slung themselves, in hammocks of their own making, from various parts of her dress; rills ran from her bonnet, and her Roman nose. In such condition, Mrs. Sparsit stood hidden in the density of the shrubbery, considering what next?

Lo, Louisa coming out the house! Hastily cloaked and muffled, and stealing away. She elopes! She falls from the lowermost stair, and is swallowed up in the gulf.

Indifferent to the rain, and moving with a quick determined step, she struck into a side-path parallel with the ride. Mrs. Sparsit followed in the shadow of the trees, at but a short distance; for it was not easy to keep a figure in view going quickly through the umbrageous darkness.

When she stopped to close the side-gate without noise, Mrs. Sparsit stopped. When she went on, Mrs. Sparsit went on. She went by the way Mrs. Sparsit had come, emerged from the green lane, crossed the stony road, and ascended the wooden steps to the railroad. A train for Coketown would come through presently, Mrs. Sparsit knew; so she understood Coketown to be her first place of destination.

In Mrs. Sparsit's limp and streaming state, no extensive precautions were necessary to change her usual appearance; but, she stopped under the lee of the station wall, tumbled her shawl into a new shape, and put it on over her bonnet. So disguised she had no fear of being recognized when she followed up the railroad steps, and paid her money in the small office. Louisa sat waiting in a corner. Mrs. Sparsit sat waiting in another corner. Both listened to the thunder, which was loud, and to the rain, as it washed off the roof, and pattered on the parapets of the arches. Two or three lamps were rained out and blown out; so, both saw the lightning to advantage as it quivered and zigzagged on the iron tracks.

The seizure of the station with a fit of trembling, gradually deepening to a complaint of the heart, announced the train. Fire and steam, and smoke, and red light; a hiss, a crash, a bell, and a shriek; Louisa put into one carriage, Mrs. Sparsit put into another: the little station a desert speck in the thunderstorm.

Though her teeth chattered in her head from wet and cold, Mrs. Sparsit exulted hugely. The figure had plunged down the precipice, and she felt herself, as it were, attending on the body. Could she, who had been so active in the getting up of the funeral triumph, do less than exult? "She will be at Coketown long before him," thought Mrs. Sparsit, "though his horse is never so good. Where will she wait for him? And where will they go together? Patience. We shall see."

The tremendous rain occasioned infinite confusion, when the train stopped at its destination. Gutters and pipes had burst, drains had overflowed, and streets were under water. In the first instant of alighting, Mrs. Sparsit turned her distracted eyes towards the waiting coaches, which were in great request. "She will get into one," she considered, "and will be away before I can follow in another. At all risks of being run over, I must see the number, and hear the order given to the coachman."

But, Mrs. Sparsit was wrong in her calculation. Louisa got into no coach, and was already gone. The black eyes kept upon the railroad-carriage in which she had travelled, settled upon it a moment too late. The door not being opened after several minutes, Mrs. Sparsit passed it and repassed it, saw nothing, looked in, and found it empty. Wet through and through: with her feet squelching and squashing in her shoes whenever she moved; with a rash of rain upon her classical visage; with a bonnet like an over-ripe fig; with all her clothes spoiled; with damp impressions of every button, string, and hook-and-eye she wore, printed off upon her highly connected back; with a stagnant verdure on her general exterior, such as accumulates on an old park fence in a mouldy lane; Mrs. Sparsit had no resource but to burst into tears of bitterness and say, "I have lost her!"

Chapter XII.
Down

The national dustmen, after entertaining one another with a great many noisy little fights among themselves, had dispersed for the present, and Mr. Gradgrind was at home for the vacation.

He sat writing in the room with the deadly statistical clock, proving something no doubt—probably, in the main, that the Good Samaritan[1] was a Bad Economist. The noise of the rain did not disturb him much; but it attracted his attention sufficiently to make him raise his head sometimes, as if he were rather remonstrating with the elements. When it thundered very loudly, he glanced towards Coketown, having it in his mind that some of the tall chimneys might be struck by lightning.

The thunder was rolling into distance, and the rain was pouring down like a deluge, when the door of his room opened. He looked round the lamp upon his table, and saw, with amazement, his eldest daughter.

"Louisa!"

"Father, I want to speak to you."

"What is the matter? How strange you look! And good Heaven," said Mr. Gradgrind, wondering more and more, "have you come here exposed to this storm?"

She put her hands to her dress, as if she hardly knew. "Yes." Then she uncovered her head, and letting her cloak and hood fall where they might, stood looking at him: so colourless, so dishevelled, so defiant and despairing, that he was afraid of her.

"What is it? I conjure you, Louisa, tell me what is the matter."

She dropped into a chair before him, and put her cold hand on his arm.

"Father, you have trained me from my cradle?"

"Yes, Louisa."

"I curse the hour in which I was born to such a destiny."

He looked at her in doubt and dread, vacantly repeating: "Curse the hour? Curse the hour?"

"How could you give me life, and take from me all the inappreciable

---

1.   See the parable of Jesus in Luke 10:25–37.

things that raise it from the state of conscious death? Where are the graces of my soul? Where are the sentiments of my heart? What have you done, Oh father, what have you done, with the garden that should have bloomed once, in this great wilderness here!"

She struck herself with both her hands upon her bosom.

"If it had ever been here, its ashes alone would save me from the void in which my whole life sinks. I did not mean to say this; but, father, you remember the last time we conversed in this room?"

He had been so wholly unprepared for what he heard now, that it was with difficulty he answered, "Yes, Louisa."

"What has risen to my lips now, would have risen to my lips then, if you had given me a moment's help. I don't reproach you, father. What you have never nurtured in me, you have never nurtured in yourself; but Oh! if you had only done so long ago, or if you had only neglected me, what a much better and much happier creature I should have been this day!"

On hearing this, after all his care, he bowed his head upon his hand and groaned aloud.

"Father, if you had known, when we were last together here, what even I feared while I strove against it—as it has been my task from infancy to strive against every natural prompting that has arisen in my heart; if you had known that there lingered in my breast, sensibilities, affections, weaknesses capable of being cherished into strength, defying all the calculations ever made by man, and no more known to his arithmetic than his Creator is,—would you have given me to the husband whom I am now sure that I hate?"

He said, "No. No, my poor child."

"Would you have doomed me, at any time, to the frost and blight that have hardened and spoiled me? Would you have robbed me—for no one's enrichment—only for the greater desolation of this world—of the immaterial part of my life, the spring and summer of my belief, my refuge from what is sordid and bad in the real things around me, my school in which I should have learned to be more humble and more trusting with them, and to hope in my little sphere to make them better?"

"Oh no, no. No, Louisa."

"Yet, father, if I had been stone blind; if I had groped my way by my sense of touch, and had been free, while I knew the shapes and surfaces of things, to exercise my fancy somewhat, in regard to them; I should have been a million times wiser, happier, more loving, more contented, more innocent and human in all good respects, than I am with the eyes I have. Now, hear what I have come to say."

He moved, to support her with his arm. She rising as he did so, they stood close together: she, with a hand upon his shoulder, looking fixedly in his face.

"With a hunger and thirst upon me, father, which have never been for a moment appeased; with an ardent impulse towards some region where rules, and figures, and definitions were not quite absolute; I have grown up, battling every inch of my way."

"I never knew you were unhappy, my child."

"Father, I always knew it. In this strife I have almost repulsed and crushed my better angel into a demon. What I have learned has left me doubting, misbelieving, despising, regretting, what I have not learned; and my dismal resource has been to think that life would soon go by, and that nothing in it could be worth the pain and trouble of a contest."

"And you so young, Louisa!" he said with pity.

"And I so young. In this condition, father—for I show you now, without fear or favour, the ordinary deadened state of my mind as I know it—you proposed my husband to me. I took him. I never made a pretence to him or you that I loved him. I knew, and, father, you knew, and he knew, that I never did. I was not wholly indifferent, for I had a hope of being pleasant and useful to Tom. I made that wild escape into something visionary, and have slowly found out how wild it was. But Tom had been the subject of all the little tenderness of my life; perhaps he became so because I knew so well how to pity him. It matters little now, except as it may dispose you to think more leniently of his errors."

As her father held her in his arms, she put her other hand upon his other shoulder, and still looking fixedly in his face, went on.

"When I was irrevocably married, there rose up into rebellion against the tie, the old strife, made fiercer by all those causes of disparity which arise out of our two individual natures, and which no general laws shall ever rule or state for me, father, until they shall be able to direct the anatomist where to strike his knife into the secrets of my soul."

"Louisa!" he said, and said imploringly; for he well remembered what had passed between them in their former interview.

"I do not reproach you, father, I make no complaint. I am here with another object."

"What can I do, child? Ask me what you will."

"I am coming to it. Father, chance then threw into my way a new acquaintance; a man such as I had had no experience of; used to the world; light, polished, easy; making no pretences; avowing the low estimate of everything, that I was half afraid to form in secret; conveying to me almost immediately, though I don't know how or by what degrees, that he understood me, and read my thoughts. I could not find that he was worse than I. There seemed to be a near affinity between us. I only wondered it should be worth his while, who cared for nothing else, to care so much for me."

"For you, Louisa!"

Her father might instinctively have loosened his hold, but that he felt her strength departing from her, and saw a wild dilating fire in the eyes steadfastly regarding him.

"I say nothing of his plea for claiming my confidence. It matters very little how he gained it. Father, he did gain it. What you know of the story of my marriage, he soon knew, just as well."

Her father's face was ashy white, and he held her in both his arms.

"I have done no worse, I have not disgraced you. But if you ask me whether I have loved him, or do love him, I tell you plainly father, that it may be so. I don't know."

She took her hands suddenly from his shoulders, and pressed them both upon her side; while in her face, not like itself—and in her figure, drawn up, resolute to finish by a last effort what she had to say—the feelings long suppressed broke loose.

"This night, my husband being away, he has been with me, declaring himself my lover. This minute he expects me, for I could release myself of his presence by no other means. I do not know that I am sorry, I do not know that I am ashamed. I do not know that I am degraded in my own esteem. All that I know is, your philosophy and your teaching will not save me. Now, father, you have brought me to this. Save me by some other means!"

He tightened his hold in time to prevent her sinking on the floor, but she cried out in a terrible voice, "I shall die if you hold me! Let me fall upon the ground!" And he laid her down there, and saw the pride of his heart and the triumph of his system, lying, an insensible heap, at his feet.

END OF THE SECOND BOOK.

BOOK THE THIRD. GARNERING[1]

CHAPTER I.
ANOTHER THING NEEDFUL

LOUISA AWOKE from a torpor, and her eyes languidly opened on her old bed at home, and her old room. It seemed, at first, as if all that had happened since the days when these objects were familiar to her were the shadows of a dream; but gradually, as the objects became more real to her sight, the events became more real to her mind.

She could scarcely move her head for pain and heaviness, her eyes were strained and sore, and she was very weak. A curious passive inattention had such possession of her, that the presence of her little sister in the room did not attract her notice for some time. Even when their eyes had met, and her sister had approached the bed, Louisa lay for minutes looking at her in silence, and suffering her timidly to hold her passive hand, before she asked: "When was I brought to this room?"

"Last night, Louisa."

"Who brought me here?"

"Sissy, I believe."

"Why do you believe so?"

"Because I found her here this morning. She didn't come to my bedside to wake me, as she always does; and I went to look for her. She was not in her own room either; and I went looking for her all over the house, until I found her here taking care of you and cooling your head. Will you see father? Sissy said I was to tell him when you woke."

"What a beaming face you have, Jane!" said Louisa, as her young sister—timidly still—bent down to kiss her.

"Have I? I am very glad you think so. I am sure it must be Sissy's doing."

---

1.   I.e. gathering produce into a garner or barn. See the General Introduction p. 21.

The arm Louisa had begun to twine around her neck, unbent itself. "You can tell father if you will." Then, staying her for a moment, she said, "It was you who made my room so cheerful, and gave it this look of welcome?"

"Oh no, Louisa, it was done before I came. It was—"

Louisa turned upon her pillow, and heard no more. When her sister had withdrawn, she turned her head back again, and lay with her face towards the door, until it opened and her father entered.

He had a jaded anxious look upon him, and his hand, usually steady, trembled in hers. He sat down at the side of the bed, tenderly asking how she was, and dwelling on the necessity of her keeping very quiet after her agitation and exposure to the weather last night. He spoke in a subdued and troubled voice, very different from his usual dictatorial manner; and was often at a loss for words.

"My dear Louisa. My poor daughter." He was so much at a loss at that place, that he stopped altogether. He tried again.

"My unfortunate child." The place was so difficult to get over, that he tried again.

"It would be hopeless for me, Louisa, to endeavour to tell you how overwhelmed I have been, and still am, by what broke upon me last night. The ground on which I stand has ceased to be solid under my feet. The only support on which I leaned, and the strength of which it seemed, and still does seem, impossible to question, has given way in an instant. I am stunned by these discoveries. I have no selfish meaning in what I say; but I find the shock of what broke upon me last night, to be very heavy indeed."

She could give him no comfort herein. She had suffered the wreck of her whole life upon the rock.

"I will not say, Louisa, that if you had by any happy chance undeceived me some time ago, it would have been better for us both; better for your peace, and better for mine. For I am sensible that it may not have been a part of my system to invite any confidence of that kind. I had proved my—my system to myself, and I have rigidly administered it; and I must bear the responsibility of its failures. I only entreat you to believe, my favourite child, that I have meant to do right."

He said it earnestly, and to do him justice he had. In gauging fathomless deeps with his little mean excise-rod,[1] and in staggering over the universe with his rusty stiff-legged compasses, he had meant to do great things. Within the limits of his short tether he had tumbled about, annihilating the flowers of existence with greater singleness of purpose than many of the blatant personages whose company he kept.

"I am well assured of what you say, father. I know I have been your favourite child. I know you have intended to make me happy. I have never blamed you, and I never shall."

He took her outstretched hand, and retained it in his.

"My dear, I have remained all night at my table, pondering again and again on what has so painfully passed between us. When I consider your character; when I consider that what has been known to me for hours, has been concealed by you for years; when I consider under what immediate pressure it has been forced from you at last; I come to the conclusion that I cannot but mistrust myself."

He might have added more than all,[2] when he saw the face now looking at him. He did add it in effect, perhaps, as he softly moved her scattered hair from her forehead with his hand. Such little actions, slight in another man, were very noticeable in him; and his daughter received them as if they had been words of contrition.

"But," said Mr. Gradgrind, slowly, and with hesitation, as well as with a wretched sense of helplessness, "if I see reason to mistrust myself for the past, Louisa, I should also mistrust myself for the present and the future. To speak unreservedly to you, I do. I am far from feeling convinced now, however differently I might have felt only this time yesterday, that I am fit for the trust you repose in me; that I know how to respond to the appeal you have come home to make to me; that I have the right instinct—supposing it for the moment to be some quality of that nature—how to help you, and to set you right, my child."

She had turned upon her pillow, and lay with her face upon her arm, so that he could not see it. All her wildness and passion had subsided; but, though softened, she was not in tears. Her father was changed in

---

1.   A measuring stick used by customs officials to determine the tax due.
2.   I.e. mistrust himself more than anyone else.

nothing so much as in the respect that he would have been glad to see her in tears.

"Some persons hold," he pursued, still hesitating, "that there is a wisdom of the Head, and that there is a wisdom of the Heart. I have not supposed so; but, as I have said, I mistrust myself now. I have supposed the head to be all-sufficient. It may not be all-sufficient; how can I venture this morning to say it is! If that other kind of wisdom should be what I have neglected, and should be the instinct that is wanted, Louisa—"

He suggested it very doubtfully, as if he were half unwilling to admit it even now. She made him no answer, lying before him on her bed, still half-dressed, much as he had seen her lying on the floor of his room last night.

"Louisa," and his hand rested on her hair again, "I have been absent from here, my dear, a good deal of late; and though your sister's training has been pursued according to—the system," he appeared to come to that word with great reluctance always, "it has necessarily been modified by daily associations begun, in her case, at an early age. I ask you—ignorantly and humbly, my daughter—for the better, do you think?"

"Father," she replied, without stirring, "if any harmony has been awakened in her young breast that was mute in mine until it turned to discord, let her thank Heaven for it, and go upon her happier way, taking it as her greatest blessing that she has avoided my way."

"Oh my child, my child!" he said, in a forlorn manner, "I am an unhappy man to see you thus! What avails it to me that you do not reproach me, if I so bitterly reproach myself!" He bent his head, and spoke low to her. "Louisa, I have a misgiving that some change may have been slowly working about me in this house, by mere love and gratitude: that what the Head had left undone and could not do, the Heart may have been doing silently. Can it be so?"

She made him no reply.

"I am not too proud to believe it, Louisa. How could I be arrogant, and you before me! Can it be so? Is it so, my dear?"

He looked upon her once more, lying cast away there; and without another word went out of the room. He had not been long gone, when she heard a light tread near the door, and knew that some one stood beside her.

She did not raise her head. A dull anger that she should be seen in her distress, and that the involuntary look she had so resented should come to this fulfilment, smouldered within her like an unwholesome fire. All closely imprisoned forces rend and destroy. The air that would be healthful to the earth, the water that would enrich it, the heat that would ripen it, tear it when caged up. So in her bosom even now; the strongest qualities she possessed, long turned upon themselves, became a heap of obduracy, that rose against a friend.

It was well that soft touch came upon her neck, and that she understood herself to be supposed to have fallen asleep. The sympathetic hand did not claim her resentment. Let it lie there, let it lie.

It lay there, warming into life a crowd of gentler thoughts; and she rested. As she softened with the quiet, and the consciousness of being so watched, some tears made their way into her eyes. The face touched hers, and she knew that there were tears upon it too, and she the cause of them.

As Louisa feigned to rouse herself, and sat up, Sissy retired, so that she stood placidly near the bedside.

"I hope I have not disturbed you. I have come to ask if you would let me stay with you?"

"Why should you stay with me? My sister will miss you. You are everything to her."

"Am I?" returned Sissy, shaking her head. "I would be something to you, if I might."

"What?" said Louisa, almost sternly.

"Whatever you want most, if I could be that. At all events, I would like to try to be as near it as I can. And however far off that may be, I will never tire of trying. Will you let me?"

"My father sent you to ask me."

"No indeed," replied Sissy. "He told me that I might come in now, but he sent me away from the room this morning—or at least—" She hesitated and stopped.

"At least, what?" said Louisa, with her searching eyes upon her.

"I thought it best myself that I should be sent away, for I felt very uncertain whether you would like to find me here."

"Have I always hated you so much?"

"I hope not, for I have always loved you, and have always wished that you should know it. But you changed to me a little, shortly before you left home. Not that I wondered at it. You knew so much, and I knew so little, and it was so natural in many ways, going as you were among other friends, that I had nothing to complain of, and was not at all hurt."

Her colour rose as she said it modestly and hurriedly. Louisa understood the loving pretence, and her heart smote her.

"May I try?" said Sissy, emboldened to raise her hand to the neck that was insensibly drooping towards her.

Louisa, taking down the hand that would have embraced her in another moment, held it in one of hers, and answered:

"First, Sissy, do you know what I am? I am so proud and so hardened, so confused and troubled, so resentful and unjust to every one and to myself, that everything is stormy, dark, and wicked to me. Does not that repel you?"

"No!"

"I am so unhappy, and all that should have made me otherwise is so laid waste, that if I had been bereft of sense to this hour, and instead of being as learned as you think me, had to begin to acquire the simplest truths, I could not want a guide to peace, contentment, honour, all the good of which I am quite devoid, more abjectly than I do. Does not that repel you?"

"No!"

In the innocence of her brave affection, and the brimming up of her old devoted spirit, the once deserted girl shone like a beautiful light upon the darkness of the other.

Louisa raised the hand that it might clasp her neck and join its fellow there. She fell upon her knees, and clinging to this stroller's child looked up at her almost with veneration.

"Forgive me, pity me, help me! Have compassion on my great need, and let me lay this head of mind upon a loving heart!"

"Oh lay it here!" cried Sissy. "Lay it here, my dear."\qq

CHAPTER II.
VERY RIDICULOUS

MR. JAMES Harthouse passed a whole night and a day in a state of so much hurry, that the World, with its best glass in its eye,[1] would scarcely have recognized him during that insane interval, as the brother Jem of the honourable and jocular member. He was positively agitated. He several times spoke with an emphasis, similar to the vulgar manner. He went in and went out in an unaccountable way, like a man without an object. He rode like a highwayman. In a word, he was so horribly bored by existing circumstances, that he forgot to go in for boredom in the manner prescribed by the authorities.

After putting his horse at Coketown through the storm, as if it were a leap,[2] he waited up all night: from time to time ringing his bell with the greatest fury, charging the porter who kept watch with delinquency in withholding letters or messages that could not fail to have been entrusted to him, and demanding restitution on the spot. The dawn coming, the morning coming, and the day coming, and neither message nor letter coming with either, he went down to the country house. There, the report was, Mr. Bounderby away, and Mrs. Bounderby in town. Left for town suddenly last evening. Not even known to be gone until receipt of message, importing that her return was not to be expected for the present.

In these circumstances he had nothing for it but to follow her to town. He went to the house in town. Mrs. Bounderby not there. He looked in at the Bank. Mr. Bounderby away and Mrs. Sparsit away. Mrs. Sparsit away? Who could have been reduced to sudden extremity for the company of that griffin![3]

"Well! I don't know," said Tom, who had his own reasons for being uneasy about it. "She was off somewhere at daybreak this morning. She's

---

1.　I.e. wearing a monocle.
2.　I.e. a fence to be jumped over on horseback.
3.　Here probably meaning 'grim, vigilant guardian', by transference from the creature of classical mythology with the body of a lion and head and wings of an eagle, which keeps watch over treasure.

always full of mystery; I hate her. So I do that white chap; he's always got his blinking eyes upon a fellow."

"Where were you last night, Tom?"

"Where was I last night!" said Tom. "Come! I like that. I was waiting for you, Mr. Harthouse, till it came down as *I* never saw it come down before. Where was I too! Where were you, you mean."

"I was prevented from coming—detained."

"Detained!" murmured Tom. "Two of us were detained. I was detained looking for you, till I lost every train but the mail. It would have been a pleasant job to go down by that on such a night, and have to walk home through a pond. I was obliged to sleep in town after all."

"Where?"

"Where? Why, in my own bed at Bounderby's."

"Did you see your sister?"

"How the deuce," returned Tom, staring, "could I see my sister when she was fifteen miles off?"

Cursing these quick retorts of the young gentleman to whom he was so true a friend, Mr. Harthouse disembarrassed himself of that interview with the smallest conceivable amount of ceremony, and debated for the hundredth time what all this could mean? He made only one thing clear. It was, that whether she was in town or out of town, whether he had been premature with her who was so hard to comprehend, or she had lost courage, or they were discovered, or some mischance or mistake, at present incomprehensible, had occurred, he must remain to confront his fortune, whatever it was. The hotel where he was known to live when condemned to that region of blackness, was the stake to which he was tied. As to all the rest—What will be, will be.

"So, whether I am waiting for a hostile message, or an assignation, or a penitent remonstrance, or an impromptu wrestle with my friend Bounderby in the Lancashire manner[1]—which would seem as likely as anything else in the present state of affairs—I'll dine," said Mr. James Harthouse. "Bounderby has the advantage in point of weight; and if

---

1.   I.e. in a particularly rough and violent way.

anything of a British nature[1] is to come off between us, it may be as well to be in training."

Therefore he rang the bell, and tossing himself negligently on a sofa, ordered "Some dinner at six—with a beafsteak in it," and got through the intervening time as well as he could. That was not particularly well; for he remained in the greatest perplexity, and, as the hours went on, and no kind of explanation offered itself, his perplexity augmented at compound interest.

However, he took affairs as coolly as it was in human nature to do, and entertained himself with the facetious idea of the training more than once. "It wouldn't be bad," he yawned at one time, "to give the waiter five shillings, and throw him." At another time it occurred to him, "Or a fellow of about thirteen or fourteen stone might be hired by the hour." But these jests did not tell materially on the afternoon, or his suspense; and, sooth to say, they both lagged fearfully.

It was impossible, even before dinner, to avoid often walking about in the pattern of the carpet, looking out of the window, listening at the door for footsteps, and occasionally becoming rather hot when any steps approached that room. But, after dinner, when the day turned to twilight, and the twilight turned to night, and still no communication was made to him, it began to be as he expressed it, "like the Holy Office and slow torture."[2] However, still true to his conviction that indifference was the genuine high-breeding (the only conviction he had), he seized this crisis as the opportunity for ordering candles and a newspaper.

He had been trying in vain, for half an hour, to read this newspaper, when the waiter appeared and said, at once mysteriously and apologetically:

"Beg your pardon, sir. You're wanted, sir, if you please."

A general recollection that this was the kind of thing the Police said to the swell mob,[3] caused Mr. Harthouse to ask the waiter in return, with bristling indignation, what the Devil he meant by "wanted"?

---

1. I.e. anything violent or barbaric, by association with the ancient Britons.
2. The Inquisition, the ecclesiastical court established in mediaeval Europe to suppress heresy and which became notorious for its use of torture.
3. Thieves who assumes the clothes and manners of gentlemen to disguise their true activities.

"Beg your pardon, sir. Young lady outside, sir, wishes to see you."

"Outside? Where?"

"Outside this door, sir."

Giving the waiter to the personage before mentioned, as a blockhead duly qualified for that consignment, Mr. Harthouse hurried into the gallery. A young woman whom he had never seen stood there. Plainly dressed, very quiet, very pretty. As he conducted her into the room and placed a chair for her, he observed, by the light of the candles, that she was even prettier than he had at first believed. Her face was innocent and youthful, and its expression remarkably pleasant. She was not afraid of him, or in any way disconcerted; she seemed to have her mind entirely preoccupied with the occasion of her visit, and to have substituted that consideration for herself.

"I speak to Mr. Harthouse?" she said, when they were alone.

"To Mr. Harthouse." He added in his mind, "And you speak to him with the most confiding eyes I ever saw, and the most earnest voice (though so quiet) I ever heard."

"If I do not understand—and I do not, sir"—said Sissy, "what your honour as a gentleman binds you to, in other matters:" the blood really rose in his face as she began these words: "I am sure I may rely upon it to keep my visit secret, and to keep secret what I am going to say. I will rely upon it, if you will tell me I may so far trust—"

"You may, I assure you."

"I am young, as you see; I am alone, as you see. In coming to you, sir, I have no advice or encouragement beyond my own hope."

He thought, "But that is very strong," as he followed the momentary upward glance of her eyes. He thought besides, "This is a very odd beginning. I don't see where we are going."

"I think," said Sissy, "you have already guessed whom I left just now!"

"I have been in the greatest concern and uneasiness during the last four-and-twenty hours (which have appeared as many years)," he returned, "on a lady's account. The hopes I have been encouraged to form that you come from that lady, do not deceive me, I trust."

"I left her within an hour."

"At—!"

"At her father's."

Mr. Harthouse's face lengthened in spite of his coolness, and his perplexity increased. "Then I certainly," he thought, "do *not* see where we are going."

"She hurried there last night. She arrived there in great agitation, and was insensible all through the night. I live at her father's, and was with her. You may be sure, sir, you will never see her again as long as you live."

Mr. Harthouse drew a long breath; and, if ever man found himself in the position of not knowing what to say, made the discovery beyond all question that he was so circumstanced. The child-like ingenuousness with which his visitor spoke, her modest fearlessness, her truthfulness which put all artifice aside, her entire forgetfulness of herself in her earnest quiet holding to the object with which she had come; all this together with her reliance on his easily given promise—which in itself shamed him—presented something in which he was so inexperienced, and against which he knew any of his usual weapons would fall so powerless; that not a word could he rally to his relief.

At last he said:

"So startling an announcement, so confidently made, and by such lips, is really disconcerting in the last degree. May I be permitted to inquire, if you are charged to convey that information to me in those hopeless words, by the lady of whom we speak?"

"I have no charge from her."

"The drowning man catches at the straw. With no disrespect for your judgement, and with no doubt of your sincerity, excuse my saying that I cling to the belief that there is yet hope that I am not condemned to perpetual exile from that lady's presence."

"There is not the least hope. The first object of my coming here, sir, is to assure you that you must believe that there is no more hope of your ever speaking with her again, than there would be if she had died when she came home last night."

"Must believe? But if I can't—or if I should, by infirmity of nature, be obstinate—and won't—"

"It is still true. There is no hope."

James Harthouse looked at her with an incredulous smile upon his lips; but her mind looked over and beyond him, and the smile was quite thrown away.

He bit his lip, and took a little time for consideration.

"Well! If it should unhappily appear," he said, "after due pains and duty on my part, that I am brought to a position so desolate as this banishment, I shall not become the lady's persecutor. But you said you had no commission from her?"

"I have only the commission of my love for her, and her love for me. I have no other trust, than that I have been with her since she came home, and that she has given me her confidence. I have no further trust, than that I know something of her character and her marriage. Oh Mr. Harthouse, I think you had that trust too!"

He was touched in the cavity where his heart should have been—in that nest of addled eggs, where the birds of heaven would have lived[1] if they had not been whistled away—by the fervour of this reproach.

"I am not a moral sort of fellow," he said, "and I never make any pretensions to the character of a moral sort of fellow. I am as immoral as need be. At the same time, in bringing any distress upon the lady who is the subject of the present conversation, or in unfortunately compromising her in any way, or in committing myself by any expression of sentiments towards her, not perfectly reconcilable with—in fact with—the domestic hearth; or in taking any advantage of her father's being a machine, or of her brother's being a whelp, or of her husband's being a bear; I beg to be allowed to assure you that I have had no particularly evil intentions, but have glided on from one step to another with a smoothness so perfectly diabolical, that I had not the slightest idea the catalogue was half so long until I began to turn it over. Whereas I find," said Mr. James Harthouse, in conclusion, "that it is really in several volumes."

Though he said all this in his frivolous way, the way seemed, for that once, a conscious polishing of but an ugly surface. He was silent for a moment; and then proceeded with a more self-possessed air, though with traces of vexation and disappointment that would not be polished out.

"After what has been just now represented to me, in a manner I find it impossible to doubt—I know of hardly any other source from which I could have accepted it so readily—I feel bound to say to you, in whom

---

1. Compare Matthew 13:31-2.

the confidence you have mentioned has been reposed, that I cannot refuse to contemplate the possibility (however unexpected) of my seeing the lady no more. I am solely to blame for the thing having come to this—and—and, I cannot say," he added, rather hard up for a general peroration, "that I have any sanguine expectation of ever becoming a moral sort of fellow, or that I have any belief in any moral sort of fellow whatever."

Sissy's face sufficiently showed that her appeal to him was not finished.

"You spoke," he resumed, as she raised her eyes to him again, "of your first object. I may assume that there is a second to be mentioned?"

"Yes."

"Will you oblige me by confiding it?"

"Mr. Harthouse," returned Sissy, with a blending of gentleness and steadiness that quite defeated him, and with a simple confidence in his being bound to do what she required, that held him at a singular disadvantage, "the only reparation that remains with you, is to leave here immediately and finally. I am quite sure that you can mitigate in no other way the wrong and harm you have done. I am quite sure that it is the only compensation you have left it in your power to make. I do not say that it is much, or that it is enough; but it is something, and it is necessary. Therefore, though without any other authority than I have given you, and even without the knowledge of any other person than yourself and myself, I ask you to depart from this place to-night, under an obligation never to return to it."

If she had asserted any influence over him beyond her plain faith in the truth and right of what she said; if she had concealed the least doubt or irresolution, or had harboured for the best purpose any reserve or pretence; if she had shown, or felt, the lightest trace of any sensitiveness to his ridicule or his astonishment, or any remonstrance he might offer; he would have carried it against her at this point. But he could as easily have changed a clear sky by looking at it in surprise, as affect her.

"But do you know," he asked, quite at a loss, "the extent of what you ask? You probably are not aware that I am here on a public kind of business, preposterous enough in itself, but which I have gone in for, and sworn by, and am supposed to be devoted to in quite a desperate manner? You probably are not aware of that, but I assure you it's the fact."

It had no effect on Sissy, fact or no fact.

"Besides which," said Mr. Harthouse, taking a turn or two across the room, dubiously, "it's so alarmingly absurd. It would make a man so ridiculous, after going in for these fellows, to back out in such an incomprehensible way."

"I am quite sure," repeated Sissy, "that it is the only reparation in your power, sir. I am quite sure, or I would not have come here."

He glanced at her face, and walked about again. "Upon my soul, I don't know what to say. So immensely absurd!"

It fell to his lot, now, to stipulate for secrecy.

"If I were to do such a very ridiculous thing," he said, stopping again presently, and leaning against the chimney-piece, "it could only be in the most inviolable confidence."

"I will trust to you, sir," returned Sissy, "and you will trust to me."

His leaning against the chimney-piece reminded him of the night with the whelp. It was the self-same chimney-piece, and somehow he felt as if he were the whelp to-night. He could make no way at all.

"I suppose a man never was placed in a more ridiculous position," he said, after looking down, and looking up, and laughing, and frowning, and walking off, and walking back again. "But I see no way out of it. What will be, will be. *This* will be, I suppose. I must take off myself, I imagine—in short, I engage to do it."

Sissy rose. She was not surprised by the result, but she was happy in it, and her face beamed brightly.

"You will permit me to say," continued Mr. James Harthouse, "that I doubt if any other ambassador, or ambassadress, could have addressed me with the same success. I must not only regard myself as being in a very ridiculous position, but as being vanquished at all points. Will you allow me the privilege of remembering my enemy's name?"

"*My* name?" said the ambassadress.

"The only name I could possibly care to know, to-night."

"Sissy Jupe."

"Pardon my curiosity at parting. Related to the family?"

"I am only a poor girl," returned Sissy. "I was separated from my father—he was only a stroller—and taken pity on by Mr. Gradgrind. I have lived in the house ever since."

She was gone.

"It wanted this to complete the defeat," said Mr. James Harthouse, sinking, with a resigned air, on the sofa, after standing transfixed a little while. "The defeat may now be considered perfectly accomplished. Only a poor girl—only a stroller—only James Harthouse made nothing of—only James Harthouse a Great Pyramid of failure."[1]

The Great Pyramid put it into his head to go up the Nile. He took a pen upon the instant, and wrote the following note (in appropriate hieroglyphics) to his brother:

> Dear Jack,—All up at Coketown. Bored out of the place, and going in for camels.   Affectionately, JEM.

He rang the bell.

"Send my fellow here."

"Gone to bed, sir."

"Tell him to get up, and pack up."

He wrote two more notes. One, to Mr. Bounderby, announcing his retirement from that part of the country, and showing where he would be found for the next fortnight. The other, similar in effect, to Mr. Gradgrind. Almost as soon as the ink was dry upon their superscriptions, he had left the tall chimneys of Coketown behind, and was in a railway carriage, tearing and glaring over the dark landscape.

The moral sort of fellows might suppose that Mr. James Harthouse derived some comfortable reflections afterwards, from this prompt retreat, as one of his few actions that made any amends for anything, and as a token to himself that he had escaped the climax of a very bad business. But it was not so, at all. A secret sense of having failed and been ridiculous—a dread of what other fellows who went in for similar sorts of things, would say at his expense if they knew it—so oppressed him, that what was about the very best passage in his life was the one of all others he would not have owned to on any account, and the only one that made him ashamed of himself.

---

1.   Presumably by extension from the phrase 'monumental failure.'

CHAPTER III.
VERY DECIDED

THE INDEFATIGABLE Mrs. Sparsit, with a violent cold upon her, her voice reduced to a whisper, and her stately frame so racked by continual sneezes that it seemed in danger of dismemberment, gave chase to her patron until she found him in the metropolis; and there, majestically sweeping in upon him at his hotel in St. James's Street, exploded the combustibles with which she was charged, and blew up. Having executed her mission with infinite relish, this high-minded woman then fainted away on Mr. Bounderby's coat-collar.

Mr. Bounderby's first procedure was to shake Mrs. Sparsit off, and leave her to progress as she might through various stages of suffering on the floor. He next had recourse to the administration of potent restoratives, such as screwing the patient's thumbs,[1] smiting her hands, abundantly watering her face, and inserting salt in her mouth. When these attentions had recovered her (which they speedily did), he hustled her into a fast train without offering any other refreshment, and carried her back to Coketown more dead than alive.

Regarded as a classical ruin, Mrs. Sparsit was an interesting spectacle on her arrival at her journey's end; but considered in any other light, the amount of damage she had by that time sustained was excessive, and impaired her claims to admiration. Utterly heedless of the wear and tear of her clothes and constitution, and adamant to her pathetic sneezes, Mr. Bounderby immediately crammed her into a coach, and bore her off to Stone Lodge.

"Now, Tom Gradgrind," said Bounderby, bursting into his father-in-law's room late at night; "here's a lady here—Mrs. Sparsit—you know Mrs. Sparsit—who has something to say to you that will strike you dumb."

"You have missed my letter!" exclaimed Mr. Gradgrind, surprised by the apparition.

"Missed your letter, sir!" bawled Bounderby. "The present time is no time for letters. No man shall talk to Josiah Bounderby of Coketown about letters, with his mind in the state it's in now."

---

1.   Torturing by using a thumb-screw (comic exaggeration).

"Bounderby," said Mr. Gradgrind, in a tone of temperate remonstrance, "I speak of a very special letter I have written to you, in reference to Louisa."

"Tom Gradgrind," replied Bounderby, knocking the flat of his hand several times with great vehemence on the table, "I speak of a very special messenger that has come to me, in reference to Louisa. Mrs. Sparsit, ma'am, stand forward!"

That unfortunate lady hereupon essaying to offer testimony, without any voice and with painful gestures expressive of an inflamed throat, became so aggravating and underwent so many facial contortions, that Mr. Bounderby, unable to bear it, seized her by the arm and shook her.

"If you can't get it out, ma'am," said Bounderby, "leave *me* to get it out. This is not a time for a lady, however highly connected, to be totally inaudible, and seemingly swallowing marbles. Tom Gradgrind, Mrs. Sparsit latterly found herself, by accident, in a situation to overhear a conversation out of doors between your daughter and your precious gentleman-friend, Mr. James Harthouse."

"Indeed!" said Mr. Gradgrind.

"Ah! Indeed!" cried Bounderby. "And in that conversation—"

"It is not necessary to repeat its tenor, Bounderby. I know what passed."

"You do? Perhaps," said Bounderby, staring with all his might at his so quiet and assuasive father-in-law, "you know where your daughter is at the present time!"

"Undoubtedly. She is here."

"Here?"

"My dear Bounderby, let me beg you to restrain these loud outbreaks, on all accounts. Louisa is here. The moment she could detach herself from that interview with the person of whom you speak, and whom I deeply regret to have been the means of introducing to you, Louisa hurried here, for protection. I myself had not been at home many hours, when I received her—here, in this room. She hurried by the train to town, she ran from town to this house through a raging storm, and presented herself before me in a state of distraction. Of course, she has remained here ever since. Let me entreat you, for your own sake and for hers, to be more quiet."

Mr. Bounderby silently gazed about him for some moments, in every direction except Mrs. Sparsit's direction; and then, abruptly turning upon the niece of Lady Scadgers, said to that wretched woman:

"Now, ma'am! We shall be happy to hear any little apology you may think proper to offer, for going about the country at express pace, with no other luggage than a Cock-and-a-Bull,[1] ma'am!"

"Sir," whispered Mrs. Sparsit, "my nerves are at present too much shaken, and my health is at present too much impaired, in your service, to admit of my doing more than taking refuge in tears."

(Which she did.)

"Well, ma'am," said Bounderby, "without making any observation to you that may not be made without propriety to a woman of good family, what I have got to add to that, is that there is something else in which it appears to me you may take refuge, namely, a coach. And the coach in which we came here being at the door, you'll allow me to hand you down to it, and pack you home to the Bank: where the best course for you to pursue, will be to put your feet into the hottest water you can bear, and take a glass of scalding rum and butter after you get into bed." With these words, Mr. Bounderby extended his right hand to the weeping lady, and escorted her to the conveyance in question, shedding many plaintive sneezes by the way. He soon returned alone.

"Now, as you showed me in your face, Tom Gradgrind, that you wanted to speak to me," he resumed, "here I am. But, I am not in a very agreeable state, I tell you plainly: not relishing this business, even as it is, and not considering that I am at any time as dutifully and submissively treated by your daughter, as Josiah Bounderby of Coketown ought to be treated by his wife. You have your opinion, I dare say; and I have mine, I know. If you mean to say anything to me to-night, that goes against this candid remark, you had better let it alone."

Mr. Gradgrind, it will be observed, being much softened, Mr. Bounderby took particular pains to harden himself at all points. It was his amiable nature.

"My dear Bounderby," Mr. Gradgrind began in reply.

"Now, you'll excuse me," said Bounderby, "but I don't want to be

---

1.   An idle, nonsensical story.

too dear. That, to start with. When I begin to be dear to a man, I generally find that his intention is to come over me. I am not speaking to you politely; but, as you are aware, I am *not* polite. If you like politeness, you know where to get it. You have your gentleman-friends, you know, and they'll serve you with as much of the article as you want. I don't keep it myself."

"Bounderby," urged Mr. Gradgrind, "we are all liable to mistakes—"

"I thought you couldn't make 'em," interrupted Bounderby.

"Perhaps I thought so. But, I say we are all liable to mistakes; and I should feel sensible of your delicacy, and grateful for it, if you would spare me these references to Harthouse. I shall not associate him in our conversation with your intimacy and encouragement; pray do not persist in connecting him with mine."

"I never mentioned his name!" said Bounderby.

"Well, well!" returned Mr. Gradgrind, with a patient, even a submissive, air. And he sat for a little while pondering. "Bounderby, I see reason to doubt whether we have ever quite understood Louisa."

"Who do you mean by We?"

"Let me say I, then," he returned, in answer to the coarsely blurted question; "I doubt whether I have understood Louisa. I doubt whether I have been quite right in the manner of her education."

"There you hit it," returned Bounderby. "There I agree with you. You have found it out at last, have you? Education! I'll tell you what education is—To be tumbled out of doors, neck and crop, and put upon the shortest allowance of everything except blows. That's what *I* call education."

"I think your good sense will perceive," Mr. Gradgrind remonstrated in all humility, "that whatever the merits of such a system may be, it would be difficult of general application to girls."

"I don't see it at all, sir," returned the obstinate Bounderby.

"Well," sighed Mr. Gradgrind, "we will not enter into the question. I assure you I have no desire to be controversial. I seek to repair what is amiss, if I possibly can; and I hope you will assist me in a good spirit, Bounderby, for I have been very much distressed."

"I don't understand you, yet," said Bounderby, with determined obstinacy, "and therefore I won't make any promises."

"In the course of a few hours, my dear Bounderby," Mr. Gradgrind proceeded, in the same depressed and propitiatory manner, "I appear to myself to have become better informed as to Louisa's character, than in previous years. The enlightenment has been painfully forced upon me, and the discovery is not mine. I think there are—Bounderby, you will be surprised to hear me say this—I think there are qualities in Louisa, which—which have been harshly neglected, and—and a little perverted. And—and I would suggest to you, that—that if you would kindly meet me in a timely endeavour to leave her to her better nature for a while—and encourage it to develop itself by tenderness and consideration—it—it would be the better for the happiness of us. Louisa," said Mr. Gradgrind, shading his face with his hand, "has always been my favourite child."

The blustrous Bounderby crimsoned and swelled to such an extent on hearing these words, that he seemed to be, and probably was, on the brink of a fit. With his very ears a bright purple shot with crimson, he pent up his indignation, however, and said:

"You'd like to keep her here for a time?"

"I—I had intended to recommend, my dear Bounderby, that you should allow Louisa to remain here on a visit, and be attended by Sissy (I mean of course Cecilia Jupe), who understands her, and in whom she trusts."

"I gather from all this, Tom Gradgrind," said Bounderby, standing up with his hands in his pockets, "that you are of opinion that there's what people call some incompatibility between Loo Bounderby and myself."

"I fear there is at present a general incompatibility between Louisa, and—and—and almost all relations in which I have placed her," was her father's sorrowful reply.

"Now, look you here, Tom Gradgrind," said Bounderby the flushed, confronting him with his legs wide apart, his hands deeper in his pockets, and his hair like a hayfield wherein his windy anger was boisterous. "You have said your say; I am going to say mine. I am a Coketown man. I am Josiah Bounderby of Coketown. I know the bricks of this town, and I know the works of this town, and I know the chimneys of this town, and I know the smoke of this town, and I know the Hands of this town. I know 'em all pretty well. They're real. When a man tells me anything about imaginative qualities, I always tell that man, whoever he is, that I know what he means. He means turtle soup and venison, with a gold spoon, and that he wants to be set up with a coach and six. That's what your daughter wants. Since you are of opinion that she ought to have what she wants, I recommend you to provide it for her. Because, Tom Gradgrind, she will never have it from me."

"Bounderby," said Mr. Gradgrind, "I hoped, after my entreaty, you would have taken a different tone."

"Just wait a bit," retorted Bounderby; "you have said your say, I believe. I heard you out; hear me out, if you please. Don't make yourself a spectacle of unfairness as well as inconsistency, because, although I am sorry to see Tom Gradgrind reduced to his present position, I should be doubly sorry to see him brought so low as that. Now, there's an incompatibility of some sort or another, I am given to understand by you, between your daughter and me. I'll give *you* to understand, in reply to that, that there unquestionably is an incompatibility of the first magnitude—to be summed up in this—that your daughter don't properly know her husband's merits, and is not impressed with such a sense as would become her, by George! of the honour of his alliance. That's plain speaking, I hope."

"Bounderby," urged Mr. Gradgrind, "this is unreasonable."

"Is it?" said Bounderby. "I am glad to hear you say so. Because when Tom Gradgrind, with his new lights, tells me that what I say is unreasonable, I am convinced at once it must be devilish sensible. With your permission, I am going on. You know my origin; and you know that for a good many years of my life I didn't want a shoeing-horn, in consequence of not having a shoe. Yet you may believe or not, as you think proper, that there are ladies—born ladies—belonging to families—Families!—who next to worship the ground I walk on."

He discharged this like a Rocket, at his father-in-law's head.

"Whereas your daughter," proceeded Bounderby, "is far from being a born lady. That you know, yourself. Not that I care a pinch of candle-snuff about such things, for you are very well aware I don't; but that such is the fact, and you, Tom Gradgrind, can't change it. Why do I say this?"

"Not, I fear," observed Mr. Gradgrind, in a low voice, "to spare me."

"Hear me out," said Bounderby, "and refrain from cutting in till your turn comes round. I say this, because highly connected females have been astonished to see the way in which your daughter has conducted herself, and to witness her insensibility. They have wondered how I have suffered it. And I wonder myself now, and I won't suffer it."

"Bounderby," returned Mr. Gradgrind, rising, "the less we say to-night the better, I think."

"On the contrary, Tom Gradgrind, the more we say to-night, the better, I think. That is," the consideration checked him, "till I have said all I mean to say, and then I don't care how soon we stop. I come to a question that may shorten the business. What do you mean by the proposal you made just now?"

"What do I mean, Bounderby?"

"By your visiting proposition," said Bounderby, with an inflexible jerk of the hayfield.

"I mean that I hope you may be induced to arrange in a friendly manner, for allowing Louisa a period of repose and reflection here, which may tend to a gradual alteration for the better in many respects."

"To a softening down of your ideas of the incompatibility?" said Bounderby.

"If you put it in those terms."

"What made you think of this?" said Bounderby.

"I have already said, I fear Louisa has not been understood. Is it asking too much, Bounderby, that you, so far her elder, should aid in trying to set her right? You have accepted a great charge of her; for better for worse, for—"

Mr. Bounderby may have been annoyed by the repetition of his own words to Stephen Blackpool, but he cut the quotation short with an angry start.

"Come!" said he, "I don't want to be told about that. I know what I took her for, as well as you do. Never you mind what I took her for; that's my look out."

"I was merely going to remark, Bounderby, that we may all be more or less in the wrong, not even excepting you; and that some yielding on your part, remembering the trust you have accepted, may not only be an act of true kindness, but perhaps a debt incurred towards Louisa."

"I think differently," blustered Bounderby. "I am going to finish this business according to my own opinions. Now, I don't want to make a quarrel of it with you, Tom Gradgrind. To tell you the truth, I don't think it would be worthy of my reputation to quarrel on such a subject. As to your gentleman-friend, he may take himself off, wherever he likes best. If he falls in my way, I shall tell him my mind; if he don't fall in my way, I shan't, for it won't be worth my while to do it. As to your daughter, whom I made Loo Bounderby, and might have done better by leaving Loo Gradgrind, if she don't come home to-morrow, by twelve o'clock at noon, I shall understand that she prefers to stay away, and I shall send her wearing apparel and so forth over here, and you'll take charge of her for the future. What I shall say to people in general, for the incompatibility that led to my so laying down the law, will be this. I am Josiah Bounderby, and I had my bringing-up; she's the daughter of Tom Gradgrind and she had her bringing-up; and the two horses wouldn't pull together. I am pretty well known to be rather an uncommon man, I believe; and most people will understand fast enough that it must be a woman rather out of the common, also, who, in the long run, would come up to my mark."

"Let me seriously entreat you to reconsider this, Bounderby," urged Mr. Gradgrind, "before you commit yourself to such a decision."

"I always come to a decision," said Bounderby, tossing his hat on: "and whatever I do, I do at once. I should be surprised at Tom Gradgrind's addressing such a remark to Josiah Bounderby of Coketown, knowing what he knows of him, if I could be surprised by anything Tom Gradgrind did, after making himself a party to sentimental humbug. I have given you my decision, and I have got no more to say. Good night!"

So Mr. Bounderby went home to his town house to bed. At five minutes past twelve o'clock next day, he directed Mrs. Bounderby's property to be carefully packed up and sent to Tom Gradgrind's; advertised his country retreat for sale by private contract; and resumed a bachelor life.

Chapter IV.
Lost

THE ROBBERY at the Bank had not languished before, and did not cease to occupy a front place in the attention of the principal of that establishment now. In boastful proof of his promptitude and activity, as a remarkable man, and a self-made man, and a commercial wonder more admirable than Venus, who had risen out of the mud instead of the sea,[1] he liked to show how little his domestic affairs abated his business ardour. Consequently, in the first few weeks of his resumed bachelorhood, he even advanced upon his usual display of bustle, and every day made such a rout in renewing his investigations into the robbery, that the officers who had it in hand almost wished it had never been committed.

They were at fault too, and off the scent. Although they had been so quiet since the first outbreak of the matter, that most people really did suppose it to have been abandoned as hopeless, nothing new occurred. No implicated man or woman took untimely courage, or made a self-betraying step. More remarkable yet, Stephen Blackpool could not be heard of, and the mysterious old woman remained a mystery.

Things having come to this pass, and showing no latent signs of stirring beyond it, the upshot of Mr. Bounderby's investigations was, that he resolved to hazard a bold burst. He drew up a placard, offering Twenty Pounds reward for the apprehension of Stephen Blackpool, suspected of complicity in the robbery of Coketown Bank on such a night; he described the said Stephen Blackpool by dress, complexion, estimated height, and manner, as minutely as he could; he recited how he had left the town, and in what direction he had been last seen going; he had the whole printed in great black letters on a staring broadsheet; and he caused the walls to be posted with it in the dead of night, so that it should strike upon the sight of the whole population at one blow.

The factory-bells had need to ring their loudest that morning to disperse the groups of workers who stood in the tardy daybreak, collected round the placards, devouring them with eager eyes. Not the least eager

---

1.   In *Theogony*, Hesiod (8th century BC) describes the birth of Venus from the sea's foam.

of the eyes assembled, were the eyes of those who could not read. These people, as they listened to the friendly voice that read aloud—there was always some such ready to help them—stared at the characters which meant so much with a vague awe and respect that would have been half ludicrous, if any aspect of public ignorance could ever be otherwise than threatening and full of evil.[1] Many ears and eyes were busy with the vision of the matter of these placards, among turning spindles, rattling looms, and whirling wheels, for hours afterwards; and when the Hands cleared out again into the streets, there were still as many readers as before.

Slackbridge, the delegate, had to address his audience too that night; and Slackbridge had obtained a clean bill from the printer, and had brought it in his pocket. Oh, my friends and fellow-countrymen, the down-trodden operatives of Coketown, oh, my fellow-brothers and fellow-workmen and fellow-citizens and fellow-men, what a to-do there was there, when Slackbridge unfolded what he called the "damning document," and held it up to the gaze, and for the execration of the working-man community! "Oh, my fellow-men, behold of what a traitor in the camp of those great spirits who are enrolled upon the holy scroll of Justice and of Union, is appropriately capable! Oh, my prostrate friends, with the galling yoke of tyrants on your necks and the iron foot of despotism treading down your fallen forms into the dust of the earth, upon which right glad would your oppressors be to see you creeping on your bellies all the days of your lives, like the serpent in the garden[2]—oh, my brothers, and shall I as a man not add, my sisters too, what do you say, *now*, of Stephen Blackpool, with a slight stoop in his shoulders and about five foot seven in height, as set forth in this degrading and disgusting document, this blighting bill, this pernicious placard, this abominable advertisement; and with what majesty of denouncement will you crush the viper, who would bring this stain and shame upon the God-like race that happily has cast him out for ever! Yes, my compatriots, happily cast him out and sent him forth! For you remember how he stood here before you on this platform; you remember how, face to face and foot to foot, I pursued him through all his intricate windings; you remember how he sneaked and slunk, and

---

1.   On levels of literacy in the period, see ALTICK pp.166-72.
2.   See the story of the Fall in Genesis 3:1-21.

sidled, and splitted of straws, until, with not an inch of ground on which to cling, I hurled him out from amongst us: an object for the undying finger of scorn to point at, and for the avenging of every free and thinking mind to scorch and sear! And now, my friends—my labouring friends, for I rejoice and triumph in that stigma—my friends whose hard but honest beds are made in toil, and whose scanty but independent pots are boiled in hardship; and now, I say, my friends, what appellation has that dastard craven taken to himself, when, with the mask torn from his features, he stands before us in all his native deformity, a What? A thief! A plunderer! A proscribed fugitive, with a price upon his head; a fester and a wound upon the noble character of the Coketown operative! Therefore, my band of brothers in a sacred bond, to which your children and your children's children yet unborn have set their infant hands and seals, I propose to you on the part of the United Aggregate Tribunal, ever watchful of your welfare, ever zealous for your benefit, that this meeting does Resolve: That Stephen Blackpool, weaver, referred to in this placard, having been already solemnly disowned by the community of Coketown Hands, the same are free from the shame of his misdeeds, and cannot as a class be reproached with his dishonest actions!"

Thus Slackbridge; gnashing and perspiring after a prodigious sort. A few stern voices called out "No!" and a score or two hailed, with assenting cries of "Hear, hear!" the caution from one man, "Slackbridge, y'or over hetter in't; y'or a goen too fast!" But these were pigmies against an army; the general assemblage subscribed to the gospel according to Slackbridge, and gave three cheers for him, as he sat demonstratively panting at them.

These men and women were yet in the streets, passing quietly to their homes, when Sissy, who had been called away from Louisa some minutes before, returned.

"Who is it?" asked Louisa.

"It is Mr. Bounderby," said Sissy, timid of the name, "and your brother, Mr. Tom, and a young woman who says her name is Rachael, and that you know her."

"What do they want, Sissy dear?"

"They want to see you. Rachael has been crying, and seems angry."

"Father," said Louisa, for he was present, "I cannot refuse to see them, for a reason that will explain itself. Shall they come in here?"

As he answered in the affirmative, Sissy went away to bring them. She reappeared with them directly. Tom was last; and remained standing in the obscurest part of the room, near the door.

"Mrs. Bounderby," said her husband, entering with a cool nod, "I don't disturb you, I hope. This is an unseasonable hour, but here is a young woman who has been making statements which render my visit necessary. Tom Gradgrind, as your son, young Tom, refuses for some obstinate reason or other to say anything at all about those statements, good or bad, I am obliged to confront her with your daughter."

"You have seen me once before, young lady," said Rachael, standing in front of Louisa.

Tom coughed.

"You have seen me, young lady," repeated Rachael, as she did not answer, "once before."

Tom coughed again.

"I have."

Rachael cast her eyes proudly towards Mr. Bounderby, and said, "Will you make it known, young lady, where, and who was there?"

"I went to the house where Stephen Blackpool lodged, on the night of his discharge from his work, and I saw you there. He was there too; and an old woman who did not speak, and whom I could scarcely see, stood in a dark corner. My brother was with me."

"Why couldn't you say so, young Tom?" demanded Bounderby.

"I promised my sister I wouldn't." Which Louisa hastily confirmed. "And besides," said the whelp bitterly, "she tells her own story so precious well—and so full—that what business had I to take it out of her mouth!"

"Say, young lady, if you please," pursued Rachael, "why, in an evil hour, you ever came to Stephen's that night."

"I felt compassion for him," said Louisa, her colour deepening, "and I wished to know what he was going to do, and wished to offer him assistance."

"Thank you, ma'am," said Bounderby. "Much flattered and obliged."

"Did you offer him," asked Rachael, "a bank-note?"

"Yes; but he refused it, and would only take two pounds in gold."

Rachael cast her eyes towards Mr. Bounderby again.

"Oh, certainly!" said Bounderby. "If you put the question whether your ridiculous and improbable account was true or not, I am bound to say it's confirmed."

"Young lady," said Rachael, "Stephen Blackpool is now named as a thief in public print all over this town, and where else! There have been a meeting to-night where he have been spoken of in the same shameful way. Stephen! The honestest lad, the truest lad, the best!" Her indignation failed her, and she broke off sobbing.

"I am very, very sorry," said Louisa.

"Oh, young lady, young lady," returned Rachael, "I hope you may be, but I don't know! I can't say what you may ha' done! The like of you don't know us, don't care for us, don't belong to us. I am not sure why you may ha' come that night. I can't tell but what you may ha' come wi' some aim of your own, not mindin to what trouble you brought such as the poor lad. I said then, Bless you for coming; and I said it of my heart, you seemed to take so pitifully to him; but I don't know now, I don't know!"

Louisa could not reproach her for her unjust suspicions; she was so faithful to her idea of the man, and so afflicted.

"And when I think," said Rachael through her sobs, "that the poor lad was so grateful, thinkin you so good to him—when I mind that he put his hand over his hard-worken face to hide the tears that you brought up there—Oh, I hope you may be sorry, and ha' no bad cause to be it; but I don't know, I don't know!"

"You're a pretty article," growled the whelp, moving uneasily in his dark corner, "to come here with these precious imputations! You ought to be bundled out for not knowing how to behave yourself, and you would be by rights."

She said nothing in reply; and her low weeping was the only sound that was heard, until Mr. Bounderby spoke.

"Come!" said he, "you know what you have engaged to do. You had better give your mind to that; not this."

" 'Deed, I am loath," returned Rachael, drying her eyes, "that any here should see me like this; but I won't be seen so again. Young lady, when I had read what's put in print of Stephen—and what has just as much truth in it as if it had been put in print of you—I went straight to the Bank to say I knew where Stephen was, and to give a sure and certain promise that he should be here in two days. I couldn't meet wi' Mr. Bounderby then, and your brother sent me away, and I tried to find you, but you was not to be found, and I went back to work. Soon as I come out of the Mill to-night, I hastened to hear what was said of Stephen—for I know wi' pride he will come back to shame it!—and then I went again to seek Mr. Bounderby, and I found him, and I told him every word I knew; and he believed no word I said, and brought me here."

"So far, that's true enough," assented Mr. Bounderby, with his hands in his pockets and his hat on. "But I have known you people before to-day, you'll observe, and I know you never die for want of talking. Now, I recommend you not so much to mind talking just now, as doing. You have undertaken to do something; all I remark upon that at present is, do it!"

"I have written to Stephen by the post that went out this afternoon, as I have written him once before sin' he went away," said Rachael; "and he will be here, at furthest, in two days."

"Then, I'll tell you something. You are not aware perhaps," retorted Mr. Bounderby, "that you yourself have been looked after now and then, not being considered quite free from suspicion in this business, on account of most people being judged according to the company they keep. The post-office hasn't been forgotten either. What I'll tell you is, that no letter to Stephen Blackpool has ever got into it. Therefore, what has become of yours, I leave you to guess. Perhaps you're mistaken, and never wrote any."

"He hadn't been gone from here, young lady," said Rachael, turning appealingly to Louisa, "as much as a week, when he sent me the only letter I have had from him, saying that he was forced to seek work in another name."

"Oh, by George!" cried Bounderby, shaking his head, with a whistle, "he changes his name, does he! That's rather unlucky, too, for such an immaculate chap. It's considered a little suspicious in Courts of Justice, I believe, when an Innocent happens to have many names."

"What," said Rachael with tears in her eyes again, "what, young lady, in the name of Mercy, was left the poor lad to do! The masters against him on one hand, the men against him on the other, he only wantin to work hard in peace, and do what he felt right. Can a man have no soul of his own, no mind of his own? Must he go wrong all through wi' this side, or must he go wrong all through wi' that, or else be hunted like a hare?"

"Indeed, indeed, I pity him from my heart," returned Louisa; "and I hope that he will clear himself."

"You need have no fear of that, young lady. He is sure!"

"All the surer, I suppose," said Mr. Bounderby, "for your refusing to tell where he is? Eh?"

"He shall not, through any act of mine, come back wi' the unmerited reproach of being brought back. He shall come back of his own accord to clear himself, and put all those that have injured his good character, and he not here for its defence, to shame. I have told him what has been done against him," said Rachael, throwing off all distrust as a rock throws off the sea, "and he will be here, at furthest, in two days."

"Notwithstanding which," added Mr. Bounderby, "if he can be laid hold of any sooner, he shall have an earlier opportunity of clearing himself. As to you, I have nothing against you; what you came and told me turns out to be true, and I have given you the means of proving it to be true, and there's an end of it. I wish you good night all! I must be off to look a little further into this."

Tom came out of his corner when Mr. Bounderby moved, moved with him, kept close to him, and went away with him. The only parting salutation of which he delivered himself was a sulky "Good night, father!" With a brief speech, and a scowl at his sister, he left the house.

Since his sheet-anchor had come home,[1] Mr. Gradgrind had been sparing of speech. He still sat silent, when Louisa mildly said:

"Rachael, you will not distrust me one day, when you know me better."

"It goes against me," Rachael answered, in a gentler manner, "to mistrust any one; but when I am so mistrusted—when we all are—I cannot

---

1. I.e. since he had lost his utilitarian faith. A sheet-anchor is a ship's largest anchor used only in great emergency, and figuratively comes to mean that on which someone relies when all else has failed.

keep such things quite out of my mind. I ask your pardon for having done you an injury. I don't think what I said now. Yet I might come to think it again, wi' the poor lad so wronged."

"Did you tell him in your letter," inquired Sissy, "that suspicion seemed to have fallen upon him, because he had been seen about the Bank at night? He would then know what he would have to explain on coming back, and would be ready."

"Yes, dear," she returned; "but I can't guess what can have ever taken him there. He never used to go there. It was never in his way. His way was the same as mine, and not near it."

Sissy had already been at her side asking where she lived, and whether she might come to-morrow night, to inquire if there were news of him.

"I doubt," said Rachael, "if he can be here till next day."

"Then I will come next night too," said Sissy.

When Rachael, assenting to this, was gone, Mr. Gradgrind lifted up his head, and said to his daughter:

"Louisa, my dear, I have never, that I know of, seen this man. Do you believe him to be implicated?"

"I think I have believed it, father, though with great difficulty. I do not believe it now."

"That is to say, you once persuaded yourself to believe it, from knowing him to be suspected. His appearance and manner; are they so honest?"

"Very honest."

"And her confidence not to be shaken! I ask myself," said Mr. Gradgrind, musing, "does the real culprit know of these accusations? Where is he? Who is he?"

His hair had latterly began to change its colour. As he leaned upon his hand again, looking gray and old, Louisa, with a face of fear and pity, hurriedly went over to him, and sat close at his side. Her eyes by accident met Sissy's at that moment. Sissy flushed and started, and Louisa put her finger on her lip.

Next night, when Sissy returned home and told Louisa that Stephen was not come, she told it in a whisper. Next night again, when she came home with the same account, and added that he had not been heard of, she spoke in the same low frightened tone. From the moment of that interchange of looks, they never uttered his name, or any reference to him, aloud; nor ever pursued the subject of the robbery, when Mr. Gradgrind spoke of it.

The two appointed days ran out, three days and nights ran out, and Stephen Blackpool was not come, and remained unheard of. On the fourth day, Rachael, with unabated confidence, but considering her despatch to have miscarried, went up to the Bank, and showed her letter from him with his address, at a working colony, one of many, not upon the main road, sixty miles away. Messengers were sent to that place, and the whole town looked for Stephen to be brought in next day.

During this whole time the whelp moved about with Mr. Bounderby like his shadow, assisting in all the proceedings. He was greatly excited, horribly fevered, bit his nails down to the quick, spoke in a hard rattling voice, and with lips that were black and burnt up. At the hour when the suspected man was looked for, the whelp was at the station; offering to wager that he had made off before the arrival of those who were sent in quest of him, and that he would not appear.

The whelp was right. The messengers returned alone. Rachael's letter had gone, Rachael's letter had been delivered. Stephen Blackpool had decamped in that same hour; and no soul knew more of him. The only doubt in Coketown was, whether Rachael had written in good faith, believing that he would really come back, or warning him to fly. On this point opinion was divided.

Six days, seven days, far on into another week. The wretched whelp plucked up a ghastly courage, and began to grow defiant. "*Was* the suspected fellow the thief? A pretty question! If not, where was the man, and why did he not come back?"

Where was the man, and why did he not come back? In the dead of night the echoes of his own words, which had rolled Heaven knows how far away in the daytime, came back instead, and abided by him until morning.

CHAPTER V.
FOUND

DAY AND night again, day and night again. No Stephen Blackpool. Where was the man, and why did he not come back?

Every night, Sissy went to Rachael's lodging, and sat with her in her small neat room. All day, Rachael toiled as such people must toil, whatever their anxieties. The smoke-serpents were indifferent who was lost or found, who turned out bad or good; the melancholy mad elephants, like the Hard Fact men, abated nothing of their set routine, whatever happened. Day and night again, day and night again. The monotony was unbroken. Even Stephen Blackpool's disappearance was falling into the general way, and becoming as monotonous a wonder as any piece of machinery in Coketown.

"I misdoubt," said Rachael, "if there is as many as twenty left in all this place, who have any trust in the poor dear lad now."

She said it to Sissy, as they sat in her lodging, lighted only by the lamp at the street corner. Sissy had come there when it was already dark, to await her return from work; and they had since sat at the window where Rachael had found her, wanting no brighter light to shine on their sorrowful talk.

"If it hadn't been mercifully brought about, that I was to have you to speak to," pursued Rachael, "times are, when I think my mind would not have kept right. But I get hope and strength through you; and you believe that though appearances may rise against him, he will be proved clear?"

"I do believe so," returned Sissy, "with my whole heart. I feel so certain, Rachael, that the confidence you hold in yours against all discouragement, is not like to be wrong, that I have no more doubt of him than if I had known him through as many years of trial as you have."

"And I, my dear," said Rachael, with a tremble in her voice, "have known him through them all, to be, according to his quiet ways, so faithful to everything honest and good, that if he was never to be heard of more, and I was to live to be a hundred years old, I could say with my last breath, God knows my heart. I have never once left trusting Stephen Blackpool!"

"We all believe, up at the Lodge, Rachael, that he will be freed from suspicion, sooner or later."

"The better I know it to be so believed there, my dear," said Rachael, "and the kinder I feel it that you come away from there, purposely to comfort me, and keep me company, and be seen wi' me when I am not yet free from all suspicion myself, the more grieved I am that I should ever have spoken those mistrusting words to the young lady. And yet—"

"You don't mistrust her now, Rachael?"

"Now that you have brought us more together, no. But I can't at all times keep out of my mind—"

Her voice so sunk into a low and slow communing with herself, that Sissy, sitting by her side, was obliged to listen with attention.

"I can't at all times keep out of my mind, mistrustings of some one. I can't think who 'tis, I can't think how or why it may be done, but I mistrust that some one has put Stephen out of the way. I mistrust that by his coming back of his own accord, and showing himself innocent before them all, some one would be confounded, who—to prevent that—has stopped him, and put him out of the way."

"That is a dreadful thought," said Sissy, turning pale.

"It *is* a dreadful thought to think he may be murdered."

Sissy shuddered, and turned paler yet.

"When it makes its way into my mind, dear," said Rachael, "and it will come sometimes, though I do all I can to keep it out, wi' counting on to high numbers as I work, and saying over and over again pieces that I knew when I were a child—I fall into such a wild, hot hurry, that, however tired I am, I want to walk fast, miles and miles. I must get the better of this before bed-time. I'll walk home wi' you."

"He might fall ill upon the journey back," said Sissy, faintly offering a worn-out scrap of hope; "and in such a case, there are many places on the road where he might stop."

"But he is in none of them. He has been sought for in all, and he's not there."

"True," was Sissy's reluctant admission.

"He'd walk the journey in two days. If he was footsore and couldn't walk, I sent him, in the letter he got, the money to ride, lest he should have none of his own to spare."

"Let us hope that to-morrow will bring something better, Rachael. Come into the air!"

Her gentle hand adjusted Rachael's shawl upon her shining black hair in the usual manner of her wearing it, and they went out. The night being fine, little knots of Hands were here and there lingering at street corners; but it was supper-time with the greater part of them, and there were but a few people in the streets.

"You're not so hurried now, Rachael, and your hand is cooler."

"I get better, dear, if I can only walk, and breathe a little fresh. 'Times when I can't, I turn weak and confused."

"But you must not begin to fail, Rachael, for you may be wanted at any time to stand by Stephen. To-morrow is Saturday. If no news comes to-morrow, let us walk in the country on Sunday morning, and strengthen you for another week. Will you go?"

"Yes, dear."

They were by this time in the street where Mr. Bounderby's house stood. The way to Sissy's destination led them past the door, and they were going straight towards it. Some train had newly arrived in Coketown, which had put a number of vehicles in motion, and scattered a considerable bustle about the town. Several coaches were rattling before them and behind them as they approached Mr. Bounderby's, and one of the latter drew up with such briskness as they were in the act of passing the house, that they looked round involuntarily. The bright gaslight over Mr. Bounderby's steps showed them Mrs. Sparsit in the coach, in an ecstasy of excitement, struggling to open the door; Mrs. Sparsit seeing them at the same moment, called to them to stop.

"It's a coincidence," exclaimed Mrs. Sparsit, as she was released by the coachman. "It's a Providence! Come out, ma'am!" then said Mrs. Sparsit, to some one inside, "come out, or we'll have you dragged out!"

Hereupon, no other than the mysterious old woman descended. Whom Mrs. Sparsit incontinently collared.

"Leave her alone, everybody!" cried Mrs. Sparsit, with great energy. "Let nobody touch her. She belongs to me. Come in, ma'am!" then said Mrs. Sparsit, reversing her former word of command. "Come in, ma'am, or we'll have you dragged in!"

The spectacle of a matron of classical deportment, seizing an ancient woman by the throat, and hauling her into a dwelling-house, would have been under any circumstances, sufficient temptation to all true English stragglers so blest as to witness it, to force a way into that dwelling-house and see the matter out. But when the phenomenon was enhanced by the notoriety and mystery by this time associated all over the town with the Bank robbery, it would have lured the stragglers in, with an irresistible attraction, though the roof had been expected to fall upon their heads. Accordingly, the chance witnesses on the ground, consisting of the busiest of the neighbours to the number of some five-and-twenty, closed in after Sissy and Rachael, as they closed in after Mrs. Sparsit and her prize; and the whole body made a disorderly irruption into Mr. Bounderby's dining-room, where the people behind lost not a moment's time in mounting on the chairs, to get the better of the people in front.

"Fetch Mr. Bounderby down!" cried Mrs. Sparsit. "Rachael, young woman; you know who this is?"

"It's Mrs. Pegler," said Rachael.

"I should think it is!" cried Mrs. Sparsit, exulting. "Fetch Mr. Bounderby. Stand away, everybody!" Here old Mrs. Pegler, muffling herself up, and shrinking from observation, whispered a word of entreaty. "Don't tell me," said Mrs. Sparsit, aloud. "I have told you twenty times, coming along, that I will *not* leave you till I have handed you over to him myself."

Mr. Bounderby now appeared, accompanied by Mr. Gradgrind and the whelp, with whom he had been holding conference up-stairs. Mr. Bounderby looked more astonished than hospitable, at sight of this uninvited party in his dining-room.

"Why, what's the matter now!" said he. "Mrs. Sparsit, ma'am?"

"Sir," explained that worthy woman, "I trust it is my good fortune to produce a person you have much desired to find. Stimulated by my wish to relieve your mind, sir, and connecting together such imperfect clues to the part of the country in which that person might be supposed to reside, as have been afforded by the young woman, Rachael, fortunately now present to identify, I have had the happiness to succeed, and to bring that person with me—I need not say most unwillingly on her part. It has not been, sir, without some trouble that I have effected this; but trouble in your service is to me a pleasure, and hunger, thirst, and cold a real gratification."

Here Mrs. Sparsit ceased; for Mr. Bounderby's visage exhibited an extraordinary combination of all possible colours and expressions of discomfiture, as old Mrs. Pegler was disclosed to his view.

"Why, what do you mean by this?" was his highly unexpected demand, in great warmth. "I ask you, what do you mean by this, Mrs. Sparsit, ma'am?"

"Sir!" exclaimed Mrs. Sparsit, faintly.

"Why don't you mind your own business, ma'am?" roared Bounderby. "How dare you go and poke your officious nose into my family affairs?"

This allusion to her favourite feature overpowered Mrs. Sparsit. She sat down stiffly in a chair, as if she were frozen; and with a fixed stare at Mr. Bounderby, slowly grated her mittens against one another, as if they were frozen too.

"My dear Josiah!" cried Mrs. Pegler, trembling. "My darling boy! I am not to blame. It's not my fault, Josiah. I told this lady over and over again, that I knew she was doing what would not be agreeable to you, but she would do it."

"What did you let her bring you for? Couldn't you knock her cap off, or her tooth out, or scratch her, or do something or other to her?" asked Bounderby.

"My own boy! She threatened me that if I resisted her, I should be brought by constables, and it was better to come quietly than make that stir in such a"—Mrs. Pegler glanced timidly but proudly round the walls—"such a fine house as this. Indeed, indeed, it is not my fault! My dear, noble, stately boy! I have always lived quiet and secret, Josiah, my dear. I have never broken the condition once. I have never said I was your mother. I have admired you at a distance; and if I have come to town sometimes, with long times between, to take a proud peep at you, I have done it unbeknown, my love, and gone away again."

Mr. Bounderby, with his hands in his pockets, walked in impatient mortification up and down at the side of the long dining-table, while the spectators greedily took in every syllable of Mrs. Pegler's appeal, and at each succeeding syllable became more and more round-eyed. Mr. Bounderby still walking up and down when Mrs. Pegler had done, Mr.

Gradgrind addressed that maligned old lady:

"I am surprised, madam," he observed with severity, "that in your old age you have the face to claim Mr. Bounderby for your son, after your unnatural and inhuman treatment of him."

"*Me* unnatural!" cried poor old Mrs. Pegler. "*Me* inhuman! To my dear boy?"

"Dear!" repeated Mr. Gradgrind. "Yes; dear in his self-made prosperity, madam, I dare say. Not very dear, however, when you deserted him in his infancy, and left him to the brutality of a drunken grandmother."

"*I* deserted my Josiah!" cried Mrs. Pegler, clasping her hands. "Now, Lord forgive you, sir, for your wicked imaginations, and for your scandal against the memory of my poor mother, who died in my arms before Josiah was born. May you repent of it, sir, and live to know better!"

She was so very earnest and injured, that Mr. Gradgrind, shocked by the possibility which dawned upon him, said in a gentler tone:

"Do you deny, then, madam, that you left your son to—to be brought up in the gutter?"

"Josiah in the gutter!" exclaimed Mrs. Pegler. "No such a thing, sir. Never! For shame on you! My dear boy knows, and will give *you* to know, that though he come of humble parents, he come of parents that loved him as dear as the best could, and never thought it a hardship on themselves to pinch a bit that he might write and cipher beautiful, and I've his books at home to show it! Aye, have I!" said Mrs. Pegler, with indignant pride. "And my dear boy knows, and will give *you* to know, sir, that after his beloved father died, when he was eight years old, his mother, too, could pinch a bit, as it was her duty and her pleasure and her pride to do it, to help him out in life, and put him 'prentice. And a steady lad he was, and a kind master he had to lend him a hand, and well he worked his own way forward to be rich and thriving. And I'll give you to know, sir—for this my dear boy won't—that though his mother kept but a little village shop, he never forgot her, but pensioned me on thirty pound a year—more than I want, for I put by out of it—only making the condition that I was to keep down in my own part, and make no boasts about him, and not trouble him. And I never have, except with looking at him once a year, when he has never knowed it. And it's right," said poor old Mrs. Pegler, in affectionate championship, "that I *should* keep down in my own part, and I have no doubts that if I was here I should do a many unbefitting things, and I am well contented, and I can keep my pride in my Josiah to myself, and I can love for love's own sake! And I am ashamed of you, sir," said Mrs. Pegler lastly, "for your slanders and suspicions. And I never stood here before, nor never wanted to stand here when my dear son said no. And I shouldn't be here now, if it hadn't been for being brought here. And for shame upon you, oh, for shame, to accuse me of being a bad mother to my son, with my son standing here to tell you so different!"

The bystanders, on and off the dining-room chairs, raised a murmur of sympathy with Mrs. Pegler, and Mr. Gradgrind felt himself innocently placed in a very distressing predicament, when Mr. Bounderby, who had never ceased walking up and down, and had every moment swelled larger and larger, and grown redder and redder, stopped short.

"I don't exactly know," said Mr. Bounderby, "how I came to be favoured with the attendance of the present company, but I don't inquire. When they're quite satisfied, perhaps they'll be so good as to disperse; whether they're satisfied or not, perhaps they'll be so good as to disperse. I'm not bound to deliver a lecture on my family affairs, I have not undertaken to do it, and I'm not a going to do it. Therefore those who expect any explanation whatever upon that branch of the subject, will be disappointed—particularly Tom Gradgrind, and he can't know it too soon. In reference to the Bank robbery, there has been a mistake made, concerning my mother. If there hadn't been over-officiousness it wouldn't have been made, and I hate over-officiousness at all times, whether or no. Good evening!"

Although Mr. Bounderby carried it off in these terms, holding the door open for the company to depart, there was a blustering sheepishness upon him, at once extremely crest-fallen and superlatively absurd. Detected as the Bully of humility, who had built his windy reputation upon lies, and in his boastfulness had put the honest truth as far away from him as if he had advanced the mean claim (there is no meaner) to tack himself on to a pedigree, he cut a most ridiculous figure. With the people filing off at the door he held, who he knew would carry what had passed to the whole town, to be given to the four winds, he could not have looked a Bully more short and forlorn, if he had had his ears cropped. Even that unlucky female, Mrs. Sparsit, fallen from her pinnacle of exultation into the Slough of Despond,[1] was not in so bad a plight as that remarkable man and self-made Humbug, Josiah Bounderby of Coketown.

Rachael and Sissy, leaving Mrs. Pegler to occupy a bed at her son's for that night, walked together to the gate of Stone Lodge and there parted. Mr. Gradgrind joined them before they had gone very far, and spoke with much interest of Stephen Blackpool; for whom he thought this signal failure of the suspicions against Mrs. Pegler was likely to work well.

As to the whelp; throughout this scene as on all other late occasions, he had stuck close to Bounderby. He seemed to feel that as long as Bounderby could make no discovery without his knowledge, he was so far safe. He never visited his sister, and had only seen her once since she went home: that is to say on the night when he still stuck close to Bounderby, as already related.

There was one dim unformed fear lingering about his sister's mind, to which she never gave utterance, which surrounded the graceless and ungrateful boy with a dreadful mystery. The same dark possibility had presented itself in the same shapeless guise, this very day, to Sissy, when Rachael spoke of some one who would be confounded by Stephen's return, having put him out of the way. Louisa had never spoken of harbouring any suspicion of her brother in connexion with the robbery, she and Sissy had held no confidence on the subject, save in that one interchange of looks when the unconscious father rested his gray head on his hand; but it was understood between them, and they both knew it. This other fear was so awful, that it hovered about each of them like a ghostly shadow; neither daring to think of its being near herself, far less of its being near the other.

And still the forced spirit which the whelp had plucked up, throve with him. If Stephen Blackpool was not the thief, let him show himself. Why didn't he?

Another night. Another day and night. No Stephen Blackpool. Where was the man, and why did he not come back?

---

1.   The bog, representing spiritual discouragement, into which the hero Christian falls in John Bunyan's allegory *Pilgrim's Progress* (1678).

CHAPTER VI.
THE STARLIGHT

THE SUNDAY was a bright Sunday in autumn, clear and cool, when early in the morning Sissy and Rachael met, to walk in the country.

As Coketown cast ashes not only on its own head but on the neighbourhood's too—after the manner of those pious persons who do penance for their own sins by putting other people into sackcloth—it was customary for those who now and then thirsted for a draught of pure air, which is not absolutely the most wicked things among the vanities of life, to get a few miles away by the railroad, and then begin their walk, or their lounge in the fields. Sissy and Rachael helped themselves out of the smoke by the usual means, and were put down at a station midway between the town and Mr. Bounderby's retreat.

Though the green landscape was blotted here and there with heaps of coal, it was green elsewhere, and there were trees to see, and there were larks singing (though it was Sunday),[1] and there were pleasant scents in the air, and all was over-arched by a bright blue sky. In the distance one way, Coketown showed as a black mist; in another distance hills began to rise; in a third, there was a faint change of light of the horizon where it shone upon the far-off sea. Under their feet, the grass was fresh; beautiful shadows of branches flickered upon it, and speckled it; hedgerows were luxuriant: everything was at peace. Engines at pits' mouths, and lean old horses that had worn the circle of their daily labour into the ground, were alike quiet; wheels had ceased for a short space to turn; and the great wheel of earth seemed to revolve without the shocks and noises of another time.

They walked on across the fields and down the shady lanes, sometimes getting over a fragment of a fence so rotten that it dropped at a touch of the foot, sometimes passing near a wreck of bricks and beams overgrown with grass, marking the site of deserted works. They followed paths and tracks, however slight. Mounds where the grass was rank and high, and where brambles, dock-weed, and such-like vegetation, were

---

1.   See explanatory note to p. 61.

confusedly heaped together, they always avoided; for dismal stories were told in that country of the old pits hidden beneath such indications.

The sun was high when they sat down to rest. They had seen no one, near or distant, for a long time; and the solitude remained unbroken. "It is so still here, Rachael, and the way is so untrodden, that I think we must be the first who have been here all the summer."

As Sissy said it, her eyes were attracted by another of those rotten fragments of fence upon the ground. She got up to look at it. "And yet I don't know. This has not been broken very long. The wood is quite fresh where it gave way. Here are footsteps too.—Oh Rachael!"

She ran back, and caught her round the neck. Rachael had already started up.

"What is the matter?"

"I don't know. There is a hat lying in the grass."

They went forward together. Rachael took it up, shaking from head to foot. She broke into a passion of tears and lamentations: Stephen Blackpool was written in his own hand on the inside.

"Oh the poor lad, the poor lad! He has been made away with. He is lying murdered here!"

"Is there—has the hat any blood upon it?" Sissy faltered.

They were afraid to look; but they did examine it, and found no mark of violence, inside or out. It had been lying there some days, for rain and dew had stained it, and the mark of its shape was on the grass where it had fallen. They looked fearfully about them, without moving, but could see nothing more. "Rachael," Sissy whispered, "I will go on a little by myself."

She had unclasped her hand, and was in the act of stepping forward, when Rachael caught her in both arms with a scream that resounded over the wide landscape. Before them, at their very feet, was the brink of a black ragged chasm hidden by the thick grass. They sprang back, and fell upon their knees, each hiding her face upon the other's neck.

"Oh, my good Lord! He's down there! Down there!" At first this, and her terrific screams, were all that could be got from Rachael, by any tears, by any prayers, by any representations, by any means. It was impossible to hush her; and it was deadly necessary to hold her, or she would have flung herself down the shaft.

"Rachael, dear Rachael, good Rachael, for the love of Heaven, not these dreadful cries! Think of Stephen, think of Stephen, think of Stephen!"

By an earnest repetition of this entreaty, poured out in all the agony of such a moment, Sissy at last brought her to be silent, and to look at her with a tearless face of stone.

"Rachael, Stephen may be living. You wouldn't leave him lying maimed at the bottom of this dreadful place, a moment, if you could bring help to him?"

"No, no, no!"

"Don't stir from here, for his sake! Let me go and listen."

She shuddered to approach the pit; but she crept towards it on her hands and knees, and called to him as loud as she could call. She listened, but no sound replied. She called again and listened; still no answering sound. She did this, twenty, thirty times. She took a little clod of earth from the broken ground where he had stumbled, and threw it in. She could not hear it fall.

The wide prospect, so beautiful in its stillness but a few minutes ago, almost carried despair to her brave heart, as she rose and looked all round her, seeing no help. "Rachael, we must lose not a moment. We must go in different directions, seeking aid. You shall go by the way we have come, and I will go forward by the path. Tell any one you see, and every one what has happened. Think of Stephen, think of Stephen!"

She knew by Rachael's face that she might trust her now. And after standing for a moment to see her running, wringing her hands as she ran, she turned and went upon her own search; she stopped at the hedge to tie her shawl there as a guide to the place, then threw her bonnet aside, and ran as she had never run before.

Run, Sissy, run, in Heaven's name! Don't stop for breath. Run, run! Quickening herself by carrying such entreaties in her thoughts, she ran from field to field, and lane to lane, and place to place, as she had never run before; until she came to a shed by an engine-house, where two men lay in the shade, asleep on straw.

First to wake them, and next to tell them, all so wild and breathless as she was, what had brought her there, were difficulties; but they no sooner understood her than their spirits were on fire like hers. One of the men was in a drunken slumber, but on his comrade's shouting to him that a man had fallen down the Old Hell Shaft, he started out to a pool of dirty water, put his head in it, and came back sober.

With these two men she ran to another half-a-mile further, and with that one to another, while they ran elsewhere. Then a horse was found; and she got another man to ride for life or death to the railroad, and send a message to Louisa, which she wrote and gave him. By this time a whole village was up; and windlasses, ropes, poles, candles, lanterns, all things necessary, were fast collecting and being brought into one place, to be carried to the Old Hell Shaft.

It seemed now hours and hours since she had left the lost man lying in the grave where he had been buried alive. She could not bear to remain away from it any longer—it was like deserting him—and she hurried swiftly back, accompanied by half-a-dozen labourers, including the drunken man whom the news had sobered, and who was the best man of all. When they came to the Old Hell Shaft, they found it as lonely as she had left it. The men called and listened as she had done, and examined the edge of the chasm, and settled how it had happened, and then sat down to wait until the implements they wanted should come up.

Every sound of insects in the air, every stirring of the leaves, every whisper among these men, made Sissy tremble, for she thought it was a cry at the bottom of the pit. But the wind blew idly over it, and no sound arose to the surface, and they sat upon the grass, waiting and waiting. After they had waited some time, straggling people who had heard of the accident began to come up; then the real help of implements began to arrive. In the midst of this, Rachael returned; and with her party there was a surgeon, who brought some wine and medicines. But, the expectation among the people that the man would be found alive, was very slight indeed.

There being now people enough present to impede the work, the sobered man put himself at the head of the rest, or was put there by the general consent, and made a large ring round the Old Hell Shaft, and appointed men to keep it. Besides such volunteers as were accepted to work, only Sissy and Rachael were at first permitted within this ring; but, later in the day, when the message brought an express from Coketown, Mr. Gradgrind and Louisa, and Mr. Bounderby, and the whelp, were also there.

The sun was four hours lower than when Sissy and Rachael had first sat down upon the grass, before a means of enabling two men to descend securely was rigged with poles and ropes. Difficulties had arisen in the construction of this machine, simple as it was; requisites had been found wanting, and messages had had to go and return. It was five o'clock in the afternoon of the bright autumnal Sunday, before a candle was sent down to try the air, while three or four rough faces stood crowded close together, attentively watching it: the men at the windlass lowering as they were told. The candle was brought up again, feebly burning, and then some water was cast on it. Then the bucket was hooked on; and the sobered man and another got in with lights, giving the word "Lower away!"

As the rope went out, tight and strained, and the windlass creaked, there was not a breath among the one or two hundred men and women looking on, that came as it was wont to come. The signal was given and the windlass stopped, with abundant rope to spare. Apparently so long an interval ensued with the men at the windlass standing idle, that some women shrieked that another accident had happened! But the surgeon who held the watch, declared five minutes not to have elapsed yet, and sternly admonished them to keep silence. He had not well done speaking, when the windlass was reversed and worked again. Practised eyes knew that it did not go as heavily as it would if both workmen had been coming up, and that only one was returning.

The rope came in tight and strained; and ring after ring was coiled upon the barrel of the windlass, and all eyes were fastened on the pit. The sobered man was brought up and leaped out briskly on the grass. There was an universal cry of "Alive or dead?" and then a deep, profound hush.

When he said "Alive!" a great shout arose and many eyes had tears in them.

"But he's hurt very bad," he added, as soon as he could make himself heard again. "Where's doctor? He's hurt so very bad, sir, that we donno how to get him up."

They all consulted together, and looked anxiously at the surgeon, as he asked some questions, and shook his head on receiving the replies. The sun was setting now; and the red light in the evening sky touched every face there, and caused it to be distinctly seen in all its rapt suspense.

The consultation ended in the men returning to the windlass, and the pitman going down again, carrying the wine and some other small matters with him. Then the other man came up. In the meantime, under the surgeon's directions, some men brought a hurdle, on which others made a thick bed of spare clothes covered with loose straw, while he himself contrived some bandages and slings from shawls and handkerchiefs. As these were made, they were hung upon an arm of the pitman who had last come up, with instructions how to use them: and as he stood, shown by the light he carried, leaning his powerful loose hand upon one of the poles, and sometimes glancing down the pit, and sometimes glancing round upon the people, he was not the least conspicuous figure in the scene. It was dark now, and torches were kindled.

It appeared from the little this man said to those about him, which was quickly repeated all over the circle, that the lost man had fallen upon a mass of crumbled rubbish with which the pit was half choked up, and that his fall had been further broken by some jagged earth at the side. He lay upon his back with one arm doubled over him, and according to his own belief had hardly stirred since he fell, except that he had moved his free hand to a side pocket, in which he remembered to have some bread and meat (of which he had swallowed crumbs), and had likewise scooped up a little water in it now and then. He had come straight away from his work, on being written to, and had walked the whole journey; and was on his way to Mr. Bounderby's country house after dark, when he fell. He was crossing that dangerous country at such a dangerous time, because he was innocent of what was laid to his charge, and couldn't rest from coming the nearest way to deliver himself up. The Old Hell Shaft, the pitman said, with a curse upon it, was worthy of its bad name to the last; for though Stephen could speak now, he believed it would soon be found to have mangled the life out of him.

When all was ready, this man, still taking his last hurried charges from his comrades and the surgeon after the windlass had begun to lower him, disappeared into the pit. The rope went out as before, the signal was made as before, and the windlass stopped. No man removed his hand from it now. Every one waited with his grasp set, and his body bent down to the work, ready to reverse and wind in. At length the signal was given, and all the ring leaned forward. For now, the rope came in, tightened and strained to its utmost as it appeared, and the men turned heavily, and the windlass complained. It was scarcely endurable to look at the rope, and think of its giving way. But, ring after ring was coiled upon the barrel of the windlass safely, and the connecting chains appeared, and finally the bucket with the two men holding on at the sides—a sight to make the head swim, and oppress the heart—and tenderly supporting between them, slung and tied within, the figure of a poor, crushed, human creature.

A low murmur of pity went round the throng, and the women wept aloud, as this form, almost without form, was moved very slowly from its iron deliverance, and laid upon the bed of straw. At first, none but the surgeon went close to it. He did what he could in its adjustment on the couch, but the best that he could do was cover it. That gently done, he called to him Rachael and Sissy. And at that time the pale, worn, patient face was seen looking up at the sky, with the broken right hand lying bare on the outside of the covering garments, as if waiting to be taken by another hand.

They gave him drink, moistened his face with water, and administered some drops of cordial and wine. Though he lay quite motionless looking up at the sky, he smiled and said, "Rachael."

She stooped down on the grass at his side, and bent over him until her eyes were between his and the sky, for he could not so much as turn them to look at her.

"Rachael, my dear."

She took his hand. He smiled again and said, "Don't let 't go."

"Thou'rt in great pain, my own dear Stephen?"

"I ha' been, but not now. I ha' been—dreadful, and dree, and long, my dear—but 'tis ower now. Ah, Rachael, aw a muddle! Fro' first to last, a muddle!"

The spectre of his old look seemed to pass as he said the word.

"I ha' fell into th' pit, my dear, as have cost wi'in the knowledge o' old fok now livin, hundreds and hundreds o' men's lives—fathers, sons, brothers, dear to thousands an' thousands, an' keeping 'em fro' want and hunger. I ha' fell into a pit that ha' been wi' th' Fire-damp[1] crueller than battle. I ha' read on 't the public petition, as onny one may read, fro' the men that works in pits, in which they ha' pray'n and pray'n the lawmakers for Christ's

---

1. Carbonic gas released by coal, explosive when mixed with air, a source of danger in mines.

sake not to let their work be murder to 'em, but to spare 'em for th' wives and children that they loves as well as gentlefok loves theirs. When it were in work, it killed wi' out need; when 'tis let alone, it kills wi' out need. See how we die an' no need, one way an' another—in a muddle—every day!"

He faintly said it, without any anger against any one. Merely as the truth.

"Thy little sister, Rachael, thou hast not forgot her. Thou'rt not like to forget her now, and me so nigh her. Thou know'st—poor, patient, suff'rin, dear—how thou didst work for her, seet'n all day long in her little chair at thy winder, and how she died, young and misshapen, awlung o' sickly air as had'n no need to be, an' awlung o' working people's miserable homes. A muddle! Aw a muddle!"

Louisa approached him; but he could not see her, lying with his face turned up to the night sky.

"If aw th' things that tooches us, my dear, was not so muddled, I should'n ha' had'n need to coom heer. If we was not in a muddle among ourseln, I should'n ha' been, by my own fellow weavers and workin' brothers, so mistook. If Mr. Bounderby had ever know'd me right—if he'd ever know'd me at aw—he would'n ha' took'n offence wi' me. He would'n ha' suspect'n me. But look up yonder, Rachael! Look aboove!"

Following his eyes, she saw that he was gazing at a star.

"It ha' shined upon me," he said reverently, "in my pain and trouble down below. It ha' shined into my mind. I ha' look'n at 't and thowt o' thee, Rachael, till the muddle in my mind have cleared awa, above a bit, I hope. If soom ha' been wantin' in unnerstan'in me better, I, too, ha' been wantin' in unnerstan'in them better. When I got thy letter, I easily believen that what the yoong ledy sen and done to me, and what her brother sen and done to me, was one, and that there were a wicked plot betwixt 'em. When I fell, I were in anger wi' her, an' hurryin on t' be as onjust t' her as oothers was t' me. But in our judgements, like as in our doins, we mun bear and forbear. In my pain an' trouble, lookin up yonder,—wi' it shinin on me—I ha' seen more clear, and ha' made it my dyin prayer that aw th' world may on'y coom toogether more, an' get a better unnerstan'in o' one another, than when I were in 't my own weak seln."

Louisa hearing what he said, bent over him on the opposite side to Rachael, so that he could see her.

"You ha' heard?" he said, after a few moments' silence. "I ha' not forgot you, ledy."

"Yes, Stephen, I have heard you. And your prayer is mine."

"You ha' a father. Will yo tak a message to him?"

"He is here," said Louisa, with dread. "Shall I bring him to you?"

"If yo please."

Louisa returned with her father. Standing hand-in-hand, they both looked down upon the solemn countenance.

"Sir, yo will clear me an' mak my name good wi' aw men. This I leave to yo."

Mr. Gradgrind was troubled and asked how?

"Sir," was the reply: "yor son will tell yo how. Ask him. I mak no charges: I leave none ahint me: not a single word. I ha' seen an' spok'n wi' yor son, one night. I ask no more o' yo than that yo clear me—an' I trust to yo to do 't."

The bearers now being ready to carry him away, and the surgeon being anxious for his removal, those who had torches or lanterns, prepared to go in front of the litter. Before it was raised, and while they were arranging how to go, he said to Rachael, looking upward at the star:

"Often as I coom to myseln, and found it shinin on me down there in my trouble, I thowt it were the star as guided to Our Saviour's home.[1] I awmust think it be the very star!"

They lifted him up, and he was overjoyed to find that they were about to take him in the direction whither the star seemed to him to lead.

"Rachael, beloved lass! Don't let go my hand. We may walk toogether t'night, my dear!"

"I will hold thy hand, and keep beside thee, Stephen, all the way."

"Bless thee! Will soombody be pleased to coover my face!"

They carried him very gently along the fields, and down the lanes, and over the wide landscape; Rachael always holding the hand in hers. Very few whispers broke the mournful silence. It was soon a funeral procession. The star had shown him where to find the God of the poor; and through humility, and sorrow, and forgiveness, he had gone to his Redeemer's rest.

---

1.   Compare Matthew 2:1–10.

Chapter VII.
Whelp-Hunting

Before the ring formed round the Old Hell Shaft was broken, one figure had disappeared from within it. Mr. Bounderby and his shadow had not stood near Louisa, who held her father's arm, but in a retired place by themselves. When Mr. Gradgrind was summoned to the couch, Sissy, attentive to all that happened, slipped behind that wicked shadow—a sight in the horror of his face, if there had been eyes there for any sight but one—and whispered in his ear. Without turning his head, he conferred with her a few moments, and vanished. Thus the whelp had gone out of the circle before the people moved.

When the father reached home, he sent a message to Mr. Bounderby's, desiring his son to come to him directly. The reply was, that Mr. Bounderby having missed him in the crowd, and seeing nothing of him since, had supposed him to be at Stone Lodge.

"I believe, father," said Louisa, "he will not come back to town to-night." Mr. Gradgrind turned away, and said no more.

In the morning, he went down to the Bank himself as soon as it was opened, and seeing his son's place empty (he had not the courage to look in at first) went back along the street to meet Mr. Bounderby on his way there. To whom he said that, for reasons he would soon explain, but entreated not then to be asked for, he had found it necessary to employ his son at a distance for a little while. Also, that he was charged with the duty of vindicating Stephen Blackpool's memory, and declaring the thief. Mr. Bounderby quite confounded, stood stock-still in the street after his father-in-law had left him, swelling like an immense soap-bubble, without its beauty.

Mr. Gradgrind went home, locked himself in his room, and kept it all that day. When Sissy and Louisa tapped at his door, he said, without opening it, "Not now, my dears; in the evening." On their return in the evening, he said, "I am not able yet—to-morrow." He ate nothing all day, and had no candle after dark; and they heard him walking to and fro late at night.

But, in the morning, he appeared at breakfast at the usual hour, and took his usual place at the table. Aged and bent he looked, and quite bowed down; and yet he looked a wiser man, and a better man, than in the days when in this life he wanted nothing but Facts. Before he left the room, he appointed a time for them to come to him; and so, with his gray head drooping, went away.

"Dear father," said Louisa, when they kept their appointment, "you have three young children left. They will be different, *I* will be different yet, with Heaven's help."

She gave her hand to Sissy, as if she meant with her help too.

"Your wretched brother," said Mr. Gradgrind. "Do you think he had planned this robbery, when he went with you to the lodging?"

"I fear so, father. I know he had wanted money very much, and had spent a great deal."

"The poor man being about to leave town, it came into his evil brain to cast suspicion on him?"

"I think it must have flashed upon him while he sat there, father. For I asked him to go there with me. The visit did not originate with him."

"He had some conversation with the poor man. Did he take him aside?"

"He took him out of the room. I asked him afterwards, why he had done so, and he made a plausible excuse; but since last night, father, and when I remember the circumstances by its light, I am afraid I can imagine too truly what passed between them."

"Let me know," said her father, "if your thoughts present your guilty brother in the same dark view as mine."

"I fear, father," hesitated Louisa, "that he must have made some representation to Stephen Blackpool—perhaps in my name, perhaps in his own—which induced him to do in good faith and honesty, what he had never done before, and to wait about the Bank those two or three nights before he left the town."

"Too plain!" returned the father. "Too plain!"

He shaded his face, and remained silent for some moments. Recovering himself, he said:

"And now, how is he to be found? How is he to be saved from justice? In the few hours that I can possibly allow to elapse before I publish the truth, how is he to be found by us, and only by us? Ten thousand pounds could not effect it."

"Sissy has effected it, father."

He raised his eyes to where she stood, like a good fairy in his house, and said in a tone of softened gratitude and grateful kindness, "It is always you, my child!"

"We had our fears," Sissy explained, glancing at Louisa, "before yesterday; and when I saw you brought to the side of the litter last night, and heard what passed (being close to Rachael all the time), I went to him when no one saw, and said to him, 'Don't look at me. See where your father is. Escape at once, for his sake and your own!' He was in a tremble before I whispered to him, and he started and trembled more then, and said, 'Where can I go? I have very little money, and I don't know who will hide me!' I thought of father's old circus. I have not forgotten where Mr. Sleary goes at this time of year, and I read of him in a paper only the other day. I told him to hurry there, and tell his name, and ask Mr. Sleary to hide him till I came. 'I'll get to him before the morning,' he said. And I saw him shrink away among the people."

"Thank Heaven!" exclaimed his father. "He may be got abroad yet."

It was the more hopeful as the town to which Sissy had directed him was within three hours' journey of Liverpool, whence he could be swiftly dispatched to any part of the world. But, caution being necessary in communicating with him—for there was a greater danger every moment of his being suspected now, and nobody could be sure at heart but that Mr. Bounderby himself, in a bullying vein of public zeal, might play a Roman part[1]—it was consented that Sissy and Louisa should repair to the place in question, by a circuitous course, alone; and that the unhappy father, setting forth in the opposite direction, should get round to the same bourne by another and wider route. It was further agreed that he should not present himself to Mr. Sleary, lest his intentions should be mistrusted, or the intelligence of his arrival should cause his son to take flight anew; but, that the communication should be left to Sissy and Louisa to open; and that they should inform the cause of so much misery and disgrace, of his father's being at hand and of the purpose for which they had come. When these arrangements had been well considered and were fully understood by all three, it was time to begin to carry them into

---

1. A further reference to Lucius Junius Brutus (see note to p. 174).

execution. Early in the afternoon, Mr. Gradgrind walked direct from his own house into the country, to be taken up on the line by which he was to travel; and at night the remaining two set forth upon their different course, encouraged by not seeing any face they knew.

The two travelled all night, except when they were left, for odd numbers of minutes, at branch-places, up illimitable flights of steps, or down wells—which was the only variety of those branches—and, early in the morning, were turned out on a swamp, a mile or two from the town they sought. From this dismal spot they were rescued by a savage old postilion, who happened to be up early, kicking a horse in a fly: and so were smuggled into the town by all the back lanes where the pigs lived: which, although not a magnificent or even savoury approach, was, as is usual in such cases, the legitimate highway.

The first thing they saw on entering the town was the skeleton of Sleary's Circus. The company had departed for another town more than twenty miles off, and had opened there last night. The connection between the two places was by a hilly turnpike-road, and the travelling on that road was very slow. Though they took but a hasty breakfast, and no rest (which it would have been in vain to seek under such anxious circumstances), it was noon before they began to find the bills of Sleary's Horse-riding on barns and walls, and one o'clock when they stopped in the market-place.

A Grand Morning Performance[1] by the Riders, commencing at that very hour, was in course of announcement by the bellman as they set their feet upon the stones of the street. Sissy recommended that, to avoid making inquiries and attracting attention in the town, they should present themselves to pay at the door. If Mr. Sleary were taking the money, he would be sure to know her, and would proceed with discretion. If he were not, he would be sure to see them inside; and, knowing what he had done with the fugitive, would proceed with discretion still.

Therefore, they repaired, with fluttering hearts, to the well-remembered booth. The flag with the inscription SLEARY'S HORSE-RIDING was there; and the Gothic niche was there; but Mr. Sleary was not there. Master Kidderminster, grown too maturely turfy to be received by the

---

1.   I.e. a matinee.

wildest credulity as Cupid any more, had yielded to the invincible force of circumstances (and his beard), and, in the capacity of a man who made himself generally useful, presided on this occasion over the exchequer—having also a drum in reserve, on which to expend his leisure moments and superfluous forces. In the extreme sharpness of his look out for base coin, Mr. Kidderminster, as at present situated, never saw anything but money; so Sissy passed him unrecognised, and they went in.

The Emperor of Japan, on a steady old white horse stencilled with black spots, was twirling five wash-hand basins at once, as it is the fa-vourite recreation of that monarch to do. Sissy, though well acquainted with his Royal line, had no personal knowledge of the present Emperor, and his reign was peaceful. Miss Josephine Sleary, in her celebrated graceful Equestrian Tyrolean Flower Act, was then announced by a new clown (who humorously said Cauliflower Act), and Mr. Sleary appeared, lead-ing her in.

Mr. Sleary had only made one cut at the Clown with his long whip-lash, and the Clown had only said, "If you do it again, I'll throw the horse at you!" when Sissy was recognised both by father and daughter. But they got through the Act with great self-possession; and Mr. Sleary, saving for the first instant, conveyed no more expression into his loco-motive eye than into his fixed one. The performance seemed a little long to Sissy and Louisa, particularly when it stopped to afford the Clown an opportunity of telling Mr. Sleary (who said "Indeed, sir!" to all his ob-servations in the calmest way, and with his eye on the house) about two legs sitting on three legs looking at one leg, when in came four legs, and laid hold of one leg, and up got two legs, caught hold of three legs, and threw 'em at four legs, who ran away with one leg. For, although an ingenious Allegory relating to a butcher, a three-legged stool, a dog, and a leg of mutton,[1] this narrative consumed time; and they were in great suspense. At last, however, little fair-haired Josephine made her curtsey amid great applause; and the Clown, left alone in the ring, had just warmed himself, and said, "Now I'll have a turn!" when Sissy was touched on the shoulder, and beckoned out.

---

1.   A traditional riddle, recorded in Iona and Peter Opie's *The Oxford Nursery Rhyme Book* (Oxford: Oxford University Press, 1955), p. 151.

She took Louisa with her; and they were received by Mr. Sleary in a very little private apartment, with canvas sides, a grass floor, and a wooden ceiling all aslant, on which the box company stamped their approbation, as if they were coming through. "Thethilia," said Mr. Sleary, who had brandy and water at hand, "it doth me good to thee you. You wath alwayth a favourite with uth, and you've done uth credit thinth the old timeth I'm thure. You mutht thee our people, my dear, afore we thpeak of bithnith, or they'll break their hearth—ethpethially the women. Here'th Jothphine hath been and got married to E. W. B. Childerth, and the hath got a boy, and though he'th only three yearth old, he thtickth on to any pony you can bring againtht him. He'th named The Little Wonder of Thcholathtic Equitation; and if you don't hear of that boy at Athley'th,[1] you'll hear of him at Parith. And you recollect Kidderminthter, that wath thought to be rather thweet upon yourthelf? Well. He'th married too. Married a widder. Old enough to be hith mother. The wath Tightrope, the wath, and now the'th nothing—on accounth of fat. They've got two children, tho we're thtrong in the Fairy bithnith and the Nurthery dodge. If you wath to thee our Children in the Wood,[2] with their father and mother both a dyin' on a horthe—their uncle a retheiving of 'em ath hith wardth, upon a horthe—themthelvth both a goin' a blackberryin' on a horthe—and the Robinth a coming in to cover 'em with leavth, upon a horthe—you'd thay it wath the completetht thing ath ever you thet your eyeth on! And you remember Emma Gordon, my dear, ath wath a'motht a mother to you? Of courthe you do; I needn't athk. Well! Emma, the lotht her huthband. He wath throw'd a heavy back-fall off a Elephant in a thort of a Pagoda thing ath the Thultan of the Indieth, and he never got the better of it; and the married a thecond time—married a Cheethemonger ath fell in love with her from the front—and he'th a Overtheer and makin' a fortun."

These various changes, Mr. Sleary, very short of breath now, related with great heartiness, and with a wonderful kind of innocence, considering what a bleary and brandy-and-watery old veteran he was. Afterwards

1.   Astley's Circus (see explanatory note to p. 50).
2.   I.e. an equestrian entertainment recounting the story of the Babes in the Wood, deriving from the traditional ballad 'The Children in the Wood.'

he brought in Josephine, and E. W. B. Childers (rather deeply lined in the jaws by daylight), and the Little Wonder of Scholastic Equitation, and in a word, all the company. Amazing creatures they were in Louisa's eyes, so white and pink of complexion, so scant of dress, and so demonstrative of leg; but it was very agreeable to see them crowding about Sissy, and very natural in Sissy to be unable to refrain from tears.

"There! Now Thethilia hath kithd all the children, and hugged all the women, and thaken handth all round with all the men, clear, every one of you, and ring in the band for the thecond part!"

As soon as they were gone, he continued in a low tone. "Now, Thethilia, I don't athk to know any thecreth, but I thuppothe I may conthider thith to be Mith Thquire."

"This is his sister. Yes."

"And t'other on'th daughter. Thath what I mean. Hope I thee you well, mith. And I hope the Thquire'th well?"

"My father will be here soon," said Louisa, anxious to bring him to the point. "Is my brother safe?"

"Thafe and thound!" he replied. "I want you juth to take a peep at the Ring, mith, through here. Thethilia, you know the dodgeth; find a thpy-hole for yourthelf."

They each looked through a chink in the boards.

"Thath Jack the Giant Killer[1]—piethe of comic infant bithnith," said Sleary. "There'th a property-houthe, you thee, for Jack to hide in; there'th my Clown with a thauthe-pan-lid and a thpit, for Jack'th thervant; there'th little Jack himthelf in a thplendid thoot of armour; there'th two comic black thervanth twithe ath big ath the houthe, to thtand by it and to bring it in and clear it; and the Giant (a very ecthpenthive bathket one), he an't on yet. Now, do you thee 'em all?"

"Yes," they both said.

"Look at 'em again," said Sleary, "look at 'em well. You thee 'em all? Very good. Now, mith;" he put a form for them to sit on; "I have my opinionth, and the Thquire your father hath hith. I don't want to know what your brother'th been up to; ith better for me not to know. All I

---

1.   Eponymous hero of the traditional fairy tale.

thay ith, the Thquire hath thtood by Thethilia, and I'll thtand by the Thquire. Your brother ith one o' them black thervanth."

Louisa uttered an exclamation, partly of distress, partly of satisfaction.

"Ith a fact," said Sleary, "and even knowin' it, you couldn't put your finger on him. Let the Thquire come. I thall keep your brother here after the performanth. I than't undreth him, nor yet wath hith paint off. Let the Thquire come here after the performanth, or come here yourthelf after the performanth, and you thall find your brother, and have the whole plathe to talk to him in. Never mind the lookth of him, ath long ath he'th well hid."

Louisa, with many thanks and with a lightened load, detained Mr. Sleary no longer then. She left her love for her brother, with her eyes full of tears; and she and Sissy went away until later in the afternoon.

Mr. Gradgrind arrived within an hour afterwards. He too had encountered no one whom he knew; and was now sanguine with Sleary's assistance, of getting his disgraced son to Liverpool in the night. As neither of the three could be his companion without almost identifying him under any disguise, he prepared a letter to a correspondent whom he could trust, beseeching him to ship the bearer off at any cost, to North or South America, or any distant part of the world to which he could be the most speedily and privately dispatched.

This done, they walked about, waiting for the Circus to be quite vacated; not only by the audience, but by the company and by the horses. After watching it a long time, they saw Mr. Sleary bring out a chair and sit down by the side-door, smoking; as if that were his signal that they might approach.

"Your thervant, Thquire," was his cautious salutation as they passed in. "If you want me you'll find me here. You muthn't mind your thon having a comic livery on."

They all three went in; and Mr. Gradgrind sat down forlorn, on the Clown's performing chair in the middle of the ring. On one of the back benches, remote in the subdued light and the strangeness of the place, sat the villainous whelp, sulky to the last, whom he had the misery to call his son.

In a preposterous coat, like a beadle's, with cuffs and flaps exaggerated to an unspeakable extent; in an immense waist-coat, knee-breeches, buckled shoes, and a mad cocked hat; with nothing fitting him, and everything of coarse material, moth-eaten and full of holes; with seams in his black face, where fear and heat had started through the greasy composition daubed all over it; anything so grimly, detestably, ridiculously shameful as the whelp in his comic livery, Mr. Gradgrind never could by any other means have believed in, weighable and measurable a fact though it was. And one of his model children had come to this!

At first the whelp would not draw any nearer, but persisted in remaining up there by himself.

Yielding at length, if any concession so sullenly made can be called yielding, to the entreaties of Sissy—for Louisa he disowned altogether—he came down, bench by bench, until he stood in the saw-dust, on the verge of the circle, as far as possible, within its limits from where his father sat.

"How was this done?" asked the father.

"How was what done?" moodily answered the son.

"This robbery," said the father, raising his voice upon the word.

"I forced the safe myself over night, and shut it up ajar before I went away. I had had the key that was found, made long before. I dropped it that morning, that it might be supposed to have been used. I didn't take the money all at once. I pretended to put my balance away every night, but I didn't. Now you know all about it."

"If a thunderbolt had fallen on me," said the father, "it would have shocked me less than this!"

"I don't see why," grumbled the son. "So many people are employed in situations of trust; so many people, out of so many, will be dishonest. I have heard you talk, a hundred times, of its being a law. How can *I* help laws? You have comforted others with such things, father. Comfort yourself!"

The father buried his face in his hands, and the son stood in his disgraceful grotesqueness, biting straw: his hands, with the black partly worn away inside, looking like the hands of a monkey. The evening was fast closing in; and from time to time, he turned the whites of his eyes restlessly and impatiently towards his father. They were the only parts of his face that showed any life or expression, the pigment upon it was so thick.

"You must be got to Liverpool, and sent abroad."

"I suppose I must. I can't be more miserable anywhere," whimpered the whelp, "than I have been here, ever since I can remember. That's one thing."

Mr. Gradgrind went to the door, and returned with Sleary, to whom he submitted the question, How to get this deplorable object away?

"Why, I've been thinking of it, Thquire. There'th not muth time to lothe, tho you muth thay yeth or no. Ith over twenty mileth to the rail. There'th a coath in half an hour, that goeth to the rail, 'purpothe to cath the mail train. That train will take him right to Liverpool."

"But look at him," groaned Mr. Gradgrind. "Will any coach—"

"I don't mean that he thould go in the comic livery," said Sleary. "Thay the word, and I'll make a Jothkin[1] of him, out of the wardrobe, in five minutes."

"I don't understand," said Mr. Gradgrind.

"A Jothkin—a Carter. Make up your mind quick, Thquire. There'll be beer to feth. I've never met with nothing but beer ath'll ever clean a comic blackamoor."

Mr. Gradgrind rapidly assented; Mr. Sleary rapidly turned out from a box, a smock frock, a felt hat, and other essentials; the whelp rapidly changed clothes behind a screen of baize; Mr. Sleary rapidly brought beer, and washed him white again.

"Now," said Sleary, "come along to the coath, and jump up behind; I'll go with you there, and they'll thuppothe you one of my people. Thay farewell to your family, and tharp'th the word." With which he delicately retired.

"Here is your letter," said Mr. Gradgrind. "All necessary means will be provided for you. Atone, by repentance and better conduct, for the shocking action you have committed, and the dreadful consequences to which it has led. Give me your hand, my poor boy, and may God forgive you as I do!"

The culprit was moved to a few abject tears by these words and their pathetic tone. But, when Louisa opened her arms, he repulsed her afresh.

"Not you. I don't want to have anything to say to you!"

"Oh Tom, Tom, do we end so, after all my love!"

---

1.   A country bumpkin or joskin (slang).

"After all your love!" he returned, obdurately. "Pretty love! Leaving old Bounderby to himself, and packing my best friend Mr. Harthouse off, and going home just when I was in the greatest danger. Pretty love that! Coming out with every word about our having gone to that place, when you saw the net was gathering round me. Pretty love that! You have regularly given me up. You never cared for me."

"Tharp'th the word!" said Sleary, at the door.

They all confusedly went out: Louisa crying to him that she forgave him, and loved him still, and that he would one day be sorry to have left her so, and glad to think of these her last words, far away: when some one ran against them. Mr. Gradgrind and Sissy, who were both before him while his sister clung to his shoulder, stopped and recoiled.

For, there was Bitzer, out of breath, his thin lips parted, his thin nostrils distended, his white eyelashes quivering, his colourless face more colourless than ever, as if he ran himself into a white heat, when other people ran themselves into a glow. There he stood, panting and heaving, as if he had never stopped since the night, now long ago, when he had run them down before.

"I'm sorry to interfere with your plans," said Bitzer, shaking his head, "but I can't allow myself to be done by horse-riders. I must have young Mr. Tom; he mustn't be got away by horse-riders; here he is in a smock frock, and I must have him!"

By the collar too, it seemed. For, so he took possession of him.

Chapter VIII.
Philosophical

THEY WENT back into the booth, Sleary shutting the door to keep intruders out. Bitzer, still holding the paralyzed culprit by the collar, stood in the Ring, blinking at his old patron through the darkness of the twilight.

"Bitzer," said Mr. Gradgrind, broken down, and miserably submissive to him, "have you a heart?"

"The circulation, sir," returned Bitzer, smiling at the oddity of the question, "couldn't be carried on without one. No man, sir, acquainted with the facts established by Harvey relating to the circulation of the blood,[1] can doubt that I have a heart."

"Is it accessible," cried Mr. Gradgrind, "to any compassionate influence?"

"It is accessible to Reason, sir," returned the excellent young man. "And to nothing else."

They stood looking at each other; Mr. Gradgrind's face as white as the pursuer's.

"What motive—even what motive in reason—can you have for preventing the escape of this wretched youth," said Mr. Gradgrind, "and crushing his miserable father? See his sister here. Pity us!"

"Sir," returned Bitzer, in a very business-like and logical manner, "since you ask me what motive I have in reason, for taking young Mr. Tom back to Coketown, it is only reasonable to let you know. I have suspected young Mr. Tom of this bank-robbery from the first. I had had my eye upon him before that time, for I knew his ways. I have kept my observations to myself, but I have made them; and I have got ample proofs against him now, besides his running away, and besides his own confession, which I was just in time to overhear. I had the pleasure of watching your house yesterday morning, and following you here. I am going to take young Mr. Tom back to Coketown, in order to deliver him over to Mr. Bounderby. Sir, I have no doubt whatever that Mr. Bounderby will then

---

1. William Harvey (1578–1657), English physician, who established the role of the heart in the circulation of the blood, thus laying the foundation for modern physiology.

promote me to young Mr. Tom's situation. And I wish to have his situation, sir, for it will be a rise to me, and will do me good."

"If this is solely a question of self-interest with you—" Mr. Gradgrind began.

"I beg your pardon for interrupting you, sir," returned Bitzer; "but I am sure you know that the whole social system is a question of self-interest. What you must always appeal to, is a person's self-interest. It's your only hold. We are so constituted. I was brought up in that catechism when I was very young, sir, as you are aware."

"What sum of money," said Mr. Gradgrind, "will you set against your expected promotion?"

"Thank you, sir," returned Bitzer, "for hinting at the proposal; but I will not set any sum against it. Knowing that your clear head would propose that alternative, I have gone over the calculations in my mind; and I find that to compound a felony, even on very high terms indeed, would not be as safe and good for me as my improved prospects in the Bank."

"Bitzer," said Mr. Gradgrind, stretching out his hands as though he would have said, See how miserable I am! "Bitzer, I have but one chance left to soften you. You were many years at my school. If, in remembrance of the pains bestowed upon you there, you can persuade yourself in any degree to disregard your present interest and release my son, I entreat and pray you to give him the benefit of that remembrance."

"I really wonder, sir," rejoined the old pupil in an argumentative manner, "to find you taking a position so untenable. My schooling was paid for; it was a bargain; and when I came away, the bargain ended."

It was a fundamental principle of the Gradgrind philosophy that everything was to be paid for. Nobody was ever on any account to give anybody anything, or render anybody help without purchase. Gratitude was to be abolished, and the virtues springing from it were not to be. Every inch of the existence of mankind, from birth to death, was to be a bargain across a counter. And if we didn't get to Heaven that way, it was not a politico-economical place, and we had no business there.

"I don't deny," added Bitzer, "that my schooling was cheap. But that comes right, sir. I was made in the cheapest market, and have to dispose of myself in the dearest."

He was a little troubled here, by Louisa and Sissy crying.

"Pray don't do that," said he, "it's of no use doing that: it only worries. You seem to think that I have some animosity against young Mr. Tom; whereas I have none at all. I am only going, on the reasonable grounds I have mentioned, to take him back to Coketown. If he was to resist, I should set up the cry of Stop thief! But, he won't resist, you may depend upon it."

Mr. Sleary, who with his mouth open and his rolling eye as immovably jammed in his head as his fixed one, had listened to these doctrines with profound attention, here stepped forward.

"Thquire, you know perfectly well, and your daughter knowth perfectly well (better than you, becauthe I thed it to her), that I didn't know what your thon had done, and that I didn't want to know—I thed it wath better not, though I only thought, then, it wath thome thkylarking. However, thith young man having made it known to be a robbery of a bank, why, thath a theriouth thing; muth too theriouth a thing for me to compound, ath thith young man hath very properly called it. Conthequently, Thquire, you muthn't quarrel with me if I take thith young man'th thide, and thay he'th right and there'th no help for it. But I tell you what I'll do, Thquire; I'll drive your thon and thith young man over to the rail, and prevent expothure here. I can't conthent to do more, but I'll do that."

Fresh lamentations from Louisa, and deeper affliction on Mr. Gradgrind's part, followed this desertion of them by their last friend. But, Sissy glanced at him with great attention; nor did she in her own breast misunderstand him. As they were all going out again, he favoured her with one slight roll of his movable eye, desiring her to linger behind. As he locked the door, he said excitedly:

"The Thquire thtood by you, Thethilia, and I'll thtand by the Thquire. More than that: thith ith a prethiouth rathcal, and belongth to that bluthtering Cove that my people nearly pitht out o' winder. It'll be a dark night; I've got a horthe that'll do anything but thpeak; I've got a pony that'll go fifteen mile an hour with Childerth driving of him; I've got a dog that'll keep a man to one plathe four-and-twenty hourth. Get a word with the young Thquire. Tell him, when he theeth our horthe begin to danthe, not to be afraid of being thpilt, but to look out for a pony-gig coming up. Tell him, when he theeth that gig clothe by, to jump down, and it'll take him off at a rattling pathe. If my dog leth thith young man thtir a peg on foot, I give him leave to go. And if my horthe ever thtirth from that thpot where he beginth a danthing, till the morning—I don't know him!—Tharp'th the word!"

The word was so sharp, that in ten minutes Mr. Childers, sauntering about the market-place in a pair of slippers, had his cue, and Mr. Sleary's equipage was ready. It was a fine sight, to behold the learned dog barking round it, and Mr. Sleary instructing him, with his one practicable eye, that Bitzer was the object of his particular attentions. Soon after dark they all three got in and started; the learned dog (a formidable creature) already pinning Bitzer with his eye, and sticking close to the wheel on his side, that he might be ready for him in the event of his showing the slightest disposition to alight.

The other three sat up at the inn all night in great suspense. At eight o'clock Mr. Sleary and the dog reappeared: both in high spirits.

"All right, Thquire!" said Mr. Sleary, "your thon may be aboard-a-thip by thith time. Childerth took him off, an hour and a half after we left there latht night. The horthe danthed the polka till he wath dead beat (he would have walthed if he hadn't been in harneth), and then I gave him the word and he went to thleep comfortable. When that prethiouth young Rathcal thed he'd go for'ard afoot, the dog hung on to hith neck-handkercher with all four legth in the air and pulled him down and rolled him over. Tho he come back into the drag,[1] and there he that, 'till I turned the horthe'th head, at half-patht thicth thith morning."

Mr. Gradgrind overwhelmed him with thanks, of course; and hinted as delicately as he could, at a handsome remuneration in money.

"I don't want money mythelf, Thquire; but Childerth ith a family man, and if you wath to like to offer him a five-pound note, it mightn't be unactheptable. Likewithe if you wath to thtand a collar for the dog, or a thet of bellth for the horthe, I thould be very glad to take 'em. Brandy and water I alwayth take." He had already called for a glass, and now called for another. "If you wouldn't think it going too far, Thquire, to make a little thpread for the company at about three and thicth a head, not reckoning Luth,[2] it would make 'em happy."

---

1.   Horse-drawn coach or cart.
2.   Not including alcohol or 'lush' (slang).

All these little tokens of his gratitude, Mr. Gradgrind very willingly undertook to render. Though he thought them far too slight, he said, for such a service.

"Very well, Thquire; then, if you'll only give a Horthe-riding, a bethpeak, whenever you can, you'll more than balanthe the account. Now, Thquire, if your daughter will ethcuthe me, I thould like one parting word with you."

Louisa and Sissy withdrew into an adjoining room; Mr. Sleary, stirring and drinking his brandy and water as he stood, went on:

"Thquire, you don't need to be told that dogth ith wonderful animalth."

"Their instinct," said Mr. Gradgrind, "is surprising."

"Whatever you call it—and I'm bletht if I know what to call it"—said Sleary, "it ith athtonithing. The way in whith a dog'll find you—the dithtanthe he'll come!"

"His scent," said Mr. Gradgrind, "being so fine."

"I'm bletht if I know what to call it," repeated Sleary, shaking his head, "but I have had dogth find me, Thquire, in a way that made me think whether that dog hadn't gone to another dog, and thed, 'You don't happen to know a perthon of the name of Thleary, do you? Perthon of the name of Thleary, in the Horthe-Riding way—thtout man—game eye?' And whether that dog mightn't have thed, 'Well, I can't thay I know him mythelf, but I know a dog that I think would be likely to be acquainted with him.' And whether that dog mightn't have thought it over, and thed, 'Thleary, Thleary! Oh yeth, to be thure! A friend of mine menthioned him to me at one time. I can get you hith addreth directly.' In conthequenth of my being afore the public, and going about tho muth, you thee, there mutht be a number of dogth acquainted with me, Thquire, that I don't know!"

Mr. Gradgrind seemed to be quite confounded by this speculation.

"Any way," said Sleary, after putting his lips to his brandy and water, "ith fourteen month ago, Thquire, thinthe we wath at Chethter. We wath getting up our Children in the Wood one morning, when there cometh into our Ring, by the thtage door, a dog. He had travelled a long way, he wath in very bad condithon, he wath lame, and pretty well blind. He went round to our children, one after another, ath if he wath a theeking for a child he know'd; and then he come to me, and throwd hithelf up behind, and thtood on hith two forelegth, weak ath he wath, and then he wagged hith tail and died. Thquire, that dog wath Merrylegth."

"Sissy's father's dog!"

"Thethilia'th father'th old dog. Now, Thquire, I can take my oath, from my knowledge of that dog, that that man wath dead—and buried—afore that dog come back to me. Joth'phine and Childerth and me talked it over a long time, whether I thould write or not. But we agreed, 'No. There'th nothing comfortable to tell; why unthettle her mind, and make her unhappy?' Tho whether her father bathely detherted her; or whether he broke hith own heart alone, rather than pull her down along with him; never will be known, now, Thquire, till—no, not till we know how the dogth findth uth out!"

"She keeps the bottle that he sent her for, to this hour; and she will believe in his affection to the last moment of her life," said Mr. Gradgrind.

"It theemth to prethent two thingth to a perthon, don't it, Thquire?" said Mr. Sleary, musing as he looked down into the depths of his brandy and water: "one, that there ith a love in the world, not all Thelf-interetht after all, but thomething very different; t'other, that it hath a way of ith own of calculating or not calculating, whith thomehow or another ith at leatht ath hard to give a name to, ath the wayth of the dogth ith!"

Mr. Gradgrind looked out of the window, and made no reply. Mr. Sleary emptied his glass and recalled the ladies.

"Thethilia my dear, kith me and good-bye! Mith Thquire, to thee you treating of her like a thithter, and a thithter that you trutht and honour with all your heart and more, ith a very pretty thight to me. I hope your brother may live to be better detherving of you, and a greater comfort to you. Thquire, thake handth, firtht and latht! Don't be croth with uth poor vagabondth. People mutht be amuthed. They can't be alwayth a learning, nor yet they can't be alwayth a working, they an't made for it. You *mutht* have uth, Thquire. Do the withe thing and the kind thing too, and make the betht of uth; not the wurtht!"

"And I never thought before," said Mr. Sleary, putting his head in at the door again to say it, "that I wath tho muth of a Cackler!"

Chapter IX.
Final

It is a dangerous thing to see anything in the sphere of a vain blusterer, before the vain blusterer sees it himself. Mr. Bounderby felt that Mrs. Sparsit had audaciously anticipated him, and presumed to be wiser than he. Inappeasably indignant with her for her triumphant discovery of Mrs. Pegler, he turned this presumption, on the part of a woman in her dependent position, over and over in his mind, until it accumulated with turning like a great snowball. At last he made the discovery that to discharge this highly connected female—to have it in his power to say, "She was a woman of family, and wanted to stick to me, but I wouldn't have it, and got rid of her"—would be to get the utmost possible amount of crowning glory out of the connection, and at the same time to punish Mrs. Sparsit according to her deserts.

Filled fuller than ever, with this great idea, Mr. Bounderby came in to lunch, and sat himself down in the dining-room of former days, where his portrait was. Mrs. Sparsit sat by the fire, with her foot in her cotton stirrup, little thinking whither she was posting.

Since the Pegler affair, this gentlewoman had covered her pity for Mr. Bounderby with a veil of quiet melancholy and contrition. In virtue thereof, it had become her habit to assume a woful look, which woful look she now bestowed upon her patron.

"What's the matter now, ma'am?" said Mr. Bounderby, in a very short, rough way.

"Pray, sir," returned Mrs. Sparsit, "do not bite my nose off."

"Bite your nose off, ma'am?" repeated Mr. Bounderby. "*Your* nose!" meaning, as Mrs. Sparsit conceived, that it was too developed a nose for the purpose. After which offensive implication, he cut himself a crust of bread, and threw the knife down with a noise.

Mrs. Sparsit took her foot out of her stirrup, and said, "Mr. Bounderby, sir!"

"Well, ma'am?" retorted Mr. Bounderby. "What are you staring at?"

"May I ask, sir," said Mrs. Sparsit, "have you been ruffled this morning?"

"Yes, ma'am."

"May I inquire, sir," pursued the injured woman, "whether *I* am the unfortunate cause of your having lost your temper?"

"Now, I'll tell you what, ma'am," said Bounderby, "I am not come here to be bullied. A female may be highly connected, but she can't be permitted to bother and badger a man in my position, and I am not going to put up with it." (Mr. Bounderby felt it necessary to get on: foreseeing that if he allowed of details, he would be beaten.)

Mrs. Sparsit first elevated, then knitted, her Coriolanian eyebrows; gathered up her work into its proper basket; and rose.

"Sir," said she, majestically. "It is apparent to me that I am in your way at present. I will retire to my own apartment."

"Allow me to open the door, ma'am."

"Thank you, sir; I can do it for myself."

"You had better allow me, ma'am," said Bounderby, passing her, and getting his hand upon the lock; "because I can take the opportunity of saying a word to you, before you go. Mrs. Sparsit, ma'am, I rather think you are cramped here, do you know? It appears to me, that, under my humble roof, there's hardly opening enough for a lady of your genius in other people's affairs."

Mrs. Sparsit gave him a look of the darkest scorn, and said with great politeness, "Really, sir?"

"I have been thinking it over, you see, since the late affairs have happened, ma'am," said Bounderby; "and it appears to my poor judgement—"

"Oh! Pray, sir," Mrs. Sparsit interposed, with sprightly cheerfulness, "don't disparage your judgement. Everybody knows how unerring Mr. Bounderby's judgement is. Everybody has proofs of it. It must be the theme of general conversation. Disparage anything in yourself but your judgement, sir," said Mrs. Sparsit, laughing.

Mr. Bounderby, very red and uncomfortable, resumed:

"It appears to me, ma'am, I say, that a different sort of establishment altogether would bring out a lady of *your* powers. Such an establishment as your relation, Lady Scadgers's, now. Don't you think you might find some affairs there, ma'am, to interfere with?"

"It never occurred to me before, sir," returned Mrs. Sparsit; "but now you mention it, I should think it highly probable."

"Then suppose you try, ma'am," said Bounderby, laying an envelope with a cheque in it in her little basket. "You can take your own time for going, ma'am; but perhaps in the meanwhile, it will be more agreeable to a lady of your powers of mind, to eat her meals by herself, and not to be intruded upon. I really ought to apologise to you—being only Josiah Bounderby of Coketown—for having stood in your light so long."

"Pray don't name it, sir," returned Mrs. Sparsit. "If that portrait could speak, sir—but it has the advantage over the original of not possessing the power of committing itself and disgusting others,—it would testify, that a long period has elapsed since I first habitually addressed it as the picture of a Noodle. Nothing that a Noodle does, can awaken surprise or indignation; the proceedings of a Noodle can only inspire contempt."

Thus saying, Mrs. Sparsit, with her Roman features like a medal struck to commemorate her scorn of Mr. Bounderby, surveyed him fixedly from head to foot, swept disdainfully past him, and ascended the staircase. Mr. Bounderby closed the door, and stood before the fire; projecting himself after his old explosive manner into his portrait—and into futurity.

Into how much of futurity? He saw Mrs. Sparsit fighting out a daily fight at the points of all the weapons in the female armoury, with the grudging, smarting, peevish, tormenting Lady Scadgers, still laid up in her bed with her mysterious leg, and gobbling her insufficient income down by about the middle of every quarter, in a mean little airless lodging, a mere closet for one, a mere crib for two; but did he see more? Did he catch any glimpse of himself making a show of Bitzer to strangers, as the rising young man, so devoted to his master's great merits, who had won young Tom's place, and had almost captured young Tom himself, in the times when by various rascals he was spirited away? Did he see any faint reflection of his own image making a vain-glorious will, whereby five-and-twenty Humbugs, past five-and-fifty years of age, each taking upon himself the name, Josiah Bounderby of Coketown, should for ever dine in Bounderby Hall, for ever lodge in Bounderby buildings, for ever attend a Bounderby chapel, for ever go to sleep under a Bounderby chaplain, for ever be supported out of a Bounderby estate, and for ever nauseate all healthy stomachs, with a vast amount of Bounderby balderdash and bluster? Had he any prescience of the day, five years to come, when Josiah Bounderby of Coketown was to die of a fit in the Coketown street, and this same precious will was to begin its long career of quibble, plunder, false pretences, vile example, little service and much law? Probably not. Yet the portrait was to see it all out.

Here was Mr. Gradgrind on the same day, and in the same hour, sitting thoughtful in his own room. How much of futurity did *he* see? Did he see himself, a white-haired decrepit man, bending his hitherto inflexible theories to appointed circumstances; making his facts and figures subservient to Faith, Hope, and Charity;[1] and no longer trying to grind that Heavenly trio in his dusty little mills? Did he catch sight of himself, therefore much despised by his late political associates? Did he see them, in the era of its being quite settled that the national dustmen have only to do with one another, and owe no duty to an abstraction called a People, "taunting the honourable gentleman" with this and with that and with what not, five nights a-week, until the small hours of the morning? Probably he had that much foreknowledge, knowing his men.

Here was Louisa on the night of the same day, watching the fire as in days of yore, though with a gentler and a humbler face. How much of the future might arise before *her* vision? Broadsides in the streets, signed with her father's name, exonerating the late Stephen Blackpool, weaver, from misplaced suspicion, and publishing the guilt of his own son, with such extenuation as his years and temptation (he could not bring himself to add, his education) might beseech; were of the Present. So, Stephen Blackpool's tombstone, with her father's record of his death, was almost of the Present, for she knew it was to be. These things she could plainly see. But, how much of the Future?

A working woman, christened Rachael, after a long illness, once again appearing at the ringing of the Factory bell, and passing to and fro at the set hours, among the Coketown Hands; a woman of pensive beauty, always dressed in black, but sweet-tempered and serene, and even cheerful; who, of all the people in the place, alone appeared to have compassion on a degraded, drunken wretch of her own sex, who was sometimes seen

---

1.   See 1 Corinthians 13:13.

in the town secretly begging of her, and crying to her; a woman working, ever working, but content to do it, and preferring to do it as her natural lot, until she should be too old to labour any more? Did Louisa see this? Such a thing was to be.

A lonely brother, many thousands of miles away, writing, on paper blotted with tears, that her words had too soon come true, and that all the treasures in the world would be cheaply bartered for a sight of her dear face? At length this brother coming nearer home, with a hope of seeing her, and being delayed by illness; and then a letter, in a strange hand, saying "he died in hospital, of fever, such a day, and died in penitence and love of you: his last word being your name?" Did Louisa see these things? Such things were to be.

Herself again a wife—a mother—lovingly watchful of her children, ever careful that they should have a childhood of the mind no less than a childhood of the body, as knowing it to be even a more beautiful thing, and a possession, any hoarded scrap of which, is a blessing and happiness to the wisest? Did Louisa see this? Such a thing was never to be.

But, happy Sissy's happy children loving her; all children loving her; she, grown learned in childish lore; thinking no innocent and pretty fancy ever to be despised; trying hard to know her humbler fellow-creatures, and to beautify their lives of machinery and reality with those imaginative graces and delights, without which the heart of infancy will wither up, the sturdiest physical manhood will be morally stark death, and the plainest national prosperity figures can show, will be the Writing on the Wall,[1]—she holding this course as part of no fantastic vow, or bond, or brotherhood, or sisterhood, or pledge, or covenant, or fancy dress, or fancy fair; but simply as a duty to be done,—did Louisa see these things of herself? These things were to be.

Dear reader! It rests with you and me, whether, in our two fields of action, similar things shall be or not. Let them be! We shall sit with lighter bosoms on the hearth, to see the ashes of our fires turn gray and cold.

The End

---

1.   See Daniel 5:24–8.

Appendices: Contemporary Documents

APPENDIX A. THE COMPOSITION OF THE NOVEL

1. Agreement concerning serial publication in *Household Words*.

[Reprinted with permission from STOREY (1993) p. 911.]

28 December 1853

Present Messrs Bradbury, Evans, Forster and Wills.

Resolved That Mr. Charles Dickens is hereby engaged to write, at his earliest convenience, a story for Household Words equal in length to five single monthly numbers of Bleak House. This story is to be published in Household Words in continuous weekly portions; each of such length as Mr. Dickens, in his Capacity, as Editor, may think fit.

That for the publication of this story in Household Words, the sum of one thousand pounds, be paid to Mr. Charles Dickens by his partners in that publication, William Bradbury, Frederick Mullet Evans, John Forster and William Henry Wills. Five hundred pounds to be paid on the publication of the first weekly portion and the remaining five hundred pounds on the publication of the last weekly portion.

That the payment of one thousand pounds is not to be charged (nor any portion of it) against the profits of Household Words. Neither is it, nor any portion of it to appear in any account of the charges and expenses of that publication; it being the personal venture of the four partners before-mentioned with a view to the enlargement of the circulation of Household Words and the consequent enhancement of the value of their several shares.

That the copyright of the story for separate publication apart from Household Words in any form he may think fit to belong solely and absolutely to Mr. Charles Dickens. The proceeds of its publication in Household Words to form part of the general profits of the journal divisible in the proportions set forth in the deed of partnership.

JOHN FORSTER

2. Announcements in *Household Words* concerning the publication of the novel.

a.   **Announcement of serial publication in *Household Words*.**
[Appearing first on 4 March 1854, p. 68, and on subsequent weeks (with appropriate variations as to dates and numbers) until 5 August 1854.]

☛ *NEW TALE by Mr. CHARLES DICKENS to be published Weekly in HOUSEHOLD WORDS.*

On Wednesday, the 29th of March will be published, in Household Words, the First Portion of a New Work of Fiction, called

HARD TIMES.
BY CHARLES DICKENS.

—◆—

The publication of this Story will be continued in HOUSEHOLD WORDS from Week to Week, and completed in Five Months.

Price of each Weekly Number of HOUSEHOLD WORDS, (containing, besides, the usual variety of matter), Twopence; or Stamped, Threepence.

HOUSEHOLD WORDS, CONDUCTED BY CHARLES DICKENS, is published also in Monthly Parts and in Half-yearly Volumes.

---

b.   **Announcement of the volume publication.**
[29 July 1854, p. 596.]

On Monday, the Seventh of August, will be published, carefully revised and wholly reprinted,

IN ONE VOLUME, PRICE FIVE SHILLINGS

HARD TIMES.
BY CHARLES DICKENS.

BRADBURY and EVANS, 11, Bouverie Street.

---

3. Opening page of Dickens's working memoranda (Mems).

[Now held in the Forster Collection at the Victorian and Albert Museum, along with the manuscript and surviving proofs of the novel. Facsimiles and transcriptions of the complete Mems appear in STONE.]

[Friday January 20th 1854

Mems: Quantity

One sheet (16 pages) of Bleak House, will
make 10 pages and a quarter of Household
Words. ~~Ten~~ Fifteen pages of my writing, will make a sheet
of Bleak House.

~~A line of two more than a~~ A page and a half
of my writing, will make a page of Household
Words.

The quantity of the story to be published weekly,
being about five pages of Household Words will
require about <u>seven and a half of my
writing</u>.

[Friday January 20th 1854

Mr Gradgrind	Stubborn Things
Mrs Gradgrind	Fact
	Thomas Gradgrind's facts
	~~George~~ John Gradgrind's facts
	Hard-headed Gradgrind
	The Grindstone
	Hard heads and soft hearts
	~~The Time Grinders~~
	Mr Gradgrind's grindstone
	~~The Family Grindstone~~
	Hard Times
	The ~~universal~~ general grindstone
	Hard Times

Heads and Tales
Two and Two are Four
Prove it!
<u>Black and white</u>
According to Cocker
Prove it!
Stubborn things
~~Facts are stubborn things~~
                    Facts

~~John~~
~~Thomas~~   Mr Gradgrind's ~~grindstone~~
~~Thomas~~   ~~Mr Gradgrind's~~ grindstone
The ~~Thomas~~   Hard Times
~~These real times days~~
~~There's no~~   Two and Two are Four
~~No such thing sir~~

~~Calculations~~
~~Extremes meet~~   ~~according to Cocker~~
~~Unknown quantities~~   ~~Damaging Facts~~
Simple arithmetic   something tangible
A ~~mere~~ matter of
Calculation

Our hard-headed friend
A mere question of
figures

Rust and dust

4. Letters from Dickens touching on the writing of *Hard Times*.

[Reprinted with permission from STOREY (1993)]

a. From letter to John Forster, [20 January 1854].

I wish you would look at the enclosed titles for the *H.W.* story, between this and two o'clock or so, when I will call. It is my usual day, you observe, on which I have jotted them down—Friday! It seems to me that there are three very good ones among them. I should like to know whether you hit upon the same.

1. According to Cocker. 2. Prove it. 3. Stubborn Things. 4. Mr. Gradgrind's Facts. 5. The Grindstone. 6. Hard Times. 7. Two and Two are Four. 8. Something Tangible. 9. Our Hard-headed Friend. 10. Rust and Dust. 11. Simple Arithmetic. 12. A Matter of Calculation. 13. A Mere Question of Figures. 14. The Gradgrind Philosophy.

b. From letter to Miss Burdett Coutts, Tavistock House, 23 January 1854.

I have fallen to work again. My purpose is among the mighty secrets of the world at present; but there is such a fixed idea on the part of my printers and copartners in Household Words, that a story by me, continued from week to week, would make some unheard-of effect with it, that I am going to write one. It will be as long as five Nos. of Bleak House, and will be five months in progress. The first written page now stares at me from under this sheet of note paper. The main idea of it, is one on which you and I and Mrs. Brown have often spoken; and I know it will interest you as a purpose.

c. From letter to W.H. Wills, Tavistock House, 25 January 1854.

I want (for the story I am trying to hammer out) the Educational Board's series of question [sic] for the examination of *teachers* in schools. Will you get it.

d. From letter to John Forster, [Preston, 29 January 1854].

I am afraid I shall not be able to get much here. Except the crowds at the street corners reading the placards pro and con; and the cold absence of smoke from the mill-chimneys; there is very little in the streets to make the town remarkable. I am told that the people "sit at home and mope." The delegates with the money from the neighbouring places come in to-day to report the amounts they bring; and tomorrow the people are paid. When I have seen both these ceremonies, I shall return. It is a nasty place (I thought it was a model town); and I am in the Bull Hotel, before which some time ago the people assembled supposing the masters to be here, and on demanding to have them out were remonstrated with by the landlady in person. I saw the account in an Italian paper, in which it was stated that "the populace then environed the Palazzo Bull, until the padrona of the Palazzo heroically appeared at one of the upper windows and addressed them!" One can hardly conceive anything less likely to be represented to an Italian mind by this description, than the old, grubby, smoky, mean, intensely formal red brick house with a narrow gateway and a dingy yard, to which it applies. At the theatre last night I saw *Hamlet,* and should have done better to "sit at home and mope" like the idle workmen. In the last scene, Laertes on being asked how it was with him replied (verbatim) "Why, like a woodcock—on account of my treachery."

e. From letter to Messrs. Bradbury & Evans, Tavistock House, 9 February 1854.

I wish you would consider whether there is any thing wanting in this advertisement. It looks plain, to me.

f. From letter to Mark Lemon, Tavistock House, 20 February 1854.

Will you note down and send me any slang terms among tumblers and Circuspeople, that you can call to mind? I have noted down some—I want them in my new story—but it is very probable that you will recall several which I have not got.

g. From letter to John Forster, [? February 1854].

The difficulty of the space is CRUSHING. Nobody can have an idea of it who has not had experience of patient fiction-writing with some elbow-room always, and open places in perspective. In this form, with any kind of regard to the current number, there is absolutely no such thing.

h. From letter to Messrs. Bradbury & Evans, Tavistock House, 7 March 1854.

Throughout Hard Times, will you arrange when you get the corrected revises back from me (I now send those of the two first parts) to have *then* pulled, for my reference copy at work, a proof folded in any easy form for reference that may not give much trouble to your people. I want to avoid the botheration, both of the long slips, and of having to cut my working copy out of the Nos. week by week.

i. From letter to Emile de la Rue, Tavistock House, 9 March 1854.

It was considered, when I came home, such a great thing that I should write a story for Household Words, that I am at present up to the eyes in one. It is to be published in Household Words, weekly, through five months, and will be altogether as long as five Nos. of Copperfield or Bleak House. I did intend to be as lazy as I *could* be all through the summer, but here I am with my armour on again.

j. From letter to Peter Cunningham, Tavistock House, 11 March 1854.

Being down at Dover yesterday, I happened to see the Illustrated London News lying on the table, and there read a reference to my new book which I believe I am not mistaken in supposing to have written [sic] by you.

I don't know where you may have found your information, but I can assure you that it is altogether wrong. The title was many weeks old, and chapters of the story were written, before I went to Preston or thought about the present Strike. The mischief of such a statement is twofold. First, it encourages the public to believe in the impossibility that books are produced in that very sudden and Cavalier manner (as poor Newton used to feign that he produced the elaborate drawings he made in his madness, by winking at his table); and Secondly in this instance it has this pernicious bearing: It localizes (so far as your readers are concerned) a story which has a direct purpose in reference to the working people all over England, and it will cause, as I know by former experience, characters to be fitted on to individuals whom I never saw or heard of in my life.

I do not suppose that you can do anything to set this mis-statement right, being made; nor do I wish you to set it right. But if you will, at any future time, ask me what the fact is before you state it, I will tell you, as frankly and readily as it is possible for one friend to tell another, what the truth is and what it is not.

k. From letter to Miss Burdett Coutts, Tavistock House, 17 March 1854.

It is a mercy O did not seriously hurt herself. A lady-friend of ours broke her leg at about the same time in very much the same manner. Do you think it would be good for her to hear half an hour of my new story? It contains the dawn of the idea and is not at all distressing—yet. If you would like it, as the publication begins tomorrow fortnight, I would come up any evening in the meantime, except Wednesdays.

l. From letter to Charles Knight, Tavistock House, 17 March 1854.

I have read the article with much interest. It is most conscientiously done, and presents a great mass of curious information condensed into a surprisingly small space.

I have made a slight note or two here and there, with a soft pencil, so that a touch of indiarubber will make all blank again.

And I earnestly entreat your attention to the point (I have been working upon it, weeks past, in Hard Times) which I have jocosely suggested on the last page but one. The English are, so far as I know, the hardest worked people on whom the sun shines. Be content if in their wretched intervals of leisure they read for amusement and do no worse. They are born to the oar, and they live and die at it. Good God, what would we have of them!

m. From letter to W.H. Wills, Tavistock House, 18 April 1854.

I am in a dreary state, planning and planning the story of Hard Times (out of materials for I don't know how long a story), and consequently writing little.

n. From letter to Mrs. Gaskell, Tavistock House, 21 April 1854.

I have no intention of striking. The monstrous claims at domination made by a certain class of manufacturers, and the extent to which the way is made easy for working men to slide down into discontent under such hands, are within my scheme; but I am not going to strike. So don't be afraid of me. But I wish you would look at the story yourself, and judge where and how near I seem to be approaching what you have in your mind. The first two months of it will shew that.

o. From letter to Henry Cole, Tavistock House, 17 June 1854.

Although I date from here [Tavistock House], I have in fact retreated to Boulogne to pass the summer in the society of your friend Mr. Gradgrind and the others, free from the disturbances of London. [...]

I often say to Mr. Gradgrind that there is reason and good intention in much that he does—in fact, in all that he does—but that he over-does it. Perhaps by dint of his going his way and my going mine, we shall meet at last at some half-way house where there are flowers on the carpets, and a little standing-room for Queen Mab's Chariot among the Steam Engines.

p.   From letter to Thomas Carlyle, Villa du Camp de droite, Boulogne, 13 July 1854.

I am going, next month, to publish in One Volume a story now coming out in Household Words, called Hard Times. I have constructed it patiently, with a view to its publication altogether in a compact cheap form. It contains what I do devoutly hope will shake some people in a terrible mistake of these days, when so presented. I know it contains nothing in which you do not think with me, for no man knows your books better than I. I want to put in the first page of it, that it is inscribed to Thomas Carlyle. May I?

q.   From letter to W.H. Wills, Boulogne, 14 [13] July 1854.

I am so stunned with work, that I really am not able (in sending off my own parcel hurriedly) to answer your questions—I mean, not able to consider them. I doubt if there will not be too much of Hard Times, to admit of the conclusion all going in together. There will probably be either 14 or 15 sides of my writing. But the best thing will be for me to come over with it, the moment I have finished. *On Wednesday night at a quarter past ten,* I hope to be at London Bridge. But if I should find on Monday (though I hardly expect it) that I can come on Tuesday night instead, I will let you know as much by Monday's post.

The MS now sent, contains what I have looked forward to through many weeks.

The advertisement will simply be

On such a day will be published

Complete in One Volume, price five shillings,

HARD TIMES

By Charles Dickens.

I will send B & E the two first books in your returned parcel.

r.   From letter to John Forster, Boulogne, 14 July 1854.

I am three parts mad, and the fourth delirious, with perpetual rushing at *Hard Times*. I have done what I hope is a good thing with Stephen, taking his story as a whole; and hope to be over in town with the end of the book on Wednesday night. [...] I have been looking forward through so many weeks and sides of paper to this Stephen business, that now—as usual—it being over, I feel as if nothing in the world, in the way of intense and violent rushing hither and thither, could quite restore my balance.

s.   From letter to W.H. Wills, Boulogne, 17 July 1854.

I am happy to say that I have finished Hard Times this morning. I purpose coming over tomorrow, arriving at London Bridge at a quarter past 10 at Night. Will you tell Cooper to be there, in waiting for me.

**t.   From letter to Henry Carey, Tavistock House,
24 August 1854.**

To interest and affect the general mind in behalf of anything that is clearly wrong—to stimulate and rouse the public soul to a compassionate or indignant feeling that it *must not be*—without obtruding any pet theory of cause or cure, and so throwing off allies as they spring up—I believe to be one of Fiction's highest uses. And this is the use to which I try to turn it.

**u.   From letter to The Hon. Mrs. Richard Watson, Tavistock
House, 1 November 1854.**

Why I found myself so "used up", after Hard Times, I scarcely know. Perhaps because I had intended to do nothing in that way for a year, when the idea laid hold of me by the throat in a very violent manner; and because the compression and close condensation necessary for that disjointed form of publication, gave me perpetual trouble. But I really was—tired!—which is a result so very incomprehensible that I can't forget it.

**v.   From letter to Charles Knight, Tavistock House,
30 [December] 1854.**

My satire is against those who see figures and averages, and nothing else—the representatives of the wickedest and most enormous vice of this time—the men who, through long years to come, will do more to damage the real useful truths of political economy, than I could do (if I tried) in my whole life—the addled heads who would take the average of cold in the Crimea during twelve months, as a reason for clothing a soldier in nankeen on a night when he would be frozen to death in fur—and who would comfort the labourer in travelling twelve miles a day to and from his work, by telling him that the average distance of one inhabited place from another in the whole area of England, is not more than four miles. Bah! What have you to do with these!

Appendix B. Contemporary Reviews of the Novel

1. Unsigned *Athenæum* (12 August 1854) No. 1398 p. 992.

[Prestigious weekly literary review (1828–1921) with a wide circulation, then edited by W. Hepworth Dixon; brief comments in the 'Our Library Table' series.]

The idea of Mr. Dickens's last story, 'Hard Times,' is a good idea:—but is scarcely wrought out with Mr. Dickens's usual felicity. The purpose is to show that Fact is not everything to man; and that the spiritual longings of our nature are not to be neglected with impunity. In its essence, this is a poetical conception; and it required for its due exhibition an ideal framework. Mr. Dickens has been pleased to give it a prosaic framework and to people it with very repulsive and vulgar characters. Considered as a work of Art, this is its great defect. A story, the form of which was poetical, and the characters of which were removed from common-place alike in their graces, their humours, and their pathos—as, for example, are those in 'The Tempest' and in 'The Midsummer Night's Dream'—might have been invented by the literary artist, in which all the morals proposed by Mr. Dickens as a necessary part of the education of young people could have been established without the straining and the violence which many persons will reasonably object to in 'Hard Times.' The case of Fancy *versus* Fact is here stated in prose, but without the fairness which belongs to a prose argument. A purely ideal treatment was needed for such a purpose. Many persons—and most certainly those for whose reproof the tale is written—will fail to see that the education of Fact, as opposed to the education of Fancy—of the Reason without due notice of the Emotions—of the Intellect without reference to the Imagination—leads of necessity to the results pourtrayed in Louisa and Tom Gradgrind. If not of necessity, why seek to substitute the general by the incidental? The many will object—unless Mr. Dickens goes so far as to assert that the girl came to the brink of shame, and the boy went over it, because they had not been allowed to read fairy tales and see strolling players in their youth—as we think he will scarcely venture to do—that the story teaches nothing at all, and that therefore the moral machinery in it fails. That 'Hard Times,' like everything that Mr. Dickens writes, is full of humour, observation, knowledge of manhood, will not be gainsaid. It has the beauties and the vices of his style. It abounds in passages bright and glowing—

delicate in their humour—and subtle in their fancy; but these passages are found in close relationship to others coarse, violent, and awkward. Altogether the tale is readable, though it lacks moral interest; and the puppets of the play move and speak like living creatures, though the mind refuses to allow that they are fitting messengers of the poetical truth with the delivery of which they appear to be charged. Fancy asks an ideal advocate.

2. Unsigned *Examiner* (9 September 1854) pp. 568–9.

[Radical then liberal weekly review of politics and literature (1808–81), edited from 1847 by Dickens's friend and biographer John Forster, who wrote this piece.]

[...]

So far as the purpose of *Hard Times* involves the direct raising of any question of political economy, we abstain from comment upon it. In a tale, especially a very short one, clearly and powerfully written, full of incident and living interest, it is difficult to find room for a sufficiently full expression of opinion upon details, in the working of a given principle. The principle emphatically laid down by Mr Dickens in the story before us is one to which every sound heart responds. We cannot train any man properly unless we cultivate his fancy, and allow fair scope to his affections. We may starve the mind upon hard fact as we may starve the body upon meat, if we exclude all lighter diet, and all kinds of condiment. To enforce this truth has been the object of the story of *Hard Times,* and its enforcement is not argumentative, because no thesis can be argued in a novel; but by a warm appeal from one heart, to a hundred thousand hearts quite ready to respond. The story is not meant to do what fiction cannot do—to prove a case; its utmost purpose is to express forcibly a righteous sentiment. To run anywhere into a discussion of detail would have checked the current of a tale, which, as it stands, does not flag for the space even of a page. Wherever in the course of it any playful handling of a notion of the day suited the artist's purpose, the use made of it has been artistic always, never argumentative.

Hard Times, in fact, is not meant to be fought through, prosed over, conned laboriously, Blue Book in hand. Is the heart touched with a lively perception of the true thought which pervades the work from first to last—then the full moral purpose of it is attained. The very journal in which the novel appeared is itself a complete answer to any man, who, treating in a hard-fact spirit all the fanciful allusions of the novelist, should accuse Mr Dickens of attacking this good movement and the other, or of opposing the search after statistical and other information by which only real light can be thrown on social questions. What is *Household Words* but a great magazine of facts? And what one is there, of all those useful matters of detail which the novelist has by some readers been supposed to treat with disrespect, which he has not, as conductor of that journal, carefully and fully urged upon the public notice? In his character of journalist Mr Dickens has from the first especially laboured to cultivate the kindly affections and the fancy at the same time with the intellect, and that is simply what he asks men in 'these times' to do. But because he knows that facts and figures will not be lost sight of by the world, he leaves them, when he speaks as a novelist, to take care of themselves, and writes his tale wholly in the interests of the affections and the fancy.

And with unbroken satisfaction will those finer qualities in its readers fasten upon it. The personal regard which Mr Dickens inspires by his books will here have no abatement. Again he garners for himself the first fruits of the harvest of kindliness sown broadcast in all his writings. It is not necessary to review *Hard Times*. When we have said that the remarkably close texture of the story, the carefulness of its elaboration, and the unsuperfluousness of its details, as well as its whole interest, are far more perceptible now that it can be read as a book, than when it was known only as a series of chapters, we have reported all that calls for report from us. A new sense of its design and beauty in its various particulars is awakened by the reading of it as a whole. The homely grace and tenderness of Rachel [sic] appeals with more quiet effect, the unobtrusive pathos of her intercourse with Stephen is deepened, and if possible we are more impressed by what is shown of the working man's wrongs and delusions in connection with the truth and constancy of his nature. [...]

3. Unsigned *Gentleman's Magazine* (September 1854) No. 42 pp. 276–8.

[Long-standing general interest monthly; the review, of which only the last third is reproduced here, covers both Lectures on Education delivered at the Royal Institution (see App. C 10) and *Hard Times*.]

[...]

Among the remaining lectures we incline to rate most highly Professor Paget on Physiology, and Dr. Hodgson on Economic Science. In the very able lecture delivered by the latter are some remarks on Mr. Dickens' latest work, "Hard Times," which seem to us just and well put.

Mr. Dickens is sufficiently exaggerative to throw discredit on his truths; but yet that there should be scope and room for such a tale at all—that, not among the ignorant of schools only, but among many who have had experience of them, there should be a feeling that, on the whole, he has got hold of a fact and a dangerous tendency which those who love their fellow-creatures should not be slow to perceive, is one of the signs of the times, and we have no desire to ignore it. We feel confident that political economists and that many educators of the people rely by far too much on intellectual information and clearness in a certain round of facts, for the improvement of the poor. The great fault we are disposed to find with Mr. Dickens, besides his unreasonable exaggerations and unnatural characters, is that he does not paint something higher and better for our example and help. He is right, surely, in his perception of the cold cheerlessness of the facts of a calculating bodily life; but he should show what may be done by more genial cultivation. He tells us what is evil, but there is scarce a word of good. We have ourselves many and obstinate rebellings against the class of educators who want to keep the poor wholly within the circle of "useful" facts. The poor man needs, as much as any one, amusement, enjoyment, ideas beyond his immediate vision; but this requires to be shewn in a better way than by finding fault with the short-comings of our time. We trust examples will be given as the world goes on of greater sympathy between the classes of society. No one has yet felt or done half so much for this desirable end as that charming writer and thinker, Mr. Helps. May he not grow tired of the task, but give us more and more reason to bless the author of the "Claims of Labour" and "Companions of my Solitude."

4. Unsigned *British Quarterly Review* (October 1854) Vol. XX No. 40 pp. 581–2.

[Nonconformist evangelical quarterly (1845–86), with a wide coverage including theology, literature, politics and science.]

In this story, Mr. Bounderby, of Coketown, is a great mill owner, who prides himself on having risen from the lowest imaginable condition, and on having made himself the great man he is. Mr. Gradgrind, of the same town, is a specimen of the severe economist school, living in a region of statistics, who sees in human beings only so many pieces of mechanism, to be weighed or measured according to certain mechanic laws, the substance of which laws, fairly and briefly translated is, that man's mission in this world is to take the best possible care of number one. The working of this philosophy in the domestic relations of the philosopher is not pleasant. His eldest son becomes a coarse-minded rascal. His eldest daughter marries unhappily, being influenced so to do by the false philosophy of her father. In the course of the story the quarrel between masters and men comes up, and if the picture of a master in Mr. Bounderby is not very flattering, as little so is the picture of the orator who gets the ear of the workmen, and puts them on wrong courses. Among the men is an honest fellow whose wife has become the burden of his existence from habits of intoxication. The woman is sunk in filth and offensiveness. The man would know why the poor man may not have a divorce in such cases, in common with the rich man, and why he should not be allowed to marry again.

These are the main features of the story. Its faults are the faults common to Mr. Dickens' authorship—the faults of one-sidedness and exaggeration. There is a class of men resembling Mr. Bounderby, but he is, in our judgement, an exaggeration of even the worst in his class. Moreover, the class of millowners, and of such as have risen from an humble origin, who acquit themselves most humanely and honourably, is much greater than the class which Mr. Bounderby is made to represent; and to depict the worst man of a class so that he can hardly fail to be taken as a sample of the whole, is to become chargeable with what would be described, applied to individuals, as falsehood and calumny. As to the picture of the economical school, who see the whole duty of man in buying in the cheapest market and selling in the dearest, we believe there are not a few of them fully as bad as the picture here given of them. They are men without bowels. Concerning the divorce question—we could wish that divorce were available in the case of the poor as of the rich on the one ground which the New Testament permits, but if Mr. Dickens can suppose that it would be for the benefit of the working classes that our laws should deem the plea of incompatibility a sufficient ground for divorce, all we can say is, that we think he is more at home in delineating character than he would be as a legislator. In this story, again, as in all his works, Mr. Dickens has his characters of great moral beauty, but care seems to be taken that this beauty of character shall come into existence, not only apart from any religious influences, but in circumstances most alien to such influences. His best condition of humanity is a condition without religion, a condition that does not need religion. When he does introduce that element, it is an element of cant and hypocrisy, not as a matter rooted in honest convictions, and taking with it pure and noble tendencies. Mr. Dickens may not mean to teach his readers to distrust and ignore everything religious by this one-sided and unfair course of authorship, but this is the lesson which multitudes of his readers are imperceptibly, but steadily learning, as they sit at his feet, and we could wish him, for his own sake, to remember that for all this he is responsible. We loathe the cant of religiousness quite as much as Mr. Dickens does, and we see it where it is as much as he does. But are we all to become atheists, practically at least, if not avowedly, because the world has its hypocrites in religion, as in everything besides? Theologians, however, have themselves to thank for much of this mischief. It is rarely their manner to do justice to poor human nature, which, faulty as it may be, often gives signs of noble qualities; and these romancings about it are a not unnatural reaction against their harsh and narrow dogmatisms concerning it.

5. Unsigned *Rambler* (October 1854) Vol. II Pt. 10 pp. 361–2.

[Liberal Catholic monthly review, succeeded by the *Home and Foreign Review*; this piece in the 'Miscellaneous Literature' section by the editor, Richard Simpson.]

This is a reprint, in one volume, of a tale which has already appeared in "Household Words." Thomas Gradgrind, a hard-headed magnate of Coketown (in the manufacturing districts), with the aid and advice of his friend Josiah Bounderby, a banker, hard-headed, hard-hearted, and purse-proud, educates his two eldest children, Louisa and Tom, on facts and figures, to the entire exclusion of tastes and affections. The system bears fruit. Louisa, in callous misery, sacrifices herself in marriage to Bounderby, thirty years her senior, and is only saved from the snares of a seducer by a timely flight to her father's roof. Tom turns thief, and robs the safe in the Bounderby bank, where he is a clerk, but escapes to die abroad in wretchedness, having succeeded in throwing suspicion on an innocent man, Stephen Blackpool, a weaver, who, in hot haste to clear himself, pitches headlong down an old mine-shaft, and is so mangled that, as soon as rescued, he expires. This dreary framework is filled in by the loves of Stephen, who, in his youth, married a drunkard, from whom, to his and Mr. Dickens' disgust, neither death nor the laws will divorce him; and Rachel [sic], a fellow "hand" of pattern goodness, who is his guiding star. A star of the same kind is supplied to poor Louisa, in her trouble, by Sissy Jupe, the daughter of a clown in Sleary's horseriding troupe, the latter dividing the comic business of the tale with Mrs. Sparsit, a sort of brownholland edition of Volumnia in our author's "Bleak House," who acts as housekeeper to Mr. Bounderby. Here and there we meet with touches not unworthy of the inventor of "Pickwick;" but, on the whole, the story is stale, flat, and unprofitable; a mere dull melodrama, in which character is caricature, sentiment tinsel, and moral (if any) unsound. It is a thousand pities that Mr. Dickens does not confine himself to amusing his readers, instead of wandering out of his depth in trying to instruct them. The one, no man can do better; the other, few men can do worse. With all his quickness of perception, his power of seizing salient points and surface-shadows, he has never shown any ability to pierce the depth of social life, to fathom the wells of social action. He can only paint what he sees, and should plan out his canvas accordingly. No doubt great evils exist in manufacturing towns, and elsewhere; but, nevertheless, steam-engines and power-looms are not the evil principle in material shape, as the folly of conventional humanitarian slang insists on making them. The disease of Coketown will hardly be stayed by an abstinence from facts and figures; nor a healthy reaction insured by a course of cheap divorce and the poetry of nature. In short, whenever Mr. Dickens and his school assume the office of instructors, it is, as Stephen Blackpool says, "aw a muddle! Fro first to last, a muddle!"

6. Unsigned *South London Athenæum and Institution Magazine* (October 1854) Vol. I No. 2 p. 115.

[Recently-founded metropolitan quarterly review; a lengthy review, of which only the opening paragraph is reproduced here.]

For the first time we rise from the perusal of one of Mr. Dickens' works thoroughly disappointed. Introduced to us at a time when the Preston Strike claimed an attention second only to the never-ending Eastern Question, its name was suggestive of the author's intention of dealing with that unhappy struggle; the opening chapters were plainly indicative of a crusade against the purely utilitarian tendencies of the day, while, with the history of Stephen Blackpool, one of the blots on our civilisation—the present law of divorce—seemed destined to receive its death-blow from the hand that unmasked and laid bare the iniquities of Yorkshire Schools, Doctors Commons, and the Court of Chancery. It is possible Mr. Dickens proposed for himself more than he could accomplish in one work. It is more than probable, that had either of the above themes received his undivided attention, he would have produced three good books, and "have done the state some service."

[...]

7. Unsigned *Westminster Review* (October 1854) Vol. VI No. 12 pp. 604–6.

[Quarterly radical intellectual review (1824–1914), established by Jeremy Bentham and James Mill (father of J.S. Mill) and originally entitled the *London and Westminster Review*; a long article in the 'Contemporary Literature' section by Jane Sinnet, of which only the opening paragraphs are reproduced here. (Authorial footnotes are omitted.)]

"Hard Times" decidedly reads better in a volume than it did in detached chapters; we can hasten over those parts which are painful to dwell upon towards those of more pleasing interest.

When it was announced, amid the strikes and consequent derangements of commerce, that Mr. Dickens was about to write a tale in "Household Words" to be called "Hard Times," the general attention was instantly arrested. It was imagined the main topic of the story would be drawn from the fearful struggle which was being then enacted in the north, in which loss of money on the one side and the pangs of hunger on the other, were the weapons at command. The inner life of those great movements would, it was thought, be exhibited, and we should see the results of the wrongs and the delusions of the workmen, and the alternations of hope and fear which must from day to day have agitated him at the various crises of the conflict, delineated in many a moving scene. Mr. Dickens—if any one—it was considered, could be intrusted with this delicate task, and would give us a true idea of the relations of master and workman, both as they are and as they might be. Some of this is done in the book now before us, only this purpose is subordinated and made incidental to another, which is to exhibit the evil effects of an exclusive education of the intellect, without a due cultivation of the finer feelings of the heart and the fancy. We suppose it is in anticipation of some change of the present educational system for one that shall attempt to kill "outright the robber Fancy," that Mr. Dickens launches forth his protest, for we are not aware of such a system being in operation anywhere in England. On the contrary, it is the opinion of various continental professors, very competent to form a judgment on this subject, that more play is given to the imagination and will by the English system of instruction than by any other. If we look to our public schools and universities, we find great part, too great part, we think, of the period of youth and adolescence devoted to the study of the mythology, literature, and history of the most poetic people of all time. The "gorgeous Tragedies" of Athens,

> "Presenting Thebes' or Pelops' line,
> Or the tale of Troy divine,"

under the name of the Greek Play, have produced no slight consumption of birch-rod in this country. In almost every school in the kingdom, passages of our finest poets are learned by heart; and Shakespeare and Walter Scott are among the Penates of every decent family. If there are Gradgrind schools, they are not sufficiently numerous to be generally known. Now, at the very commencement of "Hard Times," we find ourselves introduced to a set of hard uncouth personages, of whose existence as a class no one is aware, who are engaged in cutting and paring young souls after their own ugly pattern, and refusing them all other nourishment but facts and figures. The unpleasant impression caused by being thus suddenly intro-duced into this cold and uncongenial atmosphere, is never effaced by the subse-quent charm of narrative and well-painted characters of the tale. One can have no more pleasure in being present at this compression and disfigurement than in witnessing the application of the boot—nor in following these poor souls, thus intellectually halt and maimed, through life, than in seeing Chinese ladies hob-bling through a race. It is not then with the truth Mr. Dickens wishes to enforce, but with the manner in which it is enforced, that we find fault. It was possible to have done this in a less forbidding form, with actors whom we should have rec-ognised as more natural and less repulsive than the Gradgrinds, Bounderbys, and Crakemchilds [sic]; to have placed in contrast persons educated after an ordinary and *practicable* plan, and persons of higher aesthetic training; but, at the same time, the task would have required a deeper acquaintance with human nature. The most successful characters in "Hard Times," as is usual with Mr. Dickens, are those which are the *simplest* and least cultivated. Stephen Blackpool, Rachel [sic] and Sissy, Mr. Thleary of the 'horth-riding', and his single-hearted troupe, all act and talk with such simplicity of heart and nobleness of mind, that their appearance on the stage is a most welcome relief from the Gradgrinds, Bounderbys, Sparsits, &c., who are all odd characters portrayed in a quaint style; and we regret that more of the story is not devoted to objects who are so much more within Mr. Dickens's power of representation. Stephen Blackpool, with his rugged steadfastness, sturdy truth, upright bearing, and fine Northern English dialect, smacking strongly of the old Saxon, is a noble addition to the gallery which already contained the bluff John Browdie, the Yarmouth boatmen, and so many other fine portraits. The gentle lowly grace of Rachel [sic], and her undeviating instinct of what is right and good, make her a fit companion to the worn and much-wronged Stephen. The story of their unfulfilled love, and its sad catastrophe, is a truly pathetic episode of humble life. But when Mr. Dickens leaves his lowly-born heroes and heroines, and weaves personages of more cultivated natures into his plots, the dif-ference of execution is very marked. [...]

8. Unsigned *Blackwood's Edinburgh Magazine* (April 1855) Vol. LXXVII No. 474 pp. 453–4.

[Scottish conservative monthly miscellany (1817–1980); the comments on *Hard Times* reproduced here form a parenthesis to a lengthy and generally favourable survey of Dickens's literary career by novelist and journalist Margaret Oliphant.]

[...] Mr Dickens is the favourite and spoiled child of the popular heart. There is a long ring of applause echoing after him wherever it pleases him to go; but for the sake of his great and well-deserved reputation, we think it would be well for Mr Dickens to discover on which foundation it is that he stands most secure.

And in this volume before us, the latest work he has given to the world—*Hard Times*—we discover, not the author's full and many-toned conception of human life, its motives and its practices,—not the sweet and graceful fancy rejoicing in her own creations, nor the stronger and graver imagination following the fate of her complete idea, rather as a chronicler than a producer of the events which its natural character and qualities call forth,—but the petulant theory of a man in a world of his own making, where he has no fear of being contradicted, and is absolutely certain of having everything his own way. We have seldom seen a more lamentable *non sequitur* than *Hard Times*. A story written in direct illustration of some preconceived idea is seldom successful as a story. Beyond an Eastern apologue, a distinct and professed allegory or parable, fiction breaks down when it is bound within these certain limits, and compelled to prove and to substantiate a theory. This, which is the proper work of reason, is by no means the business of the poetic faculty, and Pegasus is too restive a steed to be bound to the plough; but in this case the theory is so over-strained and unnatural, the cause is so perfectly inadequate to the results attributed to it, that the original objection increases tenfold. The name of the book and the period of its publication alike deluded the public. We anticipated a story, certainly sad—perhaps tragical—but true, of the unfortunate relationship between masters and men which produced the strike of Preston; and this most legitimate subject, at once for public inquiry and for the conciliating and healing hand of genius, to whom both belligerents were brother, might have well employed the highest powers. The sketch of Stephen Blackpool, too, and of Rachel [sic], his ministering angel, seemed to indicate this larger purpose early in the tale. But no; Stephen Blackpool is only introduced to bring out the greater villainy of the wretched little rogue of the story, and to be made a forced example, in his domestic circumstances, of the unequal pressure of the law upon the rich and poor—and, in his death, of the carelessness and neglect to which so many lives are sacrificed; while the real object of the book is, to prove that the teaching of universal knowledge, the instruction in all the "ologies," the education which arbitrarily imposes fact and puts down fancy, is a system which makes very poor villains of our sons, and very wretched wives of our daughters, and that the perfectly opposite system of no education at all, save the natural growth of the sentiments and affections, produces angels, not only of goodness, but of wisdom and judicious courage almost unparalleled. In short, the conclusion of the story is this: shut out all *Arabian Nights*, all imagination, fancy, poetry, from your schoolroom—rear your boy on the dry pabulum of facts and sciences (yet there once was wonderful poetry in these same sciences), and your boy will rob the bank and become a dissipated little provincial scoundrel, as mean as he is guilty; whereas you have only to bind him apprentice to the horse-riding instead, and have him trained among the delightful idealities of the circle, to make everything that is kind-hearted, noble, and unselfish of this very boy.

This lame and impotent conclusion, and not the great question between the "hands" and their employers, is the end and aim of Mr Dickens in writing *Hard Times*. The book is more palpably a *made* book than any of the many manufactured articles we have lately seen. It is neither born out of the natural fruition of a mind and fancy always astir—nor, after it has begun to be, do its characters and events proceed with the natural compulsion and impulse of life. If Mr Dickens forgets himself now and then, and remembers the craft of which he is a master, by running into a natural exhibition of nature and life, he draws up immediately under the hard necessity of holding by his text and proving his theory. To say that the story was without character or without interest would not be true; but we are sure that every reader really admiring the fine genius of Mr Dickens must, in the annoyance and regret with which he read, have almost overlooked the inalienable gifts of the writer. Stephen Blackpool and his womanly pure-hearted Rachel [sic] are beautifully sketched; there is distinctness and identity in Louisa, perfect reality and truth in Tom, who represents a large class of whelps, and a very clever outline in Mr James Harthouse. We can make nothing of the impossible Sissy, but we have no doubt that Mr Sleery's [sic] company of horse-riders are drawn to the life. When we have said all this, we still leave undiminished our condemnation of the book,—a story made on the didactic principle, with all its events forced into proofs of an untenable theory, and with almost the only life among its personages, which thoroughly interest us, thrown away, forsooth, to show the evils of that carelessness, which, in great matters and little matters, from Balaklava to the Lancashire coal-pits, is undoubtedly becoming a rather remarkable feature in our national character.

But we are very glad to leave *Hard Times* and Mr Dickens' individual theories for Mr Dickens' real works, the broad foundation on which his fame stands sure. [...]

Appendix C. On Industrialization: Commentary

1a. Unsigned (Thomas Carlyle) 'Signs of the Times' *Edinburgh Review* (June 1829) Vol. XLIX No. 98.

[Thomas Carlyle (1795–1881), Scottish social historian and political philosopher. The essay attacks the mechanistic and materialistic spirit of the age.]

Were we required to characterise this age of ours by any single epithet, we should be tempted to call it, not an Heroical, Devotional, Philosophical, or Moral Age, but, above all others, the Mechanical Age. It is the Age of Machinery, in every outward and inward sense of that word; the age which, with its whole undivided might, forwards, teaches and practises the great art of adapting means to ends. Nothing is now done directly, or by hand; all is by rule and calculated contrivance. For the simplest operation, some helps and accompaniments, some cunning abbreviating process is in readiness. Our old modes of exertion are all discredited, and thrown aside. On every hand, the living artisan is driven from his workshop, to make room for a speedier, inanimate one. The shuttle drops from the fingers of the weaver, and falls into iron fingers that ply it faster. The sailor furls his sail, and lays down his oar; and bids a strong, unwearied servant, on vaporous wings, bear him through the waters. Men have crossed oceans by steam; the Birmingham Fire-king has visited the fabulous East; and the genius of the Cape, were there any Camoens now to sing it, has again been alarmed, and with far stranger thunders than Gamas. There is no end to machinery. Even the horse is stripped of his harness, and finds a fleet fire-horse yoked in his stead. Nay, we have an artist that hatches chickens by steam; the very brood-hen is to be superseded! For all earthly, and for some unearthly purposes, we have machines and mechanic furtherances; for mincing our cabbages; for casting us into magnetic sleep. We remove mountains, and make seas our smooth highway; nothing can resist us. We war with rude Nature; and, by our resistless engines, come off always victorious, and loaded with spoils.

What wonderful accessions have thus been made, and are still making, to the physical power of mankind; how much better fed, clothed, lodged and, in all outward respects, accommodated men now are, or might be, by a given quantity of labour, is a grateful reflection which forces itself on every one. What changes, too, this addition of power is introducing into the Social System; how wealth has more and more increased, and at the same time gathered itself more and more into masses, strangely altering the old relations, and increasing the distance between the rich and the poor, will be a question for Political Economists, and a much more complex and important one than any they have yet engaged with.

But leaving these matters for the present, let us observe how the mechanical genius of our time has diffused itself into quite other provinces. Not the external and physical alone is now managed by machinery, but the internal and spiritual also. Here too nothing follows its spontaneous course, nothing is left to be accomplished by old natural methods. Everything has its cunningly devised implements, its preëstablished apparatus; it is not done by hand, but by machinery. Thus we have machines for Education: Lancastrian machines; Hamiltonian machines; monitors, maps and emblems. Instruction, that mysterious communing of Wisdom with Ignorance, is no longer an indefinable tentative process, requiring a study of individual aptitudes, and a perpetual variation of means and methods, to attain the same end; but a secure, universal, straightforward business, to be conducted in the gross, by proper mechanism, with such intellect as comes to hand. Then, we have Religious machines, of all imaginable varieties; the Bible-Society, professing a far higher and heavenly structure, is found, on inquiry, to be altogether an earthly contrivance: supported by collection of moneys, by fomenting of vanities, by puffing, intrigue and chicane; a machine for converting the Heathen. It is the same in all other departments. Has any man, or any society of men, a truth to speak, a piece of spiritual work to do; they can nowise proceed at once and with the mere natural organs, but must first call a public meeting, appoint committees, issue prospectuses, eat a public dinner; in a word, construct or borrow machinery, wherewith to speak it and do it. Without machinery they were hopeless, helpless; a colony of Hindoo weavers squatting in the heart of Lancashire. Mark, too, how every machine must have its moving power, in some of the great currents of society; every little sect among us, Unitarians, Utilitarians, Anabaptists, Phrenologists, must have its Periodical, its monthly or quarterly Magazine;—hanging out, like its windmill, into the *popularis aura*, to grind meal for the society.

With individuals, in like manner, natural strength avails little. No individual now hopes to accomplish the poorest enterprise single-handed and without mechanical aids; he must make interest with some existing corporation, and till his field with their oxen. In these days, more emphatically than ever, 'to live, signifies to unite with a party, or to make one.' Philosophy, Science, Art, Literature, all depend on machinery. No Newton, by silent meditation, now discovers the system of the world from the falling of an apple; but some quite other than Newton stands in his Museum, his Scientific Institution, and behind whole batteries of retorts, digesters, and galvanic piles imperatively 'interrogates Nature,'—who, however, shows no haste to answer. In defect of Raphaels, and Angelos, and Mozarts, we have Royal Academies of Painting, Sculpture, Music; whereby the languishing spirit of Art may be strengthened, as by the more generous diet of a Public Kitchen. Literature, too, has its Paternoster-row mechanism, its Trade-dinners, its Editorial conclaves, and huge subterranean, puffing bellows; so that books are not only printed, but, in a great measure, written and sold, by machinery.

National culture, spiritual benefit of all sorts, is under the same management. No Queen Christina, in these times, needs to send for her Descartes; no King Frederick for his Voltaire, and painfully nourish him with pensions and flattery: any sovereign of taste, who wishes to enlighten his people, has only to impose a new tax, and with the proceeds establish Philosophic Institutes. Hence the Royal and Imperial Societies, the Bibliothèques, Glypothèques, Technothèques, which front us in all capital cities; like so many well-finished hives, to which it is expected the stray agencies of Wisdom will swarm of their own accord, and hive and make honey. In like manner, among ourselves, when it is thought that religion is declining, we have only to vote half-a-million's worth of bricks and mortar, and build new churches. In Ireland it seems they have gone still farther, having actually established a 'Penny-a-week Purgatory-Society'! Thus does the Genius of Mechanism stand by to help us in all difficulties and emergencies, and with his iron back bears all our burdens.

These things, which we state lightly enough here, are yet of deep import, and indicate a mighty change in our whole manner of existence. For the same habit regulates not our modes of action alone, but our modes of thought and feeling. Men are grown mechanical in head and in heart, as well as in hand. They have lost faith in individual endeavour, and in natural force, of any kind. Not for internal perfection, but for external combinations and arrangements, for institutions, constitutions,—for Mechanism of one sort or other, do they hope and struggle. Their whole efforts, attachments, opinions, turn on mechanism, and are of a mechanical character.

[...]

To us who live in the midst of all this, and see continually the faith, hope and practice of everyone founded on Mechanism of one kind or other, it is apt to seem quite natural, and as if it could never have been otherwise. Nevertheless, if we recollect or reflect a little, we shall find both that it has been, and might again be otherwise. The domain of Mechanism,—meaning thereby political, ecclesiastical or other outward establishments,—was once considered as embracing, and we are persuaded can at any time embrace, but a limited portion of man's interests, and by no means the highest portion.

To speak a little pedantically, there is a science of *Dynamics* in man's fortunes and nature, as well as of *Mechanics*. There is a science which treats of, and practically addresses, the primary, unmodified forces and energies of man, the mysterious springs of Love, and Fear, and Wonder, of Enthusiasm, Poetry, Religion, all which have a truly vital and *infinite* character; as well as a science which practically addresses the finite, modified developments of these, when they take the shape of immediate 'motives,' as hope of reward, or as fear of punishment.

Now it is certain, that in former times the wise men, the enlightened lovers of their kind, who appeared generally as Moralists, Poets or Priests, did, without neglecting the Mechanical province, deal chiefly with the Dynamical; applying themselves chiefly to regulate, increase and purify the inward primary powers of man; and fancying that herein lay the main difficulty, and the best service they could undertake. But a wide difference is manifest in our age. For the wise men, who now appear as Political Philosophers, deal exclusively with the Mechanical province; and occupying themselves in counting-up and estimating men's motives, strive by curious checking and balancing, and other adjustments of Profit and Loss, to guide them to their true advantage: while, unfortunately, those same 'motives' are so innumerable, and so variable in every individual, that no really useful conclusion can ever be drawn from their enumeration. But though Mechanism, wisely contrived, has done much for man in a social and moral point of view, we cannot be persuaded that it has ever been the chief source of his worth or happiness. Consider the great elements of human enjoyment, the attainments and possessions that exalt man's life to its present height, and see what part of these he owes to institutions, to Mechanism of any kind; and what to the instinctive, unbounded force, which Nature herself lent him, and still continues to him. Shall we say, for example, that Science and Art are indebted principally to the founders of Schools and Universities? Did not Science originate rather, and gain advancement, in the obscure closets of the Roger Bacons, Keplers, Newtons; in the workshops of the Fausts and the Watts; wherever, and in what guise soever Nature, from the first times downwards, had sent a gifted spirit upon the earth? Again, were Homer and Shakspeare members of any beneficed guild, or made Poets by means of it? Were Painting and Sculpture created by forethought, brought into the world by institutions for that end? No; Science and Art have, from first to last, been the free gift of Nature; an unsolicited, unexpected gift; often even a fatal one. These things rose up, as it were, by spontaneous growth, in the free soil and sunshine of Nature. They were not planted or grafted, nor even greatly multiplied or improved by the culture or manuring of institutions. Generally speaking, they have derived only partial help from these; often enough have suffered damage. They made constitutions for themselves. They originated in the Dynamical nature of man, not in his Mechanical nature.

Or, to take an infinitely higher instance, that of the Christian Religion, which, under every theory of it, in the believing or unbelieving mind, must ever be regarded as the crowning glory, or rather the life and soul, of our whole modern culture: How did Christianity arise and spread abroad among men? Was it by institutions, and establishments and well-arranged systems of mechanism? Not so; on the contrary, in all past and existing institutions for those ends, its divine spirit has invariably been found to languish and decay. It arose in the mystic deeps of man's soul; and was spread abroad by the 'preaching of the word,' by simple, altogether natural and individual efforts; and flew, like hallowed fire, from heart to heart, till all were purified and illuminated by it; and its heavenly light shone, as it still shines, and (as sun or star) will ever shine, through the whole dark destinies of man. Here again was no Mechanism; man's highest attainment was accomplished Dynamically, not Mechanically.

Nay, we will venture to say, that no high attainment, not even any far-extending movement among men, was ever accomplished otherwise. Strange as it may seem, if we read History with any degree of thoughtfulness, we shall find that the checks and balances of Profit and Loss have never been the grand agents with men; that they have never been roused into deep, thorough, all-pervading efforts by any computable prospect of Profit and Loss, for any visible, finite object; but always for some invisible and infinite one. The Crusades took their rise in Religion; their visible object was, commercially speaking, worth nothing. It was the boundless Invisible world that was laid bare in the imaginations of those men; and in its burning light, the visible shrunk as a scroll. Not mechanical, nor produced by mechanical means, was this vast movement. No dining at Freemasons' Tavern, with the other long train of modern machinery; no cunning reconciliation of 'vested interests,' was required here: only the passionate voice of one man, the rapt soul looking through the eyes of one man; and rugged, steel-clad Europe trembled beneath his words, and followed him whither he listed. In later ages it was still the same. The Reformation had an invisible, mystic and ideal aim; the result was indeed to be embodied in external things; but its spirit, its worth, was internal, invisible, infinite. Our English Revolution too originated in Religion. Men did battle, in those old days, not for Purse-sake, but for Conscience-sake. Nay, in our own days, it is no way different. The French Revolution itself had something higher in it than cheap bread and a Habeas-corpus act. Here too was an Idea; a Dynamic, not a Mechanic force. It was a struggle, though a blind and at last an insane one, for the infinite, divine nature of Right, of Freedom, of Country.

Thus does man, in every age, vindicate, consciously or unconsciously, his celestial birthright. Thus does Nature hold on her wondrous, unquestionable course; and all our systems and theories are but so many froth-eddies or sand banks, which from time to time she casts up, and washes away. When we can drain the Ocean into mill-ponds, and bottle-up the Force of Gravity, to be sold by retail, in gas jars; then may we hope to comprehend the infinitudes of man's soul under formulas of Profit and Loss; and rule over this too, as over a patent engine, by checks, and valves, and balances.

Nay, even with regard to Government itself, can it be necessary to remind any one that Freedom, without which indeed all spiritual life is impossible, depends on infinitely more complex influences than either the extension or the curtailment of the 'democratic interest'? Who is there that, 'taking the high *priori* road,' shall point out what these influences are; what deep, subtle, inextricably entangled influences they have been and may be? For man is not the creature and product of Mechanism; but, in a far truer sense, its creator and producer: it is the noble People that makes the noble Government; rather than conversely. On the whole, Institutions are much; but they are not all. The freest and highest spirits of the world have often been found under strange outward circumstances: Saint Paul and his brother Apostles were politically slaves; Epictetus was personally one. Again, forget the influences of Chivalry and Religion, and ask: What countries produced Columbus and Las Casas? Or, descending from virtue and heroism to mere energy and spiritual talent: Cortes, Pizarro, Alba, Ximenes? The Spaniards of the sixteenth century were indisputably the noblest nation of Europe: yet they had the Inquisition and Philip II. They have the same government at this day; and are the lowest nation. The Dutch too have retained their old constitution; but no Siege of Leyden, no William the Silent, not even an Egmont or De Witt any longer appears among them. With ourselves also, where much has changed, effect has nowise followed cause as it should have done: two centuries ago, the Commons Speaker addressed Queen Elizabeth on bended knees, happy that the virago's foot did not even smite him; yet the people were then governed, not by a Castlereagh, but by a Burghley; they had their Shakspeare and Philip Sidney, where we have our Sheridan Knowles and Beau Brummel.

These and the like facts are so familiar, the truths which they preach so obvious, and have in all past times been so universally believed and acted on, that we should almost feel ashamed for repeating them; were it not that, on every hand, the memory of them seems to have passed away, or at best died into a faint tradition, of no value as a practical principle. To judge by the loud clamour of our Constitution-builders, Statists, Economists, directors, creators, reformers of Public Societies; in a word, all manner of Mechanists, from the Cartwright up to the Code-maker; and by the nearly total silence of all Preachers and Teachers who should give a voice to Poetry, Religion and Morality, we might fancy either that man's Dynamical nature was, to all spiritual intents, extinct, or else so perfected that nothing more was to be made of it by the old means; and henceforth only in his Mechanical contrivances did any hope exist for him.

To define the limits of these two departments of man's activity, which work into one another, and by means of one another, so intricately and inseparably, were by its nature an impossible attempt. Their relative importance, even to the wisest mind, will vary in different times, according to the special wants and dispositions of those times. Meanwhile, it seems clear enough that only in the right coördination of the two, and the vigorous forwarding of *both*, does our true line of action lie. Undue cultivation of the inward or Dynamical province leads to idle, visionary, impracticable courses, and, especially in rude eras, to Superstition and Fanaticism, with their long train of baleful and well-known evils. Undue cultivation of the outward, again, though less immediately prejudicial, and even for the time productive of many palpable benefits, must, in the long-run, by destroying Moral Force, which is the parent of all other Force, prove not less certainly, and perhaps still more hopelessly, pernicious. This, we take it, is the grand characteristic of our age. By our skill in Mechanism, it has come to pass, that in the management of external things we excel all other ages; while in whatever respects the pure moral nature, in true dignity of soul and character, we are perhaps inferior to most civilised ages.

1b. Thomas Carlyle *Chartism* (1839) Ch. 2.

[*Chartism* concerns the condition of the industrial and agricultural working-classes and the causes of class conflict. This chapter is entitled 'Statistics' and attacks utilitarian methods of calculating social progress. (The footnote is the author's.)]

A witty statesman said, you might prove anything by figures. We have looked into various statistic works, Statistic-Society Reports, Poor-Law Reports, Reports and Pamphlets not a few, with a sedulous eye to this question of the Working Classes and their general condition in England; we grieve to say, with as good as no result whatever. Assertion swallows assertion; according to the old Proverb, 'as the *statist* thinks, the bell clinks!' Tables are like cobwebs, like the sieve of the Danaides; beautifully reticulated, orderly to look upon, but which will hold no conclusion. Tables are abstractions, and the object a most concrete one, so difficult to read the essence of. There are innumerable circumstances; and one circumstance left out may be the vital one on which all turned. Statistics is a science which ought to be honourable, the basis of many most important sciences; but it is not to be carried on by steam, this science, any more than others are; a wise head is requisite for carrying it on. Conclusive facts are inseparable from inconclusive except by a head that already understands and knows. Vain to send the purblind and blind to the shore of a Pactolus never so golden: these find only gravel; the seer and finder alone picks up gold grains there. And now the purblind offering you, with asseveration and protrusive importunity, his basket of gravel as gold, what steps are to be taken with him?—Statistics, one may hope, will improve gradually, and become good for something. Meanwhile it is to be feared, the crabbed statist was partly right, as things go: 'A judicious man,' says he, 'looks at Statistics, not to get knowledge, but to save himself from having ignorance foisted on him.' With what serene conclusiveness a member of some Useful-Knowledge Society stops your mouth with a figure of arithmetic! To him it seems he has there extracted the elixir of the matter, on which now nothing more can be said. It is needful that you look into his said extracted elixir; and ascertain, alas, too probably not without a sigh, that it is wash and vapidity, good only for the gutters.

Twice or three times have we heard the lamentations and prophecies of a humane Jeremiah, mourner for the poor, cut short by a statistic fact of the most decisive nature: How can the condition of the poor be other than good, be other than better; has not the average duration of life in England, and therefore among the most numerous class in England, been proved to have increased? Our Jeremiah had to admit that, if so, it was an astounding fact; whereby all that ever he, for his part, had observed on other sides of the matter, was overset without remedy. If life last longer, life must be less worn upon, by outward suffering, by inward discontent, by hardship of any kind; the general condition of the poor must be bettering instead of worsening. So was our Jeremiah cut short. And now for the 'proof?' Readers who are curious in statistic proofs may see it drawn out with all solemnity, in a Pamphlet 'published by Charles Knight and Company,'*—and perhaps himself draw inferences from it. Northampton Tables, compiled by Dr. Price 'from registers of the Parish of All Saints from 1735 to 1780;' Carlisle Tables, collected by Dr. Heysham from observation of Carlisle City for eight years, 'the calculations founded on them' conducted by another Doctor; incredible 'document considered satisfactory by men of science in France:'—alas, is it not as if some zealous scientific son of Adam had proved the deepening of the Ocean, by survey, accurate or cursory, of two mud-plashes on the coast of the Isle of Dogs? 'Not to get knowledge, but to save yourself from having ignorance foisted on you!'

The condition of the working man in this country, what it is and has been, whether it is improving or retrograding,—is a question to which from statistics hitherto no solution can be got. Hitherto, after many tables and statements, one is still left mainly to what he can ascertain by his own eyes looking at the concrete phenomenon for himself. There is no other method; and yet it is a most imperfect method. Each man expands his own hand-breadth of observation to the limits of the general whole; more or less, each man must take what he himself has seen and ascertained for a sample of all that is seeable and ascertainable. Hence discrepancies, controversies, wide-spread, long-continued; which there is at present no means or hope of satisfactorily ending. When Parliament takes up 'the Condition-of-England question,' as it will have to do one day, then indeed much may be amended! Inquiries wisely gone into, even on this most complex matter, will yield results worth something, not nothing. But it is a most complex matter; on which, whether for the past or the present, Statistic Inquiry, with its limited means, with its short vision and headlong extensive dogmatism, as yet too often throws not light, but error worse than darkness.

[...]

---

* An Essay on the Means of Insurance against the Casualties of &c. &c. London, Charles Knight and Company, 1836. Price two shillings.

1c. Thomas Carlyle *Past and Present* (1843)
Bk. III Ch. 9.

[*Past and Present* compares social and spiritual conditions in contemporary industrial England unfavourably with those in a twelfth
century abbey. This chapter, entitled 'Working Aristocracy', addresses
the responsibilities of modern capitalists ('Working Mammonism'),
and to a lesser extent of landowners ('Unworking Dilettantism'),
towards industrial and agricultural labourers.]

A poor Working Mammonism getting itself 'strangled in the partridge-nets of an
Unworking Dilettantism,' and bellowing dreadfully, and already black in the face,
is surely a disastrous spectacle! But of a Midas-eared Mammonism, which indeed
at bottom all pure Mammonisms are, what better can you expect? No better;—if
not this, then something other equally disastrous, if not still more disastrous.
Mammonisms, grown asinine, have to become human again, and rational; they
have, on the whole, to cease to be Mammonisms, were it even on compulsion,
and pressure of the hemp round their neck!—My friends of the Working Aristocracy, there are now a great many things which you also, in your extreme need,
will have to consider.

The Continental people, it would seem, are 'exporting our machinery, beginning to spin cotton and manufacture for themselves, to cut us out of this market
and then out of that!' Sad news indeed; but irremediable;—by no means the saddest news. The saddest news is, that we should find our National Existence, as I
sometimes heard it said, depend on selling manufactured cotton at a farthing an
ell cheaper than any other People. A most narrow stand for a great Nation to base
itself on! A stand which, with all the Corn-Law Abrogations conceivable, I do not
think will be capable of enduring.

My friends, suppose we quitted that stand; suppose we came honestly down
from it, and said: "This is our minimum of cotton-prices. We care not, for the
present, to make cotton any cheaper. Do you, if it seem so blessed to you, make
cotton cheaper. Fill your lungs with cotton-fuz, your hearth with copperas-fumes,
with rage and mutiny; become ye the genial gnomes of Europe, slaves of the
lamp!"—I admire a Nation which fancies it will die if it do not undersell all other
Nations, to the end of the world. Brothers, we will cease to *under*sell them; we
will be content to *equal*-sell them; to be happy selling equally with them! I do
not see the use of underselling them. Cotton-cloth is already two-pence a yard or
lower; and yet bare backs were never more numerous among us. Let inventive
men cease to spend their existence incessantly contriving how cotton can be made

cheaper; and try to invent, a little, how cotton at its present cheapness could be somewhat justlier divided among us! Let inventive men consider, whether the Secret of this Universe, and of Man's Life there, does, after all, as we rashly fancy it, consist in making money? There is One God, just, supreme, almighty: but is Mammon the name of him? With a Hell which means 'Failing to make money,' I do not think there is any Heaven possible that would suit one well; nor so much as an Earth that can be habitable long! In brief, all this Mammon-Gospel, of Supply-and-demand, Competition, Laissez-faire, and Devil take the hindmost, begins to be one of the shabbiest Gospels ever preached on Earth; or altogether the shabbiest. Even with Dilettante partridge-nets, and at a horrible expenditure of pain, who shall regret to see the entirely transient, and at best somewhat despicable life strangled out of it? At the best, as we say, a somewhat despicable, unvenerable thing, this same 'Laissez-faire;' and now, at the *worst,* fast growing an altogether detestable one!

"But what is to be done with our manufacturing population, with our agricultural, with our ever-increasing population?" cry many.—Aye, what? Many things can be done with them, a hundred things, and a thousand things,—had we once got a soul, and begun to try. This one thing, of doing for them by 'underselling all people,' and filling our own bursten pockets and appetites by the road; and turning over all care for any 'population,' or human or divine consideration except cash only, to the winds, with a "Laissez-faire" and the rest of it: this is evidently not the thing. 'Farthing cheaper per yard:' no great Nation can stand on the apex of such a pyramid; screwing itself higher and higher; balancing itself on its great-toe! Can England not subsist without being *above* all people in working? England never deliberately purposed such a thing. If England work better than all people, it shall be well. England, like an honest worker, will work as well as she can; and hope the gods may allow her to live on that basis. Laissez-faire and much else being once well dead, how many 'impossibles' will become possible! They are 'impossible,' as cotton-cloth at two-pence an ell was—till men set about making it. The inventive genius of great England will not forever sit patient with mere wheels and pinions, bobbins, straps and billy-rollers whirring in the head of it. The inventive genius of England is not a Beaver's, or a Spinner's or Spider's genius: it is a *Man's* genius, I hope, with a God over him!

Supply-and-demand? One begins to be weary of such work. Leave all to egoism, to ravenous greed of money, of pleasure, of applause:—it is the Gospel of Despair! Man *is* a Patent-Digester, then: only give him Free Trade, Free digesting-room; and each of us digest what he can come at, leaving the rest to Fate! My unhappy brethren of the Working Mammonism, my unhappier brethren of the Idle Dilettantism, no world was ever held together in that way for long. A world of mere Patent-Digesters will soon have nothing to digest: such world ends, and by Law of Nature must end, in 'over-population;' in howling universal famine, 'impossibility,' and suicidal madness, as of endless dog-kennels run rabid. Supply-and-demand shall do its full part, and Free Trade shall be free as air;—thou of the shotbelts, see thou forbid it not, with those paltry, *worse* than 'Mammonish' swindleries and Sliding-scales of thine, which are seen to be swindleries for all thy canting, which in times like ours are very scandalous to see! And Trade never so well freed, and all Tariffs settled or abolished, and Supply-and-demand in full operation,—let us all know that we have yet done nothing; that we have merely cleared the ground for doing.

Yes, were the Corn-Laws ended tomorrow, there is nothing yet ended; there is only room made for all manner of things beginning. The Corn-Laws gone, and Trade made free, it is as good as certain this paralysis of industry will pass away. We shall have another period of commercial enterprise, of victory and prosperity; during which, it is likely, much money will again be made, and all the people may, by the extant methods, still for a space of years, be kept alive and physically fed. The strangling band of Famine will be loosened from our necks; we shall have room again to breathe; time to bethink ourselves, to repent and consider! A precious and thrice-precious space of years; wherein to struggle as for life in reforming our foul ways; in alleviating, instructing, regulating our people; seeking, as for life, that something like spiritual food be imparted them, some real governance and guidance be provided them! It will be a priceless time. For our new period or paroxysm of commercial prosperity will and can, on the old methods of 'Competition and Devil take the hindmost,' prove but a paroxysm: a new paroxysm,—likely enough, if we do not use it better, to be our *last*. In this, of itself, is no salvation. If our Trade in twenty years, 'flourishing' as never Trade flourished, could double itself; yet then also, by the old Laissez-faire method, our Population is doubled: we shall then be as we are, only twice as many of us, twice and ten times as unmanageable!

All this dire misery, therefore; all this of our poor Workhouse Workmen, of our Chartisms, Trades-strikes, Corn-Laws, Toryisms, and the general down-break of Laissez-faire in these days,—may we not regard it as a voice from the dumb bosom of Nature, saying to us: Behold! Supply-and-demand is not the one Law of Nature; Cash-payment is not the sole nexus of man with man,—how far from it! Deep, far deeper than Supply-and-demand, are Laws, Obligations sacred as Man's Life itself: these also, if you will continue to do work, you shall now learn and obey. He that will learn them, behold Nature is on his side, he shall yet work and prosper with noble rewards. He that will not learn them, Nature is against him; he shall not be able to do work in Nature's empire,—not in hers. Perpetual mutiny, contention, hatred, isolation, execration shall wait on his footsteps, till all men discern that the thing which he attains, however golden it look or be, is not success, but the want of success.

Supply-and-demand,—alas! For what noble work was there ever yet any audible 'demand' in that poor sense? The man of Macedonia, speaking in vision to an Apostle Paul, "Come over and help us," did not specify what rate of wages he would give! Or was the Christian Religion itself accomplished by Prize-Essays, Bridgewater Bequests, and a 'minimum of Four thousand five hundred a year?' No demand that I heard of was made then, audible in any Labour-market, Manchester Chamber of Commerce, or other the like emporium and hiring establishment; silent were all these from any whisper of such demand;—powerless were all these to 'supply' it, had the demand been in thunder and earthquake, with gold Eldorados and Mahometan Paradises for the reward. Ah me, into what waste latitudes, in this Time-Voyage, have we wandered; like adventurous Sindbads;— where the men go about as if by galvanism, with meaningless glaring eyes, and have no soul, but only a beaver-faculty and stomach! The haggard despair of Cotton-factory, Coal-mine operatives, Chandos Farm-labourers, in these days, is painful to behold; but not so painful, hideous to the inner sense, as that brutish godforgetting Profit-and-Loss Philosophy, and Life-theory, which we hear jangled on all hands of us, in senate-houses, spouting-clubs, leading-articles, pulpits and platforms, everywhere as the Ultimate Gospel and candid Plain-English of Man's Life, from the throats and pens and thoughts of all but all men!—

Enlightened Philosophies, like Molière Doctors, will tell you: "Enthusiasms, Self-sacrifice, Heaven, Hell and such like: yes, all that was true enough for old stupid times; all that used to be true: but we have changed all that, *nous avons changé tout cela!*"

So scandalous a beggarly Universe deserves indeed nothing else; I cannot say I would save it from Annihilation. Vacuum, and the serene Blue, will be much handsomer; easier too for all of us. I, for one, decline living as a Patent-Digester. Patent-Digester, Spinning-Mule, Mayfair Clothes-Horse: many thanks, but your Chaosships will have the goodness to excuse me!

2. Andrew Ure *The Philosophy of Manufactures: or, an Exposition of the Scientific, Moral, and Commercial Economy of the Factory System of Great Britain* (1836) Ch. 1 'General View of Manufacturing Industry' pp. 6–8 & 17–9.

[Andrew Ure (1778–1857), utilitarian surgeon, a staunch supporter of the manufacturers and opponent of landed interests. *The Philosophy of Manufactures* is an extravagant encomium on the material and moral progress represented by the mechanization of labour. (Authorial footnotes are omitted.)]

This island is pre-eminent among civilized nations for the prodigious development of its factory wealth, and has been therefore long viewed with a jealous admiration by foreign powers. This very pre-eminence, however, has been contemplated in a very different light by many influential members of our own community, and has been even denounced by them as the certain origin of innumerable evils to the people, and of revolutionary convulsions to the state. If the affairs of the kingdom be wisely administered, I believe such allegations and fears will prove to be groundless, and to proceed more from the envy of one ancient and powerful order of the commonwealth, towards another suddenly grown into political importance than from the nature of things.

In the recent discussions concerning our factories, no circumstance is so deserving of remark, as the gross ignorance evinced by our leading legislators and economists, gentlemen well informed in other respects, relative to the nature of those stupendous manufactures which have so long provided the rulers of the kingdom with the resources of war, and a great body of the people with comfortable subsistence; which have, in fact, made this island the arbiter of many nations, and the benefactor of the globe itself. Till this ignorance be dispelled, no sound legislation need be expected on manufacturing subjects. [...]

The blessings which physico-mechanical science has bestowed on society, and the means it has still in store for ameliorating the lot of mankind, have been too little dwelt upon; while, on the other hand, it has been accused of lending itself to the rich capitalists as an instrument for harassing the poor, and of exacting from the operative an accelerated rate of work. It has been said, for example, that the steam-engine now drives the power-looms with such velocity as to urge on their attendant weavers at the same rapid pace; but that the hand-weaver, not being subjected to this restless agent, can throw his shuttle and move his treddles at his convenience. There is, however, this difference in the two cases, that in the factory, every member of the loom is so adjusted, that the driving force leaves the attendant nearly nothing at all to do, certainly no muscular fatigue to sustain, while it procures for him good, unfailing wages, besides a healthy workshop *gratis*: whereas the non-factory weaver, having everything to execute by muscular exertion, finds the labour irksome, makes in consequence innumerable short pauses, separately of little account, but great when added together; earns therefore proportionally low wages, while he loses his health by a poor diet and the dampness of his hovel. [...]

The constant aim and effect of scientific improvement in manufactures are philanthropic, as they tend to relieve the workmen either from niceties of adjustment which exhaust his mind and fatigue his eyes, or from painful repetition of effort which distort or wear out his frame. At every step of each manufacturing process described in this volume, the humanity of science will be manifest.

[...]

In my recent tour, continued during several months, through the manufacturing districts, I have seen tens of thousands of old, young, and middle-aged of both sexes, many of them too feeble to get their daily bread by any of the former modes of industry, earning abundant food, raiment, and domestic accommodation, without perspiring at a single pore, screened meanwhile from the summer's sun and the winter's frost, in apartments more airy and salubrious than those of the metropolis, in which our legislative and fashionable aristocracies assemble. In those spacious halls the benignant power of steam summons around him his myriads of willing menials, and assigns to each the regulated task, substituting for painful muscular effort on their part, the energies of his own gigantic arm, and demanding in return only attention and dexterity to correct such little aberrations as casually occur in his workmanship. The gentle docility of this moving force qualifies it for impelling the tiny bobbins of the lace-machine with a precision and speed inimitable by the most dexterous hands, directed by the sharpest eyes. Hence, under its auspices, and in obedience to Arkwright's polity, magnificent edifices, surpassing far in number, value, usefulness, and ingenuity of construction, the boasted monuments of Asiatic, Egyptian, and Roman despotism, have, within the short period of fifty years, risen up in this kingdom, to show to what extent, capital, industry, and science may augment the resources of a state, while they meliorate the condition of its citizens. Such is the factory system, replete with prodigies in mechanics and political economy, which promises, in its future growth, to become the great minister of civilization to the terraqueous globe, enabling this country, as its heart, to diffuse along with its commerce, the life-blood of science and religion to myriads of people still lying "in the region and shadow of death."

3. P. Gaskell *Artisans and Machinery: The Moral and Physical Condition of the Manufacturing Population Considered with Reference to Mechanical Substitutes for Human Labour* (1836) Ch. 2 'Factory System ...' pp. 65–8.

[P. Gaskell was a surgeon and social critic who idealized eighteenth century village life. A revised and expanded version of his earlier work *The Manufacturing Population of England* (1833), *Artisans and Machinery* condemns the factory system for destroying the social and moral ties of family which were fostered under domestic manufacturing. (Authorial footnotes are omitted.)]

This disruption of all the ties of home is one of the most fatal consequences of the factory system. The social relations which should distinguish the members of the same family are destroyed. The domestic virtues, man's natural instincts, and the affections of the heart, are deadened and lost. The feelings and actions which should be the charm of the fire-side—which should prepare young men and young women for fulfilling the duties of parents—are displaced by a selfishness utterly repugnant to all such sacred obligations. Tenderness of manner—solicitude during sickness—the foregoing of personal gratification for the sake of others—submission to home restraint—these are partially lost, and their place occupied by individual independence—private avarice—the withholding assistance, however slight, from those around them, who have a natural claim upon their generosity, based solely upon sordid motives,—with a gradual extinction of those sympathies and feelings, which are alone fitted to afford happiness—a wearing away of the more delicate shades of character, leaving nothing but attention to the simple wants of nature, in addition to the depraved appetites which are the result of other circumstances connected with their condition;—and in the end reducing them, as a mass, to a heartless assemblage of separate and conflicting individuals, each striving for their "own hand", uninfluenced by the more gentle, the more noble, and the more humanized cares, aspirations, and feelings, which could alone render them estimable as fathers, mothers, brothers and sisters.

[...]

It has been truly observed, and not less beautifully than truly, that "heaven is around us in our infancy." This might have been extended, and said, that "heaven is around and within us in our infancy;" for the happiness of childhood springs full as much from an internal consciousness of delight, as from the novelty of its impressions from without. Its mind, providing the passions are properly guided, is indeed a fountain of all that is beautiful—all that is amiable—overflowing with joy and tenderness; and its young heart is a living laboratory of love, formed to be profusely scattered on all around it.

The very copiousness of its sensations, however, prevents stability in their direction, if not carefully tended; and if its heart and mind have capabilities for exhibiting and lavishing the treasures of their awakening energies, they are, from their very immaturity, more easily warped and misdirected. The hacknied quotation, "just as the twig is bent," &c. is not the less true for being hacknied. Most unhappily, every thing which goes on before the eyes of the unfortunate factory children is but too well calculated to nip in the bud—to wither in the springtime of its growth—the flower which was springing up within them, to adorn and beautify their future existence.

4a. 'A' (J.S. Mill) 'Bentham' *London and Westminster Review* (August 1838) Vol. XXIX.

[John Stuart Mill (1806–73), English liberal philosopher and economist, strongly influenced by Bentham who was a friend of his father, James Mill. In this controversial piece in the chief radical organ, together with its companion essay on 'Coleridge' (March 1840), Mill distances himself from the mechanistic aspects of Bentham's thought.]

In the brief view which we have been able to give of Bentham's philosophy, it may surprise the reader that we have said so little about the first principle of it, with which his name is more identified than with anything else; the "principle of utility," or, as he afterwards named it, "the greatest-happiness principle." It is a topic on which much were to be said, if there were room, or if it were in reality necessary for the just estimation of Bentham. On an occasion more suitable for a discussion of the metaphysics of morality, or on which the explanations necessary to make an opinion on so abstract a subject intelligible could be conveniently given, we should be fully prepared to state what we think on this subject. All we intend to say at present is, that we are much nearer to agreeing with Bentham in his principle, than in the degree of importance which he attached to it. We think utility, or happiness, much too complex and indefinite an end to be sought except through the medium of various secondary ends, concerning which there may be, and often is, agreement among persons who differ in their ultimate standard; and about which there does in fact prevail a much greater unanimity among thinking persons, than might be supposed from their diametrical divergence on the great questions of moral metaphysics. As mankind are much more nearly of one nature, than of one opinion about their own nature, they are much more easily brought to agree in their intermediate principles, *vera illa et media axiomata,* as Bacon says, than in their first principles: and the attempt to make the bearings of actions upon the ultimate end more evident than they can be made by referring them to the intermediate ends, and to estimate their value by a direct reference to human happiness, generally terminates in attaching most importance, not to those effects which are really the greatest, but to those which can most easily be pointed to and individually identified. Those who adopt utility as a standard can seldom apply it truly except through the secondary principles; those who reject it, generally do no more than erect those secondary principles into first principles.

We consider, therefore, the utilitarian controversy as a question of arrangement and logical subordination rather than of practice; important principally in a purely scientific point of view, for the sake of the systematic unity and coherency of ethical philosophy. Whatever be our own opinion on the subject, it is from no such source that we look for the great improvements which we believe are destined to take place in ethical doctrine. It is probable, however, that to the principle of utility we owe all that Bentham did; that it was necessary to him to find a first principle which he could receive as self-evident and to which he could attach all his other doctrines as logical consequences: that to him systematic unity was an indispensable condition of his confidence in his own intellect. And there is something further to be remarked: whether happiness be or be not the end to which morality should be referred—that it be referred to an *end* of some sort, and not left in the dominion of vague feeling or inexplicable internal conviction, that it be made a matter of reason and calculation, and not merely of sentiment, is essential to the very idea of moral philosophy; is, in fact, what renders argument or discussion on moral questions possible. That the morality of actions depends on the consequences which they tend to produce, is the doctrine of rational persons of all schools; that the good or evil of those consequences is measured solely by pleasure or pain, is all of the doctrine of the school of utility, which is peculiar to it.

In so far as Bentham's adoption of the principle of utility induced him to fix his attention upon the *consequences* of actions as the consideration determining their morality, so far at least he was in the right path: though to go far in it without wandering, there was needed a greater knowledge of the formation of character, and of the consequences of actions upon the agent's own frame of mind, than Bentham possessed. His want of power to estimate this class of consequences, together with his want of the degree of modest respect (a far different thing from blind deference) due to the traditional opinions and feelings in which the experience of mankind on that part of the subject lies embodied, render him, we conceive, a most unsafe guide on questions of practical ethics.

He is chargeable also with another error, which it would be improper to pass over, because nothing has tended more to place him in opposition to the common feelings of mankind, and to give to his philosophy that cold, mechanical, and ungenial air which characterizes the popular idea of a Benthamite. This error, or rather one-sidedness, belongs to him not as a utilitarian, but as a moralist by profession, and in common with almost all professed moralists, whether religious or philosophical: it is that of treating the *moral* view of actions and characters, which is unquestionably the first and most important mode of looking at them, as if it were the *sole* one: whereas it is only one of three, by all of which our sentiments towards the human being may be, ought to be, and without entirely crushing our own nature cannot but be, materially influenced. Every human action has three aspects: its *moral* aspect, or that of its *right* and *wrong*; its *aesthetic* aspect, or that of its *beauty*; its *sympathetic* aspect, or that of its *lovableness*. The first addresses itself to our reason and conscience; the second to our imagination; the third to our human fellow-feeling. According to the first, we approve or disapprove; according to the second, we admire or despise; according to the third, we love, pity, or dislike. The *morality* of an action depends on its foreseeable consequences; its beauty, and its lovableness, or the reverse, depend on the qualities which it is evidence of. Thus, a lie is *wrong*, because its effect is to mislead, and because it tends to destroy the confidence of man in man; it is also *mean*, because it is cowardly—because it proceeds from not daring to face the consequences of telling the truth—or at best is evidence of want of that *power* to compass our ends by straightforward means, which is conceived as properly belonging to every person not deficient in energy or in understanding. The action of Brutus in sentencing his sons was *right*, because it was executing a law essential to the freedom of his country, against persons of whose guilt there was no doubt: it was *admirable*, because it evinced a rare degree of patriotism, courage, and self-control; but there was nothing *lovable* in it; it affords no presumption in regard to lovable qualities, unless a presumption of their deficiency. If one of the sons had engaged in the conspiracy from affection for the other, *his* action would have been lovable, though neither moral nor admirable. It is not possible for any sophistry to confound these three modes of viewing an action; but it is very possible to adhere to one of them exclusively, and lose sight of the rest. Sentimentality consists in setting the last two of the three above the first; the error of moralists in general, and of Bentham, is to sink the two latter entirely. This is preeminently the case with Bentham: he both wrote and felt as if the moral standard ought not only to be paramount (which it ought), but to be alone; as if it ought to be the sole master of all our actions, and even of all our sentiments; as if either to admire or like, or despise or dislike a person for any action which neither does good nor harm, or which does not do a good or a harm proportioned to the sentiment entertained, were an injustice and a prejudice. He carried this so far, that there were certain phrases which, being expressive of what he considered to be this groundless liking or aversion, he could not bear to hear pronounced in his presence. Among these phrases were those of *good* and *bad taste*. He thought it an insolent piece of dogmatism in one person to praise or condemn another for a matter of taste: as if men's likings and dislikings, on things in themselves indifferent, were not pregnant with the most important inferences as to every point of their character; as if a person's tastes did not show him to be wise or a fool, cultivated or ignorant, gentle or rough, polished or coarse, sensitive or callous, generous or sordid, benevolent or selfish, conscientious or depraved.

Connected with the same topic are Bentham's peculiar opinions on poetry. Much has been said, for which there is no foundation, about his contempt for the pleasures of imagination, and for the fine arts. Music was throughout life his favourite amusement; painting, sculpture, and the other arts addressed to the eye, he was so far from holding in any contempt, that he occasionally recognizes them as means employable for important social ends; though his ignorance of the deeper springs of human character prevented him from suspecting how profoundly such things enter into the moral nature of man, and into the education both of the individual and of the race. But towards poetry in the narrower sense, that which employs the language of words, he entertained no favour. Words, he thought, were perverted from their proper office when they were employed in uttering anything but precise logical truth. He says, somewhere in his works, that "quantity of pleasure being equal, push-pin is as good as poetry:" but this is only a paradoxical way of stating what he would equally have said of the things which he most valued and admired. Another aphorism is attributed to him, which is much more characteristic of his view of this subject: "All poetry is misrepresentation." Poetry, he thought, consisted essentially in exaggeration for effect: in proclaiming some one view of a thing very emphatically, and suppressing all the limitations and qualifications. This trait of character seems to us a curious example of what Mr. Carlyle strikingly calls "the completeness of limited men." Here is a philosopher who is happy within his narrow boundary as no man of indefinite range ever was; who flatters himself that he is so completely emancipated from the essential law of poor human intellect, by which it can only see one thing at a time well, that he can even turn round upon the imperfection and lay a solemn interdict upon it. Did Bentham really suppose that it is in *poetry* only that propositions cannot be exactly true, cannot contain in themselves all the limitations and qualifications with which they require to be taken when applied to practice? We have seen how far his own prose propositions are from realizing this Utopia: and even the attempt to approach to it would be incompatible not with poetry merely, but with oratory, and with popular writing of every kind. Bentham's charge is true to the fullest extent; all writing which undertakes to make men *feel* truths as well as *see* them, does take up one point at a time, does seek to impress that, to drive that home, to make it sink into and colour the whole mind of the reader or hearer. It is justified in doing so, if the portion of truth which it thus enforces be that which is called for by the occasion. All writing addressed to the feelings has a natural tendency to exaggeration; but Bentham should have remembered that in this, as in many things, we must aim at too much, to be assured of doing enough.

4b. J.S. Mill *Principles of Political Economy* (1848) Bk. IV Ch. 7 §1–2 pp. 313–21.

[*Principles of Political Economy* concerns the progress of democratic institutions as well as abstract economic theory; this chapter, entitled 'On the Probable Futurity of the Labouring Classes', attacks the concept of the dependence of the lower on the higher classes.]

§I. [...]

Considered in its moral and social aspect, the state of the labouring people has latterly been a subject of much more speculation and discussion than formerly; and the opinion that it is not now what it ought to be, has become very general. The suggestions which have been promulgated, and the controversies which have been excited, on detached points rather than on the foundations of the subject, have put in evidence the existence of two conflicting theories, respecting the social position desirable for manual labourers. The one may be called the theory of dependence and protection, the other that of self-dependence.

According to the former theory, the lot of the poor, in all things which affect them collectively, should be regulated *for* them, not *by* them. They should not be required or encouraged to think for themselves, or give to their own reflection or forecast an influential voice in the determination of their destiny. It is supposed to be the duty of the higher classes to think for them, and to take the responsibility of their lot, as the commander and officers of an army take that of the soldiers composing it. This function, it is contended, the higher classes should prepare themselves to perform conscientiously, and their whole demeanour should impress the poor with a reliance on it, in order that, while yielding passive and active obedience to the rules prescribed for them, they may resign themselves in all other respects to a trustful *insouciance,* and repose under the shadow of their protectors. The relation between rich and poor, according to this theory (a theory also applied to the relation between men and women) should be only partly authoritative; it should be amiable, moral, and sentimental: affectionate tutelage on the one side, respectful and grateful deference on the other. The rich should be *in loco parentis* to the poor, guiding and restraining them like children. Of spontaneous action on their part there should be no need. They should be called on for nothing but to do their day's work, and to be moral and religious. Their morality and religion should be provided for them by their superiors, who should see them properly taught it, and should do all that is necessary to ensure their being, in return for labour and attachment, properly fed, clothed, housed, spiritually edified, and innocently amused.

This is the ideal of the future, in the minds of those whose dissatisfaction with the present assumes the form of affection and regret towards the past. Like other ideals, it exercises an unconscious influence on the opinions and sentiments of numbers who never consciously guide themselves by any ideal. It has also this in common with other ideals, that it has never been historically realized. It makes its appeal to our imaginative sympathies in the character of a restoration of the good times of our forefathers. But no times can be pointed out in which the higher classes of this or any other country performed a part even distantly resembling the one assigned to them in this theory. It is an idealization, grounded on the conduct and character of here and there an individual. All privileged and powerful classes, as such, have used their power in the interest of their own selfishness, and have indulged their self-importance in despising, and not in lovingly caring for, those who were, in their estimation, degraded by being under the necessity of working for their benefit. I do not affirm that what has always been must always be, or that human improvement has no tendency to correct the intensely selfish feelings engendered by power; but though the evil may be lessened, it cannot be eradicated, until the power itself is withdrawn. This, at least, seems to me undeniable, that long before the superior classes could be sufficiently improved to govern in the tutelary manner supposed, the inferior classes would be too much improved to be so governed.

I am quite sensible of all that is seductive in the picture of society which this theory presents. Though the facts of it have no prototype in the past, the feelings have. In them lies all that there is of reality in the conception. As the idea is essentially repulsive of a society only held together by the relations and feelings arising out of pecuniary interests, so there is something naturally attractive in a form of society abounding in strong personal attachments and disinterested self-devotion. Of such feelings it must be admitted that the relation of protector and protected has hitherto been the richest source. The strongest attachments of human beings in general, are towards the things or the persons that stand between them and some dreaded evil. Hence, in an age of lawless violence and insecurity, and general hardness and roughness of manners, in which life is beset with dangers and sufferings at every step, to those who have neither a commanding position of their own, nor a claim on the protection of some one who has—a generous giving of protection, and a grateful receiving of it, are the strongest ties which connect human beings; the feelings arising from that relation are their warmest feelings; all the enthusiasm and tenderness of the most sensitive natures gather round it; loyalty on the one part and chivalry on the other are principles exalted into passions. I do not desire to depreciate these qualities. The error lies in not perceiving, that these virtues and sentiments, like the clanship and the hospitality of the wandering Arab, belong emphatically to a rude and imperfect state of the social union; and that the feelings between protector and protected, whether between kings and subjects, rich and poor, or men and women, can no longer have this beautiful and endearing character, where there are no longer any serious dangers from which to protect. What is there in the present state of society to make it natural that human beings, of ordinary strength and courage, should glow with the warmest gratitude and devotion in return for protection? The laws protect them, wherever the laws do not criminally fail in their duty. To be under the power of some one, instead of being as formerly the sole condition of safety, is now, speaking generally, the only situation which exposes to grievous wrong. The so-called protectors are now the only persons against whom, in any ordinary circumstances, protection is needed. The brutality and tyranny with which every police report is filled, are those of husbands to wives, of parents to children. That the law does not prevent these atrocities, that it is only now making a first timid attempt to repress and punish them, is no matter of necessity, but the deep disgrace of those by whom the laws are made and administered. No man or woman who either possesses or is able to earn an independent livelihood, requires any other protection than that which the law could and ought to give. This being the case, it argues great ignorance of human nature to continue taking for granted that relations founded on protection must always subsist, and not to see that the assumption of the part of protector, and of the power which belongs to it, without any of the necessities which justify it, must engender feelings opposite to loyalty.

Of the working classes of Western Europe at least it may be pronounced certain, that the patriarchal or paternal system of government is one to which they will not again be subject. That question has been several times decided. It was decided when they were taught to read, and allowed access to newspapers and political tracts. It was decided when dissenting preachers were suffered to go among them, and appeal to their faculties and feelings in opposition to the creeds professed and countenanced by their superiors. It was decided when they were brought together in numbers, to work socially under the same roof. It was decided when railways enabled them to shift from place to place, and change their patrons and employers as easily as their coats. The working classes have taken their interests into their own hands, and are perpetually showing that they think the interests of their employers not identical with their own, but opposite to them. Some among the higher classes flatter themselves that these tendencies may be counteracted by moral and religious education; but they have let the time go by for giving an education which can serve their purpose. The principles of the Reformation have reached as low down in society as reading and writing, and the poor will not much longer accept morals and religion of other people's prescribing. I speak more particularly of our own country, especially the town population, and the districts of the most scientific agriculture or the highest wages, Scotland and the north of England. Among the more inert and less modernized agricultural population of the southern counties, it might be possible for the gentry to retain, for some time longer, something of the ancient deference and submission of the poor, by bribing them with high wages and constant employment; by insuring them support, and never requiring them to do anything which they do not like. But these are two conditions which never have been combined, and never can be, for long together. A guarantee of subsistence can only be practically kept up, when work is enforced and superfluous multiplication restrained, by at least a moral compulsion. It is then, that the would-be revivers of old times which they do not understand, would feel practically in how hopeless a task they were engaged. The whole fabric of patriarchal or seignorial influence, attempted to be raised on the foundation of caressing the poor, would be shattered against the necessity of enforcing a stringent Poor-law.

§2. It is on a far other basis that the well-being and well-doing of the labouring people must henceforth rest. The poor have come out of leading-strings, and cannot any longer be governed or treated like children. To their own qualities must now be commended the care of their destiny. Modern nations will have to learn the lesson, that the well-being of a people must exist by means of the justice and self-government [...] of the individual citizens. The theory of dependence attempts to dispense with the necessity of these qualities in the dependent classes. But now, when even in position they are becoming less and less dependent, and their minds less and less acquiescent in the degree of dependence which remains, the virtues of independence are those which they stand in need of. Whatever advice, exhortation, or guidance is held out to the labouring classes, must henceforth be tendered to them as equals, and accepted by them with their eyes open. The prospect of the future depends on the degree in which they can be made rational beings.

There is no reason to believe that prospect other than hopeful. The progress must always be slow. But there is a spontaneous education going on in the minds of the multitude, which may be greatly accelerated and improved by artificial aids. The instruction obtained from newspapers and political tracts is not the best sort of instruction, but it is vastly superior to none at all. The institutions for lectures and discussion, the collective deliberations on questions of common interest, the trades unions, the political agitation, all serve to awaken public spirit, to diffuse variety of ideas among the mass, and to excite thought and reflection in a few of the more intelligent, who become the leaders and instructors of the rest. Although the too early attainment of political franchises by the least educated class might retard, instead of promoting, their improvement, there can be little doubt that it has been greatly stimulated by the attempt to acquire those franchises. It is of little importance that some of them may, at a certain stage of their progress, adopt mistaken opinions. Communists are already numerous, and are likely to increase in number; but nothing tends more to the mental development of the working classes than that all the questions which Communism raises should be largely and freely discussed by them; nothing could be more instructive than that some should actually form communities, and try practically what it is to live without the institution of property. In the meantime, the working classes are now part of the public; in all discussions on matters of general interest they, or a portion of them, are now partakers; all who use the press as an instrument may, if it so happens, have them for an audience; the avenues of instruction through which the middle classes acquire such ideas as they have, are accessible to, at least, the operatives in the towns. With these resources, it cannot be doubted that they will increase in intelligence, even by their own unaided efforts; while there is reason to hope that great improvements both in the quality and quantity of school education will be speedily effected by the exertions of government and of individuals, and that the progress of the mass of the people in mental cultivation, and in the virtues which are dependent on it, will take place more rapidly, and with fewer intermittences and aberrations, than if left to itself.

From this increase of intelligence, several effects may be confidently anticipated. First: that they will become even less willing than at present to be led and governed, and directed into the way they should go, by the mere authority and *préstige* of superiors. If they have not now, still less will they have hereafter, any deferential awe, or religious principle of obedience, holding them in mental subjection to a class above them. The theory of dependence and protection will be more and more intolerable to them, and they will require that their conduct and condition shall be essentially self-governed. It is, at the same time, quite possible that they may demand, in many cases, the intervention of the legislature in their affairs, and the regulation by law of various things which concern them, often under very mistaken ideas and suggestions, to which they will demand that effect should be given, and not rules laid down for them by other people. It is quite consistent with this, that they should feel respect for superiority of intellect and knowledge and defer much to the opinions, on any subject, of those whom they think well acquainted with it. Such deference is deeply grounded in human nature; but they will judge for themselves of the persons who are and are not entitled to it.

5. Arthur Helps *The Claims of Labour: An Essay on the Duties of the Employers to the Employed* (1844) Ch. 1 'Masters and Men' pp. 33–6.

[Sir Arthur Helps (1813–75), philanthropist and writer. *The Claims of Labour* is addressed to employers of both domestic servants and factory hands, and is an extended appeal for the exercise of Christian benevolence in all relations between masters and men.]

Having spoken of some of the duties of private persons, we come now to the great employers of labour. Would that they all saw the greatness of their position. Strange as it may sound, they are the successors of the feudal barons, they it is who lead thousands to peaceful conquests, and upon whom, in great measure, depends the happiness of large masses of mankind. As Mr. Carlyle says, "The Leaders of Industry, if Industry is ever to be led, are virtually the Captains of the World; if there be no nobleness in them, there will never be an Aristocracy more." Can a man, who has this destiny entrusted to him, imagine that his vocation consists merely in getting together a large lump of gold, and then being off with it, to enjoy it, as he fancies, in some other place: as if that which is but a small part of his business in life, were all in all to him; as if indeed, the parable of the talents were to be taken literally, and that a man should think that he has done his part when he has made much more gold and silver out of little? If these men saw their position rightly, what would be their objects, what their pleasures? Their objects would not consist in foolish vyings with each other about the grandeur or the glitter of life. But in directing the employment of labour, they would find room for the exercise of all the powers of their minds, of their best affections, and of whatever was worthy in their ambition. Their occupation, so far from being a limited sphere of action, is one which may give scope to minds of the most various capacity. While one man may undertake those obvious labours of benevolent superintendence which are of immediate and pressing necessity, another may devote himself to more remote and indirect methods of improving the condition of those about him, which are often not the less valuable because of their indirectness. In short, it is evident that to lead the labour of large masses of people, and to do that, not merely with a view to the greatest product of commodities, but to the best interests of the producers, is a matter which will sufficiently and worthily occupy men of the strongest minds aided by all the attainments which cultivation can bestow.

I do not wish to assert a principle larger than the occasion demands: and I am, therefore unwilling to declare that we cannot justly enter into a relation so meagre with our fellow-creatures, as that of employing all their labour, and giving them nothing but money in return. There might, perhaps, be a state of society in which such a relation would not be culpable, a state in which the great mass of the employed were cultivated and considerate men; and where the common interests of master and man were well understood. But we have not to deal with any such imaginary case. So far from working men being the considerate creatures we have just imagined them, it is absolutely requisite to protect, in the most stringent manner, the interests of the children against the parents, who are often anxious to employ their little ones most immaturely. Nay more—it is notorious that working men will frequently omit to take even the slightest precaution in matters connected with the preservation of their own lives. If these poor men do not demand from you as Christians something more than mere money wages, what do the injunctions about charity mean? If those employed by you are not your neighbours, who are?

6. Friedrich Engels *The Condition of the Working Class in England in 1844* (1845; trans. Florence Wischnewetzky/Institute of Marxism–Leninism, Moscow, 1887/1892) Ch. 3.

[Friedrich Engels (1820–95), German socialist and co-founder with Karl Marx of modern Communism, who lived in Manchester in 1843–4 and from 1849. This passage, from a chapter entitled 'The Great Towns', describes living conditions in the proletarian areas of Manchester. (Authorial footnotes are omitted.)]

Manchester lies at the foot of the southern slope of a range of hills, which stretch hither from Oldham, their last peak, Kersallmoor, being at once the racecourse and the Mons Sacer of Manchester. Manchester proper lies on the left bank of the Irwell, between that stream and the two smaller ones, the Irk and the Medlock, which here empty into the Irwell. On the right bank of the Irwell, bounded by a sharp curve of the river, lies Salford, and farther westward Pendleton; northward from the Irwell lie Upper and Lower Broughton; northward of the Irk, Cheetham Hill; south of the Medlock lies Hulme; farther east Chorlton on Medlock; still farther, pretty well to the east of Manchester, Ardwick. The whole assemblage of buildings is commonly called Manchester, and contains about four hundred thousand inhabitants, rather more than less. The town itself is peculiarly built, so that a person may live in it for years, and go in and out daily without coming into contact with a working people's quarter or even with workers, that is, so long as he confines himself to his business or to pleasure walks. This arises chiefly from the fact, that by unconscious tacit agreement, as well as with outspoken conscious determination, the working people's quarters are sharply separated from the sections of the city reserved for the middle class; or, if this does not succeed, they are concealed with the cloak of charity. Manchester contains, at its heart, a rather extended commercial district, perhaps half a mile long and about as broad, and consisting almost wholly of offices and warehouses. Nearly the whole district is abandoned by dwellers, and is lonely and deserted at night; only watchmen and policemen traverse its narrow lanes with their dark lanterns. This district is cut through by certain main thoroughfares upon which the vast traffic concentrates, and in which the ground level is lined with brilliant shops. In these streets the upper floors are occupied, here and there, and there is a good deal of life upon them until late at night. With the exception of this commercial district, all Manchester proper, all Salford and Hulme, a great part of Pendleton and Chorlton, two-thirds of Ardwick, and single stretches of Cheetham Hill and Broughton are all unmixed working people's quarters, stretching like a girdle, averaging a mile and a half in breadth, around the commercial district. Outside, beyond this girdle, lives the upper and middle bourgeoisie, the middle bourgeoisie in regularly laid out streets in the vicinity of the working quarters, especially in Chorlton and the lower lying portions of Cheetham Hill; the upper bourgeoisie in remoter villas with gardens in Chorlton and Ardwick, or on the breezy heights of Cheetham Hill, Broughton, and Pendleton, in free, wholesome country air, in fine, comfortable homes, passed once every half or quarter hour by omnibuses going into the city. And the finest part of the arrangements is this, that the members of this money aristocracy can take the shortest road through the middle of all the labouring districts to their places of business, without ever seeing that they are in the midst of the grimy misery that lurks to the right and the left. For the thoroughfares leading from the Exchange in all directions out of the city are lined, on both sides, with an almost unbroken series of shops, and are so kept in the hands of the middle and lower bourgeoisie, which, out of self-interest, cares for a decent and cleanly external appearance and can *care* for it. True, these shops bear some relation to the districts which lie behind them, and are more elegant in the commercial and residential quarters than when they hide grimy working men's dwellings; but they suffice to conceal from the eyes of the wealthy men and women of strong stomachs and weak nerves the misery and grime which form the complement to their wealth. So, for instance, Deansgate, which leads from the Old Church directly southward, is lined first with mills and warehouses, then with second-rate shops and alehouses; farther south, when it leaves the commercial district, with less inviting shops, which grow dirtier and more interrupted by beer houses and gin palaces the farther one goes, until at the southern end the appearance of the shops leaves no doubt that workers and workers only are their customers. So Market Street running south-east from the Exchange; at first brilliant shops of the best sort, with counting-houses or warehouses above; in the continuation, Piccadilly, immense hotels and warehouses; in the farther continuation, London Road, in the neighbourhood of the Medlock, factories, beerhouses, shops for the humbler bourgeoisie and the working population; and from this point onward, large gardens and villas of the wealthier merchants and manufacturers. In this way anyone who knows Manchester can infer the adjoining districts, from the appearance of the thoroughfare, but one is seldom in a position to catch from the street a glimpse of the real labouring districts. I know very well that this hypocritical plan is more or less common to all great cities; I know, too, that the retail dealers are forced by the nature of their business to take possession of the great highways; I know that there are more good buildings than bad ones upon such streets everywhere, and that the value of land is greater near them than in remoter districts; but at the same time I have never seen so systematic a shutting out of the working class from the thoroughfares, so tender a concealment of everything which might affront the eye and the nerves of the bourgeoisie, as in Manchester. And yet, in other respects, Manchester is less built according to a plan, after official regulations, is more an outgrowth of accident, than any other city; and when I consider in this connection the eager assurances of the middle class, that the working class is doing famously, I cannot help feeling that the liberal manufacturers, the 'Big Wigs' of Manchester, are not so innocent after all, in the matter of this sensitive method of construction.

I may mention just here that the mills almost all adjoin the rivers or the different canals that ramify throughout the city, before I proceed at once to describe the labouring quarters. First of all, there is the Old Town of Manchester, which lies between the northern boundary of the commercial district and the Irk. Here the streets, even the better ones, are narrow and winding, like Todd Street, Long Millgate, Withy Grove, and Shude Hill, the houses dirty, old, and tumble-down, and the construction of the side streets utterly horrible. Going from the Old Church to Long Millgate, the stroller has at once a row of old-fashioned houses on the right, of which not one has kept its original level; these are remnants of the old pre-manufacturing Manchester, whose former inhabitants have removed with their descendants into better-built districts, and have left the houses, which were not good enough for them, to a working-class population strongly mixed with Irish blood. Here one is in an almost undisguised working men's quarter, for even the shops and beerhouses hardly take the trouble to exhibit a trifling degree of cleanliness. But all this is nothing in comparison with the courts and lanes which lie behind, to which access can be gained only through covered passages, in which no two human beings can pass at the same time. Of the irregular cramming together of dwellings in ways which defy all rational plan, of the tangle in which they are crowded literally one upon the other, it is impossible to convey an idea. And it is not the buildings surviving from the old times of Manchester which are to blame for this; the confusion has only recently reached its height when every scrap of space left by the old way of building has been filled up and patched over until not a foot of land is left to be further occupied.

[...]

The south bank of the Irk is here very steep and between fifteen and thirty feet high. On this abrupt slope there are planted three rows of houses, of which the lowest rise directly out of the river, while the front walls of the highest stand on the crest of the rise in Long Millgate. Among them are mills on the river, in short, the method of construction is as crowded and disorderly here as in the lower part of Long Millgate. Right and left a multitude of covered passages lead from the main street into numerous courts, and he who turns in thither gets into filth and disgusting grime, the equal of which is not to be found—especially in the courts which lead down to the Irk, and which contain unqualifiedly the most horrible dwellings which I have yet beheld. In one of these courts there stands directly at the entrance, at the end of the covered passage, a privy without a door, so dirty that the inhabitants can pass into and out of the court only by passing through foul pools of stagnant urine and excrement. This is the first court on the Irk above Ducie Bridge—in case any one should care to look into it. Below it on the river there are several tanneries which fill the whole neighbourhood with the stench of animal putrefaction. Below Ducie Bridge the only entrance to most of the houses is by means of narrow, dirty stairs and over heaps of refuse and filth. The first court below Ducie Bridge, known as Allen's Court, was in such a state at the time of the cholera that the sanitary police ordered it evacuated, swept, and disinfected with chloride of lime. [...] Since then, it seems to have been partially torn down and rebuilt; at least looking down from Ducie Bridge, the passer-by sees several ruined walls and heaps of *débris* with some newer houses. The view from this bridge, mercifully concealed from mortals of small stature by a parapet as high as a man, is characteristic for the whole district. At the bottom flows, or rather stagnates, the Irk, a narrow, coal-black, foul-smelling stream, full of *débris* and refuse, which it deposits on the lower right bank. In dry weather, a lone string of the most disgusting blackish-green slime pools are left standing on this bank, from the depths of which bubbles of miasmatic gas constantly arise and give forth a stench unendurable even on the bridge forty or fifty feet above the surface of the stream. But besides this, the stream itself is checked every few paces by high weirs, behind which slime and refuse accumulate and rot in thick masses. Above the bridge are tanneries, bonemills, and gasworks, from which all drains and refuse find their way into the Irk, which receives further the contents of all the neighbouring sewers and privies. It may be easily imagined, therefore, what sort of residue the stream deposits. Below the bridge you look upon the piles of *débris*, the refuse, filth, and offal from the courts on the steep left bank; here each house is packed close behind its neighbour and a bit of each is visible, all black, smoky, crumbling, ancient, with broken panes and window-frames. The background is furnished by old barrack-like factory buildings. On the lower right bank stands a long row of houses and mills, the second row being a ruin without a roof, piled with *débris*; the third stands so low that the lowest floor is uninhabitable, and therefore without windows or doors. Here the background embraces the pauper burial-ground, the station of the Liverpool and Leeds railway, and, in the rear of this, the Workhouse, the 'Poor-Law Bastille' of Manchester, which, like a citadel, looks threateningly down from behind its high walls and parapets on the hilltop, upon the working people's quarter below.

[...]

Such is the Old Town of Manchester, and on re-reading my description, I am forced to admit that instead of being exaggerated, it is far from black enough to convey a true impression of the filth, ruin, and uninhabitableness, the defiance of all considerations of cleanliness, ventilation, and health which characterize the construction of this single district, containing at least twenty to thirty thousand inhabitants. And such a district exists in the heart of the second city of England, the first manufacturing city of the world. If anyone wishes to see in how little space a human being can move, how little air—and *such* air!—he can breathe, how little of civilization he may share and yet live, it is only necessary to travel hither. True, this is the *Old* Town, and the people of Manchester emphasize the fact whenever anyone mentions to them the frightful condition of this Hell upon Earth; but what does that prove? Everything which here arouses horror and indignation is of recent origin, belongs to the *industrial epoch*. The couple of hundred houses which belong to Old Manchester have been long since abandoned by their original inhabitants; the industrial epoch alone has crammed into them the swarms of workers whom they now shelter; the industrial epoch alone has built up every spot between these old houses to make a covering for the masses whom it has conjured hither from the agricultural districts and from Ireland; the industrial epoch alone enables the owners of these cattlesheds to rent them for high prices to human beings, to plunder the poverty of the workers, to undermine the health of thousands, in order that they only, the owners, may grow rich. In the industrial epoch alone has it become possible that the worker scarcely freed from feudal servitude can be used as mere material, a mere chattel; that he must let himself be crowded into a dwelling too bad for every other, which he for his hard-earned wages buys the right to let go utterly to ruin. This is what manufacture has achieved, and, without these workers and their poverty, this slavery would have been impossible. True, the original construction of this quarter was bad, little good could have been made out of it; but, have the land-owners, has the municipality done anything to improve it when rebuilding? On the contrary, wherever a nook or corner was free, a house has been run up; where a superfluous passage remained, it has been built on; the value of land rose with the blossoming out of manufacture, and the more it rose, the more madly was the work of building carried on, without reference to the health or comfort of the inhabitants, with sole reference to the highest possible profit, on the principle that *no hole is so bad but that some poor creature must take it who can pay for nothing better.* However, it is the Old Town, and with this reflection the bourgeoisie is comforted.

7. Unsigned (Charles Dickens) 'On Strike'
Household Words (11 February 1854)
Vol. VIII No. 203 pp. 553–9.

[*Household Words*, a weekly entertainment magazine founded by Dickens in 1850 and reaching a broad middle-class readership, included essays on contemporary social issues as well as fiction, sketches and verse. At the end of January 1854, Dickens briefly visited the Lancashire mill town of Preston, site of a bitter and protracted industrial dispute, and produced this anecdotal account of what he saw. The opening, describing Dickens's train journey to Preston during which he encounters 'a friend of the Masters', is omitted. (The strike itself collapsed at the end of April after thirty-seven weeks, due to a falling off of strike contributions from outside and a gradual drift of operatives back to the mills.)]

When I got to Preston, it was four o'clock in the afternoon. The day being Saturday and market-day, a foreigner might have expected, from among so many idle and not over-fed people as the town contained, to find a turbulent, ill-conditioned crowd in the streets. But, except for the cold smokeless factory chimneys, the placards at the street corners, and the groups of working people attentively reading them, nor foreigner nor Englishman could have had the least suspicion that there existed any interruption to the usual labours of the place. The placards thus perused were not remarkable for their logic certainly, and did not make the case particularly clear; but, considering that they emanated from, and were addressed to, people who had been out of employment for three-and-twenty consecutive weeks, at least they had little passion in them, though they had not much reason. Take the worst I could find:

> "FRIENDS AND FELLOW OPERATIVES,
> "Accept the grateful thanks of twenty thousand struggling Operatives, for the help you have showered upon Preston since the present contest commenced.
>
> "Your kindness and generosity, your patience and long continued support deserve every praise, and are only equalled by the heroic and determined perseverance of the outraged and insulted factory workers of Preston, who have been struggling for some months, and are, at this inclement season of the year, bravely battling for the rights of themselves and the whole toiling community.

"For many years before the strike took place at Preston, the Operatives were the down trodden and insulted serfs of their Employers, who in times of good trade and general prosperity, wrung from their labour a California of gold, which is now being used to crush those who created it, still lower and lower in the scale of civilization. This has been the result of our commercial prosperity!—*more wealth for the rich and more poverty for the Poor!* Because the workpeople of Preston protested against this state of things,—because they combined in a fair and legitimate way for the purpose of getting a reasonable share of the reward of their own labour, the *fair dealing* Employers of Preston, to their eternal shame and disgrace, *locked up their Mills,* and at one fell swoop deprived, as they thought, from twenty to thirty thousand human beings of the means of existence. Cruelty and tyranny always defeat their own object; it was so in this case, and to the honor and credit of the working classes of this country, we have to record, that, those whom the rich and wealthy sought to destroy, the poor and industrious have protected from harm. This love of justice and hatred of wrong, is a noble feature in the character and disposition of the working man, and gives us hope that in the future, this world will become what its great architect intended, not a place of sorrow, toil, oppression and wrong, but the dwelling place and the abode of peace, plenty, happiness and love, where avarice and all the evil passions engendered by the present system of fraud and injustice shall not have a place.

"The earth was not made for the misery of its people; intellect was not given to man to make himself and fellow creatures unhappy. No, the fruitfulness of the soil and the wonderful inventions—the result of mind—all proclaim that these things were bestowed upon us for our happiness and well-being, and not for the misery and degradation of the human race.

"It may serve the manufacturers and all who run away with the lion's share of labour's produce, to say that the *impartial* God intended that there should be a *partial* distribution of his blessings. But we know that it is against nature to believe, that those who plant and reap all the grain, should not have enough to make a mess of porridge; and we know that those who weave all the cloth should not want a yard to cover their persons, whilst those who never wove an inch have more calico, silks and satins, than would serve the reasonable wants of a dozen working men and their families.

"This system of giving everything to the few, and nothing to the many, has lasted long enough, and we call upon the working people of this country to be determined to establish a new and improved system—a system that shall give to all who labour, a fair share of those blessings and comforts which their toil produce; in short, we wish to see that divine precept enforced, which says, 'Those who will not work, shall not eat.'

"The task is before you, working men; if you think the good which would result from its accomplishment, is worth struggling for, set to work and cease not, until you have obtained the *good time coming,* not only for the Preston Operatives, but for yourselves as well.

> "By Order of the Committee.
> "Murphy's Temperance Hotel, Chapel Walks,
> "Preston, January 24th, 1854."

It is a melancholy thing that it should not occur to the Committee to consider what would become of themselves, their friends, and fellow operatives, if those calicoes, silks, and satins, were *not* worn in very large quantities; but I shall not enter into that question. As I had told my friend Snapper, what I wanted to see with my own eyes, was, how these people acted under a mistaken impression, and what qualities they showed, even at that disadvantage, which ought to be the strength and peace—not the weakness and trouble—of the community. I found, even from this literature, however, that all masters were not indiscriminately unpopular. Witness the following verses from the New Song of the Preston Strike:

> "There's Henry Hornby, of Blackburn, he is a jolly brick,
> He fits the Preston masters nobly, and is very bad to trick;
> He pays his hands a good price, and I hope he will never sever,
> So we'll sing success to Hornby and Blackburn for ever.

> "There is another gentleman, I'm sure you'll all lament,
> In Blackburn for him they're raising a monument,
> You know his name, 'tis of great fame, it was late Eccles of honour,
> May Hopwood, and Sparrow, and Hornby live for ever.

> "So now it is time to finish and end my rhyme,
> We warn these Preston Cotton Lords to mind for future time.
> With peace and order too I hope we shall be clever,
> We sing success to Stockport and Blackburn for ever.

"Now, lads, give your minds to it."

The balance sheet of the receipts and expenditure for the twenty-third week of the strike was extensively posted. The income for that week was two thousand one hundred and forty pounds odd. Some of the contributors were poetical. As,

> "Love to all and peace to the dead,
> May the poor now in need never want bread.
> three-and-sixpence."

The following poetical remonstrance was appended to the list of contributions from the Gorton district:

> "Within these walls the lasses fair
> Refuse to contribute their share,
> Careless of duty—blind to fame,
> For shame, ye lasses, oh! for shame!
> Come, pay up, lasses, think what's right,
> Defend your trade with all your might;
> Fer if you don't the world will blame,
> And cry, ye lasses, oh! for shame!
> Let's hope in future all will pay,
> That Preston folks may shortly say—
> That by your aid they have obtain'd
> The greatest victory ever gained."

Some of the subscribers veiled their names under encouraging sentiments, as Not tired yet, All in a mind, Win the day, Fraternity, and the like. Some took jocose appellations, as A stunning friend, Two to one Preston wins, Nibbling Joe, and The Donkey Driver. Some expressed themselves through their trades, as Cobbler Dick, sixpence, The tailor true, sixpence, Shoemaker, a shilling, The chirping blacksmith, sixpence, and A few of Maskery's most feeling coach makers, three and threepence. An old balance sheet for the fourteenth week of the Strike was headed with this quotation from MR. CARLYLE. "Adversity is sometimes hard upon a man; but for one man who can stand prosperity, there are a hundred that will stand adversity." The Elton district prefaced its report with these lines:

> "Oh! ye who start a noble scheme,
> For general good designed;
> Ye workers in a cause that tends
> To benefit your kind!
> Mark out the path ye fain would tread,
> The game ye mean to play;

And if it be an honest one,
Keep stedfast in your way!

"Although you may not gain at once
The points ye most desire;
Be patient—time can wonders work;
Plod on, and do not tire:
Obstructions, too, may crowd your path,
In threatening, stern array;
Yet flinch not! fear not! they may prove
Mere shadows in your way.

"Then, while there's work for you to do,
Stand not despairing by,
Let 'forward' be the move ye make,
Let 'onward' be your cry;
And when success has crowned your plans,
'Twill all your pains repay,
To see the good your labour's done—
Then droop not on your way."

In this list, "Bear ye one another's burthens," sent one Pound fifteen. "We'll stand to our text, see that ye love one another," sent nineteen shillings. "Christopher Hardman's men again, they say they can always spare one shilling out of ten," sent two and sixpence. The following masked threats were the worst feature in any bill I saw:

"If that fiddler at Uncle Tom's Cabin blowing room does not pay
Punch will set his legs straight.
"If that drawer at card side and those two slubbers do not pay,
Punch will say something about their bustles.
"If that winder at last shift does not pay next week,
Punch will tell about her actions."

But, on looking at this bill again, I found that it came from Bury and related to Bury, and had nothing to do with Preston. The Masters' placards were not torn down or disfigured, but were being read quite as attentively as those on the opposite side.

That evening, the Delegates from the surrounding districts were coming in, according to custom, with their subscription lists for the week just closed. These delegates meet on Sunday as their only day of leisure; when they have made their reports, they go back to their homes and their Monday's work. On Sunday morning, I repaired to the Delegates' meeting.

These assemblages take place in a cockpit, which, in the better times of our fallen land, belonged to the late Lord Derby for the purpose of the intellectual recreation implied in its name. I was directed to the cockpit up a narrow lane, tolerably crowded by the lower sort of working people. Personally, I was quite unknown in the town, but every one made way for me to pass, with great civility, and perfect good humour. Arrived at the cockpit door, and expressing my desire to see and hear, I was handed through the crowd, down into the pit, and up again, until I found myself seated on the topmost circular bench, within one of the secretary's tables, and within three of the chairman. Behind the chairman was a great crown on the top of a pole, made of parti-coloured calico, and strongly suggestive of May-day. There was no other symbol or ornament in the place.

It was hotter than any mill or factory I have ever been in; but there was a stove down in the sanded pit, and delegates were seated close to it, and one particular delegate often warmed his hands at it, as if he were chilly. The air was so intensely close and hot, that at first I had but a confused perception of the delegates down in the pit, and the dense crowd of eagerly listening men and women (but not very many of the latter) filling all the benches and choking such narrow standing room as there was. When the atmosphere cleared a little on better acquaintance, I found the question under discussion to be, Whether the Manchester Delegates in attendance from the Labor Parliament, should be heard?

If the Assembly, in respect of quietness and order, were put in comparison with the House of Commons, the Right Honorable the Speaker himself would decide for Preston. The chairman was a Preston weaver, two or three and fifty years of age, perhaps; a man with a capacious head, rather long dark hair growing at the sides and back, a placid attentive face, keen eyes, a particularly composed manner, a quiet voice, and a persuasive action of his right arm. Now look'ee heer my friends. See what t' question is. T' question is, sholl these heer men be heerd. Then 't cooms to this, what ha' these men got t' tell us? Do they bring mooney? If they bring mooney t'ords t' expenses o' this strike, they're welcome. For, Brass, my friends, is what we want, and what we must ha' (hear hear hear!). Do they coom to us wi' any suggestion for the conduct of this strike? If they do, they're welcome. Let 'em give us their advice and we will hearken to 't. But, if these men coom heer, to tell us what t' Labor Parliament is, or what Ernest Jones's opinions is, or t' bring in politics and differences amoong us when what we want is 'armony, brotherly love, and concord; then I say t' you, decide for yoursel' carefully, whether these men ote to be heerd in this place. (Hear hear hear! and No no no!) Chairman sits down, earnestly regarding delegates, and holding both arms of his chair. Looks extremely sensible; his plain coarse working man's shirt collar easily turned down over his loose Belcher neckerchief. Delegate who has moved that Manchester delegates be heard, presses motion—Mr. Chairman, will that delegate tell us, as a man, that these men have anything to say concerning this present strike and lock-out, for we have a deal of business to do, and what concerns this present strike and lock-out is our business and nothing else is. (Hear hear hear!)—Delegate in question will not compromise the fact; these men want to defend the Labor Parliament from certain charges made against them.—Very well, Mr. Chairman, Then I move as an amendment that you do not hear these men now, and that you proceed wi' business—and if you don't I'll look after you, I tell you that. (Cheers and laughter)—Coom lads, prove 't then!—Two or three hands for the delegates; all the rest for the business. Motion lost, amendment carried, Manchester deputation not to be heard.

But now, starts up the delegate from Throstletown, in a dreadful state of mind. Mr. Chairman, I hold in my hand a bill; a bill that requires and demands explanation from you, sir; an offensive bill; a bill posted in my town of Throstletown without my knowledge, without the knowledge of my fellow delegates who are here beside me; a bill purporting to be posted by the authority of the massed committee sir, and of which my fellow delegates and myself were kept in ignorance. Why are we to be slighted? Why are we to be insulted? Why are we to be meanly stabbed in the dark? Why is this assassin-like course of conduct to be pursued towards us? Why is Throstletown, which has nobly assisted you, the operatives of Preston, in this great struggle, and which has brought its contributions up to the full sevenpence a loom, to be thus degraded, thus aspersed, thus traduced, thus despised, thus outraged in its feelings by un-English and unmanly conduct? Sir, I hand you up that bill, and I require of you, sir, to give me a satisfactory explanation of that bill. And I have that confidence in your known integrity, sir, as to be sure that you will give it, and that you will tell us who is to blame, and that you will make reparation to Throstletown for this scandalous treatment. Then, in hot blood, up starts Gruffshaw (professional speaker) who is somehow responsible for this bill. O my friends, but explanation is required here! O my friends, but it is fit and right that you should have the dark ways of the real traducers and apostates, and the real un-English stabbers, laid bare before you. My friends when this dark conspiracy first began—But here the persuasive right hand of the chairman falls gently on Gruffshaw's shoulder. Gruffshaw stops in full boil. My friends, these are hard words of my friend Gruffshaw, and this is not the business—No more it is, and once again, sir, I, the delegate who said I would look after you, do move that you proceed to business!—Preston has not the strong relish for personal altercation that Westminster hath. Motion seconded and carried, business passed to, Gruffshaw dumb.

Perhaps the world could not afford a more remarkable contrast than between the deliberate collected manner of these men proceeding with their business, and the clash and hurry of the engines among which their lives are passed. Their astonishing fortitude and perseverance; their high sense of honor among themselves; the extent to which they are impressed with the responsibility that is upon them of setting a careful example, and keeping their order out of any harm and loss of reputation; the noble readiness in them to help one another, of which most medical practitioners and working clergymen can give so many affecting examples; could scarcely ever be plainer to an ordinary observer of human nature than in this cockpit. To hold, for a minute, that the great mass of them were not sincerely actuated by the belief that all these qualities were bound up in what they were doing, and that they were doing right, seemed to me little short of an impossibility. As the different delegates (some in the very dress in which they had left the mill last night) reported the amounts sent from the various places they represented, this strong faith on their parts seemed expressed in every tone and every look that was capable of expressing it. One man was raised to enthusiasm by his pride in bringing so much; another man was ashamed and depressed because he brought so little; this man triumphantly made it known that he could give you, from the store in hand, a hundred pounds in addition next week, if you should want it; and that man pleaded that he hoped his district would do better before long; but I could as soon have doubted the existence of the walls that enclosed us, as the earnestness with which they spoke (many of them referring to the children who were to be born to labor after them) of "this great, this noble, gallant, godlike struggle." Some designing and turbulent spirits among them, no doubt there are; but I left the place with a profound conviction that their mistake is generally an honest one, and that it is sustained by the good that is in them, and not by the evil.

Neither by night nor by day was there any interruption to the peace of the streets. Nor was this an accidental state of things, for the police records of the town are eloquent to the same effect. I traversed the streets very much, and was, as a stranger, the subject of a little curiosity among the idlers; but I met with no rudeness or ill-temper. More than once, when I was looking at the printed balance-sheets to which I have referred, and could not quite comprehend the setting forth of the figures, a bystander of the working class interposed with his explanatory forefinger and helped me out. Although the pressure in the cockpit on Sunday was excessive, and the heat of the room obliged me to make my way out as I best could before the close of the proceedings, none of the people whom I put to inconvenience showed the least impatience; all helped me, and all cheerfully acknowledged my word of apology as I passed. It is very probable, not-withstanding, that they may have supposed from my being there at all—I and my companion were the only persons present, not of their own order—that I was there to carry what I heard and saw to the opposite side; indeed one speaker seemed to intimate as much.

On the Monday at noon, I returned to this cockpit, to see the people paid. It was then about half filled, principally with girls and women. They were all seated, waiting, with nothing to occupy their attention; and were just in that state when the unexpected appearance of a stranger differently dressed from themselves, and with his own individual peculiarities of course, might, without offence, have had something droll in it even to more polite assemblies. But I stood there, look-ing on, as free from remark as if I had come to be paid with the rest. In the place which the secretary had occupied yesterday, stood a dirty, little common table, covered with five-penny piles of halfpence. Before the paying began, I wondered who was going to receive these very small sums; but when it did begin, the mys-tery was soon cleared up. Each of these piles was the change for sixpence, de-ducting a penny. All who were paid, in filing around the building to prevent confusion, had to pass this table on the way-out; and the greater part of the un-married girls stopped here, to change, each a sixpence, and subscribe her weekly penny in aid of the people on strike who had families. A very large majority of these girls and women were comfortably dressed in all respects, clean, whole-some and pleasant-looking. There was a prevalent neatness and cheerfulness, and an almost ludicrous absence of anything like sullen discontent.

Exactly the same appearances were observable on the same day, at a not nu-merously attended open air meeting in "Chadwick's Orchard"—which blossoms in nothing but red bricks. Here, the chairman of yesterday presided in a cart, from which speeches were delivered. The proceedings commenced with the fol-lowing sufficiently general and discursive hymn, given out by a workman from Burnley, and sung in long metre by the whole audience:

> "Assembled beneath thy broad blue sky,
> To thee, O God, thy children cry.
> Thy needy creatures on Thee call,
> For thou art great and good to all.

> "Thy bounty smiles on every side,
> And no good thing hast thou denied;
> But men of wealth and men of power,
> Like locusts, all our gifts devour.

"Awake, ye sons of toil! nor sleep
While millions starve, while millions weep;
Demand your rights; let tyrants see
You are resolved that you'll be free."

Mr. Hollins's Sovereign Mill was open all this time. It is a very beautiful mill, containing a large amount of valuable machinery, to which some recent ingenious improvements have been added. Four hundred people could find employment in it; there were eighty-five at work, of whom five had "come in" that morning. They looked, among the vast array of motionless power-looms, like a few remaining leaves in a wintry forest. They were protected by the police (very prudently not obtruded on the scenes I have described), and were stared at every day when they came out, by a crowd which had never been large in reference to the numbers on strike, and had diminished to a score or two. One policeman at the door sufficed to keep order then. These eighty-five were people of exceedingly decent appearance, chiefly women, and were evidently not in the least uneasy for themselves. I heard of one girl among them, and only one, who had been hustled and struck in a dark street.

In any aspect in which it can be viewed, this strike and lock-out is a deplorable calamity. In its waste of time, in its waste of a great people's energy, in its waste of wages, in its waste of wealth that seeks to be employed, in its encroachment on the means of many thousands who are laboring from day to day, in the gulf of separation it hourly deepens between those whose interests must be understood to be identical or must be destroyed, it is a great national affliction. But, at this pass, anger is of no use, starving out is of no use—for what will that do, five years hence, but overshadow all the mills in England with the growth of a bitter remembrance?—political economy is a mere skeleton unless it has a little human covering and filling out, a little human bloom upon it, and a little human warmth in it. Gentlemen are found, in great manufacturing towns, ready enough to extol imbecile mediation with dangerous madmen abroad; can none of them be brought to think of authorised mediation and explanation at home? I do not suppose that such a knotted difficulty as this, is to be at all untangled by a morning party in the Adelphi; but I would entreat both sides now so miserably opposed, to consider whether there are no men in England, above suspicion, to whom they might refer the matters in dispute, with a perfect confidence above all things in the desire of those men to act justly, and in their sincere attachment to their countrymen of every rank and to their country. Masters right, or men right; masters wrong, or men wrong; both right, or both wrong; there is certain ruin to both in the continuance or frequent revival of this breach. And from the ever-widening circle of their decay, what drop in the social ocean shall be free!

8.   Unsigned (Henry Morley) 'Ground in the Mill' *Household Words* (22 April 1854) Vol. IX No. 213 pp. 224–7.

[Henry Morley (1822–94), medic, journalist, and literary academic, joined the staff of *Household Words* at Dickens's invitation. The article (appearing in the same issue as Part IV—Bk. 1 Chs. 7–8—of *Hard Times*) attacks the Lancashire mill owners for circumventing the fencing and educational requirements of the Factory Act of 1844.]

"It is good when it happens," say the children,—"that we die before our time." Poetry may be right or wrong in making little operatives who are ignorant of cowslips say anything like that. We mean here to speak prose. There are many ways of dying. Perhaps it is not good when a factory girl, who has not the whole spirit of play spun out of her for want of meadows, gambols upon bags of wool, a little too near the exposed machinery that is to work it up, and is immediately seized, and punished by the merciless machine that digs its shaft into her pinafore and hoists her up, tears out her left arm at the shoulder joint, breaks her right arm, and beats her on the head. No, that is not good; but it is not a case in point, the girl lives and may be one of those who think that it would have been good for her if she had died before her time.

She had her chance of dying, and she lost it. Possibly it was better for the boy whom his stern master, the machine, caught as he stood on a stool wickedly looking out of window at the sunlight and the flying clouds. These were no business of his, and he was fully punished when the machine he served caught him by one arm and whirled him round and round till he was thrown down dead. There is no lack of such warnings to idle boys and girls. What right has a gamesome youth to display levity before the supreme engine. "Watch me do a trick!" cried such a youth to his fellow, and put his arm familiarly within the arm of the great iron-hearted chief. "*I'll* show you a trick," gnashed the pitiless monster. A coil of strap fastened his arm to the shaft, and round he went. His leg was cut off, and fell into the room, his arm was broken in three or four places, his ankle was broken, his head was battered; he was not released alive.

Why do we talk about such horrible things? Because they exist, and their existence should be clearly known. Because there have occurred during the last three years, more than a hundred such deaths, and more than ten thousand (indeed, nearly twelve thousand) such accidents in our factories, and they are all, or nearly all, preventible.

These few thousands of catastrophes are the results of the administrative kindness so abundant in this country. They are all the fruits of mercy. A man was lime-washing the ceiling of an engine-room: he was seized by a horizontal shaft and killed immediately. A boy was brushing the dust from such a ceiling, before whitewashing: he had a cloth over his head to keep the dirt from falling on him; by that cloth the engine seized and held him to administer a chastisement with rods of iron. A youth while talking thoughtlessly took hold of a strop that hung over the shaft: his hand was wrenched off at the wrist. A man climbed to the top of his machine to put the strap on the drum: he wore a smock which the shaft caught; both of his arms were then torn out of the shoulder joints, both legs were broken, and his head was severely bruised: in the end, of course, he died. What he suffered was all suffered in mercy. He was rent asunder, not perhaps for his own good; but, as a sacrifice to the commercial prosperity of Great Britain. There are few amongst us even among the masters who share most largely in that prosperity—who are willing, we will hope and believe, to pay such a price as all this blood for any good or any gain that can accrue to them.

These accidents have arisen in the manner following. By the Factory Act, passed in the seventh year of Her Majesty's reign, it was enacted, among other things, that all parts of the mill-gearing in a factory should be securely fenced. There were no buts and ifs in the Act itself; these were allowed to step in and limit its powers of preventing accidents out of a merciful respect, not for the blood of the operatives, but for the gold of the mill-owners. It was strongly represented that to fence those parts of machinery that were higher than the heads of work-men—more than seven feet above the ground—would be to incur an expense wholly unnecessary. Kind-hearted interpreters of the law, therefore, agreed with mill-owners that seven feet of fencing should be held sufficient. The result of this accommodation—taking only the accounts of the last three years—has been to credit mercy with some pounds and shillings in the books of English manufacturers; we cannot say how many, but we hope they are enough to balance the account against mercy made out on behalf of the English factory workers thus:— Mercy debtor to justice, of poor men, women, and children, one hundred and six lives, one hundred and forty-two hands or arms, one thousand two hundred and eighty-seven (or, in bulk, how many bushels of) fingers, for the breaking of one thousand three hundred and forty bones, for five hundred and fifty-nine damaged heads, and for eight thousand two hundred and eighty-two miscellaneous injuries. It remains to be settled how much cash saved to the purses of the manufacturers is a satisfactory and proper off-set to this expenditure of life and limb and this crushing of bone in the persons of their work-people.

[...]

We have not spoken too strongly on this subject. We are indignant against no class, but discuss only one section of a topic that concerns, in some form, almost every division of society. Since, however, we now find ourselves speaking about factories, and turning over leaves of the reports of Factory Inspectors, we may as well have our grumble out, or, at any rate, so far prolong it as to make room for one more subject of dissatisfaction. It is important that Factory management should be watched by the public; in a friendly spirit indeed—for it is no small part of our whole English mind and body—but with the strictness which every man who means well should exercise in judgment on himself, in scrutiny of his own actions. We are told that in one inspector's district—only in one district—mills and engines have so multiplied, during the last three years, in number and in power, that additional work has, in that period, been created for the employment of another forty thousand hands. Every reporter has the same kind of tale to tell. During the last year, in our manufacturing districts, additions to the steam power found employment for an additional army of operatives, nearly thirty thousand strong. The Factory system, therefore, is developing itself most rapidly. It grows too fast, perhaps; at present the mills are, for a short time, in excess of the work required, and in many cases lie idle for two days in the week, or for one or two hours in the day. The succession of strikes, too, in Preston, Wigan, Hindley, Burnley, Padiham, and Bacup and the other places, have left a large number of men out of employ, and caused, for a long time, a total sacrifice of wages, to the extent of some twenty thousand pounds a week. These, however, are all temporary difficulties: the great extension of the Factory system is a permanent fact, and it must be made to bring good with it, not evil.

The law wisely requires that mill-owners, who employ children, shall also teach them, and a minimum, as to time, of schooling is assigned. Before this regulation was compulsory, there were some good schools kept as show-places by certain persons; but, when the maintenance of them became a necessity, and schools were no longer exceptional curiosities, these show-places often fell into complete neglect; they were no longer goods that would attract the public. In Scotland this part of the Factory Law seems to be well worked; and, for its own sake, as a beneficial requirement. That does not seem, however, to be the case in England. All the Inspectors tell us of the lamentable state of the factory schools in this country; allowance being, of course, made for a few worthy exceptions. It is doubtful whether much good will come out of them, unless they be themselves organised by men determined that they shall fulfil their purpose. English Factory children have yet to be really taught.

> "Let them prove their inward souls against the notion
> That they live in you, or under you, O wheels!

Still, all day, the iron wheels go onward,
    Grinding life down from its mark;
And the children's souls, which God is calling sunward,
    Spin on blindly in the dark."

Here they are left spinning in the dark. Let Mr. Redgrave's account of a factory school visited by him, near Leeds, suffice to show:—

> "It was held in a large room, and the Inspector visiting it at twenty
> minutes before twelve, found the children at play in the yard,
> and the master at work in the school-room, sawing up the black
> board to make fittings of a house to which he proposed transfer-
> ring his business. The children being summoned, came in care-
> lessly, their disorderly habits evidently not repressed by their
> master, but checked slightly by the appearance of a strange gen-
> tleman. Two girls lolling in the porch were summoned in, and
> the teacher then triumphantly drew out of his pocket a whistle,
> whereupon to blow the order for attention. It was the only whole
> thing that he had to teach with. There were the twenty children
> ranged along the wall of a room able to contain seven times the
> number; there were the bits of black board, the master's arms,
> with a hand-saw, and a hammer for apparatus, and there were
> the books, namely, six dilapidated Bibles, some copy books, one
> slate, and half-a-dozen ragged and odd leaves of a 'Reading made
> Easy.' To such a school factory children were being sent to get
> the hours of education which the law makes necessary. Doubt-
> less, that sample is a very bad one, but too many resemble it."

"They know the grief of man but not the wisdom," these poor childish hearts. They are now rescued from day-long ache and toil; we have given them some leisure for learning, though, as yet but little more than the old lesson to learn.

9. **Harriet Martineau** *The Factory Controversy:*
A Warning against Meddling Legislation (1855)
pp. 35–38 & 43–47.

[Harriet Martineau (1802–76), utilitarian English writer and social
reformer. The attack in *Household Words* of April 1854 on the disregard of mill owners for the life and welfare of their operatives (see
preceding extract) was followed up by four further essays of a similar nature in 1855 ('Fencing with Humanity', 14 April; 'Death's
Cyphering-Book', 12 May; 'Deadly Shafts', 23 June; and 'More
Grist to the Mill', 28 July). Martineau angrily defended the owners in this article which was rejected by the *Westminster Review* but
appeared as a pamphlet sponsored by the National Association of
Factory Occupiers of Manchester. Dickens and Morley replied con-
temptuously on 19 January 1856 in 'Our Wicked Mis-statements'
(*Household Words* Vol. XIII No. 304 pp. 13–19).]

[...] A good many people have wondered before that Mr. Dickens, who has such
a horror of Poor-law reform, and who acted the part of sentimental philanthropist in "Oliver Twist," by charging the faults of the repealed law upon the new
one, and other devices common to that order of pleaders, should have fallen foul
afterwards of the prison reformers and the African missionaries, and certain other
philanthropic adventurers. But there was the excuse that he was a novelist; and
no one was eager to call to account on any matter of doctrine a very imaginative
writer of fiction. It might be a pity, as a matter of taste, that a writer of fiction
should choose topics in which political philosophy and morality were involved;
but the criticism was willingly restricted to this. But Mr. Dickens himself changed
the conditions of his responsibilities and other people's judgments when he set
up "Household Words" as an avowed agency of popular instruction and social
reform. From that time, it was not only the right but the duty of good citizens to
require from him some soundness of principle and some depth of knowledge in
political philosophy. It is not within our scope now to show how conspicuous
has been Mr. Dickens's proved failure in the department of instruction upon which
he spontaneously entered. We need refer to only a single instance out of many,—
as his Tale of "Hard Times." On this occasion, again, the plea of those who would
plead for Charles Dickens to the last possible moment is that "Hard Times" is
fiction. A more effectual security against its doing mischief is that the Tale, in its
characters, conversations, and incidents, is so unlike life,—so unlike Lancashire

or English life,—that it is deprived of its influence. Master and man are as unlike life in England, at present, as Ogre and Tom Thumb: and the result of the choice of subject is simply, that the charm of an ideal creation is foregone, while nothing is gained in its stead. But a much greater responsibility is incurred by Mr. Dickens, in the more recent papers in "Household Words," in which this Factory Controversy is treated of. Who wrote the papers we do not know, and it is of no importance to inquire. Mr. Dickens is responsible for them and, whoever may be his partner in the disgrace of them, he alone stands before the world as answerable for their contents.

[...]

We must say that a mission to Borrioboola-Gha is an innocent enterprise, in comparison with that which Mr. Dickens has undertaken on behalf of meddling and mischievous legislation like that of the fencing clauses of the Factory Acts. If we had room, and if our object was to convict the humanity-monger in "Household Words" of all his acts of unfairness and untruth, we should go into the case of the boy in Mr. Cheetham's factory, who, in defiance of remonstrance, thrust himself into the extremity of danger, and was killed on the instant; and of the overlooker at Bury, George Hoyle, aged 50, of whom his comrades said at the inquest, "It was entirely his own fault; the shaft was quite out of the way of everybody, and unless a person willfully did something that he ought not to do, he could not be injured by that shaft." Again, "He was very venturesome; the shaft is quite entirely out of the way of every person, and could not do any harm, unless a person went wilfully into danger."—*Report of Association*, page 21. The people in the mill shouted to him to come down, and had done so often before; and when he was killed, the exclamation was, "It is just what I lippened of." Such cases as these, set off with ironical descriptions of spilt brain, puddles of blood, crushed bones, and torn flesh, are exhibited as spectacles for which the masters are answerable, and which they obstinately prefer to an expenditure of a few shillings to make all safe. If Mr. Dickens really believes in such a state of things as he describes, he should not meddle with affairs in which rationality of judgment is required; and if he can be satisfied to represent the great class of manufacturers— unsurpassed for intelligence, public spirit, and beneficence—as the monsters he describes, without seeking knowledge of their actual state of mind and course of life, we do not see how he can complain of being himself classed with the pseudo-philanthropists whom he delights to ridicule. He has exposed philo-criminal, and philo-heathen cant; but his own philo-operative cant is quite as irrational as either, while it has the distinction of being far more mischievous. The danger is less than it was. In Luddite times, Mr. Dickens might have been answerable for the burning of mills and the assassination of masters; and if no deadly mischief follows now, it will be because the workers understand their own case better than he does. The benevolence of their employers, educating them long before the Factory Law made education compulsory, and feeding them in times of hardship, has generated a mutual understanding, and a common intelligence, which go far to render Mr. Dickens's representations harmless; but not for this is his responsibility the less. If the names of Dickens and Jellyby are joined in a firm as humanity-mongers in the minds of his readers, the gentleman may resent being so yoked with a noodle; but the lady might fairly plead that her mission had no mischief in it, if no good,—no exciting of fierce passions and class hostilities through false principles and insufficient knowledge. In conceit, insolence, and wilful one-sidedness, the two mission-managers may compare with each other; but the people of Borrioboola-Gha could hardly be so lowered and insulted by any ministrations of Mrs. Jellyby as the Lancashire operatives would be if Mr. Dickens could succeed in reviving on their behalf the legislation which their ancestors outgrew some centuries ago.

Are there any readers who still feel some lingering doubt, akin to Mr. Horner's confident avowal,—that he cannot for the life of him see why the millowners do not put up casings or hooks, rather than stand out at such cost of every kind? Let us remind such doubters, in the first place, that very high authorities have pronounced those methods of fencing dangerous; and that the workers themselves have so objected, in several cases, to their use, as to cause their removal. Again, it is seen to be untrue that the mill occupiers have refused to fence their shafts. What they have done is ascertaining what the law really means, in the apprehension of the Judges. In one case we find it decided that height constitutes a sufficient fence; and in another, that the erection of mules immediately under the shaft is an all-sufficient compliance with the law. While such facts as these should not be forgotten, there are more important considerations still; those which involve the principles of legislation. If men and women are to be absolved from the care of their own lives and limbs, and the responsibility cast on anybody else by the law of the land, the law of the land is lapsing into barbarism. If the charge is thrown upon the employers of industry, they will retire from occupations so intolerably burdened. That will be one consequence; and it seems to be agreed by the common sense of all concerned who have any common sense that our manufactures must cease, or the Factory Laws, as expounded by Mr. Horner, must give way. Are we, it may be asked, to stop, leaving one particular interest under the incubus of a special law, while the Common Law suffices for all others? Or are we to go on in the course of special legislation; and if so, where are we to stop? The Common Law provides securities against injuries from neglect or mismanagement in the regular course of the employments of workpeople of all orders.

If the law is to be extended, as in the case of the mill-workers, to the prevention of "*all* accidents" from any instrument which can hurt or destroy, we must proceed to obviate all the dangers of life by law. Every landlord who erects cottages for his labourers must be legally compelled to put up fireguards, lest the children should be burnt. Every owner of houses must fence all the windows with gratings, lest people should fall out. At present, a silly servant here and there gets outside a window to clean it, against the most positive prohibition; and when the mistress comes home, she finds that the poor creature, who has taken advantage of her absence to disobey orders, has been impaled on the area rails, and is dying at the hospital. Mr. Horner and Mr. Dickens are bound to do their best to procure a law for putting up gratings at every window in the kingdom. But nothing is more certainly proved than that such laws do not work. Rash people get killed, whatever their neighbours do to save them. The law might decree that every country gentleman must surround every tree in his park with a chevaux-de-frise, to prevent "all accidents" by boys climbing; but boys would climb nevertheless, and now and then one would be killed. What would be said of the justice of throwing the spilt brain and smashed skull of the sufferer in the face of the owner of the land on which the accident happened? Yet this would be no more than Mr. Horner and Mr. Dickens have done in the case of disobedient servants who have met their deaths by going out of the way of their proper employments. As the Special Report observes—the keeper of the Zoological Gardens, whose "occasional duty" it was to feed the Cobra Capella, put it to his nose, was bitten, and died. Who calls for punishment on his employer, or believes that any special law is needed for the protection of his fellow-servants?

It appears to us that the public are under great obligations to the National Association of Factory Occupiers, for undertaking the important but difficult task of ascertaining,—first, what the law is, as between factory employers and their workers; and next, what it ought to be. The bad principle which they are exposing, and the good one which, it is to be hoped, they will insist upon, are as important to all other interests as to those of the manufacturing classes. [...]

10. W.B. Hodgson 'On the Importance of the Study of Economic Science as a Branch of Education for All Classes' in *Lectures in Education Delivered at the Royal Institution of Great Britain* (1855) pp. 296–304.

[William Ballantyne Hodgson (1815–80), English lawyer and political economist. The lecture, delivered in June 1854, deplores Dickens's attempts in *Hard Times* (then still appearing in *Household Words*) to discredit the science whose social benefits he advocates, in a lengthy parenthesis which forms the second part of the extract reproduced here. (Authorial footnotes are omitted.)]

[...]
One more analogy [between the Physiological and the Economic Sciences] I would briefly note. We know how common quack medicines are. Why is this? Because, through ignorance of physiological laws, people are silly enough to believe that any nostrum can exist potent to repair, as by a magic spell or incantation, the evil results of their own neglect of health and its conditions. To such people, talk about air and exercise, and washing, and regular diet, and early hours, and temperance, and alternation of labour and rest, is very uninteresting and commonplace. To a similar class of persons, discourse on diligence and economy, and forethought and integrity, is very dull. 'What is the use of all your chemistry,' said the old lady, 'if you cannot take the stain out of my silk gown?' And by tests not less narrow and erroneous are the teachings of science, whether economical or physiological, often tried. But a change is coming over the public estimate of the latter, at least in this respect. *Prevention* is being ever more thought of than *cure* or, in technical phrase, the *prophylactic* claims, and now receives, more attention than the *therapeutic* portion of the physician's art. Pure water, and fresh air and light are now, almost for the first time, really recognized as the fundamental and indispensable conditions of health; and baths, and drains, and ventilators, and wash-houses, are fast encroaching on the domain of the blister and the lancet, the pill and the black draught. Now, what systems of the treatment of disease are to Sanitary Physiology, Poor-laws and Charitable Institutions and Criminal Legislation are to Economic Science. It aims at preventing the evils which those seek to deal with as they arise. The attempt may never quite succeed; but its success will be exactly proportioned to the vigour and unanimity with which it is made. It seeks to treat the source of the disease, rather than the mere symptoms. It is only as the former

is removed that the latter will disappear. By all means let no palliative be neglected in the meantime, but let no cure be expected therefrom. Efforts to *perfect* systems of poor-laws, or criminal laws, however excellent or useful, must be abortive, because the very existence of the evils which these address is abnormal; and it is for the removal of these wens and blotches on the social system that we must strive, not for their mere abatement by topical applications, or the rendering of them symmetrical and trim. Wisdom and Benevolence here meet, and are at one.

Yet persons are not wanting who meet our desire that Economic Science should be taught to all, and especially to the young, by the cry that 'it tends to make men selfish.' In reply, I will not content myself with saying, in the words of Shakspere, 'Self-love is not so vile a sin as self-neglecting.' I go much further, and assert that this teaching, if properly conducted, has precisely the opposite tendency. Its great purpose is, to show how the community is enriched by the industry of the individual, and how the value of individual industry is measured by its result in enriching the community. It wholly disowns and condemns every mode of enriching the individual at the general expense, or even without the general advantage. Thus, the merchant who brings a commodity, say tea, from a country where it is cheap to one where it is dear, and gains a profit by the transaction, fulfils the conditions of Economic Science. He serves at once the community in which he lives by bringing an article from a place where it is less, to a place where it is more, wanted; and the community with which he trades by giving them in exchange for the article they sell something that they value more. But the man who enriches himself at the gaming-table, or by other means more or less resembling the picking of pockets, does injury, not service, to the community. He is wholly out of the pale of Economic Science; he may be a *chevalier d'industrie,* in the French sense, but Economic Science disowns his industry, and condemns him as a wasteful consumer of what others have produced. It teaches every man to look on himself as a portion of society, and widens, not narrows, his views of his own calling.

And here I cannot but express my deep regret that one to whom we all owe, and to whom we all pay, so much gratitude, and affection, and admiration, for all he has written and done in the cause of good—I mean Mr. Charles Dickens— should have lent his great genius and name to the discrediting of the subject whose claims I now advocate. Much as I am grieved, however, I am not much surprised, for men of purely literary culture, with keen and kindly sympathies which range them on what seems the side of the poor and weak against the rich and strong, and, on the other hand, with refined tastes, which are shocked by the insolence of success and the ostentation incident to newly-acquired wealth, are ever most apt to fall into the mistaken estimate of this subject which marks most that has yet appeared of his new tale, *Hard Times*. Of wilful misrepresentation we know him to be incapable; not the less is the misrepresentation to be deplored. We have heard of a young lady who compromised between her desire to have a portrait of her lover, and her fear lest her parents should discover her attachment, by having the portrait painted very unlike. What love did in the case of this young lady, aversion has done in the case of Mr. Dickens, who has made the portrait so unlike, that the best friends of the original cannot detect the resemblance. His descriptions are just as like to real Economic Science as 'statistics' are to 'stutterings,' two words which he makes one of his characters not very naturally confound. He who misrepresents what he ridicules, does, in truth, not ridicule what he misrepresents. Of the lad Bitzer, he says, in No. 218 of *Household Words*:—

> "Having satisfied himself, on his father's death, that his mother had a right of settlement in Coketown, this excellent young economist had asserted that right for her with such a steadfast adherence to the principle of the case, that she had been shut up in the workhouse ever since. It must be admitted that he allowed her half a pound of tea a year, which was weak in him: first, because all gifts have an inevitable tendency to pauperize the recipient; and, secondly, because his only reasonable transaction in that commodity would have been to buy it for as little as he could possibly give, and to sell it for as much as he could possibly get; it having been clearly ascertained by philosophers that in this is comprised the whole duty of man—not a part of man's duty, but the whole."—(p. 335.)

Here Economic Science, which so strongly enforces *parental* duty, is given out as discouraging its moral if not economic correlative—*filial* duty. But where do economists represent this maxim as the whole duty of man? Their business is to treat of man in his industrial capacity and relations; they do not presume to deal with his other capacities and relations, except by showing what must be done in their sphere to enable any duties whatever to be discharged. Thus it shows simply that without the exercise of qualities that need not be here named again, man cannot support those dependent on him, or even himself. If it do not establish the obligation, it shows how only the obligation can be fulfilled.

Let me once more recur to physiology for an illustration. The duty of preserving one's own life and health will not be gainsaid. Physiology enforces this duty by showing how it must be fulfilled. But, if one's mother were to fall into the sea, are we to be told that physiology forbids the son to leap into the waves, and even peril his own health and life in the effort to save her who gave him birth? Physiology does not command this, it is true; this is not its sphere; but this, at least, it does,—it teaches and trains to the fullest development of strength and activity, that so they may be equal for every exigency—even one so terrible as this; and so precisely with Economic Science.

Again, we are told it discourages marriage:—

> "'Look at me, ma'am,' says Mr. Bitzer. 'I don't want a wife and family. Why should they?'
>
> 'Because they are improvident,' said Mrs. Sparsit.
>
> 'Yes, ma'am, that's where it is. If they were more provident, and less perverse, ma'am, what would they do? They would say, "While my hat covers my family," or "while my bonnet covers my family," as the case might be, ma'am, "I have only one to feed, and that's the person I most like to feed."'—(p. 336.)

Does this mean that men or women ought to rush blindly into the position of parents, without thinking or caring whether their children can be supported by their industry, or must be a burden on that of society at large? If not, on what ground is prudent hesitation, in assuming the most solemn of all human responsibilities, a subject for ridicule and censure? Is the condition of the people to be improved by greater or by less laxity in this respect?

But not merely are we told that this teaching (which, by the way, scarcely exists in any but a very few schools), tends to selfishness, and the merging of the community in the individual; it has, it seems, also, a quite opposite tendency to merge the individual in the community, by accustoming the mind to dwell wholly on *averages*. Thus, if in a city of a million of inhabitants, twenty-five are starved to death annually in the streets, or if of 100,000 persons who go to sea, 500 are drowned, or burned to death, we are led to believe that Economic Science disregards these miseries, because they are exceptional, and because the average is so greatly the other way! Now, though in comparison of two countries, or two periods, such averages are indispensable, Economic Science practically teaches everywhere to analyze the collective result into its constituent elements,—in a word, to *individualize*. It teaches, for example, that every brick, and stone, and beam of this building, of this street, of this city, has been laid by some individual pair of hands; and it urges every man to work for himself, and to render his own industry ever more productive, surely not to rest in idle contemplation of the average of industry throughout the land. It is his duty to swell, not to reduce that average. So with prosperity. I am quite unable to see what tendency the knowledge of that average can have to discourage the effort to increase it. Besides, it is a fundamental error to confound mere statistics with economic science, which deals with *facts* only to establish their connections by way of cause and effect, and to interpret them by *law.*

But were it otherwise, with what justice can economic instruction be charged with destroying imagination, by the utilitarian teaching of 'stubborn facts.' Why should either exclude the other? I can see no incompatibility between the two. By all means let us have poetry, but first let us have our daily bread, even though man is not fed by that alone. It is the *Poet* Rogers who says, in a note to his poem on *Italy,* 'To judge at once of a nation, we have only to throw our eyes on the markets and the fields. If the markets are well supplied, and the fields well cultivated, all is right. If otherwise, we may say, and say truly, these people are barbarous or oppressed.' Destitution must be removed for the very sake of the higher culture. If we would have the tree fling its branches widely and freely into the upper air, its roots must be fixed deeply and firmly in the earth. But enough of this subject, on which I have entered with pain, and only from a strong sense of duty. The public mind alas! is not enlightened enough to render such writing harmless.

11. John Ruskin 'Unto This Last: Essay I: The Roots of Honour', *Cornhill Magazine* (August 1860) Vol. II No. 8 pp. 155–9.

[John Ruskin (1819–1900), English art historian and social critic, who followed Carlyle in rejecting social and aesthetic arrangements under capitalism and preferring those of the Middle Ages. *Unto This Last* is an attack on political economy in general and the theories of J.S. Mill in particular; this extract concludes with a footnote claiming the support of Dickens's fictional writings.]

Among the delusions which at different periods have possessed themselves of the minds of large masses of the human race, perhaps the most curious—certainly the least creditable—is the modern *soi-disant* science of political economy, based on the idea that an advantageous code of social action may be determined irrespectively of the influence of social affection.

Of course, as in the instances of alchemy, astrology, witchcraft and other such popular creeds, political economy has a plausible idea at the root of it. "The social affections," says the economist, "are accidental and disturbing elements in human nature; but avarice and the desire of progress are constant elements. Let us eliminate the inconstants, and, considering the human being merely as a covetous machine, examine by what laws of labour, purchase, and sale, the greatest accumulative result in wealth is obtainable. Those laws once determined, it will be for each individual afterwards to introduce as much of the disturbing affectionate element as he chooses, and to determine for himself the result on the new conditions supposed."

This would be a perfectly logical and successful method of analysis, if the accidentals afterwards to be introduced were of the same nature as the powers first examined. Supposing a body in motion to be influenced by constant and inconstant forces, it is usually the simplest way of examining its course to trace it first under the persistent conditions, and afterwards introduce the causes of variation. But the disturbing elements in the social problem are not of the same nature as the constant ones: they alter the essence of the creature under examination the moment they are added; they operate, not mathematically, but chemically, introducing conditions which render all our previous knowledge unavailable. We made learned experiments upon pure nitrogen, and have convinced ourselves that it is a very manageable gas: but, behold! the thing which we have practically to deal with is its chloride; and this, the moment we touch it on our established principles, sends us and our apparatus through the ceiling.

Observe, I neither impugn nor doubt the conclusion of the science if its terms are accepted. I am simply uninterested in them, as I should be in those of a science of gymnastics which assumed that men had no skeletons. It might be shown, on that supposition, that it would be advantageous to roll the students up into pellets, flatten them into cakes, or stretch them into cables; and that when these results were effected, the re-insertion of the skeleton would be attended with various inconveniences to their constitution. The reasoning might be admirable, the conclusions true, and the science deficient only in applicability. Modern political economy stands on a precisely similar basis. Assuming, not that the human being has no skeleton, but that it is all skeleton, it founds an ossifiant theory of progress on this negation of a soul; and having shown the utmost that may be made of bones, and constructed a number of interesting geometrical figures with death's-head and humeri, successfully proves the inconvenience of the reappearance of a soul among these corpuscular structures. I do not deny the truth of this theory: I simply deny its applicability to the present phase of the world.

This inapplicability has been curiously manifested during the embarrassment caused by the late strikes of our workmen. Here occurs one of the simplest cases, in a pertinent and positive form, of the first vital problem which political economy has to deal with (the relation between employer and employed); and, at a severe crisis, when lives in multitudes and wealth in masses are at stake, the political economists are helpless—practically mute: no demonstrable solution of the difficulty can be given by them, such as may convince or calm the opposing parties. Obstinately the masters take one view of the matter; obstinately the operatives another; and no political science can set them at one.

It would be strange if it could, it being not by "science" of any kind that men were ever intended to be set at one. Disputant after disputant vainly strives to show that the interests of the masters are, or are not, antagonistic to those of the men: none of the pleaders ever seeming to remember that it does not absolutely or always follow that the persons must be antagonistic because their interests are. If there is only a crust of bread in the house, and mother and children are starving, their interests are not the same. If the mother eats it, the children want it; if the children eat it, the mother must go hungry to her work. Yet it does not necessarily follow that there will be "antagonism" between them, that they will fight for the crust, and that the mother, being strongest, will get it, and eat it. Neither, in any other case, whatever the relations of the persons may be, can it be assumed for certain that, because their interests are diverse, they must necessarily regard each other with hostility, and use violence or cunning to obtain the advantage.

Even if this were so, and it were as just as it is convenient to consider men as actuated by no other moral influences than those which affect rats or swine, the logical conditions of the question are still indeterminable. It can never be shown generally either that the interests of master and labourer are alike, or that they are opposed; for, according to circumstances, they may be either. It is, indeed, always the interest of both that the work should be rightly done, and a just price obtained for it; but, in the division of profits, the gain of the one may or may not be the loss of the other. It is not the master's interest to pay wages so low as to leave the men sickly and depressed, nor the workman's interest to be paid high wages if the smallness of the master's profit hinders him from enlarging his business, or conducting it in a safe and liberal way. A stoker ought not to desire high pay if the company is too poor to keep the engine-wheels in repair.

And the varieties of circumstance which influence these reciprocal interests are so endless, that all endeavour to deduce rules of action from balance of expediency is in vain. And it is meant to be in vain. For no human actions ever were intended by the Maker of men to be guided by balances of expediency, but by balances of justice. He has therefore rendered all endeavours to determine expediency futile for evermore. No man ever knew, or can know, what will be the ultimate result to himself, or to others, of any given line of conduct. But every man may know, and most of us do know, what is a just and unjust act. And all of us may know also, that the consequences of justice will be ultimately the best possible, both to others and ourselves, though we can neither say what *is* best, or how it is likely to come to pass.

I have said balances of justice, meaning, in the term justice, to include affection,—such affection as one man *owes* to another. All right relations between master and operative, and all their best interests, ultimately depend on these.

We shall find the best and simplest illustration of the relations of master and operative in the position of domestic servants.

We will suppose that the master of a household desires only to get as much work out of his servants as he can, at the rate of wages he gives. He never allows them to be idle; feeds them as poorly and lodges them as ill as they will endure, and in all things pushes his requirements to the exact point beyond which he cannot go without forcing the servant to leave him. In doing this, there is no violation on his part of what is commonly called "justice." He agrees with the domestic for his whole time and service, and takes them;—the limits of hardship in treatment being fixed by the practice of other masters in his neighbourhood; that is to say, by the current rate of wages for domestic labour. If the servant can get a better place, he is free to take one, and the master can only tell what is the real market value of his labour, by requiring as much as he will give.

This is the politico-economical view of the case, according to the doctors of that science; who assert that by this procedure the greatest average of work will be obtained from the servant, and therefore the greatest benefit to the community, and through the community, by reversion, to the servant himself.

That, however, is not so. It would be so if the servant were an engine of which the motive power was steam, magnetism, gravitation, or any other agent of calculable force. But he being, on the contrary, an engine whose motive power is a Soul, the force of this very peculiar agent, as an unknown quantity, enters into all the political economist's equations, without his knowledge, and falsifies every one of their results. The largest quantity of work will not be done by this curious engine for pay, or under pressure, or by help of any kind of fuel which may be supplied by the chaldron. It will be done only when the motive force, that is to say, the will or spirit of the creature, is brought to its greatest strength by its own proper fuel: namely, by the affections.

It may indeed happen, and does happen often, that if the master is a man of sense and energy, a large quantity of material work may be done under mechanical pressure, enforced by strong will and guided by wise method; also it may happen, and does happen often, that if the master is indolent and weak (however good natured), a very small quantity of work, and that bad, may be produced by the servant's undirected strength, and contemptuous gratitude. But the universal law of the matter is that, assuming any given quantity of energy and sense in master and servant, the greatest material result obtainable by them will be, not through antagonism to each other, but through affection for each other; and that, if the master, instead of endeavouring to get as much work as possible from the servant, seeks rather to render his appointed and necessary work beneficial to him, and to forward his interests in all just and wholesome ways, the real amount of work ultimately done, or of good rendered, by the person so cared for, will indeed be the greatest possible.

Observe, I say, "of good rendered," for a servant's work is not necessarily or always the best thing he can give his master. But good of all kinds, whether in material service, in protective watchfulness of his master's interest and credit, or in joyful readiness to seize unexpected and irregular occasions of help.

Nor is this one whit less generally true because indulgence will be frequently abused, and kindness met with ingratitude. For the servant who, gently treated, is ungrateful, treated ungently, will be revengeful; and the man who is dishonest to a liberal master will be injurious to an unjust one.

In any case, and with any person, this unselfish treatment will produce the most effective return. Observe, I am here considering the affections wholly as a motive power; not at all as things in themselves desirable or noble, or in any other way abstractedly good, I look at them simply as an anomalous force, rendering every one of the ordinary political economist's calculations nugatory; while, even if he desired to introduce this new element into his estimates, he has no power of dealing with it; for the affections only become a true motive power when they ignore every other motive and condition of political economy. Treat the servant kindly, with the idea of turning his gratitude to account, and you will get, as you deserve, no gratitude, nor any value for your kindness; but treat him kindly without any economical purpose, and all economical purposes will be answered; in this, as in all other matters, whosoever will save his life shall lose it, whoso loses it shall find it.*

★   The difference between the two modes of treatment, and between their effective material results, may be seen very accurately by a comparison of the relations of Esther and Charlie in *Bleak House,* with those of Miss Brass and the Marchioness in *Master Humphrey's Clock.*

The essential value and truth of Dickens's writings have been unwisely lost sight of by many thoughtful persons, merely because he presents his truth with some colour of caricature. Unwisely, because Dickens's caricature, though often gross, is never mistaken. Allowing for his manner of telling them, the things he tells us are always true. I wish that he could think it right to limit his brilliant exaggeration to works written only for public amusement; and when he takes up a subject of high national importance, such as that which he handled in *Hard Times,* that he would use severer and more accurate analysis. The usefulness of that work (to my mind, in several respects the greatest he has written) is with many persons seriously diminished because Mr. Bounderby is a dramatic monster, instead of a characteristic example of a worldly master; and Stephen Blackpool a dramatic perfection, instead of a characteristic example of an honest workman. But let us not lose the use of Dickens's wit and insight, because he chooses to speak in a circle of stage fire. He is entirely right in his main drift and purpose in every book he has written; and all of them, but especially *Hard Times,* should be studied with close and earnest care by persons interested in social questions. They will find much that is partial, and, because partial, apparently unjust; but if they examine all the evidence on the other side, which Dickens seems to overlook, it will appear, after all their trouble, that his view was the finally right one, grossly and sharply told.

Appendix D. On Industrialization: Fiction

1. Harriet Martineau *A Manchester Strike*
(*Illustrations of Political Economy* No. 7) (1832)
Ch. 1 'The Week's End.'

[One of twenty-five slim didactic novels issued between 1832 and 1834 and illustrating economic principles in action. Here, in a scene at a public house frequented by workers in the cotton mills preceding a strike, the hero Allen, searching for his drunken friend Field, encounters the hard-line trade unionist Clack, and Bray, a former co-worker who was dismissed after an earlier strike and now earns his bread as a travelling entertainer.]

It required no great sagacity to prophesy that Field would be found at the Spread-Eagle. He varied his excursions a little, according to times and seasons; but those who knew his ways, could easily guess at which of his haunts he might be expected when missing from home. When he stole out before getting to his loom in the morning, or after leaving it late at night, he generally stepped only to the dram-shop, for a glass of gin to warm him for his work, or to settle him to his sleep, as his pretence was: but when he had finished his piece and got his pay, he felt himself at liberty to go to the Spread-Eagle and have a carouse, from which he returned in the dark, sometimes reeling on his own legs, sometimes carried on other men's shoulders. This habit of drinking had grown upon him with frightful rapidity. He had, a year before, been described by his employers as a steady, well-behaved lad. He had fallen in love with Sally and married her in a hurry, found her temper disagreeable and his home uncomfortable, tried in vain to keep her in order, and then, giving up all hope, took to drinking, and would not tolerate a word of remonstrance from any one but his old friend Allen.

There were more customers this evening at the Spread-Eagle than was usual even on Saturdays. Allen was warmly welcomed as he entered, for it was supposed he came to keep company with his companions from the same factory. Almost all present were spinners and power-loom weavers under the firm of Mortimer and Rowe; and the occasion of their assembling in greater numbers than usual, was the reduction of wages which had that day taken place. Room was made for Allen as soon as he appeared, a pipe and pot of porter called for, and he was welcomed to their consultation. But Allen looked round instead of taking his seat, and inquired for Field. The landlord pointed to a corner where Field lay in a drunken sleep under a bench.

"Let him lie," said one. "He is too far gone to be roused."

"What concern is it of yours?" cried another. "Come and listen to what Clack was saying."

"You shirked us in the street," said a third: "now we have caught you, we shall not let you go."

The landlord being really of opinion that Field had better lie where he was for an hour or two, Allen sat down to hear what was going on.

Clack turned to him to know what their masters deserved for lowering their wages.

"That depends upon circumstances," replied Allen. "Be they much to blame or little, something must be done to prevent a further reduction, or many of us will be ruined."

"Shake hands, my fine fellow!" cried Clack. "That was just what we had agreed. It is time such tyranny was put down, and we can put it down, and we will."

"Gently, gently," said Allen. "How do you think of putting it down?"

"Why should not we root out the one who is the most of a tyrant, and then the others may take warning before it is too late? We have nothing to do but to agree."

"No easy matter sometimes, friend."

"Stuff! we have agreed before upon a less occasion, and when there was danger in it. Had not we our combinations, when combination was against the law? and shall not we have them again now that the law lets us alone? Shall we be bold in the day of danger and shrink when that day is over?"

"Well, well, neighbour: I said nothing about being afraid. What would you have us agree to do?"

"To root out Messrs. Mortimer and Rowe. Every man in our union must be sworn not to enter their gates; and if this does not frighten the masters and make them more reasonable, I don't know what will."

"And if instead of being frightened, the masters unite to refuse us work till we give up our stand against Mortimer and Rowe, what are we to do then?"

"To measure our strength against theirs, to be sure. You know they can't do without us."

"Nor we without them; and where both parties are so necessary to each other, it is a pity they should fall out."

"A pity! To be sure it is a pity; but if the masters drive us to it, the blame rests with them."

"I hope," said a timid-looking man, Hare by name, who had a habit of twirling his hat when silent, and of scratching his head when he spoke, "I hope, neighbour, you will think what you are about before you mention a strike. I've seen enough of strikes. I had rather see my children on the parish than strike."

Clack looked disdainfully at him, and said it was well that some dove-like folks had not to manage a fight against the eagle. For his part, he thought any man ought to be proud of the honour of making a stand against any oppression; and that he had rather, for his own share, have the thanks of the Union Committee than wear Wellington's star. Would not his friend Allen say the same?

No. Allen agreed with Hare so far as thinking that there could be few worse evils than a strike; but at the same time, it was an evil which might become necessary in certain cases. When, convinced that it was necessary in defence of the rights of the working-man, he would join in it heart and hand; but never out of spite or revenge,—never to root out any master breathing.—So many agreed in this opinion, that Clack grew more eager than ever in defending himself and blaming the masters in question.

"Dare any one say," he cried, "that the Dey of Algiers himself is a greater tyrant than Mortimer would be if he dared? Does not he look as if he would trample us under foot if he could? Does not he smile with contempt at whatever is said by a working-man? Does not he spurn every complaint, and laugh at every threat? and if he takes it into his lofty head to do a kindness, does not he make it bitter with his pride?"

"All true, Clack, as every body knows that works for Mortimer; but—"

"And as for Rowe," interrupted the talker, "he is worse, if possible, in his way."

"I don't know," said Hare, doubtfully. "Mr. Rowe came once and talked very kindly with me."

"Aye, when he had some purpose to answer. We are all, except you, Hare, wise enough to know what Rowe's pretty speeches mean. You should follow him to the next masters' meeting, man, and hear how he alters his tone with his company. The mean-spirited, shuffling knave!"

"Well, well, Clack: granting that Mortimer is tyrannical and Rowe not to be trusted,—that does not alter the case about rooting them out. To make the attempt is to acknowledge at the outset that the object of our union is a bad one: it will fill the minds of the operatives with foul passions and provoke a war between masters and men which will end in the destruction of both. Whenever we do strike, let it be in defence of our own rights, and not out of enmity to individuals among our employers."

Clack muttered something about there being shufflers among the men as well as the masters; to which Allen replied that the way to make shufflers was to use intimidation. The more wisdom and moderation there was in the proceedings of any body of men, the better chance there was of unanimity and determination. He repeated that, as long as the Union of which he was a member kept in view the interests of the body of operatives, he would be found ready to do and to sacrifice his share: but as soon as it should set to work on other objects, he should withdraw at all risks.

Before he had done speaking, the attention of his companions was called off by an unexpected addition to their company. Music had been heard gradually approaching for some minutes, and now the musician stood darkening the door and almost deafening the people within with the extraordinary variety of sounds he produced. An enormous drum was strapped across his body; a Pan's pipe employed his mouth, and his hat, with a pointed crown and a broad brim, was garnished with bells. A little girl, fantastically dressed, performed on the triangle, and danced, and collected halfpence from the bystanders. While the musician played a jig, jerking his head incessantly from side to side, nobody thought of looking particularly at him: but when he turned to the company within doors and set his little companion to sing to his playing

"Should auld acquaintance be forgot,"
several of the debaters began to fancy that they knew the face and figure of the musician. "It is—yes, it certainly is Bray!" said one to another; and many a hand was held out to him.

"I thought you were not likely to forget old acquaintance, even if they come in a new dress," said Bray, laughing heartily, and proceeding to deposit his decorations with one or another of his former companions. He put his hat on Allen's head, slipped the strap of his drum over Clack's shoulders, and gave the triangle to Hare.

"Come," said he, "let us have a concert. It is my turn to see spinners turn strollers. Come, Allen, shake your head, man, and let us hear what comes out of it."

"How we have wondered," exclaimed Allen, "what had become of you and yours! Is that poor little Hannah that used to be so delicate?"

"The same that your good wife nursed through the measles. She would hardly know her now."

Allen shook his head.

"Ah, I see what you mean," said Bray. "You had rather see her covered with white cotton flakes than with yellow ribands; but remember it is no fault of mine that she is not still a piecer in yonder factory; and I don't know that I need call it my misfortune any more than my fault. Look how strong and plump she is! so much for living in the open air, instead of being mewed up in a place like an oven. Now, don't take off the hat on purpose to shake you head. What can a man do—" and looking round, he appealed to the company, "what can a proscribed man do but get his living, so as not to have to ask for work?"

A loud clapping and shuffling of feet was the answer to his question. The noise half roused the drunken man in the corner, who rolled himself over to the terror of little Hannah, who had got as far as she could out of the way of the smokers, among whom her father had been so well received. Allen rose to go, having some hope that Field might be safely set on his legs again by this time. He asked Bray whether he meant to stay in the neighbourhood, and where he would lodge.

"You must stay," cried one, "and play a tune before your old masters' gates."

"You must stay," said another, "and see how we manage a strike now-a-days."

"A strike! Are you going to try your strength again? You will make me wish I was one of you still; but I can head the march. Stay? Yes, I'll stay and lead you on to victory. Hurra! I'll go recruiting with my drum. I'll manage to meet Mortimer, when I have a procession a mile long at my heels!"

"You lay by your drum on Sundays, I suppose?" said Allen.

"Yes, yes. We keep within and take our rest on Sundays. It is as great a treat to us to sit within doors all day once a week, as it is to some other folks to get into the green meadows. If the landlord can give us lodging, you will find us here in the morning, Allen."

"Let Hannah go home with me, Bray. I know my wife will be glad to see her and to hear her story, and this is no place for a child. If I can rouse yon sleeper, I will go now, and send my wife with a cloak or something to hide the child's frippery, and then she will spend tomorrow in a fitter place than in a public-house."

Bray sat gravely looking at his child for a few moments, and then started up, saying that he would undertake to rouse the sleeper. Blowing the Pan's pipe close by his ear made him start, and a rub-a-dub on the drum woke him up effectually: so that he was able, cross and miserable, to crawl homewards with the help of Allen's arm, and to be put to bed by his wife, with the indistinct dread in his mind of a terrible lecture as soon as he should be in a condition to listen to it.

2. Frances Trollope *Life and Adventures of Michael Armstrong: The Factory Boy* (1840) Ch. 22. 'Miss Brotherton Sets off on her Travels ....'

[Frances Trollope (1780–1863), writer from the 1830s of a long sequence of popular social novels, and mother of Anthony Trollope, novelist. In their search for the boy hero Michael Armstrong who, like Dickens's Oliver Twist, has become lost in the proletarian underworld of workhouses and factories, Mary Brotherton and her lady companion visit the industrial North of England and are conducted around a cotton mill. (Authorial footnotes are omitted.)]

It was not difficult in this first stage of their expedition to follow exactly the plan that had been laid down. The two ladies professed themselves to be travellers, anxious to see all objects of curiosity, and particularly the factories, which were, as they observed, so famous throughout all the world. The master of the hotel where they lodged exerted himself with the utmost civility to gratify so natural a desire, and Mrs. Tremlett and Mary were accordingly promenaded, on the following morning, through one of the largest establishments of the town. It is probable, from the drowsiness of the public mind on the subject, that many travelling strangers who are in like manner led by a skilful official through the various floors of a factory, retire from the spectacle they present without having any feeling of sympathy excited by the cursory glance they have thrown over the silent unobtrusive little beings, one moment of whose unchanging existence they have been permitted to witness. It is the vast, the beautiful, the elaborate machinery by which they were surrounded that called forth all their attention, and all their wonder. The uniform ceaseless movement, sublime in its sturdy strength and unrelenting activity, drew every eye, and rapt the observer's mind in boundless admiration of the marvellous power of science! No wonder that along every line a score of noise-less children toiled, unthought of, after the admirable machine. Strangers do not visit factories to look at them; it is the triumphant perfection of British mechanism which they come to see, it is of that they speak, of that they think, of that they boast when they leave the life-consuming process behind them. The more delicate, and (alas!) living springs by which the GREAT ARTIFICER has given movement to the beings made in his own image, are not worth a thought the while. The scientific speculator sees nothing to excite his intellectual acumen in them; he hardly knows that they are there, but gazes with enthusiasm and almost reverence on the myriads of whirling spindles amidst which they breathe their groans, unheeded, and unheard.

But it was not thus that Mary won her way through the whirling hissing world of machinery into which she now entered for the first time in her life. The hot and tainted atmosphere seemed to weigh upon her spirits, as well as upon her lungs, and the weary aspect of the Drakes, and the failing joints of Edward Armstrong became fearfully intelligible as she watched the children (and she watched nothing else) who dragged their attenuated limbs along. Then it was that Mr. Bell's tremendous statement of the number of suffering beings thus employed came with full force upon her mind. She would have given years of existence at that moment, could she have believed it false. Two hundred thousand little creatures, created by the abounding mercy of God, with faculties for enjoyment so perfect, that no poverty short of actual starvation can check their joy so long as innocence and liberty be left them! Two hundred thousand little creatures, for whose freedom from toil during their tender years the awful voice of nature has gone forth, to be snatched away, living and feeling, from the pure air of heaven, while the beautiful process is going on by which their delicate fabric gradually strengthens into maturity,—taken for ever from all with which their Maker has surrounded them for the purpose of completing his own noblest work—taken and lodged amidst stench and stunning, terrifying tumult,—driven to and fro, till their little limbs bend under them—hour after hour, day after day—the repose of a moment to be purchased only by yielding their tender bodies to the fist, the heel, or the strap of the overlooker! All this rushed together upon poor Mary's heart and soul, and, turning deadly pale, she seized the arm of her friend to save herself from falling.

"Terrible hot day!" roared their conductor, in the hideous scream by which some human voices can battle successfully with the din of machinery.

Fortunately, they were near the door of the room, and Mrs. Tremlett, urging her steps forward, now brought her to an open window outside it. The fresh air, so carefully excluded within, soon revived her: the colour returned to her lips, and having remained silently inhaling the breeze for another minute or two, she signified her wish to proceed.

"Not now, Mary! Pray, not now!" said the frightened Mrs. Tremlett. "Indeed, indeed, you have not the strength for it!"

Mary gave her one steady look, and opposition ceased; for it said as plainly as look could speak—"Is it thus that I shall find Michael Armstrong?"

"For a moment I felt the heat oppressive," said Miss Brotherton, in a voice of very steady composure. "But I am quite sure the sensation will not return. I came to * * * on purpose to see the factories, my dear friend, and, indeed, you must not disappoint me."

"The young lady's right," replied their conductor. "She'll never see the like of our mills, you may depend upon that. Why all the machinery in the known world put all together won't equal one of our spinning-mills. There is nothing in creation to compare to it; and I don't question but the young lady heard as much before she come. So it would be altogether wrong to disappoint her of the sight of 'em."

"Thank you," said Mary. "Are we to go up stairs now?"

"Yes, if you please, miss. We have got seven stories here, and, thank God, all is busy just now, one as the other, from the bottom to the top."

3. 'Charlotte Elizabeth' (Mrs. Tonna) *Helen Fleetwood* (1841) Ch. 7 'Setting to Work.'

[Mrs. Charlotte Elizabeth Phelan/Tonna (1790–1846), evangelical novelist and philanthropist. The village orphan Helen Fleetwood has been adopted into the pious Green family, who earn their living from farming and fishing. Poverty following the death of Mr. Green forces the family to remove to the city and the children to seek factory work alongside their relatives, the Wrights.]

Long before morning had broke on the dull misty town of M. the widow Green and her family arose to pray, preparatory to the departure of the two girls. Gladly would the aged woman have accompanied them to the innermost scene of their labours, but this, she had been assured, was out of the question. However, to send them alone through the streets was not to be thought of; and after seeing them swallow a few mouthfuls of bread, she took Helen's arm, grasped Mary by the hand, and closely followed by the two boys, who would not remain, softly quitted the house.

The air was frosty, and consequently to them more congenial than the foul, dank atmosphere that usually prevailed in those pent-up thoroughfares. It breathed comparative refreshment, and imparted some buoyancy to their spirits. Helen was entering on her future task with a clearer view of its probable evils than any other of the party had taken; but strengthened by a determination to do and to suffer uncomplainingly whatever might be before her. She had spoken truly her prevailing thought when reminding the widow of the cross that every Christian must needs bear, and of their past exemption from all deserving the name. She now realized the daily taking up of that cross, and her only solicitude was to be found following Christ under its burdens. She would indeed have preferred any species of drudgery among the rural scenes that floated before her mind's eye, with their endearing recollections, in all the heightened beauty of deep contrast; but had the choice been hers, she would not for one moment have entertained a thought of deserting the post of sacred duty beside her benefactress, for the sweetest delights of her own loved native hamlet. In all Helen's pictures of earthly happiness, that family ever occupied the foreground; and an enjoyment unshared by them was a dream that never entered the affectionate girl's imagination.

Poor Mary, who intended to work such wonders in the factories by her unflinching resistance of all aggressive doings, did not feel quite so resolute under the chilling influence of a raw dark morning, as when, in her snug bed, she had watched the flickering candle that cast its ray on the page her grandmother was studying. Gladly would she have been spared the trial that now drew near; but no outward sign of such misgivings was apparent. On the contrary, she endeavoured to trip with a gait as lively as when bounding along the eastern cliff towards old Buckle's shed; but that was impossible. However, she bore up with a sprightly air, frequently turning to cheer her brothers with the promise of bringing home at night a full, true, and particular account of her expected adventures through the day.

At length they reached the mill, and there they found a pale, sleepy, little crowd, who, like themselves, were somewhat too early, shivering in the ungenial air. A large lamp was burning over the entrance-gate, and the morning's light had begun to throw a doubtful streak across the sky, blending with its sickly glare. Many curious eyes examined the strangers, and some questions were directed to Mary, whose communicative looks invited them. 'You are too smart,' said a little girl, surveying her dress; 'I doubt your fine clothes won't hold long.'

'Fine clothes!' responded Mary, in astonishment. 'I never wore fine clothes in my life; and this is my common milking-dress.'

'It's too good for the mill,' rejoined the other; and the bystanders confirmed her assertion, both by their words and appearance. Mary stoutly maintained her ground. 'Neatness and cleanliness are never out of place,' she said; 'they make the poorest child look respectable; and so my granny has often told me.'

A burst of rude laughter followed this speech, and the voice of a grown lad exclaimed, 'You'll soon forget your granny's sayings, and learn things more to the purpose, my fine little madam.'

The next moment the gate was thrown open, and a sort of rush ensued, in the midst of which the Wrights were seen elbowing their way. Phoebe cast a glance of disdain on her relations as she passed, and took no farther notice. John nodded; but Charles, after apparently overlooking them, and hurrying on, stole back, as if more than half reluctant to have anything to do with them, and in a hesitating manner said, 'I promised Sarah to see you in; so come along, for I can't stop a minute.'

At the door, the widow was told that she must go no further, unless she had work in the mill: and so great was the press just then, that she scarcely knew how the girls had been disengaged from her retentive grasp, and borne inward by the living tide, while she, with the boys, was obliged to turn back.

[...]

In the evening, Mary commenced her promised recital. 'When Charles Wright hurried us away from you, granny, I was so dizzy with the crowd about us that I hardly know how we managed. He behaved civilly, for him, and took us to a man and said something; and the man bade us come along with him. So Charles left us, and we went on, and all I could make out was that I should be a piecener.'

'What is a piecener?' said James.

'Oh, you'll hear presently. Well, after going through a good many places that I could make little out of, it was so dusk, and we walked so fast, we came to a room, and the man put me in there, and went off with Helen, before I knew what I was about, and what a sight I saw? Nothing ever frightened me so much.'

'Why, you said nobody should frighten you in the mills,' remarked Willy.

'Nobody did frighten me, though the man that took me from the other, looked as cross and spoke as gruff as old Buckle; but only think, boys, what it must be to see ever so many great big things, frames upon carriages on each side of the room, walking up to one another, and then walking back again, with a huge wheel at the end of each, and a big man turning it with all his might, and a lot of children of all sizes keeping before the frame, going backwards and for-wards, piecening and scavenging—why, we all stared yesterday, when that Mr. South said there was no sitting down; but nobody would even think of it. Move, move, everything moves. The wheels and the frames are always going, and the little reels twirl round as fast as ever they can; and the pulleys, and chains, and great iron works over-head, are all moving; and the cotton moves so fast that it is hard to piece it quick enough; and there is a great dust, and such a noise of whirr, whirr, whirr, that at first I did not know whether I was not standing on my head.'

'How funny!' said James, laughing, 'but what was your work like?'

'Why you see, the frame goes sloping up so, and the bottom edge is not so high as this little table; and the upper edge has got two rows of little rollers, and over them several other rows, that stand up; and there are a great many cotton threads reaching from the bottom to the top of the frame; and while the machine moves about, the threads go running up, and twist round the little rollers above.

Now the threads being thin and fine, they often break, and I have to keep a great watch, to get hold of the two ends when one breaks, and put them together, the same as in spinning.'

'It is spinning,' said Helen.

'Yes, it is; but not a bit like Mrs. Barker's wheel and distaff, with only one thread to mind. The man at the wheel is the spinner, and when the frame comes up the room he has to set his hand against it and push it back, which is pretty hard work. The joining, or piecening, is easy enough when you get used to it.'

'And what is scavenging?'

'Oh, that made me laugh. You see, bits of cotton wool will stick to the thread, and they mustn't go on the reels; so there is a little girl huddled up under the frame and she snatches off all the loose wool, and throws it down so fast! and when the machine runs back, if the little scavenger did not bob and duck, and get very low, she would have a fine knock on the head.'

'Poor thing!' said Helen, 'she can never stretch herself out, hardly; and she is almost choked and smothered in the dust of the light cotton bits that she has to pull and scatter about her.'

'I did not think of that,' replied Mary, 'it amused me to see her so frightened and all in a bustle, so I laughed, and the spinner laughed to see me; and he is like old Buckle, not so cross as he looks.'

'Did the scavenger laugh?' asked James.

'No; she seemed angry, and muttered: I am sorry I was so thoughtless, granny, I will not laugh any more at her.'

'I hope not, my dear: all this is new to you, but you may find it very fatiguing before long; and then how would you like to be laughed at by others?'

'Nobody shall laugh at me.'

'You could not prevent it, Mary. Remember how often I have told you, that the choice of what we are to be and to suffer is not in our own hands. It becomes us all, at all times, to submit humbly to whatever God sees fit to lay upon us; and to help our companions to do the same.'

'Yes, granny; I will always submit to God; but I need not let my fellow-creatures domineer over me.'

'If the Lord makes them the means of afflicting us, Mary, it is to Him we submit. But we may not reason about it, since we have a positive command, "Submit yourselves one to another." "Be clothed with humility." "Resist not evil." There are many more such passages in the Bible.'

Mary said nothing, but she looked unconvinced. Helen remarked, 'There is no resisting in a mill, for nobody can stop the great wheels always kept going by the steam. My work is among much bigger machines than Mary's, in the carding-room, where the cotton is pulled out and prepared for the spinners.'

'Do you walk about?' asked Willy.

'Yes, a good deal. There is plenty of bustling, and crowding, and hurrying, but the work does not seem very hard. Phoebe Wright is in the same room.'

'Is she civil?' Mary inquired.

'I hope I shall do nothing to make her otherwise,' answered Helen: and the widow felt that the question had been evaded. In fact, Phoebe could not restrain for a single day her bad feelings against the girl whom she had scoffingly introduced among her new companions as a mighty great saint; who sang psalms by way of payment for above a dozen years' board, lodging, and clothing, which a silly old woman had given her at the expense of her own grandchildren, now forced to leave a respectable home in the country, and to work in the factories for bread. The first part of the information of course excited much laughter, the latter no less indignation: and poor Helen found herself at once marked out for the contempt and dislike of the people around her. She hoped it might wear off; but whatever ensued she resolved in the strength of the Lord to submit, and never to grieve her friends by communicating the trial to which their kinswoman had subjected her.

4. Mrs. Stone (Elizabeth Stone) *William Langshawe, the Cotton Lord* (1842) Vol. II Ch. 15 'The Lover's Revenge.'

[Elizabeth Wheeler Stone (1803–1883?), writer, daughter of the owner of the *Manchester Chronicle*. Like Elizabeth Gaskell's *Mary Barton*, *William Langshawe* describes the murder of a factory owner's son in vengeance by a member of a trade union, both stories being loosely based on the death of Thomas Ashton in 1831. Reproduced here is a general attack on the activities of the cotton spinners' union, a passage which precedes the melodramatic account of the initiation of a new member into the union. (The footnotes are the author's.)]

One of the most extraordinary and, to strangers, one of the most incomprehensible excrescences appended to the general system of the cotton manufactures is, the formation, organization, and far-extending power of "The Union." True it is that most other trades have their Unions, or Associations, or Brotherhoods, so called, for the protection of the operative or mechanic; but the Union of the cotton spinners has been, and, for aught we know, may still be, of infinitely more power or importance than any other in the kingdom: they have absolutely passed laws, levied contributions, and published their proceedings at their annual or half-yearly meetings, or "parliaments," with as much formality as the supreme legislative assembly of the kingdom could have assumed. And their power over an immense portion of the manufacturing population has been enormous and *fearful*. And though the spinners themselves do not, in fact, form a greater proportion than one-tenth of the whole mass employed in cotton mills, still is their labour so absolutely necessary to the working of these establishments that they do in fact control the whole: and if they refuse to work themselves, it follows, necessarily, that the remaining nine tenths of the manufacturing population are thrown out of work also.

It would be in contradiction to all experience of human nature to suppose that the immense power which these operatives thus, according to the necessity of things have, and which power is multiplied to the nth by their regular organization, and the laws of their "Union,"—it were absurd to suppose that this power is never exerted *except* for the protection of the operative from an oppressive or illiberal master. Far otherwise, indeed, is the fact. Men, master manufacturers, excellent in themselves, and beneficent and liberal masters, have been reduced to the very verge of ruin by the "turn outs," which the Spinners' Union has ordered. Readers who have not happened to reside in the "Manufacturing Districts," may be surprised to learn that, on an intimation from the leaders of the "Spinners' Union," who may have some cause, real or imaginary, of dissatisfaction with some of the masters, "all hands" will strike: that is to say, every workman, of whatever description, employed in or about the delinquent factories, will, on a certain appointed day, at a certain appointed hour, leave off working, and neither threats nor entreaties on the part of their masters can induce them to do a hand's-turn till the oracles of the Union permit them to work again. Picquets, regular soldierlike picquets, are set to watch the condemned mills; and if any well-disposed men venture still to their work, *they do it at the risk of their lives.* Hundreds and thousands of men have turned out often, not because they had the slightest cause of dissatisfaction themselves, but because it was the will of the Union.* These Unions are systematically supported from month to month, from year to year, by the weekly, rigidly exacted contributions of the members; therefore they have generally a standing fund from which to support those operatives who "turn out" at their bidding. During one "strike" (for so these turn-outs are called,) within the small circumference of a circle of scarcely three miles in diameter, not less than from thirty to forty thousand souls—men, women, and children—husbands and mothers, brothers and sisters, abandoned their employment, and by that act threw out of weekly circulation something like fifteen thousand pounds; and forced into the same vessel as themselves, and compelled as allies, the shopkeepers and tradespeople of every class who depended on their custom for subsistence. To every member of this immense multitude who had subscribed to the "Union," that Union declared it would pay ten shillings weekly: and, for a time, it fulfilled its promise.

---

*   Mr. Chappel, a Manchester manufacturer, stated in evidence before the Factory Commission, that in October, 1830, the whole of his spinners, whose average wages were 2*l.* 13*s.* 5*d.* weekly, turned out at the instigation of the delegates of the Union. That his men declared they had no fault to find with wages, work, or master; but that the Union insisted on their "striking."

These delegates waited on this gentleman to dictate conditions, without which, they said, neither his own spinners, *nor any others,* should work for him again. These modest conditions were,—that the men should have a considerable increase of wages; that they should not be fined for bad work, or for not conforming to the general regulations of the mill.

These conditions being declined, watches were set on every avenue to the mill, and for many weeks all workmen were effectually prevented from entering.

Thus, while the orators of the political clubs and the scribes of the Radical newspaper press were declaiming on the slavery and the long-protracted toil of the factory operative—whilst ill-judging "philanthropists" were sighing over the much-exaggerated sorrows of the manufacturing labourers, these same people were not only devoting the night hours, which, it might be imagined, with "slaves, o'erworn with toil," were best and naturally given to the pillow,—to midnight meetings of committees and delegates, but they were absolutely giving weekly, systematically, and readily, a considerable portion of the money "wrung from their sinews" to support all the arrangements of a "Trade's Union," with its liberally-stipended secretaries, delegates, and treasurers, and rout of inferior officers.

Though these turn-outs were generally begun with peaceable professions, and an expressed desire only to obtain the redress of some specified "grievance," they often ended in riot, tumult, and insubordination of the most extreme kind. Immense multitudes would assemble, riots would ensue, factories would be burned to the ground; the windows of private houses (of those connected, or supposed to be, with obnoxious cotton-men) would be shattered; those gentlemen, how inoffensive or estimable soever, or their families, dare not appear abroad, or if they did it was in danger of life and limb. Civil power being totally unavailing to quell these demonstrations, military force would necessarily be called in, and blood-shed and misery would ensue.*

There has been murder,—not hasty slaying in hot blood, but cool, deliberate, well-"proven" murder, committed at the behest of the leaders of the "Spinners' Union."

---

* This picture is not in one iota exaggerated—rather otherwise. I and mine are totally "innocent of cotton;" I have not, I never had, a relative connected with the manufacture. Yet has it been my lot more than once to see my father, a man of unimpeachable honour and of great humanity, go out when my mother has been all but hopeless of his safe return; and I remember frequently the whole front of our house being shuttered and barricadoed, and soldiers or policemen quartered in the hall, whilst we were huddled for safety in the breakfast-room at the back of the house. This was during the tumults and riots consequent on different "strikes."

5a. Benjamin Disraeli *Coningsby* (1844)
(i) Bk. III Ch. 4.

[Benjamin Disraeli (1804–81), 1st Earl of Beaconsfield, novelist,
Conservative M.P. from 1837, and Prime Minister 1868 and 1874–
80. *Coningsby*, which concerns the social obligations of landed aris-
tocrats and manufacturers, was the first of a trilogy of novels of the
1840s describing contemporary political and social conditions. Here,
there is a brief depiction of the model of a responsible landowner,
in the person of Mr. Lyle, who has revived the feudal custom of
alms-giving on his estates.]

Far as the eye could reach there spread before them a savage sylvan scene. It wanted,
perhaps, undulation of surface, but that deficiency was greatly compensated for
by the multitude and prodigious size of the trees; they were the largest, indeed,
that could well be met with in England; and there is no part of Europe where
the timber is so huge. The broad interminable glades, the vast avenues, the quantity of deer browsing or bounding in all directions, the thickets of yellow gorse
and green fern, and the breeze that even in the stillness of summer was ever playing over this table-land, all produced an animated and renovating scene. It was
like suddenly visiting another country, living among other manners, and breathing another air. They stopped for a few minutes at a pavilion built for the purposes of the chase, and then returned, all gratified by this visit to what appeared
to be the higher regions of the earth.

As they approached the brow of the hill that hung over St. Geneviève, they
heard the great bell sound.

'What is that?' asked the Duchess.

'It is almsgiving day,' replied Mr. Lyle, looking a little embarrassed, and for
the first time blushing. 'The people of the parishes with which I am connected
come to St. Geneviève twice a-week at this hour.'

'And what is your system?' inquired Lord Everingham, who had stopped,
interested by the scene. 'What check have you?'

'The rectors of the different parishes grant certificates to those who in their
belief merit bounty according to the rules which I have established. These are
again visited by my almoner, who countersigns the certificate, and then they present
it at the postern-gate. The certificate explains the nature of their necessities, and
my steward acts on his discretion.'

'Mamma, I see them!' exclaimed Lady Theresa.

'Perhaps your Grace may think that they might be relieved without all this ceremony,' said Mr. Lyle, extremely confused. 'But I agree with Henry and Mr. Coningsby, that Ceremony is not, as too commonly supposed, an idle form. I wish the people constantly and visibly to comprehend that Property is their protector and their friend.'

'My reason is with you, Mr. Lyle,' said the Duchess, 'as well as my heart.'

They came along the valley, a procession of Nature, whose groups an artist might have studied. The old man, who loved the pilgrimage too much to avail himself of the privilege of a substitute accorded to his grey hairs, came in person with his grandchild and his staff. There also came the widow with her child at the breast, and others clinging to her form; some sorrowful faces, and some pale; many a serious one, and now and then a frolic glance; many a dame in her red cloak, and many a maiden with her light basket; curly-headed urchins with demure looks, and sometimes a stalwart form baffled for a time of the labour which he desired. But not a heart there that did not bless the bell that sounded from the tower of St. Geneviève!

5b. Benjamin Disraeli *Coningsby* (1844)
(ii) Bk. IV Ch. 3.

[In this second extract from *Coningsby*, we see Disraeli's depiction of the model of the responsible capitalist in the person of the Lancashire mill owner Mr. Millbank.]

In a green valley of Lancaster, contiguous to that district of factories on which we have already touched, a clear and powerful stream flows through a broad meadow land. Upon its margin, adorned, rather than shadowed, by some old elm-trees, for they are too distant to serve except for ornament, rises a vast deep red brick pile, which though formal and monotonous in its general character, is not without a certain beauty of proportion and an artist-like finish in its occasional masonry. The front, which is of great extent, and covered with many tiers of small windows, is flanked by two projecting wings in the same style, which form a large court, completed by a dwarf wall crowned with a light, and rather elegant railing; in the centre, the entrance, a lofty portal of bold and beautiful design, surmounted by a statue of Commerce.

This building, not without a degree of dignity, is what is technically, and not very felicitously, called a mill; always translated by the French in their accounts of our manufacturing riots, 'moulin;' and which really was the principal factory of Oswald Millbank, the father of that youth whom, we trust, our readers have not quite forgotten.

At some little distance, and rather withdrawn from the principal stream, were two other smaller structures of the same style. About a quarter of a mile further on, appeared a village of not inconsiderable size, and remarkable from the neatness and even picturesque character of its architecture, and the gay gardens that surrounded it. On a sunny knoll in the background rose a church, in the best style of Christian architecture, and near it was a clerical residence and a schoolhouse of similar design. The village, too, could boast of another public building; an Institute where there were a library and a lecture-room; and a reading-hall, which any one might frequent at certain hours, and under reasonable regulations.

On the other side of the principal factory, but more remote, about half-a-mile up the valley, surrounded by beautiful meadows, and built on an agreeable and well-wooded elevation, was the mansion of the mill-owner; apparently a commodious and not inconsiderable dwelling-house, built in what is called a villa style, with a variety of gardens and conservatories. The atmosphere of this somewhat striking settlement was not disturbed and polluted by the dark vapour, which, to the shame of Manchester, still infests that great town, for Mr. Millbank, who liked nothing so much as an invention, unless it were an experiment, took care to consume his own smoke.

5c. Benjamin Disraeli *Sybil* (1845) Bk. I Ch. 5.

[*Sybil* is the second novel in Disraeli's trilogy, and centers on class conflict between the rich and poor. Here we witness a key encounter in the grounds of the derelict monastery Marney Abbey, between Charles Egremont, younger brother of the arrogant landowner Lord Marney, and the Chartist Walter Gerard, father of the heroine, along with his atheist companion Stephen Morley.]

'You lean against an ancient trunk,' said Egremont, carelessly advancing to the stranger, who looked up at him without any expression of surprise, and then replied, 'They say 'tis the trunk beneath whose branches the monks encamped when they came to this valley to raise their building. It was their house, till with the wood and stone around them, their labour and their fine art, they piled up their abbey. And then they were driven out of it, and it came to this. Poor men! poor men!'

'They would hardly have forfeited their resting-place had they deserved to retain it,' said Egremont.

'They were rich. I thought it was poverty that was a crime,' replied the stranger, in a tone of simplicity.

'But they had committed other crimes.'

'It may be so; we are very frail. But their history has been written by their enemies; they were condemned without a hearing; the people rose oftentimes in their behalf; and their property was divided among those on whose reports it was forfeited.'

'At any rate, it was a forfeiture which gave life to the community,' said Egremont; 'the lands are held by active men and not by drones.'

'A drone is one who does not labour,' said the stranger; 'whether he wear a cowl or a coronet, 'tis the same to me. Somebody I suppose must own the land; though I have heard say that this individual tenure is not a necessity; but, however this may be, I am not one who would object to the lord, provided he were a gentle one. All agree that the Monastics were easy landlords; their rents were low; they granted leases in those days. Their tenants, too, might renew their term before their tenure ran out: so they were men of spirit and property. There were yeomen then, sir: the country was not divided into two classes, masters and slaves; there was some resting-place between luxury and misery. Comfort was an English habit then, not merely an English word.'

'And do you really think they were easier landlords than our present ones?' said Egremont, inquiringly.

'Human nature would tell us that, even if history did not confess it. The Monastics could possess no private property; they could save no money; they could bequeath nothing. They lived, received, and expended in common. The monastery, too, was a proprietor that never died and never wasted. The farmer had a deathless landlord then; not a harsh guardian, or a grinding mortgagee, or a dilatory master in chancery: all was certain; the manor had not to dread a change of lords, or the oaks to tremble at the axe of the squandering heir. How proud we are still in England of an old family, though, God knows, 'tis rare to see one now. Yet the people like to say, "We held under him, and his father and his grandfather before him": they know that such a tenure is a benefit. The abbot was ever the same. The monks were, in short, in every district a point of refuge for all who needed succour, counsel, and protection; a body of individuals having no cares of their own, with wisdom to guide the inexperienced, with wealth to relieve the suffering, and often with power to protect the oppressed.'

'You plead their cause with feeling,' said Egremont, not unmoved.

'It is my own; they were the sons of the people, like myself.'

'I had thought rather these monasteries were the resort of the younger branches of the aristocracy,' said Egremont.

'Instead of the pension list,' replied his companion, smiling, but not with bitterness. 'Well, if we must have an aristocracy, I would rather that its younger branches should be monks and nuns than colonels without regiments, or housekeepers of royal palaces that exist only in name. Besides, see what advantage to a minister if the unendowed aristocracy were thus provided for now. He need not, like a minister in these days, entrust the conduct of public affairs to individuals notoriously incompetent, appoint to the command of expeditions generals who never saw a field, make governors of colonies out of men who never could govern themselves, or find an ambassador in a broken dandy or a blasted favourite. It is true that many of the monks and nuns were persons of noble birth. Why should they not have been? The aristocracy had their share; no more. They, like all other classes, were benefited by the monasteries: but the list of the mitred abbots, when they were suppressed, shows that the great majority of the heads of houses were of the people.'

'Well, whatever difference of opinion may exist on these points,' said Egremont, 'there is one on which there can be no controversy: the monks were great architects.'

'Ah! there it is,' said the stranger, in a tone of plaintiveness; 'if the world but only knew what they had lost! I am sure that not the faintest idea is generally prevalent of the appearance of England before and since the dissolution. Why, sir, in England and Wales alone, there were of these institutions of different sizes, I mean monasteries, and chantries and chapels, and great hospitals, considerably upwards of three thousand; all of them fair buildings, many of them of exquisite beauty. There were on an average in every shire at least twenty structures such as this was; in this great county double that number: establishments that were as vast and as magnificent and as beautiful as your Belvoirs and your Chatsworths, your Wentworths and your Stowes. Try to imagine the effect of thirty or forty Chatsworths in this county, the proprietors of which were never absent. You complain enough now of absentees. The monks were never non-resident. They expended their revenue among those whose labour had produced it. These holy men, too, built and planted, as they did everything else, for posterity: their churches were cathedrals; their schools colleges; their halls and libraries the muniment rooms of kingdoms; their woods and waters, their farms and gardens, were laid out and disposed on a scale and in a spirit that are now extinct; they made the country beautiful, and the people proud of their country.'

'Yet if the monks were such public benefactors, why did not the people rise in their favour?'

'They did, but too late. They struggled for a century, but they struggled against property, and they were beat. As long as the monks existed, the people, when aggrieved, had property on their side. And now 'tis all over,' said the stranger; 'and travellers come and stare at these ruins, and think themselves very wise to moralise over time. They are the children of violence, not of time. It is war that created these ruins, civil war, of all our civil wars the most inhuman, for it was waged with the unresisting. The monasteries were taken by storm, they were sacked, gutted, battered with warlike instruments, blown up with gunpowder; you may see the marks of the blast against the new tower here. Never was such a plunder. The whole face of the country for a century was that of a land recently invaded by a ruthless enemy; it was worse than the Norman conquest; nor has England ever lost this character of ravage. I don't know whether the union workhouses will remove it. They are building something for the people at last. After an experiment of three centuries, your gaols being full, and your treadmills losing something of their virtue, you have given us a substitute for the monasteries.'

'You lament the old faith,' said Egremont, in a tone of respect.

'I am not viewing the question as one of faith,' said the stranger. 'It is not as a matter of religion, but as a matter of right, that I am considering it: as a matter, I should say, of private right and public happiness. You might have changed, if you thought fit, the religion of the abbots as you changed the religion of the bishops: but you had no right to deprive men of their property, and property moreover which, under their administration, so mainly contributed to the welfare of the community.'

'As for community,' said a voice which proceeded neither from Egremont nor the stranger, 'with the monasteries expired the only type that we ever had in England of such an intercourse. There is no community in England; there is aggregation, but aggregation under circumstances which make it rather a dissociating than a uniting principle.'

It was a still voice that uttered these words, yet one of a peculiar character; one of those voices that instantly arrest attention: gentle and yet solemn, earnest yet unimpassioned. With a step as whispering as his tone, the man who had been kneeling by the tomb had unobserved joined his associate and Egremont. He hardly reached the middle height; his form slender, but well-proportioned; his pale countenance, slightly marked with the small-pox, was redeemed from absolute ugliness by a highly intellectual brow, and large dark eyes that indicated deep sensibility and great quickness of apprehension. Though young, he was already a little bald; he was dressed entirely in black; the fairness of his linen, the neatness of his beard, his gloves much worn, yet carefully mended, intimated that his faded garments were the result of necessity rather than of negligence.

'You also lament the dissolution of these bodies,' said Egremont.

'There is so much to lament in the world in which we live,' said the younger of the strangers, 'that I can spare no pang for the past.'

'Yet you approve of the principle of their society; you prefer it, you say, to our existing life.'

'Yes; I prefer association to gregariousness.'

'That is a distinction,' said Egremont, musingly.

'It is a community of purpose that constitutes society,' continued the younger stranger; 'without that, men may be drawn into contiguity, but they still continue virtually isolated.'

'And is that their condition in cities?'

'It is their condition everywhere; but in cities that condition is aggravated. A density of population implies a severer struggle for existence, and a consequent repulsion of elements brought into too close contact. In great cities men are brought together by the desire of gain. They are not in a state of cooperation, but of isolation, as to the making of fortunes; and for all the rest they are careless of neighbours. Christianity teaches us to love our neighbour as ourself; modern society acknowledges no neighbour.'

'Well, we live in strange times,' said Egremont, struck by the observation of his companion, and relieving a perplexed spirit by an ordinary exclamation, which often denotes that the mind is more stirred than it cares to acknowledge, or at the moment is able to express.

'When the infant begins to walk, it also thinks that it lives in strange times,' said his companion.

'Your inference?' asked Egremont.

'That society, still in its infancy, is beginning to feel its way.'

'This is a new reign,' said Egremont, 'perhaps it is a new era.'

'I think so,' said the younger stranger.

'I hope so,' said the elder one.

'Well, society may be in its infancy,' said Egremont, slightly smiling; 'but, say what you like, our Queen reigns over the greatest nation that ever existed.'

'Which nation?' asked the younger stranger, 'for she reigns over two.'

The stranger paused; Egremont was silent, but looked inquiringly.

'Yes,' resumed the younger stranger after a moment's interval. 'Two nations; between whom there is no intercourse and no sympathy; who are as ignorant of each other's habits, thoughts, and feelings, as if they were dwellers in different zones, or inhabitants of different planets; who are formed by a different breeding, are fed by a different food, are ordered by different manners, and are not governed by the same laws.'

'You speak of—' said Egremont, hesitatingly.

'The Rich and the Poor.'

6a. Elizabeth Gaskell *Mary Barton* (1848) (i) Ch. 16 'Meeting between Masters and Workmen.'

[Mrs. Elizabeth Gaskell (1810–65), English provincial novelist, whose father and husband were both ministers of the Unitarian Church. *Mary Barton* was her first novel, which, like several of its successors, describes conditions in the industrial North and pleads for a spirit of reconciliation between conflicting social classes. Here we witness a meeting of striking mill workers in a public house in Manchester held to hear the intransigent masters' answer to a demand for an increase in wages. Desperate from poverty and provoked by an agitator from London, the workers' violent anger turns from the 'knobsticks' (labourers brought in from outside to break the strike) to the masters themselves. The outcome is a terrible oath which binds John Barton, the father of the heroine, to assassinate Harry Carson, the callous son of a mill owner.]

Towards seven o'clock that evening, many operatives began to assemble in a room in the Weavers' Arms public-house, a room appropriated for "festive occasions," as the landlord, in his circular, on opening the premises, had described it. But, alas! it was on no festive occasion that they met there this night. Starved, irritated, despairing men, they were assembling to hear the answer that morning given by the masters to their delegates; after which, as was stated in the notice, a gentleman from London would have the honour of addressing the meeting on the present state of affairs between the employers and the employed, or (as he chose to term them) the idle and the industrious classes. The room was not large, but its bareness of furniture made it appear so. Unshaded gas flared down upon the lean and unwashed artisans as they entered, their eyes blinking at the excess of light.

They took their seats on benches, and awaited the deputation. The latter, gloomily and ferociously, delivered the masters' ultimatum, adding thereto not one word of their own; and it sank all the deeper into the sore hearts of the listeners for their forbearance.

Then the "gentleman from London" (who had been previously informed of the masters' decision) entered. You would have been puzzled to define his exact position, or what was the state of his mind as regarded education. He looked so self-conscious, so far from earnest, among the group of eager, fierce, absorbed men, among whom he now stood. He might have been a disgraced medical student of the Bob Sawyer class, or an unsuccessful actor, or a flashy shopman. The impression he would have given you would have been unfavourable, and yet there was much about him that could only be characterized as doubtful.

He smirked in acknowledgment of their uncouth greetings, and sat down; then glancing round, he inquired whether it would not be agreeable to the gentlemen present to have pipes and liquor handed round, adding, that he would stand treat.

As the man who has had his taste educated to love reading, falls devouringly upon books after a long abstinence, so these poor fellows, whose tastes had been left to educate themselves into a liking for tobacco, beer, and similar gratifications, gleamed up at the proposal of the London delegate. Tobacco and drink deaden the pangs of hunger, and make one forget the miserable home, the desolate future.

They were now ready to listen to him with approbation. He felt it; and rising like a great orator, with his right arm outstretched, his left in the breast of his waistcoat, he began to declaim, with a forced theatrical voice.

After a burst of eloquence, in which he blended the deeds of the elder and the younger Brutus, and magnified the resistless might of the "millions of Manchester," the Londoner descended to matter-of-fact business, and in his capacity this way he did not belie the good judgement of those who had sent him as delegate. Masses of people, when left to their own free choice, seem to have discretion in distinguishing men of natural talent; it is a pity they so little regard temper and principles. He rapidly dictated resolutions, and suggested measures. He wrote out a stirring placard for the walls. He proposed sending delegates to entreat the assistance of other Trades' Unions in other towns. He headed the list of subscribing Unions, by a liberal donation from that with which he was especially connected in London; and what was more, and more uncommon, he paid down the money in real, clinking, blinking, golden sovereigns! The money, alas! was cravingly required; but before alleviating any private necessities on the morrow, small sums were handed to each of the delegates, who were in a day or two to set out on their expeditions to Glasgow, Newcastle, Nottingham, &c. These men were most of them members of the deputation who had that morning waited upon the masters. After he had drawn up some letters, and spoken a few more stirring words, the gentleman from London withdrew, previously shaking hands all round; and many speedily followed him out of the room, and out of the house.

The newly appointed delegates, and one or two others, remained behind to talk over their respective missions, and to give and exchange opinions in more homely and natural language than they dared to use before the London orator.

"He's a rare chap, yon," began one, indicating the departed delegate by a jerk of his thumb towards the door. "He's getten the gift of the gab, anyhow!"

"Ay! ay! he knows what he's about. See how he poured it into us about that there Brutus. He were pretty hard, too, to kill his own son!"

"I could kill mine if he took part wi' the masters; to be sure, he's but a step-son, but that makes no odds," said another.

But now tongues were hushed, and all eyes were directed towards the member of the deputation who had that morning returned to the hotel to obtain possession of Harry Carson's clever caricature of the operatives.

The heads clustered together, to gaze at and detect the likenesses.

"That's John Slater! I'd ha' known him anywhere, by his big nose. Lord! how like; that's me, by G—d, it's the very way I'm obligated to pin my waistcoat up, to hide that I've getten no shirt. That *is* a shame, and I'll not stand it."

"Well!" said John Slater, after having acknowledged his nose and his likeness; "I could laugh at a jest as well as e'er the best on 'em, though it did tell again mysel', if I were not clemming" (his eyes filled with tears; he was a poor, pinched, sharp-featured man, with a gentle and melancholy expression of countenance), "and if I could keep from thinking of them at home, as is clemming; but with their cries for food ringing in my ears, and making me afeard of going home, and wonder if I should hear 'em wailing out, if I lay cold and drowned at th' bottom o' th' canal, there,—why, man, I cannot laugh at aught. It seems to make me sad that there is any as can make game on what they've never knowed; as can make such laughable pictures on men, whose very hearts within 'em are, so raw and sore as ours were and are, God help us."

John Barton began to speak; they turned to him with great attention. "It makes me more than sad, it makes my heart burn within me, to see that folk can make a jest of striving men; of chaps who comed to ask for a bit o' fire for th' old granny, as shivers i' th' cold; for a bit o' bedding, and some warm clothing to the poor wife who lies in labour on th' damp flags; and for victuals for the childer, whose little voices are getting too faint and weak to cry aloud wi' hunger. For, brothers, is not them the things we ask for when we ask for more wage? We donnot want dainties, we want bellyfuls; we donnot want gimcrack coats and waistcoats, we want warm clothes; and so that we get 'em, we'd not quarrel wi' what they're made on. We donnot want their grand houses, we want a roof to cover us from the rain, and the snow, and the storm; ay, and not alone to cover us, but the helpless ones that cling to us in the keen wind, and ask us with their eyes why we brought 'em into th' world to suffer?" He lowered his deep voice almost to a whisper.

"I've seen a father who had killed his child rather than let it clem before his eyes; and he were a tender hearted man." . . .

He began again in his usual tone. "We come to th' masters wi' full hearts, to ask for them things I named afore. We know that they've getten money, as we've earned for 'em; we know trade is mending, and they've large orders, for which they'll be well paid; we ask for our share o' th' payment; for, say we, if th' masters get our share of payment it will only go to keep servants and horses—to more dress and pomp. Well and good, if yo choose to be fools we'll not hinder you, so long as you're just; but our share we must and will have; we'll not be cheated. *We* want it for daily bread, for life itself; and not for our own lives neither (for there's many a one here, I know by mysel', as would be glad and thankful to lie down and die out o' this weary world), but for the lives of them little ones, who don't yet know what life is, and are afeard of death. Well, we come before th' masters to state what we want, and what we must have, afore we'll set shoulder to their work; and they say, 'No.' One would think that would be enough of hard-heartedness, but it isn't. They go and make jesting pictures on us! I could laugh at mysel', as well as poor John Slater there; but then I must be easy in my mind to laugh. Now I only know that I would give the last drop o' my blood to avenge us on yon chap, who had so little feeling in him as to make game on earnest, suffering men!"

A low angry murmur was heard among the men, but it did not yet take form or words. John continued—

"You'll wonder, chaps, how I came to miss the time this morning; I'll just tell you what I was a-doing. Th' chaplain at the New Bailey sent and gived me an order to see Jonas Higginbotham; him as was taken up last week for throwing vitriol in a knob-stick's face. Well, I couldn't help but go; and I didn't reckon it would ha' kept me so late. Jonas were like one crazy when I got to him; he said he could na' get rest night or day for th' face of the poor fellow he had damaged; then he thought on his weak, clemmed look, as he tramped, footsore, into town; and Jonas thought, maybe, he had left them at home as would look for news, and hope and get none, but, haply, tidings of his death. Well, Jonas had thought on these things till he could not rest, but walked up and down continually like a wild beast in his cage. At last he bethought him on a way to help a bit, and he got the chaplain to send for me; and he tell'd me this; and that th' man were lying in the Infirmary, and he bade me go (to-day's the day as folk may be admitted into th' Infirmary) and get his silver watch, as was his mother's, and sell it as well as I could, and take the money, and bid the poor knob-stick send it to his friends beyond Burnley; and I were to take him Jonas's kind regards, and he humbly axed him to forgive him. So I did what Jonas wished. But bless your life, none on us would ever throw vitriol again (at least at a knob-stick) if they could see the sight I saw to-day. The man lay, his face all wrapped in clothes, so I did not see *that*; but not a limb, nor a bit of a limb, could keep from quivering with pain.

He would ha' bitten his hand to keep down his moans, but couldn't, his face hurt him so if he moved it e'er so little. He could scarce mind me when I telled him about Jonas; he did squeeze my hand when I jingled the money, but when I axed his wife's name he shrieked out, 'Mary, Mary, shall I never see you again? Mary, my darling, they've made me blind because I wanted to work for you and our own baby; oh, Mary, Mary!' Then the nurse came, and said he were raving, and that I had made him worse. And I'm afeard it was true; yet I were loath to go without knowing where to send the money. . . . So that kept me beyond my time, chaps."

"Did you hear where the wife lived at last?" asked many anxious voices.

"No! he went on talking to her, till his words cut my heart like a knife. I axed th' nurse to find out who she was, and where she lived. But what I'm more especial naming it now for is this,—for one thing I wanted you all to know why I weren't at my post this morning; for another, I wish to say, that I, for one, ha' seen enough of what comes of attacking knob-sticks, and I'll ha' nought to do with it no more."

There were some expressions of disapprobation, but John did not mind them.

"Nay! I'm no coward," he replied, "and I'm true to th' backbone. What I would like, and what I would do, would be to fight the masters. There's one among yo called me a coward. Well! every man has a right to his opinion; but since I've thought on th' matter to-day, I've thought we han all on us been more like cowards in attacking the poor like ourselves; them as has none to help, but mun choose between vitriol and starvation. I say we're more cowardly in doing that than in leaving them alone. No! what I would do is this. Have at the masters!" Again he shouted, "Have at the masters!" He spoke lower; all listened with hushed breath—

"It's the masters as has wrought this woe; it's the masters as should pay for it. Him as called me coward just now, may try if I am one or not. Set me to serve out the masters, and see if there's aught I'll stick at."

"It would give the masters a bit on a fright if one of them were beaten within an inch of his life," said one.

"Ay! or beaten till no life were left in him," growled another.

And so with words, or looks that told more than words, they built up a deadly plan. Deeper and darker grew the import of their speeches, as they stood hoarsely muttering their meaning out, and glaring, with eyes that told the terror their own thoughts were to them, upon their neighbours. Their clenched fists, their set teeth, their livid looks, all told the suffering which their minds were voluntarily undergoing in the contemplation of crime, and in familiarizing themselves with its details.

Then came one of those fierce terrible oaths which bind members of Trades' Unions to any given purpose. Then, under the flaring gaslight, they met together to consult further. With the distrust of guilt, each was suspicious of his neighbour; each dreaded the treachery of another. A number of pieces of paper (the identical letter on which the caricature had been drawn that very morning) were torn up, and *one was marked*. Then all were folded up again, looking exactly alike. They were shuffled together in a hat. The gas was extinguished; each drew out a paper. The gas was re-lighted. Then each went as far as he could from his fellows, and examined the paper he had drawn without saying a word, and with a countenance as stony and immovable as he could make it.

Then, still rigidly silent, they each took up their hats and went every one his own way.

He who had drawn the marked paper had drawn the lot of the assassin! and he had sworn to act according to his drawing! But no one, save God and his own conscience, knew who was the appointed murderer.

6b. Elizabeth Gaskell *Mary Barton* (1848) (ii) Ch. 37 'Details connected with the Murder.'

[In this second extract from *Mary Barton* , we see an argument leading to reconciliation between the mill owner Mr. Carson, whose son has been murdered, and the friends of John Barton, the murderer, after the latter's death. The son Harry Carson had attempted to seduce Barton's daughter Mary, which had led to her lover Jem Wilson being arrested for his murder. However, the discussion clearly reveals that the motives underlying the crime were social and political rather than personal.]

"Then you believe that Barton had no knowledge of my son's unfortunate—," he looked at Jem, "of his attentions to Mary Barton. This young man, Wilson, has heard of them, you see."

"The person who told me said clearly she neither had, nor would tell Mary's father," interposed Jem. "I don't believe he'd ever heard of it; he weren't a man to keep still in such a matter, if he had."

"Besides," said Job, "the reason he gave on his death-bed, so to speak, was enough; 'specially to those who knew him."

"You mean his feelings regarding the treatment of the workmen by the masters; you think he acted from motives of revenge, in consequence of the part my son had taken in putting down the strike?"

"Well, sir," replied Job, "it's hard to say: John Barton was not a man to take counsel with people; nor did he make many words about his doings. So I can only judge from his way of thinking and talking in general, never having heard him breathe a syllable concerning this matter in particular. You see he were sadly put about to make great riches and great poverty square with Christ's Gospel"— Job paused, in order to try and express what was clear enough in his own mind, as to the effect produced on John Barton by the great and mocking contrasts presented by the varieties of human condition. Before he could find suitable words to explain his meaning, Mr. Carson spoke.

"You mean he was an Owenite; all for equality and community of goods, and that kind of absurdity."

"No, no! John Barton was no fool. No need to tell him that were all men equal to-night, some would get the start by rising an hour earlier to-morrow. Nor yet did he care for goods, nor wealth; no man less, so that he could get daily bread for him and his; but what hurt him sore, and rankled in him as long as I knew him (and, sir, it rankles in many a poor man's heart far more than the want of any creature-comforts, and puts a sting into starvation itself), was that those who wore fine clothes, and eat better food, and had more money in their pockets, kept him at arm's length, and cared not whether his heart was sorry or glad; whether he lived or died,—whether he was bound for heaven or hell. It seemed hard to him that a heap of gold should part him and his brother so far asunder. For he was a loving man before he grew mad with seeing such as he was slighted, as if Christ Himself had not been poor. At one time, I've heard him say, he felt kindly towards every man, rich or poor, because he thought they were all men alike. But latterly he grew aggravated with the sorrows and sufferings that he saw, and which he thought the masters might help if they would."

"That's the notion you've all got," said Mr. Carson. "Now, how in the world can we help it? We cannot regulate the demand for labour. No man or set of men can do it. It depends on events which God alone can control. When there is no market for our goods, we suffer just as much as you do."

"Not as much, I'm sure, sir; though I'm not given to Political Economy, I know that much. I'm wanting in learning, I'm aware; but I can use my eyes. I never see the masters getting thin and haggard for want of food; I hardly ever see them making much change in their way of living, though I don't doubt they've got to do it in bad times. But it's in things for show they cut short; while for such as me, it's in things for life we've to stint. For sure, sir, you'll own it's come to a hard pass when a man would give aught in the world for work to keep his children from starving, and can't get a bit, if he's ever so willing to labour. I'm not up to talking as John Barton would have done, but that's clear to me, at any rate."

"My good man, just listen to me. Two men live in a solitude; one produces loaves of bread, the other coats,—or what you will. Now, would it not be hard if the bread-producer were forced to give bread for the coats, whether he wanted them or not, in order to furnish employment to the other: that is the simple form of the case; you've only to multiply the numbers. There will come times of great changes in the occupation of thousands, when improvements in manufactures and machinery are made. It's all nonsense talking,—it must be so!"

Job Legh pondered a few moments.

"It's true it was a sore time for the hand-loom weavers when power-looms came in: them new-fangled things make a man's life like a lottery; and yet I'll never misdoubt that power-looms, and railways, and all such-like inventions, are the gifts of God. I have lived long enough, too, to see that it is a part of His plan to send suffering to bring out a higher good; but surely it's also a part of His plan that so much of the burden of the suffering as can be should be lightened by those whom it is His pleasure to make happy, and content in their own circumstances. Of course it would take a deal more thought and wisdom than me, or any other man has, to settle out of hand how this should be done. But I'm clear about this, when God gives a blessing to be enjoyed, He gives it with a duty to be done; and the duty of the happy is to help the suffering to bear their woe."

"Still, facts have proved, and are daily proving, how much better it is for every man to be independent of help, and self-reliant," said Mr. Carson thoughtfully.

"You can never work facts as you would fixed quantities, and say, given two facts, and the product is so and so. God has given men feelings and passions which cannot be worked into the problem, because they are for ever changing and uncertain. God has also made some weak; not in any one way, but in all. One is weak in body, another in mind, another in steadiness of purpose, a fourth can't tell right from wrong, and so on; or if he can tell the right, he wants strength to hold by it. Now to my thinking, them that is strong in any of God's gifts is meant to help the weak,—be hanged to the facts! I ask your pardon, sir; I can't rightly explain the meaning that is in me. I'm like a tap as won't run, but keeps letting it out drop by drop, so that you have no notion of the force of what's within."

Job looked and felt very sorrowful at the want of power in his words, while the feeling within him was so strong and clear.

"What you say is very true, no doubt," replied Mr. Carson; "but how would you bring it to bear upon the masters' conduct,—on my particular case?" added he, gravely.

"I'm not learned enough to argue. Thoughts come into my head that I'm sure are as true as Gospel, though maybe they don't follow each other like the Q.E.D. of a Proposition. The masters has it on their own conscience,—you have it on yours, sir, to answer for to God, whether you've done, and are doing all in your power to lighten the evils that seem always to hang on the trades by which you make your fortunes. It's no business of mine, thank God. John Barton took the question in hand, and his answer to it was NO! Then he grew bitter and angry, and mad; and in his madness he did a great sin, and wrought a great woe; and repented him with tears of blood, and will go through his penance humbly and meekly in t'other place, I'll be bound. I never seed such bitter repentance as his that last night."

There was a silence of many minutes. Mr. Carson had covered his face, and seemed utterly forgetful of their presence; and yet they did not like to disturb him by rising to leave the room.

At last he said, without meeting their sympathetic eyes—

"Thank you both for coming,—and for speaking candidly to me. I fear, Legh, neither you nor I have convinced each other, as to the power, or want of power in the masters, to remedy the evils the men complain of."

"I'm loath to vex you, sir, just now; but it was not the want of power I was talking on; what we all feel sharpest is the want of inclination to try and help the evils which come like blights at times over the manufacturing places, while we see the masters can stop work and not suffer. If we saw the masters try for our sakes to find a remedy,—even if they were long about it, even if they could find no help, and at the end of all could only say, 'Poor fellows, our hearts are sore for ye; we've done all we could, and can't find a cure,'— we'd bear up like men through bad times. No one knows till they have tried, what power of bearing lies in them, if once they believe that men are caring for their sorrows and will help if they can. If fellow creatures can give nought but tears and brave words, we take our trials straight from God, and we know enough of His love to put ourselves blind into His hands. You say, our talk has done no good. I say it has. I see the view you take of things from the place where you stand. I can remember that, when the time comes for judging you; I sha'nt think any longer, does he act right on my views of a thing, but does he act right on his own. It has done me good in that way. I'm an old man, and may never see you again; but I'll pray for you, and think on you and your trials, both of your great wealth, and of your son's cruel death, many and many a day to come; and I'll ask God to bless both to you now and for evermore. Amen! Farewell!"

Jem had maintained a manly and dignified reserve ever since he had made his open statement of all he knew. Now both the men rose, and bowed low, looking at Mr. Carson with the deep human interest they could not fail to take in one who had endured and forgiven a deep injury; and who struggled hard, as it was evident he did, to bear up like a man under his affliction.

He bowed low in return to them. Then he suddenly came forward and shook them by the hand; and thus, without a word more, they parted.

There are stages in the contemplation and endurance of great sorrow, which endow men with the same earnestness and clearness of thought that in some of old took the form of Prophecy. To those who have large capability of loving and suffering, united with great power of firm endurance, there comes a time in their woe, when they are lifted out of the contemplation of their individual case into a searching inquiry into the nature of their calamity, and the remedy (if remedy there be) which may prevent its recurrence to others as well as to themselves.

Hence the beautiful, noble efforts which are from time to time brought to light, as being continuously made by those who have once hung on the cross of agony, in order that others may not suffer as they have done; one of the grandest ends which sorrow can accomplish; the sufferer wrestling with God's messenger until a blessing is left behind, not for one alone but for generations.

It took time before the stern nature of Mr. Carson was compelled to the recognition of this secret of comfort, and that same sternness prevented his reaping any benefit in public estimation from the actions he performed; for the character is more easily changed than the habits and manners originally formed by that character, and to his dying day Mr. Carson was considered hard and cold by those who only casually saw him, or superficially knew him. But those who were admitted into his confidence were aware, that the wish that lay nearest to his heart was that none might suffer from the cause from which he had suffered; that a perfect understanding, and complete confidence and love, might exist between masters and men; that the truth might be recognized that the interests of one were the interests of all, and, as such, required the consideration and deliberation of all; that hence it was most desirable to have educated workers, capable of judging, not mere machines of ignorant men; and to have them bound to their employers by the ties of respect and affection, not by mere money bargains alone; in short, to acknowledge the Spirit of Christ as the regulating law between both parties.

Many of the improvements now in practice in the system of employment in Manchester, owe their origin to short, earnest sentences spoken by Mr. Carson. Many and many yet to be carried into execution, take their birth from that stern, thoughtful mind, which submitted to be taught by suffering.

6c. Elizabeth Gaskell *North and South* (1855) Vol. II Ch. 13 'Promises Fulfilled.'

[*North and South*, which was serialized in *Household Words*, from 2 September 1854, three weeks after the last episode of *Hard Times*, contrasts the experience of its heroine Margaret Hale in Helstone, a Southern country village, and Milton, a Northern industrial city. Here we see an uncomfortable interview between the stubborn manufacturer Mr. Thornton and the radical worker Higgins, which is brought about by Margaret who has formed an uneasy friendship with both and wishes to reconcile their conflicting positions.]

It was not a favourable hour for Higgins to make his request. But he had promised Margaret to do it at any cost. So, though every moment added to his repugnance, his pride, and his sullenness of temper, he stood leaning against the dead wall, hour after hour, first on one leg, then on the other. At last the latch was sharply lifted, and out came Mr. Thornton.

'I want for to speak to yo', sir.'

'Can't stay now, my man. I'm too late as it is.'

'Well, sir, I reckon I can wait till yo' come back.'

Mr. Thornton was half-way down the street. Higgins sighed. But it was no use. To catch him in the street was his only chance of seeing 'the measter;' if he had rung the lodge bell, or even gone up to the house to ask for him, he would have been referred to the overlooker. So he stood still again, vouchsafing no answer, but a short nod of recognition to the few men who knew and spoke to him, as the crowd drove out of the millyard at dinner-time, and scowling with all his might at the Irish 'knobsticks' who had just been imported. At last Mr. Thornton returned.

'What! you there still?'

'Ay, sir. I mun speak to yo."

'Come in here, then. Stay, we'll go across the yard; the men are not come back, and we shall have it to ourselves. These good people, I see, are at dinner,' said he, closing the door of the porter's lodge.

He stopped to speak to the overlooker. The latter said in a low tone—

'I suppose you know, sir, that that man is Higgins, one of the leaders of the Union; he that made that speech in Hurstfield.'

'No, I didn't,' said Mr. Thornton, looking round sharply at his follower. Higgins was known to him by name as a turbulent spirit.

'Come along,' said he, and his tone was rougher than before. 'It is men such as this,' thought he, 'who interrupt commerce and injure the very town they live in: mere demagogues, lovers of power, at whatever cost to others.'

'Well, sir! what do you want with me?' said Mr. Thornton, facing round at him, as soon as they were in the counting-house of the mill.

'My name is Higgins'—

'I know that,' broke in Mr. Thornton. 'What do you want, Mr. Higgins? That's the question.'

'I want work.'

'Work! You're a pretty chap to come asking me for work. You don't want impudence, that's very clear.'

'I've getten enemies and backbiters, like my betters; but I ne'er heerd o' ony of them calling me o'er-modest,' said Higgins. His blood was a little roused by Mr. Thornton's manner, more than by his words.

Mr. Thornton saw a letter addressed to himself on the table. He took it up and read it through. At the end, he looked up and said, 'What are you waiting for?'

'An answer to th' question I axed.'

'I gave it you before. Don't waste any more of your time.'

'Yo' made a remark, sir, on my impudence: but I were taught that it was manners to say either "yes" or "no," when I were axed a civil question. I should be thankfu' to yo' if yo'd give me work. Hamper will speak to my being a good hand.'

'I've a notion you'd better not send me to Hamper to ask for a character, my man. I might hear more than you'd like.'

'I'd take th' risk. Worst they could say of me is, that I did what I thought best, even to my own wrong.'

'You'd better go and try them, then, and see whether they'll give you work. I've turned off upwards of a hundred of my best hands, for no other fault than following you and such as you; and d'ye think I'll take you on? I might as well put a firebrand into the midst of the cotton-waste.'

Higgins turned away: then the recollection of Boucher came over him, and he faced round with the greatest concession he could persuade himself to make.

'I'd promise yo', measter, I'd not speak a word as could do harm, if so be yo' did right by us; and I'd promise more: I'd promise that when I seed yo' going wrong, and acting unfair, I'd speak to yo' in private first; and that would be a fair warning. If yo' and I did na agree in our opinion o' your conduct, yo' might turn me off at an hour's notice.'

'Upon my word, you don't think small beer of yourself! Hamper has had a loss of you. How came he to let you and your wisdom go?'

'Well, we parted wi' mutual dissatisfaction. I wouldn't gi'e the pledge they were asking; and they wouldn't have me at no rate. So I'm free to make another engagement; and as I said before, though I should na' say it, I'm a good hand, measter, and a steady man—specially when I can keep fro' drink; and that I shall do now, if I ne'er did afore.'

'That you may have more money laid up for another strike, I suppose?'

'No! I'd be thankful if I was free to do that; it's for to keep th' widow and childer of a man who was drove mad by them knobsticks o' yourn; put out of his place by a Paddy that did na know weft fro' warp.'

'Well! you'd better turn to something else, if you've any such good intention in your head. I shouldn't advise you to stay in Milton: you're too well known here.'

'If it were summer,' said Higgins, 'I'd take to Paddy's work, and go as a navvy, or haymaking, or summut, and ne'er see Milton again. But it's winter, and th' childer will clem.'

'A pretty navvy you'd make! why, you couldn't do half a day's work at digging against an Irishman.'

'I'd only charge half-a-day for th' twelve hours, if I could only do half-a-day's work in th' time. Yo're not knowing of any place, where they could gi' me a trial, away fro' the mills, if I'm such a firebrand? I'd take any wage they thought I was worth, for the sake of those childer.'

'Don't you see what you would be? You'd be a knobstick. You'd be taking less wages than the other labourers—all for the sake of another man's children. Think how you'd abuse any poor fellow who was willing to take what he could get to keep his own children. You and your Union would soon be down upon him. No! no! if it's only for the recollection of the way in which you've used the poor knobsticks before now, I say No! to your question. I'll not give you work. I won't say, I don't believe your pretext for coming and asking for work; I know nothing about it. It may be true, or it may not. It's a very unlikely story, at any rate. Let me pass. I'll not give you work. There's your answer.'

'I hear, sir. I would na ha' troubled yo', but that I were bid to come, by one as seemed to think yo'd gotten some soft place in yo'r heart. Hoo were mistook, and I were misled. But I'm not the first man as is misled by a woman.'

'Tell her to mind her own business the next time, instead of taking up your time and mine too. I believe women are at the bottom of every plague in this world. Be off with you.'

'I'm obleeged to yo' for a' yo'r kindness, measter, and most of a' for yo'r civil way o' saying good-bye.'

Mr. Thornton did not deign a reply. But, looking out of the window a minute after, he was struck with the lean, bent figure going out of the yard: the heavy walk was in strange contrast with the resolute, clear determination of the man to speak to him. He crossed to the porter's lodge—

'How long has that man Higgins been waiting to speak to me?'

'He was outside the gate before eight o'clock, sir. I think he's been there ever since.'

'And it is now'—

'Just one, sir.'

'Five hours,' thought Mr. Thornton; 'it's a long time for a man to wait, doing nothing but first hoping and then fearing.'

7. Currer Bell (Charlotte Brontë) *Shirley* (1849) Ch. 8 'Noah and Moses.'

[Charlotte Brontë (1816–55), novelist, eldest of the three literary Brontë sisters, largely educated at home in rural Yorkshire. Set earlier in the century at the time of the Luddite disturbances, *Shirley* is the second of her three published novels, and the only one to deal explicitly with the problems of industrialization and class conflict. Here, following the arrest of one of the wreckers which occurs during a confrontation between the stubborn mill owner Mr. Moore and a delegation representing the workmen who have been dismissed to make way for the new machinery, we see an interview between Moore and Farren, an honest workman, followed by a scene showing the poverty in which Farren's family is now forced to live.]

Stepping backwards, facing the foe as he went, he guarded his prey to the counting-house. He ordered Joe Scott to pass in with Sugden and the prisoner, and to bolt the door inside. For himself, he walked backwards and forwards along the front of the mill, looking meditatively on the ground, his hand hanging carelessly by his side, but still holding the pistol. The eleven remaining deputies watched him some time, talking under their breath to each other: at length one of them approached. This man looked very different from either of the two who had previously spoken: he was hard-favoured, but modest, and manly-looking.

"I've not much faith i' Moses Barraclough," said he, "and I would speak a word to you myseln, Mr. Moore. It's out o' no ill-will that I am here, for my part; it's just to mak' an effort to get things straightened, for they're sorely a crooked. Ye see we're ill off—varry ill off: wer families is poor and pined. We're thrown out o' work wi' these frames: we can get nought to do: we can earn nought. What is to be done? Mun we say, wisht! and lig us down and dee? Nay: I've no grand words at my tongue's end, Mr. Moore, but I feel that it would be a low principle for a reasonable man to starve to death like a dumb creatur':—I will n't do't. I'm not for shedding blood: I'd neither kill a man nor hurt a man; and I'm not for pulling down mills and breaking machines: for, as ye say, that way o' going on 'll niver stop invention; but I'll talk—I'll mak' as big a din as ever I can. Invention may be all right, but I know it isn't right for poor folks to starve. Them that governs mun find a way to help us: they mun mak' fresh orderations. Ye'll say that's hard to do:—so mich louder mun we shout out then, for so much slacker will t' Parliament-men be to set on to a tough job."

"Worry the Parliament-men as much as you please," said Moore; "but to worry the mill-owners is absurd; and I, for one, won't stand it."

"Ye're a raight hard 'un!" returned the workman. "Will n't ye gie us a bit o' time?—Will n't ye consent to mak' your changes rather more slowly?"

"Am I the whole body of clothiers in Yorkshire? Answer me that!"

"Ye're yourseln."

"And only myself; and if I stopped by the way an instant, while others are rushing on, I should be trodden down. If I did as you wish me to do, I should be bankrupt in a month: and would my bankruptcy put bread into your hungry children's mouths? William Farren, neither to your dictation, nor to that of any other, will I submit. Talk to me no more about machinery; I will have my own way. I shall get new frames in to-morrow:—If you broke these, I would still get more. *I'll never give in.*"

Here the mill-bell rang twelve o'clock: it was the dinner hour. Moore abruptly turned from the deputation and reentered his counting-house.

His last words had left a bad, harsh impression: he, at least, had "failed in the disposing of a chance he was lord of." By speaking kindly to William Farren,— who was a very honest man, without envy or hatred of those more happily circumstanced than himself; thinking it no hardship and no injustice to be forced to live by labour; disposed to be honourably content if he could but get work to do,—Moore might have made a friend. It seemed wonderful how he could turn from such a man without a conciliatory or a sympathising expression. The poor fellow's face looked haggard with want: he had the aspect of a man who had not known what it was to live in comfort and plenty for weeks, perhaps months past: and yet there was no ferocity, no malignity in his countenance: it was worn, dejected, austere, but still patient. How could Moore leave him thus, with the words "I'll never give in," and not a whisper of good-will, or hope, or aid?

Farren, as he went home to his cottage—once, in better times, a decent, clean, pleasant place, but now, though still clean, very dreary, because so poor—asked himself this question. He concluded that the foreign mill-owner was a selfish, an unfeeling, and, he thought, too, a foolish man. It appeared to him that emigration, had he only the means to emigrate, would be preferable to service under such a master. He felt much cast down—almost hopeless.

On his entrance, his wife served out, in orderly sort, such dinner as she had to give him and the bairns: it was only porridge, and too little of that. Some of the younger children asked for more when they had done their portion—an application which disturbed William much: while his wife quieted them as well as she could, he left his seat and went to the door. He whistled a cheery stave, which did not, however, prevent a broad drop or two (much more like the "first of a thunder-shower" than those which oozed from the wound of the gladiator) from gathering on the lids of his grey eyes, and plashing thence to the threshold. He cleared his vision with his sleeve, and the melting mood over, a very stern one followed.

He still stood brooding in silence, when a gentleman in black came up—a clergyman, it might be seen at once; but neither Helstone, nor Malone, nor Donne, nor Sweeting. He might be forty years old: he was plain-looking, dark-complexioned, and already rather grey-haired. He stooped a little in walking. His countenance, as he came on, wore an abstracted and somewhat doleful air; but, in approaching Farren, he looked up, and then a hearty expression illuminated the preoccupied, serious face.

"Is it you, William? How are you?" he asked.

"Middling, Mr. Hall; how are *ye*? Will ye step in and rest ye?"

Mr. Hall, whose name the reader has seen mentioned before (and who, indeed, was vicar of Nunnely, of which parish Farren was a native, and from whence he had removed but three years ago to reside in Briarfield, for the convenience of being near Hollow's Mill, where he had obtained work), entered the cottage, and, having greeted the good wife and the children, sat down. He proceeded to talk very cheerfully about the length of time that had elapsed since the family quitted his parish, the changes which had occurred since; he answered questions touching his sister Margaret, who was inquired after with much interest; he asked questions in his turn, and at last, glancing hastily and anxiously round through his spectacles (he wore spectacles, for he was short-sighted) at the bare room, and at the meagre and wan faces of the circle about him—for the children had come round his knee, and the father and mother stood before him—he said abruptly— "And how are you all? How do you get on?"

Mr. Hall, be it remarked, though an accomplished scholar, not only spoke with a strong northern accent, but, on occasion, used freely north-country expressions.

"We get on poorly," said William: "we're all out of work. I've selled most o' t' household stuff, as you may see; and what we're to do next, God knows."

"Has Mr. Moore turned you off?"

"He has turned us off; and I've sich an opinion of him now, that I think, if he'd tak' me on again to-morrow, I wouldn't work for him."

"It is not like you to say so, William."

"I know it isn't; but I'm getting different to mysel': I feel I am changing. I wadn't heed, if t' bairns and t' wife had enough to live on; but they're pinched— they're pined—"

"Well, my lad, and so are you; I see you are. These are grievous times; I see suffering wherever I turn. William, sit down; Grace, sit down; let us talk it over."

And in order the better to talk it over, Mr. Hall lifted the least of the children on to his knee, and placed his hand on the head of the next least; but when the small things began to chatter to him he bid them "Whisht!" and, fixing his eyes on the grate, he regarded the handful of embers which burnt there very gravely.

"Sad times!" he said, "and they last long. It is the will of God: His will be done! but He tries us to the utmost."

Again he reflected.

"You've no money, William, and you've nothing you could sell to raise a small sum?"

"No; I've selled t' chest o' drawers, and t' clock, and t' bit of a mahogany stand, and t' wife's bonny tea-tray and set o' cheeney 'at she brought for a portion when we were wed."

"And if somebody lent you a pound or two, could you make any good use of it? Could you get into a new way of doing something?"

Farren did not answer; but his wife said quickly, "Ay, I'm sure he could, sir; he's a very contriving chap, is our William. If he'd two or three pounds, he could begin selling stuff."

"Could you, William?"

"Please God," returned William deliberately, "I could buy groceries, and bits o' tapes, and thread, and what I thought would sell, and I could begin hawking at first."

"And you know, sir," interposed Grace, "you're sure William would neither drink, nor idle, nor waste, in any way. He's my husband, and I shouldn't praise him; but I *will* say there's not a soberer, honester man i' England nor he is."

"Well, I'll speak to one or two friends, and I think I can promise to let him have £5 in a day or two: as a loan, ye mind, not a gift: he must pay it back."

"I understand, sir: I'm quite agreeable to that."

"Meantime, there's a few shillings for you, Grace, just to keep the pot boiling till custom comes. Now, bairns, stand up in a row and say your catechism, while your mother goes and buys some dinner: for you've not had much to-day, I'll be bound. You begin, Ben. What is your name?"

Mr. Hall stayed till Grace came back; then he hastily took his leave, shaking hands with both Farren and his wife: just at the door, he said to them a few brief but very earnest words of religious consolation and exhortation: with a mutual "God bless you, sir!" "God bless you, my friends!" they separated.

8a. Charles Kingsley *Yeast* (1850)
Ch. 13 'The Village Revel.'

[Charles Kingsley (1819–75), clergyman and novelist, vigorous proponent of Christian Socialism. His first two works of fiction were concerned with the sufferings of the working classes and argued passionately for social reform. First serialized in *Fraser's Magazine* in 1848, *Yeast* concerns material and spiritual poverty in rural England. Here we see a discussion between the hero Lancelot, the carefree son of a landowner in search of a social role, and Tregarva, a radical Cornish game-keeper who has recently been unjustly dismissed from his post, as they go together to visit the local village fair.]

At dusk that same evening the two had started for the village fair. A velveteen shooting-jacket, a pair of corduroy trousers, and a waistcoat, furnished by Tregarva, covered with flowers of every imaginable hue, tolerably disguised Lancelot, who was recommended by his conductor to keep his hands in his pockets as much as possible, lest their delicacy, which was, as it happened, not very remarkable, might betray him. As they walked together along the plashy turnpike road, overtaking, now and then, groups of two or three who were out on the same errand as themselves, Lancelot could not help remarking to the keeper how superior was the look of comfort in the boys and young men, with their ruddy cheeks and smart dresses, to the worn and haggard appearance of the elder men.

'Let them alone, poor fellows,' said Tregarva, 'it won't last long. When they've got two or three children at their heels, they'll look as thin and shabby as their own fathers.'

'They must spend a great deal of money on their clothes.'

'And on their stomachs too, sir. They never lay by a farthing; and I don't see how they can, when their club-money's paid, and their insides are well filled.'

'Do you mean to say that they actually have not as much to eat after they marry?'

'Indeed and I do, sir. They get no more wages afterwards round here, and have four or five to clothe and feed off the same money that used to keep one; and that sum won't take long to work out, I think.'

'But do they not in some places pay the married men higher wages than the unmarried?'

'That's a worse trick still, sir; for it tempts the poor thoughtless boys to go and marry the first girl they can get hold of; and it don't want much persuasion to make them do that at any time.'

'But why don't the clergymen teach them to put into the savings banks?'

'One here and there, sir, says what he can, though it's of very little use. Besides, every one is afraid of savings banks now; not a year but one reads of some breaking and the lawyers going off with the earnings of the poor. And if they didn't, youth's a foolish time at best; and the carnal man will be hankering after amusement, sir—amusement.'

'And no wonder,' said Lancelot; 'at all events, I should not think they got much of it. But it does seem strange that no other amusement can be found for them than the beer-shop. Can't they read? Can't they practise light and interesting handicrafts at home, as the German peasantry do?'

'Who'll teach 'em, sir? From the plough-tail to the reaping-hook, and back again, is all they know. Besides, sir, they are not like us Cornish; they are a stupid pig-headed generation at the best, these south countrymen. They're grown-up babies who want the parson and the squire to be leading them, and preaching to them, and spurring them on, and coaxing them up, every moment. And as for scholarship, sir, a boy leaves school at nine or ten to follow the horses; and between that time and his wedding-day he forgets every word he ever learnt, and becomes, for the most part, as thorough a heathen savage at heart as those wild Indians in the Brazils used to be.'

'And then we call them civilised Englishmen!' said Lancelot. 'We can see that your Indian is a savage, because he wears skins and feathers; but your Irish cottar or your English labourer, because he happens to wear a coat and trousers, is to be considered a civilised man.'

'It's the way of the world, sir,' said Tregarva, 'judging carnal judgment, according to the sight of its own eyes; always looking at the outsides of things and men, sir, and never much deeper. But as for reading, sir, it's all very well for me, who have been a keeper and dawdled about like a gentleman with a gun over my arm; but did you ever do a good day's farm-work in your life? If you had, man or boy, you wouldn't have been game for much reading when you got home; you'd do just what these poor fellows do,—tumble into bed at eight o'clock, hardly waiting to take your clothes off, knowing that you must turn up again at five o'clock the next morning to get a breakfast of bread, and perhaps a dab of the squire's dripping, and then back to work again; and so on, day after day, sir, week after week, year after year, without a hope or a chance of being anything but what you are, and only too thankful if you can get work to break your back, and catch the rheumatism over.'

'But do you mean to say that their labour is so severe and incessant?'

'It's only God's blessing if it is incessant, sir, for if it stops, they starve, or go to the house to be worse fed than the thieves in gaol. And as for its being severe, there's many a boy, as their mothers will tell you, comes home night after night, too tired to eat their suppers, and tumble, fasting, to bed in the same foul shirt which they've been working in all the day, never changing their rag of calico from week's end to week's end, or washing the skin that's under it once in seven years.'

'No wonder,' said Lancelot, 'that such a life of drudgery makes them brutal and reckless.'

'No wonder, indeed, sir: they've no time to think; they're born to be machines, and machines they must be; and I think, sir,' he added bitterly, 'it's God's mercy that they daren't think. It's God's mercy that they don't feel. Men that write books and talk at elections call this a free country, and say that the poorest and meanest has a free opening to rise and become prime minister, if he can. But you see, sir, the misfortune is, that in practice he can't; for one who gets into a gentleman's family, or into a little shop, and so saves a few pounds, fifty know that they've no chance before them, but day-labourer born, day-labourer live, from hand to mouth, scraping and pinching to get not meat and beer even, but bread and potatoes and then, at the end of it all, for a worthy reward, half a crown a week of parish pay—or the workhouse. That's a lively hopeful prospect for a Christian man!'

'But,' said Lancelot, 'I thought this new Poor Law was to stir them up to independence?'

'Oh, sir, the old law has bit too deep: it made them slaves and beggars at heart. It taught them not to be ashamed of parish pay—to demand it as a right.'

'And so it is their right,' said Lancelot. 'In God's name, if a country is so ill-constituted that it cannot find its own citizens in work, it is bound to find them in food.'

'Maybe, sir, maybe. God knows I don't grudge it them. It's a poor pittance at best, when they have got it. But don't you see, sir, how all poor-laws, old or new either, suck the independent spirit out of a man; how they make the poor wretch reckless; how they tempt him to spend every extra farthing in amusement?'

'How then?'

'Why, he is always tempted to say to himself, "Whatever happens to me, the parish must keep me. If I am sick it must doctor me; if I am worn out it must feed me, if I die it must bury me; if I leave my children paupers the parish must look after them, and they'll be as well off with the parish as they were with me. Now they've only got just enough to keep body and soul together, and the parish can't give them less than that. What's the use of cutting myself off from six-penny-worth of pleasure here, and sixpenny-worth there. I'm not saving money for my children, *I'm only saving the farmers rates.*" *There* it is, sir,' said Tregarva; 'that's the bottom of it, sir,—"I'm only saving the farmers' rates. Let us eat and drink, for to-morrow we die!"'

'I don't see my way out of it,' said Lancelot.

'So says everybody, sir. But I should have thought those members of parliament, and statesmen, and university scholars have been set up in the high places, out of the wood where we are all struggling and scrambling, just that they might see their way out of it; and if they don't, sir, and that soon, as sure as God is in heaven, these poor fellows will cut their way out of it.'

'And blindfolded and ignorant as they are,' said Lancelot, 'they will be certain to cut their way out just in the wrong direction.'

'I'm not so sure of that, sir,' said Tregarva, lowering his voice. 'What is written? That there is One who hears the desire of the poor. "Lord, Thou preparest their hearts and Thine ear hearkeneth thereto, to help the fatherless and poor unto their right, that the man of the earth be no more exalted against them."'

'Why, you are talking like any Chartist, Tregarva!'

'Am I, sir? I haven't heard much Scripture quoted among them myself, poor fellows; but to tell you the truth, sir, I don't know what I am becoming. I'm getting half mad with all I see going on and not going on; and you will agree, sir, that what's happened this day can't have done much to cool my temper or brighten my hopes; though, God's my witness, there's no spite in me for my own sake. But what makes me maddest of all, sir, is to see that everybody sees these evils, except just the men who can cure them—the squires and the clergy.'

'Why surely, Tregarva, there are hundreds, if not thousands, of clergymen and landlords working heart and soul at this moment to better the condition of the labouring classes!'

'Ay, sir, they see the evils, and yet they don't see them. They do not see what is the matter with the poor man; and the proof of it is, sir, that the poor have no confidence in them. They'll take their alms, but they'll hardly take their schooling, and their advice they won't take at all. And why is it, sir? Because the poor have got in their heads in these days a strange confused fancy, maybe, but still a deep and a fierce one, that they haven't got what they call their rights. If you were to raise the wages of every man in this country from nine to twelve shillings a week to-morrow, you wouldn't satisfy them; at least, the only ones whom you would satisfy would be the mere hogs among them, who, as long as they can get a full stomach, care for nothing else.'

'What, in Heaven's name, do they want?' asked Lancelot.

'They hardly know yet, sir; but they know well what they don't want. The question with them, sir, believe me, is not so much, How shall we get better fed and better housed, but whom shall we depend upon for our food and for our house? Why should we depend on the will and fancy of any man for our rights? They are asking ugly questions among themselves, sir, about what those two words, rent and taxes, mean, and about what that same strange word, freedom, means. Right or wrong, they've got the thought into their heads, and it's growing there, and they will find an answer for it. Depend upon it, sir, I tell you a truth, and they expect a change. You will hear them talk of it to-night, sir, if you've luck.'

'We all expect a change, for that matter,' said Lancelot. 'That feeling is common to all classes and parties just now.'

Tregarva took off his hat.

' "For the word of the Lord hath spoken it." Do you know, sir, I long at times that I did agree with those Chartists! If I did, I'd turn lecturer to-morrow. How a man could speak out then! If he saw any door of hope, any way of salvation for these poor fellows, even if it was nothing better than salvation by Act of Parliament!'

'But why don't you trust the truly worthy among the clergy and the gentry to leaven their own ranks and bring all right in time?'

'Because, sir, they seem to be going the way only to make things worse. The people have been so dependent on them heretofore that they have become thorough beggars. You can have no knowledge, sir, of the whining, canting, deceit, and lies which those poor miserable labourers' wives palm on charitable ladies. If they weren't angels, some of them, they'd lock up their purses and never give away another farthing. And, sir, these free schools, and these penny clubs, and clothing clubs, and these heaps of money which are given away, all make the matter worse and worse. They make the labourer fancy that he is not to depend upon God and his own right hand, but on what his wife can worm out of the good-nature of the rich. Why, sir, they growl as insolently now at the parson or the squire's wife if they don't get as much money as their neighbours, as they used to at the parish vestrymen under the old law. Look at that Lord Vieuxbois, sir, as sweet a gentleman as ever God made. It used to do me good to walk behind him when he came over here shooting, just to hear the gentle kind-hearted way in which he used to speak to every old soul he met. He spends his whole life and time about the poor, I hear. But, sir, as sure as you live he's making his people slaves and humbugs. He doesn't see, sir, that they want to be raised bodily out of this miserable hand-to-mouth state, to be brought nearer up to him, and set on a footing where they can shift for themselves. Without meaning it, sir, all his boundless charities are keeping the people down, and telling them they must stay down, and not help themselves, but wait for what he gives them. He fats prize-labourers, sir, just as Lord Minchampstead fats prize-oxen and pigs.'

Lancelot could not help thinking of that amusingly inconsistent, however well-meant, scene in *Coningsby*, in which Mr. Lyle is represented as trying to restore 'the independent order of peasantry,' by making them the receivers of public alms at his own gate, as if they had been middle-age serfs or vagabonds, and not citizens of modern England.

'It may suit the Mr. Lyles of this age,' thought Lancelot, 'to make the people constantly and visibly comprehend that property is their protector and their friend, but I question whether it will suit the people themselves, unless they can make property understand that it owes them something more definite than protection.'

Saddened by this conversation, which had helped to give another shake to the easy-going complacency with which Lancelot had been used to contemplate the world below him, and look on its evils as necessaries, ancient and fixed as the universe, he entered the village fair, and was a little disappointed at his first glimpse of the village green. Certainly his expectations had not been very exalted; but there had run through them a hope of something melodramatic, dreams of Maypole dancing and athletic games, somewhat of village-belle rivalry, of the Corin and Sylvia school; or, failing that, a few Touchstones and Audreys, some genial earnest buffo humour here and there. But there did not seem much likelihood of it. Two or three apple and gingerbread stalls, from which draggled children were turning slowly and wistfully away to go home; a booth full of trumpery fairings, in front of which tawdry girls were coaxing maudlin youths, with faded southernwood in their button-holes; another long low booth, from every crevice of which reeked odours of stale beer and smoke, by courtesy denominated to-bacco, to the treble accompaniment of a jigging fiddle and a tambourine, and the bass one of grumbled oaths and curses within—these were the means of relaxa-tion which the piety, freedom, and civilisation of fourteen centuries, from Hengist to Queen Victoria, had devised and made possible for the English peasant!

'There seems very little here to see,' said Lancelot, half peevishly.

'I think, sir,' quoth Tregarva, 'that very thing is what's most worth seeing.'

8b. Charles Kingsley *Alton Locke* (1850) Ch. 10 'How Folk turn Chartists.'

[*Alton Locke* depicts the miseries of London tailors after the intro-duction of the 'sweating' system of production—the contracting out of tailoring work on piecework rates at starvation level. The epony-mous hero and narrator tells the story of his experiences as appren-tice tailor and proletarian poet, and his intellectual conversion from Calvinism to Chartism and finally to Christian Socialism. Here we see his reaction to a Chartist meeting to which he has been taken by his fellow tailor Crossthwaite, after sweating has been introduced by their employer.]

'Well, Alton! where was the treason and murder? Your nose must have been a sharp one, to smell out any there. Did you hear anything that astonished your weak mind so very exceedingly, after all?'

'The only thing that did astonish me was to hear men of my own class—and lower still, perhaps some of them—speak with such fluency and eloquence. Such a fund of information—such excellent English—where did they get it all?'

'From the God who knows nothing about ranks. They're the unknown great—the unaccredited heroes, as Master Thomas Carlyle would say—whom the flunkeys aloft have not acknowledged yet—though they'll be forced to, some day, with a vengeance. Are you convinced, once for all?'

'I really do not understand political questions, Crossthwaite.'

'Does it want so very much wisdom to understand the rights and the wrongs of all that? Are the people represented? Are you represented? Do you feel like a man that's got any one to fight your battle in Parliament, my young friend, eh?'

'I'm sure I don't know—'

'Why, what in the name of common sense—what interest or feeling of yours or mine, or any man's you ever spoke to, except the shopkeeper, do Alderman A— or Lord C— D— represent? They represent property—and we have none. They represent rank—we have none. Vested interests—we have none. Large capitals—those are just what crush us. Irresponsibility of employers, slavery of the employed, competition among masters, competition among workmen, that is the system they represent—they preach it, they glory in it.—Why, it is the very ogre that is eating us all up. They are chosen by the few, they represent the few, and they make laws for the many—and yet you don't know whether or not the people are represented!'

We were passing by the door of the Victoria Theatre; it was just half-price time—and the beggary and rascality of London were pouring in to their low amusement, from the neighbouring gin-palaces and thieves' cellars. A herd of ragged boys, vomiting forth slang, filth, and blasphemy, pushed past us, compelling us to take good care of our pockets.

'Look there! look at the amusements, the training, the civilisation, which the Government permits to the children of the people!—These licensed pits of darkness, traps of temptation, profligacy, and ruin, triumphantly yawning night after night—and then tell me that the people who see their children thus kidnapped into hell are represented by a Government who licenses such things!'

'Would a change in the franchise cure that?'

'Household suffrage mightn't—but give us the Charter, and we'll see about it! Give us the Charter, and we'll send workmen into Parliament that shall soon find out whether something better can't be put in the way of the ten thousand boys and girls in London who live by theft and prostitution, than the tender mercies of the Victoria—a pretty name! They say the Queen's a good woman—and I don't doubt it. I wonder often if she knows what her precious namesake here is like.'

'But really, I cannot see how a mere change in representation can cure such things as that.'

'Why, didn't they tell us, before the Reform Bill, that extension of the suffrage was to cure everything? And how can you have too much of a good thing? We've only taken them at their word, we Chartists. Haven't all politicians been preaching for years that England's national greatness was all owing to her political institutions—to Magna Charta, and the Bill of Rights, and representative parliaments, and all that? It was but the other day I got hold of some Tory paper, that talked about the English constitution, and the balance of queen, lords, and commons, as the "Talismanic Palladium" of the country. 'Gad, we'll see if a move onward in the same line won't better the matter. If the balance of classes is such a blessed thing, the sooner we get the balance equal, the better; for it's rather lopsided just now, no one can deny. So, representative institutions are the talismanic palladium of the nation, are they? The palladium of the classes that have them, I daresay; and that's the very best reason why the classes that haven't got 'em should look out for the same palladium for themselves. What's sauce for the gander is sauce for the goose, isn't it? We'll try—we'll see whether the talisman they talk of has lost its power all of a sudden since '32—whether we can't rub the magic ring a little for ourselves and call up genii to help us out of the mire, as the shopkeepers and the gentlemen have done.'

****

From that night I was a Chartist, heart and soul—and so were a million and a half more of the best artisans in England—at least, I had no reason to be ashamed of my company. Yes; I too, like Crossthwaite, took the upper classes at their word; bowed down to the idol of political institutions, and pinned my hopes of salvation on 'the possession of one ten-thousandth part of a talker in the national palaver.' True, I desired the Charter, at first (as I do, indeed, at this moment), as a means to glorious ends—not only because it would give a chance of elevation, a free sphere of action, to lowly worth and talent; but because it was the path to reforms—social, legal, sanatory, educational—to which the veriest Tory—certainly not the great and good Lord Ashley—would not object. But soon, with me, and I am afraid with many, many more, the means became, by the frailty of poor human nature, an end, an idol in itself. I had so made up my mind that it was the only method of getting what I wanted, that I neglected, alas! but too often, to try the methods which lay already by me. 'If we had but the Charter'—was the excuse for a thousand lazinesses, procrastinations. 'If we had but the Charter'—I should be good, and free, and happy. Fool that I was! It was within, rather than without, that I needed reform.

And so I began to look on man (and too many of us, I am afraid, are doing so) as the creature and puppet of circumstances—of the particular outward system, social or political, in which he happens to find himself. An abominable heresy, no doubt; but, somehow, it appears to me just the same as Benthamites, and economists, and high-churchmen, too, for that matter, have been preaching for the last twenty years with great applause from their respective parties. One set informs the world that it is to be regenerated by cheap bread, free trade, and that peculiar form of the 'freedom of industry' which, in plain language, signifies 'the despotism of capital'; and which, whatever it means, is merely some outward system, circumstance, or 'dodge' *about* man, and not *in* him. Another party's nostrum is more churches, more schools, more clergymen—excellent things in their way—better even than cheap bread, or free trade, provided only that they are excellent—that the churches, schools, clergymen, are good ones. But the party of whom I am speaking seem to us workmen to consider the quality quite a secondary consideration, compared with the quantity. They expect the world to be regenerated, not by becoming more a Church—none would gladlier help them in bringing that about than the Chartists themselves, paradoxical as it may seem—but by being dosed somewhat more with a certain 'Church system,' circumstance, or 'dodge.' For my part, I seem to have learnt that the only thing to regenerate the world is not more of any system, good or bad, but simply more of the Spirit of God.

About the supposed omnipotence of the Charter, I have found out my mistake. I believe no more in 'Morison's-Pill-remedies,' as Thomas Carlyle calls them. Talismans are worthless. The age of spirit-compelling spells, whether of parchment or carbuncle, is past—if, indeed, it ever existed. The Charter will no more make men good, than political economy, or the observance of the Church Calendar—a fact which we working men, I really believe, have, under the pressure of wholesome defeat and God-sent affliction, found out sooner than our more 'enlightened' fellow-idolaters. But at that time, as I have confessed already, we took our betters at their word, and believed in Morison's Pills. Only, as we looked at the world from among a class of facts somewhat different from theirs, we differed from them proportionably as to our notions of the proper ingredients in the said Pill.

9. 'A Friend of the People' (Fanny Mayne)
Jane Rutherford, or the Miners' Strike (1854)
Ch. 1 'The Town.'

[Fanny Mayne (dates unknown), journalist and novelist. According to the author's preface, the purpose of the novel, which was first serialized in her own journal the *True Briton* in 1853, was 'to warn the working classes against the inevitable evil consequences of *strikes* and *turn-outs*.' Here, in the opening of the novel, following the general introduction of the Somerset mining community of Horsley, there is a description of a meeting of the striking colliers being addressed by their leader Jonathan Rutherford, the father of the heroine. (Authorial footnotes are omitted.)]

The colliers have struck! Some time since they asked to have their wages raised, and they were promised that such should be the case, but, somehow or other, the middle-men have made an arrangement to counteract this promise on the part of the proprietor. Now it is the second week since they have worked or received any wages, and they have met together for the purpose of considering and discussing 'their grievances.' One of their number, apparently a leader, is in the act of addressing his fellow-workmen. Let us draw near and hear what he has to say. Not less than five hundred miners are deeply listening to every word which he utters, interrupting him only by occasional mutterings of reproach against the authors of their 'wrongs.'

The speaker is a man apparently about fifty years of age, with thick, grizzled hair, standing up in distinct patches from his head, and so coarse in its texture as more to resemble a door-mat than a head of hair. His face is long, thin, and sallow; its ordinary expression is cunning and subdued, and on the whole, unprepossessing; but he is now speaking with considerable vehemence and energy of lungs and muscles, accompanied by a somewhat fierce and repulsive smile spreading over his whole countenance. He has on the usual Sunday dress of the collier in part, very long blue coat with very large brass buttons—not the brightest in the world—and very greasy-looking serge trousers, with the pockets unbuttoned and hanging down so as to show a dark triangle of greasy lining.

The miner is no dandy anywhere; and, while his toilsome occupation and ruder habits render him insensible to the love of dress peculiar to other classes of society in many of its various phases, his other characteristics are no less peculiar and distinctive. No one can mistake the expression of a collier's countenance any more than they can his clothes or his figure. At first sight you know he is a miner. A sort of earthen, yellow, mole-like cast of countenance, with sunken peering eyes, great development of bone and muscle, especially about the shoulders and hips, and legs so small that they seem scarcely to have enlarged or elongated since they left the cradle. This is especially observable in the best workmen, those who are employed in the side veins of coal, where very often the whole of their day's work is performed while lying flat on their sides or backs, using their 'pick' (axe) above their heads. Certainly, the colliers are by no means of the Adonis school! But there are, with all their deficiency in personal attractions, many clever men among them: some shrewd, sharp, worldly, and far-seeing men, in spite of their mole-like life; some spiritual-minded, and intelligent, and pious men. And of these latter, apparently, a far greater proportion than we find among agricultural laborers—probably arising from the fact of their realising the idea that their life is continually in the hands of their fellow-creatures—that one careless use of an unshaded light, one trap-boy asleep at his post, one hitch in drawing up or letting down the rope to which they are clinging like bees, may send them into eternity at once. And yet more, that from their childhood many of them study the Word of God, and thus their mental powers are expanded, even if their souls receive not the spiritual gift. The only alleviation, indeed, of the little trapper-boy's eight long weary hours, as he sits behind the doors, is the being able to obtain a candle-end now and then from one of the colliers or *deaden folk,* by which he can read his Bible, generally his whole library, for a quarter of an hour. Some of them are also preachers. Jonathan Rutherford, the leader, who is now addressing his companions, is one of the latter. He is very fond of 'speaking a few words for the edification of the unconverted,' he says; and many shrewd, worldly-wise, and crafty words he can also speak at other times—not altogether to edification. Jonathan Rutherford belongs to no particular sect. He is not a Wesleyan as the greater part of his comrades are; nor an Independent—nor a Swedenborgian—nor a Churchman. No, he is a man to himself: he joins no congregation; he prays with no sect; he knows little enough of doctrinal Christianity, although he has texts by the score at his fingers' ends; he says he worships God according to his own fashion. The probability is that he does not worship any God at all except one whom he has fashioned in himself and for himself.

Let us draw near, for he is now addressing the mob, and truly there is a kind of rude and singular eloquence in his words and gestures; while his ungainly form and diminutive stature grows polished and enlarged before our eyes as we listen to the energetic language that flows from his lips.

'Men and fellow-laborers—There is not under the broad canopy of heaven so ill-used a class of men as we colliers. Condemned from our earliest childhood to work in dark and dismal mines, far removed from the air and sunshine which the universal Disposer of all things has given for the free use of all. Condemned, I say, to work from our earliest childhood in the dark bosom of God's earth, subjected to perils within the mine, and perils in ascending from or descending to our work. Condemned to perpetual changes of atmosphere calculated to try the strongest constitutions; and subject to more diseases than even the frail flesh of man is usually heir to. Condemned to work for low wages—and these badly paid— the collier, I say, is the most ill-used man under the open canopy of heaven. Men and fellow-laborers—I wish to speak to you of our wrongs. I need not remind you of them. I need not remind you that we have been working task work for low wages, and that, in addition to this, our employers have, like the Pharaohs of old, cheated us in the work itself. I need not tell you of the twenty-six hundred-weight counted as twenty. I need not remind you of our wages being paid in very dear goods; and, though that practice has lately been abandoned by many of our employers, yet that still they adhere to the system of paying our wages at the beer-houses kept by tenants of our employers—who are in many cases themselves also brewers—so that the young and inexperienced among us are tempted to ruin their souls, as well as starve their families, by indulging in drink.'

Here was a fine opportunity for a little preaching, which Jonathan Rutherford did not fail to make use of, for he was a rigid teetotaller in profession (we will say nothing of that with which his tumbler of hot water at home was privately flavored every night) and self-righteous and domineering in his generation. The opportunity, therefore, was not to be lost of setting before his hearers the iniquity of drunkenness, and this, accompanied, as it was usual in Jonathan Rutherford's speeches, by abundance of worldly wisdom, demonstrated in showing forth the infallible consequences of drinking.

When he had run on for some minutes or more, saying many things that were true, some worldly truths, and some divine truths, and many more things that were neither worldly nor divine truths, though he proclaimed them as such— quoting from proverbs, whether English, American, or translated, they were all the same in Jonathan's idea, all propounded by Solomon, he thought; so that he would as soon have said 'thus saith the Holy Bible,' to introduce

'More are drowned in the wine-cup than in the ocean,'
as he would to

'Look not upon the wine when it is red,' etc.

At last, however, he returned again to his theme—the ill-usage of the colliers. Had we had time to take down his words, our readers might not, perhaps—unless with exemplary patience—have easily gathered the real subject of complaint.

We will give it, therefore, briefly in our own way; for Jonathan Rutherford, in his not very logical or luminous speeches, as in his professions and actions, was very much like a hero of past times, accounted by some a mighty saint, and by others a wonderful hypocrite—we allude to Oliver Cromwell. In short, we will give our friend Jonathan the credit of being a 'Cromwell guiltless of his country's blood,' though only in deed, not in will; for, if by any means he could have stirred up his comrades to more than a mere passive resistance to the authorities, he certainly would have done so.

The case stands thus. The colliers thought that they were underpaid. Everything around them was rising in price. The necessaries of life were daily and weekly becoming dearer, but the wages of many of them were still low—too low, they said, to enable any but the best workmen to do more than barely supply their wives and families with the necessaries of life, though, somehow or other, most of the men, and many of the women too, managed to spend a full quarter of their weekly earnings at the ale-house or gin-shop, while a smaller portion was for the most part paid to the union.

Now, though Jonathan was one of the best workmen, if not the very best, in the mine; and, consequently, had never earned less than eighteen shillings a-week, yet he could not resist the temptation of taking the lead in this matter.

A deputation, headed by him, had, therefore, waited upon the leading proprietor in London, and induced him to address a letter to the manager, instructing him to raise the miners' wages. But, when the next Saturday night came—though the price of labor stood higher—the earnings of each man were less rather than more; because, henceforth, instead of being paid twenty-two per hundredweight to the twenty, twenty-six was to be counted as twenty.

On the following Monday, before going to work, the men demanded whether such was to be the system for the future. On being answered in the affirmative the whole gang at once struck. Their example was followed in the afternoon by the other gang, and, within four days, by the colliers in all the surrounding pits; so, by the end of the week preceding that on which our tale commences, five hundred men, besides lads and boys, were hanging about. On this evening, they were gathered together on the hill to hear the exhortation of their leader, previous to the expected arrival of the lordly proprietor to spend his Easter in the country.

Drunk and half-maddened by his fierce and intoxicating words—more than if they had been partaking of strong drink; ready to commit any outrage; ill at ease themselves in their own minds, and full of foreboding as to what may be the final consequences of their strike; no wages coming in on the morrow to take to their wives, and nothing laid by in a time of prosperity upon which to fall back for subsistence! Verily, the men of Horsley are in an evil case. Is there no kind hand stretched forth to help them? We shall see.

Explanatory Notes

Book I

Chapter 2: Murdering the Innocents

44   *'Very well then ...' ... 'You know what a horse is.'*

    See Dickens's letter to W.H. Wills reproduced in App. A 4c. The Lancasterian and Bell systems, the dominant methods of mass elementary education from the beginning of the century, which were in competition because of their links to the Nonconformist and Established churches respectively, were in fact very similar in form. Both depended, perhaps inevitably given that several hundred children were often taught in one large room by only a couple of teachers, on a mechanical style of rote learning under a hierarchy of 'monitors' appointed from among the older or more advanced pupils. HAMMOND pp. 171–9 describes the methods in detail; the specimen dialogues between monitors and pupils reproduced there from contemporary Manuals have many points of similarity with Dickens's satire here. Bitzer's definition of a horse is also reminiscent of the style of factual information appearing in the publications of the Society for the Diffusion of Useful Knowledge aiming at working-class readers from the 1820s; see, for example the *Store of Knowledge* (1842) by Charles Knight, publisher to the Society and an acquaintance of Dickens.

46   *'Very well,' ... '... This is fact. This is taste.'*

    Here the specific object of the satire at the expense of the 'government officer' is the Board of Trade's Department of Practical Art, founded after the Great Exhibition of 1851 to oversee art education, promote sound industrial design, and establish museums of art, with the utilitarian Henry Cole as its General Superintendent and its headquarters in Marlborough House. In 1853 the Department was expanded to form the Department of Science and Art, and in 1856 responsibility passed from the Board of Trade to the Committee of Council on Education; the Marlborough House exhibits went on to form the basis of the Victoria and Albert Museum. *Household Words* had earlier attacked the dogmatic policies of the original Department as revealed in a short-lived display at Marlborough House exposing what were claimed to be errors in taste, in Henry Morley's 'A House full of Horrors' *Household Words* VI 141, 4 December 1852, pp. 265–70. See COLLINS (1963) pp. 156–8, ODDIE pp. 43–6, and Janet Minihan *The Nationalization of Culture* (London: Hamish Hamilton, 1977) pp. 96–137.

47   *He and some one hundred ... taught much more!*

    On the development of a national teacher-training scheme on the basis of the 1846 Minutes of the Committee of Council on Education under Sir James Kay-Shuttleworth, see HAMMOND pp. 203–16 and COLLINS (1963) pp. 148–53. The first group of 'Queen's Scholars' (teachers trained under the scheme) entered schools in 1853.

Chapter 3: A Loophole

49   *called Coketown in the present faithful guide-book*
      On the question of whether Coketown is intended to represent Preston or another
      Lancashire cotton town, see Dickens's letter to Peter Cunningham, reproduced in
      App. A 4j.

50   *He had reached the neutral ground ... Journey to Brentford*
      Dickens had previously described visits to Astley's (1786–1893), the foremost Eng-
      lish circus troupe, in 'Astley's' in *Sketches by Boz*, *The Old Curiosity Shop* Ch. 34, and
      Bleak House Ch. 21. On the general outlines and specific details of Dickens's depic-
      tion of the circus in the novel, see SCHLICKE (1985) pp. 137–89. For example, in
      relation to this paragraph he traces the details of acts in the Astley repertoire en-
      titled 'The Swiss Maid and the Tyrolean Lover' and 'Billy Button, or The Tailor's
      Ride to Brentford' (pp. 157–61).

Chapter 4: Mr. Bounderby

55   *your district schools and ... your whole kettle-of-fish of schools*
      'District schools' were special residential establishments for pauper children, replacing
      workhouse schools in some boroughs; 'model schools' could refer to a number of
      'show-case' establishments, including factory schools before they became compul-
      sory under the 1844 Factory Act (see App. C 8), and charitable 'Ragged Schools' for
      the poor from the mid 1840s; 'training schools' presumably refers to the training
      colleges recently set up to train the new 'Queen's Scholars' (see explanatory note to
      p. 47).
          More generally on developments in schools and schooling in the period, see
      HAMMOND pp. 168–216 and COLLINS (1963) *passim*.

Chapter 5: The Key-note

61   *acts of parliament ... religious by main force*
      The attack here may also be on the voluntary societies within the Church of Eng-
      land which pressured Parliament to vote substantial sums of money to build new
      churches in the rapidly expanding industrial towns and cities, but it is principally
      directed at the strict Sabbatarian movement within both the Established and Non-
      conformist churches, which strenuously opposed national and local moves to open
      leisure facilities on Sundays. See HAMMOND pp. 229–36 and 258–62. Earlier, in
      the pamphlet *Sunday under Three Heads* (1836), Dickens had bitterly attacked Sir
      Andrew Agnew's Sunday Observance Bill of the same year, largely because it sought
      to impose restrictions only on the leisure activities of the poor. Note also the anti-
      Sabbatarian jibe on p. 285.

62   *the experienced chaplain of the jail*
      According to COLLINS (1962) pp.141ff., the butt here is specifically the Rev. John
      Clay, reformist chaplain of Preston Gaol from 1821 to 1858.

Chapter 6: Sleary's Horsemanship

68   *missed his tip*

The meaning of this and other items of circus slang in what follows is carefully explained for the reader in the dialogue. On Dickens's sources for this usage, note his letter to Mark Lemon reproduced in App. A 4f.

71   *seven year old.*

Here the manuscript continues with the following passage, excluded from all printed editions of the novel beginning with the serialization in *Household Words*:

> "Did the canvass, more or less every day of the year till I was out of
> my time," said Childers. Seeing Mr. Gradgrind at a loss, he explained
> very clearly by a circular motion of his hand that doing the canvass
> was synonymous with riding round the ring.

72   *these seven years.*

Here the manuscript continues with the following sentence, excluded from all printed editions of the novel beginning with the serialization in *Household Words*:

> If she had been apprenticed, she would have been doing the gar-
> lands in an independent way by this time.

Chapter 8: Never Wonder

86   *Now, besides very many babies ... never to wonder.*

This paragraph satirizes paternalistic attitudes toward the working-classes within both Nonconformism and utilitarianism, and there were indeed ideological connections between the two, as HOUSE argues (pp. 74–6). Obviously 'the eighteen denominations' refers back to the 'eighteen religious persuasions' of page 65, that is, the various Nonconformist churches. But many of the details in the later 'Body number one ... two ...three ... four' point towards more secular utilitarian organizations. The 'leaden little books' written by 'Body number three' sound like Harriet Martineau's *Illustrations of Political Economy* in twenty-five slim volumes (1832–4)—see App. D 1.

At the end of the paragraph, the manuscript continues with the following passage, excluded from all printed editions of the novel beginning with the serialization in *Household Words*:

> and all the babies agreed in wondering on their own accounts. There-
> fore it is perhaps not absolutely wonderful if their wondering faculty
> sometimes went into dangerous directions and got itself imposed
> upon.

87   *of common men and women!*

Here the manuscript continues with the following sentence, excluded from all printed editions of the novel beginning with the serialization in *Household Words*:

> Facts and figures were not always all sufficient for them as they would
> have been for good machines.

87   *There was a library in Coketown ... this unaccountable product.*
Compare the article on the Manchester Free Library's report on its first year of operation 'Manchester Men at their Books' in *Household Words* VIII 195, 17 December 1853, pp. 377–9. For general accounts of the development of public libraries and popular reading habits in the period, see HAMMOND pp. 314–56 and ALTICK pp. 188–259.

Chapter 10: Stephen Blackpool

101   *"Ah, lad! 'Tis thou?"*
With little detailed local knowledge, Dickens attempts to reproduce Lancashire dialect in the dialogues between Stephen and Rachael. According to EASSON, in writing such dialogue Dickens had recourse to John Collier's *A View of the Lancashire Dialect* (1770).

102   *in his innermost heart.*
Here the manuscript continues with the following sentence, excluded from all printed editions of the novel beginning with the serialization in *Household Words*:
> It may be one of the difficulties of casting up and ticking off human figures by the hundred thousand that they have their individual varieties of affection and passions which are of so perverse a nature that they will not come under any rule into the account.

Chapter 11: No Way Out

110   *"Why, you'd have to go to Doctors' Commons ... Perhaps twice the money."*
On divorce procedures in England before the Matrimonial Causes Act of 1857, see STONE pp. 183–346.

Chapter 13: Rachael

123   *the muddle cleared awa'.*
Here the manuscript continues with the following passage, excluded from all printed editions of the novel beginning with the serialization in *Household Words*, by far the most substantial and significant cancellation in the text. Some of the cancelled material reappears in Stephen's second interview with Bounderby (see pp. 180–1), but the passage also contains the only account of Stephen's promise to Rachael to which unexplained references remain on pp. 172, 178, and 188:
> "Thou'st spokken o' thy little sister. There agen! Wi' her child arm tore off afore thy face!"
>
> She turned her head aside, and put her hand up to her eyes.
>
> "When doest thou ever hear or read o' *us*—the like o' *us*—as being otherwise than onreasonable and cause o' trouble? Yet think o' that. Government and gentlemen comes down and mak's report. Fend off the dangerous machinery, box it off, save life and limb, don't rend and tear human creeturs to bits in a Christian country! What follers? Owners sets up their throats, cries out, "Onreasonable! Inconven-

ient! Troublesome!" Gets to secretaries o' states wi' deputations, and nothing's done. [Here, a footnote was added on the galley proofs: 'See Household Words vol. IX page 224, article entitled GROUND IN THE MILL.'] When do *we* get there wi' *our* deputations, god help us! we are too much int'rested and nat'rally too far wrong t' have a right judgement. Happly we are; but what are they then? I' th' name o' th' muddle in which we are born and live and die, what are they then?"

"Let such things be, Stephen. They only lead to hurt. Let them be."

"I will, since thou tell'st me so. I will. I pass my promise."

See the extracts from the noted article, by Henry Morley, and Harriet Martineau's reaction in App. C 8 & 9. More generally on the cancelled passage and the controversy over factory fencing, see K.J. Fielding and Anne Smith 'Hard Times and the Factory Controversy: Dickens vs Harriet Martineau' in NISBET pp. 22–45, and Peter W.J. Bartrip 'Household Words and the Factory Accident Controversy' Dickensian 75 (1979) pp.17–29.

Book II

Chapter 1: Effects in the Bank

144   *The wonder was ... on several occasions.*
On the various Factory Acts and public health regulations imposing duties on factory and mill owners in the first half of the nineteenth century, see HAMMOND pp. 181–2, 193–4, and 282–313.

148   *ascertained by philosophers ... not part of man's duty, but the whole*
For an indignant reaction to this sardonic summary of the principles of Political Economy, see W.B. Hodgson's comments reproduced in App. C 10.

Chapter 2: Mr. James Harthouse

158   *First of all, you see our smoke ... in Great Britain and Ireland.*
For a similar satire on a mill-owner defending the benefits of smoke, see BRIGGS (1963) p.147. There were various national and local measures to control the output of smoke from domestic and factory chimneys in the early Victorian period, but few had any real bite, although there was widespread recognition of the negative effects on public health. While *Hard Times* was still running as a serial, *Household Words* carried 'Smoke or No Smoke', an essay by Dickens attacking smoke pollution in general and in particular pointing out the limitations of Lord Palmerston's Smoke Abatement Act of 1853 (*Household Words* IX 223, 1 Jul 1854, pp. 464–6).

Chapter 4: Men and Brothers

170   *the United Aggregate Tribunal*
No Trade Union of this name existed; it is probably a parody of the utopian socialist Robert Owen's project of a Grand National Consolidated Trades Union which was intended to embrace the whole of labour. The Combination Laws of 1799 and 1800 which prohibited the formation of craft unions were repealed in 1824–5, though combinations remained restrained by common law against conspiracy.

Chapter 9: Hearing the Last of It

223   *his parliamentary cinder-heap … the national dust-yard*
I.e., Parliament is being compared to the piles of disposed household refuse accumulating in Victorian cities and Gradgrind to one of the scavengers who lived on them. As can still be seen today in the British English word 'dustbin' (i.e. receptacle for household refuse), 'dust' was often a euphemism; given the state of urban sanitation in the mid-century, human waste would have been a likely component of the garbage piles. The image is repeated on pp. 231 and 240, and is one of the controlling metaphors of *Our Mutual Friend*, Dickens's last completed novel. On Dickens's generally negative attitude towards Parliament and its business, see HOUSE pp. 170–224.

Book III

Chapter 1: Another Thing Needful

250   *"Lay it here, my dear."*
Here the manuscript continues with the following brief paragraph, excluded from all printed editions of the novel beginning with the serialization in *Household Words*:

> Louisa's tears fell like the blessed rain after a long drought. The sullen glare was over, and in every drop there was a germ of hope and promise for the dried-up ground.